DRAKEMASTER

DRAKEMASTER

E. C. Ambrose

GUARDBRIDGE BOOKS
ST ANDREWS, SCOTLAND

Published by Guardbridge Books,
St Andrews, Fife, United Kingdom.

http://guardbridgebooks.co.uk

ISBN: 978-1-911486-69-5

For Sherry Peters,
who coached me back from the brink.

CHAPTER ONE

The Year of the Snake, Yin Earth Cycle
1257 AD

The king goes hunting
Dark stars burn
In the next ten days, catastrophe

The characters inscribed on the bone were ancient, hard to decipher, and Zhencai had likely misread them. At least this bone did not suggest sacrificing sheep or beheading prisoners to remedy the coming catastrophe. No matter. The ten days the bone referred to had passed a thousand years before: either catastrophe had come, or it had not. He crumbled the brittle bone into the mortar on the floor by his knees, and ground it into powder.

Four ranks of dead, laquered monks, each in the lotus position, each with his head bowed, filled the tiers before Zhencai. They were dead, he knew, in spite of the abbot's insistence they had attained a state of sarira: living Buddahood. All the dead monks had narrow faces and thin arms beneath the layers of gold or red lacquer on their stretched skin. Coils of smoke rose from incense sticks in stone burners, and flowers drifted in bowls of water next to the altar. Paintings of the bodhisattvas adorned the crumbling walls, giving signs of blessing, their bellies wrinkled with deprivation, their faces as serene as the dead monks they watched over.

As a child he viewed the ritual of sarira as a pinnacle of spiritual attainment—the elderly monk entering a higher state, eternally meditating; as a young warrior who knew the satisfaction of physical achievement, he suspected the ritual was vanity. The process stank of geomancy, a worldly magical practice that had no place in the Buddha's teachings.

Nonetheless, the sarira tower was a peaceful place to work, especially while the rest of the Cloud Mountain Monastery fretted over what would happen when the Mongols reached the mountains. Fuss, worry, crowds—all things Zhencai became a monk to avoid. Thankfully the sarira tower could only be reached by a very long stair even the most diligent novices hated. Zhencai smiled over his work. Years ago, when he had been the martial master, he made his pupils climb that stair daily. On their knees.

He ground another scapula from his basket of old bones, all riddled with the cracks and inscriptions of ancient prophecies.

Zhencai's own body revealed age spots, aches, the faltering of the flesh, leaving him with a growing understanding of the impermanence the Buddha spoke of. His methodical grinding became a meditation, the work of his muscles grinding away his sense of himself, so that he could maintain a detached awareness of the world.

A bird had taken a liking to Master Liu's stiff, pointed hat. Its pecking had damaged the monk's lacquered coating, a breach that could lead to the rotting of the revered flesh underneath. Zhencai would have to take care of the cracks. He stretched, looking one way over his shoulder, then the other, to relieve the strain in his back.

Framed by bodhisattva paintings, holes pierced through the one plain wall and soft stains of rust marked a pattern on the floor, showing where an old gearwork had been removed when the monastery claimed this place from the geomancers. The floor remained uneven, as if the device's removal had weakened the stone. One of the broad slabs by the feet of the lowest rank of sarira tipped slightly upward, a change from his last visit.

Rising, Zhencai prowled over, prodding the edge of the stone with his toe. He pushed it back into place.

It groaned and settled with a series of clicks that startled Zhencai into pulling back his foot. The bird launched from the hat of Master Liu who swayed to the side. Scowling, Zhencai stepped up to right the sarira, folding his waxy, supple arms back into place and adjust the brocade over the dead monk's shoulders.

Something else shifted behind him, and Zhencai turned, prepared to adjust Master Deng, the next sarira along the rank.

Master Deng's bald head nodded upward, and Zhencai retreated, wondering what process of the dried flesh caused movement after more than a hundred years, or if his pressing on the shifted stone had disturbed the body.

Then the dead monk shook back the long fabric from his withered hands and wiped at his eyes, blinking them open.

Zhencai leapt away, hands held lightly before him, balanced on his toes. He felt absurd, preparing to do battle with a dead monk, yet his heart drummed in his chest, suddenly too tight to breathe.

The dead monk stretched out skeletal hands to drag one of the bronze bowls of water from the side of the altar. Sloshing water and flowers over his brocade and down his robe, Master Deng brought the bowl to his lips and drank a few swallows, waited, drank again. At last, Master Deng's black eyes swiveled in their gilded sockets, then focused on Zhencai. The sunken flesh of his face worked hard and tiny cracks formed in the lacquer, then a raspy breath parted his lips.

"What is the year?" Master Deng breathed.

Master Deng spoke an older dialect, but not so different that he could not be understood. Zhencai wet his own lips and steadied his breathing, "Master, it is the year of the Snake."

The dead monk gave a hollow, hard breath, his bald head swinging about. "Where is the device that should have woken me?"

"Forgive me, Master," said Zhencai, "but we have no devices here."

With a gravelly sound of irritation, Master Deng rose on feeble legs and wobbled. Zhencai, feeling rather wobbly himself, offered himself as a prop. Whatever else the sarira was, he was clearly Zhencai's elder, and his senior.

A skeletal hand clutched Zhencai's shoulder with surprising strength, bony fingers digging in, and with a leathery creak, Master Deng stepped down beside him. When the dead monk straightened, his head crested a little below Zhencai's own. The dry, black eyes stared at him.

"Thank you. Your robes suggest you are no senior here, although your age suggests you should be."

"I lack spiritual discipline," Zhencai told him, taking a deep breath to steady himself. "I have been set to learn by your example, Master."

"Ha!" When the dead monk cracked out a laugh, flecks of golden paint fell away. "If you seek enlightenment, ask them." He thrust a finger toward the remaining sarira. "Year of the Snake. That's good. Which cycle?"

"The Yin Earth cycle, Master," Zhencai began, prepared to say more, but Master Deng interrupted.

"Yin Earth?" The barely visible brows leapt. "Bah. Then I am late. Has it already happened?"

"I cannot say, Master, perhaps if you—"

"You'd know! Even if you'd been a hermit here as long as I have, you would know the kind of ruin I'm talking about." Master Deng pushed off and lurched toward the arch at the front of the pagoda.

Mountains framed the misty distance where the silver thread of the river embroidered the plains beyond. Towering pines shaded the narrow stairs along the pathway to the monastery below. A few peaks distant, the observatory tower showed pale against the blue of the sky, and Master Deng squinted in that direction. "Take my device, would you," he muttered.

"Please, Master, I have studied in this valley all of my life, but I do not know about your device, or the trouble you mentioned."

"Su Sung—at least you will have heard of him? He made the emperor's clock at Kaifeng, its predictions were meant to counter the decadence of the emperor's children?"

Zhencai gave a short nod. "It was dismantled when the capital moved south, after the Jurchen conquest. One hundred sixty years ago, Master."

"Dismantled." The monk ran a hand over his bare scalp, his narrow shoulders sinking. "They dismantled—Buddha's hand—what wouldn't they do?" His brows crinkled as if he would weep, but had no tears. "You should have seen it. Four stories high, with figures that played music every hour on tiny drums and clever little flutes. The top story had devices for tracking the stars, bound into a system so the clock moved in perfect time with the heavens." His hands moved as he spoke, tracing the tower of the clock in the air before him, outlining complex devices and tiny sculptures as if he could pick them up with his thin fingers. "Ah, you should have seen it. It was almost as beautiful as mine." His eyes tracked a distant cloud with a curious shape, inauspicious and worrisome. "One hundred sixty years."

"Who are you, Master?" Zhencai asked. Certainly he was not a former abbot as Zhencai had been told when he first entered the sarira temple.

The monk's lips showed darkly through the broken mask of golden paint. "Forty years a monk, fifty, is it? You might at least have read the scrolls, novice."

Zhencai rejected the sting. "I might, Master, if they had not been taken to the city, to be studied by the scholars there."

"Decadent indeed," Master Deng snorted. "A monastery without any scrolls. A fifty-year novice with no knowledge of the past—and Su Sung's greatest achievement taken to bits by tiny minds. For a moment, I thought the Mandate of Heaven had already brought ruin upon you all. I thought I was too late, novice. Now I see that I am nearly right on time." Master Deng gave a sharp bow and strode away, his steps shaky, but his back as stiff as a warrior's lance. He made for a narrow ledge that led to a hermit's chamber on the other side of the peak.

Zhencai watched his hobbling progress, his awe returning as the sarira monk's prayer beads clinked and his sandals slapped between the bushes toward the ancient way. Swinging back, Zhencai stared at the empty place among the dead masters, then ran his gaze over those remaining, no longer certain they were dead—no longer certain of anything. He was about to follow the old man to see where the Buddha's hand might lead him, when, from the monastery far below, the great bronze bell rang out, long before dinner. It rang with urgency, and Zhencai's heart fell. Catastrophe, the old bone said—and here it was: the Mongols had found them at last.

CHAPTER TWO

"Hurry up!" barked Wang Lin Yo, the Cathayan overseer, as Dailus and the other slaves trudged barefoot up the narrow path muddied by the hundred soldiers who had already passed that way. A few bodies, monks and Mongols both, scattered the slope below, dead in the fighting or from the fall. Dailus's stomach churned, but he scanned the area anyhow, looking for a way to escape. The mountainous terrain meant fewer people, which would work in his favor, if he knew anything of how to survive in the wild, but still… If he stopped looking, he might miss the chance when it came.

Ahead, the path turned between two peaks shaggy with pines, mist still lurking beneath them. From the mist rose a white wall pierced by a round gate and topped with a narrow edge of those brown, half-loaf tiles Cathayans preferred. Above the wall rose the rooftop of the heathen temple, a dizzying pile of square roofs with upswept corners, each embellished with a series of creatures, like the gargoyles on the new cathedral back home, but gilded and gleaming in the early light.

The next man stumbled into him, and Dailus muttered an apology as he trotted to catch up, cradling his wrist so the weight of his slave bracelet didn't send him off-balance into the chasm. No escape now, not with so many slaves and soldiers about.

Bloody trails marked the courtyard beyond the arch and a few soldiers still worked there, pushing the bodies into heaps at either side, the golden-yellow robes of the dead streaked crimson. The Tatars plucked arrows from the corpses, wasting nothing.

"Here!" Wang Lin Yo pointed his thick arm toward a smaller building. "We need this taken down and broken up. It's too big to carry or drag, not down that path."

The crew of eighteen men, Dailus included, bowed and turned, wiping mud from their scarred hands. Each took one of the hammers Wang Lin Yo had carried up rather than risk a slave with a tool of his own. The overseer had been a slave himself before his advancement, so he knew what they'd be thinking. Dailus hefted the hammer in both hands, his bracelet wearing a groove into his forearm. A few blows from a hammer like that, and slave bracelets could disappear into the mud, and slaves themselves could disappear into the countryside, lost among their countrymen.

Except for Dailus. He stood head and shoulders taller than most, even if his pale skin hadn't marked him out. Tatars said Cathayans used the same word for "stranger" as for "ghost," pointing to him when they explained. Pale as a fish belly, pale as old bones, as a newborn's rump. Then they laughed and laughed and Yusen, his master, could pretend himself a man for having captured the pale giant and hauling him here. No, even without his bracelet, Dailus stood out too much to hope for freedom by running away. He would have to look harder for escape—or work harder on behalf of the khan, as Wang Lin Yo had, earning higher status and less supervision.

Carrying his begrudged hammer, Dailus followed the others, unable to avoid the blood that marked the stones, up to the steps of the little open structure. At one end, two ropes suspended a thick log, a man's body sprawled beneath it, his head missing. Swallowing bile, Dailus fought the urge to cross himself.

Four groups of slender pillars supported another peaked roof, sheltering a bell. Dailus froze at the sight of it. Tall as a man, half as broad as it was tall, the huge bronze bell hung a few feet from the ground. Mad, heathen figures marked the surface all over with lines of writing in between and all manner of decorations to frame them: flames and orbs, filigreed bats and writhing, wingless dragons. The bell…he flashed his glance back to the hanging log. A man standing on the steps could swing that log and strike this extraordinary thing! What might it sound like? He imagined the shape of the sound moving through him, deep and resonant, echoing in the valley, lingering in the bronze.

Wang Lin Yo's hand smacked the back of Dailus's head. "Get to work! Or do you want another pounding, Fishbelly?"

Dailus bowed quickly.

"Add that body to the stack." The man jabbed his finger at the corpse, then he swung about to study the bell. "Tang! Climb up there and loosen that coupling. Let's break this thing—the khan needs his firedrakes when we get to Kaifeng."

The imagined peal of the bell vanished into Dailus's clenched, always-empty stomach. He tucked the hammer through his belt and moved toward the corpse, ducking the log to wrap his arms under the dead monk's shoulders. The other slaves grumbled and gestured about how to reach the coupling in question. Among them, Jian Ho, the closest thing Dailus had to a friend, stood silent as if in mourning for the bell. In a matter of hours, it would be broken into shards, ready to haul away and melt down so the khan could get his firedrakes. The shadow of the log hung over Dailus and his burden, and his heart raced. He could do it, as if by accident, slipping in the blood, stumbling and righting himself, exactly as they expected of a great oaf like him. Did he want another pounding? No—his face and stomach still ached from the last one. But to think of the bell dying without singing once more…

Dailus gathered the dead monk and hauled him upward. A few scant inches too far and he backed into the log, leaning into it as if he didn't expect it to move, then lurching away, slipping down the steps. The crew laughed as he dropped the monk. He caught hold of the log, strained for a moment as if to stop it, pulling it back from the bell, and pushed as he let go, his bloody hands slipping, flung wide, ridiculous. And then, sublime.

The log struck hard and the bell rang, a single brilliant note that seized him low in the gut and quivered through his body. His bare feet felt the sound in the stone steps beneath him, every tiny hair of his skin tingling with it.

"Sorry, sorry, sorry," he said—in threes, to show he really meant it—as he dropped to his knees and smacked his forehead into the mud at Wang Lin Yo's feet. The overseer kicked him back again with a growl.

"Monkey! Can't even be trusted to drag out the dead. Why Yusen thought to take a lump like you is beyond the sages." He snorted, but Dailus repeated his apologies, twice more, and the overseer merely pointed at the body.

Jian Ho caught Dailus's eye with the flash of a smile, as if he knew exactly what had happened, then both men got to work. Jian Ho had been a sculptor before his capture. No doubt he admired the images on the bell just as much as Dailus admired the thing itself. The vast temple bell still rang in Dailus's ears—in his entire body, if truth be told—when the khan arrived. A few captains in their furs and leathers galloped in first, then Möngke Khan himself, the horsetail dangling from his peaked helmet the only sign of his Tatar origins. Below that, the khan was all Cathay silks and brocades the Holy Roman Emperor himself would envy. Powerfully built, the khan bestrode his horse as if it were his throne, sword and bow hanging ready at his sides. Dailus dropped his gaze and took up his burden, dragging the headless monk, trusting his hunched posture would allow him to escape notice.

Instead of moving on toward the temple, the khan swung down from his horse and stomped closer. Dailus dropped the corpse and fell once more to his throbbing knees, bowing his head.

"These aren't geomancers!" The khan shouted. "Where's Batzorig?" He prodded the body with his foot, smearing a little blood on his fancy boot as someone hurried to fetch the general.

Dailus turned over the word "geomancers." He thought he had translated it right. Two years gave him a fair grasp of the language of his captors, but the words the khan used combined the earth and witchcraft or magic. Earth witches? Mud witches? Dailus fell back on Latin, what little he had of it from working at various churches, and settled for "geomancers," as something like "those who make magic from the earth."

"Here, my lord. What is your will?" Batzorig bowed low and straightened, hands spread, ready for the khan's command.

"These are yellow monks—Buddhists. They're not geomancers."

"Oh. Are you certain, my lord?"

"Have you found any compasses or symbols?"

Batzorig glanced around at the bodies, the temple, the soldiers—anywhere but at the khan. "You said they would have sanctuaries, high in the mountains. That they would be like monks."

"Like monks! Not be monks. We can't go about the countryside slaughtering everyone we find, not if we want to govern this place for ourselves. No wonder Kaifeng is in revolt!" The khan slapped his thighs. "Didn't you send your scouts?"

"Only one was available, and he seemed…" The general shook his head.

One scout, the one that nobody employed unless he had to: Dailus's own master.

"It does not matter. I have failed you. A thousand apologies, my lord." Batzorig bowed his head, shoulders slumping.

"At least tell me that none have escaped to spread word of this?"

"None, my lord." Again, the general glanced around, his eyes briefly settling on the opposite mountaintop, where another peaked structure could be seen, linked to the temple by a thread of steps. "Absolutely."

"Thank the Eternal Sky for that! Tell your men they may take booty, then put this place to the torch."

"My lord, look there—so much bronze." Batzorig pointed to the huge bell across the yard just as the crew succeeded in de-coupling it. It fell with a resounding crash against the stones beneath, cracking several, Dailus noted. Even in death, the bell had power. Jian Ho cringed from the damage. A strange man, that one, but their strangeness brought them together—shunned by the other men.

Wang Lin Yo, silent as the khan berated his general, spoke up at last. "With this bronze, Master Sheng can make four or five firedrakes, at least, my lord khan!"

The khan's eyes lit up as if reflecting the glow of his firedrakes, then his light faded and he gave a sigh. "You have not heard? Sheng fell from his horse, struck by a dart, so the shaman tells me. He's dead—assassinated. We need those firedrakes at Kaifeng, but without a master..." He rolled a shrug. "How long do you think the city can withstand a siege? If we bring up reinforcements or wait for a new master to cast the firedrakes?"

Batzorig dropped to one knee and sketched in the mud, a long, wriggling line, a few swooping marks, a square. "They have the river, my lord. If we could divert it, take their water, we could re-gain our advantage."

"If the river was their only water source, and even then it would take months for them to run out—they've been planning this a long time, stockpiling fire lances. If the rebels have friends in the South to send reinforcements—or if they reach the geomancers—we might lose the entire region." The khan stomped, splashing the muck, and Dailus flinched. "Without Sheng." The khan shook his head, the horsetail slapping his shoulders.

"There must be somebody else who could do it, my lord?"

Wang Lin Yo's brow furrowed, his priveleged position threatened without a drakemaster to supply.

Dailus's heart thundered in his chest, and he spoke a Hail Mary under his breath. Sheng, who ran the entire bronze-casting operation—killed! Leaving the army with a lengthy siege instead of a brief and glorious victory powered by firedrakes belching stone to shatter the walls of their enemy. The Tatars hated to wait. Dailus would have no hide left when Wang Lin Yo and Yusen had taken out their fury over that. What then? Would he ever get the chance to go home? Firedrakes: great hollows of bronze to contain an explosion instead of a voice. Like bells of fire.

Dailus swallowed hard and said, "My lord khan." He winced even as he spoke, tucking his body even closer to the ground, his hands pressed to the mud.

"What's that?" the khan said. "Speak up, slave, did you dare to address me?"

"Yes, my lord khan." Dailus tried a sidelong glance.

"What are you? What is this?"

At a gesture from the khan, two of the captains grabbed Dailus's arms and hauled him up. He sagged between them, trying to disguise his height.

Wang Lin Yo bowed repeatedly. "Forgive me, my lord! Please, please, please forgive me! Surely there was no intent to disturb your reverent person—"

The khan thrust out his hand, folding back his over-long silken sleeve and grabbed Dailus's chin, lifting his head to stare into his face. "A European?"

"Just a slave, my lord," Wang Lin Yo babbled, "He belongs to Kurdun—that is, to Yusen, your—that is—" The flustered overseer almost blundered into Yusen's past, into the things they never spoke of. He bowed again, and opened his mouth, but the khan cut him off with a look, still gripping Dailus's chin with work-hardened fingers.

Dailus's jaw ached where the khan's grip overlaid his earlier beating, but he refused to lower his gaze. Let the khan seen him as strong, capable of what he was about to propose.

"No wonder it dared to speak to me. Europeans have no discipline. And Yusen, well, you could hardly expect him to take a firm hand." The khan gave a short chuckle, echoed by Batzorig and a few of the men.

"No, my lord, certainly not." Wang Lin Yo's voice dared amusement.

"Certainly not, but when you are given the charge of him, I expect you to do better." The khan released Dailus and stepped back.

"Yes, my lord." Wang Lin Yo spun about almost too fast to see and slammed his foot into Dailus's chest.

Gasping for breath, Dailus staggered against the grip of the Tatar captains. He floundered, but he would not fall. This was his first chance in two years to rise above the wretched place he'd been given. "A b—bronze caster, my lord. I c-cast bronze."

Wang Lin Yo landed another kick that shot pain through Dailus's chest and sent him tumbling free of the captains' grasp to writhe on the ground. The words over his head came and went on echoes of pain, as if the bell's great log had struck his own breast.

"A bronze caster? Is this true?"

"So Yusen claimed. The slave is disgusting, my lord, but not without knowledge. At first I had to hit him just to make him shut up."

Huddled on the earth, fist pressed against his heart, Dailus wished he had absorbed those lessons. His chest radiated pain with every half-breath. He had seized the chance to improve his lot, and now he would die for it.

"Any others? Anyone else you have with knowledge? Then he'll have to do. At least, he'll have to try." The khan chuckled again. "Yusen might have finally redeemed himself with this. Beneath the Eternal Sky, Batzorig, would you ever have imagined such a thing?"

"No, my lord." The general offered a short laugh of his own. "What is your will?"

"Send for Yusen and tell him to haul his slave down to the plains, to General Munkjar's tumaan. Wang Lin Yo's crew will follow with more bronze. In the meantime, Yusen and his slave will make us a firedrake worthy of the khanate." The khan's grin lit his round face and brightened his eyes. "Or they'll be shot from one."

CHAPTER THREE

The long light of the setting sun cast the astronomical instruments into strange shadows that interlaced like gears across the floor. They lapped at Bao Xing's tiny feet as she bent over her charts and paper, her brush furiously moving, her long fingers spotted with ink. She had to finish her measurements, finalize the astronomical chart and understand what the stars were trying to tell her. The Celestial Throne shone brightly, orange and gleaming among the vivid stars around it, but the pattern of the Dark Lance looked wrong. The other celestial weapons surrounding it in the pattern might mute the effect of this worrisome sign, but one of the wandering stars edged toward it, moving backward. If she were right, it would ring the Lance and signal the advent of a radiant energy that would damage the Imperial Palace and devastate the Han people. Terrible danger could be coming, more terrible even than the Mongols, if such were possible. Last night's observations were obscured by an inauspicious cloud, but she had the historical record—her father's and grandfather's observations going back for decades, surely she could—

"Bao Xing!"

She jerked at the voice, and her pen left a few drops of ink across her careful work. "Yes, Papa!"

"What do you see? Are they coming?"

"Just a moment, I'm almost done, Papa." She blotted the drops, but too quickly, and one of them smeared the characters of the pole star, the emperor's star, into something else entirely.

"There is no more time for that, Bao Bao." His voice drew nearer, then his shadow fell alongside hers, merging with the circular shadows of the astronomical instruments. At his approach, the compass needle shivered on a water bowl engraved with the pattern of the stars.

Bao Xing blinked back tears. His hand stroked her hair, then rested too heavily against the back of her neck and she looked up, following his gaze. Across the valley, smoke curled and flames danced where the Cloud Mountain monastery stood. A dark file of soldiers moved back toward the river far below, but another, smaller group pressed onward, up the steep track to Bao Xing's own quiet peak.

When the soldiers came, all of this—her father, their instruments, their scrolls and diagrams—all could be gone in moments, and he wanted her to leave, to dress in boy's clothing, smear her face and vanish into the country, leaving the tower and their observations, to be burned or broken at the soldiers' will. There had to be another way.

"Here, Papa, the chart isn't ready yet, I know, but the signs suggest there's danger. Look at the way the clouds circle at the Dark Lance—"

Her father reached out and took the brush from her hand, setting it back on the inkstone. "Bao Bao. There is no time any more for signs. Even if there were a greater danger than the army at our mountain, there is no one we could warn."

"But Papa—"

He settled his thin hand against her face, warm, comforting, too frail. "You must take your eyes from the sky and look to the earth, Bao Bao. You have to go."

She pressed his hand to her cheek. "If they don't find something worth taking here, some treasure, they'll kill you."

"The only treasure I have is you," he told her, "and I am not afraid to die."

"And the work will be unfinished." She turned on her stool to face him. "Who will carry on, if not for us? You once told me that the future of the land might rest on this."

"Even if we knew on what day, at what hour a thing might come to pass, how would we act upon it? We, alone, are not enough to stop some great catastrophe. Even if we knew the Dark Lance would strike, the emperor moved south. We could not reach him."

"Then we should have gone with him!"

The shadow of grief passed her father's face. Her mother had been dying when the last of the emperor's family fled. She had been too weak to travel, and they dare not move her. Mother had wanted Bao Xing, at least, to go with the imperial court, even if it must be a distant and diminished court.

"Go. This last time, Bao Xing, be a dutiful daughter and leave your father to his fate."

Bao Xing lowered her head, her fingers hesitating over the brush, then taking up the handle of the cane that hung from the side of her work table. She propped herself on it and made her cautious way to the stairs, inching down them. When her father wasn't there, she usually dropped to her bottom and bumped her way down as she had when she was a child but young ladies of marriageable age could not behave in such a way. Bao Xing descended as far as the second floor, outside the door they never opened, the room where her mother had died. Bao Xing used to pause and glare on the long, tedious way up the stairs. Her courtly mother's wish for her future had crippled her, binding her feet to make her the perfect bride. After Mother's death, Papa couldn't bring himself to let Bao Xing go, and so it was her father's gifts she took up instead, her father's work she pursued and her father's dreams she took into her heart. Her mother's dream had given her nothing but pain and sorrow.

Carved into the closed door, Double Happiness suggested the devotion her parents had known in their own marriage. Bao Xing had rejected all of that, stuck only with her miniature feet as a reminder of what might have been. Hide herself as a boy, and she would hobble through the mountains, begging for her keep, doing what she must to honor her family.

She blinked away tears, picturing her father, dead, picturing her mother, dead years before, her face made up perfectly, her paint, her hair complimenting her great beauty. Her mother was pleased, at least, not to grow old and ugly, but to pass from the world at the summit of her splendor.

A dutiful daughter. Her father said she was his only treasure. Might there be another way to show her duty, and to honor her father, a way where they both could live, and even continue their urgent work? Perhaps by setting aside her father's legacy, she could preserve it, and him.

Bao Xing put out her hand and opened the door. It creaked inward and she hobbled through into her mother's domain, a foreign place of rich fabrics, delicate embroideries, bottles of paints and drawers full of gold and pearl combs to pin up the silken darkness of one's hair. Bao Xing closed the door behind her and sat at the table, taking up a bronze mirror that showed her weak reflection, startled to find the faint image of her own mother staring back. In the years she had been her father's daughter, she had become her mother's as well. The time had come to reveal it.

Bao Xing worked as carefully as she ever had on any chart of stars.

She dressed in a robe so fine it caught upon the roughness of her hands. She painted her face with pearl dust into a pale, perfect moon. She applied rouge to her lips and cheeks and tweezed away her brows, drawing them in perfect form. She combed back her long hair and twisted it into careful knots, tucking in a series of golden combs shaped like butterflies that jingled with jewels. At her ears, she hung a pair of enormous pearls. On her tiny feet, she wore a pair of slippers that showed months of stitches worked in silk. She shook down the sleeves of the gown so the silk draped well beyond her fingertips, signaling that she was a woman who had no need of work—and concealing her ink-stained fingers. With every stitch of clothing and brush of color, she concealed her heart, trying to embody her mother's perfection: a beautiful, painted corpse.

Outside, footfalls sounded, voices shouted, someone pounded on the door of the house. Her father hurried down the stairs, but Bao Xing opened the chamber before he had passed the landing. He stumbled to a halt, gasping. "Bao Xing?"

"Tell them my name, Papa. Tell them I am for the khan—the khan and no other." She stared hard at his widened eyes and gripped the carved cinnabar of her cane so tightly the carving ground into her palms.

"They will take you away." His eyes glistened. "What will become of you?"

She didn't want to think of that. Invoking the khan should be enough to protect her. She hoped. Bao Xing swallowed. "I will be his and you will be in peace. The prophecy of the Dark Lance, Papa. You told me that our very world depended upon it. The truth must be found."

He gave her a quick, fierce embrace, and hurried down before her, shouting, "I am coming, please forgive my lateness."

With her mother's serenity, Bao Xing descended the stairs, leaving her father's world behind her, surrendering the stars.

CHAPTER FOUR

Clad in a loin cloth and his slave bracelet, Dailus sweated along with the crew to shift the huge iron handle into place. Two-ended, with a great ring at the center to carry the crucible, the thing was as long as four men and took at least six on each end to maneuver it. He waved and pointed, gesturing carefully to steer the men. So close to the furnace, the roar of the flames made speech impossible, and the heat drove all moisture from his eyes and body. Panting, longing for water, Dailus forced himself up the two steps to glance into the molten bronze. Its surface shimmered and shifted, brighter than the sun, with streams of darker imperfections resting on top like black islands.

With another gesture, he summoned one of the men to hand him a long iron paddle. The man sauntered over and retrieved it, using it as a prop for his slow walk back. Dailus glared and snapped, and the rest of the crew snickered. Wang Lin Yo must be distracted for them to flout Dailus's authority, knowing he could not personally enforce it with a whip. At last, the other slave offered up the tool, letting it sway so that Dailus must lunge to grab it, and the heat on his left side became briefly unbearable. He flinched back, gripping the rod with both hands, his muscles trembling. If he fell in, the whole project was ruined—but at least, he thought with grim humor, they could beat him no longer. He balanced carefully, scanning behind him to make sure the area was clear.

The other slave bounced back a little, withdrawing his hands as if he had been pretending to push Dailus into the crucible. He couldn't hear their laughter over the sound of the fire, but he saw the flash of bright teeth, and his friend Jian Ho's scowl. With an expression as commanding as he could muster, Dailus gestured the man back, out of the dangerous area. Balancing the weight of the paddle so he wouldn't fall in, Dailus crouched and leaned, scooping the slag from the surface. With a practiced pivot, he swung about and rapped the paddle against the steps, shaking free a few splashes of molten metal.

Someone shrieked. Dailus dropped the scoop on the landing and spun about. The insubordinate slave danced away from the steps, his too-long trousers on fire.

Two of the others grabbed a cauldron of water for quenching and started forward, prepared to douse the man and likely steam the flesh from his body.

"No! No water! Drop down!" Dailus sprang from the landing, catching himself hard, still shouting, realizing too late that he was shouting in Lithuanian and fumbling for the right words in the Chin language. At last, his long legs were good for something. He ran hard, out-pacing the water-bearers, and leapt on the burning man, toppling him to the grass, smothering the flames, though the slave struggled beneath him.

Pushing himself to his knees, breathing hard, Dailus watched the man scramble away.

"He tries to kill me!" the slave bleated in Chin-accented Tatar, jabbing a finger at Dailus. His fellows dropped the cauldron and hurried to his side, inspecting the seared skin of his thigh. "Twice, he tries this! He throws the metal on me, then leaps on me to break my neck."

A horse stamped forward, its rider giving a sharp crack of his whip. "Don't be a fool. He saved your life, first, by ordering you back, next by putting out the flames." Yusen stared down at the blubbering slave and snapped his whip again.

The man fell silent, dropping his gaze, and the others lowered their heads as well.

"Yes, he's a disgusting fishbelly, but he is also the khan's drakemaster, and he rules over you." Yusen thrust the end of his whip toward the men on the ground, then swung it about to take in the entire crew. "If he does wrong, I'll take it from his flesh. Until then, you listen to him." With a final crack of the whip, his mount flattening its ears, Yusen motioned them back to work.

Catching his breath, Dailus clambered to his feet, half-hoping the other slaves would snicker or stare, showing their defiance to Yusen, and earning the stripes he so clearly longed to deliver. But they remembered the Tatar's lash and returned quietly to their places. Still hesitating, Dailus glanced toward the base of the stairs. If he returned to his post to finish scooping out the slag, his head would rise above Yusen's—even with his master mounted. His master was a dwarf: not with legs too short and head too large, like some dwarfs Dailus remembered from the Feast of Fools at Vilnius. Rather, Yusen had the proportions of a child, well-formed if too muscular for youth. Thick black hair hung to his shoulders, framing a face too young to be battle-scarred as it was, yet his spirit was anything but childlike. Yusen defended him to the others only to prove his ownership: if Dailus went astray, it would, indeed, be taken from his flesh, drakemaster or no.

"How long until you pour it?" Yusen's child-like voice broke Dailus's concerns.

"A few minutes, only—I need to clear the last of the slag, Captain."

"The khan wishes to watch. I shall bring him. You'll wait to pour until we return."

"Of course, Captain." When the horse turned and trotted away, Dailus straightened, his heart still too quick, and dusted off his hands and legs.

This time, when he climbed up to the landing, the other slaves stood well back, most of them to either side of the huge iron handle ready to lift on his command. Not unlike the crew of his foundry back home. A pang of sadness struck him, but he resumed cleaning the surface of the molten metal and rehearsed in his head the next few steps.

A few paces away, a deep pit held the ceramic mold for the huge firedrake. It rested muzzle down, with a core mold inside to create the walls of the barrel. At the top, a funnel-shaped opening waited for the hot metal to stream inside. The crew would use the handle to pick up the scorching crucible and carry it those few steps. Dailus himself would manipulate a rod at the back to guide the crucible and tip it. Not unlike his own foundry, except that he had never cast a bell as large as a man. The crucible would be devilishly heavy and every man on the crew would be needed, including a few to help him steer it. A wrong step, a fumble, and the bronze would spill or the slaves would die. Dailus sighed. A wrong step or a fumble, and the slaves would die in any case. Even if they survived the accident—some of them would not survive their masters' fury.

The surface of the bronze moved beneath him, dazzling and pure. Dailus straightened and summoned one of the others to take the paddle. In grand procession, the khan and his personal guard rode up, clad in brocades, leathers and furs. Dailus, his lean, tall form high upon the steps, his modesty barely appeased by the strip of cloth bound about his loins, felt more conspicuous than ever. Among the khan's elite, Yusen stretched himself tall, his feet sticking out to the sides of a horse bigger than the other men's mounts, yet he beamed, his eyes bright. He looked like the only child at a courtly Twelfth-night. Dailus shook off the thought. After two years, he still couldn't think of his master as a man, however young.

Dailus gave a brief bow and indicated that the horsemen should stay on the far side of the casting pit. They arrayed themselves to ensure the khan had the best view.

With a few claps and a circling motion, Dailus gathered the crew and they took up the iron handle. He descended and hauled the wooden steps back from the furnace, scraping a pathway in the coal dust, soot and rough bits of slag that surrounded the furnace. At his direction, the slaves brought the handle up and fitted it under the crucible's lip, then grunted, hauling it up. They staggered the few steps toward the waiting mold. Dailus ran forward, finding the long, hooked rod where it lay ready and crouched to fit it to the base of the crucible. The vessel glowed with the bronze and spit out sparks. Together, the crew marched forward, straining against the weight in their shoulders, wincing against the heat.

Wang Lin Yo stood to one side, brow furrowed, displeased to have any part of his authority transferred to another, much less to a slave. He had risen from their ranks himself, and hoarded his hard-earned rights.

The crucible drew close to, then over the pit. Dailus summoned Jian Ho to take his post for a moment while he hurried to the side. He crouched, eying the narrowing gap between the lip of the crucible and the open funnel of the mold below.

"Hold!" he shouted, thrusting up both arms for emphasis, then ran back to his rod.

"Go!" Dailus shouted. He, Jian Ho, and his other assistant pulled hard on their rod so the crucible swung upward and liquid fire poured down, a few sparks tumbling aside. Tendrils of moisture steamed and sizzled, the smell of the hot metal searing their nostrils.

They pulled hard against the crucible's weight, struggling to keep the spout aligned. Dailus dug in his heels, his back, arms and legs aching with the tension. Jian Ho shrieked and slipped, his feet giving way, his body tumbling.

Dailus shifted, stuck out a foot and shoved the flailing man, shifting his direction to keep him away from the pit, nearly sliding under himself.

With a growl, Wang Lin Yo threw himself toward the rod at their back, adding his strength and weight as he took hold.

A golden, glowing dome of bronze capped the mold and Dailus released his tension. He tried to shout a command to the others, but his throat had gone completely dry, his lips chapped by the heat, so it was Wang Lin Yo who confirmed the order as they eased off and staggered back, the crucible much lighter now, their muscles trembling. They replaced the crucible, the handle striking ground with a clang as the men moved back, slumping, wiping their sweaty hands on their equally sweaty thighs.

Jian Ho, too, moved away from the pit, looking slightly dazed and haunted as he glanced toward the glow and steam, the fiery pit into which he'd nearly fallen. Dailus walked to meet him. "Jian Ho, are you hurt?"

The young man shook his head quickly, met his eye, then swiftly bowed his head. "Thank you, master. Thank you, thank you."

"No need." Dailus spread his hands.

"Yes, there is," Jian Ho said fiercely, still staring at the ground, his slave bracelet quivering with his intensity. "They would have us forget that we are men, that our skills, our hearts, our lives mean something. Twice today, you have shown them wrong. A third time, and it will be hard for any man of judgment to treat you as they do. Three lives in the span of a day and the very earth shall tremble. You should be master, even if they will never say so."

Again, he bowed, and Wang Lin Yo approached, growling low in his throat.

Dailus reached out and rested his hand lightly on Jian Ho's bent back, feeling the instant tension that shot through the young slave. "Jian Ho hurt his back in his fall."

"He should have told me, slave," said the overseer. "Not that we waste healing needles on such as you. Go on." He gave a flick of his hand, and Jian Ho hurried away to rejoin the crew. "For a moment, I thought I saw a slave bow to another slave."

Dailus bowed to the overseer. "I understand how it might have been perceived so, overseer." He kept his head down, sinking a little in his shaky knees to make himself smaller. "Permit me to check on the mold?"

"Don't think I have forgotten your own rudeness put you here, fishbelly."

"No, overseer." Bowing himself out of Wang Lin Yo's presence, Dailus moved toward the mold. Did that count, in Jian Ho's strange pronouncement, as a third life, or merely the same one twice? Dailus's fingers twitched to cross himself. Heathen superstitions, that was all. Walking to the edge of the pit, Dailus knelt to examined the bulge at the top of the casting. It looked well-formed, likely the metal had gone all the way down. He prowled the edge of the pit, studying it from all sides, bowing lower as he passed Yusen and the khan, then returning to kneel before the khan.

"Speak."

"My lord, the work appears sound. We must wait at least a day before we open the mold."

"A day!" the khan protested, but his voice rang with delight. "What a sight that was, to see those men pouring the sun itself into my firedrake. You've done well. Yusen! There are dancing girls tonight. Come to my ger, and bring your man."

"Thank you, my lord," answered Yusen's strange voice.

With a flurry of cheers, the khan and his captains rode away, kicking their mounts to a race through the campsite of this tumaan back to the royal encampment.

The flush of the khan's praise settled over Dailus's aching back, and he smiled to himself as he straightened and walked slowly away.

CHAPTER FIVE

Hidden among the dancing girls of the invader's ger, Ming Lun gathered the strands of information all around her. Her bowed head and innocent demeanor did not prevent her quick eyes from glancing, her mind from counting. Six male servants at the doors to the outside, and to the smaller tent where others prepared the food. Five female servants seeing to platters of roasted lamb and little bowls of salt and spices. Seventeen men seated on cushions or rugs across the central hearth, arrayed according to their rank. The dwarf occupied a place of honor, shifting about and squaring his shoulders constantly to appear taller than he was. His slave lurked behind him, nearly invisible, in spite of the disparity in their heights. An enslaved drakemaster to replace the dead man: a turn she had not anticipated, but not one that would stand in her way. The other sixteen men—one of them the khan himself—were another matter. Even dressed in dancing robes, her face painted, her lips smiling, she was too conspicuous to take her chance tonight.

A servant at the door admitted a stocky Han man, a whip bound at his side. The overseer of slaves. "My lord khan," said the man, bowing low. "What is your will?"

"You have served me well, Wang Lin Yo. I know you have family further west and the desire to visit them, to pay respect to your ancestors, yes?"

The overseer gave a nod.

"I cannot spare you until we have dealt with the rebels at Kaifeng, but I give you this as my promise." He held out a flat plaque of silver as big as his palm and covered with symbols. "This paizi gives you free passage through all the lands of the khan. When Kaifeng is subdued, you have my leave to visit the graves of your ancestors."

The overseer accepted the paizi, bowing very low indeed, the pass gripped in his hand. Reward for his complicity with their conquerors. "Thank you, my lord khan. I vow to see Kaifeng in rubble."

The khan roared with laughter and waved him off. The drakemaster watched his overseer depart, tracking that bit of silver with a greedy stare.

"Enough business. Airag! And dancing!" the khan shouted.

A Han girl brought up the jug of airag, pouring the clear drink first for the khan, then for the dwarf, then for the other captains. The dwarf was honored, indeed, though Ming Lun knew this was both new and tenuous. It depended upon his ownership of the drakemaster, and the khan could take that away at any moment.

Among them, the seventeen men of the khan's company had sixteen bows, at least twenty seven knives visible, and four axes. Three of the captains refused airag and sat stiff as statues. Dangerous men. Seven of them had been sipping from their own little jugs already. A nuisance. Dangerous only to the pretty virgins who would dance with her. Two of the men were Mandarins, educated Han bureaucrats who aided the conqueror in administering the lands he seized. One of them avoided looking at her. Her imperial contact, clearly unskilled at deception and unworthy of such a prominent role. The other was a tall man with ink-stained hands who carried himself too lightly for a mere scholar. One to watch.

The khan himself, expansive and lightly armed, counted on his guard to defend him. He tipped his head to laugh, exposing his throat above his brocade collar. He leaned over, balancing with his hand, exposing a side of his ribcage. At the right angle, a blade little longer than her hand could pierce his heart. A series of movements flashed through her mind: herself in motion, her dancing costume swirling about her, confusing the eye. She rounded the fire, circled as if too fast, dropped to one knee and slid the knife between his ribs, just at the right angle—the dropped knee would provide that. If she kept moving, she could circle again the other side and be out the door before they noticed he was dead. Alas that killing the khan was not her mandate, not tonight.

The dwarf and his slave sat close by. If she took the chance, they would likely see her, but they were also the least credible opponents. The sliding glances and smirks of the other men showed her this. Unworthy of respect, easy to eliminate. If she had seen the pair together, in the court of the emperor, Ming Lun might have taken them for acrobats, a deliberate pairing of large and small meant to add humor and excitement to a tumbling routine.

Nearby, a drum started a steady beat. Ming Lun withdrew her flute and started to play. At the high note, the six girls of the School of the

Soaring Lark rose up together, smooth and elegant. They bent to the side, draping their long sleeves, smiling just as she had taught them, then they began to dance, tiny, mincing steps for their little feet, their bodies lithe as willows, bending and dipping. They worked their sleeves from side to side, sometimes taking them up and holding them taut, sometimes wafting them as if on a breeze. Their unison was perfect. It should be, for all the work she had put into it.

Ming Lun changed her tune to a more languorous one, and the girls turned their backs, exposing their pale necks and upswept hair, peeking over their shoulders like nervous brides. The audience roared and the khan slapped his thigh. At his side, the dwarf gawked up at the girls, as if he had never seen such a thing. Likely, with his stature and his low position in the army, he had rarely been so close to beautiful women. Behind him, the drakemaster's eyes slid shut, his head tipping, his straw-colored hair bobbing over his face. His lean, powerful hands rested in his lap, his fingers drifting away from the slave bracelet that left a patch of pale, hairless skin on his left arm.

How close could she get to her target? Ming Lun rose, stepping carefully as part of the dance, and turned a circle with the others. Still playing her flute, she moved around the raised hearth, keeping the girls between herself and the men, making her eyelashes flutter.

"Their feet," the dwarf murmured, sticking out one of his own little feet, still larger than those of the dancers.

"Lotus blossom feet, they're called. Are they not beautiful?" The khan laughed again. "Except for that one."

Ming Lun continued to play, though one note came rather shrill. At the dwarf's back, the drakemaster startled awake, as if he suddenly realized his danger. Ming Lun controlled her breathing as the man's eyes briefly met hers. The slave's round eyes were pale jade, a shade she had never seen before, striking and wrong. A foreigner, a ghost. What if he had supernatural skills?

"What are you?" The khan slapped his hands together, and the girls of the Soaring Lark stumbled to a halt, glancing at their leader.

Gracefully lowering her flute, Ming Lun gave an elegant bow with a sweep of her sleeve that brushed the floor. She answered in Mongolian, her words hesitant and rough. "I am dance teacher, my lord, nothing more."

"With feet like that? You must plod like a camel."

Ming Lun kept her face averted, heat rising at her throat. Perhaps she ought to have taken her chance at the khan. "Surely you correct, my lord."

"Show me—I am curious to see how a camel dances!"

Bowing again, Ming Lun replaced the flute in her broad sash and nodded to the drummer. The girl with the drum started a new rhythm, much faster, much sharper.

Ming Lun took a deep breath, fluttered a hand before her face, and brought her mind to its other state.

She danced the part of the River Dragon, sinuous and strong, her arms sharply up, now whipping out as she spun, her big, ugly feet slamming the ground, propelling her up in a leap, sliding down so that she lunged forward, baring her teeth with the rush of winter floods.

She fueled that rage with memory: the first time she had ever seen a Mongol.

At the age of three, Ming Lun barely fit into the wooden child-minder, but her mother had stuck her into it then hurried around the farmhouse bundling up their sleeping mats and piling food onto cloths that she tied securely. She paused from time to time, out of breath, to rub her pregnant belly, and Ming Lun redoubled her wailing and reaching, but Mama only clucked her tongue and lurched into motion again.

The door banged open, and Papa was there, shouting. Two men came behind him, and his back suddenly bristled with feathery sticks. Arrows, she knew now, but the child-Ming could only gape at the armored strangers who burst into the room, her father's body still hanging from the door by the arrows that slew him. Mama started weeping. As if, even then, she had been sensitive for a cue, Ming Lun started crying, too, her arms stretching.

The strangers growled and jabbed their bows, resembling bears with their guttural speech and furred clothing. Mama held out a bundle of food, grinning madly, a smile almost more frightening than the men themselves.

The Mongols laughed, and one of them put away his bow, shoving her mother until she lay on the table nearby, pleading. The man prodded her belly, scowling, then he swept a big knife from his belt, big as the one Papa used on watermelons, and he sliced it across her mother's throat. They scooped up the bundles of food and glanced around the house. One of them stared at Ming Lun, the bloody knife still in his grip beneath the armload of food, then he shrugged and stomped out.

Trapped in the child-minder, Ming Lun stretched toward her mother's hand, twitching on the tabletop nearby, their fingers separated by a handspan, never to meet.

Now, almost thirty years later, she danced for the enemy with wicked strength, concealing her hatred in the perfection of her movement, planning when to strike her next blow against them. She arched and twisted, swaying through the breezes of springtime, her fingertips stroking the air, her face uplifted in an imitation of joy. Summer's long drought brought slow, careful paces, a series of movements that imitated peasants at work. At last, the harvest festivals had her leaping, landing without sound, kicking out, spiraling, her sleeves outflung into a whirlwind of color that fluttered down as she struck the final pose, chin thrust up, fingers poised. She lowered herself into a half-split that allowed her forehead, ever so lightly, to touch the sole of her upturned foot, her knee bent before her, her spine arched, then rising in a sweep of her head.

For a moment, the men sat silent. The drakemaster's vivid eyes caught hers, his lips parted, nearly smiling.

"What was that?" the khan demanded. "Opera? We don't have opera dancing here. Go back to the other side—nobody wants to see that!" The seven drunk captains laughed, the dwarf snickered. The slave behind him gripped his bracelet and dropped his gaze, his cheeks lightly flushed, straw-colored hair parting against his too-pale neck.

Ming Lun rose up in a fluid motion, plucked free her flute and began a new, sprightly tune that called the girls out for another roar of approval. She receded among them and turned her gaze from the drakemaster's throat.

Ming Lun's overlarge feet carried her back to the musicians, but she played the trill that would finish the dance, and the girls all swept into their final poses.

The Mongols roared again and slapped their thighs. The girls, trotting back to their resting place, tittered behind their draped sleeves.

"My lord," said one of the captains, rising and bowing until the khan acknowledged him. "If it is beauty you seek tonight, then forget all you see here. I have a gift for you, a treasure found in the mountains and brought here with greatest care, in a seat carved of sandalwood."

"My kind of treasure." The khan raised his bowl of airag. "Pray, deliver your gift."

A pair of servants swept aside the draped curtain across the ger's broad entrance and more of them carried a sedan chair to the edge of the carpet where they set it down, opening the door. A miniature foot stepped out, clad in a tiny, delicate slipper of red silk embellished with butterflies and flowers. The tip of a cinnabar cane accompanied this, then the lady rose from within the chair, a little wobbly. Dressed as elegantly as a lady of court, her movements betrayed her as a country girl, but likely only to Ming Lun's experienced eye. The lady stepped carefully forward, using her richly carved cane—itself a treasure—the skirt and sleeves of her gown trailing upon the rug, displaying an opulent wealth her family had likely gone bankrupt to provide. Her hair, twisted into careful knots, tinkled with ornaments of gold and pearl, but her face—Ai! Her face was exquisite. Her make-up was inexpert, but adequate, for it had little work to enhance her sculpted eyes and well-framed mouth.

Again, a hush fell over the men, then the khan slapped his thigh, and the others hooted and stamped their heels against the ground. The dwarf swallowed hard and kept blinking as if he could not believe his eyes. Seduction would be highly effective there, possibly even for Ming Lun, if it proved worthwhile to sway him, perhaps to separate him from his slave.

"Well done, captain! Well done indeed. Come, my pretty, let us see you."

Swaying as she moved, the lady crossed the carpet with a breath of perfume and a rustle of silk. The lady bowed slightly before the khan; beauty excused almost anything, in Ming Lun's experience. She turned a slow circle, not ungraceful in spite of being untutored. The family would have done better to save their money on fancy canes and slippers and get the girl a proper instructor instead. Her mother, at least, should have done something about the defect.

The khan stood up and circled round her himself. "What's your name?"

"My father called me Bao Xing," the lady answered in a high, sweet voice.

"'Treasure star', isn't that what it means? An unusual name, yet it suits you." He reached out to run his thumb along the lady's jaw and sigh. "I have a rule that I only take wives and concubines from my own people, lady, though for you, I am tempted to break it."

The men around him hollered, but the lady's face, tipped away, betrayed a sudden flinch of concern. So the beauty had a plan to seduce the khan himself, and now she failed it.

"My lord khan," the beauty said carefully, "my father has little but his tower. He sent me here to join your household, in the hopes that you will trouble his own humble place no further."

Ming Lun resettled on her knees, letting her glance flick around the ger again, catching the pale slave staring at her, unsure who dropped their eyes first. Could he possibly know why she was here? How had she betrayed herself? Ming Lun's spine felt tight as a bowstring.

"I am sure we can find a place for you at court, my dear," the khan said kindly. "Do you sing? Dance? Play an instrument?" He gave a snort of disbelief at the shake of her decorated head. "What talents do you have?"

"I can read and write in the Mandarin script, my lord," she answered hesitantly. "I can both write and recite poetry, I am familiar with all of the classics, and I can read—" she broke off.

"Reading again? You've already said that." An indulgent chuckle swept the room.

"The stars, my lord. I can read the stars."

"No matter—my wives can teach you some useful skills, if need be. If not, well, you can bloom in my palace garden." He beamed at her, and she bowed again. "Come, sit by me." With a pushing gesture, he indicated that the dwarf should move. The man vacated his own cushion, relegating his slave to the latticework at the back of the ger.

"Yes, my lord, certainly," the little man said, his queer voice catching the beauty's ear so that she tipped her head, gave a twitch like a stuck deer, and then settled onto the offered cushion, gripping her cinnabar cane too tightly on her lap. If Ming Lun had not been watching so closely, she might have missed the sparkle of tears that edged the corners of Bao Xing's eyes.

CHAPTER SIX

Yusen stared down at the spectacular creature who now occupied the cushion he had coveted for years. All of his life, he had been shut out of places like this, and now he found the khan's ger as packed with wonders as he had ever imagined. Bao Xing was stunning. The dancing girls were lovely, graceful and giggling. Even their teacher displayed great skill. The spicy grease of the lamb clung to his teeth to be sucked on and enjoyed as he witnessed all of this.

"Yusen! Still on your feet? Perhaps you wish to dance for us?"

Flustered, Yusen shook his head. "No, my lord, I just—" but the other men snickered, and Yusen found himself rudely returned to the world he tried at every moment to leave behind.

"A story then? Come, bring out your slave."

Yusen gestured toward the bell maker who unfolded himself from the back wall and edged around the lady to come to Yusen's side, slouching, and sinking to his knees, to touch his forehead to the ground. At least the man had some humility. Yusen needed to keep a sharp eye lest the khan's notice returned his slave to his arrogant beginnings. "I am humbled and honored, my lord, that you have allowed my slave to serve in the great work."

"Stand up. Come on, all the way." The khan flapped his hand impatiently, urging the bell maker to his feet.

Very slowly, head still bowed, the slave rose up. He kept his spine bent, his knees slightly bent, and still he towered over Yusen, causing a spark of pride that lifted Yusen's chin. Yusen, of all people, had captured a giant.

"All the way," the khan growled, and the slave complied, straightening himself with a tiny sigh, until he reached his full height, eyes forward, nearly double Yusen's own height.

The other men shared glances, twitched their eyebrows, and stifled their laughter.

"Tell us how this happened, Yusen. How did you come to be the master of such a creature?" The khan's eyes, too, twinkled.

"I was a scout with the tumaan of your noble cousin, Batu, in the expedition to the west. I was there at the great victory of the river

Danube—" He stumbled over the foreign word. "Not far to the north, those people were building one of their god-houses, a great place of piled stones to capture spirits in." He used his hands to sketch out what he had seen.

"To one side, my lord, I noticed a foundry not unlike your own, and men working there. I was alone, seeking a ford or bridge along the river, so I had no others to aid me."

"Very brave! Go on."

Yusen swelled beneath the praise. "I knew such workers could be of use in the army, so I watched a long time, until I identified their leader. That night, as the workers began to go home to their stone houses, the leader stayed, to inspect his castings. I rode down hard and stretched my bow. I didn't want to kill him, but to capture him for your honor." He mimed stretching the bow, rising in the stirrups and sighting along the arrow, then let it fly.

"I struck his leg before he ever knew I was coming. He shouted, but his companions were far off then. When they turned to see what had happened, quickly I shot them, too, but they had nothing to offer the armies of the khan, and so I killed them.

"The bell maker tried to escape me. He cried aloud for the aid of their hanged god and formed signs against me. He even took up one of the rods he used at the furnace as a weapon, but I circled my horse, and his injured leg could not support him in a pivot like that. When he fell, I struck him—again, careful to preserve him for your army. I dragged him up onto my horse and bound his hands and feet to the saddle, then rode with him east, as hard as I could." Yusen added a silent prayer of gratitude to the Eternal Sky for the strength of his horse Tsang to carry them both, and the swiftness that brought them back out of enemy lands.

"When I reached Batu's tumaan, I did not reveal the man's skill—I feared that your kinsman might rather keep such a one for himself. I only asked the aid of the shaman to tend his wound so he would not die of it before I brought him to you.

"It was months before we could return to the motherland, and then months again to follow where you had gone, my lord." Yusen bowed his head slightly, as if acknowledging his leader, but bile stung his throat. Should he now tell how the khan's ministers had laughed at him and prevented him from offering his prize? No, better not to sour the moment.

"During that time, the bell maker healed, and I encouraged him in our language, as well as that of the Chin prisoners. I offered his service to Wang Lin Yo under Master Sheng to learn how firedrakes are made, and he has served well there. Much as I regret the fall of your justly famous drakemaster, I also give thanks to the Eternal Sky that his death gave the chance to bring my slave to your attention."

The khan tapped his finger on his thigh. "As I recall, it was the slave himself who did that. I had thought you would teach him better manners. Still and all, it was boldly done, Yusen. Tomorrow, we shall see the results of his labor, and see if your boldness bears fruit. Tomorrow, yes, slave?"

The bell maker cleared his throat and answered, "Yes, my lord." Still staring at the wall straight ahead of him.

"So we know how you came to be here. Do you know how Yusen came to be?" The khan leaned forward, that sparkle still playing about his eyes, and Yusen's bowels clenched. If the khan hadn't been so close, he'd have given his slave a gentle kick to remind him to keep silent.

The bell maker's tawny head tipped, he frowned.

"Answer me—do you know? He's told us your story, have you heard his?"

"No, my lord?"

"I thought not." The khan grinned.

The slave's head sank a little lower, and Yusen braced himself for what came next.

"Will you tell it yourself, Yusen? Oh, but you've already told us one, and a very fine one at that." The khan lost his smile. "Very well, then, I shall tell it myself. No matter it is, after all, rather—short."

Even now, the khan would not allow him to escape his past. One of the captains snickered, and Yusen prepared for another humiliation, as if asking his slave such questions were not bad enough, as if a slave deserved any notice of his master's history.

"Years ago, some people in the eastern clans rose up against their Great Khan, my uncle Ogodei, son of Chinggis Khan himself!" A few cheers and stomps greeted the name of the supreme ruler. "These clans, considered loyal for so long, thought they might prefer a khan of their own. They were defeated in a great battle, but some of the leaders escaped into the mountains. Scouts tracked these traitors, these rebels who shared blood even with the khan himself, and so they found them, but the traitors were outnumbered so they faced the khan's justice."

The khan clapped his hands together, his eyes keen. "Chinggis Khan himself had made the law. The family of a traitor should be slain along with him, down to anyone taller than a cart wheel."

Kurdun. The word for wheel, the name that haunted Yusen from that day to this. At his side, the giant gave a little quiver of interest, and Yusen's hands clenched. He tucked them into the sleeves of his del. He could not show fury to the khan, of all people, nor would he reveal how this humiliation burned.

"Yusen was a middle son of that family, blood relative of the khan, but he stood no taller than a wheel. And has never grown an inch from that day forward." The khan stared at Yusen, reminding him not only of his lack of height, but also of his place as a traitor, a man to be suspected, to be watched and questioned and slain, regardless of his height, if he should ever say or do the wrong thing.

At last, the khan clapped his hands again and laughed. "So, not as good a story as yours, drakemaster. Sit, sit—shall we have another dance?"

The slave trailed Yusen to the pillows at the far side, there being no room by the khan any more, and they sat. Yusen's head pulsed, and he felt the stares of all the others who might not have heard the tale before, who looked down on him now, not only for his height, but for the past. He regretted the airag that scorched his throat and made his stomach queasy. When the first of the other captains rose to take his leave, Yusen rose likewise, bowing low, and stalked out into the night, his slave trailing at his heels. His horse knelt at a nudge, and Yusen sprang into the saddle. Nearby, a cart full of the khan's supplies waited to be unloaded, firelight silhouetting its wheels.

"Hand," he snapped. After a heartbeat, the slave offered his hand, the bracelet gleaming dully. Yusen hooked a chain through the loop on the bracelet and kicked his horse into a canter, the slave's long legs working to keep pace.

When they reached Yusen's small and ragged ger, on the far side of the furthest tumaan, Yusen slid down from his horse, seized the slave's wrist and dragged him inside, dropping him to his knees. In the feeble light of the stars outside and the coals of the brazier within, he caught the glint of the slave's pale eyes, still higher than his own.

"Two years! And you haven't learned to keep your mouth shut." Yusen grabbed the slave's jaw, bending his back until he had the advantage of height. He squeezed, grinding his short, strong fingers into the other man's cheeks. "I should cut out your accursed tongue, bell maker. Then the bell would sound no more."

And the khan's drakemaster would be unable to call his orders, to direct his men, to do the great work that might bring glory on them both. Yusen flung him down, letting him sprawl face first on the mats. He closed a lock through the bracelet's loop, chaining his slave to a post sunk in the ground.

"What will it take for you to learn?"

"Master," the slave said, barely a whisper from his unseen face.

"Quiet." Yusen turned to his gear and located a stiff bamboo cane. "Take off your trousers."

For a moment, the slave lay still. The trousers and shirt—too short as any of their clothing would be—were new for their dinner with the khan. Yusen gave a menacing growl, and the slave wriggled to comply, his free hand fumbling at the ties, shoving until he'd managed to kick the trousers down around his knees, and lay there breathless.

Yusen smacked the cane across the slave's bare thighs. The flesh twitched, and the man stifled a yelp, drawing his free hand back up to his concealed face. That first blow landed very near the round, puckered scar where Yusen's arrow had taken him down. It was Yusen's right, his duty, even, to ensure that his slave knew how to behave among the Mongols. The captains already thought Yusen too small and too weak, more a child than a man—what must they think if he could not even handle the slave he had captured? Lash after lash crossed the slave's skin, raising nasty red welts. The slave had lost weight in the two years since his capture, and the lines of his lean muscles showed clear beneath his skin. Working under the hot sun in nothing more than a loincloth had made him nearly as bronze as the metals he cast. Such punishments had been more satisfying when the slave was still as pale as a fishbelly and the red marks stood out like a calligraphy of shame, signaling to all that Yusen was the master.

Yusen gave another sharp lash and winced without sound. Such punishments had been more satisfying when the slave's big, stupid, never-shut mouth had not talked him into a place as the khan's drakemaster, had not brought Yusen to the khan's side, to eat with him, to share his airag and to see the most beautiful woman in the world.

The cane dangling from his hand, Yusen stared down at his slave. Laid out along the ground, the man's body looked tall and awkward, his thighs tracked with anger, his shoulders shaking and the breath shuddering from his narrow chest. His free hand covered his face and Yusen could not tell if he was weeping with the pain, or covering his mouth so that he made no sound. His chained arm stretched out, his hand gripped around the chain, knuckles white with clinging.

Yusen's own breath shuddered, his shadow stretching as it crossed the stricken slave, for once, towering over him. Never in his life had he felt so small.

CHAPTER SEVEN

Beneath the smoky sky on the outskirts of Kaifeng, Zhencai tensed, taking his stance, then forced himself to relax and master his breathing. His hands—hard as iron—circled slowly before him and came to rest. He pushed his qi into the backs of his eyes as if he could project it before him, shooting forth his will like arrows into the hearts of his enemies.

"Give up, old man!" shouted the Mongol, waving his sword back and forth. "Your hands can't match my blade."

The fires of the Mongol camp, the camp Zhencai had painstakingly snuck around, after managing to dodge the army these past two weeks, lit the Mongol watchman from behind as if he were a demon, firelight glancing off his conical helmet and the plates that wrapped his chest. No, even the arrow of Zhencai's will could not pierce such metal. In that case, his hands must do. The young man's two companions lounged back, grinning, laughing. They passed between them a jug of something they had stolen from the wreckage of some other place, waiting to see their bold leader chop the head from another monk. Zhencai's qi grew hot and his teeth clenched as he forced it down. Too attached. A man too attached to the world could never master the emptiness required to move swiftly and surely. He shifted a little to his back foot, taking another breath. Release attachments, and allow the enemy to become him, to flow to him, through him, and be defeated.

Taking his movement for retreat, the young Mongol lunged forward with a low sweep of the sword.

By the time the breeze of its coming sliced the air, Zhencai was gone. With a swoosh of his loose pants and a twist of his hips, the monk stepped aside, seized the Mongol's wrist, and delivered the entire strength of his body into a blow with his other hand, straight to the elbow of the extended arm. His iron hand cracked into the joint, power rushing from his muscles through the other man's bone. The wrist wrenched back as bones ground. The young man howled, his momentum carrying him past, out of his own control. Zhencai guided his movement with a turn of his body, swinging him down to tumble across the ashen yard, screaming, sword dragging useless.

With a shout of his own, one of the other Mongols dropped the jug and brought up his blade. His fellow leapt with him, the pair automatically separating, forcing Zhencai to divide his attention. The first was a gangly youth, his hands still too big for his body, his training good, but his muscles untuned, like an instrument untempered by time. The second prowled, bulky with strength, keeping his center low and hard to unbalance.

Slicing his hands together through the air and back again, Zhencai pivoted with them, tracking the first with his eyes. When the second took a sharp breath, Zhencai transferred his weight to his forward foot in a lean as if he would lunge, then swung his rear foot off the ground in an arc that smacked his bare foot into the stocky man's chest, his sword still raised above his head.

The breath puffed from his lungs as he staggered. His glance shifted in spite of his shock, revealing the skinny boy's position. Zhencai let his kick carry him around and down, dropping to swing his foot again just above the earth. Still, the skinny boy's blade nicked his cheek as he thrust forward to take advantage of Zhencai's exposed back.

The boy recovered well, already retracting his blade for a backswing, but Zhencai's hand shot out, his fingers extending, and rammed upward as the boy stood over him. He channeled his force and felt a little queasy as his hardened fingers, locked together into a weapon, struck the boy's testicles and ground his soft flesh.

The boy yelped, his fighting stance destroyed. Zhencai brought him down sideways with a casual tap to the back of his knee.

Grunting, the stocky man gripped his sword tighter. Jumping his skinny friend, he came on again. "Come on, old man—I'll send you to your nirvana! If it's nothingness you crave, I'll give it to you."

Their eyes met, and the force of the young man's qi shone with a ferocious passion. Anger slew form. It slew more warriors than a naked blade. They circled, Zhencai trying to draw the Mongol toward his writhing, cursing companions, hopeful of a distraction, a goad for the swordsman's anger, but this was no mere boy on his first campaign. The Mongol's blade cut and poked, herding Zhencai toward empty ground, away from the city, closer to the encampment.

"You can't stand against me, against the whole of the Mongol army, you fool. I've stripped the silks from a hundred monks and my saddlebags bulge with the heads of golden Buddhas." The Mongol pounced and dodged, the flat of his blade smacking Zhencai's arm as they met and parted.

"No—not a hundred monks, a hundred and eight!" The Mongol let out a cackle of laughter.

A hundred and eight, the sacred number. Zhencai growled and lunged. Clumsy! His iron fist missed its target but the Mongol's sword opened a gash on his thigh. He barely escaped losing a leg. Anger slew form. Zhencai retreated, struggling for breath, for poise.

"No pagoda gardens for them," said the Mongol, then rushed forward. Another flurry of blows, a slash that cut Zhencai's sleeve. "Well, aside from the ones I killed there."

In the pagoda garden. The graveyard. Zhencai remembered the quiet stone pillars splashed with blood, dead monks strewn about, their guts spilling onto the carefully tended ground, their bowels releasing. At the sound of the bell, Zhencai turned away from Master Deng and left his duty on the mountain top. He bounded down the long steps to come to that scene—the slaughter of his brethren, the temple already burning, the Mongols already victorious. Zhencai considered attacking them, one man against the dozens of the Mongol party. Then he considered Master Deng, the dead gilded monk who spoke of scrolls and danger, who stood up and walked away into the hills. The only clues Zhencai possessed from their brief talk pointed toward history, and the scrolls sent to Kaifeng. The Buddha's hand pointed him toward this mystery—it was not one he could simply abandon. Not as he must abandon the spirits of the dead.

Snarling, he burst forward, into the Mongol's attack. The Mongol's heavy-lidded eyes sprang wide, his sword coming down, but Zhencai's careless action carried him under, his head slamming the other man's chest. They went down together in a graceless sprawl, the sword slapping his back, the Mongol's free hand grabbing the neck of his robe.

Wrestling with a man whose people considered wrestling one of the highest manly arts. Stupid! Zhencai's stomach churned as he twisted, punched and tried to break free. He rammed his iron fist against the Mongol's throat, and the man gagged, his arms loosening. Zhencai focused his qi, trying to regain his detachment and punched again, harder. The

Mongol had wriggled beneath him, half-rising. His fist found the Mongol's temple.

Zhencai's blow wrenched the man's head around. His neck gave a crunch like a handful of twigs snapped to start a fire. The Mongol's arms went limp and all his qi evaporated, his eyes gazing at nothing.

Pushing away from the body, Zhencai stumbled on his wounded leg, winced and righted himself, then put on a stern attitude. He settled his face into impassive lines, the open readiness of the abbot—whose guts stained the pagodas of the memorial garden. Zhencai thrust away that vision, drawing up other memories of the abbot, pretending for a moment that he could ever become as wise. His iron hands throbbed as he formed the gesture of blessing for the dead, his lips trembled as he formed the name of the Buddha.

The broken-armed Mongol merely huddled on the ground, weeping and moaning. The other one—still gasping—made as if to struggle up, but Zhencai, still imagining himself as someone else, stared him down, his hands poised for another blessing.

Recognizing the threat, the skinny boy subsided, but his hand groped about for his sword.

Zhencai kicked it away as he departed, tall and proud and fierce, wearing the aspect of his old teacher until he rounded the city wall away from the camp, hidden from his audience. His wounded leg trembled, his wrists and forearms aching, all his years of training for the strength of iron coming to this, that he was nearly beaten by three boys because he could not control his own will. What good to pretend himself powerful, wise, compassionate? Zhencai's body ached from his battering victory, and his spirit ached from his failure. The city of Kaifeng hunched in the night, gripped by fear, surrounded by the Mongol army save for the river that still flowed beyond. Zhencai searched for a way inside, to bind his wound, to find the scrolls that could tell him the truth about Master Deng. Detachment, his abbot preached: do not be disturbed by possible outcomes, as if it were so easy for a man to give up hope, or even despair.

In a few days, Kaifeng would be besieged, battered by an army she could not hope to withstand. Within the month, Kaifeng would stand as open, empty and broken as Zhencai himself. Before that happened, he must find the missing scrolls and learn about Su Sung's astronomical clock, the device the dead monk had mentioned. Was this merely another form of attachment? Zhencai had given up Nirvana to pursue it. Years ago, when young Zhencai complained of the hardships at the monastery, the abbot answered with a story:

A stonecutter went to select stones for a monument to honor his ancestors and reach into the heavens. When he found a good stone, he placed it upon his back. Before long, he carried many, many stones. As he went, his back bowed and he shrank beneath his growing burden. When he could no longer carry them, he gave up his burden. And it was he, himself, who reached to the heavens.

"He died, Father Abbot, is that what it means?" Zhencai asked.

"A man carries many burdens in this world of suffering."

"So he built the monument, and that's how he did it, by giving honor." The abbot smiled. "Honor itself can be a burden."

"He can't have just given up—a man can't achieve Nirvana that way."

Forming the sign of blessing, the abbot said, "Perhaps it was his attachment to outcomes that he set aside."

Picturing the abbot on that long-ago day, Zhencai imagined pity and indulgence in the old man's eyes. Last time he had seen him, the abbot lay sprawled in the pagoda garden, his eyes open to the sky, his burden given up, his Nirvana achieved. On the mountain above, nearly two dozen gilded monks watched over their valley, every hand in a posture of blessing, in eternal contemplation. Zhencai had always imagined the abbot one day joining them. He never imagined that one of them might leave, nor that it would fall to Zhencai to learn the reason why.

CHAPTER EIGHT

"Mistress," whispered one of Ming Lun's girls, focusing on the country beauty across the tent.

Ming Lun set down the case of flutes as she arranged their belongings in the tent they'd been assigned. "What is it?"

"Her…the lady. She has feet like mine, hasn't she? Like all of ours—well, not yours." The girl gripped opposite sleeves with her pale hands. "I thought we wouldn't see any—"

"Hush." Ming Lun gently tapped the girl's forehead. "We all must settle for the night, even the lady."

Across the broad tent, one of the few Chinese tents in the Mongol encampment, Bao Xing swayed, her glance flicking in each direction. Taking in her surroundings as Ming Lun herself might do?

But no. The beauty was still crying, very gently, and flicked her eyes as a way to clear the tears without taking her hands from their very long sleeves. As Ming Lun watched, the lady finally did, sweeping back her sleeves impatiently and wiping her eyes. The tips of her right-hand fingers looked dark in the lantern's light, as if she spent all day at calligraphy. Had she mentioned that among her catalog of unladylike skills? A mystery, this doll-like creature who wore a disguise as surely as did Ming Lun—but not a mystery for her to solve.

"Oh!" sighed one of the other girls. "She's so sad. What if she has had to leave her lover to come here?" Two others joined in the sighing, and Ming Lun thrust her hand sharply across their vision.

"She is a lady, not an opera. She has left no lover. Neither is she likely to spring upon horseback and conquer an army." Ming Lun drew back her hand and struck a pose like the heroine of that famous story, making her gaze fierce and her hand like a sword. The girls giggled. "To bed, all of you. Here's your posset." She took a clay jar from the brazier where she had warmed it and gave each of them a sip as they nestled into their mound of blankets.

As the last girl swallowed, she clung to the jar, resisting Ming Lun's attempt to cork it. "We should give some to the lady, too, so she can sleep."

"Oh, yes," murmured the others, nodding and making little pushing gestures with their eyes and hands.

Ming Lun sighed as if put-upon, but the suggestion suited her own needs. "It's expensive, you know."

"We are dancing for the khan, now, Lun." The girl squared her shoulders and pushed up her small breasts. "There will be greater rewards, won't there?"

The School of the Soaring Lark should have been dancing for the emperor, for the Son of Heaven himself, not for these invaders, but Ming Lun laughed. "Indeed there will." The reward of stopping the invaders, for one. She bowed gracefully and moved to where Bao Xing had just settled onto a low mattress, her cane resting across her knees as she reached to remove the golden ornaments from her hair. Two of the pins stuck out of her mouth as she wrestled with a third one, her drawn-on brows arching up at Ming Lun's approach. Letting go her hair with one hand, she plucked the pins from her lips, but before she could speak, Ming Lun deftly took hold of the butterfly comb still tangled in her hair, and slipped it free, handing it over with a smile.

Bao Xing clutched the ornaments tightly. "Thank you."

Her speech indicated she had been far from court these last years. Ming Lun smiled. "My dancers suggested you might need help sleeping tonight. I brew them this posset, to ease their minds. Would you like a sip?"

Bao Xing's tumbled hair stroked the cane in her lap. "I might need that. Thank you again."

Ming Lun sank to her knees before the other woman. "They're very curious about you. We rarely meet anyone else with lotus-blossom feet, much less anyone who's not a dancer."

Bao Xing flinched away, depositing the combs into a silken pouch at the head of her bed. "It was my mother's work."

A beauty who did not prize what made her so? Curious indeed. "And now you are to live in the palace of the khan. Your mother must be proud."

"I should light incense at an altar in her name." Bao Xing flicked away another tear. Ink on her fingers, most definitely. "Thank you for your kindness."

"You are in the women's realm now, lady. Take comfort." Ming Lun held up the jar, and Bao Xing sniffed its mouth, then took a careful swallow. Her hair released from its elaborate tracing, Bao Xing lay down and stared upward, as if she could see something past the silken roof.

"A story?" suggested a small, piping voice from the mounds of blankets, a plea immediately echoed by a half-dozen more. Even Xiajin, the instrumentalist, looked eagerly toward their leader.

These foolish girls, all orphans like her, spoke of her almost like a mother, and she wondered if any of them would light incense at an altar for her. The idea of herself, flat-footed, aging Ming Lun, as an honored ancestor, was worthy of laughter, and they did not even know the truth.

"Long ago," Ming Lun began, and the girls huddled together, bright-eyed, as she spread her arms, then swept a rippling hand across the air to show the passage of time, "the empire had grown weak with gold and luxury. Ah!" She leapt in place and settled lightly, earning a gasp. "You wonder how it is possible, how luxury leads to weakness. Well, my children, know this: when a man has too much, he cannot tend to it all, and so he grows flabby." She let her muscles relax, dropping into a loose-limbed, fat-man walk, rolling about the small space between their blankets and the lady's couch. The girls giggled, and even Bao Xing gave a tiny smile.

"Can a flabby man fight?" She tried to marshal her wobbly limbs into a warrior's stance, but collapsed again to their great delight. "Can a flabby man make strong children?" She gave a little thrust of her hips, and the girls, scandalized, but at an age where they must know of such things, covered their mouths beneath huge eyes. "Can a flabby man think clearly enough to run his empire?" She rubbed her fingers on the top of her head, plucked her chin, then mimed raising a giant goblet instead, quaffing the contents, then leering at Bao Xing, eyebrows wriggling. "He cannot!" Ming Lun snapped herself back to strength.

"And so, this flabby man, this man who claimed the mantle of the Son of Heaven, had a great party, in the gardens of this very city, this Kaifeng, upon whose plains we now are camped." Her hands sketched out the towers, the pagodas, the streams and pathways of the garden, then she walked through them, imagining the flowering cherries, nodding to imaginary ladies, and to real girls.

"But when he arose from his throne to greet his many guests, a fox leapt up and sat there in his place." With a sinuous movement, and a spring that landed her on fingertips and toes, squatting in imitation of the fox, Ming Lun licked a paw and panted. Giggling.

Ming Lun swirled herself back up again. "And those present whispered that this flabby man would be undone—and so he was! Barbarians swept down from the plains like a sandstorm to overwhelm his throne, and he was neither warrior nor thinker, and so his empire began to unravel like a silk cocoon." She imagined the cocoon, then stretched the thin thread between her fingers, riveted by it.

"Wait—what was the other thing?" She held that imaginary thread. "I said a flabby man could not think, that he could not fight—what was the other thing he might not do?"

Lots of giggling now, then one of the girls blurted, "Sire great children!"

"Ah! But perhaps he did…" She followed the invisible strand of silk to its bright and distant end. "He did, indeed! Among his weak and flabby children, there was a boy no older than yourselves—younger, even! And this boy, with his clever nurse and clever mother, escaped the fall of his father's family, and rode south as quick as ever he might.

"There, in the land of silk and of rice, this clever boy claimed a new empire. He built it of stone and law, he built it with great halls for justice, and great temples for the ancestors, and great walls to keep it safe. He learned of all his father had forgotten, and he taught it to his children. He taught them of beauty, yes, and luxury, but he taught them, too, of war and wisdom, and he defied the fox that stole his father's throne. And his grandchildren defy it still." She repeated the movements of the fox, then mimed the warrior, slaying the thief and standing proud. A long breath, then she sank into a curtsey to the girls' applause.

"Now, to bed!"

"Will we ever go there?" murmured one yawning child. "To the south?"

Was Bao Xing a follower of the Son of Heaven, a believer in the lark? Her tears and her bound feet suggested that she was. Still… Ming Lun leaned very close to the little dancer and whispered, "Perhaps, if we are lucky, the south will come to us."

Turning away, she made a great show of laying out her own

bedclothes near the doorway and finding places for their trousseau of costumes and instruments.

By the time Ming Lun glided back to her little dancers, most of them were already snoring lightly, dreaming their way into story.

She went about settling the rest of their belongings, until not a sliver of a drowsy eye could be seen beneath the flutter of lashes, even of the lady across the way. As she worked, she thought of another story entirely.

Years ago, in the School of the Falling Waters, an orphan named Ming Lun wept for the parents she would never know, parents slain by the Mongols, and a dancing mistress kept her strong with stories. She had no family to honor, and so her devotions turned to the Han people, and the man who should lead them. A dancer showed her how to be proud, to be graceful, to be silent—to move swiftly and be invisible among men, listening, learning. Few of the dancers could be so resolute, so detached that they turned easily from dancing in the light to sliding through the darkness, but Ming Lun could. She never understood what her mistress was listening for, why she did not turn these whispers to the ruin of their enemies, and so Ming Lun turned to other masters whose mandate came down from the emperor himself. At this, she excelled, passing even the final test—the test that left her body sore, her breasts aching, her place among the larks secured in blood and flesh. She gave up a woman's pride, a virgin's treasure, fashioning herself into a whore at the behest of her masters, in service to the Son of Heaven.

Nine months later, she entered an apprenticeship of knives and powders, codes and secrets. A warrior's skills overlaid the dancer's. Her mistress professed service to the Han people, but would never condone this transformation. No matter. Ming Lun honored what she learned from her dance mistress, founding a new school in honor of the lark. That duty led her to the khan's encampment where she could fulfill a greater cause.

She silently took up the flute case again. Her fingers traced the form of a dragon carved into the side until they came to the hidden catch and squeezed it open. From the muffled compartment below, she took a different flute, a packet of darts that fit inside the binding at her sleeve, and a pair of hair-picks joined by a deceptively light chain. These she worked into her braid, separating them so the chain did not jingle. Hard to know what she might need when she found the drakemaster. He nearly nodded off at the khan's celebration, so likely he would sleep deeply enough to be taken without even waking. Perhaps a long, thin needle to the heart, or, a brush of poison in a sensitive place that could mimic another kind of death. She had not anticipated the Mongol shaman would notice the dart-prick that took down the last drakemaster: a risk, aiming for the man instead of the horse, but she couldn't have been certain that he would die when the horse fell.

The army lay so near Kaifeng, and the bronze had been poured for the great firedrake to break the gates. If she had the chance, she should slay the weapon as well as its master.

Ming Lun replaced the case and stepped between the girls, heading for a loose corner of the tent where it abutted another tent for the khan's female attendants. Crouching low, Ming Lun slid outside. She froze a long moment, listening. Leather creaked, closer than the giggles of men and women at play, or the groan of wind in the tent ropes.

She hurried in shadows toward the front of the tent. There, in the moonlight, stood a figure she nearly took for a child, but for the soldier's del and glint of a weapon. Yusen: the dwarf Mongol, despised by all the rest. He shifted his weight from one foot to the other, turned as if to go, then looked back again, scowling.

Where had he left his troublesome slave?

Ming Lun retraced her steps, rounded the far corner of the tent, then stepped away from it, ducking her head, letting hurried footsteps carry her directly into him.

"Ai!" She covered her mouth immediately, letting her eyes go wide. "Forgive me, Captain." She heavily accented her Mongolian, stumbling over the words. She made as if to dodge past, but the little man caught her arm.

"Where are you going at this hour?" he demanded, his other hand already at his sword.

"Please, Captain," she said, sinking closer to his level, leaning toward him. "I think you know what a woman might do at such an hour."

Yusen caught his breath and stepped away, keeping her at arm's length.

"Surely, you would not begrudge one of your countrymen his passion." She sank a little further, tilting her face to look up into his shadowed eyes. "I cannot entertain in here—"she nodded toward the women's tent—"surrounded by dancing girls and the khan's women. As it was, the other captain's slaves saw a show of his... skill during my visit." She tried a slender smile. His eyes flicked when she mentioned slaves, then narrowed. She guessed rightly: he, too, had his slave in his ger.

"All the ladies sleep in there?"

"The newcomers, yes. I hope it is not forbidden for me to... entertain. I hope you will not reveal me." She turned her captured arm so her fingers rested on his chest. His heart thundered beneath her touch. Good.

He stared down at her, his face difficult to read, folds of skin at the corners of his eyes adding more shadows. Unlike other dwarfs she had seen, Yusen's body was well-proportioned in the way of a child rather than long of torso. His hand held the strength of a fighting man, his arms muscular. She could escape him if need be. None expected such strength or speed from a woman.

"Of course, if you, too, need entertainment, Captain, we might aid each other." She let the tip of her tongue linger on her parted lips, tipping her head up. It was hard to maintain the posture, but the very image of a woman looking up to him might be enough.

He glanced back to the tent, then gave a tug that drew her to her feet. "Come." He let go of her immediately and set off down the long aisle of tents, dodging the silken ropes and the round stones that held them taut.

Elated by her success, Ming Lun followed, watching everything, ensuring she could find her way back—or out. Her instinct about him had been right; he knew too little of the company of women. Her lack of classic beauty served her well: men readily believed her desperate, absent the wiles learned by more refined women. She prided herself on how few of them ever realized their mistake.

Moonlight limned the larger, more colorful silk pavilions of Chinese design, and the round felt ones of the Mongols. The night hummed with the sound of snoring men, guards playing at knucklebones, and somewhere, the two-stringed, horse-headed fiddle that passed for music. They angled west, approaching the guardposts of the khan's encampment, a pair of armed men at a small fire.

"Who?" one of the men called out, then, with a startled laugh, "Cartwheel! Finished your business already?"

The other man tapped him with a sword tip and waved it toward Ming Lun, who stood back, her head lowered. "Looks to me like he's bringing some business back to the ger."

"Surely even a washerwoman could do better than him. His weapon can't be more than a chopstick!"

Both men snorted with laughter.

Yusen marched straight ahead, his back as stiff as a spear even as the guardsmen chuckled in his wake. Then, barely missing a stride, the little man slipped free his sword with a spin that smacked the flat of the blade across the bigger man's knee. The guard landed in the dirt with a yelp as Yusen resheathed his sword and resumed his stride. "Next time, mind your own weapon!"

Trailing after, Ming Lun smiled to herself. A graceful, well-executed maneuver, reminding the others that they might not appreciate the height of the little man's blade. Given his status in the ranks here, might he be open to recruitment? She would inquire in that direction when she had him comfortably in bed. The question of what else they might do there crossed her mind, but she did not dwell on it. Some dances she performed from memory, others must be improvised.

Between the camps of the khan's army, they passed the rough-hewn roofs of workshops and armories, through the acrid smell of heated metal and singed straw. She added this to the map of the encampment in her mind. The next camp they entered was more sparsely guarded, facing as it did, the khan's own encampment. Good.

The difficulty with slaying the drakemaster or ruining his weapons tonight would be that Yusen would know she had been here. Some atmospheric poison in a brazier might take the drakemaster and Yusen both, but the border guards were aware of her destination. Ming Lun's hopes deflated. She could gain access to the drakemaster, but to take advantage of it would ruin her place in the khan's encampment.

A group of slaves lay sleeping in the shadow of a broad roof, one of them on his side, staring at Yusen and Ming Lun as they passed. Young, Chinese. She hoped she wouldn't have to kill him. Yusen's ger stood close by the workshops.

Saying, "Wait here," Yusen flicked open the cloth door and went inside.

Perhaps he prepared himself or his bedding—he had not likely expected female companionship tonight. Light grew at the edge of the door flap.

Inside, a muffled voice said, "Master?" with that curious accent that could only be the pale slave. Ming Lun's breath caught. So close!

"Quiet," Yusen ordered.

She waited outside, pacing a little, as the moon tracked across the stars. What would Bao Xing, star-reader, say about the sky tonight? Ming Lun cared only when the sky was bright enough to light a path—or dark enough to conceal one. Finally the door flap opened, and Ming Lun stepped forward, but the Mongol emerged, letting the door close behind him. He thrust something toward her.

"Give it to Bao Xing, the khan's new… gift." Then he fumbled at a pouch and handed over a coin as well. "Here's for your trouble." He stared at her darkly. "Don't tell her it's from me."

She nearly dropped the paper-wrapped packet as she accepted the coin, then stood, dumbfounded, when the door flap closed behind him, leaving her standing in the gloom, no closer than she had been to the drakemaster. He dragged her all the way here, to carry a gift for another woman? No matter: he had shown her the place, all that remained was to devise the means. At the time of her choosing one man, or both of them, could be dead.

CHAPTER NINE

Dailus woke with a start, trying to remember why he'd woken earlier. In spite of the stinging pain in his thighs, he had slept after Yusen's beating—one grim advantage of his enslavement was this ability to fall asleep regardless of circumstance. Yusen returned in the middle of the night, fired up his lantern and clattered about, and Dailus, after a single inquiry, remained silent until his master doused the light and sleep returned.

Wincing, Dailus tugged his trousers back up, trying to ease the fabric over the welts of his caning. The chain lay free of his left wrist—Yusen often unlocked it when he had trouble sleeping, so that Dailus could rise promptly and prepare his food. Dailus scrambled up to find the sack of grain and the pot and set about making his master's morning meal. On a raised bed draped with woolen blankets, Yusen slept facing the center of the ger. The ferocity eased from his face, leaving frown lines as if they had been painted on by one of those dancers.

Ah, the dancers! While everyone marveled over the other woman's tiny feet, Dailus found himself enthralled by the dancer who moved so readily through grace and power. Surely, it had been the most unChristian display he had ever witnessed—this was no courtly dance of lords and ladies, nor even the carefree delight of Mayday—and yet... no wonder men were tempted when they visited the east, and why so many who rode off on Crusade returned with a different light in their eyes. Women so bold—dancing barefoot, wearing trousers—would not be countenanced by the patriarchs of his home.

While his master lightly snored, their porridge bubbling on the brazier, Dailus pressed his hands together and tried to remember how to pray. "Hail Mary, full of grace..." but when he closed his eyes, the face he saw was dark and round, with slanting eyes, the costume heavily embroidered, the ankles bared and feet poised for dancing. "Our Father who art in Heaven..." he whispered fervently, clasping the tiny cross he had made from the flashing that edged a failed casting. Pray that yesterday's casting would be good. Perfect. Head bowed, the scent of cooked barley moistening his throat, Dailus acknowledged what woke him: excitement. Quite simply, he couldn't wait to open the mold.

How long had it been since such a chance awaited? This was the last mold made by Master Sheng, the slain Drakemaster. The mold seemed heavier than need be, with a core likely to float during the casting. He did all he could to ensure that the core would stay in place and centered, but an image formed behind his closed eyelids: a trough-like mold, poured on its side. Master Sheng had made some models that way—why not a full-sized firedrake? With an opening at the side where the balls would be set in, he could better control the position of the bore. The top-down mold, more similar to his own bell-making days, appealed, but might not be the right choice. What thunder would that great bell make now, in its new form?

He hoped he'd never need another mold. Last night, the khan gave Wang Lin Yo, a former slave, a paizi—the pass to depart from the khan's encampment, once Kaifeng had fallen. If Dailus and his casting succeeded, was it possible he, too, might earn his freedom? It was a wonder he had slept at all.

Blankets shifted, and Dailus dropped his hands from prayer, slipping the cross away. He gave the pot a stir, then scooped most of it into an engraved metal bowl for Yusen. How such a small person ate so much food, Dailus had no idea. At home, they'd have said he would be growing soon.

Dailus lifted his own bowl, but his throat constricted, his eyes blurred with a memory of Anya. *"Am I taller, Daddy? Surely I am!"* bobbing up on her tip-toes, bouncing and dancing, the Mayday flowers still sprinkled in her hair. *"I need more sugarcakes if I'll ever be as tall as you!"*

The bowl trembled in his hands, and Dailus blew on it, but the barley smelled bitter, tainted by the heathen hands that harvested it, by the heathen master who carried it.

"Today, bell maker!"

Dailus blinked a few times and looked up to acknowledge his master's words. Yusen's ill-humor after the celebration had entirely fled, replaced by a nervous energy in his eyes and fingers that brought Dailus's daughter back to mind. Thousands of miles away. Gripping his bowl, Dailus forced himself to drink the porridge and dispel the memory.

"Will we fire it today, or must we wait?"

We—as if Yusen owned the work the same way he owned the worker. "If the casting is true, master, and does not need cleaning, it might be fired today."

"Excellent. Perhaps the khan will..." but his triumphant grin tipped sideways and he resumed shoveling down his porridge.

Perhaps the khan would what? Taunt them again with women they could not touch? Force them to humiliate each other in front of all the captains? What part of the evening's entertainment made Yusen's sourness return? Perhaps the khan would leave them blessedly in peace. Perhaps—though Dailus dare not articulate this save in his deepest heart—perhaps the khan would one day let him go.

"May I go to the casting pit, master?"

Yusen wiped his mouth on his sleeve. "Yes, of course. I'll be there soon."

Dailus crept on his knees to where his pitiful work clothes waited in a pile and shrugged out of the silk tunic and trousers he had been given last night. A few flecks of blood clung to the trousers, along with the stinging welts reminding him it could have been worse. Dailus drank from the pitcher by the brazier, noting wearily that it needed refilling. He carried it into the dawn, to refill it at the well. This done, Dailus relieved his bladder at the nearest trench, and finally, his chin lifting and stride lengthening, walked to the casting pit.

The crew slaves stirred, grumbling in several languages, but he ignored them, stepping up to the edge of the pit. Yes, the overflow at the top still looked good, solid and cool, without the grainy texture that foretold disaster. Then his chest tightened, and Dailus dropped to his knees, leaning closer. A crack cut the ceramic mold from the second iron band to the third, dust and chips sprinkling the bands, down to the murky depth of the pit where a stone as big as his head rested alongside the mold.

Dailus sat back on his heels, sucked in a breath at the pain from his thighs, and pushed himself up again. "The ladder." He spun about. "I need the ladder."

Jian Ho dropped his bowl near the communal porridge pot and hurried to help him. Fetching the ladder, they stuck it down into the hole. Jian Ho steadied the top while Dailus climbed down, running his hand along the side of the mold. The crack spread in all directions, clearly showing the impact factures, but the metal inside? He wriggled his fingers into the crack and touched bronze, apparently smooth. No way to judge the damage until they had it free, except that clearly the mold could never be used again.

"What is it, fishbelly?" Wang Lin Yo stared down at him.

"A stone fell in last night and cracked the mold." Or someone had thrown it, a thought frightened and infuriated him at the same moment. Could a drunken soldier have kicked the stone off a nearby rope and never noticed?

"And the khan's firedrake?"

"I can't tell. We'll need to raise it."

The overseer glared down at him. "Very well. Stay there to fix the chains."

Within moments, the crew braced a frame over the top of the hole and fed down four chains to attach to the lowest band and lift the monstrously heavy mold free of the pit. Dailus worked on the chains, setting the hooks, stepping aside as the slaves above drew up the ladder to get it out of the way. They took hold of the chains above, Wang Lin Yo shouting the count to time their pulling. The huge thing swayed above Dailus, blocking most of the sky, and he wondered how much the overseer hated him. Not enough, surely, to drop the khan's firedrake on his head. A thousand pounds of ceramic and bronze could crush him like an ant beneath a heel.

At last, it swung ponderously out of the way, the crew hurrying to steady it.

Dailus's shoulders eased when Jian Ho reappeared, and he lowered the ladder to release the drakemaster from the pit. By the time he emerged, they already had the mold open, the cracked side splitting the rest of the way with a scraping sound like broken bone. Dailus hurried over, Jian Ho at his back and Wang Lin Yo blocking his view. "Please, overseer." He tamed his voice to politeness with only moderate success as the overseer's glare suggested.

Yusen and a few other Mongols gathered nearby, and Dailus spared them a bow as he squeezed close to the firedrake. It gleamed in the light of the new dawn, and he stared down the barrel as if sighting it against an enemy. And there, in the light of the brand new day, a tell-tale bulge and dip. A mis-cast bell might sound wrong. It might crack under the strain of tolling. A mis-cast weapon might explode and kill them all, but how could he tell if the flaw were dangerous?

Dailus motioned everyone away from the firedrake where it rested in a sling of ropes, the ruined mold in pieces on the ground. He rested his ear on the metal and gave the side a rap with his knuckles. The bronze responded with a dull resonance, not the clean, pure echo of a centered bore and thick wall, but the off-note of a problem. Dailus sagged against the side of the firedrake, his cheek resting against the metal.

"What is it?" Wang Lin Yo dragged Dailus up by the shoulder. "It is beautiful, fishbelly, why do you flop?"

"That stone cracked the mold before the metal cooled." He ran his hand over the spot. "Some of the metal shifted, leaving a weak spot."

The overseer shoved Dailus against the bronze, and it made a hollow sound that shivered through Dailus's spine. "Careless! Did you not inspect the grounds for stones?"

"They are on the tents, every rope." Dailus gestured toward the tents all around them, their sides held taut by stones, save one where the rope dangled loose without its stone anchor,

Yusen's head appeared on the other side of the firedrake, upside down in Dailus's view. Wang Lin Yo pulled Dailus up and slammed him against the firedrake again, hard enough that it jarred his teeth. "What will you do about it, fishbelly?"

"Another, a new one," he gulped. "We break up this one and re-melt it."

"But you have no molds, only models." All three of them glanced toward the drakemaster's workshop with its broad tables and miniature firedrakes.

"How long will it take?" Yusen interrupted.

"He would need to make a new mold," Wang Lin Yo replied. "If he even has the skill. Besides, this one seems perfectly sound. There is plenty of metal to sustain a charge."

"And if it explodes?" Dailus struggled to escape the overseer's grip.

"I was the overseer for Master Sheng, who knew more of casting than you ever will."

Yusen slapped the butt of his whip against the bronze near Dailus's head, staring at the overseer. "It is hardly his fault if someone kicks a stone into a pit. He has said he can make a new mold and so he will. The khan will require more than one in any case." He shifted his hard gaze to Dailus. "How long?"

A month, Dailus wanted to say, but the overseer's fingers dug into his flesh and his head still rang. "A week at least. I have the models. We can use a different kind of mold, an easier one."

"Fine. In the meantime, we test fire this one." Wang Lin Yo released him to slide to his knees on the ground beside the flawed firedrake.

"We could be killed, overseer."

"Not you, fishbelly, your assistants will fire it. That way, you can account for it to the khan." Wang Lin Yo strode away, pointing. "Jian Ho! You and these others must get the firedrake cleaned and ready to fire, tonight at the latest."

Christ and all his saints. Dailus pushed himself up, backing away from the firedrake to allow the others to get to work: polishing the bore, removing flashing from the air holes, fitting the wooden structure to support its great weight during firing. He walked over to Master Sheng's workshop, where few had trespassed since the Master's death. Sheng's models looked like a series of little vases, bulbous at one end to contain the explosion, with decoration like the painting on the old bamboo weapons these bronze ones replaced. Dailus hoped—he prayed—he was wrong about the flaw. In the meantime, he had a single day to create a model that would convince the khan to let him live if Sheng's last firedrake blew into a dozen shards.

Finding a brush and inkstone, Dailus ground out a bit of ink in the Chinese fashion, and dripped water into it, then started sketching on the tabletop. Some of the other weapons in Sheng's workshop—older things and things seized from the cities they had conquered—featured a side-opening which must be covered with a panel during firing, but could make the pouring and loading much easier. Whatever he developed must be impressive, beautiful as well as effective. The walls of the bore must be just the right thickness. But the exterior? As long as it did not impinge upon the central bore, it could be anything that would please the khan. Dailus sketched a few of the curly clouds the Tatars preferred—the Eternal Blue Sky—and what else? of course, horses. He drew them galloping down the side of the weapon, adding little flourishes like fire from their hooves. If the khan approved the design, he might ask for supplies to gild the fiery hooves—surely that would please the khan.

Across the yard, Wang Lin Yo directed the sawing, scraping and banging that would result in a wagon to carry the weapon. The crew of slaves, mostly farmers and craftsmen in their former lives, struggled to keep up with his demands. The overseer's hurry to please his Tatar masters would get them killed. Dailus dropped his brush and walked over, bowing very deeply indeed. "Honored overseer, may I have Jian Ho to help with the new model?"

"He's a key assistant—take one of the others."

"With greatest respect, overseer, he is also a sculptor."

Wang Lin Yo prodded Dailus's shoulder with the end of his whip. "He is a slave. As are you. You all do what I tell you."

"For the glory of the khan."

"Yes, of course, for the glory of the khan!" The overseer's mustache trembled. "Take him."

Together, Dailus and Jian Ho dug clay and crafted the model, talking little, focusing on the work before them. His assistant knew without asking the urgency of the project, and so they made the model a little bigger than usual, a fine display piece. Dailus roughed out running horses, but Jian Ho refined them into the local style, adding stripes about the legs, and a certain ferocity to their eyes to match the fire of their hooves. Both wilted with exhaustion by the time they were ready to carry it to a drying rack before firing it solid. Between the two of them, they lifted it more gently than a baby and placed it well back from the edges so it had no danger of falling. Clay caked their trembling hands, but they stood a moment looking at their creation, only clay, but already beautiful.

Across the distant camp, from the broken farmhouse the firedrake tenders used to perfect their aim, echoed a shattering roar, then a deafening silence followed by screaming.

They glanced at each other, then they ran.

CHAPTER TEN

On a low rise facing the ruined farm, Yusen sat his mount uneasily, and Tsang shifted her hooves in turn, reflecting her master's troubled state. He stroked her tawny neck, clucking under his breath. The slave seemed so certain this firedrake wouldn't work, while the overseer insisted it would be fine. Still, the overseer stood well back, close to Yusen's position, to supervise the test. The great firedrake, not yet fully polished on the outside at any rate, rested in a cradle of wood, with a half-dozen slaves clustered about it. One of the khan's firedrake tamers packed in the charge of black powder and a small, round stone. At last, they stood to the back and one of their number fetched the lantern.

Wang Lin Yo's grin faded as the sound of riders approached. The overseer bowed. A small party led by the generals Munkjar, the khan's armsmaster, and Batzorig, his field general, approached, with goshawks resting on saddle-mounted perches, on their way to hunt. The lesser generals and their tumaans camped miles away, closer to the city, where they built siege devices and made a show of strength to intimidate the rebels. The rebels had no idea the Mongol army's true strength, nor of the weapons they would bring to bear. So why was Yusen nervous? What if his slave was right about the firedrake? Yusen wished the generals had chosen a different path for their evening ride.

He bowed his head to them as they rode up, and Munkjar stared flatly back at him, as he had been staring at Yusen most of his life, waiting. "Why has the khan not been informed of this test?"

"It is a preliminary firing, sir, to be sure the weapon can sustain a charge." Yusen's throat felt scoured by the fine grit of the local earth, by the hard black stare of the general. "When it has been fully polished and prepared, then it will be worthy of the khan's attention."

"And what of mine?"

"I thought you had other business, general." Yusen glanced over the horses and hawks. "Are your animals used to such a sound? It can be startling."

The hawk on Munkjar's saddle, its head hidden beneath a leather hood, swiveled its blind gaze this way and that. He summoned one of his soldiers with a flick of his hand, and transferred the bird to the soldier's fist. "Take the hawks to my ger. I will hunt another day."

"Very good, general." The rest of the party turned for camp.

"Another time, then," Batzorig said. "Suits me—I have a cask of rice wine my men found for me. Join me after, if you'd like." Batzorig raised a hand in farewell as he followed the soldiers.

Yusen sat perfectly erect, and Tsang obligingly pricked her ears, the image of a battle-ready mount. Truly, he had bred her well. "Thank you for your time, general."

Munkjar merely grunted. "Where's your drakemaster?"

"The mold for this firedrake was damaged. The drakemaster is working on new models and molds for the glory of the khan."

Another grunt. The man communicated less than a horse.

"Do you wish to give the order, general?" Wang Lin Yo suggested.

"Go ahead."

The three of them gazed down the slope toward the firedrake. A smaller outbuilding stood between, decaying, a wooden barrel still standing beneath the eaves to catch the rain. Beyond the weapon, in a swath of dying wheat, stood three damaged walls of a red-painted farmhouse, its disintegrating roof a home for bats or doves, but no longer for men. The slaves positioned the firedrake pointing at the tallest remaining wall a short ride distant. The soldier nodded when Wang Lin Yo raised his arm and let it fall.

Bringing a reed up to the lantern, the soldier transferred a spark to the touch hole in the bronze weapon, then covered his head as the slaves already had.

With a tremendous flash and a boom that rolled across the shallow valley, the firedrake thundered flame and burst asunder. Shards as big and red as foxes flew out to the sides and the cradle crashed to the ground, trapping the soldier beneath it, screaming. Fire sparked in the dry wheat and two other men, likewise pinned or wounded by blackened metal lay shrieking on the ground as the flames kindled toward them. The four men who were able ran, stumbled, scrambled away. Munkjar's horse leapt into motion, fleeing the rending and screaming, and he wrenched its neck about, growling as he controlled the animal.

Wang Lin Yo cursed, smacking his fist into his palm, then turned from the ruin, shouting, "Drakemaster!"

At the nudge of Yusen's heels, Tsang launched herself down the hill. Yusen's jaw clenched, and he saw not the dry, dusty plain of China, but the green tumble of hills and stones where his family prayed for safety. After months of hunting, the khan's men had found them. Down below, people were screaming, burning—trapped in their camp by fires, his mother's ger already collapsing with her still inside. A younger version of Munkjar watched them burn, the torch still in his grip. Yusen's father dropped his sword, still sheathed.

"We have done nothing! Our family honors the khan, we—" arrows slammed into him from three sides and he collapsed to his knees, blood bubbling.

Yusen and his brothers, already running to douse the flames, turned back toward their father. Arrows sliced them down, save Yusen, thirteen seasons, but not yet growing like a yearling foal. Dodging ahead, Yusen reached his father's side, his father's sword. Fury swept over him, and he grasped the hilt, but his father's hand locked him in its grip. "Live," his father breathed. "Live and show... our family's honor."

At his back, women's voices screamed, flames roared, before him, the dark, steady gaze of the khan's captain: Munkjar.

Yusen's heart, too, roared. Tears blurred his eyes, but he forced them away, his hands spread—as his father's had been.

A soldier trotted out, sword in hand, but Munkjar frowned. "They are the khan's blood. Best obey the khan's law."

The soldier caught Yusen by the throat and hauled him toward the family's wagon, half-loaded in their hopes of escape. He shoved Yusen's back against the wheel, gripping his chin to pin him there. Munkjar lazily swung his leg down from the saddle and reached the ground with a chink of metal-plate armor. With a long, even stroke, he drew his sword, the gleaming length of it crossing Yusen's vision. The smell of roasting flesh and smoke permeated the air, his saliva going dry as he realized it was his mother's flesh he smelled. If not for the hand gripping his mouth, he would have vomited.

Munkjar laid the sword over Yusen's head, resting the flat on the rim of the wheel at his back. He gave a soft cluck of his tongue. "Looks like we'll have to save this one. At least until he grows a little more." Both men stepped back, releasing him, and Munkjar said, "Add the boy to your hundred. Let me know when he's tall enough, and I'll shorten him then."

He pivoted on his heel and sauntered across the camp, stopping to get a handful of Yusen's father's hair and pull back his head. His sword swung hard, bit deep, and the body collapsed with a thud. "The khan will be pleased to see his justice done, and his grandsire's law obeyed." The head dangling from his hand, Munkjar strolled back to his horse.

Now, Yusen bared his teeth into the smoke and rode hard, closing the short distance to the farmhouse, the flames of the burning wheat briefly searing him as he went, the screams of the trapped men briefly invading his head. He reached down—too short, still, always, too short—and turned Tsang for another try. She cornered as if they rode down an enemy, and he slipped one foot from the stirrup, crouching along her side, swinging his hand down. There! He gripped the edge of the rain barrel, its metal rim carving into his palm as he heaved it up. Not far, he couldn't carry it, couldn't lift it completely, but he did not need to drag it far.

Off-center, his fingers wound into Tsang's mane—*his father's dark hair gripped in Munkjar's fist*—Yusen galloped back toward the flames. His hand twitched, his arm already aching, by the time he got close enough and shoved the dragging barrel over.

Water splashed out, sizzling onto the flaming grass. It smoldered and hissed.

Yusen hauled himself back into the saddle, blood oozing from his right fist and let Tsang ease her pace. "Slaves! Get back here and free those men!" He cantered a wide circle around the men, who had run up to the overseer as if he would save them. "Get back," Yusen said again. One of the slaves handed Wang Lin Yo a long shard of split bronze which it had taken both his arms to carry.

Tsang and Yusen herded the slaves back down.

Voices rumbled behind them, just far enough away for their meaning to be a mystery. The four uninjured slaves hauled the broken remains off of the three downed men and started two of them limping up the slope. The third lay with his chest caved in, blood pooling from his mouth, his eyes already going dull.

Yusen turned away.

Atop the slope, two other men had arrived, one of them moving to help the injured men, the other bowing before Wang Lin Yo, his shaggy pale hair a good match for the old wheat, his hands spread, and his voice low. Munkjar glared down at them from his dancing mount, its eyes still rolling white.

Wang Lin Yo raised the shard of metal in his hand and lashed out, cracking it across the drakemaster's face in a spray of blood. Munkjar's horse danced back from the violence. The overseer reached down to line up the slave for another blow.

At a kick, Tsang launched forward and Yusen shouted, "No." They pushed past the group of injured men and mounted the slope. "No," Yusen repeated, low and hard. "He is the khan's drakemaster, and you do not beat him senseless."

Wang Lin Yo retreated a little from the horse's hooves, and Yusen stopped her precisely between the two men.

"He must be held accountable." The overseer's face reddened, his glance darting toward the general. "His duty—"

"Is to the khan and to his weapons. Yours is to the khan, and to his slaves. Duty is more than discipline. Discipline is more than beatings, do you understand? The khan's property and mine have been damaged today by you. It's enough. It does not happen again." Tsang stood still as stone beneath him. Discipline. Her strong legs defended his slave. Duty. Protecting what was his. As his father tried to do. Honor.

Munkjar chuckled. "I see your education in my tumaan has taken hold."

Yusen stared down at the overseer until the man stalked away, barking at the slaves, demanding to know about their injuries.

"When was the last time I measured you?" Munkjar said in that same laconic tone.

"Hand," Yusen ordered, then, with a sharp glance over his shoulder, "I am taking the khan's drakemaster for treatment by the shaman, so that he may present the khan with his new weapons as soon as possible." He aimed his fist down to where the drakemaster hunched on the ground, not opening his palm, not wanting to show his own injury. "Hand," he repeated.

Shakily, the giant rose, wobbling on his too-long legs, slowly extending his left arm, his right hand pressed to the side of his head, blood streaming down his jaw and dripping to the ground.

Yusen hooked the chain onto the slave's bracelet, then caught the slave's wrist and guided his hand to the front of the saddle, holding his fingers to the solid edge, keeping his own small, dark hand on top of the slave's pale one. At the softest cluck, Tsang walked forward, slow and graceful, leading them away, the smell of smoke fading, the smell of blood still strong.

Several times during the walk, the drakemaster faltered, and Tsang paused, ears switching, until Yusen gave her the nudge or cluck that moved them onward. The slave's hand beneath his trembled, and he held on tight. Soldiers glanced up as they walked by until they noticed Yusen's scowl and looked away. Soon enough, the entire tumaan would hear of the explosion—those who had not already connected the sound they heard with the failure of the latest firedrake. He hoped his slave's injury would not prevent him getting to work on new ones. That, or he would have the overseer stitched into a hide and beaten to a bloody mess: Wang Lin Yo pushed them into this, then made the drakemaster pay for his own haste, but Yusen had allowed it. He had forgotten his own duty, and that knowledge burned behind his eyes. Surely the overseer, the khan's trusted workman, would not willfully place his crew in the path of an explosion. Yusen had been wrong, and he would be lucky not to be taken to task for his mistake. Perhaps, in the end, it had been a good thing to have Munkjar witness their scene.

This thought made Yusen's scalp tingle as if he could feel the shadow of the sword, or, worse yet, feel the chill weight of it at the top of his head, feel the balance shift toward the hilt as he finally stood just tall enough to die.

Ahead the peaked tent of a shaman rose up on the outskirts of camp. He had remembered rightly, though this tent was new, its occupant unknown to him. No matter—any shaman should be able to search the slave's eyes and probe his scalp and see to his health.

Tsang stopped at the slightest shift in his weight, and Yusen leapt lightly down on the wrong side, briefly crowding the drakemaster against the horse's side. "Stay," he told the slave. "She will be steady."

The flap of the shaman's tent opened and a head poked out—wizened and narrow, so thin it was nearly skeletal. The eyes narrowed, searched him again, flaring, narrowing as if the shaman could not decide if he were intrigued by Yusen, or irritated by him. Yusen knew both responses. "I meditate," the shaman said in a strange accent. "What do you want?"

"The khan's drakemaster is injured. He needs treatment."

The eyes twitched again. "That slave?"

"My slave." Yusen tried to sort the shaman's accent into any of the tribes. "He is the khan's drakemaster. One of the weapons exploded."

The shaman made a rumble of interest, ducked back inside and rustled about his tent for a moment.

Yusen unhooked the chain, then caught the slave's wrist in his grip, taking his faltering weight and leading him a little forward, then down to kneel on a deer hide spread before the tent. He glanced around and, finding nothing of use, fetched the waterskin from his saddle and splashed it over the left side of the drakemaster's face, peeling away his protective hand, gripping him as he flinched from the water. Roughly cleaned, the wound angled from the slave's eye across his jaw, a short cut and an area of bruising. Yusen ran an appraising finger, pressing lightly along the brow and eye socket down to the jaw. The drakemaster gasped and flinched, trying to pull away, but no bones shifted under the pressure. The pain of the cut and the ache of the spreading bruise would be awful, and it would hurt him to eat, possibly for days, but the blow did less damage than a higher blow might have—the foreigner's height had spared him that. Maybe they did not need the shaman's aid after all.

"Nothing broken. Did you lose teeth?" Yusen asked.

The slave started to shake his head, stifled a cry, and mumbled, "No." His hand moved back up toward his face, hesitated, cradled his jaw.

"You make the khan's weapons?" The shaman emerged from his tent with a little bundle of oddments, a piece of bone, a leather pouch, some sort of wooden containers, and a pillow clutched under his elbow. This he dropped and sat down on with a groan, tucking his sandaled feet under his rough hide clothing. Sandals?

Yusen squatted alongside his slave, opposite the injury. The drakemaster's jade-colored eyes shifted to glance at him, the left eye rimmed in red, changing shape as the flesh swelled around it. Please the Eternal Sky it would not swell shut. Satisfied now that his slave was not seriously injured, Yusen faced the shaman as he spread his little array of items.

The shaman's skeletal thinness—dark skin stretched over obvious bones and feeble muscles—disturbed him. His skin had a peculiar glow about it, as if flecks of gold hid in the creases. Sandals. Not boots. That strange accent, as if he barely spoke Mongolian at all. "Where are you from?" Yusen asked.

"The mountains," the shaman answered. He leaned forward, studying the drakemaster's face. "And he—not from here."

"I captured him on the campaign to Budapest. He made bells for their towers."

The shaman picked up the broken bone he had carried out and waved it with one hand. "How the khan's weapons? How you make them?"

The slave barely parted his lips. "Not well enough." His fingers tightened into fists. "Next time, better."

The pain of speaking tightened the slave's well-muscled arms and shoulders and trembled in his hands.

"Do you have herbs for the pain?" Yusen demanded. "He must be able to work on the new weapons."

The shaman's tongue darted out, wetting his lips. "Not here." His hand roved over his things. Where were the bundled herbs, or the incense? He hadn't even lit a fire. Yusen fingered the hilt of his sword.

"You are good weapons?"

The slave expelled a sharp breath, and Yusen leaned forward. "He will be better than Master Sheng, for the glory of the khan. Who are you?"

"I shaman!" said the shaman, waving the broken bone. "I speak spirits, I know secrets!"

"I know lies." Yusen's sword slashed free, the drakemaster scrambling backward from his path. "You are no shaman—who are you?"

In spite of his age, the shaman leapt up, flailing his arms. "Is crazed! Is crazed whelp of a dog!" He danced away from Yusen, shrieking. Clusters of soldiers, returning from patrols or practices hesitated, and a few tramped toward the disturbance.

"Ai, Cartwheel, are you robbing a shaman, now?" called one of the commanders. "Watch that he doesn't put a curse on you—or on that fine horse of yours."

Yusen froze, sword in hand, still between the shaman and his property. What if the man were simply a tribal shaman from a different place, where they practiced different rituals? He couldn't be sure. He couldn't take the chance. Foolish to provoke the man; foolish, too, to allow him any closer to the drakemaster. No worthy kind of shaman forced a man to speak whose jaw had been nearly split moments before. Gritting his teeth, Yusen slid his sword back into the sheath and flicked his fingers in blessing. "I was rash. Forgive me. I think the slave will be fine."

The shaman pointed his bone sharply at Yusen and chattered in a language he did not recognize. The setting sun caught the hints of gold in his skin—had the man bathed in a stream with golden silt? Was that a key to his magic? Yusen didn't want to find out. He flicked his fingers again, adding a bow. "Again, forgive me. We took you from meditation. A mistake. We go now." The shaman's absurd speech was beginning to affect Yusen as well. He turned his back—a brave gesture? A foolish one?—and helped the drakemaster to his feet, latching his hand back onto the saddle, patting the horse's neck. "Not far," he muttered, then mounted up.

The shaman bobbed his head, then again at their audience, and swiftly ducked back into his tent. A skinny arm emerged a moment later to drag in the deerhide and everything on it.

Once they arrived at Yusen's ger, the drakemaster stumbled to his place and sank down, first to his knees, then lying on his back, eyes closed, breath catching. Yusen stared down at him. It had been a long time, even granted Wang Lin Yo's severe beatings, since his slave was so badly off that he did not even try to honor his master or perform his duties. Rummaging through his own things, Yusen found a packet of herbs and set that to steeping, then he located a clean swatch of silk to staunch the blood. His rough fingers snagged on the fine threads, and he thought of Bao Xing, the khan's treasure. He found a length of cotton instead. He dropped this on the slave's hand—no sense in chaining him tonight—and placed a bowl of the herb brew near his head. "Drink it for the pain."

The slave did not open his eyes. His fingers gathered in the cloth and brought to his face, pressing. His lips parted, and he breathed, "Master."

Better. Yusen wrapped his own palm, changed to a clean del, and thought a long moment of his duty. Finally, he rose and left the ger to find Munkjar, his general, and tell him of the false shaman, but when he passed by the place, the tent was gone, and only a bit of trampled grass showed where it had been.

"Scared him off, I guess," said the commander of the nearby troop. "Imagine you, scaring anyone that much! But then, a child could've snapped that man like a dry stick for the fire, maybe even you could've done it."

Yusen asked, "Did he come with your hundred?"

"The shaman? He arrived around the quarter-moon, said a vision brought him to serve the khan."

"To serve the khan? That's what he said?"

The fellow shrugged. "Near enough. Something about the order of heaven."

Yusen prodded a bit of the flattened ground, noticing a few drops of blood. His, or the slave's? Should he tell Munkjar anyhow? He thought of the shadow of the sword upon his head, and turned away.

CHAPTER ELEVEN

Bao Xing fumbled a hair pick and poked her own finger, a spot of red appearing in the midst of the ink stain already there. She was not used to all of the details it took to make her a lady, and no matter how she tried to organize them, they did not make sense to her. All of the pearls and combs, the paint-pots and tiny brushes scattered a low table, a disordered sky in which she could never seem to identify the proper constellation of tools.

"Come, come!" The fleshy woman's pouty lips did little to elevate her appeal. "The khan's wives are waiting."

"Perhaps they would appreciate an entertainment." Ming Lun gave a graceful bow of the sort Bao Xing should be able to execute; the thought of it made her queasy. She would fall over and ruin all the work of her hair and face.

The queens' servant looked doubtful, but gave a sharp wave of her hand, and Ming Lun lead her dancers past in a flutter of silks and whispers.

Bao Xing fixed the pins in her hair as the music in the next tent began. She groped and found her cane, holding on a little too tight to her father's gift. The cane had been her grandfather's and several ancestors before him. Its carvings of trees, mountains and stairs made her think of home with piercing sadness, then firm resolve. Home survived because she was here instead of fleeing into the hills. Once the soldiers had taken her, they left the observatory intact, left her father alone in their excitement to deliver her to the khan. She must make the best of it.

Then she slipped her hand under the pouch that held her combs and slid free the strange gift she had found upon waking. The round amulet just about filled her palm. Slightly bent and blackened by age or fire, it consisted of three layers of bronze held together with a pin at the center. The back plate had a loop at the top for the amulet to be hung, and the front of it bore a pattern of dots. Over that, a second layer had a tracery of swooping lines, then a simple, crooked pointer. The plates must once have turned in relation to each other, the middle plate serving to mark something on the plain of dots below, and the long pointer to take readings. What was it and who had sent it? It came wrapped in a scrap of fabric, cotton, well-woven, but not embellished, lightly soiled as if washed many times. How had it even arrived at her bedside in the middle of the night? Bao Xing did not know, but its pattern of dots and arcs looked tantalizingly familiar.

Next door, the music rose to a trill of completion, and Bao Xing slid the amulet away, rising carefully and passing through a vestibule, into the tent proper, beckoned by the woman-servant and flanked by a few others.

The drummer rapped out a complex rhythm and the dancers sighed, their pretty faces drooping. "The Mandate of Heaven? Must we dance it, Lun?" one of them whispered.

Ming Lun flared her eyes at them. "It is the most important dance that we perform, and you must know it flawlessly. Come." She swept them forward, this time taking the floor along with the girls and leading them through a series of precise stomps and pivots. Bao Xing's feet throbbed just looking at them. At least the dance was slow enough for regal movement, but she could barely walk up stairs on her Golden Lotus feet, and these girls were dancing.

Bao Xing lifted her eyes to the women who watched them, bored, lips pursed. A few of the women looked on politely, but the others sipped their bowls of tea and toyed with the edges of their Mongolian robes. While the dancers wore flowing layers of silk, the queens and their daughters wore narrow garments of brocade, stiff with gold and red edging. Almost all wore blue in some variation, most with patterns of clouds. Their eyes had drooping corners, their noses looked sharp, their hands—displayed for all to see—were roughened by riding. Furs decked their cushions and draped their shoulders as if they had just come from the hunt, or as if it were winter, not summer at all. They looked barbaric and strange, roughly shaped.

The dance ended and the girls all curtseyed and trotted past Bao Xing back to their own tent.

"You are our husband's new treasure?" said an older woman who sat on a pile of cushions at the center of the group. Rings of silver shone on every finger, and silver coils marked her throat and ears. Atop all this, she wore a tall, conical hat embellished with pearls.

Bao Xing moved forward, bowed, and settled on her knees before the queens. Three, at least, were queens, the others princesses or ladies, she knew that much. "Thank you for your kind welcome," she said carefully, the strange language feeling thick and blocky on her tongue.

One of the younger women, her glossy braid trailing down into her lap said, "It's a good thing he doesn't take concubines from the Chin, I think, Qutuqui, or a few of our friends should find themselves with lots of time for stitching."

The older queen smiled too widely, without showing any teeth. "Indeed, Chubei. Although she looks too willowy for use."

The women laughed, and Bao Xing, struggling to follow their rough speech, tried a smile herself.

"Then give me the training of her," Chubei offered. "She needs help with language, and she must learn everything of the household if she's to become a part of it."

"Beh." Qutuqui leaned back and waved for more tea. "She'll still be Chin. A bauble to decorate the hall when the khan entertains ambassadors. He's already thinking who to give her to."

Chubei flicked this away and held out her hand to Bao Xing. "Come by me, lady. The khan has said you are to remain with us, to learn from each other. What's your name?"

"Bao Xing." She rose and, receiving a nod from the senior queen, went to Chubei's side.

"Sit, sit. Ceremony comes with time."

"Please quiet yourself," Qutuqui said. "There are many more offerings to view."

Chubei pressed a finger to her lips, but her eyes twinkled. She drew Bao Xing down beside her and whispered, in careful Chinese, "I should like to have a friend among the Chin. You will be my friend?"

"Yes," Bao Xing answered, though, in truth, she did not know how. She and her father lived in the tower alone after her mother's death, after imperial commissions ceased to arrive and they had to dismiss their servants. A runner from the nearest village brought them food when her father lit the lantern to signal for it, otherwise, they descended only to walk to the temple on holy days or to light incense at their ancestors' graves. Bao Xing had never had a friend.

The tall, keen-eyed Mandarin she had noticed in the khan's ger entered, bowing to the queens, a scribe's desk and pens in his hand. His eyes lit briefly on her, and he inclined his head, with a trace of a smile. "Queen Qutuqui, ladies, I have been asked to catalog the khan's new acquisitions, to see if there is anything of note."

"Get on with it, Guowei," the senior queen said, waving him away.

Guowei settled easily, preparing his things with the care of a scholar, as her father might, two dozen years earlier, when he was still strong. Bao Xing took her eyes from the Mandarin, trying to focus, on what it meant to be a woman of the khan's household.

A succession of gifts followed her arrival—bolts of silk fabrics, vessels of wine or fine oils, spices and perfumes, and cinnabar carvings, a few statues of the Buddha or the sages, taken from temples in the mountains and given to the khan and his wives.

If an offering excited them, the queens all leaned forward and shouted or bargained for it. In this fashion, Chubei wrapped herself in a bolt of blue cloth and draped a sable fur about her shoulders. She held a lapful of trinkets—nothing as fine as the senior women took, but she delighted in each and every one, holding up a cuff of gold for Bao Xing's admiration. Was this what it was to be a friend? Bao Xing mustered her smile and pretended the jewelry and paint-pots were star charts and instruments, and suddenly caught her breath.

"What is it?" Chubei asked. "Do you like this one so much?" She held up a silver comb decorated with bits of lapis. "It's nothing compare to yours, but you may have it." She offered it to Bao Xing, who uncovered a pale hand to accept it. "But what's happened to your fingers? Is it frostbite?"

"Ink. From calligraphy."

"Oh, I should like to see some of that. Do you have the tools? No matter, I can send you some, or maybe take something from this next offering." She scooted forward to examine the chests being carried in by a group of young men.

Bao Xing clung to the comb, but imagined the amulet instead, with its pattern of spots and arcs of bronze: some sort of star-chart, it had to be! Yet the pattern of stars resembled no constellations she knew. Unless... she pictured it in detail. It might be! The one slightly larger mark connected with those others. Suppose the larger marks were brighter stars, and the lines showed some other astronomer's idea of their patterns. If she broke those lines and drew new ones, that bright star might be the Celestial Throne, and the patterns around it could be the Weapons, including the Dark Lance she had watched for so long. How far had the amulet been carried? And the disks rotated to read one's position—a traveler's device from a foreign country, which now had travelled to her hand.

Chubei thrust into her lap a portable writing desk complete with paper, brushes, and a block of ink.

The next chest held a mound of scrolls and books, some already torn. Bao Xing craned her neck to see if she recognized the contents. Guowei, too, came forward, his relaxed gaze transformed in an instant to that of a hunter. He reached out to touch the books, his ink-stained fingers stroking over the scrolls. "By your leave, khatun, I will take these to the khan's archive at Xuzhou."

"Take the lot of them, Guowei, I know you have a great interest in boring things," Qutuqui yawned broadly, and the others laughed. "I feel the need for a ride."

Too late, they had slammed the lid on the chest full of books and carted it away. Guowei bowed deeply, his eyes tracking the chest, then flicking back to Bao Xing, an eyebrow curving with curiosity. Was she, too, of interest to the archivist? Bao Xing lowered her gaze to her lap as Guowei and the porters departed with their chest of treasures.

"What fun. It's time to go riding—but perhaps later you can show me your writing?"

"Riding? With those feet? And she can't even see her hands." Qutuqui, already on her feet planted her fists at her back. "Come, Chubei, let your new pet relax as she is accustomed."

"Ooh, I hadn't thought of your feet." Chubei blinked at the pointed toes of Bao Xing's tiny slippers. "Will you show me those, too? But later—first, riding! Goodness, it's so stifling in here." Chubei bounced up and followed the senior women toward the sunlit door.

Left among the servants, Bao Xing stood up and returned to her own place, taking the writing kit along. At her desk, she pulled out the amulet, prodding the moveable disc with her finger. If she could shift it, she could make out the patterns and see if her guess were true. No, it would not move, but perhaps... Bao Xing found a little jar of hair oil among her things and set to work. The tiny eyebrow brushes fit very nicely to clean the crevices on the plates, and the oil brought out markings on the edge and back, characters in a language she did not recognize, blunt vertical things unlike the elegant strokes of proper writing. Using a corner of the cloth wrapping, she rubbed and polished the amulet until it shone. Still, the gnomon—for that is what the pointer must be—did not turn. Her fingers weren't strong enough to flatten the plate, and she had little else to work with.

Ming Lun followed her chattering dancers in from the outside, the girls complaining of her rigorous practice as they changed out of their dancing clothes to simple trousers and tunics. The leader put away their instruments and chided them from time to time, but otherwise indulged their litany of complaint.

"A thousand pardons," Bao Xing began, and Ming Lun swung to face her in an instant. Startled by the speed of her response, Bao Xing gave a tiny laugh, then held up the disk. "This is bent. I wonder if you might be able to make it flat?"

Ming Lun took it between her strong hands, studying it briefly. "A family heirloom?" She squatted to place the amulet on an unused hearthstone at the tent's center.

"I don't know. It arrived last night."

Had that been a note of interest in Ming Lun's breath? "Someone delivered it here," Bao Xing prompted.

"No one came after I went to bed." In a moment, Ming Lun offered back the amulet. "It will not be perfect, lady, but it is improved."

Bao Xing cradled the amulet and gently turned the dial, watching the curved lines move across the plain of stars. The Celestial Throne indeed. Her heart raced.

"Were you well-received by the queens?"

Bao Xing forced herself to pay attention to the other woman. "Yes, I think so."

Ming Lun's head tipped a little to one side. "The khatun, the chief queen, hates you already. She thinks you are too beautiful to remain in her husband's household without drawing his notice. The youngest one, Chubei? She wants something from you, or some advantage she thinks you can give. Be wary until you know what that is."

Clutching the amulet, Bao Xing blinked. "She said she wanted a Chinese friend."

"Chinese and Mongols are not friends, lady. Mongols do not know what friends are." She made another of those startling turns, her split robe swaying in the breeze. For a moment, Bao Xing had thought the dancer might become her friend, but perhaps neither one of them knew a thing about friendship.

CHAPTER TWELVE

Zhencai moved against the rush in the streets of Kaifeng. The city occupied a rich plain along the river, just out of the shadow of the mountains, and had once served as the capital of the empire, a truth that still shone in its broad streets and thick walls. Two days ago, a great explosion echoed across the plain and put the citizens in an uproar, adding more soldiers to the wall, readying weapons of their own, tensing for the attack. Yesterday, he merely waited for the senior monk to acknowledge his visit after showing his monk's pass that should grant him entry to any temple or shrine, but the senior monk, too, prepared for battle. Today, Zhencai felt the wheel of Dharma turning—how long before the Mongols swarmed them? Part of his training was to dispel illusions: to think Kaifeng would withstand the Mongols was illusion indeed, yet he understood why the citizens could not relax and await their fate, the death that waited for all.

A pilgrim's house gave him space for sleeping, and a bit to eat, but the host watched him sidelong. When he asked how Zhencai had entered the city, Zhencai replied, "Monks have power," and the host asked for his blessing on the house and on his family.

His fingertips and toes still ached from exercising that power. There were said to be sages in the mountains further west—sages who followed the Dao and could fly, among other claims. His faith in the Buddha provided much, but wings were not among his blessings. He relied on the blessings of strength, persistence, and silence, but it was no blessing he uttered when he tumbled over the top of the wall after his climb. He knelt in the darkness a long moment, poised for any response. None came. Instead, he walked the wall until he found a soldier, startling the young man, and demanded to see his commander.

With a bow and a blessing, Zhencai informed the commander that his defenses were inadequate. It hovered on his tongue to offer training, but the soldiers carried fire lances and smelled of black powder, and he doubted they would value his skills. When it came to street-fighting, they might regret their lack.

Midway through town, soldiers and peasants built a barricade of salvaged stones, furnishings and columns from abandoned houses. Fine yellow dust rose into the air along with shouted orders, shouted anger.

"We cannot lift anything more!" a woman shouted at a soldier nearer the top of the heap. "We're exhausted as it is!"

"Then just let the Mongols sweep through town. If this barricade falls, how long will you have to escape on the river then?"

"You can't keep driving us! We are not slaves—why else do we defy the Mongols?" Tears streaked the yellow dust that caked her face.

Zhencai took a pose of blessing, and waited, drawing the qi into his heart, gazing as if he, too, could see the river.

The soldier noticed him first, then a ripple of silence spread from Zhencai's place, until the woman, turned, ready to snap, and bowed instead.

"Strife brings you nothing. In silence, you will find the way," Zhencai said.

She pressed her lips together, then nodded wearily, and waved to the men behind her. They passed along another column, grunting with effort, straining to push it up to where the soldier waited, and Zhencai moved on, diverted from his path to an alleyway that cut across the city. He followed the turns past the barred gates of houses full of fear, coming out into a square, where suddenly the gates were gone. A large, rectangular building occupied one wall, surmounted with strange symbols—a star, a candlestick with many arms. An emperor centuries in the grave had invited these strangers to China to share their knowledge, but they stayed for their trade and had been here ever since. They did not give to the monastery, not money nor food nor children to be monks, and so, strangers they remained.

Turning from that quarter, Zhencai bounced up lightly to spot the pagoda and reorient himself.

"Many pardons, brother, are you here for me?"

Zhencai landed in a fighting stance, then took his hands up to blessing. A young man stood before him, in the loose trousers and tunic of any workman, save for the round cap on his head, with its rim of curly lambskin. Zhencai blinked. Not lambskin, his hair, dark and curly so it bounced when he hurried forward. His face, too, looked different from other Chinese, his nose more forward, his lips more full.

"For you?" Zhencai asked. "No. I was diverted from the way by a barricade."

"Diverted from the way?" A grin broke the young man's face. "If you followed the Way—" he flared his eyes to indicate emphasis, "wouldn't that be a problem?"

Humor. He referred to the Dao, 'the way'. An idea associated with the discredited geomancers and their attachment to the world. Zhencai gave a slight bow. "Perhaps it would. I follow the Buddha's way, and today, it leads me to the pagoda."

"Oh, I can lead you there," said the young man. "I am Li Andao. Speaking of the Way." His smile returned then vanished.

Zhencai walked beside Andao, matching his long strides. The young man's hands moved constantly as he spoke. "I need to go there myself. I've been trying to for days, weeks, even, but they… they don't listen to me at the monastery."

Perhaps because he talked too much. Zhencai knew where the monastery lay, from yesterday's visit during which he had spoken little, befitting their contemplation, but they had not listened to him either. Had the Buddha's hand drawn him to where this young man waited? Zhencai was content to follow, to see where meeting Andao might lead.

Andao's curly hair bobbed, his round cap threatening at any moment to fly from his head, as he brought them through another series of alleys and to the great gate of the monastery, which stood open barely enough for a man to slide through sideways. Andao slid inside. When Zhencai entered, the young man's hands were already explaining to a tall man with protruding ears: Benmo, one of the senior monks.

"I found this man wandering near the synagogue, looking for you—I suppose he just had directions to the temple—and I thought we could come together, and I could—"

"Brother," said the monk, bowing as Zhencai slipped inside.

Zhencai bowed in return. "Brother."

"The Monastery of Cloud Mountain is no more?"

"It is gone, Brother. I believe I, alone, remain of the monks there."

Andao's hands flopped in the air, his face furrowed as he looked on. "You know each other."

Zhencai inclined his head. "My home was a child of this temple."

"But you said it is no more…" his hands at last clasped each other. "I'm sorry."

"Death is not a reason for sorrow," Zhencai said, reminding himself.

"The khan's brother Khubilai favors the teachings of Buddha. He gave his authority to the removal of all trace of the geomancers and allowed us to keep their temples." Benmo slipped his hands into his sleeves. "This is very disturbing news." He glanced at Andao then back. "Join us for tea." Benmo led them past pools and bamboo plantings along the house of the Buddha. Here, Zhencai paused a moment to give a very deep bow. Inside, its head barely visible among the rafters, sat an enormous figure of the Buddha, all painted gold, its face serene. It reminded him of the gold-painted sarira who rose up and walked away, and he hurried to catch up. Andao flashed him another smile, even more excited than before, if such were possible.

Beneath the roof of the open-walled room, they sat on square cushions, silent while a novice prepared the small table for tea. Silent, except for Andao. "I hope you see, brother, why it's so important to move the scrolls. If they destroyed the monastery in the mountains, what's to stop them destroying yours? The synagogue has a vault, it's very safe, very secret." He pressed his palms together, as if in a deliberate effort to be still. "Please let us help you."

"All things end," Benmo began, but Andao interrupted, as if they had already had this argument and he knew what followed. "No! Not learning, not study, not books. Knowledge must go on."

The senior monk's mouth drew down, and Zhencai said, "Peace. First tea, then conversation."

"You don't understand," said Andao, matching Zhencai's tone as if Benmo couldn't hear him, "he's never let me past the door before. If I don't speak now, when will I?"

"When the time comes," Zhencai answered more firmly, placing his hand palm down on the table.

The two monks met eyes across the table, the slightest lift of Benmo's brows suggesting both amusement and long-suffering patience. Zhencai answered with a turn of his hand—turning the wheel back to youth, when they might have had as much wildness as this young man, and their eyes smiled.

At last, the novice placed a steaming pot between them, and Benmo poured tea into three bowls. He raised his bowl and took a long swallow. The others followed, the tea too strongly brewed: the novice must have been distracted and waited too long.

Benmo sipped again, then carefully set down his bowl. "The Teachings of the Buddha should remain under the care of the Buddha."

With a rap of his bowl on the table, Andao leaned in, his hands already moving, but Zhencai held up his palm for patience.

Andao gave him barely a glance. "Your Buddha house in the mountains didn't save your monastery, did it?"

The scrolls had already been removed from Cloud Mountain, much to the consternation of Master Deng. That was the entire reason Zhencai had come to Kaifeng. His store of patience, never very deep, began to trickle dry. "You are no monk, and it is only of the Buddha's great compassion you are allowed to drink tea and sit with us at all."

The young man's face grew red, his lips parting, but Zhencai tapped his wrist. "If you value learning, you must have learned to listen."

Shoulders sagging, Andao clamped his jaw on whatever he wanted to say.

"The Teachings of the Buddha are not the only books here," Zhencai observed.

Benmo's eyebrows twitched.

"I seek the records of Cloud Mountain, to learn about the sarira monks."

"A curious time to become interested in history."

"The Buddha's hand directs me along a strange path, Brother. I do not know where it leads."

"We do not search the future."

"As is fitting. That way lies suffering. Will you permit me to understand the past?"

Benmo reached for the pot and poured more tea, his hand steady. Finally, he nodded.

Zhencai nodded his acknowledgement, then reached for his tea.

"What about the books, the other books?" Andao asked.

"Nothing will be taken from here. I can see that you suffer with each denial—please permit me not to cause you such suffering again."

The young man's eyes narrowed as he thought through what the monk was saying.

"There are seven rooms of books and scrolls," Benmo said. "I do not know where the history you seek may be found."

Seven rooms! Zhencai felt as deflated as Andao must feel. How long before the Mongols battered down the gates and flooded the streets with blood? "Will you permit me an assistant, to sort through the texts and find them?"

Benmo's mouth tipped down again, slender acknowledgement of the world beyond the walls. "The monks of the gate will know to expect you. The library chambers begin near the Buddha's right hand." Benmo rose, summoning the novice to clear the table.

Andao scrambled up, with a cursory bow, "Brother, please, you must—"

Zhencai caught his knee, giving a squeeze that made him gasp and sink back down. "If you are to be my assistant, you must learn patience."

The young man gave a faltering laugh. "I don't want to just look at the books, I want to save them. My people are doing what we can for the city, and it is my task to save as many books as possible, all kinds!" He tossed his hands about, carelessly slapping Zhencai's shoulder. "Sorry."

"You are closer now than you have been before, yes?"

"Yes, thank you, I am, but…" Andao sighed. "Yes. I've done what I can outside of here. Maybe if I help you, I can convince him to let some of the books go. We're not stealing them, we'll bring them back."

Zhencai smacked his palm over a closed fist, causing the young man to flinch and stop talking. "If you are going to be my assistant, you must be quiet."

"Fine."

Rising in a single movement, Zhencai lead the way toward the Buddha house, pausing to let Andao catch up—he rose as if he never sat on the floor, like a prince. Pausing by the pond, Zhencai said, "You can read."

He snorted. "Of course. My people value learning above almost anything."

Taking a leaf of bamboo, Zhencai dipped it in the water and drew a few symbols, in an older script. "I am looking for sarira, the Cloud

Mountain Monastery, Master Deng." The characters faded. "Devices, a clock made by Su Sung." A few more characters.

"A clock?"

Zhencai dropped the leaf. "Any of these symbols together might be the histories I seek."

"Yes, fine. Where is the library?"

They set out at the back of the Buddha house, toward the chambers at the Buddha's right hand. They entered a chamber full of shelves stacked with bamboo books, paper books, parchments, and the crisscross openings that held scrolls. Dust filtered through the sun from small windows set high up. The most sacred scrolls, the Teachings, stood out, their handles decorated with tassels, painted red and rimmed with gold. That single wall they need not search, leaving twenty-seven walls and seven floors worth of bins, baskets and chests.

"You begin at the far end. I shall begin here. Bring me whatever you find."

For once, Andao made no reply, and Zhencai turned to look at him. The young man's lips parted with awe. "Just look at them—look at all of them."

Imagining how long it might take made Zhencai weary and glad of the young man's energy and clear enthusiasm for the task. Whoever his people were, they did, indeed value learning. Hopefully Andao's enthusiasm would not lead him to spend hours poring over ancient texts when they might have only days before the Mongol army sent all seven chambers up in flames.

CHAPTER THIRTEEN

Wang Lin Yo stayed close on Dailus's shoulder as they moved through the sheds toward the enclosed building where the khan's soldiers mixed black powder—a secret recipe Dailus was not to know. Ahead of him, broad-chested, flat-nosed General Munkjar bore down on the soldier who led them all.

"How could it get wet? We built four walls, not merely a roof. Don't you store the ingredients in barrels?"

"Yes, sir, I don't know, sir," the soldier stammered. "And with a lock," he added.

Munkjar growled.

Dailus's jaw ached and he absently rubbed the fading bruise wincing at the tenderness of the cut at its heart. Five days. He rarely paid the sensations any mind anymore, except at moments like this, when Wang Lin Yo's breath heated the back of his neck and the general—who spent more time around the workshop than he ever had during Master Sheng's tenure—seemed restless. Now this, the discovery that one of the critical components had gotten wet.

The four of them stopped at the powder building and the soldier fumbled the key as he let them in. Inside, he pulled a series of sticks, permitting daylight through small windows—no lanterns or torches could be allowed. A high table ran down one wall, with a series of mortars and bowls on top and a fine scale at the center. Beneath this and lining the wall opposite stood ranks of sealed barrels, and it was to these the soldier led his general.

Munkjar inspected the place, top to bottom. "How could they get wet?" He felt the outside of one barrel. "It's only wet inside." Pivoting on his heel, he rapped up and down the walls. "Someone must have come in and done it. When? Who?"

"Lock!" The soldier thrust out the key in a trembling hand.

"I can see that."

Munkjar's keen eyes settled on Dailus and the overseer, and both men bowed. "Two days ago, the ceramics kiln did not fire properly for your models. Before that, the stone in the pit—an accident, or so I imagined. Someone does not wish the khan to have his firedrakes."

"General, we shall post men around the workshops and buildings," Wang Lin Yo replied.

"Since clearly my soldiers are not sufficient."

Clearly they were not: whoever had damaged their things worked inside the camp, not beyond the general's perimeter. Every delay won him time before testing his new firedrake, and increased the aggravation of the Tatar command.

Wang Lin Yo bowed again. "Certainly they are, general, certainly—"

Before the overseer could utter the third and most certain of the certainly's, Munkjar thrust his finger toward the door. "Locked, as this man so cleverly states. Still locked today when he came to make charges to test the model. Yet the powder is wet inside. Whatever happened to the powder might have happened any time between the last firing and today. I will bring the shaman to investigate. There may be powers beyond that of men."

"Certainly," Wang Lin Yo echoed.

"We must replace the material that is ruined. Fortunately," he smiled thinly, "this component is local. One of my captains will lead the crew to mine it. We can perform the test tomorrow or the next day."

"Very good, general."

So the saboteur knew they needed the powder, but not how to cause the greatest delay. Why not fire the entire building and have done? Because then the general would know—certainly—that the delays were not merely a string of coincidences.

"I repaired the kiln, general," Dailus said, softly, in case it was not his time to speak, but the general gave a nod. "I used brick from the old furnace, and the firing will be complete tonight, then the mold needs to cool very carefully."

"How long until the casting, then?"

"Three days, general, unless—"Dailus cut himself off. He did not seek any further problems. "If my master permits it, I will sleep by the kiln, to keep it safe."

At the mention of Yusen, the general's lip curled. "I will command it. Do not speak of these things, not until we can be sure of what's happened."

They bowed their agreement and Munkjar swept away, sending another soldier to find the shaman, ordering the removal of the ruined powders.

Yusen readily agreed to Dailus sleeping by the kiln, no doubt eager to ensure success. Dailus caught himself rubbing his face again, and remembered the hazy pain of that afternoon: Yusen's hand, small as a child's, strong as a man's, gripping his own at the edge of the saddle, keeping him grounded; Yusen shouting and threatening a shaman, of all people; Yusen berating Wang Lin Yo for striking him to begin with, speaking of duty beyond discipline. The overseer's duty to his slaves as well as to his khan. He hated the unfairness of this blow more than any other, and hated that Yusen clearly recognized the injustice, yet both Yusen and the overseer allowed Munkjar to blame Dailus. Yusen defended him, and all the slaves, as property. Dailus hated that, in particular.

Duty beyond discipline. What duty did Dailus have to the slaves who followed his bidding? Could he have prevented the death and the injuries by insisting the flawed weapon not be fired? Perhaps, more than anything, he hated that Yusen's words might just as well have been for him.

"There will be more guards, more soldiers, drakemaster, and my ger is just beyond the furnaces—you know I do not sleep well. Do not think you can get away with thieving or mischief." Yusen wagged a finger at him, a sight so bizarre Dailus might have laughed.

"I wish only to serve, master," Dailus said, the customary bend coming to his back and knees, trying to keep his head low.

The little man seemed to consider this. "Serve well, and the khan may reward us."

There was only one reward Dailus wanted from the khan: his freedom, but he was hardly going to reveal that to Yusen. A silver tablet like the one earned by Wang Lin Yo would give him passage through the khan's territory. Surely even his skill would not be worth the khan's effort to come after him if he never returned. Times this seemed a slender hope, but hope was all he had.

After sharing an evening meal with the rest of the crew, Dailus made up a pallet of straw near the kiln and brought his thin blanket from Yusen's ger to lie beneath the stars.

Sometime later, he woke, shivering, to find the stars were gone.

Blinking, Dailus cleared his vision. A ragged shadow blocked the sky and a man knelt over him. In the middle of the night, Jian Ho knelt at his side, holding what seemed to be a parasol.

"What are you doing?" Dailus whispered.

"An ill-favored star streaked the sky tonight. Its light would sicken you."

"I'll be fine. Go back to sleep. Wait—where did you get this?" He put up his hand. Slats of bamboo and slivers of cast-off wood supported a blanket no warmer than Dailus's own.

"You must heed the omens," Jian Ho whispered back. "The sky is dangerous. As the heavens move they bring more dangers together, worse than any firedrake."

"Not worse than ours, surely. Go back to sleep, Jian Ho. I'll want your help with cleaning the mold."

"You need protection." The makeshift parasol shook with Jian Ho's concern.

"I need sleep. And more blankets would be nice." Yusen's ger had been warm all the time, felt walls trapping the heat of their sleeping bodies or the brazier.

With a sigh, Jian Ho reached up and drew the blanket off of the parasol to cover Dailus's long legs. "What about you?" Dailus asked.

Jian Ho's smile glinted in the starlight. "I sleep with the others. It is warm enough."

Jian Ho showed no hurry to leave, so Dailus wrapped one blanket around his shoulders, rolled over and stared at his assistant until he bowed, and departed toward the largest shed where the other men snored. Near the powderhouse, the shaman still chanted, and a scent of incense drifted on the breeze. Surrounded by heathens, idolaters, Dailus murmured the Lord's Prayer and squeezed shut his eyes.

A muffled sound startled him awake and Dailus scrambled up, the pre-dawn grey still looming over all. The noise came again, bleating and moaning like a child—no, not a child, never that, then a thrashing rattle of armor or tools. Dailus took off running. Behind him the newly placed guards roused themselves while, the slaves, like Dailus, rose quickly, ready for action. The thrashing came from Yusen's ger. Without thinking, Dailus caught the door flap and pulled it open. Gloom hung in the air beyond and Yusen staggered, his feet tangled in his blanket, the brazier already tipped on its side and hot coals sizzling. Yusen stepped on one and let out a shriek, the violence of his reaction sending a wave of smoke in Dailus's direction.

Dailus started coughing, retreating, but without dropping the flap. "Here, Master," he croaked. "Master—the door!" He coughed again and his eyes stung with the smoke.

Inside, Yusen cursed then stumbled again on the threshold—a beating offense, if it had been Dailus's feet. Dailus shot out a hand and grabbed his master's arm, pulling him through and dropping the flap again. "Burning!" Yusen shrieked, struggling against Dailus's hand. "Mama!"

The Mongol's eyes streamed tears, red-rimmed, and swollen nearly blind. Even in his panic, his desperate shouts wheezed from a clenched throat, his powerful body doubling up and thrashing as he fought for voice.

"Mama?" called one of the nearby soldiers. "Told you he was too young for the army!" They laughed.

Dailus caught Yusen about the shoulders, fighting him to drag him away from the ger and whatever had spoiled the air inside. Together, they dropped beside one of the basins set out against the danger of fire. Dailus splashed water into his master's face, then his own, hanging over the edge, panting.

Breaking free of him, Yusen gasped at the clean air, scrubbing his arm over his damp face and snatching Dailus' blanket to drench it and smother himself all over again.

"What's happened?" Wang Lin Yo loomed over them. At his side stood an old man draped in ribbons and dangling with bones. The shaman.

"Black magic." The old man bobbed his ribboned hat. "I felt it in the night, and now, see how it afflicts him."

Dailus gulped at the air, thinking of Jian Ho's dangerous stars. His eyes stung, but not badly, and he had been exposed to whatever it was for only a moment. His master must be in agony. Hunched and breathless beside the basin, Yusen held the wet cloth to his face, sucking at drops of water, shaking. Between one heartbeat and the next, Dailus felt the strength of fear run from his body. Why had he leapt up so quickly? A few more minutes in the tainted ger and Yusen might be dead.

"Black magic. The general must be informed." Wang Lin Yo dispatched a soldier.

Gradually, Yusen mastered himself, bleary-eyed, and pushed to his feet, his hair dripping down his back. "The smoke. Something in the smoke." He breathed heavily, barely audible.

"Why curse him? He's cursed enough as it is," muttered one of the soldiers—probably the same one who heard Yusen calling for his mother.

The little captain fixed him with a dangerous glare from his swollen eyes, his hand automatically swinging to his side. No sword. "No one knows my curse better than I," Yusen rasped.

The soldiers and slaves parted as Munkjar, still tightening his belt, moved through. He came up to the basin, caught Yusen's chin and tipped back his head to study his face, then let him go. "It wasn't meant for him, but the khan's drakemaster slept outside last night." He swiveled to bow slightly toward the shaman. "Black magic could account for all of this, but did the spirits reveal the face of the witch?"

Wavering side to side, ribbons whispering, the shaman said, "My vision quest fell short when I heard all this bother." He shook his shaggy head. "Have there been no other reports? No one has seen any strange behavior or found any markings of witchcraft?"

Like a man who held a parasol at night? Was Jian Ho's behavior strange enough for sorcery? Had anyone else noticed it? Dailus kept his head bowed and prayed for a heathen.

"The drakemaster's assistant," said one of the slaves: the man who always taunted Dailus, whose violation of the dangerous area by the stairs had gotten him burned the day of the first casting. He huddled, forehead to the ground, in an abasement to the general.

"What is it? What have you seen?"

The slave called out without looking up. "He sleeps to the south. He chants. He gathers things, useless things. Jian Ho, general. He's wrong in the head."

Wang Lin Yo grunted. "I've seen such behavior, but I did not think of magic."

Dailus swallowed his prayer. "If he meant to kill me, general, he's had a thousand chances. We've worked together on the new firedrake—without him, the model wouldn't be ready in time, the molds would be—"

"So perhaps this is why. He seeks to displace you, to have himself made drakemaster in your stead."

"No, general, he's a sculptor, he doesn't care for weapons!" Dailus started to his feet.

"Where is this Jian Ho?" Munkjar swiveled and stared, searching the bent backs of the huddled slaves. A few of them edged aside, leaving Jian Ho exposed at the edge. He twisted a little as two soldiers grabbed his arms and pulled him up, dragging him to meet the general. "You. Are you a geomancer?"

"No, general, they are a legend." Jian Ho darted a glance up. "Destroyed years ago."

"Why do you sleep facing south?"

Jian Ho swallowed hard. "Auspicious winds, general."

"From the south—because the so-called Son of Heaven, the little emperor of China wills it so?" Munkjar slapped his face. "Do you know the punishment for black magic?"

Jian Ho caught his lip between his teeth, his eyes flickering.

"Let me remind you." Munkjar held out his hand. One of the soldiers placed in his palm a thick club.

"General, please," Dailus lunged toward them, hands pleading, "I know this man. Of all of them, he would not harm me, nor any of my work."

"Yusen." The general looked back over his shoulder. "I begin to wonder if the magic has already taken hold on your slave."

A soldier grabbed Jian Ho's tunic. The frayed material tore, and he stripped it from the slave's body, then reached for his trousers.

"Kneel." Yusen caught Dailus's right arm and twisted it back, adding a kick that half-way dropped him already. Dailus fell to his knees to relieve the pressure enough to think of some way to get them to leave Jian Ho alone. Yusen pinned Dailus's wrist at his back. Yusen's other hand slipped to his robe and brought a short knife to Dailus's throat. "Black magic is a capital crime, slave, you know what that means?" He spoke low, his voice harsh from the tainted smoke.

The point of the blade dug in beneath Dailus's beard. He stared as they stripped Jian Ho.

"Are you a geomancer?" Munkjar demanded again, then the club swung and cracked Jian Ho's right leg. The slave screamed, staggering against his captors' grip. He shook his head desperately.

"It can't be stopped once it begins," Yusen murmured.

"Have you used black magic to destroy the weapons of the great Khan?" the general demanded.

The club swung again with a crack of bone and a spray of blood.

"It has to," Dailus breathed urgently. "Master, it's not true."

"The general does not care what is true. He delivers this message to everyone—to his soldiers, to the slaves and servants. So they understand discipline."

Dailus flicked his glance up, his master's head not far above his own, at that word. "I owe him a duty."

Yusen's enflamed eyes flinched, the knife turning in his hand, the flat of the blade pressing to Dailus's throat. "Who is Anya?"

The name cut Dailus as surely as the knife would have and he did not answer, her bright eyes and laughter suddenly springing to his heart. Two years he had been gone. What did she look like now? And little Matteus? Would they even remember him?

"You speak at night," Yusen continued under his breath, watching his general break Jian Ho's bones. "You speak your own tongue, calling this name."

If Dailus spoke for Jian Ho, if he fought for his assistant, for his friend, for the only good man he had ever met in this God-forsaken place, he would never see his daughter again.

"Your duty to him is nearly done," said Yusen as the club cracked ribs. "That is not your only duty."

Munkjar called for a felt, and a soldier laid it on the ground, a panel left over from someone's ger. They finally released Jian Ho's broken arms and let his blood-soaked body tumble to the felt, almost as if they cared. Dailus barely breathed.

"Munkjar is my foster father. He raised me, he taught me to fight."

This briefly caught his attention as they rolled the felt. Two soldiers brought out big, curving needles and stitched it closed around Jian Ho's battered form, his flesh still twitching, his chest still struggling to rise.

Yusen released Dailus and slipped the blade away. "The truth does not matter—only the khan. Bring my horse—I will ride to the river."

CHAPTER FOURTEEN

As Dailus led Tsang from the little paddock where she always stood ready, he wildly imagined leaping upon her back. Galloping through the numb slaves and eager soldiers to scoop up Jian Ho and ride away with him. But to where? They'd never get out of the encampment. Even if they did—Tsang was a fine horse, no doubt about that—but no barber nor surgeon nor saint could repair what the general had done to Jian Ho's body. It would take too many miracles, and Dailus had yet to witness a single one.

He held the stirrup while Yusen pulled himself up to the saddle, hooking the chain to Dailus's bracelet as if this was a natural thing, and it was. This was the life they had both grown used to. Yusen strutting on his horse, Dailus trudging or running or limping at his side, his arm stretched awkwardly between them. Only once had Yusen ever allowed him to grip the saddle, an unexpected kindness, followed up by bandages and healing herbs. A master's duty to his slave.

The camp drained away, soldiers in formations, slaves in ragged, worried rows, Wang Lin Yo cracking his whip over them.

Munkjar and the other Mongol leaders mounted as well, and the general took up a rope bound around a lump at the end of Jian Ho's woolen shroud. Binding his ankles, or his throat? Dailus's breath constricted. Pray the Lord Jian Ho was already dead. The felt bundle dragged as Munkjar nudged his horse into motion. Yusen angled his mount to the far right, along a column of soldiers. Far enough away that they could not see the dragging. Down a slope, a narrow, swift river hurried to join the larger river flowing past the doomed city of Kaifeng. At a bluff overlooking this, the procession stopped and Munkjar rode through to the edge, dropping the rope. "For the crime of black magic, perpetrated in the khan's own encampment, against the weapons and devises of the khan, and against his craftsmen who made them. We carry out the judgement of the great Eternal Sky!"

The felt bundle bumped down the slope and landed with a splash and a sudden thrashing.

Dailus doubled over, bile burning his throat. He hunched against the horse's side, his shoulder brushing Yusen's leg. He barely noticed when the chain slipped free. "Your duty here is done," his master told him. "Go back and finish the khan's work."

Remembering to bow, Dailus turned and stumbled past the crowd. They watched, enthralled, soldiers murmuring bets as to when the bundle would sink or how many times it would bob to the surface before it was lost to view. Stretching his legs, Dailus ran, head down, panting for breath. Tatars indeed; the knights of Tartarus, the clergymen of home had called them, the knights from Hell.

He paused to retch into a ditch where the Tatars pissed away their drink, but his stomach was so clenched and empty that little came. A few more soldiers hurried in the other direction, eager not to miss the judgement of the Eternal Sky. Dailus stepped aside, bowing to let them pass, and finally reached the yard of workshops. He moved automatically toward the drakemaster's workbench. Master Sheng's. Now his own. He would need to train a new assistant. Had he really done his duty to Jian Ho, a man who thought only to protect him, in spite of his bizarre methods? Dailus leaned on the table, head hanging. What did he care for the Tatar madman's meaning of duty anyhow? He was a good Christian, in spite of everything, wasn't he? Why struggle with the death of a heathen, a heathen witch, no less?

On the bench one of the cast bronze models gleamed, reflecting a hairy face with sunken eyes, a man his own children or wife would not recognize. The reflection moved and stretched, and Dailus stared at the patch of shadow lurking behind him.

"If you've come to kill me, then have done already. Otherwise, for God's sake, leave me alone." He pushed away from the table as the reflected shadow hesitated, then straightened as well. Dailus turned to find the powerful dance-mistress standing before him. He expected an assassin, maybe a saboteur, but this?

She ducked her head and covered her lips in that Cathayan way, but he could see the smile that crinkled her eyes. She spoke the rough tongue of the Tatars with little grace. "What say—'to kill you?' Surely I misunderstand."

"They've gone to drown my friend." His chest constricted—he hadn't meant to say it, but the words shot out, burning his tongue as if he were the firedrake about to shatter into a dozen pieces. His jaw ached and he rubbed at the scab. "Whoever you're looking for isn't here."

In her long, black robe, her face framed by the silky black sweep of her hair like a wimple, she resembled a nun—but the gleam at her eyes and the sinuous sway of her movement dispelled that image.

Footsteps, hoofbeats returned from the direction of the river, and the woman's glance darted away, her posture suddenly alert.

"You! Woman!" Munkjar called. The hoofbeats accelerated as the woman dodged around the end of the table.

Even quick and graceful as she was, she couldn't outrun the general's horse and all of his soldiers. No—they would not kill another, not today.

Dailus ducked beneath the table to come between her and the general, bowing as low as he might. "Forgive me, general." He cleared his throat as the other captains rode up, stirring the dust, eager for another thrill. "I asked her to come, to celebrate the completion of the firedrake mold. I did not," he paused, at a loss for how to refer to Jian Ho's death without fury, "I hoped I would have the chance…"

"Is bad time, yes?" the woman said behind him.

Munkjar leaned in his saddle, the rope draped casually over the neck of his horse, ready for binding. "Her? You are a slave, a foreigner."

"Is it forbidden?" Dailus bowed more deeply. "Forgive me, general, I did not know."

The general sat back and scrubbed a hand over his face as if wearied by the day, then laughed. "How would you pay her? You don't think even a creature like that dances for free."

Some of the other men chuckled, and one said, "Well, general, she's already danced for Yusen."

At that, Munkjar turned in his saddle to spot Yusen at the fringe of the mounted men. "Yusen! I thought you were still a child!" He grinned as Yusen's face took on that still, cold expression that put Dailus in mind of the bronze furnace: dark, right up until it washed with liquid fire. "My son," the general continued, still jovial, "why didn't you tell me you needed company? Surely we might have found a suitable Mongol girl? One about eight seasons might make a good fit." Turning his back to Yusen's petrified fury, Munkjar leaned his elbows on his saddle frame. "Still and all, the Chin whore and the fishbelly slave might make for a good show."

The men's grins and jibes quieted at the sound of a woman's muffled laughter. At Dailus's side, she dropped into a very low courtesy and rose again, covering her giggles. "Ai, general, another show I have, yes? Now is bad time."

She tipped her head to look up at Dailus, then sprang up on her toes and ran her fingers through his beard, stroking beneath the cut on his cheek and letting her hand trail down his throat. "This one, maybe I no money. I wish see if he so hairy down below."

Dailus's skin shivered, his muscles tightening at her touch, her palm resting on his chest. As he stared down at her, all was silence—the Tatars roaring with silent laughter, the horses shifting on silent hooves. Her dark eyes warmed with laughter, her lips—concealed by her hand, at least in profile toward the Tatars, hinted at a sharp smile as if they two shared a secret jest. Not beautiful? Dailus could not imagine a man who believed it. Still, if she had been willing to lie with Yusen, of all Tatars, then she must be nearly as despised as he.

She broke their gaze at last, dipped into another courtesy, then strolled away, the back collar of her robe sliding a little downward to reveal a crescent of bare skin at the back of her neck.

For a moment, he wished she really had come to help him celebrate, his loins tightening as well—then guilt flushed the feeling away. Jian Ho was dead. Dailus lied to save her the same fate, and now he stood like a callow youth, forgetting his family, his faith, his damnable duty. Lusting for a heathen? He had strayed from the Lord for too long.

"Back to work, drakemaster." Munkjar summoned Wang Lin Yo with an impatient gesture. "If there is any further sign of magic, tell me immediately."

"Yes, general." The overseer bowed, then cracked his whip. "Back to work!"

Soldiers dispersed to their camps, to their morning meal and daily duties, honing weapons, talking over plans. Dailus needed this firedrake to work. Not only that, but to impress the khan, to be so effective it would be worth his freedom.

"Overseer," Dailus said, offering a slight bow. "Bring the leader of the wood carving crew." Wang Lin Yo scowled a little at such a command, but Dailus was beginning to see how things were done in these parts. He claimed his authority, carefully, but firmly. Both of them had a duty to the khan. Yusen walked his horse around the workshops, keeping a watchful eye: the firedrake was too important to risk further damage to the khan's drakemaster.

The overseer rounded up the others and returned as Dailus finished his sketch. "Here. Instead of building just a big trough at one angle, we can use these wedges to change the angle, so we can fire the weapon from different places or distances. This—"he tapped the drawing—"is a pivot. If a few men put their weight here, the firedrake can tip up and the wedges be moved underneath."

The overseer grunted, then started issuing commands for how much lumber they would need and doling out the carving tools from another of the locked sheds. Locked, so he would not find one of those tools protruding from his skull.

The khan would have his firedrake, and someday soon, please God, Dailus would have his freedom.

CHAPTER FIFTEEN

Zhencai rose from the floor, stifling a groan as his back spasmed. He gathered the armload of scrolls into their bin and performed a series of movements, squaring his shoulders, twisting his spine, leaping to face one way, then the other. Up in the mountains, he performed daily martial practice as well as meditation and his duties with the sarira, but it was hard to resist the urgency that pervaded Kaifeng, to slow down in order to maintain his spiritual balance. He barely slept, but only entered a deeper meditation to restore his mind before he returned to the search. He began to wonder if that was enough when he thought he saw Master Deng, of all people, passing outside the gate when he let in Andao after the morning prayers.

Benmo and the other senior monks still signaled their disapproval of the stranger's admittance, and Zhencai's talk of the Buddha's guiding hand did not convince them. Zhencai accepted Andao's ignorant intrusions and foreign beliefs as part of his own burden of worldly suffering, but he hoped they would promptly find what they sought and part company.

"What are you doing? Is it Wu shu?" The young man appeared in the doorway, carrying a sheaf of bamboo pages. "What do you call that movement?"

Wu shu, the practice of the spiritual warrior, not the practice of the ignorant and rash. "It is called, 'old man rising.' Have you found something?"

"This is about the sarira ceremony, it details everything—the herbs, how to bless the urn, how long to wait before you open it—are they just, well, dead in there?" The young man shuddered, but his face glowed with eagerness to know.

"They enter a state of prolonged meditation in harmony with the Buddha nature. I know about the sarira ceremony." Zhencai spread his hands. "But it is a good find." He accepted the sheaf of pages, flicking through them. Newer, brighter pages sat at the back, and he turned toward the light from outside to examine them.

Andao lingered in the doorway, then slouched back to the third chamber where he had been working.

Thunder rumbled, very long, very low, and the building trembled beneath Zhencai's feet. Swirling eddies of dust flitted through the sunlight. Outside a few novices likewise paused. The floor shivered with the rumbling as it advanced. Not thunder, but hooves. How many? Zhencai's breath slowed. He gathered his qi, poised and waiting, until the thunder ceased with a single blast of a horn.

The novices huddled and whispered, then one of them sprinted back and started climbing, catching hold of a red pillar and scrambling up to the roof of the monks' hall. He craned his neck a moment, then hurried on until he climbed over the low balcony at the second level of the pagoda towering over the monastery.

Worldly matters should not intrude upon the work of monks. The world was coming. Zhencai flipped through the bamboo pages: lists of ingredients, drawings of urns and temples, sacred prayers, a list of names and the honors due to them. List of names. Zhencai studied the characters, turning until he reached the right period, and finding a page for Master Deng, exactly as if he had been a true sarira. Deflated, Zhencai read of the Master's work as abbot, the praise of his leadership, his wisdom in recognizing the worldly corruption of the geomancers and urging their expulsion, his devotion to the mandate of heaven, and to… but the mandate of heaven was a thing of the world, not of the Buddha. Zhencai plucked the page out of the stack. With a bamboo book like this one, a man wishing to alter the text could simply make a page and add it. That made it easy to keep an ongoing record, but hard for Zhencai to know when any given leaf was written. That couldn't be what Master Deng himself sought among the papers, but it confirmed the dead monk had been more than a vision.

"There are a thousand thousand of them! But I don't know if they will attack—they are so far from the walls, and besides, they have brought a statue!" called a young voice from far away.

The novice hung far over the top railing at the highest level of the pagoda, pointing in the direction of the city gates.

"A statue? What does it look like?" cried one of the others down below.

"It's bronze and has a special wagon to carry it. It is tall, but it's lying down right now—how it shines!"

The Mongols stayed back from the walls out of fear of the fire lances of Kaifeng, that was no mystery. As for the statue the novice observed, the Mongols had not arrived in force to bring an offering to the Buddha. Zhencai took two steps out into the yard. "What are they doing with the statue?"

"A few men are around it. They are leaning it up and down—oh, they've stopped, but it's still lying down. They have a ghost, too, a very tall one! A man is lighting a candle at the statue, I think it may be—"

Thunder roared as if an avalanche came down from the mountains. Bricks or stone broke, tiles crashed, and people began screaming.

Zhencai whirled and sprang lightly up the steps into the library. "Andao! Andao, you should go."

The young man appeared, breathless, a pile of scrolls in his arms. "Go? But we haven't found it."

"I have renounced the world, as have the other monks. You have family, outside. The Mongols are at the gates of Kaifeng."

"They are very strong gates," Andao said. "Look at this, I found some records of the old city. I remember my grandfather telling me—"

Zhencai cut him off with a sweep of his hand, but the bamboo sheaf he still held, its wooden covers unbound, tumbled from his grasp and pages flew in a startled flock to scatter on the floor. Haste. The world required haste, but his quest required stillness.

Andao set aside his scrolls and knelt to help gather up the bamboo pages. "Will it be safer, out there?"

"More dangerous, but your family is there. Do you have no safe places?" Zhencai glanced up as they reached for the same page.

"The synagogue? The vault of the books?" Andao laughed nervously, his curls bobbing. "My father wants me to become a rabbi. How better to continue my studies than to be locked in with all of our books?" He dropped Zhencai's gaze and picked up the page between them. "Master Deng." His long finger traced underneath the characters of the name.

"I have read it." Zhencai studied the young man before him; with his fine bones and lack of knowledge, he would likely be among the first casualties. The teachings of compassion warred against the teachings of detachment.

"This… looks like a diagram of something." Andao pointed to a faint pattern of lines.

The lines formed a grid, as if for a child to practice forming his characters, but set on an angle to the edge of the page, and they could only be seen when the page tilted a certain way against the light. It was exactly the sort of pattern a novice might carve with the edge of his fingernail when he was set to read the history of the sarira monks as an inducement to focus, perhaps copying out the shape of the shelves he saw before him in the scriptorium. "They will lock the monastery gate very soon. If you remain inside, it may be that you will not see your family again."

"Most of them have already gone," he murmured. "But this is our home. So much will be lost." Andao placed the page carefully on the stack, tracing over it with his fingers.

A second explosion rocked the building so hard that a few scrolls slid down from the wall of sacred teachings. Zhencai rose up and hurried to replace them, giving a series of brief prayers as he did so. When he turned back, Andao was gone.

In the yard, the bell began to ring, calling the monks to prayer. The gates might already be locked—what if Andao could not get out? Zhencai sprinted from the library, darting between the pillars of the Buddha house and sliding past the procession of monks as they entered, with a brief bow to Benmo who escorted the aged abbot. With a burst of speed, he ran for the gate. A pair of junior monks wrestled with a long bar, the third of three that sealed the gate. The smaller door beside it, round as the one at Cloud Mountain had been, remained for the moment unsealed.

"A thousand pardons, brothers." Zhencai inclined his head and accepted their deeper bows as their senior. "Has a young man with curling hair passed here?"

"We have been at our work, Brother. Someone was at the door a moment ago, but outside."

Zhencai grasped the big round handle and twisted it to draw back the latch and pull the door partially open.

"Brother, we must be sure everything is locked."

"I will lock this when I am done. You may go to your prayers." Zhencai adopted the stiff tone of the martial master, and the young monks bowed, then hurried away to join the ranks moving inside the temple.

Glancing outside, Zhencai found a scene of frantic movement. A soldier ran by toting an armload of fire lances—long poles with incendiary tips, while a woman hustled three children in the other direction. A group of stocky youths clustered on a corner huddled and whispered as if planning their own defense, and a spider-thin old man slipped into an alleyway. Master Deng! Could it be? Zhencai ran across the yard and stopped at the alley which led between a pair of courtyard houses. Where had the old man gone?

"Master!" Andao's voice rang with fevered excitement, and he waved a scroll as he ran across the square. "Master—those markings on the bamboo page, a map, it showed the place—look!" He stopped short and unfurled part of the scroll. From where Zhencai stood, it was hard to make out the designs. A series of drawings marched across the scroll with hundreds of characters packed between. The drawings looked like buildings, but for round parts at the top, but then, some of the drawings showed only strings of dots like beads. "Is this what you're looking for?"

If the brothers of the monastery saw him outside the walls with one of their scrolls, they would be furious. "You can't bring that out. Let me—"

The impact against his back knocked the words from his throat, the breath from his body, and Zhencai collapsed to his knees, struggling to fill his chest at the same time he centered his qi.

Someone shouted behind him, and the young men from the corner swarmed Andao like locusts, leaping into Wu shu stances, feet connecting, hands outthrust. Andao shrieked in their midst.

"The scroll, you fools!" shouted the voice from behind again. "Only the scroll matters!" A foot connected with Zhencai's shoulder, knocking him aside.

Zhencai allowed himself to fall and roll with the blow, reducing its impact and leaving him, palms and toes to the earth, ready for action. Before he had the chance to spring—still gasping for breath—his assailant ran by, arms waving from a nondescript robe of dark cloth. Master Deng: his skin still glittered.

Ignoring the slight grind at his shoulder, Zhencai leapt after him. He forced a running meditation, a focus of the qi into the center of his chest, warming him and letting him draw a deeper breath.

In the knot of men ahead, one of them broke out, scroll in hand and smeared with blood. Master Deng snatched it from him, with the barest thanks.

Why was Master Deng lurking outside the monastery with a gang of toughs? Looking for the chance to steal this secret scroll, this plan worth waiting a hundred and sixty years, worth beating a scholar in the street. In that moment Zhencai could take it. For that moment, time hung suspended.

Master Deng's gold-tinged hands cradled the scroll, its bar plain and red, the reinforced margin where it opened painted with a scene of mountains as if it were a landscape painting ready to be hung. The ancient monk's eyes gleamed as well, as he grinned in triumph. His lean body hunched over the scroll, a snake bending over a hare in avarice all-too-worldly. Blood smeared the back of the scroll and one edge had a hanging flap as if it had been damaged being torn from Andao's grip. The scroll contained knowledge worth killing for, knowledge that might be found in no other place, that might lead the world to sorrow or to Nirvana. When the moment was done, Master Deng would take that knowledge and vanish with his mystery, until it was too late to understand what he was doing and stop him.

Behind Master Deng, six men in the wrapped trousers of the poorest farmers, their bare chests taut with muscle, assumed the classic postures of Wu shu—although not the refined practice of the monastery. This one had his feet set and arms extended, that one had one foot chest-high in the act of kicking. At their center, barely visible, Andao arched backward from that foot, his round cap flying from his head, chin stretched aside and blood splashing from his lips, the fist of another attacker indenting his cheek and twisting him away. Four other men stood ready for their turn, some in profile, one with a sneer so sharp he looked a demon, waiting to revel in the sacrifice.

"Meet me across the river when you are through here, at the old bridge," said Master Deng, and turned away with the scroll. "None may live who have seen this."

The leader of Andao's attackers gave a nod in acknowledgement of

Master Deng's command, and stepped up to the attack. In that moment, Zhencai must choose to pursue the Master and take back the knowledge he had been searching for, that scroll worth killing for. Or to stay and defend the man they were killing.

All was decay and ruin. All men died—knowledge went on. In that terrible span between heartbeats, Zhencai saw all of this, and chose.

CHAPTER SIXTEEN

Dailus lowered his hands from his ears and squinted through the smoke of the blast. The gates of the city hung off-kilter, one with a great rend in the wood. One more shot should do it, a little lower and to the left, beneath the huge, peaked tower. Defenders on the walls and the tower balconies shot arrows toward the army in undisciplined swarms, all of them falling well short. After each blast from the firedrake, Munkjar led a small force of horsemen to charge toward the gate as if commencing the onslaught. Then the horsemen turned like the tide and swirled back up the slope, drawing the arrows of the Kaifeng archers, depleting their supply and howling in glee.

The air smelled of flame, smoke, and the stinging powder. Dailus tapped the barrel of the firedrake gently—warm, but not dangerously so, and it still sang with the exquisite resonance of a bell well-cast. Tatar-style clouds embellished the upper portion; below ran the herd of horses he and Jian Ho had modelled, the horses of the sun. They gleamed, highly polished, seeming to gallop in the sunlight. The khan's delight extended to giving Dailus thin sheets of gold which he applied to the modeled flames, and a vial of quicksilver to dissolve any bits of gold out of place so they could later be reclaimed. Jian Ho the sculptor could have been proud of such workmanship, and Dailus's careful gilding honored his memory, a delicate process worthy of works in honor of God. Briefly, Dailus imagined him in Heaven, viewing the glory of the work they had made together. But Jian Ho was a heathen, an idolater whose execution for witchcraft would be seen as only just in the minds of the priests back home.

Dailus made a sharp movement with his hand, held up his fingers, then swiveled his arm to indicate the aim. The khan's firedrake tamers glanced back toward the gate and got to work, quickly shifting the wedges and shoving the barrel, then bringing up the pouch that contained their precious powder. They accepted his advice on aim merely because of the new system of angles, but the firing was their task. Dailus stepped back, his ears slightly ringing from the last one.

For the first time since his capture, when his own clothes had been stripped away to humiliate him, to heal his leg and deprive him of any sign of home, Dailus wore trousers that actually reached his ankles and a tunic with sleeves that brushed his hands. Made of sturdy blue cotton, the new garments had edges of patterned silk, no doubt the remnants of a lady's sewing project, but finer than anything he'd worn before. Ordered by the khan to honor the first successful test of his firedrake, the clothes had been delivered to Yusen's ger that morning.

Yusen dressed in his finest silk tunic and padded del beneath the tiny chest and back plates that armored him. On his knees, Dailus had tightened the thongs that held it all together, keeping his master safe. Even Tsang had silver fittings on her bridle and saddle today, snorting and tossing her ears as she stood on the hill beside him. Many of the other soldiers wore silver belts, all of the same type, and Yusen eyed these as if he wanted to steal one from the waist of one of his fellows. It meant something. Everything around him seemed to mean something to the Tatars, and especially to his master, but Dailus fervently hoped that soon, it would all be meaningless to him. Today, perhaps even with this next shot of the firedrake, he might win the pass to his freedom.

They brought up the lantern and took a straw to light the hole. Dailus pressed his hands over his ears. He'd been tempted to stuff them with wool as the firedrake tamers did, but that resonance of good metal reassured him too much.

At his side, the firedrake roared and spat its stone in a blast of smoke and flames.

The gate tower shuddered, then crumpled in a mound of stone, taking archers and soldiers into its ruin. The left-hand gate groaned backward and toppled, the right-hand one following it down in a shattering of wood. A mass of soldiers waiting inside scattered from the collapse, some of them trapped beneath it, arms flailing at the broken beams.

In the deafness that followed, Dailus did not hear the roar of the Tatars around him, but their mouths and their eyes widened with excitement. Munkjar's charge galloped full-force into the breach, and the soldiers of Kaifeng scrambled to re-group as the Tatar army poured through the wall. At both sides of the Tatar advance, ranks of mounted archers faced outward, shooting to the sides, felling defenders from the walls and balconies inside.

A hand clamped his shoulder and gave it a shake. Dailus glanced up into the round and jovial face of the khan himself, his furred helmet topped by a switching tail of horsehair. "Well done!" the khan shouted down at him. "Excellent! Never has a firedrake taken out a structure so directly." Still grinning, he gave Dailus a last slap on the shoulder, even as Dailus was deciding whether to bow and how low, then the khan directed the crew to aim the weapon again, continuing the destruction of the city wall.

Yusen rode in the second wave, which Dailus gathered was an improvement on his usual rank in fighting situations. Since his scouting talents were not required during a siege or city fight, the little man had requested other service and had been granted it. Dailus watched him ride by on the outside of his group, very exposed, but high on his horse, his bow in his hands. Arrow after arrow he launched, but each one with precision now that the massed defenders had broken up to fight. Dailus watched until he could not find him in the fray, hoping to see an arrow strike him in return. Was it sinful to pray for the death of a heathen?

Just as it seemed the swarm of Tatars would overwhelm the city, a phalanx of soldiers emerged from the street alongside the wall. They thrust long lances with burning ends, carving into the ranks of horsemen. They punched a hole through the stream of Tatars, drawing more soldiers forward, the smell of burning flesh and the screams of horses filling the air.

The khan howled his fury and shook his sword, then the firedrake rang again with destruction and another section of wall collapsed, interrupting the stream of soldiers within. Dailus moved on with the firedrake, helping to drag it alongside the wall, hot, dusty, tiring work, once more the slave now that the drakemaster was not needed. Wang Lin Yo's crew hauled cartloads of stones and fresh powder. The khan decreed that no rebel city should stand. When the city was first conquered a couple of years before, the khan had allowed the wall to stand, to better defend his new prize, but with its rebellion, it lost that distinction. Their orders were to demolish the length of the wall and leave whatever buildings they could reach in rubble.

The firedrake crew left behind screams and war-cries as they moved along, and the time between firings gave the weapon a chance to cool down. Even then, if Dailus checked it and found it still too hot, they waited—restlessly—on his word. Wang Lin Yo glared down at him as he took the chance to squat in the shade of the firedrake's carriage. The overseer no doubt remembered the day he forced an early firing and the khan's soldier died. Avoiding his stare, Dailus tried to wipe the soot and yellow dust from his new clothing, but the stains smeared until his blue tunic looked a muddy green. The simple loincloth might have been a better choice, but he could not bring himself to give up his clothes, no matter how he sweated.

The drake tamers pointed and argued with each other, loudly to be heard over the stuffing in their ears, and Dailus pushed himself up, sighting along the barrel. Inside the walls stood a many-layered temple, rising up like an evergreen tree, but with deep red pillars and golden demon faces on the ends of the upswept beams.

"—to destroy monasteries. We must leave it—and we must leave this entire section of wall. It is the back wall of the monastery."

"The khan wishes the city destroyed," the other soldier shouted back.

"His brother Khubilai is Buddhist, we have to leave it! What say you, overseer?"

Wang Lin Yo crossed his arms, his whip tucked under, and gave a long sigh. "This is for the khan to say, not I. Who runs fast?" He glanced at Dailus and his brows sank. "You. Go ask the khan what should be done about temples."

Dailus gave him a quick bow and trotted down the hill, Wang Lin Yo shouting, "Hurry!"

His back ached and his legs throbbed from the hard labor of the morning—or was it afternoon, now, for his stomach ached as well. At the entrance to the city, the quiet surprised him. From the streets beyond, shouts echoed and weapons clashed, but the defenders lay dead around the gates and the Tatar invasion had moved on to the more difficult street fighting. Smoke billowed from buildings in the densely-packed center, tracking the progress of the assault. Most of the mounted soldiers had withdrawn, and the foot-soldiers took over. Tatar archers now occupied the balconies he could see, aiming down into the streets.

The Tatar khan sat his tall white horse, laughing and cheering. By nightfall the city would be done.

***

Yusen galloped down the street, letting Tsang have her head, keeping himself upright, firing arrow after arrow. The wind whistled beneath his helmet, his thighs gripping his saddle, armor jingling—and all, all, gloriously alive. The air smelled of blood and powder and echoed with the cries of the defeated rebels. It had been too long since Yusen had ridden into battle. For years, he rode out ahead, alone, shunned by the other warriors for his size and his family. No matter how much information he brought, how far he rode, how fast or how much ground he covered and still came back alive, Munkjar merely accepted the information as his due and dismissed Yusen to his ger to wait out the battle which followed, or sent him on to scout some other mission, days away from their line of march. Even that had been the pattern of the great Eternal Sky, for just such a fool's mission brought him to the foundry where his slave worked casting bells. His capture of that one man had brought him here, galloping in the sunshine, for once surrounded by his fellow warriors, for once, a part of them.

Yusen reached again for his quiver and found it empty. He drew his sword instead, pointing toward the inside and indicating that he should exchange places with another archer to resume the task. The three men abreast and behind him flicked dark glances his way. One rolled his eyes and kicked his horse to close up the gap—the gap that Yusen should have ridden into. They were leaving him on the edge, exposed to enemy archers with no means of returning fire.

Heart racing now with anger rather than battle-joy, Yusen leaned against Tsang's neck, ducking very low. An arrow slipped over, straight through the place where he should have been. Unhooking his foot from his stirrup, Yusen swung sideways, dropping down behind her, one hand caught up in her mane, peeking beneath her neck.

With a yelp and a crash, one of the men beside him fell, his horse twisting against the sudden pull on her reins. Yusen shot out his sword and cut the reins, letting her jerk her head up and regain her stride.

The street widened, accommodating a threshing mass of warriors and rebels. His short reach would avail him little in such a combat, but there might be another way to fight. The acrid smell of fire lances reached him, from the west. When he reached the square, Yusen pushed Tsang in that direction, skirting combat. Ahead, a street opened between buildings, but a huge mound of furniture and urns blocked it, shored up with planks. A group at the top of the barricades handed down fire lances to rebels who came up alongside the barricade. A pair of rebel soldiers guarded the brazier they used to light the incendiary tips of their weapons. Sheathing his sword, Yusen pulled himself in tight to the horse's side, dropping the reins and wrapping his arm around the slave's chain that hung from the pommel to hold on. One hand free, both small feet sharing a single stirrup, he allowed Tsang to trot closer, tossing her head, wandering.

A man received his firelance from the people on the barricade, lit it at the brazier and turned toward the battle. Tsang trotted behind the rebel, apparently riderless. Yusen swung out his arm, wrapping the chain around the rebel's neck and dragging him away. The man's face turned livid then blue, tongue protruding as he feebly slapped at Yusen's arms and shoulders with the staff of his firelance. Yusen grabbed the weapon before the dead man dropped it, and released his enemy to tumble down with the other corpses.

He kept the firelance low, though Tsang set her ears back and snorted, then he swung her back toward the barricade, and pulled himself to the saddle once more, galloping past the rebels, the firelance heavy in his hand. A sword slapped at him, and a few arrows swished around him. Even the archers who saw him took a moment to calibrate their aim for a man so small.

Grinning, Yusen smacked the firelance into the barricade, dragging it along the furniture, especially any upholstered pieces where straw stuck out of the seams. Someone screamed from the top of the mound. An arrow grazed Tsang's hip and she stumbled. Yusen thrust the firelance deep into the barricade, then galloped past, plunging through the outskirts of battle while the barricade blazed behind him.

He had not gone far when Tsang's hooves suddenly struck grass instead of cobbles. The pleasure garden! Trails wound about through cages of animals that shrieked with strange cries. Would setting them free aid the khan or hinder him? The animals were just as likely to kill Mongols as rebels, so he let them be, though a huge tiger eyed him as he passed. Near its cage stood a long staff with a spiked tip flecked with blood, probably a tool for feeding the beast, but also a weapon long enough to be used from horseback. Yusen plucked it from the ground under the golden stare of the captured beast.

Turning about to check Tsang's wound, Yusen found it was shallow—a long cut that oozed blood down her leg, but should heal well. They emerged from the willows to one of the most remarkable things he had ever seen. There, in a courtyard by the river, stood a huge series of rings, one inside the other, cast of bronze and supported by sculpted dragons. Bronze, for the khan's firedrakes. Excellent. He would be wanting more after today's victory. Yusen rode in a circuit around the thing. Chinese words covered its base, along with images of the moon and the twelve animals of the sky. An astronomical device then. Bronze for the khan's weapons, yes, but first, words and stars, for the lady's eye. The sun glowed down on him, the Eternal Sky blessing this glorious day.

***

Zhencai's flying kick slammed the first assailant straight to the ground, where Zhencai landed on his chest, bringing the qi down to his feet with a crack of bone. Breath and blood and life puffed from the downed man's lips. Throwing up his hand, Zhencai blocked a fist, pushing it aside and jabbed his own hand in beneath the man's jaw, making his fingers like iron. With a choking sound, the man staggered aside from the blow, gulping for air, then floundering on the ground as Zhencai knocked him down.

Andao lay there already, curled into himself, a bloody arm wrapped, trembling, over his head. The trembling was his only sign of life.

A sidelong kick caught Zhencai's knee, but he flexed and turned with it, dropping down, trapping the foot and pulling the attacker toward him. The attacker's other foot snagged on one of the fallen, twisting out from under him with an awkward wrenching. Still, his hand snaked out toward Zhencai, landing a hard blow against Zhencai's ribs.

He gave the captured foot an extra twist. The assailant howled as his ankle ground.

The other three advanced, one on either side, one circling with a long knife that sliced at Zhencai's back. Distantly feeling the pain, he dropped away from the blow onto both hands and pushed himself into a handspring, his old bones protesting, his muscles straining. Clearly, it had been too long since he practiced that discipline. Spinning about, Zhencai set his stance and found that his move had more than the desired effect: they hadn't expected it from an old man.

The sounds of horses and the clash of massed fighting echoed from the narrow streets. From the corner of his eye, Zhencai saw Master Deng pause beneath an awning and strip off his nondescript robe. Beneath, he wore the del and felt boots of a Mongol. Tucking the scroll into his del, he slipped away.

Zhencai brought his awareness to the space between his eyes, and made the sign of blessing as the three attackers shifted before him. The one with the knife held it up, sneering, letting Zhencai's blood drip onto his hand.

"The old man got what he came for, why wait?" one of them blurted, his glassy eyes twitching toward the sounds of battle. "Let's go to the bridge and get paid."

As if the question alone were enough, the second man spun about and ran away as fast as he could, slipping on spilled blood and running all the faster.

"Buddha will still take you in," Zhencai said.

"When we're dead," spat the man with the knife, then he lunged.

"So be it." Shifting at the hips, Zhencai allowed the blade to slice close to his chest, caught the man's wrist and shoved the back of his shoulder with his other hand.

Bone cracked and cartilage tore, the man's sneer twisting into grimace of pain. His knife rattled from his grip. Zhencai landed a hard kick to his spine and dropped him. Still, the man turned about, bringing up his off-hand to hook Zhencai's foot. Placing his head in range of the other foot. Zhencai transferred his balance, drew down his qi and planted his foot solidly in the other man's temple. He crumpled without a sound.

One remained, dancing on his toes, hands held out, eyes dancing, too.

"Buddha will still take you," Zhencai repeated, softly.

The tremors of his eyes took over his body, and the young man nodded weakly, then fell to his knees and kowtowed at Zhencai's feet. With a brief blessing for the attacker, Zhencai slid past him and dropped to one knee himself, passing a hand over Andao's skull, along his spine, feeling the ragged breath and rapid heartbeat. He gathered Andao against his chest and rose, staggering slightly. The fight had taken too much, today. Still, he would have enough. He pushed hard into his toes and ran across the square to the small door he had promised to lock. "Come!" he called over his shoulder, and the last attacker stumbled to his feet, nodded and broke into uneven motion, trying to follow him.

The sound of hoofbeats echoed from the direction of the river, then a spear lodged in the young man's chest, blood blossomed from his lips and he fell forward. The Mongols were here.

Zhencai slammed the door with his foot, leaned against it, scraping his cut back, and pushed his weight against the latch to slide it home. He lay Andao on a bed of moss beside the pool. The young man's eyes, golden-brown and bright, unlike his own near-black gaze, flickered up to meet him. "That was…what…" he mumbled something in another language, then, "amazing. Thank you."

"Where are you hurt?"

"Everywhere." Andao's mobile fingers twitched along his own limbs. He winced and prodded. "Maybe not broken." With a groan, he shifted onto his back, his hand returning to his head where blood matted his curly hair. "Outside, the Mongols."

"I do not think they will attack the temple," said Zhencai, but he remembered his own abbot slain in the graveyard, his own temple burning.

"Everything else."

For a moment, they were silent. The Buddha house echoed with the low thrum of chanting monks. The ground echoed with the tramping of feet, and the stamping of horses. Beyond the wall, screams, curses, cracking bones and clashing weapons. Smoke billowed up across the city, and the khan's great weapon voiced periodic thunder that shook the pagoda and sent bits of plaster and pots to rocking.

"All is ruin and decay. It is the way of the world," Zhencai murmured. "Life is suffering."

"My family!" Andao shouted, then he got his hands under him and rolled over. Clutching alternately at his bloody head and battered stomach, he dragged himself to a step and tried to get his feet under him. One shoe was missing, his toes bloody, likely trampled during the fight. He dug in his heel and pushed himself up, grabbing the edge of a vast urn. His knee crumpled, and he slid back down, still clinging to the urn, letting his head fall against it, sobbing.

Zhencai brought his feet into lotus position and his fingers into a pose of acceptance. Andao's broken weeping faded as Zhencai focused within. Aches now emerged from his battle, and he ignored them. Blood seeped down his back, hot, then cool, the sting of the cut merely another sensation among many.

"The scroll? The device." Andao's voice cracked. "They took it."

This required no answer. Zhencai had made his choice.

"Why does a monk want a weapon?"

This question fit nothing in Zhencai's knowledge, so he remained silent. Monks did not use weapons, at least, in his discipline, though he knew of others where sword and spear training might apply. Master Deng was no monk. His false record in the book of the sarira was only meant to convince others he was.

Andao lifted his head at last, smeared blood from his face, and pointed his bloody finger at Zhencai. "You set me to look for that scroll, so tell me why! Tell me why you wanted a weapon."

"I do not," he answered. "The Buddha's hand guided me toward the mystery of Master Deng and what he was seeking. The design on the scroll, it was a weapon?"

Breathing heavily, Andao turned until his back rested against the urn, his hands limp at last. "Something to do with the stars, with rivers of mercury and signs of death." He took a few deeper breaths. "You didn't know."

"I knew the man who took it, that is all."

Andao bent forward, too quickly, cradling his stomach. Zhencai edged closer. "Let us find herbs and bandages. You need rest to recover."

The curly head shook slightly. "What if he uses it? Is he on our side?"

More questions that had no bearing: Zhencai had no side, except that he wished the fighting would stop. "It is only a plan. Even should he wish to use it—"

"No! The weapon is already made. It's hidden, like the plan. I read that much." Andao gasped for breath, his shoulders trembling. "Have to stop him, have to… find… use…"

Whose side was Master Deng on? Certainly not the side of peace.

He hid for over a century among the sarira and wore the trappings of a Buddhist monk of high order. Until he appeared here, with men to search a monastery or to attack its inhabitants, to get back what he wanted. And when he had it, he wore the clothing of a Mongol. Another disguise. Could such a man be trusted with a weapon like the one Andao described?

Andao reached out to the broad stones of the walkway and dragged a bloody finger in a series of short movements. "On the scroll, the seal."

"*The Mandate of Heaven,*" he wrote. Then, "*By fire, by flood, by star. To fertilize the land in ashes, and be born again in blood.*"

"We have to," Andao breathed.

By Buddha's hand, and Andao's blood, Zhencai made the choice. He had been set upon this road, seeing the false monk, meeting Andao, finding and losing the scroll. Propelling him out of the monastery, into the world. Born again in blood.

CHAPTER SEVENTEEN

As the soldier bowed before her, Bao Xing gaped at the back of his head. "Come to the khan? But why?"

What could it mean? After days of living among the ladies, struggling to learn their ways, this sudden command to attend the khan, and the day after his destruction of Kaifeng… no, after his great victory. Bao Xing swallowed, trying to contain her own feelings. She had given herself into the Mongols' possession, from now on all that mattered was the khan. When the boredom of women's talk or the frustration of her isolation needled her, Bao Xing gazed at the sky and imagined the placement of the stars, the sinister creeping of the signs toward the Dark Lance. She imagined her father up in the mountains staring skyward as well, studying the same celestial phenomenon. She came here, to the Mongols, so that his work could go on. Even if she could no longer participate, the idea that they both watched the same sky consoled her loneliness.

"I do not question the command of the khan, lady," the soldier told her. "A sedan chair is coming for you. You may bring an attendant. This is all I know, lady." The angle of his head indicated he was staring at her feet, her tiny slippers protruding from the hem of her gown. She pulled them in, and his head tipped further, shoulders hunching as if in apology.

An attendant? Bao Xing's gaze swept the tent, her disordered bedding, her lap desk strewn with bits of paper and the low seat she occupied on one side, and the perfectly tidy belongings of the dancing girls opposite. Ming Lun sat there, her back to Bao Xing, as she directed the young women in a braiding technique using bundles of silk threads. To Bao Xing, the series of knots and silks looked like a great tangle waiting to happen, but she had never had such a patient teacher as Ming Lun.

"Mistress?"

The dance teacher turned her head. "Yes, my lady?"

"I am asked to go to the khan, but I may bring an attendant. Will you come with me?"

The older woman smiled gently and wound up the reel of silk she was using. "Of course, my lady. Give me a few moments to prepare."

Bao Xing completed her own preparations, painting on her eyebrows and painting her lips, twisting and pinning her hair with pearls and butterflies, her only concession was to slide the amulet on its silken cord around her neck and bury it beneath the layers of her gowns.

With economical movements, Ming Lun shrugged out of her simple dark overdress and found a long, elegant one with embroidered edges, binding this with a very long braided belt and hanging a few pouches from that. She took up her hair in braids and pins, not as elaborate as Bao Xing's, but with a pleasing symmetry. She pulled on long boots just as the sedan chair arrived.

Six young men—three ahead and three behind—set down the thick bars that carried the lacquered chair, deep black gilded with chrysanthemums and phoenix, symbols of the empress. Which imperial city had they stolen it from? It might well date from the Northern capital at Kaifeng itself. Perhaps the city mourned its imperial past, and thus could not settle beneath the Mongol yoke as it should. That might explain its rebellion. Bao Xing walked over with the help of her cane, and Ming Lun's strong hand helped her into the covered box, then she got in to the seat opposite and one of the bearers shut the door.

At a short command, the chair rose up and moved smoothly away from the ladies' tents. Small windows with spindles allowed a segmented view of all they passed—for now, the endless tents of the Mongol army. Her father claimed the Mongols, like all the would-be conquerors before them, would simply fade into the greatness of China, but Bao Xing saw their greed, their brutality, their sheer numbers, and she could not imagine them fading like old ink from the page of history.

"Thank you for the invitation, my lady," said Ming Lun. "It is rare I have the chance to see anything beyond the inside of a tent."

"I am glad of the company. I don't know... I can't think..." Bao Xing studied the handle of her cane, the ebony wood that curved up from the cinnabar decoration.

"You fear that the khan seeks female company." Ming Lun leaned forward. Already, their knees nearly brushed in the cramped space, and she lightly touched Bao Xing's hand. "It is not so fearsome as might be thought."

"You have—? But you are not married." Bao Xing immediately regretted this outburst, and her cheeks warmed. She knew the dance mistress came and went at odd hours sometimes, and wished she had the courage to do likewise, so that she might see the stars.

"In my village, a woman must have a beautiful voice in order to be married. Or she must have tiny feet."

"My mother saw to that."

"I did not know my mother."

"Oh!"

Ming Lun patted her hand again. "I have my own duty, a duty I discovered. A married woman is in this box all the time." She glanced at the inside of the sedan chair, with its silk paintings and tiny windows. "She cannot choose where to go or when. She cannot choose how to spend her time, but must be always waiting on her husband."

Thinking of her parents' mutual devotion, Bao Xing said, "I think there can be more to marriage than a box."

"Never expect more than a box, my lady, and you shall never be disappointed."

"That seems a rather bitter perspective."

"From my view upon the world, my lady, bitterness is justified." Ming Lun tipped her head to direct Bao Xing's view out the window. Flies buzzed and a ripe, rotten smell reached through the spindles. They passed a shadow and back into the sun. Bao Xing leaned toward the window, steadying herself with her fingers between the spindles. They had passed a great mound she did not recall from her visits to Kaifeng as a girl. Lumps and branches protruded from the mound, or rather, heads and arms and legs, a great heap of bodies. As she watched, Mongol soldiers dragged a few more to add them to the heap, but these ones had no heads. A pile of rubble followed on this—the ruins of the gate tower, but this, too, sprouted hands in unlikely places, fingers thick with death and dark with blood. Bao Xing's stomach soured. She pressed a hand over her mouth, but she forced herself to see what war had done.

The prophecy of the Dark Lance spoke to this. The Dark Lance scorched the sky with its great tail of fire and burned the light of the benevolent stars. The time of the Dark Lance was a time of chaos and dying, and her father believed it was coming. If he could work out when and give warning, surely some of the ill effects would be mitigated. Long ago, astronomers worked with geomancers on a way to avoid the poison of a ruined star, but the geomancers were no more, and astronomers like her father had only the power to predict and not to change.

But this … it was as if the Dark Lance already destroyed the power of the skies. As above, so below: that was the oldest tenet of culture, that the land would reflect the sky, and any disharmony there would play out here upon the earth. What dread star shone upon the birth of the Mongols?

Streets of empty, broken buildings followed, with Mongols overseeing little clumps of survivors, some on their knees, pleading, some weeping, some staring, vacant-eyed as a Mongol struck off their heads in a spray of blood. Young women, their clothing torn or gone altogether, moved like ghosts, hobbling on tiny feet. Without their slippers, their feet were hideous, deformed, the toes bent sharply under, the instep too high, bent into shape. Some of them had bindings that flapped like shrouds as they walked.

"They must be stopped," Ming Lun murmured, her fists clenched.

"What?"

The dancer blinked a few times and shook her head, her pins and chains tinkling together. "Forgive me, lady. I said I should like to stop. The ride makes me a little dizzy." She touched her hand to her forehead, smiling faintly.

Bao Xing sat up very straight. "No, mistress, that is not what you said."

"I only mean that the rebels should stop. The sooner they accept the rule of the Mongols, the safer we shall be."

Narrowing her eyes, Bao Xing pressed the point, her voice falling very low. "I do not think that is what you meant."

Black eyes stared back at her. "I serve the Great Khan now, my lady, as do you."

"What about the south?" Bao Xing breathed. "I imagine the rebels expect some support from the emperor."

The dark gaze flicked away. "The Son of Heaven may be concerned about the North, but I do not think he will intervene directly."

"The empire left Kaifeng with a promise to return. Even the capital city of the south is only temporary."

"Even in a very old nation, one hundred sixty years is a long time for a temporary thing."

Bao Xing studied her companion, the intense stillness of the dancer's form in spite of her off-hand manner of speech. "You are very well educated about history, mistress."

That brought a glint of teeth. "Many of my dances are historical, my lady. The steps and the movements remind us of things long ago and better left that way. And my own teacher had a deep love of the classics."

The classics, of course. A safe subject while history, apparently, was not. "I dearly miss having anything to read myself," Bao Xing said. "I am afraid to ask. The khan's archivist, Guowei, quickly claims any books, and Chubei and the other queens seem little interested in words."

Ming Lun laughed, a little sound of brightness in the enclosed space. "Indeed. They are interested in riding—both horses and men—and they care little for the culture of the Han people."

"The Han people." Ming Lun was a rebel, even if she had never done anything about it.

The sedan chair stopped and slowly settled to the ground, and both women leaned to their windows. Bao Xing gave a little gasp. Towering groves of willow surrounded them in a green and dappled cascade of sunlight. The snarls and strange cries of wild beasts rang around them, and the smell of smoke competed with the sweetness of flowers. Close by, the river murmured along its banks and fountains trickled in channels of stone.

One of the bearers opened the door, and Ming Lun stepped down first, reaching up to help Bao Xing out of the sedan chair. They stepped into another world, as if the bearers had carried them directly from the shelter of the ladies' tent to this lush garden by the river. They stood in an open space, with a high-arching bridge across the river to one side. The river itself, usually yellow with silt, looked red and lumpy and Bao Xing looked away. A cluster of men and horses moved forward, but they seemed hardly worth her attention compared with what stood between: an immense armillary sphere—a series of rings inside each other with the central one so tall that she could easily have stood inside of it. The bronze gleamed dully, green with age, and supported on sculptures of four writhing dragons. A round set of marble steps lead up to the dragons with a few weeds and clinging patches of moss. Her father spoke of instruments as great as this, but she never imagined she would see one.

Bao Xing took a few steps forward, then heard a hiss from Ming Lun, who was bowing deeply. Bao Xing arrested her excitement and bowed as well.

"I see you find the place as enchanting as my scout imagined. Perhaps I should bring my wives down for a visit. We could use such a place at the capital, eh, Batzorig?" The khan rubbed his hands together, glancing about.

"Certainly, my lord khan. But perhaps it is best the queens wait until the city has been tidied." The general stood stiffly to one side.

"Come, come—what do you think?" The khan waved them to rise, and Bao Xing straightened, smiling a little behind her hand.

The khan's retinue included a few other captains, and the dwarf she had seen at his ger the first night of celebration, who now watched her with a fascination that made her a little frightened. Behind him, as ever, stood the ghost. Today, the gaunt giant looked even more ghostly. His jade eyes seemed bleached of color and smears of darkness beneath made them more pale. His facial hair poked out in all directions, pale as well, framing his mouth, bent as if he were about to be ill. He looked a curse, and Bao Xing imagined her mother whispering charms to ward off evil and prayers to the ancestors to send the ghost's eyes away. But the ghost's eyes focused through her, through the world to something terrible beyond.

Bao Xing turned away, ducking that vacant stare. She assembled the words in Mongolian. "This place very beautiful, and many thanks you, Great Khan."

The khan grinned and laughed, then spoke carefully as well, in Chinese. "Many thanks you, as well! With such a beauty to frame, the garden shines more fair. What do you make of this?" He pointed to the astronomical device, and Bao Xing hurried toward it, her cane rapping, her little feet moving in their mincing steps.

She ran her free hand along the largest circle, then gave a little push to one of the inner rings. It groaned with age and unoiled hinges, but rotated slowly at her whim. "It is an armillary sphere, my lord khan, for noting the movements of the stars. Here, this ring shows the rising and setting of the sun, and these determine the path of eclipses—when the sun shall go dark, about every generation. And this ring shows the twenty-eight celestial mansions—" She stopped short, cheeks warming so that she was grateful for the white paint that concealed her blush. "Forgive me, my lord. I have not before seen a monumental instrument so fine." She bowed again, the laughter of men piling up all around her.

"Oh, you are a treasure, no doubt. Do you suppose my wives have any idea? What a heap of nonsense to keep in a woman's head." The khan's broad Chinese stumbled over words and might have gotten them wrong, but she did not think so. "Pity that Guowei's already heading back to Xuzhou. I'm sure he would have some insight."

Bao Xing stared at the ground. Bronze characters embellished the stone at her feet, set in level with the surface. She slowly bent down and swept away a scattering of old leaves.

"What do the words say? They are instructions for its use?" The khan and a few of his party moved closer. The ghost remained, swaying, as if their presence had been the only thing keeping him upright, then came up and bowed at the khan's insistent gesture. The dwarf did not need to stoop at all to see the words at her feet.

"It is a memorial inscription, my lord." She swept a little more, leaning too far, and caught herself on her cane, straightening. She read, *"To mark the worthy and sorrowful union of the watchers of stars*—astronomers—*with the movers of earth"*—(geomancers, she thought, but did not say). *"In the order of celestial purity. As above, so below.* And the date, about one hundred sixty years ago, my lord."

"Is that it? Hardly seems worth the effort."

"There are more words on the other side, lady," said a soft, high voice. The dwarf gestured.

She moved slowly around the great sphere, watching the changing views supplied by its rings. The various planes held markings for taking accurate measurements, but something about the rings bothered her. Perhaps she was unused to seeing them on such a scale. By the time she reached the other side, the dwarf had scraped away the moss to reveal the engraved characters.

"In time of peace, the sun shines by day, auspicious stars by night. In time of war, shed darkness over all. As above, so below." Strange, that repetition, like a refrain to a song, the ancient reminder of the link between heavens and earth, through the intermediary of the Son of Heaven, the emperor himself. Strange, too, that there was no emperor's name associated with

the inscription. At the time, however, the family claiming the imperial city had no truly imperial standing, though they pretended they did. She wished she could go back up the mountain and ask her father about the sphere and its curious inscription. A scraping sound drew her attention, as the dwarf worked in a circular path, removing the rest of the moss. He revealed a series of dots and lines, the representations of constellations, but no more words. She followed, looking at the diagrams, then back up at the device.

From this side, the unusual feature stood out: a bronze tube attached to the horizon ring. From the other side, she had seen only the bump of the end of this tube. It must be for sighting the stars, well, a particular star, in any case—likely the Imperial star itself. She tilted her head and peered into it. At the moment, in daylight, it sighted a distant mountain. The mountain might be used to track the positions of stars, though with such a device, it seemed unnecessary—backward, even—to depend on geographical features. The mountain did have a pleasing, auspicious shape, but so did many others, no doubt. She set her hands on the ring and tried to push it into position, but it did not groan or shift. Too long without moving. A little oil might do the task, as it had on the amulet she wore beneath her robes.

She used the ring for balance, peering around to see where it might be oiled. Unlike the other ring, this one was attached directly to the frame. Bao Xing shook her head with a little tingle of gold, then she hesitated. There, at the center of the sphere by the model of the earth and moon, was another tiny addition: an inconspicuous string of stars; her father's and grandfather's obsession, the harbinger of evil: the Dark Lance ringed by a wandering star.

CHAPTER EIGHTEEN

"What do you say, Drakemaster? Will it yield enough bronze to cast another firedrake?"

The lady gasped, but controlled herself quickly.

Dailus stared through the rings of the sculpture, watching the bodies that drifted on the river, their hair tangled, their faces bloated and clothing stained with blood, bile and smoke. God help him if he ever made another firedrake.

Yesterday, as he followed his magnificent creation on its slow circuit of the city, destroying the walls so no rebel could shelter there again, he surged with pride at every shot, every accurate strike and every use of his system for raising the barrel. Every gleam of the sun upon the graven horses and clouds warmed his own heart. The rumble of its blast resonated through the bronze for long moments afterward, and he could even tell by the sound if the barrel were getting too warm and they needed to give time for it to cool. The firedrake felt like a living beast, a beast almost of his own blood, raised by his hand, his partner and servant just as Yusen's beloved horses were to him. He knew its mood, its voice, its hunger. It hungered for death.

Last night, when it became too dark to fire and all that remained was for the Tatars to find and subdue the last of the rebels, Dailus and his crew returned to camp, triumphant. Even the slaves were given airag, allowed to drink, to cheer, to dance around their braziers, and Wang Lin Yo let his eyes half-close and his lips half-smile, maybe thinking of his paizi, the pass that would grant him freedom. Again, Dailus and Yusen went to the khan's ger for feasting and dancing girls. Dailus drank little, preferring to keep his wits, especially around drunken Tatars, but he let himself relax, enjoying the dance mistress's graceful athletic movement.

Then a gong banged outside, and the gathered men rose and trooped out of the ger. A ring of torches illuminated the moment, snapping red and glowing gold—like the brightness of the firedrake's voice, Dailus thought. Then, in a moment, he was sober.

"You, too, deserve some reward," the khan was saying. "I save myself for my wives and concubines, but we must show these rebels some discipline." His magnanimous hand offered girls. Women. Many of them barely old enough for marriage, as old as those dancing girls or the khan's Cathayan treasure-woman. They stood in ragged rows, clutching what remained of their clothing, hiding their faces with their hands, or behind curtains of hair. They wept and sniffled. They shrieked when a Tatar seized their hair and tipped their heads back for a look at their hidden faces. They shrieked the more when the soldiers dragged them off or carried them, when the soldier's rough hands clasped their waists or shoulders, or cradled the backs of their necks with command.

Munkjar strode among them, disdaining the littlest, and taking the arm of an older woman, tugging her in the direction of his own ger. She glanced back, whimpering, her feet dragging, then stumbled along with him, her skin looking cold in the firelight.

"What do you like? Little ones? First time for them is very exciting, eh?" The khan pointed to a cluster of girls around Anya's age, hiding their minimal breasts, shrinking into themselves.

"No," said Dailus, faint with horror.

"Older then—just ripe." The khan laughed and pointed. "Not so many choices there. Or maybe some experience? Here, these ones have been taken from rebel husbands. These need to learn the meaning of duty and discipline. Even should their husbands defy their lord khan, they must remember I defend this country and I make the laws here." He thumped his chest.

The women flinched. Fewer by the moment as other men made their choices. A pair of soldiers wrangled over one girl, and finally agreed which would have her first. The second man chose his own, and they all went off together.

Yusen was nowhere to be seen. He must have already chosen and taken his reward. Would he be in the ger even now, deflowering a child, or disciplining another man's wife? Dailus closed his eyes, but he pictured his master taking Anya by the hand, laying her down on a woolen robe and brushing back her golden hair—Dailus turned away from the khan, staggered to his knees and vomited.

The khan laughed uproariously, as if this were the greatest jest he'd ever known. "Take your time then, but they'll all be well-used by morning, better to claim yours now! Give her to the other slaves if you want." Still laughing, the khan returned to his ger, shouting to clear the place of soldiers, shouting for his youngest wife, Chubei, to help him celebrate.

Ignored by the others, Dailus slunk away in the darkness, stumbling back toward Yusen's ger, then remembering his master's absence at the giving of women, he angled toward the workshop. He curled on his blankets beneath the work table. The slaves' celebration wound down to drunken murmurs and bursts of song, hiccups, and snoring. Elsewhere in camp, drums beat and men still shouted. Women cried, and Dailus clamped his arms over his head, curled on his side tight as he could, yet he could not block the sounds he could not hear. All around him in the darkness stood the evidence of his creation: models in brass and ceramic, molds and sketches, the faintest smell of power and of smoke.

He need not take a woman by force that night. In his own way, he had forced them all, for his firedrake that destroyed their defenses. He shattered the walls and allowed the tide of Tatars to rush in among them, to slaughter their men, burn their houses and steal themselves and their daughters. For what? For the merest hope of his own freedom. Even were the slave-band gone from his wrist and he a thousand miles from Cathay, he would never be free of their tears. He gripped the band. Yusen and the khan enslaved his body, but he himself had bound his soul. He should wear that band for the rest of his days, to remember what he had become. Murderer, destroyer, drakemaster.

"Cha! Drakemaster!" The khan snapped his fingers in Dailus's face, drawing him back from the memory. "This should be an easy one, eh? Easier than breaking bells for certain."

Dailus forced himself to look at the device. "Yes, easier, my lord," he rasped. He had eaten nothing, drunk nothing since purging himself last night. The young Cathayan woman continued her perusal of the device, fascinated by something deep in the workings, but Dailus pushed his feet up the steps. He tapped one of the rings. It sang dully, connected too tightly, but the next one gave a beautiful note, and the one after that, higher, and the one after that, as if the rings were tuned as an instrument of music even more than of the stars. He ran his hands along the frame that held it. His slave bracelet clinked against it.

The wingless dragons that supported the frame astonished him. Carved in every detail, with sharp-edged claws and ranks of scales, sinuous bodies and clasping limbs, they looked ready to leap from their mountings and tumble about. As long as a man was tall, but coiled in a lively fashion, they crouched one at each direction, mouths open and keen eyes staring. Even his trained eye had trouble finding the markings of molds or any flaw in casting. If the talents of these long-gone sculptors turned to cathedrals and saints, what a work they might have made to the glory of God! If Jian Ho had lived, what would he have made of this? Cathay held such arts that his own country could never match. To sculpt a beast with such live and vigor, to cast it so perfectly. Somewhere in this city lived the descendants of the artists, the apprentices of their apprentices. Rather, they had lived, until Dailus turned his art against them and blasted their homes to Hell. Drakemaster.

"The metal is good quality?"

"The best, my lord." Dailus's hand lingered on the dragon's mouth.

A wave summoned one of the soldiers with the silver belts—the khan's personal guard. "Bring up Wang Lin Yo and his crew—if they've recovered from their night. Tell them to break up the whole thing, the letters as well. We might need every scrap if the rebels aren't through." The khan pointed toward the inscription on the base. The soldier bowed and mounted his horse. In a few hours, the magnificent device would be scrap, piled in a cart and borne away to cast more firedrakes.

Dailus could go back with it. If he worked fast, he could break the molds and perhaps destroy the models. Without getting hold of the hammers Wang Lin Yo guarded, he could not think how to ruin the great firedrake itself.

Across the rings from him, the young woman sighed, her shoulders sinking. She spoke of the thing as a work of knowledge, while he viewed it as a work of art. In days it would become a weapon of war, and neither of them could stop it. Someone had been trying to stop it all along. Someone spoiled the powder and sabotaged the molds. Someone assassinated the last drakemaster, thinking, as had the khan, that it would take months to replace him.

Dailus trailed back down the steps. Beyond a screen of bamboo rose the ruined city, houses and towers smoldering, corpses rotting, dogs and rats feasting in the alleys, and soldiers toiling to clean the streets. The ragged women of Kaifeng—those who had survived the night—crept back to what remained of their homes. Were they still strong enough to weep, still living enough to bleed?

"What about the temple?" the khan was saying to one of his men.

"By your command, my lord, the monastery has not been harmed."

The khan growled a little. "Has it been searched? Any rebels must be found, even if they hide at the feet of their god. If any are found, then seize their bells as well—anything we can use."

"Yes, my lord."

Dailus walked the edge of the cobbled plaza. Near the sedan chair, the dance mistress waited, head tipped demurely, but her eyes flicked up as he prowled by. Heathens. Idolaters. Foreign temptresses no better than Delilah. The Holy Church would not decry a single death he had caused, nor pity a single woman who had been defiled. Their own holy knights had done the same in driving out the heathens in Jerusalem. This crusade was one of heathens upon heathens—let them all die and their places, their rights, their wealth, be claimed by god-fearing men.

The half-circle bridge rose up before him, cool and bright in white marble, leading to a little island with a pretty pavilion at its heart. Dailus climbed slowly up the steep bridge. Heathens had made it. Heathen architects and builders worked out how the arch must be shaped, and how to raise it over a river. Heathen masons crafted the stones and heathen sculptors like Jian Ho had carved them. Heathen ladies and heathen lords walked this bridge and spoke heathen poems in their uncouth tongue. In their heathen temples, idolaters worshipped a gilded god.

In the quick water as the river narrowed beneath the bridge, between the garden and the island beyond, a heathen child's body drifted by. Her face was dark, her eyes were bright, her hair was long and shining.

Yusen had seized Dailus for this, that his skills could be turned to the khan's great crusade and enable the Tatars to destroy whatever resistance they met on their path to the glory of the Eternal Sky. Dailus knew of no others in the army or among the slaves who could do what he did. The assassin of the last drakemaster had assumed as much, but never imagined a slave would claim the task, nor had the khan imagined a slave would be capable of it. Without Dailus, they could make no more weapons.

A slave he remained. Even if the khan took him from Yusen into his own household, every day his art and knowledge would destroy a few more sculptures, a few more cities, a few more hundred or thousand lives. Even if he one day earned his freedom, he would have paid in the coin of heathen lives. He clung to the slave band at his wrist.

God forgive him. Jesus and Mary and all the saints forgive him. Anya, dear Anya, forgive him too, on behalf of a thousand heathen girls who would not be touched by Tatar hands.

Dailus placed his hands on the marble baluster, climbed up, and jumped. He prayed as he fell, prayed as his back slammed the water, prayed as the silt of Cathay and the blood of her people rushed into his mouth, as the sun vanished in the gloom over his head.

CHAPTER NINETEEN

Yusen drank in Bao Xing's every graceful gesture, the way her eyes flared with delight and discovery, and then her face sank into a frown of concentration. Sunlight gave her hair the sheen of silk, and she pressed her hand for a moment to her breast, the cloth of her gown outlining the amulet he had sent her, the one his father brought back from his own campaigns far to the southwest. She wore it so close to her skin that it thrilled him just to see her hand press against it. On this glorious morning, Yusen stood in the pleasure garden of a city he had helped to conquer, both by his own prowess, and through his seizure of the bell maker whose labor broke the gates. In that moment, he felt a thousand feet tall, soaring in the khan's laughter, in the army's victory, in the lady's beauty, in the strength of his own body—small though it was, it had served him well.

It was not until the bearer's shout broke his concentration that he knew something was wrong, and not until he followed them, running, up the half-round bridge that he realized what had happened. The slave was trying to escape. His initial splash was a ripple in the river's current. Yusen roared his rage, a pitiful, too-high sound.

"Get after him! Someone bring him back!" The khan thundered up along with them, fists clutching his thickly embroidered del, his horsetail crest waving.

The soldiers and bearers swallowed and looked anywhere but at the river—likely the khan was the only one among them who could swim, and he only could because his grandfather, Chinggis himself, had thrown the boys in, assuming that old story could be believed. Yusen leaned close against the balusters, looking between. The slave's pale hair broke the surface some distance away already, then sank back again, his pale hands wafting nearby. Stupid, to jump from a bridge when he seemed no better at swimming than the rest of them.

The dance mistress sprang up to the rail and dove in. She surfaced right away, her strong arms cutting through the water, her big feet kicking behind her, pushing hard and fast with the current to catch up.

The soldiers gave a cheer, but already, the glimpse of the slave's hair was rounding a bend, the woman straining to close the gap. In moments, both would be out of sight.

Yusen turned and dropped to one knee before the khan. "My lord, I shall bring him back. Wherever they land, whether he is alive or dead, my lord, I shall return him to you for the khan's justice."

The khan's eyes narrowed in his round face. "You do that, scout. If that woman pulls him up alive, I will grant her the freedom of the empire. And if you fail me, scout, woe be to you, no matter your size. No cartwheel will defend you from my wrath."

With a bow of his head, Yusen rose and sprinted back down, nearly losing his balance on the arch of the bridge. He stumbled and caught himself before he ran into the lady Bao Xing, her face once again a painted mask as she stared down at him, her red lips pursed. As he ran for his horse, Yusen could hear the crumbling of his own dreams, the precarious glory of the day shattered in front of all this company—his slave escaping in broad daylight, humiliating him before the khan and before the lady. He became once again tiny and ridiculous, a monkey with no tail or a child with no minder. Vaulting into Tsang's saddle, Yusen galloped back through the gates of the garden and along the battered and bloody streets of Kaifeng. Even passing the intersection where he had burned the barricade brought him no joy. Outside the ruined walls, he turned sharply east, skirting the mound of bodies the soldiers were building, and rode until he found the river again, glimpsed between clusters of net-strewn hovels and rickety docks.

He pushed between these to the riverside, Tsang snorting and prancing beneath him. The river widened here and a few bodies gathered against the dock footings. Whatever boats there may have been were gone, taken by rebels not brave enough to fight. The bend channeled most of the floating debris of battle, the burned wood and ruined furnishings, toward the other bank far away. In the scruffy brush on the other side, he caught glimpses of hidden boats and thought he saw movement, but couldn't be sure. An arm flashed from the water—the woman still swam, then she went under and he saw the slave's head, bedraggled with weeds and water. The current drove them away.

Yusen gritted his teeth. It would not be so easy, then. Very well. He turned his mount and kept riding, a little faster than the river flowed.

Clearly, he had been lax in his duty to his slave, allowing him to join the celebrations, to join this morning's party without proper supervision. Didn't the drakemaster know what would happen to him when he was caught? Yusen had been too enchanted with the lady and with his own cleverness in having her brought there. Now, even if he brought the slave back alive, the khan might have to torture and kill him just to ensure the discipline of the others. The drakemaster understood nothing. Together they had risen in comfort and power, and together, they could have risen very far indeed. Apart, they would both be punished. The sentence for a man of the khan's blood was to be rolled into a felt and drowned rather than allow a drop of the royal blood to be spilled. Already, Yusen's breath grew short, his face hot and stifled as if pressed into the wool.

There! A broad road to the right-hand, to cross the river. Yusen turned and pushed hard. Tsang gave him the speed he asked for, laying back her ears and stretching her neck, then snorting wildly when he pulled her up short. She stumbled and danced to the side, kicking herself back to balance.

A bridge abutment started from the street, only to break off at the edge of the water, with bits of rubble and vacant footings dotting the path it would have taken, all the way to the broken end on the other side. Thick ropes stretched between the fragments, down low to prevent the passage of boats trying to flee the city. Similar ropes would be strung across above Kaifeng as well.

Stroking Tsang's neck, Yusen walked her in a slow circle, glancing back at the river that thwarted him. Where was the nearest bridge? This one had been ruined by the rebels to thwart the khan's army. Yusen growled under his breath. The current suggested they would wash up on the other side. It would be best if he crossed below them, in case they were pushed far downstream, but the nearest bridge might be upstream, in fact, where the river narrowed. It would take time that he did not want to give.

Accepting the burden, Yusen rode back toward camp.

He first visited the grand ger where the general presided, hoping Munkjar would be busy with the remains of Kaifeng. No such luck. A pair of guards announced his arrival, and the familiar broad shoulders and bright armor greeted him as Munkjar turned. "Has the khan tired of you already?"

"I have a commission to bring back an escaped slave, general. I ask you to issue a scout's share." He stared past the general, as if the felt panels on the wall fascinated him. A few servants busied themselves folding bedding and polishing weapons.

Munkjar strolled up beside him, then glanced sharply down as if surprised by his size. "You seemed taller last night at the khan's ger. What slave has escaped?"

"The drakemaster, general."

Clapping his hands, the general roared with laughter. "Your only slave and the only thing you've ever done right in this army? Oh, you are a fine one to speak of discipline, my little Cartwheel." Munkjar snorted his laughter still and rubbed his eyes. "And the khan trusts you to bring him back? Here I thought your trip to the pleasure garden was sure to be boring. Who knew what I've been missing."

Munkjar rounded the ger to his portable desk, but hesitated over the sheaf of papers there. "How do we know you'll even return?"

Yusen's jaw ached from clenching. "My ger and my falcons will remain, general. I hope they will be cared for in my absence."

The general rifled his papers and plucked out one, adding a stamp of his personal sign. "There, a scout's share of grains and what other stores you need."

"I'll need a prisoner's board."

Munkjar scrawled a few more words on the page and handed it to a waiting Chin clerk. "I don't know that we have arrows to suit your… strength, but you may take them as well." The general strolled back, his boots quiet on the carpets beneath. "And if you don't return, I shall have the pleasure of hunting you, Cartwheel. As once I hunted your father." He shifted, his arm lifting as if to test the measure of Yusen's height once more, but Yusen ducked him with a bow, and turned away.

At his ger, he collected what he would need in the wilderness, recreating the bundles he had taken apart when he joined the tumaan with his slave, thinking to settle in and enjoy their new position. From the deepest part of his pack, he found the worn fur pouch that contained a few remembrances of his home, still, on the rare occasions he opened the pouch, smelling faintly of smoke. He tucked it into a satchel that would be strapped to one of his spare mounts along with the supplies the general issued.

Yusen touched the doorway of his ger, a painted frame with clouds for the Eternal Sky, mountains for the bones of the earth, eagles in between, for the souls of his family. Closing his eyes, he rested his forehead against the wood. In memory, their screams echoed in the burning camp, he could hear his father's final words, urging him to fulfill the duty they owed to their khan, the duty his father had betrayed and for which his entire family had been punished. Long ago, he raced through training, mastering sword and horse and bow to prove his worth before Munkjar's measure found him tall enough to slay. The honor of his family rested on his shoulders. This morning, standing in the sun at the side of the khan, he had felt so close to their redemption, now all of those hopes were drowned. His father had betrayed him by betraying the khan. Now his slave, too, had betrayed him. Munkjar stood ready to betray him yet again. It was too much.

He should make an offering, find an oovo where he could pray, or go to the shaman to ask for the thing he had never dared before: a vision of his future. Already he had taken too much time.

He took up the lead ropes for his four spare mounts and gathered the horses for travel. At least a day and night, more if he must search every bit of brush and tiny island near the other bank where the body might wash up. And if he did not find it, then it was better never to return. No, that was unacceptable. He vowed upon the eagles and the spirits they carried, that he would find the missing slave if he had to dam the river and search its mud for the drakemaster's remains, the slave bracelet still marking the over-long bones of his arm. His khan would see that he cared for honor and for duty. His khan would know, and Munkjar's sword be sheathed forever. At last, he would stand proud and claim his family's name. In this, Yusen vowed, he would not fail.

CHAPTER TWENTY

The meditative air of the monastery felt oppressive as smoke wafted on the breezes around them. Zhencai sat with the other monks, bowed with them, chanted with them, his prayer beads filtering slowly through his fingers, but he wondered what lay outside. When his mind should empty of all but the Buddha spirit, worldly concerns haunted him. Andao rested on a pallet in the novices' chamber with herbed poultices on his wounds, his ribs and arm wrapped, his gaze roving the outside wall as if he could see the city beyond. The novices climbed the pagoda once more, but furtively lest they be mistaken for archers and shot from the tower. They reported that many buildings still stood, especially down by the gardens and the old imperial structures, the things the Mongols would preserve for their own use. The last Mongol governor had been killed and his staff expelled, the rebellion which had brought upon the city this latest calamity. *In the next ten days, catastrophe.* Just as the ancient bone predicted.

Banging echoed through the courtyard into the Buddha house where they all sat, a hundred shaven heads, bowed over their hands, their beads clicking. The banging came again, and someone outside shouted, "Open the gate or we shall break it in. The general Batzorig demands entrance!"

Zhencai's throat clenched. If the monastery were found to be harboring any rebels, they could all be punished.

Benmo's deep-set eyes found his, then the senior monk rose languidly, bowed to the aged abbot and moved very slowly toward the door. "I pray your patience, general. I come to let you in."

Zhencai bowed more swiftly and sprang, sprinting toward the novices' chamber. But what could he do? Where could Andao be hidden? He had no doubt his brother monks would stand upon the Buddha's mercy rather than allow the young man to be slain, but to do so would condemn them all—and allow Master Deng and his weapon the freedom of destruction that the Mongols so enjoyed.

In the dim chamber, Andao lay awake. "Master," he said, his voice more even after a night's rest and many cups of tea.

In a monastery of open-walled chambers and a hundred men, there was only one place to hide him. "I must shave your head."

"What?" Andao pushed himself up, wincing, nearly sliding back again, and Zhencai caught his shoulder, helping him to sit.

"The Mongols are here and they will kill you. Unless they believe you are one of us."

"I can't—I can't pretend to be—to worship—no! I can't do it. Hashem forbids it." He gasped and fumbled for the cup of cool tea at his side.

"Hashem. This is your leader?"

The curly head shook. "Hashem is the creator of my people." He glanced heavenward.

"He is your god."

"We don't say that word for him."

"He forbids you to be shaven."

"Yes." He gazed into the cup, but the reflections trembled.

Zhencai sat back on his heels. He thought he had found the solution to Andao's safety, but this foreign god had strange ways.

"You think it will save me?" Andao whispered.

"I believe this."

"Fine." He set aside the cup and bowed his head, but a few tears dripped to fall upon the stone or land in the tea. "My sisters, my mother left the city weeks ago. My father—everyone else is already dead, aren't they."

Zhencai took out a long, sharp knife. "I believe this also." He took hold of Andao's curly locks, rough and springy. Normally, this was a ritual between a senior monk and a novice entering the monastery. The Buddha of his compassion would not mind, yet it still felt strange to ply the blade and scrape away a swath of Andao's hair. "Your Hashem. Does he welcome your people into Nirvana?"

"He will. On the day when all rise up to join Him." Andao swallowed hard. "If their bodies are intact." His shoulders trembled.

Andao's god clearly required more compassion if such a matter as a burned body or missing limb would keep his people from Nirvana. Zhencai worked to shave Andao's hair.

From the first courtyard, footfalls marched and voices echoed.

Zhencai forced his hand to move slowly and evenly, the last patch of curls tumbling to the ground where he shoved them underneath the bedding.

"Here—what's this?" A Mongol marched into the room. "Not at your prayers, brothers?"

Andao went rigid, and Zhencai gave a brief bow. "This novice was injured yesterday when the ground shook. I have been preparing herbs for his comfort."

Squatting down, the Mongol grabbed Andao's shoulder and shook him. "Look at me, boy—look at me!"

Trembling, Andao turned his head.

"He looks to me as if he's been fighting." The Mongol's dark gaze fell upon Zhencai.

Zhencai spread his hands. "Our order practices martial discipline. This novice has not excelled in that. Yesterday's experience suggests that poor balance is to blame."

"Show me something. Now. One of your tactics." The Mongol soldier gave them room, beckoning with a dagger in his fist.

Zhencai rose, his joints stiff after yesterday's excitement and a long morning of ritual.

"Him. I want to see him do it."

Letting the blankets fall from his lap, Andao rose unsteadily, the Mongol staring at him. He wore simple trousers and his tunic had been taken for cleaning, leaving his thin chest bare save for his bandages. Zhencai stepped back, out of the soldier's line of sight. He held his hands in the sign of blessing. Andao's gold-flecked glance darted at him and back to the soldier, his throat working and lips trembling. Hesitantly, he lifted his hands and echoed Zhencai's movement as he repeated the gesture.

"Show him the iron hand strike," Zhencai suggested, miming the movement—slicing a hand backward then thrusting forward sharply, open palm, fingers clamped together.

Andao tried to stand as Zhencai stood, gathered himself and swung his arm about. His habit of flailing his hands as he spoke at least gave him some ease of movement, but the gesture looked weak, the attack of a scholar, not a warrior. "No!" Zhencai shouted. "Again!"

Andao flinched and stumbled back. He placed his feet again in imitation of a martial stance, drew a deep breath that made him wince, and tried again.

Zhencai drew up his qi and centered it at his hips, striding forward, pushing past the Mongol as if the soldier meant nothing at all. "No, no, no." He caught Andao's hands and formed them into blessing, then pressed down on his thighs, forcing him lower.

Whimpering, the young man tried to sink down as Zhencai demanded. "Lower! Lower! Here—your arm is like iron." He seized Andao's arm and held it out to the side as if preparing for the strike. "Have you heard nothing? Have you done nothing all of these months?" he barked.

"Please, master." Andao's voice cracked.

"Here, brother, there's no need—" the soldier began.

"No need? You are a warrior yourself." Zhencai pointed to the Mongol. "Discipline of the body is essential to discipline of the spirit."

"Yes, but he's injured—he can barely stand." The Mongol waved his free hand at Andao. "Surely he can recover before he—"

"Ai!" Zhencai smacked a closed fist into his palm. "Does your general Batzorig allow you such luxury? Surely he does not or your army should not be so powerful."

The soldier squared his shoulders. "Well, not luxury, but for injuries, there's some… accommodation."

"The Buddha's service requires no less." Zhencai bowed deeply. "Forgive me that you have not seen the strength of spirit that we should reveal. I assure you, this boy will work hard until he is worthy."

"Yes, of course." The Mongol backed away, frowning, his mustache wriggling as he considered Zhencai and his hapless student, clearly thinking one or both must be utterly mad. He turned and went down the steps, crossing toward the library chambers where a group of soldiers routed through the scrolls.

Zhencai swung about, lunging to catch Andao as his fragile balance collapsed. The young man's bald head pitched forward against Zhencai's chest. Alive, alive! Letting him back onto the pallet, Zhencai shifted them away from the open wall. He refilled the cup of tea and offered it to Andao's pale lips. "Drink, please. Rest."

Andao drank and laughed without sound. "Rest? Master, you coddle me." His eyes closed, his lids slightly lavender with the veins beneath his skin. "When do we begin my training?" He cradled his bandaged arm against his chest.

"Forgive me. The soldier doubted us, and I sought to prove what I claimed." Zhencai held Andao's wrist, counting his rapid pulse, and watching his breathing.

"No." Andao opened his eyes. "I have to learn this if I'm going to help you find the weapon." Again, he almost laughed. "If I'm going to stay alive."

"This discipline is no easy thing." Zhencai planted his fists on his thighs. "And I am no worthy teacher."

"You beat six men last night, master."

Zhencai shook his head. "That is not all a monk must be."

"I can't be a monk, I just need—" Andao's voice faltered and he took another swallow. "I came here seeking knowledge. I need to know how to live. Help me. Show me how."

"I cannot teach you strength without the strength of the Buddha. I cannot teach you discipline without the quiet of the Buddha. These things are not in pieces, they are everything together." His hands rose up and shaped the blessing. "They contain each other."

Andao regarded him for a long moment. "I wish I could contain some of you."

Zhencai sat back on his heels, all words taken from him. He was the least of monks, the one so undisciplined that his abbot sent him to sweep the sarira temple like a novice, the one who could not sit meditation without thinking of the world. He knew the body, yes, he knew how to use it and even how to teach its use, in order to turn away from its needs as it became strong enough to sustain the spirit, that was all. Why should anyone wish to have a piece of him?

But Andao's spirit so clearly needed sustenance. Who else, in such a time and place, could teach him anything at all?

"I am no sage," Zhencai told him. "I am not a master, but I will teach you what I know." A smile flickered to Andao's lips, but Zhencai put up a finger in warning. "The Buddha will be present, as he is in all things. He will be in my teachings and he will be in my spirit, and I leave it to you and your Hashem to meditate on what that means." He took note of Andao's willowy frame and scholar's hands. "It will be hard—very difficult. The novice must be willing to eat bitter."

Andao set aside his cup, and a flash of the power of his qi came suddenly to his eye. "Master, no one knows more of eating bitter than a Jew. We have entire holidays for eating bitter." He drew a deep, shuddering breath. "When do we begin?"

CHAPTER TWENTY-ONE

Dailus convulsed and curled into himself as the devils of Hell assailed him with their punching hands and clawing fingers. He came to, coughing and choking, branches dragging at his clothes and powerful hands pounding on his back. They let up abruptly as he spat out water and wiped his face, finally blinking open his eyes. His throat and chest seared with pain, as if he had swallowed fire not ash, but the place was too dim and dense with rugged vegetation to be Hell. All of which meant he was not dead. He shivered and plucked a weed from his beard. Beyond the thicket, the river rumbled past without him.

"Then you are alive," a woman said in Mongolian.

Dailus caught his breath. He twisted onto his back, pushing the hair from his eyes.

The dancer knelt over him, her glossy hair hanging in wet ringlets from the combs and pins that remained, her keen gaze dodging away. "Rest, get your breath."

She rose up and moved through the underbrush followed by a soft snapping of twigs and rustle of grasses. Dailus pushed himself to sitting, his back against an ancient tree trunk mired in the dirt. In moments, she returned, crouching as she ran. "No, not safe. Still too close." She seized his hand and dragged him to his feet, pulling him along in spite of himself.

Dailus hurried with her, stumbling, still shaky. They passed a little clump of Cathayans, including a boy who brandished a knife at him, but the woman tugged him onward. Other eyes watched them, haunted with fear, hiding from the Tatars. From Dailus, though they knew it not. He saw an old man, slender as a skeleton, a woman sheltering a group of children, a few men with the round caps and curling hair he associated with Jews. For a moment, in these glimpses of faces that could not be, Dailus started to think he might be in Hell after all, along with the heathen rebels he had killed and whomever else defied the Lord.

They splashed into a rivulet, and the woman hesitated, glancing back at him. "You don't swim."

"No," he told her.

She dragged him after her along the edge of the water, finding a narrow log and letting go of him to glide across it on small, precise steps, turning to wait for him on the other side. Dailus shook his head. "I can't do that."

The woman curled her hand imperiously, holding her arm outstretched. "You cannot swim either, yet you escape by leaping into a river. Why so?"

"I wasn't trying to escape." The long grooves of the tree bark looked slippery. Her years of dancing served her well.

Taking a few steps back onto the log, she held out her hand. "That did not kill you. Nor will this."

Dailus set one foot then the other on the log, his toes sticking off one side, his heels to the other, his arch painfully draping the narrow wood. His hips swayed wildly, the log bouncing, and his hand flailed. He caught at her, gripping her wrist and she his.

He inched toward her across the log, she stood steady as a tree, bending her knees to balance them both. He wet his lips, tasting the grit of silt, surely only imagining the blood. "Why did you save me?"

"No one truly wishes to die."

"Few so truly deserve it." With a flurry of steps, he reached the other bank, and she released him to find his balance. He bent, hands on knees, catching his breath and coughing again.

"Come." She threaded her way between clumps of brush, old logs, and the occasional bit of furniture or carved stone left over from flood season.

Dailus stumbled after her, pushing things out of his way, ducking branches and beating back the twigs that tried to snare him. "Who are you?"

"I am Ming Lun." A name, but no answer. She slid between the branches and trotted along stones and logs.

"I'm Dailus," he told her, but she might be too far ahead to hear him.

They crossed another stream, and Dailus, panting and weak in the knees, called out, "I can't, I'm too tired."

Instantly, she appeared again, her fingers occupied with twining her hair. She finished the twist and pinned the lock in place. Over the course of their hike, he had been scraped, bruised and stumbling, and she had been fixing her hair. Dailus shook his head and sank to his knees. "I'm sorry. You go on." His head bowed, and her bare feet hesitated, then trotted off again. For a moment, his heart gave a lurch, but truly, she should look after herself. Should he be grateful to a person who saved his life when he himself sought to be rid of it? There on his knees, Dailus pressed his palms together, his limbs trembling. What if her rescue meant he had a chance at redemption? Did God want him to show mercy to the heathens, or did God allow him to live so that he could continue his work of destruction?

With a swish of her skirts, the woman emerged from a different direction. "Here is better. It's very close." She gave a little nod of encouragement.

Dailus left his prayer in God's hands, or maybe, in hers, and followed a few more steps. A tree stump the size of an ox rested on its side, the roots tangling with decades of flood debris to form a partial cave of wood and reeds, pierced with flecks of sunlight. "Better," he agreed and sank against the tree trunk, shivering.

She darted about to one side then another and returned with dry twigs and branches, then scraped a little pit in the dirt and laid a fire. From one of the pouches at her waist—its top twisted to hold out water—she plucked a few small items and struck sparks into the grasses curled at the center of the fire. She leaned down as if to worship the sparks, and pursed her lips as if to kiss them as she blew them into life. Her every movement spoke efficiency, grace, and control.

Dailus scooted closer to the fire, rubbing his hands over the flames, staring into it, rather than stare at her.

"I am sorry I have no cloak or blanket for you," she told him.

"Why did you save me?"

She sat back on her heels. "To return what you have done for me. Do you not think the Mongols would have killed me, as they did that other man, if you had not spoken for me?"

"I thought they might." The stream where they had drowned Jian Ho likely fed into this great river. How far down had his body been washed?

"So I am quit of your debt."

"Then you should go."

She gave a little shrug. "Perhaps, but I am hungry, and you have the fire." With another quick movement, she vanished back into the brush. He would not have thought the afternoon sun would allow such a disappearance, yet it was so. Dailus moved closer to the fire. As his shivering subsided, Dailus let his eyes slide shut.

He had a wife back at home, a plump woman with golden hair and skin like his—Marietta. Everyone agreed it was a good match, and it brought him Anya and Matteus. Marietta's fortitude and piety seemed attractive enough, in spite of her complaints when his work took him to another town to cast bells or other fittings easier to make on site. He kept her in good wool for spinning, with the brightest of dyes, and a few luxuries the other women of the village could envy—engraved buckles for bodices, laces from Hungary, when he could get them. He tried to imagine her pinning up her hair with picks of gold and strings of pearls, wearing a blouse of silk or boots of wool with turned-up toes. He tried to imagine even seeing her again, but he was too weary for the image to come clear.

Dailus startled awake in late afternoon gloom, to the watery smell of fresh fish and Ming Lun's voice hissing, in the Cathayan language, "Who are you and why have you followed us?"

"Take care," a man answered in a curious dialect. "I only wish to speak to him when he wakes."

"You know who he is."

"The khan's drakemaster, of course. I must congratulate him on finding his freedom."

Dailus kept his eyes squeezed shut. Freedom? Was it true? He was across the river, without a Tatar for miles, only his foreign face and his slave's bracelet to mark who he was. Free.

"Fine. But first, you clean fish." Something wet slapped the ground, and the man gave a startled grunt. "You do know how?"

"I haven't cleaned a fish for… a very long time."

At that strange pause in the man's voice, Dailus opened his eyes and sat up, dusting off the silt and debris. Across the fire, holding a large fish, sat the ancient skeletal shaman, the one Yusen threatened to kill. Dailus drew back. "I've seen this man before—last time I met him, he was dressed as a shaman of the Mongols—"

"And now, I find him sitting by the fire, watching you sleep." She turned her knife deftly from slitting the fish's stomach to pricking the old man's throat. He froze, the fish in his own hands slithering to the ground. "Who are you, old man? What do you want?"

"I am called Master Deng, and I want to speak to the drakemaster. I think he may be the man I need." He spread his hands. "If I meant him harm, I could have killed him as he slept."

"Perhaps." She swung the knife back, carving deftly into the fish. "What do you say, drakemaster? Will you listen to him?"

Still recovering from the speed with which she took aim on the old man, then resumed her task, Dailus replied, "I don't see why not."

She spread the fish open and spiked them up over the fire with longer sticks.

Master Deng narrowed his eyes at her. "I need a clever and able craftsman, to aid me in repairing… a device."

Dailus took a moment to process his words, seeking meanings equivalent in his own language. When he spoke with the dancer, they referred to things he already knew, or things that were clear from their context, but the old man used strange language and spoke in an unfamiliar accent. "I may need you to speak slowly, father. I have not all the words of your tongue."

The old man scrutinized him. "I hope you have enough. Let us find out. The device I speak of was built many years ago, and has not been operated since then. I hope it is in good condition and needs only slight maintenance. Before I say more, I must know that you, neither of you, support the Mongols' cause?"

Dailus shuddered. "I curse the day I ever aided it."

The woman shrugged, and went on with preparing some roots which she set alongside the coals. She relaxed into this role, going about the preparations for their meal, as if her earlier knife work had been merely a cooking demonstration.

As the old man spoke, Ming Lun moved more into the background, finding broad leaves to use as plates and fetching water from the stream, letting the silt settle out before offering it around.

Master Deng smoothed a patch of ground beside the fire, but not too close, then slowly withdrew a long scroll from his robe. "This device represents the height of learning from both astronomers and geomancers, a union of their skills in the service of the Mandate of Heaven." He spread the scroll upon the ground, pinning its corners with small stones. "Your people must know how the stars can rule the destiny of man or country?"

Dailus nodded distractedly, crouching over the scroll.

"This device harnesses that power. It can be focused to draw down the energy of auspicious stars into the earth."

All around the diagram marched rows of Cathayan calligraphy, incomprehensible swirls and checks of dark ink. The drawings detailed a scaffold about three stories tall, with stairs going up inside like a bell tower, but entirely of wood. At its side rose a large column of disks, each with figures or markings, as if it were the face of a clock, but placed on a cylinder rather than a circle. Interesting. That made the gearing more direct. Also interesting. A great water wheel drove a series of interlocking rings and gears behind the dials. On the top of all rose a hollow sphere like the one in the pleasure garden, a device for marking the passage of the stars, or so the young woman claimed. Opaque boxes surrounded that, with discs and thin threads that connected them all over the machine. Another diagram showed a further series of rings and gears—settings, of some kind, and levers. This apparatus sat below the hollow sphere. He recognized some of the symbols, the Cathayan script, that pointed to various parts as markings he had seen on the barrels, packets and boxes of supplies he used in casting the firedrakes. The connecting threads were marked with the symbol for gold, while the base of the machine showed quicksilver.

Beyond the central plan, the drawings looked more theoretical, patterns of dots and lines that reminded him of the constellations, but not in any structure he recognized. Some of these were marked in red, the color of joy to the Cathayans, and others underscored in black.

"Wait a minute." Dailus pointed to a configuration in black. "If you can harness the light of the good stars, what about the bad ones?"

The old man smiled. "Those, too. With this device and the formulas of geomancy, we can direct that power against our enemies, and send the entire Mongol army up in flames." He steepled his fingers. "So, drakemaster, will you join me? Will you help me to scald these barbarians to ashes and build our land anew?"

CHAPTER TWENTY-TWO

Ming Lun took the fish from the fire and peeled out their spines, laying the cooked meat on the long leaves she had gathered, allowing her focus on the meal to make her invisible to the men, as such things always did. She stacked a few pieces of root alongside, pulled a wooden container from one of her pouches and sprinkled herbs onto the roots. Keeping her head bowed, she offered a meal to each of the men. She had positioned herself exactly opposite the fire where its light revealed the drawings and words in perfect detail. The dangling seal referred to the Order of Celestial Purity, and held a symbol of stars that reminded her of the paintings in the chamber where she first learned to dance.

"This array—" Master Deng tapped a sketch of circles and triangles that seemed to impress the men, "allows the light to be focused using special stones. Some of them are permanent, gathering the power of the stars into a constant fire that is carried through gold. The Golden Serpent—it strikes fast as an adder." He traced the lines connecting those circles at the top to the rest of the machine. "Other stones can be rotated, depending on the desired effect. The cranks here direct the power to where we choose on a map down below. Once the focus is set, this dragon lever keeps it sealed into a radiant circle of golden energy. The geomancers developed these mechanisms for storage and transmission, while the astronomers created our machinery for tracking celestial indicators. If the astronomical sighting tube above is aligned with the stone, it will transmit the energy of the stars wherever you choose." He tapped the top of the diagram and traced the path of its energy downward, through the focusing apparatus. "The Mongols are camped around the Yellow River. Imagine if the Mongol army could be utterly destroyed."

Dailus's eyes flared, pale in the flickering light. "They've occupied Cathay for decades, yes? There must be Mongols all over."

The old man shrugged. "Most of them are here, and around the palace at Xuzhou. Now that they have broken the rebellion at Kaifeng, they will move south again, to attack the rest of the empire. We must stop them before they reach the Yangtze River, if we can."

Dailus flinched at the mention of Kaifeng, but it was the old man's idea of the south that Ming Lun needed to hear, to understand who he worked for, ideally without revealing herself. She murmured, "I hear the empire remains strong in the south, to rise like a lark with the new dawn."

The old man's gesture dispelled her words. "It is the last blood of a weak bloodline, but it is what we have." He tapped the first large drawing with a skeletal finger. "Su Sung's design inspired this. His entire commission in building that clock was to track the birth of worthy imperial children. Imagine, this great work devoted to the whelping of imperial brats, and what is worse, he failed." All of this was directed at Dailus—the old man ignored her reference to the lark as if it meant nothing. "Perhaps in your land there are better ways to ensure a worthy successor?"

Dailus shook his head vaguely. "A child of the granduke is worthy because he is the grand duke's child."

This term granduke? grand duke? must be like an emperor in the ghost country where he came from.

"But if he has many children," Master Deng prompted, "then how does he choose?"

This seemed to puzzle the foreigner, and he shrugged. "The oldest becomes the next grand duke."

"Then he must have fine clocks as well, to know which of his children is oldest."

Dailus laughed suddenly. "Everyone knows, his wife knows."

The old man pressed his fingertips into his bald pate. "Your emperor has only one wife? What of his concubines?"

"He is a Christian man," Dailus replied, as if another foreign word explained everything.

"I don't know what is this Christian." The old man plucked a few bits from his plate and stuffed them in his mouth. Apparently he did not notice the herbs she had sprinkled on top. Good.

"Christian—people who believe in Christ—" Dailus took a few bites as well, licking the juices from his fingertips. Such long, strong fingers. "We are the followers of God—the only God. He has only one church, his followers have only one wife. No concubines at all, if they are true believers."

The old man snorted and wiggled his fingers for Ming Lun to pass over the water skin so he could drink deeply. "That needs re-filling, woman." To Dailus he said, "I cannot imagine any emperor foolish enough to breed with only one woman. The empire is too important to be entrusted to such a random thing as an only wife's only child. What if she can't even have any?"

"Then the duke would have no heirs. Or he might petition the Pope to ask if he can set her aside and have a new wife."

"Ah! Two wives." Master Deng thrust his finger at the sky.

"Not at the same time." Dailus darted a glance toward Ming Lun. "Thank you for this." He lifted his plate and a smile parted his thick straw-colored beard. She gave a little nod, took up the water skin and moved back through the reeds toward the river's edge. He should not be looking at her. Let him focus on the old man's plan. Was he looking at her now? Watching her walk away, watching for her to return? When she danced, she had been watched by men who asked her price and never knew how much they really paid for the services she gave and the information she took. Sometimes, watched by men who derided her, taunting her large feet or her old-fashioned style. She knew how to get them to pay attention when she wanted it, and how to become uninteresting. But this man watched her with a hunger that knew no price. She had no idea what to make of it, or if she wanted it to continue, but it warmed her throat, and taking his hand in hers made her feel stronger. Caring for him did not irritate her the way that caring for the little dancers so often did. He had need of her—as they did—but also gratitude for her, which they never did… She held the waterskin under the surface, using a mat of reeds to strain away the silt as it filled. Gratitude. Even her imperial contacts never showed that.

His eyes flicked up as she re-entered their little clearing, and they warmed with more than fire. Ming Lun settled into her place, picking at morsels of fish and eating slowly. She had hoped not to rescue the drakemaster only to have to kill him. She already had one plan in action, and Master Deng's design suggested other possibilities.

"—truly only one wife and a single heir, then I can see why the Mongols so easily overran your country."

"Your emperor has dozens, hasn't he? But that hasn't helped him!"

"Because the bloodline is weak, as I said." Master Deng's lips spread thinly, the smile of a snake. "That is why we did not act sooner. When the emperor's family fled from Kaifeng, we choose to wait, to see if a worthy successor would arise. The wait was not meant to be so long." He glared at his own thin wrist and scratched at a flake of gold clinging inside his thumb, then reached up to stifle a yawn and frowned. "The Mongol advance has been too fast. I should have been awakened before now, but I can only proceed in the time before me. I should like to have your help."

Dailus, too, suppressed a yawn and shook himself as he set aside the bare leaf where his dinner had been. "These machines track the stars, yes? These dials reveal timing, while the gold threads carry radiant energy." He traced over the structure from the circles on the top down the face of the device. "The array focuses power—"

"Like the body of your firedrake gathering the explosion to direct its force."

Dailus glanced at him, wary, and shifted the slave bracelet further up his arm. A series of parallel scars showed where it had torn into his flesh time and again. He stretched his long arm and pointed. "You say a map will allow you to aim it, to destroy the Mongols. How can you strike only Mongols?"

Master Deng blinked, but otherwise remained precisely as he was.

Dailus regarded him across the fire. "We want to break the Mongol army, but we can't simply kill everyone on the map." He waved his hand to indicate a vast area. "Thousands of people live along the river, yes? Hundreds of thousands. At least as many as there are Mongols."

"The soil will be no good for farming when this is done, not for a long time. When it is clean again, there will be new farmers." He pressed his fingertips together and gave a tiny shrug.

Dailus withdrew his hands as well, the fingers of the right hand stroking over his slave bracelet, then letting it settle back into the scars. "You're asking me to kill them all. All the Mongols and their soldiers, all the farmers, all their wives and children and heathen priests and pagan temples and merchants and soldiers and thieves and sinners. I'm sorry, but the answer is no."

"Are you—" Master Deng began, but Dailus's long, strong arms cut through the rising smoke.

"No! I won't do it. I pray to God you won't either. You don't know how it weighs on your soul." Dailus looked away, leaning back against the wood, then slumping more deeply. He could no longer keep his eyes open.

In a moment, his breath evened into sleep.

Master Deng gave a snort of irritation and plucked the stones from the corners of the scroll, letting it snap back into place. He rose, swaying a little, his cheeks distending and eyes half-closed as he suppressed a yawn of his own, then he staggered off into the darkness without another word.

Ming Lun had hoped for the other way about, that the spindly old man would succumb first to her herbal mixture and leaving her to offer Dailus the chance to aid the Son of Heaven, but he had emphatically rejected Master Deng, even when the man's offer included the deaths of every Mongol who had ever hurt him. He would be no more receptive to killing them in the service of the Emperor, not today in any case. So be it. She knew her duty. The Mongols knew she had come after him. They would not rest until they knew his fate. It might be more kind to kill him quickly than to allow him to be found.

She slipped free a short, sharp blade and knelt down at his side.

For such a big man, he took up so very little ground, his long limbs pulled close as if he were again a child, his shaggy wheat-colored hair fallen back from his face, revealing the sharp angle of his nose and the planes of his cheeks. His jade-ghost eyes remained shut, his lips parted as he breathed. His wounded, angry voice echoed in her mind. Even if the Mongols found him, he would never again forge the weapons they craved. Laying the knife close to his hands, where he would find it when he woke, Ming Lun slipped away into the darkness. She should take the drakemaster's life, but Master Deng had showed her another tool.

When she found the old man, sleeping beneath an old bridge footing, she even felt so moved as to toss a stone and chase away the two men creeping already toward him, no doubt intent on robbing him and slitting his throat. No, Master Deng need not die today, in spite of his lack of faith in the emperor. He only need give up his plan and return it to the Son of Heaven who would better know how to employ it. Her deft hands stroked into his robe, slipped free the scroll, then she was on her way: South, toward home and Empire.

CHAPTER TWENTY-THREE

Zhencai and Andao retreated in shadow after the stone flew at them from the darkness. Andao rubbed his back where the stone had struck him. "How did you move out of the way so quickly?"

Zhencai said, "I felt the breath of the stone upon my cheek."

Around them, a few clumps of refugees slumbered beneath the scruffy trees or watched them, trembling, afraid at any moment of Mongol retribution. Zhencai made the sign of blessing, and some of the watchers relaxed. Motioning for Andao to follow, Zhencai started forward. They had been waiting among the refugees since midafternoon, still wet from clinging to the ropes as they crossed the river. They hoped Master Deng's words to his hirelings were not merely empty, and were rewarded finally by seeing the skeletal old man stagger into the flood plain around the ruined bridge and collapse at the base of the pier. They waited a moment longer, only to be struck by stones as they moved toward him. Then someone else went to the sleeper instead and ran away. His remaining hireling, perhaps, taking his money or slaying his master?

One of them should check Master Deng and find the scroll, and the other go after the stranger at least far enough to see who it was and which way he went. Both tasks required stealth Andao did not possess, but his younger eyes would serve better in seeing the stranger. "Andao, follow that person."

"Right."

Andao ran off, clumsy and panting already. At least it would not be hard for Zhencai to find him again. While his apprentice departed, Zhencai crept up to where Master Deng slept. Deng's scrawny throat trembled with breath, so the stranger had not killed him at any rate. Zhencai ran his careful hands down the old man's robe, then along his back in case he had concealed the scroll. This seemed unlikely, given the near-drunken way he had stumbled toward the bridge and now snored soundly in spite of two different people investigating his presence. If Master Deng had ever been a monk, he had not trained under so rigorous an approach as Zhencai's own monastery.

In the direction of the old road, someone shouted, and Zhencai pulled back. Andao was in trouble. Zhencai drew a deep breath, centering his qi and pushing it to his legs. He ran, pumping hard along the slope of the bridge until he reached the old road surface, his toes digging briefly against the paving stones and launching him ahead. Strength and warmth flowed through him. Up ahead, something crashed through the bushes. Andao. A yelp, then a louder crash.

Zhencai put on a burst of speed and sprang into the brush at the side of the road. At the bottom of a short slope, Andao scrambled to his feet, dusted off, and glanced up. "Master! This way." He pointed.

"He has the scroll," Zhencai said.

"He threw another rock," Andao said. "If he hears I'm after him, he'll try to stop me. Then you can fight him."

Zhencai gave a nod, and let Andao lead. His apprentice was no monk, but neither was he a fool. He understood his limitations but was using them against their opponent.

After the thin brush and twisted pistachio trees along the road, the land spread out beneath the stars, showing a few farm houses and other structures, many of them ruined in the years of war and still empty—or empty again. Zhencai caught a glimpse of someone dodging toward a cluster of buildings, then Andao's long, awkward frame lunging after. Zhencai looped to the side, back toward the river, then at an angle along a tumbled stone wall that connected with the farmyard buildings.

"Ai! Stop!" Andao shouted somewhere up ahead.

Zhencai sprang to the top of the wall and ran along it, then up over a broken gate, his bare toes spreading to balance on the tile. He nearly didn't make the short jump from there to the top of the farmhouse wall, his left ankle striking and scraping. Suffering was a part of the world, but that made it sting no less. He crouched down as he ran along the rooftop, to a balcony on the only building tall enough to have one, then dropped down to a lower roof. Ahead, a gap, and a shout from Andao, followed by coughing. In the yard below, near a long barn, his apprentice doubled over, waving away a cloud.

Clad in trousers with a split robe over the top, the stranger spun away, releasing an old sack as it expelled its dusty contents. The scroll stuck from the back of the stranger's sash, a narrow, pale streak in the gloom.

With a mighty thrust, Zhencai launched himself into the yard, rolling and bouncing up again in the stranger's path. He pushed away the ache in his shoulder from the awkward landing, and the persistent sting of his ankle.

The stranger hissed, dancing back from his sudden appearance. His opponent was light and slender, moving with admirable grace and speed, and a bit of darkness coiled around—her head. The stranger was a woman, her hair looped and pinned up with gold.

She spun low and lashed out with a dagger, which Zhencai easily leapt. She had grace and speed, but would have little training.

"I have no wish to harm you. Give up the scroll." Zhencai had not touched a woman for forty years—he hoped he would not have to do so now. He rested lightly on his toes, forming the sign of blessing, his hand before his lips.

"What do you know of it?" She shifted back and forth, weaving like a novice, perhaps expecting him to be intimidated by her blade.

"We are here for the sake of the Buddha's compassion."

She shook her head, and her laughter echoed the tinkle of the chains that decorated her hair. "Forgive me, holy one, I have known too little of compassion."

"Then allow us to reveal it to you." He lowered his hand into an invitation to learn and share their knowledge. "Sit with us."

"Why would I trust you?" Her gaze flicked back to Andao, who wiped his face and smothered a cough.

Zhencai tried a smile. "We have no wish to hurt you, or even to prevent your passage, but we cannot allow the scroll to depart."

"You cannot pay what it's worth."

"If it's money you want, then perhaps an arrangement can be met."

"Money is not close to what I want." She leapt, her heel slamming into his shoulder and spinning him around. She darted past while he was catching his balance, but he launched after her, still breathless in surprise, and slid his leg across her path.

Forced to change course or fall, she spun about to face him, any sense of feminine vulnerability vanishing into the solid stance and smooth execution of the practiced warrior.

This observation, too, Zhencai removed from his thought. Now that he saw what he faced, he had no time for surprise. The Buddha forgive him, he must no longer see her as a woman. He pivoted and prepared his qi, strengthening the fingers of his right hand into a weapon.

Zhencai focused on watching her core, seeking the signs of movement that would help him anticipate her. Her hips swayed, then her leg soared out in an unexpected leap, her foot striking hard into his side.

The breath flew from him, and he slid back, absorbing the blow and the grunt that followed. She let that foot swing about, hit the ground, and lift her into the air, an elegant spin that lined up the dagger with his chest.

Zhencai dropped and rolled, snatching for her support leg. He missed, but caused her to stumble.

"You are Shaolin. Is it not against your order to touch a woman?" She recovered quickly, stalking forward, hand outstretched as if in warning and dagger held at the ready.

"Who are you?" said Andao from the darkness.

"A dancer." She launched herself in a series of spins.

Zhencai reached out from stillness, and seized her arm, but the dagger carved a line across his scalp and he let go, blood streaming into his eyes. Enough—enough! A dancer could not strike him so readily. It could not be. He turned with her, letting her spin take her toward the path and escape, then he pushed hard into a spring and flew over her head—she was small and keeping low. He thrust out his hand—iron fist—and smacked her spine. Shifting his hand, he seized her collar.

The dancer twisted beneath him, but he snatched the scroll from her belt and released her, dodging away.

"Master!" Andao bleated, and Zhencai stopped short, dropping into a stance of readiness and sweeping back his leg.

She leapt over this attempt, and something flashed gold in her hand—a thin length of chain with a sharp pick at its end. Her hair released, its chain wrapped Zhencai's throat, the pick scratching his skin.

He joined in the dance with a turn unwrapping the chain, letting its sharp anchor swing free.

She snatched the scroll—as deftly as he had done—but without the strength to match his. Their hands pressed side by side, neither willing to let go. Her off-hand still held the pick at the other end of the chain, and she drove it into the flesh between his thumb fingers.

The pressure point sent a shot of pain straight down his arm that even his iron hand could not withstand. His grip spasmed open, and she drew back the scroll as if it were an arrow and she held the bow. Zhencai's hand tremored in the air in its absence.

She smiled, a flash of teeth in the darkness, then she tumbled to the ground, Andao landing on top of her, crushing the breath from her as he lay full-length, pinning her arms.

Recovering with a stumble in the right direction, Zhencai snatched back the scroll and thrust it into the front of his tunic. He seized her wrist, finding a pressure point of his own, and twisted back her hand, then caught the chain she had used against him.

"Ai!" she whimpered beneath Andao. "Poisoned," her breath hissed.

Zhencai tossed it away. Instead, he tugged off her sash and bound her wrist to her opposite ankle. Andao wriggled out of the way while his master completed the task, securing both hands and feet. The position would strain her shoulders, no doubt, but she had shown herself flexible enough to handle it. Both men moved back, breathing heavily, as the dancer struggled with her bonds, then let her head rest against the ground.

"Poison—what kind?" Andao demanded.

"Poisonous," she muttered.

Zhencai glanced at his hand, blood dripping down his fingers, the wound throbbing.

"Free my hands, and I will find you the antidote."

Andao moved toward her, then said, "No. Tell me where it is."

"If you have poisoned me, dancer, then why should you now preserve me?" Zhencai asked. Still, he kept his hand down, the blood flowing free and taking any poison with it.

"I have no wish to slay monks." She let her head flop down. "Buddha forgive me." Or at least that was what Zhencai imagined he had heard.

"At least turn her so that she can speak."

Andao rolled the woman to her side, facing them. She shook her head and blew out a breath, trying to clear the strands of dark hair that hung into her face.

"Please, honored one, allow me to help you." She wet her lips. "The poison is not meant for monks, but for drunken men, for men who know nothing of compassion." She gazed up at him.

"Tell me where to find the antidote," Andao repeated.

She tipped her chin awkwardly, indicating her lower side. "These pouches. Take care—they are snug to open." She wriggled a little further onto her back so that he could reach the pouches, but the position must have ground at her bent arms and legs. Zhencai considered whether they should release her, or bind her in a way—

Her dagger flashed up in her hand, her other hand gripping the back of Andao's neck as she held the blade to his throat. She rose slowly onto her knees, pushing Andao with her, the dagger biting his neck. The cut sash dangled from her wrists. "I do not wish to harm either of you, but I will do so, have no doubt. Please, honored one, remove the scroll from your robe."

Andao's eyes danced with fear. From his robe, Zhencai withdrew the length of the scroll, holding it at one end, the stiff parchment and lacquered rod solid in his grip.

"Hand it to your apprentice. He may have to carry it until I see fit to release him."

Zhencai, still moving slowly, took a half-step forward, extending the scroll. With the movement, he drew his qi along his side, up into his arm, forging the scroll into an extension of his bones. Andao reached toward him to receive it.

With a rush of speed, Zhencai shoved the scroll beneath the woman's hand, driving back the knife. Andao writhed to the other side, grappling with the hand that held him. She tried to bring up the knife, but Zhencai caught her wrist with his off-hand and twisted it back. Something snapped and a sheen of tears flooded her eyes, but she made no sound. A man held each arm, pinning her to the ground, her feet still trapped beneath her.

They shared a look over her body, her chest heaving with shallow breaths, then Zhencai tipped up his chin toward the barnyard where a series of pillars separated the long building into spaces. Together, they walked her backward, trying to be no more firm than they had to be—at least, Zhencai was trying, Andao's jaw looked hard as iron, blood trickling down his throat. Andao pulled off his belt and bound her hand to the nearest pillar, then scouted the yard and came back with rope.

Before he tied off her hand to the next pillar, Zhencai probed the length of her arm, noting her wince. It was not the wrist, but a lower bone that had broken. He used the remainder of her own sash to bind the injury, supporting the broken bone against its neighbor, then tying her hand to the pillar so that she stood spread between them, staring at him. "I will not forget this, honored one."

"Then you'd best remember that he even bound up your injury, and that he tried to offer you compassion, but you attacked him." Andao's hands flew, releasing the anger that he carried in his jaw. "All we wanted was the scroll—you're the one who made him fight you for it."

"Hush," said Zhencai. Andao stalked away, his breathing catching. He still bore the injuries of his last fight, and perhaps his own Hashem, too, spoke against the touching of women. "Amito fu." Zhencai made the sign of blessing, and the dancer finally looked away, her throat working as she tried to conceal her pain. She held too much pride in her fighting; no doubt she wept as much for her defeat as for her broken arm.

Zhencai followed Andao into the darkness, tapped his shoulder with the scroll, and led him away. When they were out of sight of the farmyard, he turned again, crossing the old road, heading West up the river. At last he allowed the pain of his aches and injuries to return. He could not ignore his aging body forever. "There is a monastery in the high mountains, a place of healing I think the Mongols have not found. There, we may learn more about these matters."

"What about the poison?"

Zhencai smiled faintly. "Do you believe there was poison?"

"But she said that she…" For a moment, they walked in silence. "She said she would give you the antidote so that we'd let her go." His voice held a note of suppressed fury. "I can't believe she lied to you after you offered her compassion."

The wound at his hand needed no poison to be painful and to make him hope they would meet no further dangers, for a few days at least. He needed to tend his wound, but he hesitated to linger close to that dangerous dancer. Her bindings would not hold her long. "They disdain compassion most, who are most in need of it. Those lie the loudest who are most afraid of the truth."

"Aren't you angry?"

Angry? He had touched a woman for the first time in forty

years—not only that, but touched her in anger, but he remained silent, and knew himself for a liar as he led the way into the mountains.

CHAPTER TWENTY-FOUR

Bao Xing frowned at the tangle of silk in her fingers, leading down to the patch of cloth she was meant to be embroidering. Somewhere nearby, one of the serving girls plucked at a high-pitched lute and sang in a voice so sweet it made Bao Xing want to howl from its very tedium.

"Oh dear, Bao! What can be done with you?" Chubei examined the tangled thread. "Perhaps you should keep with calligraphy? What about painting—can you paint?"

"I will try," Bao Xing replied, dropping the mess of thread and fabric. Chubei laughed, a sound meant to be kind, perhaps, but always sounding a little sharp to Bao Xing's ear.

"Qutuqui's ladies have been painting in the garden, perhaps they can show you?" Chubei took her hand and tugged her toward the garden, causing Bao Xing to stumble, her cane clicking as she tried to keep up with her friend's hurried steps. Chubei hurried everywhere, and nothing seemed to slow her down. Since they arrived at Xuzhou, the Mongol queen's excitement grew over every chamber, passageway and courtyard in the palace. The palace ground might have sustained a dozen villages, yet Bao Xing understood that this was only a way-station, an old imperial palace they used when they did not wish to ride all the way home. Still, it was much more comfortable than the tents, especially the high Chinese-style beds with their round openings, flowing curtains and thick mattresses—so much easier than rising from the floor every morning.

In the garden, the Mongolian ladies clustered near a patch of blooming flowers. To one side, an elegant setting showed a curious stone, deeply pitted, with jutting peaks like a mountain. Bao Xing moved to one end of the stone while Chubei arranged for her to have painting materials. The stone's rough surface resembled the wrinkles defining an old man's face with a dark hollow for an eye. The whole world lived inside of that stone, it seemed, with each facet revealing more.

"Isn't it queer, having such a huge garden, then putting rocks all over it? I like the streams and bridges, though, and those little houses." Chubei pointed beyond a cluster of drooping larch trees toward a tea house. "If we get rid of this rock, we could have another one of those right here, so much easier than crossing the stepping stones."

Bao Xing smiled politely. The queen's chatter expanded her knowledge of their language, so that was useful, but it would be some time before she could speak very much of it. For the next awkward hour, Bao Xing held a stylus and drew butterflies. She imagined them moving in little constellations, scattered through the sky of this garden, then one of them, a deep purple butterfly, circled a stalk of grass, reminding her of the work she had abandoned in her father's observatory. It had been too long since she had had a chance to study the stars. Was that wanderer indeed circling the Dark Lance? Distracted, she had painted a series of dots—the pattern of the Dark Lance, with the path of the wandering star imposed on top. Bao Xing crumpled the page and tried to focus on the butterflies and flowers, the things of beauty, not the warnings of despair.

In her mind, they soared and fluttered, showing off their colorful wings. On her paper, they flattened into smudges of ink, all the grace removed, as if she had swatted them with a book while she sat reading.

At last, the servants fetched them into their dining hall, a private one for the ladies of court, to slurp their soup and nibble at dumplings alongside tangy strips of pickled vegetables. The dumplings of Mongolia had thick dough and dark meat filling, rather than light pork and cabbage or spiced fish, but the queens often had all sorts, both their own and Chinese dishes—another thing to be grateful for.

But Bao Xing was most grateful when the queens took their ride, and she was released to go her own way. Her little feet swayed her to the library every day. They had arrived here eight or nine days ago, and she had followed a cartload of scrolls into a hall intended for other use. There, the Mandarin Minister of Archives Guowei graciously accepted her utility as a literate person, and permitted her to aid in sorting, bundling and stacking the manuscripts brought in from Mongol raids across the north of China. More often than not, Guowei would be summoned away to write letters for the khan or undertake some other duty, and Bao Xing served her true purpose: finding out everything she could about the Dark Lance, and the making of the instrument she had seen in Kaifeng. What was the meaning of its strange inscription referring to both astronomers and geomancers? And why had one of its rings been fixed, with a sighting tube that did not even point to the sky? Her heart ached, knowing the instrument lay broken in shards, possibly already melted for weapons. After the slave's escape, the khan's fury slowly dissipated, and the royal family moved on to the palace while the army re-exerted control over the ruins of Kaifeng.

Today, Bao Xing pushed back the curtain and entered the library as quietly as she might. Guowei stood over a high table with a mound of scrolls, snapping them open, glancing down at the contents, letting them snap shut again. "Here," he barked as she came in. "These can be put away. Not so messy this time." His eyes lifted, and he gave a tight smile that removed some of the sting of his rebuke.

"Forgive me." She gathered them into one arm, steadying her cane with the other. "I was rushing yesterday when I heard the gong for dinner."

In spite of his manner, Guowei clearly cared for the books as much as she did, and both of them relaxed into their own language after struggling with the sharper sounds of Mongolian. "Next time, leave the manuscripts out and find their places the next day. Or perhaps you would wish to join myself and the other ministers for dinner? When the khan does not require our company, we have our own hall and our own cooks." He leaned toward her. "No mutton! And plenty of vegetables." He glanced around, as if afraid of being overheard, then whispered, "Some of them aren't even pickled."

Bao Xing giggled behind her hand. "Thank you for the offer. I would need to discuss it with my mistress."

"Do that." His eyes twinkled: fine, dark eyes with a few wrinkles at their corners, so they crinkled when he smiled, rare though that was. He dressed in austere and practical robes, with edges of brocade and broad cuffs folded back so he could use his hands. In here, she, too, turned back her sleeves, letting the extra fabric drape over her elbows. Bao Xing moved between the bins and piles toward another table with a chair where she usually did her sorting.

These scrolls held a familiar mixture of Buddhist scripture, Confucian classics, and household advice, and Bao Xing could see why Guowei had let them roll up again so quickly. She readily found places for them among the low bins near her table. In the morning, Guowei's servants would push the bins over and shelve the works that she had sorted. That done, Bao Xing opened the lid of the next chest on the pile and took out a sheaf of bamboo pages with Buddhist mantras. They needed a new ribbon, so she sorted one from among her supplies and bound the stack, then placed them with the scriptures. The next manuscript—a handful of pages with a burnt corner, held an image of a string-and-spot pattern she recognized as one of the Celestial Mansions. This, she slid onto the shelf beneath her table to examine later, though excitement tingled in her fingertips.

She pulled another stitched packet of papers from the chest: an inventory of farmland and the families who had owned it, hundreds of years ago. "Minister? How are the history shelves arranged?"

"Mmm?" Guowei looked up from his perusal of a complicated diagram. "Mostly by location. Where is the history from?"

"These are chests from Henan province, Minister."

"From Kaifeng? I'll take a look at those. Here." He lifted a basket of scrolls from a corner where they'd obviously been sitting a long time, and shuffled over with them, balancing the weight on her table as he slid the chest out of the way. "I believe these are all paintings, but we must be sure. If they are merely paintings, send them to the queens' gallery."

Bao Xing watched him stump away with the heavy chest, deflated. What was his interest in the history of Kaifeng? Or did he not think her capable of sorting histories? Instead, he left her with paintings, uninspired landscapes and boring birds.

Across the room, Guowei crooned over the chest, shuffling the land documentation to one side, and plucking out a thicker sheaf bound with silk. The front page held a painting of a gate and the tower that topped it. Kaifeng, an architectural history.

Her heart raced: that might be the very book she needed, but she diligently opened each scroll, noted its subject, and set aside the basket to be taken to the gallery, removing the few poems that had been mixed in.

A servant entered sometime later, carrying tea things, and Guowei waved her over to a small table near his own workspace. "Tea in the afternoon revives my tired eyes." His gaze upon her looked anything but tired, but she accepted the cup. The small, porcelain vessel nestled in her hand, its wall so thin that it felt warm all over, as if she held onto the sun.

"These things possess a rare beauty." The minister lifted his cup so the steam swirled about his nose. "In the khan's ger, the night you arrived, you said that you could not only read, but read the stars. What did you mean by that?"

"My father is an astronomer, Minister. He—" but how much should she say? So close to him now, to his masculine strength and learning, she remembered what the khan had said of her knowledge: a foolish waste of a woman's mind. What would Guowei think? She did not yet know him well enough to say—and surprised herself by the desire to know him better. "My father showed me the celestial houses and some of the other signs of the heavens. That's all."

"Mm." Guowei smiled faintly. "And it was he who named you Treasure Star. No wonder."

She stared demurely into her porcelain cup. "Surely I am nothing remarkable."

"Mm," he said again, as if he were not so sure. "Have you found anything remarkable in the scrolls so far?"

"Not today, minister, though I did find a fine painting of the celestial horses which the queens will enjoy."

Guowei sighed and took a sip of his tea. "Indeed they will. Is there anything they value so much as their horses?"

"Where would they be without them?"

His lips narrowed, and he seemed about to speak when another servant entered, bowing. "Honored Minister. The great khan requires your aid in a matter of contracts."

Sighing more heavily, Guowei set down his cup. "Very well. You will find more scrolls from that lot along the back wall, lady. I would be most grateful if you continue to work with them."

"Of course." She raised her cup to him as he departed, his strong footfalls pursuing the servant's down the corridor. At times, he did not move like a librarian, a thought that intrigued her.

The moment she was alone, Bao Xing set down her cup, a little too quickly, for it sloshed and dampened her fingers. She hurried as best she could to Guowei's table. The architectural guide to Kaifeng remained on top, and she flipped the pages quickly, scanning for references to the heavens or to the instrument. There! A small sketch of it filled one corner of a densely written page and she began to read.

The words told of a collaboration between geomancers and astronomers. Together, they would bring a new time of prosperity, linked to the stars. Very well, but this explained nothing: not what form the project took, nor why the armillary sphere's inscription described it as both great and sorrowful. Why sorrow? Did it relate to the Dark Lance image added inside the frame?

Bao Xing tapped her cane. He said the histories were arranged by place, and clearly Kaifeng, the former imperial capital, sat at the center of the mystery. She leafed through the historical collection, finding little of use there. Most of the documents came from farther north, areas the Mongols had conquered long ago. But the book of Celestial Mansions had come from the same chest, before Guowei brought it to his own desk.

Returning to her table, Bao Xing settled in her chair and removed the volume. She scanned the pages, finding a record of celestial events, including the patterns of the wandering stars, which sometimes reversed their course to draw attention to certain areas of the sky. The first lines described things she already knew, when the patterns had been seen and how they looked, and her excitement ebbed away, then, at the very end, a note from the astronomer, Chang Mailou: *it may be this very ill omen is what tarnished the hearts of the Mandarins. At least, without the arts of our cousin geomancers, they shall not resume their evil. Let the mountain keep silent and the stars remain pure.*

"What is that which so holds your interest?" Guowei crossed the room from the curtain and put out his hand.

"I thought it might be a book of fortunes, but it is not." She handed it over.

"I shall tell your fortune." Guowei held the book to his chest, propping his chin on his fist as he regarded her. "I predict you shall marry well and have many strong sons who will have your gift for learning, and many beautiful daughters who possess your fine features." He bowed briefly and returned to his desk, placing the volume alongside the other. "You did not finish your tea," he observed, then frowned and wiped a bit of moisture from his desk.

"It was too hot for me, minister. Is it better now? You haven't been gone long." She made as if to rise, but Guowei waved her back and carried the cup over to her.

As she reached out, he caught her hand and examined her fingers, his grip strong. "You have soot on your hand—and there are drops of tea on my desk. Why did you go to my desk, Bao Xing?" The wrinkles at his eyes no longer charmed her. Rather, they surrounded pools of darkness. No, not like a librarian at all.

Bao Xing thought fast, trapped, but desperate to hide her fear. "I rested my hand there when I stood up, minister, nothing more."

"Yet the pages are turned. They are not where I left them. Did the khan send you? Are you his eyes in the library, seeing what I see, reading what I read?"

"Nothing of the kind. I don't think the khan has any interest in where I go. I am a companion to his wife, nothing more."

"Will you tell him I have an interest in rebel cities?" He released her and stepped back, as forbidding as that face she imagined in the stone. He must be terrified of being seen as a traitor. In the shadow of their enemies, every Chinese man, or woman, knew that fear. He had nothing to fear from her, and so she told herself she had nothing to fear from him, in turn.

Bao Xing lay her cane across her lap and opened her hands. "Minister, please don't be so angry. Yes, I did look at the book. My family lives outside of Kaifeng, and I was curious."

"You spoke only of your father before."

"My mother always hoped the imperial court would return. She had my feet bound so I would be prepared for life at court." She edged one foot forward, letting the toe peek out. Was he as wild for a small foot as men were reputed to be?

Guowei glanced down at her foot. His fingers threaded together and gripped each other tightly. "Then you should be working under the Mistress of the Household. There is nothing here that will be of use to a lady." He bowed sharply, dismissing her back to the world of women. She had been so close to discovery, and now, she was left with nothing. Bao Xing felt the weight of this sentence as she pushed herself up, bowed in turn, and tottered away.

CHAPTER TWENTY-FIVE

A few days after Ming Lun's departure, Dailus limped to the stream he'd been following. No matter how he drank, he felt the swirl of silt through his teeth, over his tongue and wanted to vomit. How had Ming Lun strained the water she brought them? He stared into the murk, wishing he could go back to that night and beg her to stay. The next morning, Dailus had awoken feeling more refreshed than he had in a long time, the taste of roasted fish and strange herbs still clinging to his teeth. By his hand he found a short knife. He picked it up to return it to Ming Lun, and turned to find her gone. Bare coals remained of the fire, with disturbed ground where she and the old man had been, and the smooth place where Master Deng laid out his weapon, a weapon more extraordinary than any firedrake the khan could have imagined.

Of course the old man had left—Dailus could not bring himself to work on another weapon, not even one so fascinating. But Ming Lun? He had thought she…what, cared for him? At least cared he was alive—and how long did she think he could survive here alone? She had left him a knife, but he couldn't even find good drinking water.

Drops fell from his beard to ripple the water. A terrible head, smooth-skinned over lumpish features, reared up from the water—a head as large as his own, but frog-like and brown. Wide, smooth jaws gaped up at him.

Dailus cried out, falling on his rump and pushing furiously away from the edge, finding his knife and nearly fumbling it in his haste to escape.

The creature dove back down, nose first, revealing a thick, flat body and an oar-like tail that pushed it under the water, leaving ripples of its own. Dailus pressed a hand over his heart and breathed a prayer of thanks. A moment later, his stomach rumbled, and he wondered if these river creatures made good eating.

Back home, he would have gone to the market—or, more likely, sent his wife to buy eels, beans, onions and flour. After his long day at the foundry, she would have a fat eel pie ready, thick-crusted and steaming. His stomach rumbled again, and he focused on that image, Marietta's round, smiling face as she set the pie on the table between them, cutting slices for the children so their food would cool while the Grace was said. Dailus would clasp his hands together and pray, secure in his own good works, in the goodness of his wife and two fine, nearly obedient children. Perhaps there would be more—there might be already, for Marietta's courses had been a little late when he was taken—no, he tried not to think of the day Yusen ripped him from his life. He was free. Alone, in the middle of a strange land, but still free.

Dailus prayed again, this time for the Lord's guidance to get him out of Cathay. But if he starved to death because he did not know what to eat, the Lord's help would take him no further than a heathen boneyard. Very well, he must take the risk.

Pushing himself up, Dailus scanned upstream. He had stayed close to the main river since leaving the ruins of Kaifeng. When Yusen kidnapped him, he had been brought over mountains and more mountains from the west, and so, it was back to the mountains he returned. The thought of crossing them alone terrified him: if it was hard to survive down here, scrounging last year's nuts and whatever fish he could catch, how much worse would it be in the mountains? Snow clung to some of the peaks even now when spring stretched into summer. If he was to escape Cathay, he must cross them and soon. He had skirted two more cities—neither as grand as Kaifeng had been—and a few villages and farms. On one of the farms, he made two useful discoveries: the Cathayans left food in their shrines, and they would do almost anything to be rid of a hungry ghost.

Tell-tale curls of smoke rose a short distance upstream. Starting that direction, he crossed a narrow dam that diverted the stream into the farm fields. Every time he crossed the water, he remembered the grip of Ming Lun's hand and the brightness of her eye, telling him that no one truly wished to die. He stood on his own, alive and free, because of her. Sometimes, he imagined telling Anya the story of his escape from the Tatars, his flight from the very warriors of Hell. How she would cling to him and beg for more! He wouldn't speak of Jian Ho's death—no need to share his nightmares with anyone else. He would not speak of girls her own age being dragged away by soldiers, shared among them as trophies of battle. Would he speak of Ming Lun, hauling him from the depths, keeping him warm, watching over him? The sensation of her hand lingered on his skin.

It overlaid the memory of Yusen's own small hand, the day of the firedrake's failure. Why did that single act of kindness weigh so heavily in his memory? Was it even kindness, or merely, as his master had said, his duty to protect his property? Yusen had been right about the strange shaman who was no shaman: it had been Master Deng, lurking at the camp of his enemy. Dailus's throat knotted. What if Master Deng, the keeper of a secret weapon, had been dropping stones on molds and pouring water into the powder? What if Master Deng caused the problems that resulted in Jian Ho's death—even the poisoned smoke that nearly killed Yusen, the man who might have identified him?

In a few weeks, Dailus would be far away, and the problems of the heathens would no longer be his own. Neither their cruelty nor their kindness would be his concern. Ahead, a cluster of buildings rose near the stream, and he smelled the incense of another shrine. Late afternoon shadows stretched around him, and Dailus kept to their cover as he approached. Red columns supported an elegant roof with upswept corners. Inside, a row of carved stones, like gravestones, nestled together with an altar before them. Incense would be set in a pot of sand on the altar and, if he were lucky, offerings of food would be there as well.

Dailus lurked in the brush as a pair of children hurried by, hauling buckets. These, they dropped at the edge of the stream, then the older boy brought out a thick mat of reeds which he used to cover one bucket and immerse it in the water, allowing the reeds to strain out the silt. Dailus grinned. Of course—he should have thought of that! When the buckets were filled, the older boy shouldered the yoke between one pair and the younger boy grabbed the handle of the last one, stumbling a few paces, setting it down, crying out for his brother to wait, then stumbling on with his burden.

"Hurry up, shortie!" the older boy called back. "Or I'll eat your dumplings tonight!"

Their faces looked different, their homes were red and tiled, their shrines held stones without graves—but, even in Cathay, brotherhood looked exactly the same. Matteus would be five years old, old enough to carry a full bucket home from the well. Dailus steeled his nerve and slipped into the shrine. A few bowls of rice waited on the altar, some with dried fruit on top. He snatched a bowl and shoveled the rice into his mouth, savoring the tang of the sweetened fruit on top. Plums? No matter. He devoured two more before his hunger lessened, and he eyed the others. He must have the fruit, at least, and was that an offering of dried fish? Leaning over the altar like a vulture, Dailus scooped up the handful of darkened, dry flesh scraps and stuck them in the front of his tunic, held in place by his belt. Could he carry rice balls that way as well? Then he thought of the leaves Ming Lun used as dishes, and hurried back out into the lowering night. Finding a tall stalk of broad leaves, Dailus plucked a few and ran back to the shrine.

"Ai!"

He stopped short, the woman turning from the altar, her hands flying to her face.

"Ai," she breathed again, but softly. "The hungry ghost."

For a moment, Dailus stared back at her, a matronly figure with grey hair bound up off her shoulders and the plain clothing of a farmer. Two hanging lanterns illuminated the shrine, their light glinting from her frightened eyes.

"Yes, I am the hungry ghost! If I am well fed, then I won't hurt anyone." He rose up to his full height, a good two feet taller than she was, taller, even than the edge of the shrine's roof.

"Please, don't harm my family." She dropped to her knees, bowing, her head between her hands. "We thought the Mongol lied—we did not know."

Just as he was beginning to relax, this sent a shock along his spine. "Tell me about the Mongol."

"He was very small, very angry. We thought he would whip us for not knowing about you. Forgive me! Of course, we will feed you. We will leave many offerings." She hesitated, her shoulders hunched. "Will you stay very long?"

Long enough for them to tell Yusen where he was? "I will leave tonight, if you will bring me offerings of dried fish and fruits, and I will not curse this village."

"Yes, yes!" She leapt up, keeping her head bowed, and ran through the village.

Moving fast, Dailus scooped the rest of the rice into the leaves and wrapped them up, depositing them in his tunic as well. He began to look like a very well-fed ghost. He had almost decided to leave before the old woman returned, when he heard footsteps and saw her, accompanied by a younger couple, all carrying bundles bound in cloth. They started bowing right away, and Dailus moved imperiously aside, to allow them access to the shrine where they deposited their bundles on the altars, bowing repeatedly.

"Now you will leave us, yes?" the man demanded, in spite of his bent posture at Dailus's feet.

"Where did this Mongol go, the one who claimed to know me."

"Toward the mountains, but not along the river." The man pointed.

"Very good, and very good offerings."

The young woman clasped a string of beads in her hand, like a rosary. "Blessings on you, hungry ghost, and on your ancestors. May you find your rest."

"Will you… can you… keep watch over our village?" the old woman asked, but the man hissed her to silence.

Brotherhood was the same. Fears, and hopes, and prayers—all the same. By what heathen god did they bless him? Or could God's voice, God's blessing find him even here? Dailus's eyes stung. He had already defended them once, by refusing to repair a weapon that would have destroyed them. If he had the chance, he would do it again. "I will do what I can."

Bowing from his presence, the trio retreated down the road. A few murmured voices rose, a few doors opened, furtive faces peeking out, then the doors quickly shut again. These were ordinary people, not wealthy, trying to honor their ancestors by feeding them in the afterlife, and he had just threated to curse the village if they did not feed him instead? Dailus stared at the bundles. He truly needed the food, and they clearly believed feeding him would protect them, but there must be some other way he could show his gratitude. He plucked at the fraying edge of his tunic, looking at the modest houses, old grasses swaying in a breeze that carried the whispers of children, so much like his own village back home.

Dailus gathered a big handful of dry stalks, using his knife to cut them into even pieces. He pulled a few threads from the hem of his tunic and sat down, cross-legged, by the shrine, then started to string the bits of straw together, first into little squares and triangles, then binding these into shapes like houses. Yusen was ahead of him somewhere—slowing down for now might put the scout off his scent. At first, he fumbled the knots, then his hands remembered how to make them, how he had worked at his parents' side every holiday, to make the intricate straw hangings that would embellish their table.

"What are you doing?"

Dailus glanced up to find the two boys he'd seen earlier by the stream. They squatted beside the nearest house, as if afraid to be seen—but by him, or by their parents, worried about the foreign ghost?

"I'm making a blessing for your village." He kept working, the knots coming more easily. He tied on another triangle and held it up by the highest point. The open shapes of squares and triangles dangled down like little shrines, joined together in a larger one. "The bigger it is, the better will be your harvest."

"Then you'd better make a very big one!" the younger boy said.

His brother scowled. "You can't make demands of ghosts. What if he changes his mind?"

The younger boy's face fell and his shoulders drooped.

Dailus took up the next reed and waggled it. "If you bring me more, I can make it bigger."

The boy hurried off. "Stop!" his brother called after him. "You can't do that!" He jumped up to follow, but the boy gathered an armload of grasses in moments and piled them in front of Dailus who couldn't help but laugh.

Eye to eye with him, the boy reached toward his beard. "It's just like your face."

"Don't touch him!" Big brother called. Down the street, a woman cried out sharply, calling them home.

"It's fine, you can touch." Dailus ruffled up his beard with his hand.

The boy shot out his hand, furtively patting the stiff, pale hair of Dailus's beard. He grinned, then, just as his brother's hand descended to grab him, he ran off up the street, big brother in fast pursuit. A door slammed behind them, cutting off their mother's sharp rebukes. He hoped she would not be too hard on them. He'd never be able to use all the straw the boy gathered—already the light was failing—but he made a few more chambers, then bent and bound little clusters of grass into a pair of birds to circle the structure, like the two boys, playing together. This done, Dailus stood up and hung the finished work from the corner of the shrine.

It stirred in the gentle breeze, the birds flying, and he wished them a very fine harvest indeed.

Taking the bundles of food, Dailus slipped into the darkness, angling for the river since Yusen had gone for the hills. How long ago had he been here? Dailus should have thought to ask. No matter, he had food to last several days. His thieving from other shrines had marked his trail, and he might have been spotted by refugees or villagers before, in spite of his caution. He would have to stay away from people.

For the next three days, when he spoke his Grace over meals of dried fruit and fish, warming himself with a fire started by the vial of oil they had given him, Dailus asked for blessings on the family as well. They might receive the truth of God into their hearts and be saved. If such a thing could be, then let it be for good and simple people like these.

He hid close to the river by day, tucking himself into fallen trees, ruined buildings or mounds of flood debris, woken, shaking, by the sound of fishermen poling by on their flat boats, or oxen being led upon the road. He emerged one night to find the shadows even deeper than before: the river narrowed, the hills rising up to either side into formidable cliffs. A slender bridge crossed to a road that skirted the mountains to the north, at least for some distance. Dim shadows moved in that direction: horses. A few campfires marked the plain beneath the cliffside.

Swallowing hard, stifling his pounding heart, Dailus crept forward. Not the bridge, then, even if he could cross without being seen, the only paths open there made straight for the camp, or back along the river in the direction of Kaifeng and the Mongol army. Left, to where Yusen hunted the hills? No. Straight on, then, along the river trail hemmed in by the towering cliff. The trail narrowed as well, turning from packed yellow earth to smooth stone, damp from the river below and the little rivulets that trickled down the slope to his left hand. Moss grew underfoot, and Dailus slipped, grabbing for the wall. He grabbed a head, the nose jutting into his palm, and cried out, jerking back his hand, nearly stumbling back into the river, but there was no answering cry of surprise. Peering into the gloom, Dailus discerned a seated stone figure, eyes serenely shut. A niche hollowed the cliffside around the statue, leaving it in a sort of private shrine.

As his eyes adjusted, Dailus glimpsed another niche ahead, larger this time, then a few darker shadows beyond that. He moved ahead in the twilight, letting his left hand follow the pattern of niches. Statues filled every one of them, small niches piled a dozen or more high, each with its little, sitting god, then larger ones, some of them damaged by cracks in the stone, or worn down with time. The walls opened up to a broad, mossy plateau. Sunlight struck down over the mountaintops with those last, brilliant rays, illuminating hundreds upon hundreds of statues. All around him sat ranks of gods, legs crossed, arms open, eyes closed, as if an entire monastery had been turned to stone. Some sat no bigger than his hand, others towered above him. Many of the larger ones stood, carved with drapes of stone as if they wore layers of silk, their faces smiling gently, like saints, their hands upraised in a sign of blessing. Dozens of giants gazed down on him, carved with beaded necklaces and muscular legs, robustly dancing among their smaller kindred. Hundreds of tiny, simple carvings flowed up over the arches above the bigger ones, so densely arranged that they looked like patterned cloth spread upon the stone. Across the river, the sunlight picked out thousands more statues, some sharing deep coves in the stone, some set in their own shrines.

The cathedral nearest Dailus's home had been under construction for a hundred years and wasn't finished yet. He had only to make the bells, but dozens of workmen carved the statues both inside and out. How long had the Cathayans been building their cathedral cliffs? How long might it take to carve a thousand gods, sitting, standing, gazing down at him, tiny and lost among them?

Dailus lowered himself to his trembling knees. Dimly, he imagined the thunder of a priest declaiming idolatry, calling down the wrath of the Lord upon the heathens who failed to heed Him or hear the truth of His word. The heathens were meant to be poor, rude, unlearned, lost in a wasteland from which they should be grateful to be saved. Heathens—yet how could this not be a work of God? Would those thousands of sculptors, over hundreds of years dedicate themselves to such a place if they knew nothing of glory? And the carvings, even the strangest of them, held nothing evil, nothing tempting or taunting.

He pressed his hands together and gazed up at them, their faces made radiant by the glow of sunset, their hands and arms and figures made holy by the work of the dedicated hands who carved them. As he framed a prayer, Dailus felt a stirring in his bones, from his knees to the top of his skull, and all thought of glory fled. Sound moved through him and only then struck his ears in echoes along the stone pathway behind him: hoofbeats.

CHAPTER TWENTY-SIX

Lantern held low, Yusen led his horses cautiously along the narrow path, beneath the watchful eyes of so many Buddhas. His slave had come this way—Yusen had heard the cry without answer, and waited to hear a splash or some other sign of calamity. Nothing. Had he mistaken the slave's voice? No, he had heard that cry too often to doubt himself now. And there! In the mud near the edge of the path, a footprint too large for a Mongol or Chin man. He was so close now that his palms itched.

Sixteen days, the drakemaster had eluded him. For the first handful of days, Yusen could not be sure the slave wasn't merely dead, but he searched the river bank diligently and spoke to the farmers and the refugees. The boy who told him about the hungry ghost at their family shrine had almost kept back this information. His parents already assumed he was lying and punished him for eating the offerings, but Yusen's confirmation of the bearded face and pale eyes encouraged him, and the addition of a gold coin made the boy downright talkative. Yusen imagined him strutting about the village where they had beaten him for a liar, displaying his new wealth, proving himself innocent of their accusations. It was hard to judge whether they found the giant, pale thief any less a curiosity than the Mongol who hunted him, but Yusen ignored the stares and the laughter smothered behind their hands. His whip hung at his saddle, but he rode alone, and some of these people were likely rebels already, unafraid to defy their ruler, especially in the person of an undersized scout.

Yusen hurried, the string of horses trotting with him, and came out onto a broad platform that ran alongside the Buddha sculptures. He glanced around, and saw no one. At the far end, a monastery jutted from the cliffside. Yusen tethered his extra mounts to the pillar of a small shrine, to block the narrow end of the path, and leapt up on Tsang to gallop to the far end of the carven cliff. A wooden gate closed off the path along the river with heavy-looking hinges. He doubted the door could have been opened and shut to allow a visitor in the time it had taken him to get this far, not without his hearing it. Yusen rode back more slowly, glancing at the river for signs of ripples that would disturb the reflection of the dying sun. He caught sight of something and halted, staring down into the gloom, raising his lantern. One of the huge Chinese salamanders submerged into the water, its flat tail paddling it deeper.

Had that been a scuff against stone? Yusen halted, still as a statue himself, listening.

He cut across the platform toward the carvings. A vast hollow housed a number of enormous sculptures surrounded by hundreds more tiny figures. They glared down at him, hands raised in warning, great feet held up to step on him and crush him lower than a bug.

In the gloom to his left, a stone pinged down the cliff and rolled across the platform. Overhead, narrow ledges wandered up among the statues. He thought he saw movement, but it might have been the shadows shifting as his lantern reached into the gathering dark.

Suddenly, a spark from above lit one of the statues—a looming, bearded figure with wild, pale eyes. The spark soared toward the end of the path and shattered with a rush of flames. The slave had thrown a fire bomb at the horses. The tethered horses screamed and reared. Tsang cast back her ears, but Yusen urged her on. They galloped back toward the others. Yusen hooked his lantern to his saddle and slid to the ground. He threw himself at Uul, who stamped and reared. He snatched his bedding from its harness and cast his blanket down on the flames among the shards of a broken oil lamp. Catching Uul's collar, he stroked her neck, peering down her legs. She whinnied and shook her ears. Burned, but not badly. Anger flared in Yusen's heart. Not only did the slave betray him, now he attacked Yusen's horses, the only wealth and legacy he had from his family.

Behind him, more little stones pinged down the cliff. The slave was climbing. With his long legs, he could easily outpace Yusen on a ledge like that, and he already had a good start. Yusen snatched his bow and quiver from his saddle, slinging them over his shoulder, then took up the lantern. He leapt up on Tsang's back, then leapt again to the roof of the little shrine alongside. He dipped an arrow's head into the lantern's oil, and let it take fire. Arrow at the ready, he stared up into the gloom and saw movement. With a pull and a hiss, the arrow flew, a streak of flames across the distance. It briefly illuminated the man's figure a bit lower than where he had aimed, with a smaller ledge behind him. Before that arrow struck the cliff and skittered away, Yusen launched another one, unlit.

A yelp of surprise answered—surprise only, not pain, and Yusen launched another flaming arrow, aiming ahead on the same ledge, purposefully overshooting his last sighting of the slave. There—the drakemaster shrank back against one of the statues. Yusen shot again.

Gaze drawn by the flame, the slave tried to press himself into the niche of the nearest Buddha, then hurried around it, toward the other ledge.

Yusen drew another flaming arrow, shooting across the gap, even as he heard a yell and the sound of a heavy object dropping, hands or feet scrabbling for purchase. He jumped down into the saddle, riding hard for the largest alcove where the diagonal path set off, then running up it, whip in one hand and sword in the other.

The flaming arrow lodged into a crack above, showing the slave clambering up the slanting path, hand wrapping to his shoulder, staggering and bumping the cliff as he chose the widest ledge. Good choice in that he might move faster there. Bad choice, in that it gave Yusen plenty of room to work. Yusen was well-muscled, well-fed, and well-rested, and he wanted that slave as he had wanted nothing else in his life. He ran, leaping up the stone, thankful, for once, for his narrow hips and shoulders. The vagaries of the trail, now tight now broad, meant nothing to him. He unfurled his whip as the slave scrambled up one of the statues, aiming for a higher path.

"Do not make me kill you, slave!"

The drakemaster's big feet dug in, his hand reaching as he whimpered over the pain in his shoulder. Yusen's whip snapped around the man's ankle.

Injured, already off-balance, the slave fell, slithering down the statue and landing heavily on his knees. He lurched up, grabbing the whip from his end and giving a jerk.

Yusen had already let go. The slave stumbled. He took a stick from his belt, a bundle hanging from it, and swung it about. Yusen dodged, then sprang up, trapping this weapon against the cliff as he swung his sword in a neat arc, smacking the slave's outstretched elbow with the flat of the blade. The slave howled and broke his grip, moving backward up the ledge.

"Why are you chasing me! My God, can't you just let me alone?"

"You betrayed me, just as our lives got better, you threw me in the mud to be slain." Yusen advanced. "I was too gentle with you."

The slave's brittle laughter bounced from the sculptured cliffs. "Too gentle? I'd hate to see you get rough."

"You are about to." Yusen launched forward.

The slave must have heard his exertion because he grunted and pushed himself into motion, then Yusen was upon him. He jumped, tackling the tall man's legs and throwing him down to the narrow ledge between the statues.

Cursing and kicking, the slave rolled them both, pinning Yusen beneath him, but Yusen hooked his fingers through the slave's bracelet and kicked hard, shoving him aside. The slave's eyes flared as he flew sideways and off the ledge to dangle against the statues below. The last flame of the arrow above them went out. The weight of the fallen slave wrenched Yusen's arm and threatened to drag him over, but he hung on and dug in his other fingers. Dangling, the slave howled and cursed in his own language, then his twisting body stabilized. He must have found footholds. "Let me go!" he shouted, in Mongolian now. He wrenched at his arm, bringing his other hand around to grapple with Yusen's fingers. The other hand withdrew, and suddenly returned, stabbing with a short knife that carved through Yusen's sleeve and gouged his flesh.

Yusen clamped his jaw, refusing to scream. He clung to the slave's hand, pulling hard, then rolled onto his side facing the cliff edge. Grabbing a handful of the slave's wild hair with his other hand he slammed the slave's head into the rock.

The slave cried out, his body jerking and nearly falling, his knife flashing away into the darkness. Yusen rolled back, heaving with all of his strength to haul the slave up with him.

"Let me die," the slave groaned. Yusen pinned his shoulders, kneeling over him, and found his whip where it lay on the ledge. He used the long leather strap to lash the slave's hands together over his head and started to drag him down toward the road.

At a narrow patch, the slave jerked his body as if to throw them both over the edge and Yusen grabbed for him. He hitched his arm under the other man's armpit, taking a solid hold and marched steadily on in spite of the slave's thrashing.

After a long moment's peace, the drakemaster gave another dramatic surge of strength. Glancing down, Yusen let him fall. The man rolled down the short slope to the platform and lay a moment, stunned not by the fall, but by its brevity. Immediately, he tried to struggle to his feet, shaking his head and scrubbing his hands over his face to clear the blood and hair that must be obscuring his vision.

Yusen slithered down after him and let his feet slam into the man's back, knocking the breath from him.

Then he bent down and locked the man's armpit again, dragging him onward.

"Kill me now," the man moaned, or at least, Yusen assumed that's what he said.

"No."

He hauled his captive the last few lengths to where the horses waited, dropping him in the circle of lamplight. The man lay there, gasping. Blood streaked his face and straw-colored hair from scrapes across his temple and down his cheek, overlaying the scar. Scrapes tore the skin of his hands, and his fingers trembled, his palms pressed together where Yusen had bound him. His once-fine clothes hung torn and stained. He looked even thinner and more tired than before. He looked… pathetic.

Studying him, Yusen's fury nearly abated, then he turned to his horses and saw the scorched hair and raw flesh of Uul's legs. From another of his mounts, he took the prisoner board Munkjar had given him, a broad circle of wood, hinged to open across three holes—one large and two smaller. He carried this over and found the slave trying to crawl toward the river.

"You coward." Yusen caught the whip and halted the drakemaster's escape. "Is this what a man does where you come from? He hides, he runs, he tries to die? Have your people no spirit at all? You are a fishbelly."

The man stared back at him, shaking his head a little.

"Is that what your god teaches, that you should be no better than worms?" Yusen gave the board a flip so that it opened. "On your knees."

"I just want to go home!" the drakemaster shouted, but tears streaked his face. "Please."

"So do I!" Yusen shouted back at him. "On your knees." He dropped the whip and grabbed a handful of hair, hauling the man into position. "And if you had served the khan with honor, it might have happened for both of us." He pulled the heavy board up onto the slave's shoulders, wincing at the pain in his cut arm. Holding the slave's bound hands in position, Yusen slammed the board around his prisoner, the slave's neck in the largest hole, his wrists in the two smaller ones, the flesh pinched by the rough wood openings. After sliding through the metal pin to lock the circle, Yusen unwound the whip, relieving some pressure on the man's hands. A rope tied the rings on the board to a horse's harness, ensuring the drakemaster could not throw himself in the river.

"Nobody runs from the khan's army," Yusen told him. "Nobody." His hands shook and his voice trembled as he finished the task and backed away out of the circle of light, trying to find the strength to steady himself. A prisoner board would not hold him—Yusen's hands were too small. Munkjar found other ways to impose discipline.

From one of his saddlebags, Yusen plucked a leather pouch of airag and took a harsh swallow. He rested his head on Tsang's warm shoulder.

If the slave went home, then Yusen never could. His name would be reviled along with his father's, his family honor destroyed forever. What made the slave's home more valuable than his own? Nothing. And Yusen's strength and cunning had won this night. Surely the heavens granted his victory, as they had granted Chinggis Khan, his mighty ancestor, victory over so many men. In him, the blood ran true. His father was the man of broken vows: Yusen vowed to bring back the slave, and so he would, before the khan and all of his court, his vow would be fulfilled. And whatever happened then remained to the vast Eternal Sky.

Overhead, stars twinkled in the cloudless sky. A thousand crickets sang from the trees on the mountainsides and a thousand Buddhas sat in their holes of stone. He smelled the blood of his injuries and the singed horsehair, and catalogued the care that must be taken tomorrow if they were all to ride safely to the khan. The drakemaster sobbed quietly in his defeat. Yusen carried his lantern into the little shrine, deep into the heart of a cave painted with Buddhas. When he could hear the slave no longer, he shut his eyes to the Buddha's compassion and wandered the starless night of sleep.

CHAPTER TWENTY-SEVEN

Bao Xing sat very still in the middle of the brightly lit chamber as Mistress Luo prowled around her. The chamber reminded her of her mother's room, decorated with perfect embroideries of flowers and birds; edged with tables full of all manner of paints, combs and perfumes; smelling a little too much like a summer garden—but with an almost animal tang underneath, the strength of the musks that men were said to admire. She had worked very hard on her face and hair for this meeting, hoping to be told she was fine, but Mistress Luo's pitying expression said otherwise. Chubei and two of her ladies lounged nearby, whispering during the inspection.

"She has excellent bones, of course, your majesty. Her features have all of the classic attributes—her lips are perfectly shaped." Mistress Luo lifted Bao Xing's chin and turned her face. "She does well with her own paint, but really you should provide her with an assistant if she is to be shown to her best advantage." She turned her wrist and a girl brought forward a cushioned stool for Mistress Luo. "I will need to inspect your lotus blossom feet."

At that, the Mongolian ladies scooted forward on their settee and broke off their whispering. Bao Xing lifted her hem to slide forth her feet in their tiny slippers, as delicately embroidered as any of the panels that hung on the chamber walls.

"Ai! Just look at them." Mistress Luo's eyes glossed over and she reached out with trembling fingers, her nails very long and very red, to take Bao Xing's left foot in her hand. Her heel rested at Mistress Luo's fingertips, and her toe barely reached the center of the woman's palm. "They are perfect. So tiny! And the stitching of your slippers is excellent. Your mother has done very well by you, my lady, even if she did not oversee your marriage herself."

"Don't you take off the shoes to inspect them?" Chubei asked.

Mistress Luo's brow pinched. "Your majesty, it is not polite for a lady to show them to anyone but her husband."

With a sigh and a tip of her tall headdress, Chubei leaned back. "What sort of husband? The khan takes only ladies of my tribe, but some of his relatives are open. She might win one of the other blood-princes. Then she could live here or travel with the court." Chubei picked through a bowl of nuts and berries, popping some lightly into her mouth.

"Certainly she would be a prize for such a man. She might also make a fine match with one of the Mandarins—the educated gentlemen of the khan's employ."

"A servant? Surely not." Chubei tossed a handful of rejected nuts back into the bowl.

Mistress Luo pressed her hands carefully together. "Mandarins are your husband's ministers, your majesty, running the various branches of his empire. Those that Lady Bao Xing encounters here at the palace are the highest quality of men and well worthy of her attention."

One of them, Guowei, organized his library. Bao Xing thought of his warm, crinkling eyes. He was clearly a gentleman of standing and intelligence. Since her mother's death, she had not considered marriage, much less to whom she might be married. A prince of the blood—one of the descendants of the great conqueror, Chinggis Khan, hardly sounded appealing, a man who cared nothing for the heavens. The Mistress of the Household and the Mongol queen chattered on, comparing the pedigrees of various candidates, and Bao Xing's stomach churned. If she had to marry someone from the khan's household, pray the ancestors that it should be someone like Guowei, who at least had some appreciation of the things she loved.

"Please, Mistress," Bao Xing interrupted, and they stopped, both cocking their heads expectantly. "I have so long been outside of court, Mistress, that I am no fit wife for any man, much less a man of the high standing you suggest. I have so much to learn."

"Mmm. It is a wise woman who can recognize her own ignorance. We must begin as soon as possible. First, your majesty, is there a girl you can assign to tend to the lady's needs?"

"Of course." Chubei held a whispered consultation with one of the other ladies, who departed and returned a short while later with a Chin girl of about eight years. "Meili will serve you. We are off to ride. I hope your lessons proceed well!"

Meili executed an elegant bow, and Bao Xing could tell, just by watching her, that she herself had a lot to learn.

"Excellent! Attend closely…" For the next three hours, Mistress Luo instructed Bao Xing and her new maidservant on every detail of a perfect face. Then it was time for her hair, twisted and pinned so tightly that her scalp itched. Finally, she practiced walking, a skill she used in her father's tower only to mount the stairs in the evening and return again at dawn. The cane was a great help, and Mistress Luo not only admired its style and ornate carving, but also Bao Xing's facility with it.

"It is a little bold for a lady, of course, but you may be allowed a certain flourish. Again."

Bao Xing took the mincing little steps that Mistress Luo demonstrated, discovering this gait allowed her to glide along with relative ease.

"With a bit of work, my lady, you can give a tip of the heel, just so." Mistress Luo strolled past again with the aid of a slender cane of her own, and paused, the tip of her heel allowing the toe of her little shoe to peek from beneath the fine silk of her robe.

A gong echoed through the hall, and Mistress Luo broke her pose. "Ai, but we are out of time today. Come again tomorrow at the hour of the rabbit."

"Yes, Mistress." She bowed slightly, and practiced the perfect lotus blossom gait as she exited the room. Meili trailing a step behind, Bao Xing imagined happier things: the arrangement of the stars in the Weaving Girl; the movement of the wandering stars in the right season, when they maintained a true course across the sky; the cool, beautiful bronze of a well-made instrument; the even parade of black strokes across a page of white to delineate a new idea.

"Are you still thinking on fortunes, my lady?" Guowei approached along the corridor, accompanied by a few other Mandarins, their hands tucked into their sleeves.

"In a way. Mistress Luo's work may shortly result in your own prophecy coming true. Certainly she seems set upon my marriage as soon as possible."

A rumble of amusement ran through the group, and one of the younger men turned a little pink, then made bold to meet her eye.

"To marry well is a fine goal." Guowei inclined his head. "Though one I have not aspired to."

"I never aspired to more than books," she answered. "And stars."

Guowei laughed out loud. "Books and stars. I should not be surprised."

"Our supper awaits, Minister," said an older man, stroking a hand over the straining brocade that covered his stomach.

"Will you join us, my lady?"

Just to be immersed in the conversation of learned people, all in their own language, would be a pleasure. "I believe I am available, Minister," she said, "but someone will need to tell Queen Chubei."

"Really—is it quite proper?" the older man demanded.

The young one who had been eying Bao Xing said, "Isn't she the one who has been assisting you to organize the library? She has an attendant—I'm sure it would be fine."

"Run along and tell the queen, then." Guowei made a flicking gesture to the young man who sourly bowed and turned away.

"Besides," cut in another fellow, "I should like to know more about that cane." He turtled his head forward to examine it, the scholar's ties on his cap standing out stiffly to either side indicating his elevated rank.

"I do not know much myself, honored scholar. My father gave it to me, but it has been in our family for many years." She held it up across her palms, turning it gently so that he could see the winding trees and mountains carved on the cinnabar portion. The cap and end of the stick were ebony for strength, edged with gold to set off the red of the carving.

"I am the khan's overseer of mines. It is likely the talented fellow who carved this for your several-times-grandfather died of his art." The old man shuffled ahead to walk beside her. "In this form, cinnabar is relatively inert, but if you carve into it, especially to polish or drill it out as those delicate branches are drilled, you would release the poison. Mining is the worst of course, dreadful business, but so vital—well, actually, you might say that it is the refining that is worse."

At his other side, Guowei matched his pace, but flicked her a glance, then rolled his eyes skyward.

Bao Xing practiced her mincing steps, hiding her smile.

The Overseer of Mines continued, "Miners might last so long as six or eight months. Those who work in the refineries where mercury can be extracted are lucky to live so long as three months." He thrust up his fingers emphatically.

Men did not want a woman to know too much—or so Mistress Luo said—even Guowei mistrusted a woman who sought too much learning. Instead of admitting her own knowledge, Bao Xing gave a little shiver. "Oh, dear. I knew it was unhealthy, but I did not realize how deadly it could be. I do hope there's no need to descend into the mines yourself, Overseer."

"Rarely. Other officers supervise the principle mine in Henan province. Most of the workers are criminals or farmers so poor that this labor is more lucrative than farming, so you should not fear that worthy men are driven to death with such work." His face crinkled.

"And without the mercury, our clocks would be so inaccurate, especially in the north where ordinary water would freeze in the drive mechanism." Bao Xing hesitated, realizing that this statement revealed a little too much, so she tried the heel tip that would show her tiny slipper, hoping to mitigate the effect of intellect. "At least, I think that is what my father said."

"Indeed, your father was correct." said a tall man with a scarred chin, "I think the lady has probably heard enough about your specialty, Overseer."

This caused another chuckle through the group, but Guowei seemed distracted, his hands folded behind him, his eyes gazing into an unknown distance.

"Myself, I am responsible for the design and creation of the khan's navy." The taller man's broad shoulders strained his robe, and his hands looked work-worn and powerful. "But I am afraid I am already well-married, and I don't believe I can support a concubine at this time, no matter how lovely she might be."

The Overseer of Mines swatted the navy man's arm. "Tut! You mustn't dissuade her of spending more time with us, surely. There are still plenty of eligible men among us—the Minister of Finance, the Undersecretary for the Importation of Silks, the Second General of Internal Affairs, not to mention the Minister of Archives, who has a start upon the others by virtue of already having met the lady, isn't that right, Minister?"

Guowei started, then gave a short bow that made his topknot wag. "If you will forgive me, I have just had a thought that I must transcribe. I shall join you all shortly." Noticing Bao Xing's gaze upon him, he bowed again, more carefully. "Thank you, my lady, for joining us. I am sure your presence will be most enlivening." He spun on his heel and hurried toward the library, grey robe flapping with his haste.

"Perhaps he is inspired to write a poem on the subject of cinnabar," the Overseer mused. "No matter. Come, my lady, supper awaits." Bao Xing allowed herself to be escorted, thinking hard. She could do so much worse than to marry Guowei. From that evening, Bao Xing determined to make Mistress Luo's lessons her special course of study. One way and another, the library would be hers.

CHAPTER TWENTY-EIGHT

"I cannot be here," Ming Lun's imperial contact told her sharply, glancing around the tea garden. "It is too dangerous."

She bowed her head, acknowledging his words. "Forgive me, sir, but I felt this too important to leave unreported, and too complicated to transcribe in code." She cradled her injured arm close to her chest. A sling helped to support the break, but it would still take time to heal. "Also, I wished to be sure that my dancers are being well-treated."

He stared down at her, his mustache twitching with his worries. "Your leap into the river made you heroic to the Mongols—" he made a harsh sound in his throat to indicate how he felt about that, "and so the girls have been readily accepted into the khan's household. Have you a plausible story about the drakemaster? If so, you might be able to return as well."

"He would not be converted to the cause of the Son of Heaven." Ming Lun kept her eyes averted, hoping he would press her no further.

"Pity. We might have used a man of his talents. If you can identify where you left the body or bring some evidence of his death, that might serve. At least, the Son of Heaven would know that you did not deliberately fail to ruin the weapons and their maker." This little barb found home, reminding her of her attempts to do just that, attempts which ended in another man's death. The little Mongol slept too lightly for the poisoned brazier to smother him—and the drakemaster wasn't even in the tent that night. Ming Lun had failed, indeed, in that regard.

"Your daughter is well. She is being educated as you desired—why do you never ask about her?"

Another barb, this one sharper still. "She is no longer my concern."

"Ah, yes, if you had had your will, there would have been no child. Forgive me bringing it up."

And yet, he brought it up every time, if only to remind her she remained a woman, in spite of her freedom. She focused on her discovery. "I found something else, sir: the plan for a much more dangerous and elaborate weapon, a weapon the Mongols know nothing about."

"What weapon? Why was I not informed?" He perched on the bench across from her at the back of the tea garden.

"It does not belong to us, sir—not yet. I retrieved the plans from the man who had them, but they were taken from me by another."

"By whom? Who else knows about this thing?" The man pressed closer to her.

A serving girl moved past, and Ming Lun cupped the man's face, smiling as if they were a happy couple. She let her voice fall very low. "A monk and his apprentice. I don't believe they are working against us—certainly they are not with the Mongols."

"Then who else?"

His breath of confusion stroked her cheek, but his black eyes and sliver of mustache failed to warm her. Once the server had gone away Ming Lun pulled back from him. "Have you heard of the Order of Celestial Purity? It was named in the scroll I saw."

He tapped his forehead. "Yes, I remember. They were a bunch of mad old men at the time we first lost the North. They actually believed the Son of Heaven unworthy of the throne. Naturally, the imperial family disbanded the order. They have something to do with this weapon?" Her contact was young, eager, but not very bright.

"Their seal was on the scroll. I have every reason to believe that they created it."

"You should have brought it with you."

Ming Lun took a swallow of her tea to wash down her rising anger. The humiliation of being beaten and bound by monks—monks!—still stung, and now this man, who dwelled in the palace and had likely never been beaten or bound, simply informed her she should have brought it along. Indeed, she should, if only so that she could beat him about the head with it. "They are monks. They will look for other monks to pray on what to do. I was not in condition to pursue them."

He grunted and glanced at her arm. "Perhaps you are getting too old for this work."

Rattling the cup down to the tray, she aimed her stare at his face as if she could aim her hair pick into his brain: straight through the eye and dead in an instant. "Perhaps you are too young for it. The Order of

Celestial Purity—old men, you say. The man I took the scroll from was very old indeed and looked as if he had not eaten for years."

"They can't possibly still be alive, never mind still pursuing whatever plan they had in mind." The young man pushed away and rose, his brocade gown flopping down over his hands. "Well. I will report what you say, but I don't think they will be interested, except that the drakemaster is gone. Still, Kaifeng has fallen, and there is little else to stop a Mongol advance, save the mighty Yangtze."

"Or the death of the khan," Ming Lun breathed.

The young man gave a short chuckle. "You understand nothing. The khan's army buys thousands of talens of silk every year, not to mention their other needs. The khan's army is an excellent customer—we simply need them to find another target for their war."

"You don't think they would as soon own the silk, along with the weavers?"

"They can't even administer their own palace without a hundred Mandarins, and you think they would run the empire?" He bowed with an exaggerated wiggle of his head that took any respect from the gesture, then dropped a purse of coins on the table—some for her, some for the tea house. "A pleasure, as always. I hope your arm recovers well, and I shall send to the guesthouse if it is safe or desirable for you to return to your post."

Ming Lun stared at his retreating back. A few darts from her special flute, and he would fall flat on his face in the fishpond. Still, the Son of Heaven required even such functionaries as this. Every tiny lark joining the chorus.

Besides, she needed to freshen her stock of herbs and powders. She drew the purse toward her and left a few coins on the table. She had burned up her poisonous smoke, then used her sleeping blend on Master Deng and Dailus, and rather wished her bluff about poison on the hair picks had been no bluff at all, then she could bring the emperor a thing worth seeing. When she did retrieve the plan, she would not go to this boy-Mandarin, but to one of her other imperial connections, someone more likely to understand.

Ming Lun walked briskly through the city at the feet of the khan's stolen palace. Crowds of Han people mingled with Mongols, grinning and simpering, catering to the needs of their enemy. Some of them likely still thought of the Mongols as their allies, as they had been when the Emperor sought their aid to win back the North and reunite the empire, but the Mongols did not give up their claim to the territory they helped to conquer, nor did they ride their scruffy horses back to the plains where they belonged. Instead, they settled down, seizing imperial palaces and fortresses, hiring educated administrators, encouraging trade and putting down rebellions quite as if they now owned the North. But the Emperor would win it back, with Ming Lun's help.

So the Order of Celestial Purity thought the emperor had no right to rule. Interesting. Unsettling. Master Deng suggested as much when he dismissed her comment about the strength of the south. Ming Lun pushed through crowds around the market stalls, smelling leather from saddles and harness, wooly sheep for felting and flesh for eating.

In a narrow alley, she located the carved door marked with symbols for health and longevity. Inside, the cramped space stretched out long before her, one wall entirely formed of wooden drawers, the opposite wall hung with drawings of healing pathways, whole dried roots and preserved animals, including a river salamander only as big as her arm, and an entire string of penises of different kinds for handling sexual complaints—most of which, in Ming Lun's experience, amounted to how to get more of it.

"Good day, lady, and what may I offer you?" The proprietor bowed slightly, not enough to brush his cap on the opposite wall. "Do you require a prescription for your injury, or perhaps a treatment of healing needles?"

"My pantry is quite empty, sir, both of herbs and of remedies." She nudged the purse and let it jingle.

The proprietor's smile spread. "I await your needs."

She walked a little before him, tapping drawers with her good hand to indicate what she wanted, while he filled little packets with wooden scoops. "I understand you are knowledgeable about longevity," she began.

The old man smoothed his facial hair. "You say this by my beard, I gather, lady." He slid shut the most recent drawer he had opened. "Many people claim such knowledge."

"Are there ways a man could live a century or more? Two, even?" She tapped another drawer. "Three scoops of this one."

"This is very powerful—be careful never to keep it around cooking."

"Only for the barn rats," she told him and smiled.

He brought out another packet. "Longevity is the obsession of many, but few are hardy enough or persistent enough to pursue it. Some monks who have undergone certain rites are said to be meditating for centuries."

"Monks, you say? But not other men?"

Sealing the packet, he placed it in the basket he filled for her. "There is a formula I have heard of, but even this requires meditation. The formula must be taken daily for a year, and only works together with a certain substance on the skin, lacquered like a piece of furniture, lady. A man cannot move about and speak and be as a man, for the combination of herbs and lacquer slows the pulses." He pointed to a diagram on the wall which showed the track of veins within the body and the points on the skin where healing or injury could be affected. "Why should a man wish to sleep for centuries? To live a long time, yes, but to sleep it away, sitting as no more than a table or a chair?" He shrugged. "All is suffering in this realm, and we can hope for better in the next life, eh? Speaking of suffering, would you like a course of needles to speed the healing of your arm? I should be honored to assist you in recognition of your good custom."

Why should a man sleep for centuries? The old pharmacist had answered his own question: to see if things were, indeed, better in the next life. To see if an emperor might be worthy, or an enemy, too strong; to see if a plan devised in one lifetime might serve another, and find a collaborator to help him bring it about. "Thank you." She bowed slightly. "I should very much like to speed my healing." The sooner her arm was mended, the sooner she could continue her service. The emperor might think the Order of Celestial Purity disbanded, but she suspected it had only been sleeping.

The door popped open with a jingle of bells. "Papa, come see—there's a dwarf, and he's bringing a ghost! He's captured a ghost as his prisoner, come see!"

Chuckling, the pharmacist shook his head. "A dwarf with a captive ghost. What will my grandson think of next? Lady, are you quite well?"

Ming Lun tried to breathe again—tried to see why her heart felt suddenly weak. Of course, once this news reached the palace, her imperial contact would know she had not told him all the truth about the drakemaster. "A captive ghost. That must indeed be a sight." A captive ghost with startling eyes and skillful hands. Had she hoped for him to die out there, so that her conscience could be clear of this betrayal of her duty? Then why leave him a knife—why not kill him as she was meant to? It would be worse for him now, reclaimed by his brutal master.

She absently handed her payment to the proprietor and followed him and his grandson into the street. Already, word of the curious procession packed the marketplace with people, but the little boy dragged his grandfather up a narrow flight of steps and she stayed with them, gaining the balcony where household linens hung upon a line between the pillars. Looking between the sheets and towels, Ming Lun saw the little group of horses—Yusen's mounts surrounded by a few soldiers. On one of the horses, the drakemaster slumped, his head and hands protruding from a prisoner board, his legs bound to the saddle so he wouldn't fall. She squinted, but the distance made it hard to see. Blood stained his tunic beneath the shadow of the board and his fingers drooped. His ragged hair hung over his face, matted with a darkness that drew buzzing flies. How maddening to lack even the freedom to swat them away. No man truly wished to die, she had told him, yet if he had known what awaited him—if she had known, would she still believe her own words?

Her breast felt hollow. In moments, her contact would know the drakemaster lived. Surely that was the origin of her emotions. If she would stay in the graces of the Son of Heaven, then she must make amends, and quickly. She must find the plan and prove herself still worthy of a role in the fight. If nothing else, the drakemaster's miserable fate showed the cruelty of their conquerors. Even the least among the Mongols would stop at nothing to break the people they perceived as belonging to them. Her people should never belong to them. No matter what.

"Sir, if you have seen enough, I would like to begin the course of needles. I have too much to do to wait for time to heal me."

"Is that why you asked about longevity, to make more hours for the work ahead?" The old man waved for her to follow him back to the shop. "If it were me, I should take the time for reading. I am reading now the legend of the valley of the sages, where philosophers can fly."

"I want to fly!" the little boy shouted, bounding around them with his arms outstretched.

"Ai! Get off to your mother and bring back a bucket of coal. I need to warm my tools for this lady."

Still flapping, the boy ran off, the sight of him making Ming Lun's arm throb with sympathetic pain. She must be healed, so she could free him to fly as he would—so she could free them all, and scour their Mongol oppressors from the valley, and the world. If she faced again that campfire where Master Deng urged the drakemaster to join him, she would reveal herself and speak her mind, in spite of his poor opinion of the Son of Heaven. Together, they would have taken the plans to those among the Mandarins who secretly worked for the emperor, even now.

"What is it you do, lady, that is so important?" The pharmacist ushered her into a curtained chamber at the back of the shop.

"I am a dancer." She arched her neck, striking a pose. The most important performance at her command was the dance of death. She itched to be dancing again.

CHAPTER TWENTY-NINE

When Yusen's procession reached the steps of the Great Khan's palace, Munkjar waited, arms folded, eyebrows raised, staring down from a superior position on the central landing. With the drakemaster bound behind him, a phalanx of guards holding back the curious onlookers, and the swelling crowd itself, the thrill of victory flowed through Yusen. His vow, he had done it. At the base of the steps, he leapt down from Tsang's back, and a groom took her rein while he walked back to the drakemaster, bound to Uul's sister, Namar. Uul's legs remained sore, though Yusen had applied ointment to them every morning and distributed her load to the other horses. Now, they would be able to rest a while, and she would recover.

Namar twitched under her awkward load, turning her head to look at him as he worked on the knots and released the bonds of the drakemaster's legs. The slave slid to the side, but Yusen caught his arm and eased him to his knees. Excess cruelty served no purpose. Their fight at the sculpted grotto delivered his discipline for damaging his horse, and now, in front of this vast crowd, he claimed his reward for the disgrace of the slave's escape. Yusen had undone that damage with such an entrance. He stood, collecting the stares and shouts, knowing for once they stared in amazement rather than disdain.

At his feet, the slave took short, half-strangled breaths. The board fit just loosely enough, and Yusen had applied his ointment to the drakemaster's neck as well. This mode of breathing expressed the slave's defeat rather than his actual condition.

"Follow." He pivoted on his heel, mounting the stairs.

With a shuffle and a groan, the slave obeyed, limping, stumbling up the steps, sprawling when they reached the landing, the board scraping hard, arms and legs smacking the stone. Yusen waited again as Munkjar sauntered over, glancing over his head toward the slave, then focusing on Yusen's face.

"Well," the general began, but Yusen simply said, "Follow," and the slave pushed himself upward again as they climbed the last few steps. Discipline. Yusen walked slowly on, until one of the khan's fancy servants, a Mandarin, came before him and bowed. The servant had to bow especially low to be sure his head actually went below Yusen's.

The Mandarin said, "The khan has been at games, but he awaits you now in the lesser hall, if you will follow me, sir."

The Mandarin hustled away, but Yusen continued his slow pace, taking in the painted columns and tapestries that adorned the walls, listening to the slave's uneven steps and rough breathing behind him. At one point the man whimpered, and Yusen paused, studying a long painting of horses, some of them sketched in ink as a young man worked over them. "These remind me of the horses on the khan's great firedrake. Fine work."

The young man twitched, taking him in, then bent back to his painting, unsure how to respond.

The Mandarin waited at a bend in the corridor, and Yusen moved on to join him there. He began to appreciate his control over speed. Throughout Yusen's life, Munkjar cultivated the exact pace he wished, moving languidly as a tiger to dispense justice or demand that duty be observed. It exasperated Yusen to no end, but part of the point was to force others to bend to you as Yusen now made the Mandarin obey him, without the servant even intending to. Yusen had always hurried, so desperate to press onward, as if, by outrunning his past, he could escape his future. Today, he took his time.

They rounded the corner and entered a pair of huge doors studded with bronze. Inside, the khan sat on a broad throne, clad in sweaty leathers and old boots—just in from a ride. He mopped his face with a cloth. "Ah, Yusen! You have done it." The khan scrubbed his hands on his thighs and rose, stalking closer.

"Your drakemaster, my lord, apprehended while trying to escape." Yusen bowed, then turned to his slave, who already sank to his knees. The other soldiers filled in around the doors, parting for Munkjar, who contrived to look as if he arrived exactly when he intended, despite being left by Yusen on the steps.

Yusen swept the slave's hair from his face, then placed a steadying hand on the man's shoulder as he slid back the bar that closed the prisoner board. The hinge opened with a groan and a few flakes of blood, and he lifted it away to rest it on the tiled floor.

The drakemaster hunched forward, his forearms resting on the ground, and let his head down.

"Lie down," Yusen ordered. "All the way."

Slowly, the slave unfolded and stretched out on the ground, utterly abased at the boots of the khan, from his bloody, wild hair to his bare, over-sized feet.

The khan stared down at him. "I was not sure you would find him. If you found him, I was not sure you would—either of you—survive the meeting, and now here you are. Not only returning him to me alive, but apparently in working condition." He prodded the slave's side with the toe of his boot.

"My lord, it was no more than my duty to my khan." Yusen bowed and straightened, holding himself a tall as he could. His gut knotted beneath the stiff layers of his trousers and del. Would the khan commend him for his duty, or condemn him for his slave's lack of discipline?

"Clearly, such a troublesome slave should be destroyed," Munkjar said, joining them.

"I have not found him so much trouble lately, general." Yusen's mind worked furiously—would the slave return to his role as drakemaster? And if he did not, then where did that leave Yusen's quest to reinstate his family honor? "The firedrake he made at Kaifeng was a triumph for the khan's army. If he were to make more of them—"

Munkjar spread his teeth and gave a harsh sound. "Others can use his models to make more—what's to say he won't run away again?"

"There are ways." The khan walked around the slave, then held out a hand to Munkjar, who placed the hilt of a great sword into their ruler's palm. The khan lowered his arm, resting the blade at the drakemaster's ankle. "A man with severed ankles can't run."

The slave's head shook.

"It also makes for an excellent reminder to the rest of the crew."

The drakemaster tried to pull up his feet, but the khan stomped on his calf, pressing his leg down, eying the distance between the blade and the captive limb.

Yusen clenched his teeth. A man without feet couldn't run, couldn't ride—quite possibly, couldn't even survive the blow. His own ankle twitched.

"Both, do you think?"

"Certainly, my lord," Munkjar said.

The slave writhed desperately. "No! Please, no! Just kill me if you must, please don't take my feet." He rolled half to his side, hands pleading.

"Then give us something else," Yusen urged. His fingers clenched remembering the feel of the slave's bracelet as he hung on at the Buddhist grotto, as the slave begged him to let go. Would the corpse have been enough to prove himself to the khan? But there would have been no honor guard, no crowds and no future. Taking the drakemaster alive had gotten him this far. He could not let him go without a fight. "Give us something else," he said, low and urgent. "Show the khan you deserve better treatment."

The jade-green eyes stared back at him, edged white in terror over a mouth gone hard with—what? loathing or despair? "They have a weapon," the drakemaster rasped. "Worse than any I could make—worse than anything." He coughed, flopping back onto the ground.

"Water—get him a drink," Yusen demanded, and, startlingly, one of the servants obeyed, bringing over a pitcher and ladle. The girl spooned water over the slave's cracked lips to spill across his beard and the floor, but the man drank, finally lifting a hand to steady the ladle. For the past seven days, Yusen had been that servant, holding the bowl or leaf to get the slave to drink anything, to keep him alive for this moment. His heart hammered and his own throat felt dry.

"My lord, he says the Chin have a terrible weapon, worse than any firedrake."

"What weapon?" the khan asked.

"If they had any such weapon," Munkjar said, "they would surely have used it."

"Can't," the drakemaster blurted. "It's hidden, maybe damaged. I've seen the plans. It uses clocks, gearing..." his hands moved restlessly, circling the floor, shaping the image of whatever he had seen. "They use equipment to track the stars, then they have a way to capture the influence of the stars."

Munkjar snorted. "Everyone knows the stars have influence, but surely—"

"Geomancers." The drakemaster lifted his head. "They have magic."

The slave had cut off the general, as if their places were reversed. Yusen withheld his grin. The slave's information was good, vital: exactly what they both needed to survive whatever happened next.

At the mention of geomancers, the khan's eyes flared. "My shaman warned me they were dangerous, those strange men who hid in the mountains."

"But my lord—" Munkjar stopped again at the khan's raised hand.

"This must be the danger he spoke of. It seems the Chin have been outdone already, by our own shamans."

Yusen felt like shouting. Anything that could make the khan shut up the general was a thing worth shouting about. "If the slave speaks the truth, my lord," Yusen said, "we should learn more about this weapon."

The khan's brow furrowed and he nodded. "Until now, we have had only rumors about the geomancers, but enough of them to be cautious. Ask him." He pointed down, and Yusen gave a nod, sinking next to the downed man.

"Where did you see it? When?" he asked softly.

"The old man, the false shaman, he had a scroll. He found us—me—when I came out of the river." The slave wet his lips, his throat bobbing, circled by scraped skin where the board had rested. "He's looking for someone to operate it, to use it against the khan." He broke down coughing, and Yusen scooped a ladle of water, holding it to his lips. "I refused." He took a hard breath, and met Yusen's gaze. "Duty to the khan, and to the people. I refused."

The false shaman. Yusen absorbed that without blinking. He had been right about that strange old man. The man had been spying in the Mongol camp. Had he been responsible for the damage to the firedrakes and the attack on Yusen himself?

Looming over him, the khan and the general remained impassive.

"When he was asked to repair the weapon, my lord, he refused, out of his duty to yourself, and he willingly offered this information." Yusen rose up. "The weapon is no rumor—not if there is a drawing like he describes. He served you well, my lord khan. In this, and in his casting. Perhaps only the madness of battle made him leap into the river."

The khan pursed his lips, rolling his foot back and forth just a little against the slave's leg. The point of the sword he held still prodded the exposed tendon of the ankle. "True. On the other hand, it seems that our enemies have a weapon they can no longer use. They have not the skill to repair it, nor the geomancers to give it life. This is well." He smiled. "Very good news indeed. And for the palace maids, who will not have to tidy up so much blood." Grinning, he handed the sword back to Munkjar.

"Take this slave to the minister of archives and have him draw everything he remembers. Then, let us find new work for this slave, something to allow him to enjoy his ankles." He pointed to a young soldier who trotted over and bowed. "After the archives, bring this man to the mine detail. The caravan sets out tomorrow—let him mine cinnabar for the rest of his days, where no man shall tempt him with a weapon to use against us."

The soldier grabbed the slave's arm and hauled him up.

"My lord—" the drakemaster began, but the khan waved him away, and he stumbled along to this new doom.

Already, the khan turned toward Munkjar, and Yusen's moment of command slipped away—his slave was taken from him, sent to die in the mines, never more to be the master of anything, and Yusen's own amusement value ebbing as the crowd dispersed outside the door. His brief victory so quickly turned to ash.

"My lord khan," Yusen said, in his most steady voice, hoping by the time the khan turned about, that he would know what to say. What would the drakemaster have said, the man whose bold tongue had gotten them into all of this? "It is customary if a slave is transferred and cannot serve his master any longer, to grant some compensation to the owner." His voice squeaked a little, and the khan's lips hinted at a smile. At least, he maintained his value as a plaything.

"Compensation? What would serve under such circumstances?"

"The slave was my sole retainer, my lord, and he did you valuable service in the design and making of the firedrake that broke the rebels' dreams, and in bringing us word of the weapon they still hope to use against us." He drew a deep and tremulous breath, focusing on the khan, trying not to notice the way Munkjar fingered his sword. "You hold a treasure for which, unless I am wrong, you have little use." Yusen squared his shoulders and asked for what he wanted, what he had been so certain never to have. "The lady Bao Xing," he said, "I would have her to wife."

CHAPTER THIRTY

The first Bao Xing heard of her wedding was Chubei shouting outside Mistress Luo's chamber. Inside, Bao Xing jabbed her aching fingers against the strings of the pipa, trying to press hard enough to get the right sound. Instead, she produced another jangle of notes and Meili winced while Mistress Luo's fleshy face sank deeper into wrinkles. Bao Xing dropped her gaze and adjusted the tear-drop shaped instrument in her lap. "Forgive me, Mistress. I was distracted."

"As who shouldn't be, with such a racket?" The instructor flipped her silver-tipped nails toward the door, and one of her servants hurried over to ask for quiet in the halls. Bao Xing hoped for anything but quiet—she was sure she had heard her name.

"I hear you have been keeping company with the Ministers at mealtimes, Bao Xing."

"Yes, Mistress. I have been practicing the skills of culture and etiquette as you suggested."

Mistress Luo slapped the lacquered table at her side. "You have been speaking of the things of men—sciences and the law. Such talk may amuse the Mandarins, but they do not choose wives for conversation."

One of the Mandarins had revealed her—was it the Undersecretary for the Administration of Waterways who always tried to sit near her? Bao Xing's hand tightened around the neck of the pipa. "Forgive me, Mistress."

"And the Minister of Archives cares too much for his letters to be an adequate husband." Mistress Luo reached out calmly and tapped her tea cup.

Bao Xing set down the musical instrument with more force than she intended and poured a bit of strongly brewed tea into an exquisite cup—another of the skills Mistress Luo insisted that men valued—then added plain hot water to right level, according to her instructor's taste. Had her interest in the Minister of Archives been as obvious to him as it had been to Mistress Luo's informant? She hoped not. Unless such interest were itself intriguing to a man. Truly the ways of court were more confusing than trying to read the stars during a thunderstorm.

The servant trotted back from the door.

Mistress Luo sipped her tea and turned down her mouth. "This is too weak." To the servant, she said, "What is it?"

"Queen Chubei, and the khan have come."

"The khan? You should have spoken right away." Mistress Luo pushed up on her slender cane and waved Bao Xing away from the second-best settee toward a cushion on the floor. "By all means, the khan must be admitted."

The khan swept in, carrying the scent of horses and sweat, and Mistress Luo's pinched expression indicated her disapproval, likely combined with her frustration at being utterly unable to do anything about it. A phalanx of bodyguards filtered after, some standing by the door while the others lined the corridor, leaning and sneaking glances at the richly dressed chamber.

The women all bowed, but the khan slapped his thighs and laughed. "A treasure indeed! I remember the first night you came to my ger."

"She never," Chubei snapped, coming to stand just past the khan's shoulder.

His wife's pique made the khan laugh harder.

"My lord is most kind to think of me," Bao Xing said carefully in Mongolian. The language felt rough and lumpish after speaking her own language with the instructor and the Mandarins, but Mongolian had been part of her education for these last twenty days, and she noted the slight softening of Mistress Luo's eyes. For once, she had done the right thing.

"I have chosen a husband for you, a prince of the blood of Chinggis Khan." His shoulders jiggled, and he could barely contain his amusement, then burst out laughing again. "Oh, truly, this is an occasion."

"This is a disaster." Chubei planted her hands on her hips. "You can't really mean to—"

"Uh!" The khan seized his wife's buttock with one hand and pressed the fingers of the other to her lips. "Don't spoil everything. Let Qutuqui be a withered apple-face, not you." He slipped both arms around her then and pulled her close.

Bao Xing dropped her gaze immediately, but she could not miss the queen's giggle. Married. Was that what it meant to be married? To be pawed at by a man in front of so many people? Ming Lun told her to expect no more than a box. She made this bargain when she left the mountain in a sedan chair instead of on foot disguised in boy's clothing. She bargained to save her father, not imagining it could bring her so close to the knowledge he was seeking—the khan's archive was the key, but now she would not even be married to a Mandarin, much less to Guowei himself.

"Come, girl—you shall be married!"

Startled by the khan's address, Bao Xing straightened on her cushion and tried to frame a reply. "I…" she faltered and said simply, "My lord is most kind to think of me."

The khan threw back his head and roared with laughter and Chubei, who had been smiling at the khan's intimate treatment of her, lost her smile. "You won't say so later, Bao Bao. He finds his choice of a husband most amusing."

"I shall consult the astronomers to determine an auspicious day for the wedding, my lord," Mistress Luo said. She clasped her hands together over the top of her cane—meaning she wanted to slap someone, but was showing restraint.

"No need—we have already tossed the bones and read them. Tomorrow is auspicious enough, eh?"

The instructor's hands slid a little tighter over her cane. "I do not know that she can be properly prepared to be married by then, my lord."

"The couple shall live here at the palace. If her husband—" he snickered and controlled himself, "if he finds her unready, he may send her to you to finish her lessons."

"May we not at least know his year and time of birth to cast an augury for the marriage, my lord?"

If the khan noticed Mistress Luo's increasingly hard tone, he gave no sign of it, but continued to act as if the entire arrangement were some sort of jest. "In this case, I think she'd rather not know. I can't imagine the marriage bed will do well by her." The khan wiped a tear of laughter from his eye with his thumb, but broke down again in giggles, and Chubei slapped his arm. "Can she stay here tonight? I would hate for anyone to spoil her wedding day."

"Of course, my lord. There is a place for her among my other pupils. Might one inquire at what time the wedding shall occur?"

"At the hour of the Horse—most auspicious for any Mongol." He waggled his eyebrows at Bao Xing, and drew Chubei back out the door along with his other retainers.

Mistress Luo sighed very deeply, then downed the rest of her tea and carefully replaced the cup. She studied Bao Xing with a mournful expression. "My dear, I had hopes of placing you with a high minister among our own educated men. It seems the khan has other plans. Nonetheless, we shall do our duty. You need wedding attire. Come, sit here."

Mistress Luo commanded a half-dozen servants to prepare everything required: gown and cap, drapes and paints, Bao Xing standing like a doll, trying out first one costume, then another. When the flurry of activity slowed to a single scribe taking down Mistress Luo's list of demands for the wedding ceremony, Bao Xing at last donned her own gown, which now felt plain and stiff in spite of its fine weave and delicate embroidery. She sat, her tiny feet aching, clutching the cane her father had given her, and wishing her feet were big enough for her to simply run away. The thought shamed her, as it would shame her entire family back several generations.

"Mistress Luo?"

"Yes, my dear?" The mistress regarded her gently. "Do not be afraid, my dear. It is only marriage. Only a man. I am sure you can give him many sons and be a fine wife. Even if he is a barbarian. I and the other ladies of the court will stand by you to give any advice that we may."

Bao Xing attempted a smile. "If you do not have need of me, Mistress, I should like to go light incense for my mother."

"Oh, of course! I should have thought of that sooner. Yes, go along. I shall prepare a bed for you among us tonight. I shall send Meili for you when your place is ready."

"Thank you, Mistress. For everything." Bao Xing bowed and walked carefully toward the back of Mistress Luo's domain of etiquette. Here, a door led into the palace's inner courtyard. At this hour, few passed through the yard on its broad paved pathways, but bright lanterns hung from their posts and lights shone in the surrounding windows. Among the stately cedars and blooming iris stood a temple dedicated to the imperial ancestors. The engraved plaques of their names were gone, leaving the altar and lanterns with little to honor but the bare red walls. Still, the remaining Han occupants of the palace had replaced the bronze brazier and the bowl of sand for incense, and kept a small pillow for kneeling.

Before she knelt to honor her ancestors long dead, she honored her father, and looked at the sky. The Celestial Throne gleamed just above the buildings. The horizon obscured her view of the Dark Lance which would hover below it. And the wandering star could not be seen from this angle—she could not confirm her suspicion that it circled the Lance. Perhaps she could write to her father, to find out what had happened, and what he could see. For now, she remained ignorant.

Disappointed, Bao Xing lit a stick of incense at the nearest lantern, and placed it in the holder, the smoke curling about in the shapes of dragons—the year of her mother's birth. She lay her cane before her and knelt upon the cushion.

Steps came up, brushing the paving stones behind her, and Bao Xing caught her lip between her teeth. Guowei stood over her, the lanterns casting his eyes in a mysterious light and catching the corners of his smile. She started to rise, but he gestured her back, sinking to kneel beside her and light a stick of incense. To place it in the bowl, he leaned very close, his shoulder brushing her, sending a rush of warmth through her. He resumed his place, near, but not too near to suggest impropriety.

"I wondered why you did not come to supper tonight, lady." His voice sounded very deep and strong in the little shrine.

"I am to be married," she blurted, then ducked her head, her palms pressing together. "Forgive me, Minister. It has been a surprising day."

"I imagine it would be." For a moment, they knelt in silence, then he said, "We shall miss your company at table. I am sure your husband will wish to keep you for himself."

Her throat felt suddenly tight. "I am told he is a Mongol." She shuddered at the thought of the khan coming to her bed, sweaty, smelling of horses and leather, his fingers greasy with mutton.

"You have been well-bred and well-raised, lady. I am sure you will become accustomed to your duties as a wife."

"I'm sure." She squeezed her eyes shut, listening to his breath. His presence beside her was an agony. Tomorrow, she moved even further from her path, further from the books and the stars, and she could do nothing about it that would not shame her ancestors. "I do my best to honor my family, Minister."

"Mmm. Your family lived outside of Kaifeng, in the mountains?"

"My father still lives at the observatory there, but my mother moved to the spirit realm when I was eleven."

"I presume he learned his trade from his father before him." His fingers roved over the carving of her cane which lay before them.

Bao Xing smiled faintly. "My mother found prestige in the occupation, but loneliness in its location. She raised me with the hopes of finding me a better place."

Guowei smiled, too, but briefly. "I doubt your mother meant for you to marry with our conquerors."

His tone made her go still and shift a glance toward him.

"She did wish for me to marry into the court," Bao Xing said carefully. "I am given to understand my husband is of the blood of the khans."

"I am relieved to hear that our great ruler is providing you a worthy husband."

"The khan seems vastly amused by the marriage. Whatever it means, I do not think he means to honor me. I am not sure he has thought of me at all since the night I was given to him." She did not intend such bitterness, but his fingers paused on the handle of her cane. "I speak too sharply. I am sure my lord khan has the best intentions for my future."

"What of the future of China?"

Bao Xing's heart raced. She had not heard anyone else about, but his inquiries sounded too bold for the khan's own courtyard. "I cannot speak to that, Minister. I should go." She took up the cane.

"Please—I disturbed you at prayer, lady. I am the one who should leave." He guided the cane back to its place, and his fingers brushed hers. The carvings felt deep and sharp as the mountains they depicted; his fingers were hot, his eyes dark and gleaming.

Footsteps pattered behind them, and he rose, turning in a swift motion. "Ah, Meili. Your mistress is here."

"Thank you, Minister." Meili bowed, her arms laden. "This came for you, my lady, and I am to fetch you back." She held out a parcel wrapped in plain dark cotton.

Bao Xing set down both bundle and cane on the step and opened the binding. Inside rested a brick of tea and a soft pouch full of salt.

"The marriage gifts of the Mongols," Guowei said drily. "Your groom wishes to make a good impression. If we were, indeed, on the steppes, he would then try to take you from your parents' home—and your friends would try to prevent him." Guowei folded his hands together, almost as if they were tied.

If only she had friends who would do just that. Clearly, Chubei had no power to prevent the marriage—what other friends did Bao Xing have? The pouch of salt rested heavy in her palm, and she found Guowei's gaze resting on her, just as heavy, just as full of meaning she did not quite understand.

CHAPTER THIRTY-ONE

Zhencai's hand pulsed with pain when he reached out to take hold of a root and pull himself up on the next ledge. Rain streamed down his face and made him glad of his shaven head for there was no hair to block his eyes. The path they followed ran beneath mud and branches, destroyed by the occasional avalanche, but the shapes of the peaks looked familiar, and he felt sure they moved in the right direction.

"Master, I don't think this is the way," Andao called from below.

The voice, petulant and weary, grated on Zhencai's nerves. "Tell me, novice, when was the last time you visited Second Pine Monastery?"

The young man heaved a sigh and fell silent for a few more steps. Zhencai stumbled onto a broad meadow and offered his hand to assist Andao. He clamped his jaw on the pain when his apprentice gripped his hand, but said a prayer of thanksgiving when Andao was stable enough to let go. Andao braced his hands on his thighs and took a few deeper breaths, the rain running off of his scalp, then he squinted up at his master. "What if it was poisoned?"

"Then I should have been dead by now." Zhencai wrapped both of his palms, hoping to conceal the festering wound at his right thumb. Clearly, his concealment worked no better than his efforts to ignore the suffering. No better than his sense of direction: from up here, the trail had vanished completely.

"What if it were slow-acting? We assumed she was lying to free herself, what if she wasn't?" Andao reared up. His body, always lean, had lost the roundness of a city-dweller. His face, with its unusual nose and brown eyes, looked fierce.

"The moon has cycled around again to full since we left her. You are living in the past in thinking of her, and in the future in your 'what ifs'. Return to the present. Guard." Zhencai shot out his foot as he said it.

Barely warned, Andao danced back, slipped in the mud and dodged the kick only because he fell out of the way. "Master!"

Still on his toes, Zhencai regarded his apprentice. Rain sluiced between them, mist rose in curls from the stream, reminding him of Andao's once-curly hair. When Andao regained his footing, Zhencai slowly scribed an arc through the rain with his foot. An able opponent would sense that movement. Andao yelped when the foot struck his thigh. He tripped out of the way, coming to rest leaning on a dead tree, breathless.

"Master, we're lost, in the mountains." He swallowed hard, his throat bobbing, his hands waving. "You're injured. We have no more food, and there's no one to give you offerings. We are no closer to the mystery than we were when we took the scroll. That is the present." His hands spread to take in the mountains around them. "This is the present."

"No. That is worry. This is fear. Fear is never the present, it is the future." Zhencai slid his foot forward, sinking low. "Guard," he said, slowly and deliberately.

Andao scowled as he pushed off from the tree and sank into a guard position, his lanky arms held too far from his body.

Zhencai shifted into motion, slowing his every breath and muscle, sending his fist toward Andao's face, allowing him to block it, turning aside that block to lift his foot into a sharp kick, allowing Andao to pivot out of the way. This released Zhencai's fist for a second punch which slid easily under Andao's flailing hand to rap lightly on his breastbone.

Instead of striking back, Andao caught Zhencai's wrist and yanked free the binding over his palm. "Your hand is hot, Master. You're wrong: fear is the present."

Zhencai sank, shifted his foot, and brought up a kick that knocked his apprentice onto his back, watching as Zhencai's iron fist came to rest at his lips. "Your guard failed."

"I wasn't ready."

"Even when you were ready, your guard failed. You must center your qi. Where is it?"

"Everywhere, nowhere—I don't know." Andao rolled away from his master's fist and steady glare. "I always set my arms wrong."

"It is not your arms or your readiness. You have said yourself that you must always be ready."

"For you to attack me? You're supposed to be training me." Andao wiped mud from his face and flicked it away.

"I am training you. The first thing is to know your qi, and you will not even work on that. You promised that you could eat bitter."

"I am eating it!" He flung up his hands and stalked away. "I'll feast on it when you die."

"Death is another face of life," Zhencai began, but Andao spun back, his finger jabbing in accusation.

"I followed you here! I followed you to learn from you, to help you solve this mystery and stop the war, not to watch you die in the wilderness and leave me with no way home."

"A monk must forgo attachments, even to his master. Even to his brother monks."

"I'm not a monk—I can't do that. And you knew it when you took me on."

Zhencai conceded that. The area around his right thumb was swollen, the thumb itself barely mobile, and he had not found more of the herbs he had been been applying. He contemplated Andao's words. Poison? More likely, a lucky strike to a sensitive area. Even Zhencai's iron hands were not impervious to all things. The Buddha himself had died in the mountains, and so had Zhencai's abbot. Such a thing was not tragic, but to leave Andao in such a state after taking responsibility to teach him... The mistake had been in taking him on. Zhencai on his own, even injured, could travel faster and sustain himself on meditation and the leaves of the forest. His hand throbbed, and he looked into the distance. Did the Buddha demand that they suffer in the cold rain on a ledge? "When we reach Second Pine, I will meditate on what you have said, and seek advice on the best way to continue your training." Zhencai scanned the mountains around them.

Tucking his trembling hands under his arms, Andao tipped his head toward the dead tree. "Master, can we please try this way?"

"You call me 'master' and yet you question me constantly. I do not remember questioning my masters this way."

"We need to find a dry cave, then I'll shut up and listen!" His brown eyes flashed with anger, then Andao lurched away in the opposite direction.

The strength of Zhencai's qi pulsed behind his eyes. He had been the most worthless novice in the history of Cloud Mountain, but surely he had never been so willful. Of course, he came to the monastery as the gift of his parents at the age of five, with none of Andao's history. He caught up just as Andao slithered down a slope and stumbled a few paces—into the mouth of a cave. Zhencai stared after him, then made the sign of blessing, his hand cutting the rain before his face. A cave. Moments after Andao insisted upon finding one.

Keeping his footing, Zhencai trotted down and ducked inside. Goat dung scattered the floor, but further back, stones had been piled to form a half-wall, and a few pots stood on a ledge suggesting a goatherd sheltered here while tending his animals. Andao had already peeled off his soaked tunic and peered into the pots, taking a few of them to set down beside a ring of sooty stones. Lifting a scorched bronze vessel, Andao said, "I'll bring the water, Master. There is tea." He paced by, apparently taking it for granted that all of these things should be present beneath their feet as they argued. Argued? No, a monk should never argue.

Zhencai knelt by the fire ring and piled up a handful of dry dung inside it, then found his pouch with the stones to strike flames. In a few moments of striking and blowing on sparks, he had a smoldering fire, and added twigs from the goatherd's supply. A blessing of the Buddha indeed, to find such a place.

Andao walked back, cradling the bronze vessel, now half-full of water and nestled it into the fire.

"How did you know this was here?"

"My bones told me."

"Your bones are very wise." Zhencai pulled the scroll from the back of his belt and checked the oiled cloth that wrapped it. Andao held out his hand, and Zhencai allowed him to take the scroll, unrolling it on the ground.

"Will the monks know where the weapon is? and how to stop it?" Then Andao spread his hands. "Sorry. The future again."

Zhencai nodded and took the lotus position across the fire. He removed the other small scroll he always carried, the paper that established for any monastery that he was a true member of the order, and set it by the fire to dry.

"We have food, and fire," said Andao. "We're still lost. You're still injured. The present."

"The present seems more clear than it did in the past, yes?"

Andao smiled sheepishly. He traced the scroll with his eyes, tracking the characters and charts with his long fingers.

Steam rose from the pot between them. Andao resembled a figure of legend, not quite a man, and Zhencai wished he could take a very long time to meditate. His foolish, mad novice found them a cave in the mountains. Not surprising. The cave already held what they needed. This was more surprising. Still, many caves might be used by herdsmen, or might have been before the Mongols sent their soldiers to sweep the mountains.

"The device unites the heavens and the earth, those who know the stars, and those who know the ground. What does that mean, master?"

Firelight painted Andao's face with gold, like the monks Zhencai tended for so long, like the relics of the past, recalling the flash in his novice's eyes before he turned toward the cave. The flash of fury? The spark of the qi that lurked in his soul. Andao was no mere novice, his qi held something deeper. Who or what was he? What was he meant to be? The wheel turned, and Zhencai was not certain what it meant. Those who know the ground. Geomancers. "It means you are not the first to have wise bones."

"Master?" Andao tipped his head.

"The monks of Second Pine are kind, but the monks of Dragon Turns are known for healing."

Andao looked gratified that his master had chosen to take care of himself. Perhaps it was Andao who needed looking after. Zhencai appreciated Andao's help in the archives, and accepted his own role in trying to teach the youth enough to survive in this world of suffering. Now he wondered if something more had brought them together, and he hoped the monks of Dragon Turns would guide him in figuring it out. Mysteries upon mysteries. The tea steamed, the rain fell, and Andao's eyes sparkled with flecks like gold.

CHAPTER THIRTY-TWO

Yusen knelt on an embroidered cushion atop a low wooden stool, waiting. The usually soothing hum of the Moriin Huur fiddle sounded shrill today, in competition with the soft flute of the Chinese musician. He had recognized the young woman as the accompanist for the troop of dancing girls, and wondered what had become of their teacher, who had leapt into the water after the drakemaster so many days ago. On their journey to the castle, the slave spoke only when Yusen insisted on a reply, and said nothing of the woman at all. Perhaps she had drowned trying to catch the slave. Yusen commended her soul to the Eternal Sky, may she ride a fast horse through the sweet meadows of dawn.

He focused on his own familiar hands, scarred by battle, but his gaze lifted time and again to the richly clad people around him. The khan's ceremonial ger hosted the wedding—a generous gift indeed—and Yusen wanted to see this heal the breach in their family, but the khan's eyes glinted, his lips hinted at laughter, and his youngest wife soured like old milk. Crowded all around were the generals in dels decorated with gold edging and peaked caps with furry brims, and the Chin officials of the palace in their brocade robes, their own hats with ties that stuck out on the sides or crossed over, sending signals to one another with how they were worn. They looked ridiculous.

To one side, Munkjar stood in for Yusen's father, holding the bowl of airag they would drink from. Stern and proud, he betrayed none of the amusement of the other guests. He was likely scheming about how to upset Yusen's victory today. Nothing could do that: On this day, Yusen married the most beautiful woman in the world, and nothing could take that from him.

The chiming of bells announced the bride's arrival and Yusen sat up straighter. Bao Xing's pillow, at his side, had been set on the floor so that their heads should be about even when she sat. Two girls lead her by the hands, for red silk draped over her face, matching the long red gown that concealed her body. When they brought her up before him, all three bowed, and the two girls swept back the veil.

Bao Xing, straightening from her bow, blinked a few times, her eyes shining, dark pools in the pearl-white paint of her face. A Mongolian-style headdress framed her face, highlighting the shimmering darkness of her hair and the bright red of her lips. Then her gaze lifted over him, a slight crease marring her brow. Her glance returned to him, and her eyes flared wide. Her slender form shifted as if she might have fallen, her lips parted, then she turned sharply and sank down onto the pillow beside him, her breath coming in little gasps. One of her attendants revealed the familiar cane, lying it down at Bao Xing's feet, but she stared straight ahead.

Queen Chubei's scowl deepened, the khan's grin widened as he waved Munkjar over with the silver bowl. "Drink to the blessing of your union!" The khan cried. "Three times, drink and give thanks to the bright Eternal Sky."

Munkjar approached, eyes narrowing as he was forced to bow to bring the bowl first to Yusen, who dipped his fingertip and flicked a drop of the liquor in offering to the earth and sky before taking a sip. When the general bent to Bao Xing, he managed a smile, and she leaned forward, her profile smooth and lovely, cheekbones high, eyes perfectly almond-shaped.

She caught Yusen watching and looked away as he took his second drink. Was he so hideous as that?

She drank again, then Munkjar lifted the bowl to Yusen for the final sip—and tilted it too sharply so that Yusen sputtered, spilling a little stream down the front of his deep-blue marriage del. His hand clenched at his side, searching for his sword, but the general merely turned once more to the bride.

Contrary to all ritual, her hand reached out to steady the bowl, gripping it firmly, tipping it just enough, then releasing it. Munkjar's scarred jaw tightened, but he relinquished his place to Mistress Luo, whose tinkling head covered with turquoise and silver only jangled Yusen's nerves all the more. The Mistress of Ritual held out a red band of cloth, the middle of it bound into a fluffy knot. Yusen seized his end. After an instant's hesitation, Bao Xing took her end and they both rose.

The khan stifled a laugh. Yusen imagined the sight from the khan's perspective, from that of every other man present, watching a great beauty wed to a dwarf. Of course it amused them, this union of opposites.

Yusen's head reached the level of his wife's shoulder, or nearly so, a smaller difference than he had feared. He ignored the laughter by gripping the red band tighter as he started forward. Bao Xing hesitated, glancing down, and Yusen reached for her cane even as one of the Chin officials picked it up and placed it in her hand. She gave a tiny nod of thanks, and the man nodded serenely back to her. Yusen refrained from tugging the red band between them; once she had her cane, Bao Xing came readily enough. Following Mistress Luo who hobbled with a cane of her own, they exited the ger into the fading sunlight of the inner courtyard, its trees and stones looking dull by comparison to the rugs and gilded dazzle of the khan's ger. Together, they walked to the shrine at the center of the yard. He had to slow his stride to match hers—the first time he could ever remember that happening. They knelt in front of the shrine while Bao Xing lit incense, her movements graceful, her prayers silent.

The feast consisted of course after course of roasted mutton, then thin soups, then rice dumplings that stuck to his teeth. Yusen's stomach roiled as he ate—sparingly, in case his stomach rebelled altogether. When most of the eating was done, the khan lead the guests in cheering and caused wine to be poured liberally for all. Yusen sipped at his cup, and Bao Xing danced her fingers around hers, but never actually drank a drop.

Mistress Luo knelt before Yusen and Bao Xing, giving them a flat box divided into many parts and full of herbs he did not recognize. "For healing, for strength, for a good house," the woman paused, then added, "and for many sons." She let the lid fall shut and handed it to the Chin girl who followed Bao Xing everywhere.

Munkjar strode forward, carrying a saddle. "That your wife may ride at your back when you return home." Munkjar managed to make the traditional gift sound like a bit of garbage he simply hadn't time to discard. He thrust it at the Chin girl who stumbled with the unwieldy thing. The saddle wasn't new, but the wood looked to be in good condition, and the few silver ornaments gleamed dully in the light of a dozen lanterns.

That same Chin official who had picked up Bao Xing's cane now approached and bowed very low, offering a smooth and elegant cane with ivory fittings. "Befitting a lady," he said, his voice deep and sonorous as Yusen's voice could never be. "May it bring you peace and stability."

"Thank you," she whispered—the first words she had spoken all day.

Yusen stared at the Mandarin, memorizing his round face and prim lips. A few other small offerings were made—tea, rice, bottles of scent or liquor—before the gong sounded the hour of the Dog.

Once again, the Mistress of Ritual lead them down the corridor, this time to a new part of the palace where they found the khan's gift, a small apartment decorated for the marriage. At the door, the guests melted away with mumbled good wishes or drunken snorts of laughter. The Chin girl and a few of the khan's servants carried their gifts inside, then bowed many times over, and the other servants departed.

"Shall I help with your hair, lady?" the girl asked, and Bao Xing nodded, pearls twinkling.

The three of them entered the outer chamber where a woman's table, covered with all kinds of tiny things, awaited, and Bao Xing released her end of the marriage sash to walk over and sit down in front of it. The girl followed her, deftly unbinding the ties and sliding free the pins that held the wide Mongolian headdress and placing all of these things into a slender box. The girl lead Bao Xing through the arched door on the opposite wall, bowed to both of them, and departed.

Absent the cheerful guests and the shrill musicians, the room echoed with silence. Yusen missed the chirp of crickets and the swish of the grasses that he heard even back in the army encampment, not to mention the chatter and clash of too many men. The marriage sash still dangled from his hand, its central knot resting on the ground. Was that inauspicious? He gathered it into both hands and cast about briefly, then placed the unruly bundle on top of the saddle Munkjar gave them. His hands twitched to seize the saddle, his legs to run down the corridor and out to the stables, to simply ride away. A thousand other men his age dreamed of this night, the first time a woman came to their bed. Yusen simply never dreamed it would happen—not to him, certainly not with her.

What should happen next? He should leap upon the bed as a conqueror and strip her clothing from her, revealing her naked flesh. How many times around a campfire had he heard that story? The woman would shriek and try to cover herself, the soldier would pin her down and thrust inside of her until his needs were spent. She would bleed and cry: in the soldiers' stories, she then would beg for him or his friends to do it again. Yusen remembered trying to sleep as soldiers ravished the women of Kaifeng. They begged for nothing except to be left alone. That was no way to take a wife, surely.

What then? In the songs of great deeds—if women were mentioned at all—the hero would come to them softly, bringing gifts and warm embraces. The women would shed their layers of clothing and open willingly, wrapping the hero with their arms and legs, bringing him close, a seduction they shared. Yusen's near-forgotten manhood stirred, his loins tightening. Of course, in the songs, the hero then rode off on his favorite horse, ready for the next great deed. Yusen had performed his share of deeds, but never this one.

In the next room, the bed creaked, and Yusen steeled himself to face her. He stomped—then tempered his steps and walked more gently to the doorway, pushing through the drapes. Four painted silk lanterns hung in the chamber, casting strange shadows. A big rounded wooden bed filled most of the small room, tall enough to warrant a pair of steps leading into it—tradition, or another jest at Yusen's expense?

Her cane hanging from a hook at one end of the bed, Bao Xing reclined on a mound of pillows, her head resting on her arm. Relief flooded him at the thought she was sleeping. He need not face her until—then her eyes opened, and she pushed up, her face once again an image of shock. Had she forgotten whom she had married? Maybe, lying in bed as she was, she had convinced herself it was all a dream.

Yusen snatched the stiff hat from his head and shoved it onto a chest, his own chest, actually, brought from the long hall he shared with other soldiers. His own dark hair, washed and brushed that morning, hung to his shoulders and he pushed it restlessly back.

"Good evening, my husband," said Bao Xing in careful Mongolian.

Swallowing the lump in his throat, Yusen said, "Good evening." Another swallow, then he added, "My wife."

"You come closer."

Slowly, he mounted the steps and sat on the edge of the bed, an arm's length between them.

She regarded him, her fingers smoothing a circle of the cotton bedclothes. "How do I call you?"

"Yusen," he told her, then he made himself say more, "It means the ninth. For my people, it is lucky."

Nodding, she said, "You are of nine brothers?"

"And sisters. They're all dead." He fingered the round beads that formed the closure of his vest.

The silence stretched between them, then she said, "I am only one."

Racing his elder brothers to the camp, proving their best horses, bringing lambs to the ger to amuse his little nieces, wrestling in the mud and his mother's voice echoing in anger if they failed to wipe it off before they came home. Bao Xing had had none of that companionship. Even his family's constant packing and moving, keeping ahead of the khan's men, felt like a game when they were all together, the youngest never quite understanding what it meant—they were nomads after all, defined by movement. The wives of his two married brothers came with them, and all of their children, growing the family even in the face of his father's betrayal, loyal to the end.

"I don't know how to do this, how to be a husband," he blurted.

Her eyes glimmered, then she covered her mouth with her hand, her shoulders trembling. Laughing.

Yusen grabbed her wrist and pulled her hand from her lips. "No—no, if you want to laugh at me, then laugh openly—like everyone else."

Her laughter vanished, her eyelashes suddenly shimmering with tears, and he let her go, pushing back from her and pounding away back to the outer chamber.

The marriage sash slithered back to the floor as he stalked past, and Yusen scooped the saddle into his arms. She hurt him with her laughter; in his humiliation, he hurt her with his touch. He was an idiot. An ignorant fool, to be given what he so longed for and not know the first thing of what to do with it, how to treat a woman.

He lugged the saddle with him down the dim corridors, tossing it up on Tsang's back and riding the empty streets until they were both exhausted. Heart thundering, limbs weary, Yusen thought of returning to his pallet in the soldier's hall, but he couldn't bear the humiliation of that—waking up on his wedding night in the company of the soldiers, fueling another round of laughter.

Bao Xing's Chin servant girl lay curled in the corridor outside, and

Yusen stepped quietly past her, his years as a scout serving him well. He snuck into his own bridal apartment, remembering the delicate beauty of her tears, and almost summoned the strength to say he was sorry, but only one lantern remained lit in the bed chamber. Bao Xing, still in her wedding gown, curled at the far edge of the bed, breathing evenly in her sleep. She remained the most beautiful woman he had ever seen, a vision beyond what any man might dream. She made it hard to breathe, and yet, here she was, still in his bed. He would try again to reach her. He would try a thousand times.

Yusen removed his vest and del, leaving himself with the sweaty trousers he had ridden in, and climbed up to the bed. He slid beneath the covers, his head at the opposite end from hers, where he could lie, as the last lantern glowed, and gaze on her sleeping figure. His. Even if she despised him. Even if he never touched her again. Bao Xing belonged to him.

CHAPTER THIRTY-THREE

Waking to the smell of sweat and horses, Bao Xing kept her eyes shut tight, but it could not save her. She had married the little barbarian, and now she had to live with him. At least he had not tried to force himself on her when he returned—from the fury in his face and the startling power of his grip, she had felt sure he would. Rumpled bedclothes showed that her husband had already gone, leaving his ruined wedding clothes on the floor. In the front chamber someone moved about quietly, with a chink of tea things, and Bao Xing sat upright.

Tea! She was supposed to perform the tea ceremony for her husband and his family. Did he have any family? All of his siblings were dead, he had said, and his voice, too, was dead. Apparently, he had been raised by that odious general who had spilled their vile drink on the bridegroom's chest. No wonder he had learned no manners. Then she remembered the nervous laughter she tried to hide. She must improve her manners as well. Of course he had taken it badly. Still… she raised her wrist and made out the faint marks of his fingers. How could she explain, when he was glaring at her, that she, too, had no experience? She laughed because her work in the archives showed there were books for that: books that depicted in great detail what might be done between men and women. But she was just as ignorant as he about the things that passed between husband and wife.

A shadow moved past the curtain, and Bao Xing recognized Meili. She scooted to the edge of the bed to swing her feet down, the thick red gown crinkling, its folds crimped where she had slept on it. Unwrapping her sashes and cords, Bao Xing let the garment slide off her shoulders, leaving her clad in the lighter under gowns, then took her cane and moved out to where her tea sat waiting.

Meili bowed, then settled on her knees as Bao Xing came to the table. Next to her, the cane that Guowei gave as his wedding present leaned against the table. A curious gift, but her own cane with its masculine design had often raised eyebrows, perhaps he thought this would please her. After a sip of tea, Bao Xing reached out to finger the ivory handle. It felt warm and smooth, quite unlike the old wood of her own cane. She imagined Guowei's soft eyes upon her as she entered a room, using the cane he gave her, then drew back her fingers.

"Where is my husband, Meili?"

"He has gone to court, lady. The khan hears reports from his ministers today."

She picked up her chopsticks and ate a few bites of steamed cabbage and rice. "Am I to join him? Do you know?"

Meili kept her eyes down. "He said so, although I do not know if it is proper."

"Does it matter what is proper anymore? He is my husband."

The girl sighed, and Bao Xing set down her chopsticks. "What is it?

"It is so unfair, lady." Meili's head shot up. "You have the most exquisite lotus blossom feet—even Mistress Luo says so—and you are so beautiful and now you are married to that hideous dwarf!" She turned quite red and dropped into a full kowtow, her forehead touching the floor between her hands. "Forgive me, lady, for speaking ill of your husband."

Bao Xing had married no ordinary barbarian, but one who was a laughingstock even to his own people. "Meili…"

The girl glanced up uncertainly, her fingertips pressing the floor.

"When you are about your errands, you must hear rumors, things the other servants talk about or even the Mandarins."

"Oh, no, lady, I never listen to things like that." Her back hunched a little further, and Bao Xing touched her shoulder.

"I'm looking for some information, to help me in my marriage."

Meili whispered, "I wish I could help you out of your marriage, lady."

"Nevertheless, this is my duty, my fate for the time being, and I need to make the best of it. But I'd like to know why it happened to begin with. Why did the khan marry me to him?"

"Oh." Meili drew herself up as Bao Xing joined her hands in her lap. "I have heard about this. The—your husband—he owned the slave who became the khan's drakemaster. When the slave escaped, your husband swore to bring him back. Nobody thought he could do it, lady, but he brought the slave all the way here, bound on one of his horses, and gave him to the khan. He asked for you as his reward, lady. He called you a treasure the khan would never use." She turned a little pink again. "The slave has been sent to mine mercury."

The drakemaster would die in the mines, poisoned by the very air. The mineral form of cinnabar was called the Crimson Shrine for the wealth it offered—or for the souls it claimed? Her cane included carved cinnabar, and her father's story had it that the carver, her several times grandfather, had died in the making of it. Surely death—even the lingering miserable death of the mines—was a fitting end for the architect of the destruction of Kaifeng. Yet when he climbed the bridge, the drakemaster had fallen from the bridge like a stone into a chasm. Had his honor demanded his death after causing the deaths of so many?

Bao Xing's flash of anger fled, replaced by pity.

"Shall I prepare you for court, lady?"

Of course he wanted her to join him—to display the prize for which he had traded another man's life. "Yes, Meili."

The girl beamed. "Shall we use your wedding gifts? Have you seen this?" Meili pounced upon the rank of gifts arranged along the storage chest and the floor around it. The girl held up a brocade tube dangling with pearls. "Mistress Luo commissioned it and two girls stayed up all night to make it for you." It was a Mongolian-style headpiece like the ones worn by the queens, but smaller and not so grand. The pearls formed signs of the zodiac, a reference both to her name, and to the date of her wedding.

"That's a fine idea." Her eyes strayed again to Guowei's gift. To carry that, in front of everyone, would surely shame her husband. Perhaps such a wretch deserved shame—but she could not bring herself to do it. "But not the cane."

Meili's lips turned down. "I am sure it would please the minister to see you with it."

"And highly displease my husband. I shall use my old cane."

Stroking the smooth ivory, Meili lay the cane down along the chest.

It took an age before Meili declared her face and dress perfect and escorted her to court. In the large, rectangular room, one of the Mandarins spoke at length about the historical grain yield of the Henan province, allowing Bao Xing plenty of time to find her husband in the chamber—a tricky search given his stature. Aside from the queens and Mistress Luo, few other women were present. Guowei sat near the front, evidently awaiting his turn to report. He looked handsome and wise in his austere robe, his scholar's hat showing his advanced position in spite of his comparative youth. A breeze flowed from the pierced wood shutters over the windows, and Guowei glanced back, an eyebrow raised, a slight nod in her direction. His gaze shifted down, and his lips quirked toward a frown, then he returned his attention to the front of the room.

She wore the lightest musk from a collection Chubei had given her—its scent must have carried to Guowei's place. Was he so disappointed to see her with her father's old cane? He must understand, but still, her heart fell.

Yusen sat among the Mongol captains, listening to a grain report as if it were the most important thing he had ever heard. He seemed to smile, then raised a hand and gestured her toward him, pointing to a seat at his back. Bao Xing bowed in the direction of the khan, and Chubei waved cheerfully back, then mimed a yawn and rolled her eyes in the direction of the speaker. The Mongol queens were expected to follow the workings of the court, whereas Han women were meant to stay at home. Yusen's summons clearly intended for Bao Xing to behave like one of the barbarian women. Dismissing Meili, she moved across the back of the room then down among the mats to reach the seat her husband had indicated. He straightened his spine and tipped his chin up, shaking back his hair.

The Minister of Grains finally bowed and sat down, stiffly with the aid of a younger assistant, then Guowei came forward. He moved like a tiger, full of intent. "My lord, I have little to report. Progress continues on organizing your imperial collections, incorporating the new works seized from the rebel city."

The khan grunted acknowledgement and waved his hand, urging the court to move on.

"The prisoner who was sent to me did not provide any useful sketches or writings." Guowei started to bow again in closure, but the khan slapped his palms together.

"Nothing? He insisted they had a great weapon, something so powerful even his firedrakes would be mere firecrackers."

Yusen leaned forward, fingertips braced and jaw set as if he prepared to do battle.

Guowei gave an elegant shrug. "Forgive me, my lord. I tried to coax out any information he might hold, and he did make a few attempts at drawing, but the marks meant nothing. I asked your soldiers to step out of the room, in case their presence worried him, but to no avail. It is possible he was simply deranged, or, more likely, he imagined the weapon, in the hopes that you would spare him."

The khan snorted. "I appreciate your attempts, Minister. Inform me if any sign of such a thing should come to light in the archives."

"Of course, my lord." Guowei bowed back to his place and settled among the other Mandarins.

Yusen sagged, folding his arms tightly, shoulders hunching. No doubt he hoped for yet another gift of prestige from his doomed slave. General Munkjar flared his eyes, giving a fierce grin. He held his hand sideways, measuring the air, then turned back, his companions rumbling with soft laughter.

Yusen gasped as if he had suffered a blow. He shifted on his haunches and finally straightened again, giving his del a tug to smooth it out. It gave a soft, crisp sound, and he slipped a hand into the breast, the area above the belt which the Mongols used to store things in place of pouches or extended sleeves.

The Undersecretary of Silks stood before the khan, a long scroll unfurled in his hands, and read aloud, "…continued occupation of our Northern lands, the lands which your ancestors promised to aid our ancestors in recovering. You may understand, our great and powerful cousin, that concern for the occupants of those lands, many of whom have family here, weighs heavily upon the spinners, weavers, and dyers of the silk you so clearly desire. Such concerns have slowed production so that, to our immense regret, we are unable to fulfill the increased orders received by our hand beneath the new moon of the turn of Ox. We will, of course, fulfill the—"

The khan bounded up and snatched the scroll from the startled Undersecretary's hands, glaring down at it. "What is this nonsense? They're so sad they can't weave? Ridiculous! Guowei—is that truly what it says?" He thrust the scroll out and Guowei hurried up to take it, bowing, and perusing the document while the Undersecretary stood there, hands thrust into opposite sleeves, trembling. Guowei's eyes traced the text, his head tipped a little this way, then that, as if he were in conversation with the author. His robe was a bit unsettled from his quick obedience to the khan's command, and she caught a glimpse of his underrobe, patterned with flying larks.

Bao Xing felt a soft tap on her knee and dragged her attention from Guowei—reading. Yusen held a curl of paper and rested it against her knee. She took it, half-expecting to find it a note he had written. Was her husband even literate? A tear marked one edge of the paper, and a few scorch marks edged the other. The page came from a longer work, then. At the scorched edge, a painted woman wept, her body clothed in a horsehide. It illustrated the origin of silk, the white maiden becoming the silk worm that made China justly famous. The fine illustration and excellent penmanship suggested the text had come from an imperial library. She tilted it to see the strokes of the author's brush and how the painter had captured the lady's beauty, and her sadness.

Beyond her hand, she noticed Yusen's rapt attention. He watched her as eagerly as she had watched Guowei, and he gestured toward the page, with a nod of encouragement. The intensity of his stare unnerved her—reminding her of that first night when she had been introduced to the khan back in the army encampment.

Bao Xing tried a smile, resisting the urge to cover her mouth as was proper for a Han lady. It was a slight and timid expression, but Yusen grinned, then quickly turned around as if he, too, felt it improper to show his pleasure. The intense stare broken, Bao Xing allowed herself to breathe.

Apparently, when the palace at Kaifeng had been ransacked, her husband had been among the thieves, ripping up scrolls and tearing tapestries. For a moment, she was even more disgusted by him. Still, the words of Ming Lun, the lessons of Mistress Luo, the teasing remarks of her friend Chubei all added up to one thing: the power that a woman could have over a man, even where women should have no power at all. A glimpse of a tiny foot, a whiff of her perfume, and a man might do anything. Bao Xing's new position meant that she could not go anywhere near the library or its keeper. She must live now at the whim of her husband—but might he not bend to her whim as well?

Bao Xing made a little sound of delight and cradled the page in her hands as if enthralled. Before her, Yusen glanced over his shoulder, then his chin rose, his hair brushed back, and he took a deeper breath, settling in the mantle of her approval. Good. Let him earn it with more than a torn page from a vanished text. Bao Xing sat through court, dreaming of what she might take from him in exchange for her marriage.

CHAPTER THIRTY-FOUR

Over a dinner of cool stewed mutton with slithery noodles, Yusen slurped his soup and regarded his wife. A certain radiance returned to her face since he had given her the paper. Most men gave their wives jewels and silver to make them happy, but his delighted in a few smears of ink. It made him wish he, too, knew how to read, how to write, how to scribe poems worthy of her attention.

She slurped as well, displaying her enjoyment, the tip of a noodle sliding between her crimson lips before she settled back and dipped her fingers in a washing bowl. Meili, her obsequious servant, offered a cloth to dry Bao Xing's hands. They could have eaten with the court, and received their food fresh from the hands of the khan's servers, but Yusen was a keen observer of court habits: no newly married man attended a communal meal for several days, and the envy seemed greatest the longer the new husband stayed away. Yusen intended to be gone at least until the next full moon, even if his absence meant nothing like what the other men dreamed.

"My husband," she said suddenly, pressing her fingertips together.

"What is it?"

"Thank you for writing you gave." She smiled, her hand rising toward her lips, then lowering again.

Yusen accepted her gratitude, taking a sip of tea—green and flavored with some kind of burnt rice, without any milk or salt at all. The flavor wrinkled his nose and lips. "Meili—you must learn to make proper tea. I know there are yaks available for milking."

She blinked, her eyes gone round, and he leaned toward her, pointing to the cup. "Milk. Salt. For the tea."

Bao Xing spoke a quiet patter of her own language, explaining, and the girl nodded, but the fear remained as she answered. "She does not know how Mongol tea. She tries to know."

"Good, that's fine."

Meili withdrew, stacking the empty bowls on their tray, then hustling it back toward the kitchens. Bao Xing reached toward the writing desk she had dug out while he was tending to his horses that evening, her fingers specked with bits of ink already. She picked up a bit of paper and set it on the table between them. "These are things of writing. In archives. You bring me other writing? Thank you." She tried to smile again, but her brow remained furrowed. "More writing, yes?"

Yusen noted the characters she had written. "You want me to bring you more books or pages."

"These things." She traced the line of characters with her long finger, pausing at one pair of characters. "I like read them, yes?"

"These things." He gave a nod, then yawned and stood up, scowling. The top of his chest was covered with pretty things, women's jars, the marriage scarf, the cane that Mandarin had given her. Yusen swept them all off into a pile at one end, the cane giving a satisfying thunk. Much as he hated Munkjar, the general's gift was the only practical one in the lot—and Meili had lugged that to the far end of the room where Yusen stored his dirty boots and weapons in need of care. He unlocked the chest with a key that hung at his throat, then removed his belt and coiled it carefully into the chest. Someday, he would have the silver belt of the khan's tumaan. For now, he selected a different belt, and a clean del for the next day, draping these on top after he had closed and relocked the chest.

The fact that the drakemaster produced nothing of importance about the mysterious weapon rankled, but he could not let the possibility fade. If he reminded the khan of the slave's good labor, and how the drakemaster's mechanical mind had produced the firedrake, the khan would see that this warning must be heeded, and that Yusen could be vital in tracking it down. The womanly Minister of Archives claimed the slave was deranged or a liar, but Yusen had known him for over two years: the slave couldn't keep his mouth shut, but Yusen had never known him to lie. Odd, that Yusen had so much confidence in a man who had no respect for him.

When he turned back, Bao Xing remained at the table, that crease marring her brow. She picked up the page and held it out. The characters meant nothing. He had already seen them. Yusen shrugged. "It's bed time."

Bao Xing replaced the paper, very carefully smoothing it in the center of the table. She understood what he said that time, and faced it with reluctance. Yusen stomped across the room, shedding his del into the pile to be washed by his wife's servant. His trousers and undervest needed to be washed—and repaired as well, for threads dangled at the hems—but he could not bring himself to strip bare in front of his wife. Nakedness was a risk he could not afford.

"We go to shrine?" Apparently, she wanted to burn some more sticks for her dead mother.

"Go on." He should take her riding, to the nearest oovo, to leave offerings to the Eternal Sky. "Do you know how to ride?"

She stared at him.

"Horses. Can you ride a horse?" He pointed to the saddle in the corner, and she shook her head. "You'll learn." He imagined her racing through a sunlight field, her hair streaming out behind her.

She shook her head, but took up her cane and hobbled toward the door to visit with the dead.

Climbing into bed, Yusen lay awake until she returned, trying to get comfortable on the thick mattress that threatened to swallow him whole. Meili quietly greeted her mistress and followed this with the tinkling of pearls and jewelry as she prepared Bao Xing for bed. Feigning sleep, Yusen closed his eyes and remembered her entrance into court on a breeze of musk and that tinkling of jewels. For an instant, every man in the room froze, even Munkjar, casting glances from the corner of their eyes, some of them stony-faced, knowing their wives would not approve. They focused on the khan's court and the reports he received, but every one of them tracked her passage across the chamber and knew when she came to sit at Yusen's back, in all of her perfection. The bed shifted as she climbed in and moved toward her side, and he pictured instead the fear in her eyes when her laughter angered him. And that after vowing to be gentle with her. He knew how to be gentle only with Tsang, and he doubted Bao Xing would respond to a lump of sugar in quite the same way.

In the morning, after checking on his horses, Yusen sent his wife to Mistress Luo to find a suitable instructor in the Mongol language. She was very intelligent, a fast learner. The study of language would give her some occupation worthy of her mind, at least until he brought her what she wanted. For himself, he walked the corridors where the Mandarins had their offices, carrying a leather sack and looking determined. Yusen had no official reason to be in the archive, nor did he trust the archivist:

the man lied about the drakemaster. What else was he lying about? What would he do or say if he knew Yusen had been here?

And so, Yusen was a scout once more, alert and eager, though he betrayed none of it. For a little while, he stood quietly in the shadow of a pair of huge pillars as the Mandarins went about their business. The floors squeaked and groaned, the curtains at the doorways swished and slapped the walls, the corridor empty of breezes save when someone passed by. He counted the floorboards outside the archive and studied the painted cloths that draped the walls. Every hour, a servant passed with a gong to announce the time.

Around the Hour of the Goat, the Mandarins returned to their apartments to lunch, or have meals brought to their offices by Chinese servants in blue tunics and trousers. Only tea entered the archive, carried by Chinese servants, who returned later for the tray. Much later, a little group of Mandarins stopped by the door, convincing the Minister of Archives to step out with them, and they strolled off, nattering in their own tongue. Yusen tread softly, stepping over the floorboards that creaked or squealed, sliding a hand behind the curtain and sliding himself inside, letting the cloth down without a breeze or slap.

Shelves of scrolls towered above him, smelling of old paper or musty straw. Yusen followed the scent of ash to a pile of baskets and chests. He recognized the characters for the city of Kaifeng on a dangling seal and started rummaging. Some bound pages he flipped open, some of the scrolls he unfurled. Once in a while, he tucked one into the leather sack. Two had especially fine drawings and paintings, and he added those as well, until the sack weighed down even him. Satisfied, he closed the lid and turned—

Footsteps in the hall hit the eighth board near the next office, the one that groaned the softest, but only on the end near the archive. Someone spoke, raising his voice as if to a companion further away.

Catching his breath, Yusen saw no place to hide. He dropped the sack into a basket and slipped a scroll on top, then he clasped the edges of one tall shelf and scrambled quietly up, leaning into it, until he was higher than a man. Finding a half-empty bin, he squeezed into it, stepping on the scrolls. Something crinkled under his foot, but he crouched without moving as someone entered the room below and paused. The man gave a single harder breath, half a sigh, then crossed below where Yusen crouched, rustled some pages, and walked back toward the door. Yusen risked leaning forward, peering out, but the man stopped by the door and, with another puff of breath, blew out the last lantern, leaving the room in darkness as the curtain slapped the wall with his departure.

Carefully, Yusen climbed down and retrieved the sack, sliding back out into the corridor. He muttered in Mongolian as he went, casting dark looks at any servants or Mandarins who noticed him. He hefted home his sack in triumph and dropped it at Bao Xing's side. Startled already by his abrupt entrance, his wife scrambled from her desk to bow.

Her face averted, she told him, "Meili takes dishes. Already cold. Late."

Yusen's stomach growled. "She must bring more. Very hungry." He patted his stomach, then pointed at Meili. "Hurry! Food."

The girl left, the curtains swaying behind her, and Yusen pulled off his boots, rubbing his feet. The thick felt boots heated his feet during the climb, though they had been comfortable enough during the long hours of waiting. Bao Xing reached toward the sack, and he said, "Books. To read."

She glanced to where her list still sat in the middle of the table, where it had been since the previous night. Then she opened the sack, removing a scroll with a broken bar—probably broken when he had dropped it into the basket to conceal his work. Her frown deepened. She pulled out a few more, opening one to reveal a glorious illustration of the Heavenly Horses, the legendary steeds that ran so fast they sweated blood. She let the cover fall shut and set it aside, then pulled out the next one and sucked in a breath, lifting the book into the light. Grubby threads held pages of sloppy calligraphy, but his wife stroked the work as if it the pages were silver and the letters, gold.

"How?" She pointed to her list. "You read?"

Yusen snorted and shook his head. "I'm a scout." Her eyebrows squeezed together, as if the word meant nothing to her, as it might not, he realized. He didn't need to read to recognize the symbols when he saw them again. "I look..." he pointed to the list, with its meaningless patterns, then tapped his forehead. "I remember. I scout..." he mimed scanning the horizon and checking the ground. "I think of plans. I take back what I learn." He shrugged. "I tell the captains, and they tell my plan to the general as if they thought of it."

His wife sorted the documents into piles, continuing to stroke some of them, utterly ignoring others. He pulled out the one with the Heavenly Horses and tossed it onto her desk, causing a few brushes to roll down onto the floor. "Read me."

Bao Xing picked up the brushes, starting to straighten their tips, then set them into a bamboo holder and picked up the book. "You hear Chinese?"

"I hear you."

Bao Xing opened the book and began to read, carefully at first, then relaxing into it, her voice rounding the syllables of her own language, drawing out and emphasizing in a way that made him wish he understood more than a fifth of the words. The book described the travels of an imperial envoy who spent years as a captive of the enemies of the people he was meant to parlay with. The envoy took a wife and had a child before he managed to escape. Even then, his loyalty lay with his ruler. Yusen admired the man's dedication, though a better scout would have seen the envoy through safely. And of course the paintings of horses were excellent.

Meili returned, burdened with a large tray holding a covered bronze vessel and a few other things. The greasy richness of stewed mutton filled the air, and Yusen attacked his meal. The servant set down the pot nearby and took up a ladle, dipping it in, scooping, and pouring a stream of beige liquid back into the pot. Tea! And she had even learned to stir it properly.

Pushing aside the empty soup bowl, Yusen snapped at the girl to give him a smaller bowl of tea, the salty, milky brew briefly sending his memory home to the steppes, to his mother's hearth. He breathed in the scent of it, cradling it with both hands. "Good."

His wife broke off her reading when he spoke, and he addressed her next. "You learn to speak well, you attend me when I go to court, you see that my things are repaired and cleaned. Afternoons, it's cool enough, we'll go riding."

She pulled the book to her chest. "I cannot."

Yusen noted her narrow gown with its many layers underneath. "Not in those clothes. Make some riding clothes—Mongolian clothes."

"I—not clothes. Feet too small." She revealed a tiny foot clad in a slipper covered with stitching, even on the sole. With its thick heel and pointed toe it must be the most worthless shoe he had ever seen.

Yusen stretched out his own legs, slightly bow-legged from growing up on horseback, and let his foot settle next to hers. His toes stuck up past her shoe. Yusen wiggled them, their grubby flexibility contrasting with the bound-up, hidden foot of his wife. Bigger feet, even though she stood more than a head taller than he.

"Riding is not about feet, but balance. You have good balance to walk in these shoes, even with a cane. You make the clothes, and I will show you riding." He finished his tea and stood up, stretching out the muscles of his back and shoulders, still stiff after carrying the heavy sack of books, then he went through the ritual of preparing his clothes for the next morning, finding his other del and a fresh pair of trousers before going to bed.

The lanterns in the main chamber stayed lit for a long time, and he could hear the turning of pages, then his wife finally came to bed as well, accompanied by the click of her cane hanging on its peg. His clothes were clean, his wife was wise and beautiful, worthy of running a household, and her servant obeyed him, if grudgingly. He provided her the books she asked for, and she would do whatever he told her. So far, his marriage was a great success.

CHAPTER THIRTY-FIVE

Zhencai began with walking meditation, trying to push the world from his mind, trying to reject the pain. He stumbled around in a circle over and over, the pines blurring and bending, reaching out to snare him, a constant reminder of the world he must reject. Andao tried to follow, but kept kicking his master's heels or stumbling over him. Zhencai spun about, wobbling, and pointed away. "Go, novice. Perform sitting meditation until I am finished."

The young man's hands, meant to be held behind him as they walked, flashed through a series of gestures as if he couldn't figure out what he meant to say. The movements made Zhencai dizzy, and he planted his feet, thrusting his finger more insistently.

Stalking to the other side of the narrow meadow they occupied, Andao folded himself into a seated posture and gripped his hands together into something like prayer. "Master, I—"

Zhencai pulled his beads from his belt and flung them at Andao, forcing him to whip up his hand to prevent them tangling his neck. At least his reflexes were improving. The beads clattered together, and the young man drew them down into his lap. "Sutras," Zhencai barked.

"All of them?" Andao held the string of beads as if it were a snake. "A hundred and eight?"

Zhencai turned back to his pathway. Nine paces, turn, nine paces. Turn, untangle himself from a pine tree. His qi, unruly at the best of times, clattered and slid like the beads through Andao's hands. The novice didn't say sutras, of course, or rather, he did, but he said them in his own language, a droning rise and fall that buzzed around Zhencai's head louder every day.

Nine paces…no, that was ten. He didn't see the round stone that marked the other end. Or perhaps it had only been eight. He took another step.

"Master!" Andao shouted, and Zhencai pivoted, then felt his balance shift. His arms spun as his heel slid, then he cried out in pain as Andao grabbed his arm and pulled him forward. The grassy boundary of their small domain showed where a clump of earth had fallen away beneath his foot, tumbling down to the river far below.

"Your arm is like fire, Master. We cannot afford the meditations, not today."

"We cannot afford to have no meditations, especially today." He glowered, trying to clear his cloudy mind. "The more you are assailed by the world of suffering, the more you must remain detached."

"Any further delays, and you will be detached from the world! You said the Buddha opened the way to you, that his hand directed you to this mystery. You're not supposed to die before you understand it, are you?"

Zhencai's qi tumbled again, leaving him off-balance, and he bumped into his student. "Unless it is you who is meant to finish it."

With a cackle of laughter, Andao shook his head, his hands moving. "No, Master—the hand of the Buddha has nothing to do with me, unless it propelled the Mongols who ruined Kaifeng and left my people homeless. Again. My people value knowledge, almost over everything, and life. Your Buddha teaches that life and death are the same thing, that to cling to life is to cling to the world and wallow in the suffering." He hugged himself. "But if you reject the world and you never try to make things better, then everybody else suffers—you just prolong the suffering, don't you?" He flapped his hands into the sky.

Zhencai drew calming breaths, trying to master his qi. "I begin to believe that knowledge and suffering are one. Think of this—" he touched the oilcloth bound scroll, a gesture that made his arm pulse with its persistent suffering, "these people took generations of knowledge and they created a device to bind the very heavens into causing suffering. If not for their knowledge, then this machine would never be made and that suffering could never occur."

Andao mastered his hands, pressing his palms together. "And if not for your knowledge of the device, and the knowledge that others are seeking it, you, yourself would not be suffering."

Zhencai acknowledged this with the sign of blessing. Pain rolled through his arm.

"So you think we would be better off in ignorance, not knowing about this thing at all." Andao leaned over him, inspiring an urge to smack the novice's chest with an iron hand and drop him, gasping, to the ground.

"How incredibly selfish." Flaring his eyes, the young man retreated. "If we didn't know, Master Deng would have the plans—or that woman, that spy would have them, right? And some day the heavens would open with fire, the rivers would run with poison, and every man and woman and horse and beast in its path would suffer and die. That's what the scroll means, isn't it? But that's too much worldly trouble for a monk like you."

"You know nothing of monks." Zhencai's words stuck in his throat. Did the Buddha intend for him to allow so many to die, so many who would not have the peace that came from the renunciation of suffering?

"Selfish," Andao concluded. "Like wanting to die in the mountains rather than carry on with your task."

"I do not *want* to die in the mountains. I do not *want* anything." Zhencai swayed and stepped his feet a little wider apart.

"Then let's do our walking meditation walking toward Dragon Turns Mountain." Andao spoke softly this time, his fingers working together, pleading. "I'll finish the sutra beads, you'll center your qi, and we will be a little closer to knowledge than ignorance."

"You are the least obedient of novices ever to take a master."

Andao's busy hands paused in the sign of blessing, and he grinned. "How do we get to Dragon Turns, Master?"

"There—you can see the peak." Zhencai pointed along a narrow pass toward the rugged summit of Dragon Turns. "The monastery lies in a canyon hidden by old stones. The dragon leads the way." In his left hand, he took up a stout staff, the right hand tucked against his chest beneath his tunic, and started out.

CHAPTER THIRTY-SIX

Yusen's shouting awoke Bao Xing the next morning, and she scrambled out of bed, finding her robe and sliding it on before she took down her cane and hobbled to the door. In the front room, Yusen stood over a cowering servant and a broken pot, water still steaming on the floor between them.

"This is not the way to make tea! I asked for a Mongolian servant, at least for one who knew how to make tea. Clean it up and send someone who knows the job!"

The servant scuttled about, gathering broken crockery, then rushed out the door, no doubt self-conscious of the fact that, at the age of perhaps nine years old, he was as tall as the man shouting at him.

In the echoing silence, Yusen pivoted sharply, seeing her watching him. "There is soup and rice cakes. And your tea."

She briefly scanned the room: the chests, the paint and mirror, the writing desk with its stack of books alongside. "Good morning, husband. Where is Meili?"

"I sent her away. She is a thief." He dropped to kneel by the table, helping himself to a rice cake.

"A thief? What has she stolen?"

He shrugged. "Nothing I can see yet. I do not sleep well. I heard your cane click on its hook and found her lifting it off. She carried the cane that Mandarin gave you. When confronted her, she said she thought you should use the other cane, but she could have said that to you—not in the middle of the night. I sent her away. You may wish to lock your things as I do. She may come back in anger." He took a large bite of the rice cake and chewed it down, reached for his teacup, which proved to be empty, and slapped it back onto the table.

"I... why would Meili steal from me?"

Another shrug. "She is a servant, and—" he stopped, with a flicker of a glance at Bao Xing. "I believe she spies for the Mandarins. Better that she's gone."

"But—" Staring at the back of his head, Bao Xing knew it was futile, even as a weight settled into her stomach. Her husband had taken away her servant because he could—because he didn't want her to be connected with anything Chinese. He brought her books not because he cared, but because he didn't want her ever to go to the archives, and he refused to accompany her to the shrine, even during the critical first three days of their marriage. What could it mean to have such an inauspicious beginning?

Again Yusen picked up his empty cup, then he aimed it at her. "You must learn to make the tea. Here, I'll show you."

Bao Xing forced herself to sit across from him as he found an empty bowl and poured some tea from the pot into it, then topped this with almost as much milk. From a yak, apparently. The thick, white stuff swirled into the pale green of the tea, making it look like the Yellow River during the spring run-off: more silty than ever. Then he went to his chest for a pouch of salt and sprinkled in a liberal helping. "The stirring is the most important." He retrieved the ladle from under the table where it rolled as he was yelling at the hapless servant, and scooped it into the murky bowl, but rather than pour it into his cup, he poured it back into the bowl. "Many times, many times this is done." Dropping the ladle into the bowl, he pushed it toward her and gave a sharp nod.

Bao Xing took up the ladle and gave a little scoop and pour, but Yusen caught her hand. She stiffened, expecting the extraordinary strength he had used before, the first time he had touched her. Instead, he lightly guided her hand down, taking a larger scoop and lifting her hand up to pour it out, his fingers gently encouraging her hand in the right motion. Their eyes met beside the stream of milky tea, and he let her go. "Yes, again. Nine times at least."

Seven more times, she repeated the action, as if she were taking enormous embroidery stitches, pulling the silk of the tea high up to finish each one. The gesture fell into a rhythm, like embroidery, like music, unlike the smooth advance of stars. Did he know she went to the shrine at night to see the stars? Probably not.

When the tea was stirred to his satisfaction, Bao Xing poured some into the empty cup, which he drained in a few swallows and clattered back to the tray. "I go riding with other soldiers. Someone will come for the food—or just leave it in the corridor. Make sure someone will bring dinner."

"Husband," she called, and he hesitated as he rose. "Please to write my father?" She mimed using a brush.

He gave a sharp nod. "Bring it to the khan's messengers and use my name."

With that, he stood up and left. Marriage was as Ming Lun had told her, a box. At least her box had a door, and he had given permission for her to use it, at least in the service of his appetite and her letter.

Bao Xing fixed her own tea and let it cool while she picked up one of the books: the observations of Chang Mailou, an astronomer who, she believed, had a part in building of the dangerous thing alluded to by the armillary sphere at Kaifeng, and in the book she had seen at the library. Yusen the scout had done very well indeed. Everything he brought her related to the words on her list—aside from the one with many pictures of horses.

Laying the astronomer's journal on her desk, Bao Xing skimmed the text, finding date notations and sketches of celestial phenomena. The astronomer referenced the emperor's man, Su Sung, who came to discuss his astronomical clock. It sounded like a miniature of her father's own tower, and Bao Xing smiled, but her eyes stung. When she wrote to her father, she would share news of her reading—and of her marriage. A bittersweet letter to be sure.

Bao Xing's stomach rumbled, and she reached for a rice cake, then took a swallow of cold tea.

As she nibbled, she flipped the page, searching for the end of the party the astronomer was describing, wondering why Chang had even bothered to include it. Then another name caught her eye, that of her own several-times grandfather. Their host, Shou Dengho, introduced his special guests, a trio of geomancers he had talked down from the mountains, but their names had been blotted from the text. Here was the secret hinted at in bronze. She read of Su Sung's clock, and Dengho's inspiration to use it as the basis of a device to harness the power of the stars—power to heal, to refresh weakened farmland and infuse the countryside with energy. And so, together, astronomers and geomancers built themselves an extraordinary device they called the Mandate of Heaven.

Bao Xing resettled herself and flipped through a few pages of basic calculations and observations, and the dedication of the astronomical clock itself. Rumors began to reach Kaifeng of dangerous tribes along the border.

As she scanned the book, Chang remarked that work on "The Mandate of Heaven" proceeded well, and once apologized for his long absence, having forgotten his journal during the construction. He got drunk with one of the geomancers he had befriended—though someone had removed the person's name—and the fellow told him:

I'm surprised that Shou Dengho hasn't suggested that our work might be used against those the emperor perceives as his enemies. If we can enable the light of auspicious stars to shine more brightly and renew the energy of the earth itself, then we could use the light of the less auspicious stars. What then? If the incidents surrounding celestial events like the circling of the wandering stars are to be believed, then the light from an inauspicious star, even at such a great distance, can bring fire and flood, earthquake and disease. With the apparatus we are building, this power could be compounded ten or a hundredfold, just as packing the powder into a cylinder creates a much greater explosion. The geomancers have been developing a map to focus the positive light of renewal they imagine gathering. This map shows the basin of the great Yellow River as it leads to the sea, with all of its bends and as much as we can include about the surrounding area. Might the power of evil stars be used to scour the land north of the river of our enemies? Indeed it might—but not without scouring thousands of farmers, monks, and merchants in between.

"What makes you think he has not thought of this?" I demanded of the geomancers, and so we rose up together and went to demand of Shou Dengho if he had such a plan. At first, he tried to reassure us this was not true. He provided a bottle of wine to soothe us, and even drank a bowl of it himself, but we were not fooled. Then he became arrogant, thanking us for providing this means to ensure the longevity of the empire. "Yet the imperial children become weak and the empire decadent—you said so yourself!" I insisted.

This infuriated him and he threw his wine bowl at me. "You think me so short-sighted that I don't know this? All of my work, in service to a family of foxes! Our creation is for the future of all China, not for the whims of the weak."

"Then we should destroy it. At least, we should stop work on it, and ensure that word does not spread about its existence," said {the nameless geomancer}.

"A time will come when it is needed, when our device can change the fortunes of the Han people. Even if it is not today, or even tomorrow."

"In that case," I said, "We must ensure that the device can be safely used for its intended purpose. There will never be a safe time for it to be used as a weapon—surely you see that, Dengho—but its power for good must not be allowed to vanish."

"How would we ever know whom to trust with this power, if the imperial family descends into decadence," said the geomancer.

Shou Dengho paused for long thought, and I felt relieved thinking that he would understand it must be destroyed. Instead, he answered, "We shall have to be there, to judge the future for ourselves."

We laughed at this, thinking he had drunk too much as well, but in the coming days, I saw he was sincere: he had begun to consult with doctors and pharmacists. A rift opened in our company and it was clear that some supported our patron, and would try to survive into the future with him, much longer than a single lifetime. I, too, began to plan for such a survival—not for myself, but for the truth that our descendants would need to know—

"Mistress?"

She started and the book slid shut into her lap, her fingers flying to her chest.

A servant stood at the door, bowing. "Forgive me, mistress, I did call and knock, but there was no answer, and so I thought no one was here."

"Are you here for the dishes?"

"Yes, Mistress. And to bring you word from Mistress Luo who believes you may be in want of another maid."

Thank the ancestors that Mistress Luo thought of such things—of course Meili would have gone to her after Yusen threw her out. Bao Xing had missed at least one of the hourly gongs and still sat beside her cold breakfast in her dressing robe, her face clear of any paint. She must look dreadful. "I'll definitely need one. Can you bring a message to Mistress Luo that I would like to visit at—" she didn't know what the hour was, actually, so she said, "after lunch?"

Her mind spun. Imagine that the man whose cane she carried was a part of such great and terrible events. There had been few geomancers to begin with, and the Mongols hunted the handful said to remain. Her father spoke of them in the same tone he used for those poetry parties: a nostalgic feature of a life his elders recalled to him.

At the desk, she knelt and wrote him a letter, describing the journey to the palace and a few details about her life there. She started to write about her marriage, her infuriating little barbarian of a husband, but how would her father take it? When she had better adjusted to married life, she would write to him again. Instead, she described her secret research in and out of the archive, relating the prophecy of the Dark Lance to the creation of a weapon over a century ago, an event that her many-times grandfather had witnessed. Might her father have more documents about that?

Folding the paper, she sealed it and wrote her father's name and a description of the location of his observatory tower. When she set out to Mistress Luo's chambers, in the corridor of the Mandarins, she placed her letter in the hands of a scribe to be carried toward Kaifeng with the next dispatch.

Presenting herself at Mistress Luo's, Bao Xing was immediately led inside, and the instructor even rose to greet her, then said, as Bao Xing poured their tea, "Do tell me the truth, my dear, is he a dreadful little barbarian as we feared?"

"He could be worse." Bao Xing thought of his hand squeezing her wrist on their wedding night, then of the bounty of books he had brought her. He was a puzzle, and she no longer imagined she had seen all of him.

"The kitchen gossips say that he is paranoid, constantly concerned over his person, his possessions. Now it seems it is true, and poor Meili has born the blow."

They spoke about selecting a new maid, Yusen's bizarre fury at Meili, his terrible table manners. The Mongolian instructor arrived, and Bao Xing sat through endless repetitions of guttural noises meant to be words, and managed a longer conversation by the end of their session.

She employed this new skill over dinner with her husband, watching him suck the grease of his lamb from his fingers while she gripped her chopsticks. "May I go to the shrine, my husband?" she asked, after what seemed a polite interval.

"Go on," he told her, his eyes as intent as ever on herself as she rose to go.

Dusk had fallen, and Bao Xing's heart rose as she moved through the corridor and out into the yard. Once there, she tipped her head back to look at the sky. Deep blue, not yet black, but a few stars shone, and she could make out the Ox. A few steps into the yard, she heard movement behind her.

"Bao Xing—lady, is it you?" Guowei's voice stirred the darkness, then he crashed right into her.

With a cry, Bao Xing stumbled and fell, her cane toppling from her hand.

"Oh, dear—do forgive me. Here—" Guowei fussed over her, kneeling to lift her with one strong arm wrapped at her back, the other on her hand, helping her onto a nearby bench. "Are you hurt? I took a misstep on the paving stones. Let me find your cane." He cast about in the darkness as Bao Xing gripped the edge of the bench, trembling.

Her arm stung as if it had been scraped, but she the heat of his hands lingered.

"Oh, dear. Bao Xing, I am so very sorry." Guowei emerged from the twilight, holding out a short length of wood, her cane tucked under his arm. "The handle has come off of your cane. Do let me take it for repair. I'm sure it won't take long."

"Do you think so?" She reached out for it, but he was studying the end, squinting in the gloom.

"It's no good, I can barely see. I have a servant waiting in the hall, I'll have him rush it to the craftsman and bring back the other one from your chamber. I…" He wet his lips, then sank down so his face was in the light of the lamp. "I hope it will still serve you, the cane I gave you."

"I'm sure it will," she said faintly.

He bowed deeply, then hurried to the door, and she heard the music of his voice, though not the words. Guowei returned and took a bench opposite. "I am so very sorry. You've come to do your duty to your family, and I have broken your family heirloom. You must think me such an oaf."

"No, not at all. It is dark and the pavement is rough, Minister. But you are not injured?"

"No, lady, I am very well indeed." The lantern outlined his profile and lent an extra gleam to his deep eyes. It formed a little shadow by his lips as he smiled and, just at that moment, Bao Xing felt very well, too.

CHAPTER THIRTY-SEVEN

Carrying the mandarin's cane against his shoulder like a sword he meant to swing, Yusen marched down the corridor and pushed through the doors into the courtyard. The Mandarin's servant had come, explaining about the broken cane, and how she required this one to replace it. Yusen insisted on bringing it himself, his every scout's sense crying out a warning. She sat silhouetted by a single lantern, and the Mandarin sat across from her. Was this what she had been doing all these nights she visited the shrine? He had thought she merely liked to look at the stars.

"You!" He thrust the cane at the Mandarin who leapt to his feet. No, not clumsy at all, not at all night-blind. The man had deliberately broken Bao Xing's cane. Why? So that she would have to sit with him? So that she would have to use the one he gave her?

"Good evening," the Mandarin said in very good Mongolian, managing a bow, stuffing his hands into his sleeves as if he'd been planning to do something completely different with them. Strangle Yusen? Steal his wife?

"What have you done with my wife's cane?"

"Didn't my servant tell you? I asked him to deliver it for repair—"

"If it requires repair, then I should take care of it. She is my wife, and I will take care of her." He tapped his own chest, feeling shrill and ridiculous, so full of fury he could barely breathe.

"Surely, sir, your wife also deserves some consideration." The Mandarin stood very still, very tall, his back to the light, inclining his head toward Bao Xing who sat as a pale statue, her mouth pinched small and tight.

"Has he hurt you in any way?" Yusen demanded, and received a brief shake of the head. "Be glad my wife is unhurt. You did not fall by accident—you move like a warrior, not an archivist. Men like you don't stumble in the dark. They do not break things by accident."

The Mandarin tipped his head in a different way. "You know very little about me, sir, but I assure you that I hold your wife and her things in very high regard. It would pain me should anything happen to her or that which she holds dear. I grew distracted when I realized I was not alone. Such a thing could happen to anyone."

With a moment's calculation, Yusen slid forward, sweeping the cane from his shoulder and lunging onto the path between the benches. The Mandarin stepped back and to the side as Yusen slashed the cane through the spot where he'd been standing and let it crack in half against the end of the empty bench.

Bao Xing gasped, her hands pressing close against her, and he regretted her fear, but hoped she had, at least, seen the point. Without even looking, the Mandarin had easily evaded his blow, moving backwards into the darkness on the same rough paving he claimed had tripped him when he was facing the light.

"Who are you?" Yusen brandished the half of the cane he still held.

"You know who I am, surely, sir. I am Guowei, the khan's Minister of Archives. I don't understand why you are attacking me like this." Then the Mandarin sighed a little and had the gall to smile faintly as he regarded Bao Xing. "Or perhaps I do. Forgive me, sir, and lady." He bowed deeply. "I will return to perform my filial duty another time." He crossed in front of Yusen, bowed again near Bao Xing's bench and moved into the gloom. Yusen heard six, seven, eight of his long, soft paces, before the swing of the doors and the quiet rap as they shut.

"I—" his wife began, but Yusen held up his hand, stepping swiftly and silently toward the door to confirm that they were truly alone, then he returned to her.

Her glittering eyes heightened her beauty. "He breaks my grandfather's cane—by accident—and now you break my wedding gift. My husband, how do I walk home?"

Her words flamed his fury all over again, and Yusen flung away the broken cane. "Have you finished your worship?"

"I was on my way to the shrine when Guo—the minister stumbled into me."

"He didn't stumble, he did not trip, he did nothing by accident." Yusen knotted his hands into his hair. "He has stolen your cane, the one treasure you had from your family. He's taken your family from you, and you—"

Bao Xing suddenly rose. "He tries to give me! He gives cane I never use—he gives words, he gives—" she added something in her own language and flung up her hands. "He speaks as if I am a person. And you—now I cannot even walk."

Even as she said it, she wobbled. Yusen sprang forward, caught her hand and brought it to his shoulder, pressing it there. His heart thundered like a vast herd across the steppes. Her hand under his felt hot and smooth. His rough fingers would catch on her skin as if on the silk of her gown. Her hand trembled, her arm strained for freedom, then it relaxed too much, surrendering as if he had stripped the bones from her body. He had not seen what that cane meant to her. Not just an heirloom, nor a stick to lean on, the cane was her freedom. Guowei had stolen the first, and her husband had broken the second. His throat hurt. "To the shrine?"

"In thanks for what?" Her words dropped down at him like pebbles cast by a careless hand.

Nevertheless, she allowed him to support her down the path and up the few steps to the shrine where a pair of small lanterns hung. She settled on a cushion, but her eyes were raised toward the skies a long moment before she took up a stick of incense to light it. The stuff fouled his nose. Yusen stalked into the darkness, hands at his back, pacing, until she cleared her throat to signal she was ready, then he set himself again as a prop for her hand, and she trailed a step behind him, as if she, not her cane, had been broken.

At the junction between the Mandarin's offices and official chambers, and the khan's royal wing, they encountered a group of soldiers laughing as they left the royal apartments. The laughter broke up when one of them spotted Yusen, glancing down, then following Bao Xing's arm up to stare at her.

"What is it?" asked a voice from the back, then Munkjar strolled up through the group. He shifted into a bow. "Good evening, lady. I see you have found a new prop."

His wife made no reply, the pressure of her hand increasing.

"This one's uglier than the last—I suggest you seek a better craftsman."

The soldiers snickered, and Yusen stepped a little faster, but Bao Xing's small feet and restrictive gown would not allow it. He slowed to his earlier pace, the laughter of the soldiers echoing after them.

Yusen burned. He wanted to break more than just the simpering minister's wedding present. His jaw ached from the tension and his shoulders from the strain of not revealing how furious he was. Even as it shrank him in the eyes of the soldiers, the slight pressure of her hand upon his shoulder filled him with a sense of strength he had never known before. She needed him. Just for now, just for this. She hated every moment of it—that much was plain, but there must be a way to show her that he was worthy of more than this. Worthy, in some other way, of earning her touch.

Outside their chamber, a girl slept on a straw mat in the hall—a Mongolian girl, not a Chin one. She rubbed her eyes, then scrambled to a low bow. "Welcome sir and mistress," she said in his language, then again in Chinese. "I am sent of Mistress Luo, who hopes I shall be acceptable as a maid to the lady Bao Xing."

"Can you make tea?" Yusen eyed her sidelong. "The proper way, with milk."

"Yes, sir," she answered.

"Come."

The moment they passed through the curtain, Bao Xing released him and shuffled on her own to sink onto a cushion between her writing desk and her mounds of beauty things: the part of their home most clearly hers alone. She slumped, her face turned from him. The servant crept in after them, standing, waiting.

Yusen unlocked his chest, methodically performing his nightly rituals, then hesitating, hands gripped on the wooden edge. He located a small dagger which he hid beneath the front flap of his del, and another for his boot. "What's your name?"

"Selenge, sir."

"My wife will need you very much for the next few days. You'll need to cook meals here—there's a stove—" he pointed it out, though they had never used it. "Don't trust any food that someone gives you or tries to give to myself or my wife. You must shop for the ingredients, do you understand?" In an old pouch full of foul-smelling herbs, Yusen kept a number of coins, and he gave her a few, not sure what prices she might find in the market. "My wife is not to have visitors among the Mandarins, especially anyone sent by the Minister of Archives."

At that, Bao Xing's head twitched, her eyes narrowing and the golden butterflies dangling in her hair looking suddenly aggressive. She might not understand all of his words but likely she had asked for the word "archives" from her language tutor. Yusen tossed the pouch of herbs back into the chest, slammed and locked it.

Selenge met his gaze, looking slightly startled.

"I will be very busy for the next few days. I might not be here. You must arrange for water to be brought for washing, or you may take my wife to the garden to take care of that, but no place else. She may not go to the shrine, especially at night. Will you be capable of all of this, or do I need to hire another servant?"

"No, sir, I am capable," she told him, forthright and strong—not like that slithery girl Meili.

"Good."

She wore the same blue trousers and tunic as all of the servants, male or female, and stood about as tall as he.

"You'll need more clothes—can you get two more sets?"

"Yes, sir."

"Find a blanket, too. You need to sleep in the corridor."

She gave a slight bow. "Should I get them now, sir?"

"Go on—I'll be here for the night."

Selenge hurried out. She might still be a spy. Yusen considered hiring another servant anyhow, rather than rely on one provided by the Mandarins, even a Mongolian one.

"I am prisoner now, yes?" Bao Xing regarding him coolly from across the room.

"I have angered Minister Guowei. He is a liar, and we cannot trust him. We may be in danger."

"You make him angry, so I cannot leave? I cannot have visitors?" She yanked a comb from her hair, gripping it so that the teeth must be biting her palm.

"I will go find your cane, and scout the territory of our enemy. When I know more, I'll know what to do. If there is no danger, you will have your freedom."

She flung the comb at him. It struck his sleeve and tumbled to the floor. "You make me a prisoner! You make me a joke, a cripple, not even a concubine!" She yanked another pin from her hair and hurled it at him.

Yusen took a step back from the barrage, his spine curling and shoulders slumping. He had been pelted with dung before, pierced by arrows, slapped by the general and beaten by his men, and it had never hurt like this. Her missiles barely reached him, barely had the power to scratch him if they did, yet he cowered and prayed for it to stop. Stupid—a husband did not cower before his wife. How would she ever respect him, much less accept him, if he were so weak? Sucking in a breath, Yusen squared his shoulders and marched past the table, feeling something snap beneath his foot—some golden pick or butterfly or pearl-embellished trinket.

Staring down at her—barely—he said, "You understand nothing. You see nothing outside of books and pearls and Mandarins bowing and scraping! You look at me and see a stupid, ugly, ignorant dwarf. You think you're hiding this, lady, but it hangs from you like pearls. Do you think I don't know? Your only kindness to me is to not to cover your smile when I give you what you want. Go to bed!" He shoved his finger in that direction. "And I will sleep by the door like the dog you think I am."

She leaned away as he raved. Her eyes gleamed, but she knuckled away the tear, and faced him, meeting his gaze for the first time he could remember.

"You trade a man's life for me. After use his life to win your seat by the khan. You think I don't know?" She wiped her sleeve across her face, smearing away the shimmer of pearl paint and leaving a streak of her true flesh showing. "I am not a prize, not a stolen statue, or a conquered thing. You steal a man's life, steal his freedom, steal his heart to make weapons, give his life away to die—all for yourself. I must give thanks all I have, and you give thanks never once for him nor for anything. Yes, like dog! Like dog try to steal other dog's bone. What bone next, Yusen? What bone you throw me away for?"

She tore off her gowns. A thick band wrapped her breasts, the binding unravelling as she stumbled away, her naked form framed for a moment by the doorway, then she pushed through the curtain and fell onto the bed beyond. Wearing only her wrapped stockings and tiny shoes, she pulled up her feet and yanked the blankets around her. Her dim silhouette transformed from the brief and beautiful glimpse of her body to a lump of darkness.

Yusen's throat ached, his loins ached. Never, he wanted to say—never would he throw her away, but he dropped his head like a dog, one who knows he is beaten. How many times had he ridden away from Batu's tumaan, and from Munkjar's on one mission or another, and always returned, still hoping for that bone? He had thought she did not know him at all; but she knew him better than he knew himself. The knowledge settled hard into his gut. He curled onto a pair of cushions—all that it took to make him a bed, and let the darkness fill him up.

When Selenge returned and fell asleep in the corridor outside, Yusen took what he needed and, like a dog, slunk away into the night.

CHAPTER THIRTY-EIGHT

Waking in the morning to find him gone, Bao Xing accepted his absence eagerly. She left her breasts unbound beneath her morning robe and succumbed to the gentle tug of Selenge's hands as the servant brushed out her hair. The fact that Yusen approved this particular servant made Bao Xing want to get rid of her—but she needed someone, and, at the moment, she had no other. Boiling tea water over the little stove heated up the chambers and left smoke in the air. At least it was located on her husband's side of the room, and Bao Xing retreated to her own side when it was time for Selenge to brew the tea and mix up porridge.

She reached for the book she had been reading, but it was gone—along with the volume with all the pictures of horses. Did Yusen hate her so much that he took the only thing that gave her pleasure? Two of the others were gone as well, leaving her with two damaged scrolls and a volume about the manufacture of instruments, including astronomical ones. Not to go to the shrine—especially at night! She was not to see the stars at all until he returned.

Then she thought of the things she had said to him.

She had been cruelest not in what she had said, but in walking away, letting him see the body she must hide from everyone but him—and taunting him with the knowledge that he would not be close to her. She had meant to lash out at him as he had lashed out and broken the cane Guowei had given her.

Her husband, aside from being overly suspicious, was madly jealous of Guowei. She could see how that might come about. He had come upon them sitting alone in the courtyard, not even a servant to chaperone them, and he knew she went to the shrine every night—tracking the progress of the Wanderer over the Dark Lance, but he didn't know that. Finding her there with another man, he likely assumed that she met Guowei every time. It had happened once or twice, but never deliberately, at least, not on her part.

What would it be when he traded her away? A better horse? She stifled her laughter at that, and Selenge looked up from the stove. An enormous warhorse he could show off to the other soldiers as he showed her off at court, but he would need a staircase to mount the beast.

Abruptly, her laughter faded. What if he could trade her to grow taller? Last night, he had given himself as her prop and brought her home, through the laughter of those same men. She felt humiliated to need him. How much more humiliated must he have been, to be of a size to provide such a service? She had done and said things unworthy of a wife—of any man's wife, no matter how lowly.

For a moment she envisioned herself as she was meant to be that night the Mongol soldiers came: dressed in boy's clothes with padding-filled boots on her feet, escaping down the mountainside to find safety in the South, among the Han people in the empire as it should be. By now, she might have made it as far as the broad Yangtze River. She might reveal her mother's pearls and combs not as ornaments in the court of the khan, but as trade goods to buy her passage. In the court of the Son of Heaven, she could reveal herself, her perfect lotus blossom feet, and win a husband who was envied instead of scorned.

Selenge placed a cup of tea before her. Milky tea, in the Mongolian style, its surface rippling, revealing nothing of its depths.

Her father would have died that night, his beloved instruments melted into weapons to ruin Kaifeng, never to know the truth about the Dark Lance, never to know about the ancient weapon. Things she would never have learned in another place, married to a different man.

Selenge moved to a little pile of cloth near the doorway, scooped it up and went to an inner corner where she arranged the items into neat piles, then frowned. "Have my things been moved, lady? I thought to bring two pairs of clothes, but now there is only one."

"No, not I."

"Perhaps they gave me only one. No matter, lady."

A rap sounded on the wall outside, and Selenge went to the curtain.

In Chinese, a young voice said, "I bring a message for the lady Bao Xing."

Selenge stiffened. "The lady does not receive—"

"I shall take it." Bao Xing brooked no refusal. She pushed to her feet and crossed the few steps to the door.

"But the master said—"

"He did not say I could receive no messages." She thrust out her hand imperiously, and the boy outside handed over the folded paper he carried along with a small bamboo box.

"Thank you."

He grinned up at her before bowing, then hurried away.

She returned to her place and nudged the tea out of the way. "Can you also make Chinese tea?"

"Of course, lady. It requires no skill."

Bao Xing, who had spent several afternoons at Mistress Luo's learning to make tea, managed another smile. "Then it shall take you no time at all."

Selenge took away the cup, and Bao Xing called after her, "I am sorry. My husband's prohibitions have given me an ill temper."

"Yes, lady."

While the servant made tea all over again, Bao Xing opened the folded paper. "It is from Mistress Luo—how kind of her to write!" Bao Xing called out gaily as her eyes feasted on the script before her.

"My dear lady Bao Xing, if you will permit me the breach of etiquette in writing to you at all, then please allow me to apologize again for the breaking of your cane, and for the confrontation which followed. I was still flustered by our unfortunate encounter when your husband arrived, and ill-prepared to handle that conversation with the diplomacy it clearly required. Please accept this as a token of my regret. I hope that the incident will cause no further difficulty between yourself and your husband. I shall no further trouble your mind with this intrusion. Again, my apologies, Guowei."

He had bold writing, elegant, yet spare. He wrote the way that he dressed, without the ostentation of some of the other Mandarins or of the Mongols who liked to imagine they, too, were Han. Shouldn't he have mentioned returning the cane? Well, likely it took longer to repair than a single morning. He might repair the cane he gave her as well, its pieces found where Yusen had flung them.

She tucked the note into her dressing gown, then, making sure that Selenge was busy spooning porridge, she slipped open the lid of the box.

The aroma greeted her immediately: sugared plums—the sort normally reserved for celebrations.

"Lady," Selenge began, then glanced at the box and hurried forward. "The master said nothing to eat but what I prepare! Please, lady—"

Bao Xing snatched a plum and stuffed it into her mouth, sweetness exploding onto her tongue as she chewed. She had not had sugared plums since before her mother died and had forgotten the cloying sweetness that clung to her teeth.

Selenge dropped the bowl she was carrying and grabbed the box, the plums tumbling out in a sticky lump onto the floor. She grabbed those, too, dropping to her knees. "Please, lady, I hear how your husband beat his slave near to death, how he angry all the time—please do not let him be angry at me!"

The pervasive sweetness in her mouth turned sour as she looked at the frightened girl before her. Had he beaten his slave almost to death?

"I am sorry, Selenge. I don't want you to be in trouble with him, as well. He is quite…" She had been so delicate when discussing him with Mistress Luo. He was her husband, the person to whom she owed her loyalty next only to her father, but Selenge had to know. "He is a madman."

"I'm sorry," Selenge whispered, staring at the sugared plums in her hand.

"May I at least keep the box? Surely there is no harm in it?" She held out her hand, and, after a moment, the servant placed the box on her palm. "Let us do our best together not to anger him."

Selenge deposited the sugared plums into the little stove, sending up a brief burst of sweetness followed by the odor of burnt sugar.

Replacing the lid on the box, Bao Xing slid it under her writing desk and asked, "Will you help me to learn your language? This is my husband's wish, that I should learn to talk with him."

"Yes, of course, lady." Selenge brightened right away, and came to sit by her as she ate her breakfast. Together, they spoke slowly and carefully about anything they could find common words for, then Selenge set about tidying up.

"How is it you speak two languages so well?"

"Only my father is Mongolian, lady, my mother was of the Mandarin quarter." Selenge wiped her fingers quickly. "If you do not have need of me, I shall go to the market."

"Thank you—I have my books." Bao Xing patted the rather diminished pile and watched as the girl made ready and departed, then she pulled out the bamboo box and slid open the lid, releasing again the scent of sugared plums. She held it up to her face and breathed deeply. What to do with it? She must make sure her husband never noticed it. Opening the drawer in her writing desk, Bao Xing removed the soft bundle of the amulet she had been given—she never had learned by whom, but Guowei had been in the ger last night. Might it have come from him? The box was just the right size for such a thing, and putting something inside would make the box itself seem ordinary. She plucked out the square of paper at the bottom, coated on one side with something smooth, but still a bit sticky from the plums, and placed the amulet bundle inside, then hesitated.

On the sticky side, the paper held the single word "sweet." But there was writing on the back as well, a poem.

"At falcon's flight, the lark stops singing
hidden in the bush until shadows pass
together, larks sing all the sweeter—
when the shadow is gone."

A poem about birds—or not. The Mongols loved their falcons almost as much as their horses. She held the poem close, feeling insecure just in holding it, a poem of secret songs, hidden beneath a forbidden gift. Guowei reached out to her across the distance, but to what end? He could not think to seduce her—not after all that had happened, though the idea warmed her belly. Larks hidden in the bush, waiting to sing together, hiding from the falcon's shadow. She thought of Ming Lun, riding with her in the sedan chair and saying that they must be stopped. Ming Lun, who ran a dance troupe called the School of the Soaring Lark. Perhaps Ming Lun was not the only rebel she knew. Chilled, Bao Xing pulled her robe snugly over her feet. She replaced the poem under the pouch and slipped the box into her desk drawer, slapping it shut.

Thoughts of Ming Lun recalled Kaifeng in ruins, its women raped, its men slaughtered. She had come to the khan to distract his soldiers from her father, but all of the Han people were, like her, imprisoned by the Mongols. What if she could be a rebel? What if she waited, with the other larks, but not idle—she might use her position as Yusen's wife and Chubei's friend to steal their confidences and aid the Emperor in reclaiming the North. He would not intervene directly, Ming Lun had said, but surely he still cared. A vast image unfurled in her mind, like a map of the stars, with the falcon of Mongolia soaring over, its darkness blotting the glow of the imperial asterisms. How many larks might it take to overcome such a darkness and restore the empire to greatness?

She took up her pen, quickly made a little ink and found a scrap of paper. She wrote, "*A lark sings alone among falcons, she listens, hoping to join her voice to another.*" She folded the note and hurried to the door, running her hand along the top of the chests or the wall for balance. She stuck her head outside the curtain. After a moment, a pair of servants came by—"Ai! Will you help me?" They trotted over to her, two boys, bowing and waiting. "I am unwell today, unable to come out. I found this in a book from the archives. Would you return it to Minister Guowei? Thank you." She pressed her note into the hand of one of the boys, and the pair moved off together.

Letting the curtain fall, Bao Xing pressed her back to the wall and tried to master her breathing. She had not been so excited since her first star-fall, when she and her father lay on the rooftop, gazing and counting. One hundred and twenty-three stars flamed that night—she had never seen anything so beautiful.

CHAPTER THIRTY-NINE

As they walked, Zhencai stripped a bush of its berries, the tart little gems bursting between his teeth to reveal bitter seeds which he spat out. They followed a narrow track which curved around the base of a hill and joined a road. Zhencai stopped so quickly that Andao stumbled past, and swung about to look at him like a muddled ox. Zhencai held a finger to his lips, and Andao closed his mouth, listening.

A jingle of horses came from the east. Andao scrambled back and both of them pressed behind the boulder, peering through the brushy gap between stones as a trio of Mongols rode east along the road followed by a wagon driven by Chinese and trailed by a few more Mongols. The wagonload gave off the acrid odor of smelting and Zhencai covered his nose until it was long past.

"Will there be more?" Andao leaned out, looking and listening this time.

"This leads to the Crimson Shrines—there are always more soldiers." He hoped that Dragon Turns Monastery still stood. Its location should conceal it, but he had believed the same of the slender trail that lead to his own little monastery until the Mongols came there, too. "Unlikely they will send another wagon so soon. We will follow the road until we cross the ravine."

Zhencai set off quickly, the smooth footing easing his dizzy mind. The road rose steadily upward, circling the edge of a steep fall, crossing through meadows turning gold with late summertime. Wooly goats hopped up the slopes, and Zhencai imagined joining them, moving so gracefully between the heavens and the earth. The sound of trickling water led them onward, and they rounded a bend to find a moss-covered niche where a spring emerged. Beneath the waterfall, a Buddha sat with a smile upon his green-stained lips, gazing as if he saw the truth beyond the water, beyond the travelers. Zhencai bowed deeply, then sat beside the pool. For the first time in days, his qi calmed to the sound of the water, and he centered its warmth in his belly.

Andao drank noisily from the stream's fall, then wiped his mouth on his sleeve and crouched down. "Master?"

"Here is sand." Zhencai indicated where centuries of stone had worn down to a gleaming sweep of tiny particles.

"No, please no." Andao's shoulders slumped, his hands suddenly hiding.

"A few moments, then we continue. Iron hands." Zhencai clapped his own hands together, crediting the smiling Buddha that he did not show the pain.

"Iron hands." Andao sighed and knelt by the sandy verge, prodding it with his fingers. Then he drew himself up and shut his eyes. As he crouched, Zhencai mentally moved through the steps within himself. He gathered the qi at his core and made it hard, cold, strong, then brought it up with each breath higher until, with a long exhalation, he sent the energy into his fingertips. Hearing the echo of his breath in Andao's voice, Zhencai opened his eyes.

The novice shot forward one hand into the sand, grunting as his fingertips sank in, then jerking his arm back to repeat with the other hand. His shoulders rocked, his qi failing to support him. Zhencai tapped both of his apprentice's sides with his fingers. Andao sucked in a deep breath before attacking the sand again, this time remembering to turn, to bind his center into the strength of his hands. After a few strikes, he winced each time, but grit his teeth and kept going.

When they began this journey, Zhencai had searched the young man and found only loose limbs, weak muscles, a wild mind. Andao claimed his people could eat bitter, but it appeared this was his only strength. He whined, he cajoled, he tried every method to shirk, but once he began, he pushed through suffering like a woman pushed through childbirth. He had no discipline, no peace, no control, but he had something like a Buddha heart.

Zhencai was about to release him from duty when a heavy blow struck his back, and he sprawled out of his posture. Rolling onto his back, Zhencai got his staff up to defend himself. Andao splashed into the pool and sputtered, "Master, that was—" until he turned and saw the three big men confronting them.

The fact that Zhencai had not heard them coming nearly chilled the fever in his flesh.

They wore rough clothing and held their scarred knuckles in heavy fists. "All your money, all your food, or we'll drown you in the puddle."

"We don't have any food!" Andao floundered in the water.

"Guess it'll have to be money, then." The leader drew a knife from his belt and reached for Zhencai.

With a swing of his staff, Zhencai smacked the man's wrist, planting the end of the staff and heaving himself off the ground, his feet poised to slam into the man behind. Even as he launched, his right hand twitched and lost its grip. He smashed into the bandit, but fell with him. Gray rock, green moss, the black stain of moisture on stone swirled before Zhencai's face.

"Master!"

"Hand it over, boy, or you'll both go down."

"We have nothing—he's a monk." Splashing indicated Andao's movement.

Zhencai righted himself and scrambled to hands and knees. Six men confronted them. He gave a little prayer to the Buddha and blinked rapidly. No, three men—only three. He was sicker than he thought. Fumbling for his staff, Zhencai gripped an end of the wood only to have it yanked away from him. A blow stung across his back, but he rolled away before another fell. The scroll shifted in his tunic and he gripped it tight.

"There—the old man's got it." The leader advanced, still gripping his knife, and one of his companions now held the staff.

"It is a terrible time indeed if a monk may be beaten on the road. Had I any money, I would give it to you in hopes you might find peace in that." Zhencai climbed slowly to his feet, Andao sliding a hand under his elbow.

The leader growled, "Mongols stole everything from us—but they like you monks. Maybe 'cause you stole from us before them. Where'd all those golden Buddhas come from?"

Zhencai started to shift into a stable pose for their attack, but Andao tugged him back.

"Master," he whispered. "Here."

They retreated three steps, splashing across the stream, Zhencai stumbling as he resisted. "There is no need—"

"Master." Andao kept his lips at Zhencai's ear. "Wait until they cross the stream, then strike the stone." He slid his toe along an uneven stone that showed through the mud.

"I am not so old as to—"

"Please!"

Then the three men pushed across the stream. For a moment, again, Zhencai saw six. He summoned all the strength in his body and gave an enormous shout that made them hesitate as he leapt up and struck the stone his apprentice indicated, landing in a position of attack—just in case.

For a second nothing happened save a slight shiver under his foot, then the rock tipped downward, cracking the side of the pool. A tide of sand and water rushed the bandits. The one at the back tumbled onto his rump and clawed himself away while the other two slithered, screaming, over the ledge and crashed along the rocky slope below.

Straightening, Zhencai made the sign of blessing toward the fallen men. The survivor, across the stream, stared at him with enormous eyes, then threw himself down face first and clasped his hands out in pleading.

Zhencai turned, swaying, to find his apprentice watching him with eyes just as wide, but nothing of awe in his expression.

"You're sick. How much further?"

"Until the dragon turns." Zhencai waved his hand ahead of them. "Why there? Why ask me to strike there?"

"Because it was the right place. When does the dragon turn?"

"When it is the right place." Zhencai searching for the spark of Andao's qi, finding only fragments like the sparkle of a cat stroked on a warm day.

Andao's golden-brown gaze slipped away. "I don't want you to die."

"That conversation is passed." Zhencai waved it away. "I cannot tell you more than to look for the dragon." He thought to say more; instead, he closed his mouth and inclined his head, indicating Andao should take the lead. If he were wrong, he might die on this decision, but he had no further doubt: his apprentice drew the qi of the earth, and not of the spirit at all. No amount of training could make Andao a monk if he were born a geomancer.

CHAPTER FORTY

The third night after leaving his apartment, Yusen found the chance he had watched for. On a proper scouting mission, he would have taken more than three days, but for this, he dare not. He hated leaving Bao Xing alone for so long, even with a Mongolian servant. Dressed in servants' clothes, his hair bound up into a knot as if he were a Chin boy who longed to be a soldier, Yusen had moved among the servants for the last few days. His own clothes and boots remained hidden, his knives still carried close. Tonight, he helped to carry an especially grand feast into the Mandarin's hall as they celebrated the betrothal of one of their number. After bringing the first course, hearing Guowei's voice in the hall, Yusen slipped away from the others and hurried toward the Minister's private chambers. He climbed a shelf in the long corridor and out a narrow window into the courtyard rather than use a public doorway, hesitating on the ledge in case anyone was lighting incense or strolling the walkways.

Guowei's room shared a wall with the courtyard—a wall with a broad window, blocked by a pair of pierced shutters. When he helped to clear the tea things from the Minister's front room, Yusen found no sign of the cane, nor anything else of interest, but he had swept the space only with his eyes, and only as far as the locked wooden door opposite. Now, he would have time for a longer search—inside that locked room. Yusen dropped lightly inside the courtyard and crept to Guowei's window, pausing to extinguish the central lantern, leaving those by the shrine lit against the darkness. The columns of the shrine shielded their light, allowing only slender shafts to break free. In the gloom, Yusen listened. Guowei's two young assistants also moved like warriors, but Yusen heard no sign of anyone inside. Locking his fingers as high as he could through the holes in the grate, Yusen braced his feet against the wall and climbed up.

Hanging on with one hand, he slipped a blade between the shutters and moved it slowly up until it encountered resistance, then pushed until he heard a latch swing free. He continued drawing up the blade, finding another latch, before he could pry the window open just a bit. His arm ached, but he dare not swing himself inside, not yet. Faint light shone under the wooden door at the far side of the room. To his right, a shadowy bulk loomed—likely a bed. Directly below the window stood a chest, as if the man was begging for intruders. Satisfied he was alone, Yusen crept the rest of the way up and settled on the windowsill, letting his eyes adjust. A long desk filled the wall to his left, with a chair pushed back from it, and a pile of papers held down by a patch that was likely a book, and a long shaft that stood out dark against the whiteness of the pages. The cane.

Yusen glanced down again. The top surface of the chest below him looked uneven, and it might groan or squeak if he stepped on it. Instead, he crept to the left most edge of the windowsill and stuck his foot down as far as he could, to the top of the desk itself where it rested on a tall stack of drawers. He transitioned his weight there, then jumped lightly to the floor. Pausing again, listening, then he stalked over to the cane and ran his hands along it. Indeed, it was Bao Xing's. He took it up, then squinted at the book and opened the page. This was the one he had taken for his wife, the one she had been most excited about to judge by how she held it to her breast. Someone had taken it from their rooms. His anger stirred, and Yusen tamped it down. He must be methodical; anger had no place in this, not tonight. He debated for a moment, then took the book as well. When the cane was found missing, his own culpability would be clear in any case, but a relative of the khan's, even one as little esteemed as himself, could hardly be accused of stealing what belonged to his wife, or what belonged to the khan's own library.

About to depart, Yusen traced the other shapes on the desk, searching for anything he might have missed—then he transferred book and cane under his left arm, and lifted the topmost sheet of paper. He carried this to the floor in front of the door, where that thin stream of light flowed beneath. Not writing, but a drawing made of wavy, almost childish lines, meant to outline a straight tower. The circles inside of it showed a bit more skill, as if the artist had been unused to drawing with a brush. He pushed it closer to the edge and his throat clenched. He recognized that style: his own drakemaster, used to whatever techniques they employed in his own country, had trouble adjusting to the brush. A few drops of darkness stood out more deeply than the rest—not ink blots, but drops of blood, fallen as the wounded and beaten slave sketched the image he had seen. This was the plan of the weapon the drakemaster had learned about, and which he had offered to draw for the khan, the image that Guowei, reporting before the khan himself, swore did not exist. An oath that sent the slave to the mercury mines to die. Guowei was more than a liar, he was a traitor to the khan—and Yusen held the proof!

The light beneath the door flickered, a curtain sliding against a wall somewhere beyond. Sliding the drawing up, Yusen gripped it in his hand, afraid to crinkle the page and reveal himself. He retreated slowly across the room as a pair of voices entered with footsteps in the outer chamber, the two young assistants. Matching their own footfalls, Yusen backed to the outside wall, his hands full. Impossible to climb out as he had come in—he'd have to risk using the rickety chest. Still, he placed his foot as near the edge as possible, counting on the side wall to support him, balancing with his fist braced, the paper gripped tight, as he brought up the other foot and stood. Slivers of weak wood prodded his feet, and Yusen inched forward, then one of the slats gave way, sliding him sideways with a crash. The lid broke beneath him, plunging his foot into an unseen globe that shattered with the sound of pottery. Shards of wood scored along his leg. Only his low weight kept the entire surface of the chest from collapsing and sucking him in.

"Ai!" Outside the door, the footsteps ran, the lock rattled.

Yusen shoved against the broken wood, clamping his jaw against the pain as he tried to wrench himself free. Inviting burglars with a chest beneath the window? No—trapping them.

The door slammed open and two men thundered through it, swords in hand.

"Stop, thief!" One of them shouted, but the other plunged directly toward him, bent on death, not apprehension.

Yusen twisted against his trapped leg, grinding the wood deeper, and thrust forward the book he still held. The sword rammed through the pages, pushing his arm back, the sword point hovering at the level of his face.

Grabbing the cane in his right hand, page crumpled against it, Yusen yanked the book aside, opening the man's guard, and shoved the cane at his throat.

Something crunched beneath his blow, and the man staggered back, choking.

Yusen hooked the sword hilt as the man stumbled, tugging the sword from his attacker's hand. Dropping the book, he pulled free the sword, barely in time to parry the other man's blow. Now on one knee, Yusen levered his injured leg out of the chest, his back against the wall, sword up. If he tried to stand, he'd break through the lid all over again. He braced his feet at the edges of the wood for another clash of swords.

The man's blade swung for Yusen's foot, and Yusen shot out the length of his arm, plunging the sword into his attacker's sword-arm. Howling, the man ripped free.

The first man loomed up from the right, but unarmed. Yusen scrambled back, his feet breaking wood again. He hooked the cane up behind him, over the edge of the window and pulled hard to free his feet from the chest.

The second assailant thrust from the left, and Yusen defended himself, then the man's off-hand grabbed his wrist. The first man, still hacking harsh breaths, grappled with Yusen's hand on the cane. Paper tore.

Kicking the man who had trapped his arm, Yusen pulled free, but lost his sword. He grabbed the cane with both hands, pushing his feet desperately up the wall and falling down on the outside with a crack of branches and a puff of cedar. Flailing back to his feet, Yusen limped, for the farthest door and shot through it. He stumbled inside, blood slicking his left foot as he sprinted into the royal area. "My lord khan! My lord khan—traitors!" He staggered and nearly collided with one of the guards, a broad-chested Mongolian who pushed him back to arm's length.

"The khan—I've got to see him—I have proof." He waved the cane, then hesitated. Only a ripped corner remained from the sketch torn from his hand, and it held only a few dashes of ink and a spot of blood, just as likely his own.

"What is all of this shouting?" Wearing the furred hat of his office, one of the captains stared down from the khan's door.

Yusen fought for breath, then straightened, forcing himself to stand on his wounded leg. "Captain. I must see the khan. His Mandarins—his Minister of Archives has betrayed him. He's keeping secrets, about the weapon we spoke of."

"Well, it is clear you have been fighting. Possibly with a thorn bush."

The guards chuckled, but the captain waved them to silence, calling over his shoulder, "General! Your man wants to see the khan."

Women's voices whispered behind him, and Yusen glanced back. His wife stood there, just at the corner, letting it support her as she squinted at the scene. Selenge stood beside her, and a few others roused by the shouting, some carrying chopsticks from their interrupted meal.

Yusen beckoned Selenge forward and held out the cane. "For my wife."

She took it from him in cautious hands, giving a slight bow, then retreated toward Bao Xing who accepted the cane and gripped it, her knuckles pale with the strength she spent. Her eye gave that little twitch. Anger. How could Yusen, who knew that emotion so well, have missed it?

"The khan is at table," drawled Munkjar, coming to the door, then he spread his hands, "but perhaps he shall want to see this."

"He must, general." Yusen offered the shred of paper, then drew it back as the khan himself came to the door, patting his mustache with a cloth.

"What must I see, scout? What a mess you have made of yourself? And why are you traipsing about in servant's clothes?"

Yusen bowed, drawing a shaft of pain up the back of his leg. It supported him, but the wounds must be tended, and soon. "My lord khan. Three days ago, the Minister of Archives, one Guowei, contrived to steal my wife's cane—an heirloom of her family. Tonight, I went to his chambers to take it back. I found there the drawing he said did not exist, the drawing my slave—your drakemaster—made of the Chinese weapon. He concealed it from you because he is in league with the southern emperor to try to defeat us. My lord, he is a liar and a traitor."

"That's a very interesting story. What do you think, Munkjar, shall we investigate, or shall we finish our supper?"

"No!" Yusen took a step forward. "My lord, he and his men will be hiding or destroying the evidence—it has to be now!"

"Ah, my lord khan." Guowei breezed around the corner and dipped a graceful bow. "I hoped you would forgive my interrupting your meal, but I find it has already been disrupted." The Minister cocked an eyebrow at Yusen. Was he admiring the seeping wounds that gouged Yusen's leg?

"My scout, and kinsman, insists I must go to your apartment, Minister, to see some evidence he claims to have found."

The Minister gave a single, sharp laugh and his hands slid free of his sleeves. "My lord, this is why I came. I must insist that you see the evidence. Your... scout... has broken into my private chamber and destroyed a valuable and ancient collection of pottery I have been cataloging for you, my lord. If you are willing." He bowed again. "Of course, it need not be now, if you would prefer to finish your meal before you attend...?"

"On the contrary, my curiosity grows." The khan walked slowly forward, his gaze dropping to Yusen. "Show me what you have found."

Yusen's shoulders heaved with every breath, his leg twitched with pain, and his heart ached with despair. The Minister had already hidden or destroyed the evidence, letting Yusen set the scene for the greatest humiliation of his life. Clutching the useless scrap, Yusen limped toward his doom.

CHAPTER FORTY-ONE

At a loss for what else to do, Bao Xing followed the little crowd down the corridor and around the corners that would take them past the public areas of the Mandarins and into their private quarters. Spots of blood marked Yusen's passage before her, but his figure was hidden by the bulk of the other men. What under heaven had he done? He had retrieved her cane, but not through the polite means of asking for it. Instead, he vanished for days, disguised as a servant, and burglarized the Minister's bedchamber. The cane felt heavy and awkward in her hand, as if it had taken part in a sordid act, rather than being the victim of one. The handle felt a little slick, and Bao Xing's nose wrinkled. More blood.

Such a crowd certainly wouldn't fit into the Minister's rooms, so most of the guards and the gossips waited outside as Guowei bowed the khan in, followed by General Munkjar, and the pitiable figure of Yusen himself.

"Oh, my goodness, I never imagined." Chubei squeezed Bao Xing's shoulder. "How terribly embarrassing. I am so sorry. I tried to tell Möngke this would end badly, that he should not select a husband for you as a joke, but he would have his fun." She glowered.

"Lady? Will you bring the cane?" A Mongol leaned out the door, and Bao Xing passed the round doorway into Guowei's domain. She trembled a little, thinking of falcons, larks, the poems she and the Minister had been exchanging so furtively since Yusen's disappearance. Nevertheless, she caught a breath of delight at entering Guowei's home. Hanging lanterns lit a space full of comfortable furnishings—old and finely made—with rugs of delicate pattern on the floor. The scroll paintings showed mountains, ancient, twisted trees, small birds soaring freely through gardens of butterflies. No books, but perhaps he had enough of them in the archives. A wall-shelf held a few lovely porcelains and a jade figure of a dragon. Not a falcon in sight, save those the minister invited here to view the ruin her husband had caused.

In the inner chamber, she saw the books—torn to pieces and tossed about the floor and furniture. She stopped short. The Mongols stood among this devastation, Munkjar squatting to turn one fragment after another. "I see many notes here about pottery, but nothing of weaponry, my lord khan."

Beneath the open window stood a chest with its top stove in, and blood spattered on the shards of pottery revealed within, as if Yusen had jumped up and down on the chest until it broke and destroyed the contents.

"May we see the cane, lady?" The captain held out his hand.

"Here, why not be seated, lady? The events of this evening must be most distressing to you." Guowei bowed her toward the embroidered red cushion of a tall wooden chair, perhaps the very one he sat in to write to her. His hands steadied the chair as she sat down and gave up her cane to the captain.

"This is what you came for?"

Yusen spared a glance. "My wife needs it, even if it weren't an heirloom. It's how she walks."

The other Mongols looked it over and the khan shrugged. The captain handed back the cane.

"I found it on the desk, holding down some papers. When I looked more closely, I found that the papers were drawings in ink, of the kind the drakemaster used to make." Yusen waved a hand toward the desk, but whatever fury had possessed him had fled, leaving him even smaller than usual.

"Then why did you destroy them—and all of this?"

"I did not. I took the cane, and one page of the drakemaster's work to show you, but the minister's guards tore it from me when I tried to escape. They came at me with swords, my lord, with no chance to explain. Why else should they attack me if not to protect their secrets?" His voice sounded shrill, his little hands clutched into fists.

Bao Xing looked away to the torn shreds of Guowei's work, then leaned a little closer. The calligraphy on most of the pieces was unfamiliar, not his, certainly. Perhaps that of an assistant or of a work he was studying. Among the fragments, she saw two halves of a book with a fat hole through the middle of it. The journal of Chang Mailou. At least it was not badly damaged, not like the others. In fact, the silken binding cords must have been cut because the pages were not torn. Why had Yusen taken it with him from the apartment? Or had he?

"My lord, I fear that your scout has gained a mistaken impression that I have improperly spoken to his wife." Guowei moved away from the chair, his hands folded at his back. "I believe his envy led to this destruction. He wishes to stain my reputation. We had an encounter three days ago, when I tripped and caused his wife's cane to be damaged—that's why I came to have it. I planned to have a servant return it to her tomorrow. I have no wish to disrupt another man's marriage."

Bao Xing bent her head over the cane in her lap. She rather wished he did want to disturb the marriage. Every time he spoke, it sent shivers up her spine. She ran her fingers along the cane, tracing the smooth arc of its handle and the careful carving of the mountain scene that wrapped the center, down to the ebony shaft and the small brass cap that completed it. Frowning, Bao Xing traced it again. Smooth, perfectly carved. Her chest constricted. Her cane had never been broken. She had known this wood, this work, since she was six years old. It had been her daily companion, her only reminder of her family since she left her father in the mountains.

She pictured the shard of wood Guowei displayed that night in the courtyard, as if the handle had broken, but the handle was whole and the grain without blemish, patch or glue. She had never met him on purpose, but had he been meeting with her? Why? To make her husband look like more of a barbarian than he already was? Or to lure her into his rebellion against the khan? At which, she must admit, he had been succeeding.

Anger and fear warred within her heart. The night her cane was broken, or at least, Guowei claimed it was, she had been so focused on Yusen's rough treatment and her own hurt that she never considered what he'd been trying to say. Yusen was right—Guowei was a traitor and a liar. But he schemed in service to the emperor, the true Son of Heaven. If Guowei and the other larks succeeded, the Mongols would be gone, pushed from China so the Han people, her people, could be free.

"Yusen." The khan folded his arms over his chest and sighed at the forlorn dwarf before him. Yusen's topknot swept the hair back from his face, revealing his high cheekbones and strong, bleak gaze.

"What am I to do with you, my little kinsman? You have broken into the private room of my archivist, destroyed his work and his property, not to mention my own, and continue to vex me about this phantom weapon your slave claimed he saw. You disturbed us at our meal with your howling in the halls—you disgrace us at every turn. I rewarded you with a fine wife, and you think nothing of dragging her into your pettiness."

The phantom weapon. It was no phantom, or at least, it hadn't been in Chang's time. It had been real, they built it in a mountainside somewhere to the west. Bao Xing gripped the cane as if her life depended on it. Guowei lied about the cane—what if it had not been his only lie? What if his people, the larks, knew about the weapon because they intended to use it and that was why he wanted to gather all he could of the history of Kaifeng and its astronomers, including the cane her astronomer-grandfathers left behind? If Guowei had read Chang, he must know the device would kill everyone, not only the Mongols, but every monk and farmer and citizen in the path of its light. At least the rebels of Kaifeng chose their battle—they chose to fight and die in their defiance—they were not scorched by a heaven-sent fire of the stars. This rebellion with which he tempted her could lead to devastation. There must be a better way. Bao Xing had pictured herself as a spot on the vast canvas of an epic war, but she had no such strength or cunning. She had not the spirit to put a hundred thousand souls to death—even Mongol souls must have some dignity.

"Oh, my lord!" Chubei entered on a sing-song call. "If the marriage has not been consummated, you may take back the gift you have given to one who proves so very unworthy."

"An excellent suggestion, and a fitting punishment." The khan flashed a sharp grin.

Yusen flinched, his eyebrows wrinkled as if he held back tears. Blood caked his wounded leg, and he gripped one wrist behind him with the opposite hand, in whole so miserable a picture that Bao Xing looked away.

"But not enough," the khan declared. "I will honor my great ancestor's law and I will not execute him, not merely for a mad act of jealous rage, but neither will I suffer him in my presence any longer. So. I reclaim the treasure I bestowed upon you, little kinsman, and I banish you to the forest of Siberia, there to turn your skills to hunting martens. You shall serve your duty to your khan among the weasels, and other such small and stinking things."

He, too, spoke as if Yusen were a dog—or worse, and Yusen allowed every word. He had named himself a stupid, ugly, ignorant dwarf. Yet he alone had seen through Guowei's lies and done his best to show her, and now the khan. Neither stupid, nor ignorant: anyone who could memorize a page of calligraphy and return from a day's jaunt with an armload of exactly the right books could not be termed ignorant. He had risked all he was and all he had to get back her cane, clinging as if it were precious rather than keep the evidence he needed to prove himself. Foolish indeed. He risked all, and lost all—herself included—and kept her cane in spite of everything. With his hair swept back, his shoulders squared, his skin burnished by deep emotion, he was not even ugly. Not a dog, a man, one so often wounded that even he could no longer trust his own worth.

Bao Xing placed her cane deliberately on the ground, pinning a page of Guowei's supposed research. She took a step forward, parting the captain and Guowei. In her imperfect Mongolian, she said, "If I may speak, my lord khan?"

The khan gestured for her to continue.

"My husband speaks the truth. My cane is not broken, nor can I see where it has been, my lord khan." She held it out for his inspection.

Guowei narrowed his eyes. "I, too, was impressed by the skill of the craftsman who repaired it, my lady, my lord khan. The break was clean, just at the edge of the decoration." He pointed to the smooth join between cinnabar and wood, their fingers nearly touching.

What was she doing? The khan was dissolving her marriage, he might place her in the arms of the man she wanted, and the rebellion of which that man was a part. A rebellion that would use a weapon so powerful it could ruin the North she sought to save.

"The weapon the slave spoke of, the plans my husband saw, they are spoken of in these ancient books of my people, my lord khan. The weapon is true."

The khan's heavy gaze fell upon her. "And yet I hear this from whom? From a scout, desperate to save his skin, to redeem his reputation, and now from his wife? Minister, what do you know of this weapon?" He beckoned to Guowei.

Guowei cocked his head, his face hard, then he frowned. "I do recall words of great weapons in the past." He tapped his chin, then glanced around, and picked up the book of Chang Mailou, turning a few pages, then brightened. "Indeed, my lord khan. There is a tale in this volume about such plans—a tale of drunken astronomers who think they can live forever." He snorted. "Only a woman with little else to occupy her could give credence to such a tale." His glance fell upon Bao Xing, pitying.

"Her husband's madness seems infectious. When the dwarf is gone, she may return to the proper things of women," the khan declared.

Not after trying to betray the khan's Minister of Archives: Yusen's madness was infectious indeed, for she began to see the danger if all that he said were true. She had flirted with rebellion, and now rejected it. How many Mandarins loyally served the khan in exchange for luxury? How many were like Guowei, patiently scheming? How would she ever know whom to trust? No, there could be no life for her here, never again.

Bao Xing set the tip of her cane on the ground. "I thank you for your kindness, my lord khan, but marriage not so easily broken." Carefully, she knelt at Yusen's side. "Where my husband goes, I go also."

Chubei hunched beside her and spoke in a whisper. "You don't have to do this! Even if he has—" she wrinkled her nose— "taken you, surely no child could result—just look at him. You've shown your duty, but there's no need for you to suffer any more."

"Nor for my husband to suffer exile alone." Rough and crude he might be, but honorable and true. Bao Xing faced the queen. "My queen, my friend, I am resolved."

"Everyone will believe that you and he have—" she recoiled. "Have you?"

She had not even seen her husband's bare skin beyond his face, his hands, and now his feet. Everyone would think it. Bao Xing had no idea what to reply.

"Well, it seems we are done here. Let us trouble the good Minister no longer," said Munkjar, then he aimed a flick of his hand to the back of Yusen's head, the sort of blow meant to chastise a child. "On your way. You'll start north in the morning."

Yusen ignored him, bowing briefly in the direction of the khan. "My lord khan." He executed a pivot away and caught Bao Xing watching him. His face glowed, that curious mix of faint scars of age overlaying the features of a boy. No, not ugly at all—not when he was gazing at her with such rapture she felt her heart might break. For the first time, she saw him, not a hated Mongol or an unwanted husband, but a man. A man who would sacrifice anything, or everything, for her. "My lady wife."

She bowed her head, and rose, bowing again almost over him. "My lord khan."

"I am sorry to see such a treasure depart my court, especially for such little cause."

But the hint of mirth that entered his voice made her not even a little sorry. It was a court of cruelty, and she wanted no more of it.

She followed Yusen out, down the Mandarin's corridor, past the silent soldiers, servants, women, Mandarins. Whispering rose behind them, and she straightened her spine and walked on, careful and proud, using the graceful stride Mistress Luo had taught her. The crowd thinned, a few servants scurrying on ahead as if suddenly recalling the errands they had forgotten. Then Bao Xing and Yusen's steps echoed alone in the hall, hers accompanied by the tap of her cane, his halting, accompanied by the hiss of his breath every time he set down his left foot.

At a minor turning, he told her, "Wait here a moment," and took the narrow corridor, stopping at a huge urn. He fished out a bundle of clothing topped by his small felt boots and limped back. "My wife—" he clutched the clothes against his chest as if to hide the struggle of his breathing. "I know not how to be thankful for this."

Placing both hands atop her cane, Bao Xing sank down to kneel before him. "Help me stop them."

"Stop—the Mandarins?" He cocked his head, studying her.

She nodded. "Guowei, if he wants to use that weapon. It will not only be your people who die, it will be all of ours. Thousands of people. Worse than Kaifeng."

"Kaifeng was a city of rebels," he answered automatically.

"And this is a city of barbarians. It does not mean they all deserve to die."

He accepted that with a slight nod. "We cannot stop them from Siberia."

"We can decide in the morning where—"

Yusen shook his head sharply. "No—we have to leave now, tonight, as soon as possible. At least I must."

"But the khan said—"

"They'll kill me. Guowei cannot simply let me escape, nor you either, not now." He started down the hall and she rose up to follow

They reached their apartments, and Yusen put out his arm to hold her back. A sloshing sound flowed faintly from the chamber. Yusen relaxed and stepped through the curtain, holding it out of the way for Bao Xing.

At the stove, Selenge stood, stirring tea—scooping ladles up and letting it pour back into the pot. She turned as they entered, then dropped to her knees, bowing very low. "Sir and madam. I thought you might like tea."

Yusen nodded, then he moved to his chest, fumbled with the lock and retrieved a few things. He limped into the bed chamber.

Selenge and Bao Xing exchanged a glance as Bao Xing settled by her side of the table. "It was kind of you to think of him."

The girl nodded, then resumed her stirring. "I have plain tea as well for you, madam."

Leaving tonight, immediately. Bao Xing pulled a few things from her writing desk, making up a bundle of brushes, inkstone, ink brick and some small sheets of paper. She found an embroidery kit as well. It might serve to keep her occupied if she had nothing to read. Tucking these things into a sleeve, she considered what else to bring.

Yusen emerged from the other chamber, clad once again in Mongolian gear, but his left foot still bare, wrapped with the end of a bandage. The high boot would chafe his injuries. He dropped the other boot by his place at the table and walked toward the stove. "Thank you, Selenge." She filled a bowl and handed it over.

"I may have something that shows his guilt," Bao Xing said, and Yusen hesitated, the bowl at his lips. Bao Xing pulled out the box where she had been keeping Guowei's poems and opened it, but found nothing inside save the amulet. His notes were gone. Only one other person knew she had received even a single note, or would recognize the box if she came across it.

Yusen tipped up the bowl and Bao Xing shouted, "Yusen!" Her hands stretching toward him. He jerked and the bowl spilled over his hands.

"Do not think that because—"

"Please, my husband," she said, smiling, "come and bring our tea to the table. No need for you to stand."

He took a delicate teacup for her and limped over to the table, sinking down to his cushion with the softest groan of weariness, then placing the cup before her. She leaned across, pushing the box before her and speaking very quietly, "Some of my things are gone. Only Selenge knew of them."

His glance dropped to the box, to the cloth still inside of it. "The amulet?"

"No, some..." she blinked at him, then removed the amulet in its wrapping. "This was from you?"

The slightest incline of his head, then he broke his gaze and called over his shoulder, "Selenge, join us. Bring your own tea. We must talk."

"Thank you, sir, but I—"

He planted one hand on the table and pushed himself up with a wince. "Did you think I was asking? Come. Or will you drink my tea?"

"No, sir, I will make—"

"Why, is something wrong with my tea?" He lifted the bowl as she stared, then her eyes flicked to the curtained door. Yusen's head tipped a little as if listening, then he flung the bowl at Selenge and dove across the opening toward his weapons.

Selenge shrieked and lunged toward the door, but Yusen kicked out at her, dropping her to the floor as he came up with sword in hand.

For a moment, Bao Xing, still reeling from the revelation of Yusen's gift, stayed as she was, then she dropped the chain about her neck and grabbed her cane.

"Who do you work for? Who is coming?" Yusen demanded, dragging Selenge off the floor, his blade to her throat.

"No one!" she bleated. "Please, sir, I don't know what you mean!" She struggled but he held her to his chest, and placed the point of the sword at her cheek.

"No one will marry a girl who dribbles her tea from the side of her face." He pressed the point a little harder.

"Please, no, sir, I'll—"

A knife flew through the curtain. The blade plunged through her chest into his, knocking them both to the floor in a spatter of blood.

CHAPTER FORTY-TWO

The shrieking girl thrashed on top of him as pain shot through his chest and shoulder. Yusen peeled Selenge off of him, rolling her to the side, the dagger's point jutting from her back, a stream of blood staining his del above his heart. He lay her on her side, pinning her by her shoulders as she wailed, her hands clawing for the dagger. "Leave it—if you pull it, you'll die."

He blinked down at the dagger's narrow grip and recognized it as one of his own.

Yusen dragged down a breath and scrambled further from the doorway. He pressed a hand to his chest, feeling the sharp wound between breast and shoulder, but his heart still beat; his chest seared with every breath, but still he breathed. Bao Xing half-rose on the other side of the room, clutching the amulet with one hand. If he died right then, this had been a thing worth living for, the grip of her warm hand on the gift he had given. But he was not dead yet.

Selenge's agonized keening fell to a broken sobbing. Pushing himself back to the wall, Yusen strained to hear anything beyond the door. He reclaimed the sword he had lost when he fell. Even as he prepared to go, even as he worried and suspected, it was madness for them to attack now. He had already been humiliated in front of the khan, any respect he had earned stripped away in Guowei's chamber. Attacking him would bolster his claims. Then he saw his own dagger. Madness indeed: it would look as if he had gone mad and killed her.

Across the doorway, her gaze fixed to the suffering girl, Bao Xing knelt. Would they kill her, too and blame him for her death? But what could he do to prevent it?

Casting about him, Yusen found the spare bow he had brought inside to oil and a few arrows. He counted on Selenge's cries to cover his own noise as well as that of his assailants as he climbed up onto the storage drawers. The dagger had been thrown from straight-on, but the wielder wouldn't have stayed there. Which side did he choose? If he, too, acted as a scout, he would know that the right was Yusen's area, and set up diagonally opposite, near the scroll painting, expecting Yusen to go for his weapons. That is, if the attacker planned to use another throwing blade.

Bao Xing suddenly stood up with her cane and ran for the door, calling, "Don't kill me!" first in Mongolian, then in Chinese. "Don't kill me!" Words Yusen had heard in a dozen languages or more.

She flung herself past the curtain, then said, "So many! And he is so small. There are four of you, surely you can just attack him."

She understood nothing: they didn't want a real fight, not if they planned to… Yusen caught his breath. Four of them. Idiot! He was the one who did not understand: she was acting as his scout. He nocked an arrow to the string, listening, and crept as near as he could to the curtain, which still fluttered in the breeze of her passing.

A man's gruff voice answered her in Chinese, from the left, as he had suspected. He heard the words for "down" and "safe," then her cane rapped the floor. Yusen shot through the gap as the curtain waved back and heard a cry of alarm on the other side, then movement, someone cursing. He shot again. A rush of feet toward the door. Someone was coming in.

Yusen shouldered the bow and leapt down at the far end of the chest of drawers, shoving it as hard as he could. With a groan, the chest lurched across the door as the man burst through.

The intruder sprawled over the top, his head still covered by the curtain, sword arm flailing. Yusen dropped to one knee, pulled one of his knives and rammed it into the man's sword hand, pinning him to the wood. The man screamed, his mouth blowing at the curtain, his other hand straining, the whole of his big thrashing body effectively blocking his companions.

The attackers abandoned secrecy, rushing the door, one of them trying to yank the fallen man out of the way in spite of his screams. Yusen's arm barely reached across the chest of drawers, but his sword did, carving into the next one's belly. His assailant's sword skimmed over his head. Yusen thought of Munkjar and smiled. Then he vaulted onto the chest, ripping down the curtain at last.

"He's escaping!" Bao Xing shouted.

Two men remained standing, one with blood streaming down his arm from Yusen's arrow, Bao Xing crouching at his back. Close by, the other man rounded the legs of his thrashing companion. Chin men, all of them.

The nearer one swung his sword. Other soldiers always struggled with fighting Yusen, learning how low to aim and adjusting their balance for such a stance. This one aimed for the throat.

Yusen dropped down and thrust upward, slicing into the man's thigh as he overbalanced, then swinging the sword to hack into his chest from below.

The fourth man grabbed Bao Xing's arm, keeping her at his back, sword outstretched.

Yusen unslung his bow, and the man gave up all attempt to shield her, running down the corridor instead. The arrow thumped home and slammed him against the wall, sliding down in a smear of red.

Bao Xing flinched at the sound, tears sparkling on her cheeks, one hand clutching the cane, the other pressed to her mouth, but not, this time, to hide laughter.

Panting, Yusen met her eyes. "Stay here. You will be safe here."

She shook her head and hurried toward him. "They stabbed her to reach you. That is not—" words failed her, but her face flushed with anger. "If we cannot stop them in Siberia, I cannot stop them here, not alone, not knowing who to trust." Her throat worked as if she were nearly as breathless as he. "But I will slow you."

"That is why you must ride." He turned, leading the way down a side corridor and out of the palace toward the stable yards. The Mongolian quarter had been placed here specifically to grant quick access to the horses. In this case, it got them outside even as the first cry for help roused the halls. Likely, the earlier commotion worked in their favor as those with chambers nearby expected another shouting match, or possible disciplinary action against him. Outside the palace wall, a narrow stair snaked down into the lower yard. Yusen at first bounded down the steps, then paused, looking back up at his wife as she hurried after him. Every time he stopped his leg throbbed and the wound at his chest seemed to burn a little deeper. Movement was better—at least it distracted him.

At a broad patch, Bao Xing joined him, shaky, but strong. Yusen waved her to stillness, peering down into the darkness. A few lanterns lit the path for late messengers, and a few others hung about the stable yard.

Two guards leaned together at a corner, and there would be more, six on a usual night. His Chin enemies would not want to put the Mongols too far on guard by waiting at his horses, but they might well have another plan. Still, he had to take the risk: neither he nor Bao Xing could go far without those horses. They moved on, reaching the gate at the bottom of the stairs where the guards ignored him to stare at his wife and grin stupidly. The low light cast dancing shadows that concealed the blood on his clothes.

"Open the gate. I am exiled to Siberia, and I choose to go now."

That made the guards take notice. "Siberia? Do you have fur robes? You'll need them!"

The second guard chuckled. "A rabbit skin should be enough for him."

"Please, sirs," Bao Xing said, "It is hard already I leave my home, without you make it harder." Tears still shimmered on her cheeks like tiny stars, and the gate swung open, the two men bowing her through, Yusen passing like an afterthought.

"Ride safely, madam! May the Eternal Sky blanket you with sunshine," the thicker man called after.

When they reached the corral, Tsang already stood by, ears pricked at the sound of his voice. He had neither time nor strength for crooning, and simply found his saddles and lugged the first one over. At a tap on her knee, Tsang bowed and allowed him to strap the saddle on her back, then accepted the bridle with equal grace. For a moment, he rested his hand on her warm, solid neck. "Tsang," he told his wife. "She is the leader. She is beautiful, strong, clever, hard-working." Like you, he thought of adding, but did not.

Taking up the second saddle caused a burning strain at his left shoulder, tied to the hole in his chest. Not deep, he reminded himself and carried it over, the bare toes of his left foot digging into the dirt of the yard. At the fence, he gave a whistle, but it was hardly necessary. The rest of his herd emerged out of the darkness at Tsang's interest. He thought hard, then saddled Khukhree, who had an even stride and was hard to startle. He tapped her knee and motioned to Bao Xing. She approached timidly. He slid her cane into the straps meant to carry a spear, then showed her where to place her hands on the saddle for mounting. She shifted and tugged her skirts out of the way, but they still made an awkward bunch at the back of the saddle while revealing a length of leg above the ankle.

"Here. Sit on her—do nothing. She is patient." He lifted the reins into his wife's hands, then reached for her foot; she flinched and drew away from him. "For the stirrup." He took her tiny foot and slipped it into the stirrup, then ducked Khukhree's head and placed her other foot. His wife still watched him strangely as he took up the collars and packs for two other horses.

From the direction of the palace, someone shouted, and Yusen's head shot up. He flung the second pack onto Uul's back and secured it, catching her lead line to lash it quickly to the horse in front, then snatched Khukhree's lead and ran to mount Tsang, giving her a nudge. "Gates!" he shouted, and another guard, distracted by a string of lights descending the slope, came over to unhook the gate.

Yusen glanced back at Bao Xing. "Hold on. Tight." Then he kicked Tsang into motion, and they galloped out of the yard down the dirt track.

Bao Xing gave a little shriek, letting go of the reins to cling to the saddle itself, hunched over. As they approached the western gate of the city, Yusen called out, "Yam Rider! Khan's messages!"

Claiming royal privilege would be another mark against him, but compared with the rest, this would be nothing. The soldiers hurried to pull back the bar and let him pass, gaping as they realized his companion was a woman, and a terrified one at that. He pushed Tsang hard, keeping low over her neck, hanging onto Bao Xing's horse with equal fervor. Behind him, his wife let out the occasional gasp or shriek, but she clung to her mount. After a while, they settled to a steady pace, and he glanced back to find Bao Xing gazing upward, still hunched on the saddle, hanging on as instructed, her gaze drawn toward the starry sky. They passed through the army camps and settlements at the edges of town, and Yusen cut the herd toward the south, toward a narrow farmer's bridge. They slowed, and he let the rope go long, letting Tsang pick her way across the slats high above the water.

Behind him, Bao Xing gave a whimper and buried her head. Khukhree snorted and tossed her mane, her hooves clattering. Across the bridge, they turned again among the farms, and Yusen brought Bao Xing alongside him. She remained huddled until he told her, "We've crossed. No more bridges for a long time."

Trembling, she pushed herself back up to sitting and swept the hair back from her face. "Yes. This is…" she frowned, then touched her leg. "Hurts."

Yusen nodded. For someone who had never ridden, it likely would. Now that they had put some distance between them and the city, his left hand cramped around the rope, his left shoulder feeling rigid—if he let his arm swing, the pain flared between shoulder and chest so sharply he could barely breathe, and he rode without his left foot in the stirrup, mindful of the cuts that lacerated his heel and calf. "We cannot stop, not yet."

She bowed her head, but didn't argue.

They rode on into the night. Yusen led the horses down streams and through fields of cattle to disguise their path, until Bao Xing's little noises became soft whimpers of pain, and he started to look for a place to hide. Closer by the river than he would have liked, he saw an old structure, squat and walled, possibly a grain store, and turned Tsang toward it. She picked her way, as eager for a rest as either of them. At the broken wall, Yusen paused, the cramp in his leg intensifying. He leaned down to rub it, and the rope slithered from his grasp. He watched it go, curling and dropping, then, he, too was dropping, sliding from the saddle to wind up on the ground.

Yusen shut his eyes, breathing in pain, breathing out pain.

Tsang stood stolidly over him, and he put up his hand, finding her reins to drag himself to his feet.

"Yusen?" Bao Xing's voice sounded cracked and distant.

He shook off her worry, leaning on his horse as they stepped into the little compound, then turning to make sure the others followed. Almost safe. He would have liked to scout the location more thoroughly, but a Mongol who falls from his horse was not to be trusted, and he knew it.

A few paces away, Bao Xing tugged at her cane and finally got it free. Already dawn's light glowed over the wall, touching her hair with gold beyond the combs and butterflies. He urged himself over to help her, but his right leg remained rooted in place, his left knee trembling. If he walked, he would fall. Again.

Using the cane, Bao Xing tapped Khukhree's leg, and the horse bowed. His wife nearly tumbled from the saddle herself, but the high front and back kept her in place, wedged by the mess of her skirts. She wriggled her feet free of the stirrups and slid to the ground, swaying and wobbly, with a groan somewhere between exhaustion and relief. Good. Safe.

Yusen turned back toward Tsang with her saddle hung about with gear. His leg gave way, and he plunged to his knees, crying out. He caught himself on his hands, dragged them to his thigh and got his foot back under him to rise.

"Yusen—you are hurt."

His left hand resisted aiding him to stand, but he controlled it with a grimace. "Stabbed," he said. "And cut. Not serious—they hurt nothing important." He started toward the horse, dragging his left leg a little to see if that worked any better.

Silk swished against the ground, then she caught his right hand, wrapping it in her warm, soft fingers. "No, you're wrong." Her cane clattered to the ground, and she gripped his hand in both of hers. "They hurt you."

Yusen stood suspended in time, as if in a shaman's trance, the faintest glow of dawn reaching him, the unexpected grip holding him to the earth as the blessing of the Eternal Sky unfurled across the sky. This could not possibly be happening, not to him. He searched for the treachery in it, the mockery, hearing again and again the echo of her voice inside his head. *They hurt you,* as if he, himself, were something important. But there was no laughter nor cruelty in her voice. Something like pity, perhaps, the pity he remembered from a few in his early days with the Mongol army, those few able to spare a thought for a traitor's orphan who would never grow taller, never be one of them.

"Let me help you," she said.

If it had not been for the urgent grip of her hands upon his, he might have assumed the image of the shaman's journey to be true, that he had shed the flesh and drifted into another realm. As it was, he could not be certain of his mind. Pain and exhaustion washed over him like the snowstorms of winter, hazing his vision and shrouding his thoughts. But to help him, she would have to see him, the very flesh he despised. "No," he whispered. He shook his arm, reluctant to make her let go.

"You will fall again, my husband, and when your eyes close, you cannot stop me. Why did you marry me if not to have me near?"

He had never imagined that the marriage would happen, even when he dared to ask, and he had been as dazed then as he was now—but with astonishment. He had not thought as far as the marriage bed, never mind to envision a future that had her in it. As recently as last night, he had assumed she would be gone, taken from him by Guowei, then by the khan himself. Now, they rode into exile and danger together. Rather like one of those great sagas—a man, his horse, his… his woman. "I have bandages and herbs. In a bundle at Tsang's saddle, and waterskins as well."

She kept his hand a little longer as she found her cane and stood up, his hand drawn up with her, then released. She crossed to the horses, taking a moment to select the right one, and returned with the wrapped cloth packet, the waterskin slung over her shoulder. "I'll need to see the wound." She stood before him, shimmering in silks, though disarrayed, pearls glinting rosy pink with dawn. A statue like this stood in so many of those temples and houses of China, a beautiful woman, hands raised in compassion. She knelt and laid the packet on the ground, then reached out as if to take his belt. Shaking his head, Yusen tugged at the shoulders of his del, using his right hand for everything, loosening the garment and peeling it away from the dried blood at his chest. He let the sleeves slide from his arms, leaving his torso exposed, his muscles wiry rather than dense over a chest as narrow as a child's. The puckers of old arrow wounds and the lines of swords crossed his arms and shoulders. This was the nearest yet to his heart, because his attacker had wished to silence a child.

The wound gaped high up, almost at the shoulder, restricting his movement.

Bao Xing paled, but swallowed hard. "Forgive me—I have read no books for this."

"Wash it first from the waterskin, then apply some of the mixture from the smallest pouch. Can you stitch?"

"I can stitch a dragonfly, or a flower." She giggled a little, hunching up as if about to cover her face, then reminding herself to stop, and began the work he described.

The water stung and chilled him so he gasped, and her face crumpled in worry, flinching a little away from him. "I will not hurt you," he said. "I never… I told you I did not know how to be a husband."

Her long fingers stroked the poultice over his wound. "That night…" She kept her head averted, her ornaments trembling. "I did not laugh at you. I laughed because I have seen books for that, for husbands and wives. It seemed a thing I should not know from books."

From her own sleeve, she produced a sewing kit and began to thread a curved needle that might have last been used to embroider a cushion or sew a butterfly on one of her tiny shoes. Her fingers pinched his flesh together, and he held very still, using his right hand to brace his left arm and bring the edges of the wound closer. His breath fluttered the loose hairs at her forehead and surrounding her ear where a larger pearl lay against her throat.

"They have no books in the whole of Siberia. You would hate it."

She laughed again, taking the sting from the piercing pain as she embroidered his wound back together. Her laughter warmed him, her moist breath eddying against his bare skin. "Then where do we go? There may be more to learn in Kaifeng. What is left of it."

"There's one man who already knows more than we do. The drakemaster scouted that weapon as I would scout a battlefield. If the Eternal Sky blesses our fortunes, he is still alive." If Yusen dared ask any more blessings from the Eternal Sky—just then, even in his exile and disgrace, he knew he had never been more blessed.

CHAPTER FORTY-THREE

This time, Ming Lun's contact met her at a bathhouse at dawn—the Hour of the Rabbit. He claimed it was an auspicious time to bathe, but in fact it allowed him to lounge about wearing only a towel at his loins and let all the other patrons assume that she was a bath girl attending to his pleasure. He delighted in strutting before her, treating her like a whore when he could get away with it. It nearly quashed her excitement at having been contacted again, after so long, but it would not do for him to see her eagerness. She followed him meekly inside, head bowed and hands folded. The moment the door of the private chamber closed, she dropped the guise and stepped away. "There has been trouble at the palace. Your methods have not gone well."

He hung his robe on a peg and padded over to stick a toe into the recessed pool of steaming water.

"Something about the dwarf and his wife?" She found something curiously satisfying in the idea of the extravagantly beautiful Bao Xing bound in marriage with the nasty little Mongol. If she had killed him earlier, this image would be denied her. Her envy of Bao Xing's beauty was petty—she even liked the girl when they rode together in that sedan chair. In spite of her naïveté, Bao Xing was not stupid like other Han ladies Ming Lun had known.

"The dwarf burglarized a Mandarin's apartment. He broke things, destroyed documents, and saw some things he should not have seen."

"So he's dead now, yes?" The search parties of soldiers who left at dawn suggested otherwise, but she took another petty enjoyment at the contraction of the man's lips.

"He evaded two attempts last night, but he's injured. He took his wife and got his horses." His face twisted with disdain. "I doubt she goes with him willingly, but none can say if she's a hostage."

"Perhaps someone is playing a longer game. She might stay with him to track him."

He sat on the broad edge of the bath. "I don't believe that."

"Because it would mean the people you trust do not trust you. Surely that couldn't be so."

Mustache twitching he stared up at her. "Do you know more about it?"

"What do I know, I'm only a woman." She smiled, covering her mouth with her hand and fluttering her lashes. He bared his teeth at her, but she went on, "I do know that I would not have spoiled the task."

"The way you spoiled the last one? Everyone knows the drakemaster survived, Ming, that's why you haven't been sent for."

She lost any pretense of humor. "Until now. What is it you want?"

His glance slipped away, and her humor returned. "Oh, I see," she said, "It is not at all what you want—but someone else wants it. Someone wants me to go after them, is that it?"

"There's a message in my robe, instructions for you." He shrugged. "It's not a very important assignment. The dwarf is already out of favor, more so now. The story goes that he attacked a servant and when she called for help, he slaughtered the men who came to help her. The fact that she had stolen us his knife was useful in convincing the khan. So really, the task isn't worthy of much attention. I suggested you. I told them we should give you another chance." He smiled, running a hand down his bare chest, as thin and wasted as any brush-dipping Mandarin's would be. "Assuming you've recovered enough to work, of course."

Ming Lun had been standing as far from him as she could, her back to the painted wall of the little room. The bath took up most of the space, with a broad rim of tiles on two sides, the other two against the far corner. A wooden bench and a few pegs for towels or clothing completed the chamber. A single narrow door led to a walk around an inner courtyard she knew to be mostly empty. Ming Lun smiled generously. She rolled her hips in a dancer's stride for the few small steps toward the bath where he lounged upon the edge. "Thank you for helping me to regain favor and recover lost honor." When her legs brushed his, she sank down a little at her knees, bringing one knee up beside him, her dark trousers damp. He tipped his head back to regard her.

Ming Lun ran her hand along his chest, following the line he had, from his sharp shoulder to the tracery of hair beneath his navel. The towel at his loins strained with the evidence of his appreciation. She brought her other knee up, straddling his middle. "I think my arm is well enough... Would you like to find out?"

His stomach shivered at her touch, and he gave a low chuckle of appreciation. "I knew you must be quite a lover, after you and that Mongol—"

She wrapped her hand over his mouth and plunged him backward into the bath. He slapped and struggled, his eyes huge beneath the water, his legs flailing. Her thighs clamped his hips so he could neither fall in nor buck free, not with his wasted body and weak muscles. His fingers searched for purchase on her hands or garments, but she smacked them away. His jaw worked beneath her grip, his mustache pricking her. His hair flowed around his face like a nest of eels.

When his eyes could grow no larger and his chest tremble no more, Ming Lun thrust her other hand beneath the water. She cradled the back of his head, clamping his mouth and jerked him from the water again, sliding backward so she stood once more in front of him, her legs braced, his still trapped between them. "Do not mention the Mongol. I have warned you before."

His nostrils flared, dragging at the air.

"I believe my strength is adequate." Releasing him, she stepped quickly away, still facing him, until she stood at the door. Gasping and sneezing, he wiped his nose on his elbow as water streamed down his face. He clenched a fist as if he could hit her, but his superiors still had a use for her. Besides, his eye still flashed white, and she suspected both of them knew who would win.

Her arm ached a little—it might do so forever—but it had not trembled nor given way while she held him under. She gave her hands a flick, sending twin sprays of water.

"You're mad." He jabbed a finger at her.

"I am effective." She inclined her head. "Also unexpected. This confers certain advantages, would you not agree?"

Still trembling, he said, "No, I meant mad. Surely only a crazy person would abandon her child with strangers."

Mention of the child made her grow still. "You and your kind insisted that having the child would benefit the Son of Heaven. It served us nothing. If the khan himself, or even his brother Khubilai would bed a Han woman, that might, but this—no. I should never have accepted your plan. It cost me a year I will never get back, and cost the Emperor one of his most loyal servants."

"Yourself?" He barked a laugh, then leaned back on his elbows, but his legs remained tight, protective in spite of his attempt to look casual. "Then you have no interest in my other news. Beh." He shrugged and looked at the ceiling.

"In that case, I should go." Ming Lun bowed. She found the folded message in his robe and set her hand on the latch. At its click, he cleared his throat. He couldn't resist sharing, not if he thought his news would hurt her.

"Your daughter will recover. That's all." He made a little shooing motion with one hand.

Her fingers tightened on the latch. "Not long ago, you told me she did well, now you speak as if she has been ill. If you insist on needling me with the past, at least be consistent."

"She was the servant who risked her life to try to stop the dwarf. Someday, she might prove adequate to our uses." He draped his hand at his crotch.

Ming Lun cut her glance away and slipped out through the door, not allowing it to slam. The daughter she had never met began to sound a little like her. Interesting. Not that she cared for the girl, of course—she could not afford to—but still, such a development was… interesting. If her daughter resembled her in any way, then she would never allow a simpering fool like this to use her—not unless she discovered a way to use him first. Some of the other Mandarin larks were stronger, practicing martial discipline as well as studying their enemies. High time she attached herself to one of them. Chin tucked, gliding like a servant herself, Ming Lun slipped back into the wakening streets of the city.

In the meantime, she had a new mission, a trivial one as the Mandarin had said, but not an easy one. Evidently the dwarf had seen something in the Mandarin quarter which he was not to see, and so he should die. Mongol soldiers had already ridden after him, assuming him to be the perpetrator of an assault against her daughter—Ming Lun's step hesitated as she completed the script her contact had not: he said they would claim the dwarf attacked her, which meant he had not. The larks only attacked her daughter to discredit the Mongol. She moved on, cutting through the morning crowds of vendors, servants, housewives and workmen, back to the little room she kept behind a shop.

Did the Son of Heaven know His servants stabbed children? They lived so long among the Mongols that they began to resemble them. But if children must be sacrificed to remove the oppressors, how was she to judge the value of that sacrifice? The girls of Kaifeng would not hesitate to die if they knew that no other girls would be raped by their conquerors. The Mandarins gathered information from across the empire, both above and below the Mongol army—they saw more than she, and some of them could be trusted to judge, weighing lives in the balance to find the best for China.

Back in her narrow chamber, Ming Lun took out the message, a folded paper sealed with the sign of the lark. She opened it and read the elegant script inside.

"My dear Ming Lun. Permit me to address you as such though we have never met. Your information about the weapon and the plan was invaluable, and accurate, and so I have asked for you to be given the task of hunting the Mongol. Please also destroy his wife's cane, and send us any word of those plans and the man who carried them. Send a message if you have information, via the Temple of the Lark. We will soon be on the ride, to activate the weapon in service to our cause. The falcon must be brought low, and your skills are vital. May the blessings of the Son of Heaven fall richly upon you."

The message made her smile: the falcon brought low, her own skills vital. She packed her few things into a blanket and bound it to sling over her shoulder. She concealed her weapons carefully about her person, then departed, but where to go? Where would a Mongolian outcast take his Chinese bride? Would they go into hiding, perhaps back to her family—if they would take in a Mongolian son-in-law. Ming Lun paced to the temple quarter and lit incense before a statue of an angry-looking Buddhist deity, but she dedicated it to the Emperor, envisioning this tooth-gnashing deity to be one of His vengeful servants.

The miserable drakemaster had seen the plans as well, and was hauled to the palace shortly after her meeting with her contact. If the

Mongols knew about the weapon, they would do anything to try to stop it—or to seize it for themselves, so their own messenger must be discredited. More than that, he must be killed. She knew about him, knew about the weapon—the mission only appeared worthless if they believed the dwarf would go into hiding and forget the whole thing. She had watched him in the khan's ger, falling in love with a woman he could never dream of possessing. Now he had her. Anyone who believed he would give up on serving the khan because of the night's setback was deluded. They discounted the dwarf for his size, just as they discounted her for her sex. In both cases they were wrong, and they must know it before the dwarf had his hand—the hand of the khan—at the throat of the Han people. He would go to the one source he knew how to find: the drakemaster.

Half a moon ago, shortly after the dwarf's triumphant return, a wagon on its way to the mines had hauled the drakemaster away. The wagon driver, in possession of such a wonder, a pale giant enslaved by the khan, had kept him under a cloth at his side on the driver's bench.

"See the ghost! The khan's ghost!" he barked out over the streets as he drove. "Cost you a coin or a chicken!"

The Mongol guards riding along ignored his commerce, as long as the wagon kept moving, no doubt they would receive a cut of his profits. Many heard about the khan's ghost when the dwarf dragged him to the city, and some had seen him from a distance at that time, but all of these and more were willing to pay to see him up close. Ming Lun crowded alongside the wagon that day, holding up her coin with the others. The gates drew very near, and she had not yet had her turn. She fumbled in her pouch and found a bit of silver.

The driver's brows shot up, and he beckoned her, urging one of the guards to hold back the rest of the crowd. He lifted her up to the bench with one meaty hand, mindful of her injured arm, then took her coin and dropped it into his shirt to jingle among the rest. "Get closer—don't want to give anyone a free look." He grinned as she wriggled between him and the slave, then he slid the cloth back to drape across the hidden man's head and shoulders, framing him like a veil.

Dailus's face, always drawn and pale, looked pained, eyes squeezing tighter at the intrusion of light. Bruises stood out dark and angry and his breath scraped over dry lips.

"Ai—open your eyes! She's paid rich, you ghost." The driver slapped his oxen with the reins, checking the approaching gate, then reached over one hand and pried at the slave's eyes, forcing one of them open, a bloodshot white orb, the jade at its heart flicking in distress. Dailus shifted his chained wrists, but could not move far enough to do anything. Ming Lun slid under the driver's hand, forcing him away while letting him think she merely wanted to be closer.

"So pale! And such strange eyes." She adopted a sing-song tone of wonder, like a house-bound wife who never saw such wonders. She stroked his straw-colored beard as if in surprise at the color and texture of his hair. In that painful flash of his eye, she had seen no recognition, and doubted he had even noticed her in his efforts to get free of the driver's grasp. Now, he bent his face, ever so slightly, into her hand, as if he welcomed her touch.

"Kill me," he breathed, then, "No, don't—they'll kill you—you'd never escape."

"I wish I could," she whispered, sliding her thumb along his cheek.

"Ai, here's the gate—it's off with you, madam," the driver said.

"A moment longer." She offered the driver an unhidden smile—a whore's smile—before she slid him another coin. His off-hand strayed to squeeze her buttock, as she turned back to Dailus.

Sliding her hand around his head, Ming Lun kissed him gently on his bloodied lips. For an instant, his eyes flashed open, vividly green, and she slipped away. She let the driver help her down, howling with the laughter of amazement, and the nearest Mongols, the only ones who noticed her rash action, slapped their thighs and shook their heads. She swayed her hips as she walked away, becoming what they thought her: the whore who stole a kiss from a ghost. But she had not stolen it, she had given it—the only thing she had to offer that would not end in their deaths. His blood tasted of iron on her lips.

Now, so many days later, Ming Lun hurried for that same gate. The Mongol dwarf and his wife had horses, but he was injured, and she had likely never ridden before. They would be stiff and tired after last night—even a victory could sap one's strength. She herself had hidden to rest after fighting the accursed monk and his man before she could even rouse her energy to come here. They would be in a hurry, but unable to move quickly and concerned about pursuit. How would they proceed? Slowly, across a difficult landscape, or directly upon the road? They would take the road if they could—when they neared the mountains, it would be the only choice, but likely they would move through the fields until then, and that gave her time. Mandarins and palace-dwellers assumed the best way to follow someone was to do just that—coming behind—but Ming Lun's experience taught her that, if one knew the destination, a far better course was to be there first.

She bought her way onto a camel, and when it was brought to market in another town, seduced herself into a caravan going the right direction. She danced for a camp of soldiers to replace the money she had spent, and rode the back of an ox-cart past the ruins of Kaifeng. She stayed with the river through a valley lined with Buddhas—thousands of idols taking the Emperor's place in the hearts of so many, especially now when people believed the Son of Heaven lost interest in the struggles of the North. Moving quickly beyond them, Ming Lun reached a branching where the main river moved further north, toward the Mongol homeland, while a smaller tributary continued higher into the mountains. A city occupied the junction, teeming with Mongol soldiers and Han herdsmen and workers. She passed through toward the far side, where the city narrowed and the wagons carrying supplies to the mine continued on. The Mongol and his lady must pass through here, as well. At the far gate, she made herself a beggar among beggars, dirtying her hands and face, calling out for pity, and waiting two more days.

She nearly missed them, a moaning old woman riding a pack saddle, her horse led by a mounted child in scruffy peasant garb. They trailed a trio of horses piled with wrapped bundles as if moving household.

Ming Lun plucked a packet from her sleeve and turned to one of the beggars she had come to know. "Take this to Kaifeng, to the House of the Lark—do you understand?" He nodded, then grinned as she handed him a coin—and ran off to carry her message to her masters: at the mouth of the mountains, she had found her mark. They were, indeed, going for the drakemaster.

Ming Lun hurried toward the gate, to the old woman's horse,

thrusting up her hands. "In the name of pity, food, madam! By the treasured stars above!"

The woman jerked and turned her head, her horse responding with a few quick steps—a woman unused to managing such a spirited animal. A careful application of pearl paint and ink aged her face almost beyond recognition: quite an achievement to transform the greatest beauty in the North into a crone. Bao Xing hesitated, then croaked, "Do I know you?" and coughed into her hand.

Ming Lun caught the horse's girth strap and moved with her. "I am Ming Lun, the dancer. We met at the Mongol army's camp—but I hardly knew you! Are you in hiding?"

"Yes—for our lives!"

In front of them, the servant turned his head, his eyes narrowing, one hand reaching for something beneath the blanket that hid his saddle. The dwarf, and he knew her right away.

"Oh—I'll let you go." Ming Lun backed away, but Bao Xing beckoned her on and they slid through the gate together, the Mongol guards waving them by with a trickle of other locals who had to be out by sunset.

"What are you doing here?" Bao Xing asked.

Ming Lun dodged her gaze, but let her hand linger at her breast. "You will think me foolish, lady. Indeed, I am."

"You? Surely not."

Up ahead, the dwarf growled and prodded his horse a little faster.

"No, no, you must go—but I have so many questions." Ming Lun let go again, though she did not fall back. "It would be a comfort to speak with another woman." She hid a nervous chuckle.

"Indeed," Bao Xing replied, but she did not hide her own delight. "What have you done that's so foolish?"

"I am trying to rescue a ghost." Ming Lun shook her head as if she could toss away the notion. "You remember that slave, the drakemaster?" Bao Xing gasped, and a small part of Ming Lun's mind reveled in the accuracy of her guesses. Then her chest tightened as it never did when she was lying, and she murmured, "I am still haunted by his eyes."

"Yusen!"

He turned in an instant at his wife's voice, though his body betrayed a hint of weakness from his injuries. How bad had it been? How little would it take for him to die?

"She must come with us."

The Mongol's hand lingered at his saddle blanket—his sword must be beneath it, but he gave a sharp nod and turned away.

Bao Xing flashed a smile that swept away any illusion of age. "There is so much you must hear, but know this, we shall rescue your ghost together."

"Thank you, lady," Ming Lun answered but she wondered where her words had come from. She had never meant to speak the truth—never meant for it to be the truth, trying to focus on her mission. Yet every night, she still tasted his blood upon her lips and saw the hunger in his sharp, green eyes. The dwarf would die, as the Son of Heaven required, but not until he had served her purpose and brought back the ghost from his untimely tomb within the mines.

CHAPTER FORTY-FOUR

Days after their auspicious meeting with the dancer, Bao Xing shifted uncomfortably as she watched smoke coil into the sky from the cinnabar furnaces. Yusen had chosen them a site upwind of the noxious fumes, but the air tingled in her nostrils in spite of the silk wrapped over her nose and mouth. The mine occupied a narrow valley that intersected the larger one below the ledge where she and Ming Lun waited for Yusen's return. The horses had been left farther off, in a green pasture with its own small spring—Yusen forbad them access to the murky waters of the stream running below. A system of troughs carried water from beyond the mine valley down into the works and out here, fouled by the wastes of the smelters. Pine trees without needles marched down toward that tainted water, their dark trunks and dry branches reminding her of the stark calligraphy of the ancients.

"You place a great deal of trust in him," Ming Lun observed. "He's been gone three days—he may have been captured." She tended their small fire, cooking squirrels she had snared beyond the gray valley.

"There is more about my husband than others know," Bao Xing answered. "And he is an expert scout."

Ming Lun stared at her a moment, then dropped her gaze. Since seeing through their disguises several days before, Ming Lun had attended them both, acting as a servant, but watching constantly. She made clear her suspicion of Yusen—probably because he was the instrument of the drakemaster's recapture—but Bao Xing maintained the uneasy alliance between them. Ever withdrawn, the dancer spoke little about her reasons for seeking the drakemaster. Bao Xing suspected she wanted the drakemaster for some other reason entirely, but she could name that reason no more than she could recognize love.

Together, she and Ming Lun ate their meal, then banked the fire to be sure it would not glow as the sun went down. All day, Mongols moved in the valley below, bringing groups of slaves to or from the furnaces, escorting wagons loaded with cinnabar and vessels of liquid mercury. Now, as night crept over the mountains, she pillowed her head on the bundle that contained her silken gowns and lay back to watch the stars come out. Tonight the sky would begin an annual display that nearly distracted her from her true purpose: over their nights in hiding and riding, she had confirmed the worst. The wanderer was circling the Dark Lance indeed. What if they did not find the device in time?

"What do you see there?" Ming Lun asked. "Do you see the future?"

"I don't have all the skill to say what the stars mean, but I know the patterns, and I know how they return. This is a favorite time of mine—when the stars begin to fly." Overhead, pinpricks of white glittered on the deepening blue.

"Isn't that a terrible sign?"

"It is meant to be, but it's also beautiful."

At her side, Ming Lun gave a little snort. "Beauty serves no purpose."

"How can a dancer not believe in beauty?"

"Dancing is strength, it is order—" she broke off and sat up, then sprang to her feet, a knife suddenly in her hand.

Bao Xing sat up as well, finding the knife she had been given as Yusen crept into the dell where they were camped. Ming Lun backed away and sat down. Her husband's ever-weary eyes looked especially dark, and Bao Xing hurried to find the waterskins and some smoked meat from yesterday's meal. He sat stiffly, stretching his left leg out before him and drank deeply before he spoke.

"They keep a watch of ten men at the gate, probably because of the reports of bandits we heard in town. There are at least one hundred soldiers in the camp, nearly a village itself. The miners sleep in a group of sheds near the entrance. Unless they are brought to the furnaces, they do not come out into the sun. The furnaces are less heavily guarded—nobody wants to go near them. I have not seen the drakemaster, so I think he is at the mine, not the furnace." He chewed off a piece of meat.

"Any women?" Ming Lun asked.

"None, not even whores. The soldiers trade off going to town for that." He chewed thoughtfully. "We cannot ride in and demand him—we have no authority."

"What authority do we need?" Ming Lun wanted to know.

"A captain or better in the army, an order from the khan. A shaman's prophecy—we have nothing." He started to shrug, but winced, his right hand moving to cradle his left elbow between bites of meat.

"A shaman's prophecy?" Bao Xing echoed. "What if we could give them one?"

"How?"

She pointed to the sky. "In two days, the sky will rain fire."

Yusen said, "You are no shaman."

"I am an astronomer. I need no prophecy—it is true. There is a range of stars which fly at this time of year, every year. They will be at their strongest in two days. If we made a prophecy, would the soldiers believe it?"

Yusen plucked at his eyebrow. "This is not the kind of strategy I know, but I can't kill a hundred of my own people. Even if I could, I would not."

The dancer leaned forward. "Your people worship the sky, do they not? If we told them the Eternal Sky grew angry because they harbored a ghost, would they bring him out to us?"

"Who tells them?" Yusen tossed a tiny bone over his shoulder. "They won't listen to me, and Bao Xing has not enough Mongolian. And you—" he appraised her, then tipped his head. "You speak well enough, but what do you know of shaman's ways?"

"I learn quickly," said Ming Lun. "Teach me what to say, and I will ride as a shaman to the gates."

Yusen's lips edged up, just a little. "It might work. If we have no better idea." Then he rolled over into his blanket and settled for the night.

Ming Lun switched to Chinese. "Your husband is rude."

"He is tired from creeping about the rocks." Bao Xing stared at the hard curve of his back. "And he barely sleeps."

"So you have a husband who never lies with you, nor will he lie quietly and let you rest." Ming Lun patted her hand.

Bao Xing suddenly felt that a stranger had entered their bedchamber—a stranger hostile to her husband. What was it that kept him restless? She did not dare to ask. Since their marriage night, she had not asked about his past, nor had he spoken of it. "That amulet I received in the camp. Did you know it was from him?"

Ming Lun slid her hands together in her lap. "He asked me not to tell you. I think he feared you would reject any gift from him."

Slipping the amulet from beneath her jacket, Bao Xing held it up to gleam in the starlight. "He is a scout. He hears, sees, remembers. He remembered that I spoke of the stars and gave me this."

"Every man remembers such things for a woman he hopes will favor him."

Bao Xing lay back to look at the stars. "I should not be surprised you speak of all men as if they are false."

"They are. Even if your husband is better than everyone believes, lady, that only tells me that his every moment is bent upon hiding, like a spy concealing himself among his enemies."

"*Among his enemies…*" Above, the star patterns took shape in her vision, the Scholar, and the General. "He is. Perhaps they all are. Perhaps they hide themselves even from each other."

"Innocence becomes you."

Bao Xing peered at her in the darkness. "Have all men been so cruel to you, Ming, or did one hurt you beyond all others?"

Ming Lun lay under her blanket like a painting of the dead. "Some have hurt me more than others." Then a soft sound of negation. "There are none who try to aid me, none who care for my pain, not unless I am paying for healing, or he is paying me and fears I will cry out too loud."

Her words lashed into the darkness and Bao Xing flinched. "And the drakemaster?"

"His name is Dailus. No—I cannot say it as he does. He has not yet had the chance to hurt me. When he does, I'm sure he will."

Bao Xing wet her lips. "He's the first man you've met who hurts more than you."

Ming Lun lay silent for a long moment. "One night at the encampment, I was out very late. The Mongols were looking for geomancers in the camp who had been destroying things, and they accused me. Dailus lied for me, pretending he had invited me there, to lie with him."

"That's why you leapt after him into the water." Small, auspicious clouds drifted between her and the stars. The story was a romance, even if Ming Lun pretended otherwise. Under cover of the blanket of stars, Bao Xing found courage to ask, "Did you lie together after you saved him?"

Her companion laughed. "No, never. I've lain with lots of men, Bao Xing. Believe me, it's nothing special save in the getting of sons."

Her bitterness rang, and Bao Xing's hand rested on her belly. Would she ever get sons?

"It can be fun. Some men enjoy pleasuring their women because it enhances their own pleasure." Ming Lun propped her head on her hand, eyes glinting. "Haven't you ever wanted to lie with a man?"

Bao Xing thought of Guowei's wise eyes and scholar's hands, then of her wedding night, her fears confronting her husband's. "Maybe so. But I am married now."

Ming Lun smothered her laughter, kicking her feet in the air. "For most girls marriage means they will have a man, at least one. You think being married will stop him from looking? Ai, you are innocent."

As Ming Lun's glee died away, Bao Xing glanced to where her husband lay alone in the darkness. There must be more to men and women than lying and coupling and hurting each other. She had never heard of books about that. Perhaps she would write one.

"Sleep well, Bao Xing. Forgive me my old wounds."

"May they one day be healed."

Ming Lun answered with a laugh, small and lonely in the night.

CHAPTER FORTY-FIVE

In the queer twilight of the mine, a thick vein of red laced with silver tracked down into the darkness. Trickling red stone chips and seeping quicksilver, the mountain bled internally from the wound of the mine, leaving Dailus and the other miners infesting the stone like maggots devouring the decay. Dailus shook himself and stared back up the shaft toward the jagged opening of the valley above, trying to dispel the image of the festering wound. He ached in every bone, from his pounding skull to the joints of his toes, and his mouth tasted of metal all the time, a taste he could not scour away with food or water. Bile briefly served the purpose, but stung his cracked lips so badly that he had given up eating. The bloody vomit worried him more than the fact that he could not smell it.

Mastering his tremors, Dailus swung his pick against the wall, but the shaft turned in his hand and the point bounced off and tumbled him to his knees. The tool slithered from his grip. His first days in the mine, Dailus wondered why the numerous slaves did not take up their picks against the overseers, who failed Wang Lin Yo's caution in hoarding the tools. Now he knew: only a handful of the freshest men had any such strength. After a week or two, even these began to lose the accuracy of their strikes. Ah—his shaky hand found the handle and crept along it, holding on tight.

"You, what's happened?" One of the overseers approached in a halo of lantern's glow.

Dailus squinted, trying to preserve his vision—the only sense he could still manage. "Pick slid."

The Tatar overseer loomed over him, a cloth covering his nose and mouth as if that would prevent the creeping poison. "That's four times today."

Five, at least. The ringing echo of other men's work resonated with the throbbing of his skull.

The overseer caught his head and lowered the lantern to peer into Dailus's face, then released him. "Leave the pick. Get on clean-up."

Dailus bowed his head, shifting the pick to lean against the wall of the tunnel. Clean-up referred to the loading of broken ore into baskets to be carried to the smelters: a task for men no longer coordinated enough to manage tools. He grabbed a shard of cinnabar, shuffling over toward a waiting basket to drop it in, then leaned against the wall a moment before shuffling back to retrieve another stone.

The overseer moved on, checking down the tunnel before he hurried back up again to the open air. The crew kept working, slow but steady. If this tunnel failed to produce enough ore, there would be punishment. The punishment might be preferable to the work.

A Tatar nearly as tall as Dailus shuffled by with a stone in his arms and dropped it into a basket. "Tell about the ghost shaman." Tomor, that was his name. He panted a little, leaning against his own patch of wall, then spat blood on the floor.

Sighing, Dailus rested his forehead on the wall, his shoulders perpetually hunched in the tunnel. "I can't... talk and work." He pushed off toward the broken ore, but Tomor gave a whistle.

"You sit—they won't check again 'til dark."

"Tell in Chinese," said one of the others, dropping a stone in, then aiming a glare at the Tatar. Dailus recognized Xo, a brawler condemned for murder who had committed at least two more since his arrival. The others, especially the handful of Tatar prisoners, hoped Xo would die off, but the poisons worked more slowly in him, and none yet had the courage to take up a pick against him or his cohort. Or maybe it was the coordination they lacked.

"Chinese." Dailus sank to his knees, letting the roughly curved wall support him.

Tomor growled softly, but he was in a minority—the Tatars had other punishments for their countrymen.

"Both." Dailus tucked his trembling hands under his arms. Shivers racked his body, and he waited for the fit to pass, counting breaths until it did. Twenty-seven. Up from twenty yesterday. The bit of his mind still rational watched his decline. He stopped eating sooner than most, but he could still speak and mostly see. His ears rang from time to time—a distraction rather than a disability. So far.

Tomor nudged his foot. "The ghost shaman."

"One day," Dailus breathed, dredging up his Chinese, "The ghost shaman met with his students by a lake to teach them, but more students came and they did not have enough food." He broke down coughing, his chest shuddering. The wetness on his lips must be blood, but it tasted like air, like stone, like smoke, like anything. Someone pressed a gourd full of water into his lap, and Dailus drank the metallic tang of quicksilver. He spoke again, the same words, this time in the Tatar's language.

"Give me the baskets, the ghost shaman told them, and they brought out the baskets with what food they had found, a few loaves of bread and a handful of fish." He used to know how many. Stained glass windows behind an altar... somewhere... showed a plate of fish, then he pictured a broad leaf with a fish fresh from the campfire. As Dailus spoke, the workers quieted, taking turns carrying stone to listen, until the baskets were filled. "The shaman divided what little food they had between the baskets and told his students to offer it to the crowd. As the people removed the food, there was always more, until everyone had eaten his fill." Dailus finished translating and fell silent.

"Tell about the wine, that's a good story." Xo seized the water-gourd and took a long drink.

"Time to ring the bell." Dailus pointed at the full baskets.

Xo tossed the gourd back to him as Tomor rang the bell to summon those who would carry the baskets. The other prisoners hunched against the tunnel walls as the short train of carriers arrived. Some of the miners spat blood at them, and someone put out a handle to trip their leader, but the carrier, still healthy from his work above ground, dodged it, and kept walking. He dropped an empty basket, taking a full basket onto his back and turning for the surface. The miners watched them go, a movement in the gloom, then silhouettes at the top against a darkening sky. Dailus closed his eyes. The rhythm of the carriers walking made him queasy. Almost night. Thank God—he would soon have his twice-daily blessed walk in the open air.

Xo prodded his side with his foot. "Come on. The one about the wine."

"There's never any fire in your stories," Tomor complained. "What kind of shaman doesn't use fire? Or furs, or even ribbons."

"He's got so much magic, he doesn't need fire and ribbons," another Tatar suggested.

"No, he's not a shaman—he's a geomancer," said one of the

Cathayans. "Right, Xo? That's why you always tell us where the stories happen."

Dailus had given up trying to explain Jesus—why he used no fire, why a Son of Heaven wasn't an emperor, why his people had killed him. Most of his listeners enjoyed the crucifixion and resurrection though.

Xo had started it, the first night Dailus arrived at the mine. He stumbled down from the wagon with a few other prisoners. Torches flickered against the red and silver of the mine, so the veins stood out like the leading in a stained glass window of Hell. Dark faces loomed out of these pockets of light like demons indeed. Dailus, aching from the beating of his recapture, shuffled to the open structure where the miners ate their bowls of rice and slept curled around their trembling hands. Overhead, he glimpsed the stars. He slumped to his knees and pressed his hands together.

"Our Father, who art in Heaven," he began, Latin feeling foreign on his tongue.

"Hey! Hey, what are you doing, ghost?" A wiry man with scarred forearms shoved him.

"Praying." Dailus absorbed the blow as he had so many before.

"Praying? Idiot—this is how you pray." The man slammed the back of his head, shoving him face first to the ground. The other miners laughed. Dailus envisioned the days and weeks ahead, once again become the butt of everyone's joke. He rose to his full height and wiped the dirt from his face.

"My god allows a man to raise his voice to the heavens."

"Your god hasn't served you so well, dumping you here with us." The man waved a hand at Dailus, unintimidated.

"Jesus," Dailus began, half an oath, bits of parables moved through his memory, the glow of the church, his family around him. Truly, the Cathayan had the right of it—he was lost among Heathens, and no prayer or offering seemed great enough to transport him home. Tears burned: this mine, this Hell, was the end at last, the place he would die. But the oath burned as well—would he abandon his faith, no matter how poorly it served? "Jesus is the name of the son of God. He is our greatest teacher, and he said that his Father would always welcome home even the greatest sinner."

The other man laughed. "What does that mean? A sinner?"

"A criminal, someone who has trespassed or," he hesitated, frowning, "someone who rebukes the laws of god."

"So Jesus is the emperor in ghost country," someone else asked, the other miners crowding in closer, hands tucked under their arms. Blood oozed from their lips, less like demons than like the lepers the Bible spoke of, the outcasts whom Jesus most tried to help.

"No. He's a teacher, but with the spirit of God inside him."

"What is he saying?" a Mongolian demanded.

"Shut up, Tomor," the Cathayan leader said, but Dailus repeated his words in Mongolian.

"Like a shaman for the ghosts," the Mongolian said.

"What does he teach?" someone else asked.

"You were talking about sinners, bad men, like us." The Cathayan grinned, and his friends hooted and laughed, their teeth showing white and bloody.

Sinners. *Bad men, like us*—because Dailus, by his presence there, was one of them. He was a sinner indeed; he had made the weapon that broke Kaifeng, then delivered to the Mongols the plan for something even more terrible in one last bid to save himself. By the time he recovered from the pain and fear enough to understand what he had done, the chance had gone to do anything about this last betrayal. "He helps people understand what God wants by telling them stories." He tried to think of a story both Cathayans and Mongols might relate to. What did these people share with the stories of his own history? The answer, when it came to him, was obvious.

"Jesus compared God to a shepherd in the mountains, the rough country. The shepherd is tending his flock, but one of the sheep wanders away—that's the sinner, the one who strays. So God leaves his flock to search. When he finds the sinner, the one who strayed, he takes him upon his shoulders and carries him back in safety to the flock, and welcomes him home." Tears threatened, and Dailus blinked them away as he spoke again, this time in Mongolian. He had been praying for years now that God would carry him home, and had no answer.

"That was a stupid story," Tomor said. "Why would he leave the rest of his flock? What about wolves or thieves? He can't just go off for the one and leave the flock unguarded."

"You think anybody's coming to take you away, ghost?" The Cathayan jabbed his chest with his finger. "No! You're one of us forever. Tomorrow, you tell us another story."

How many days ago had that been? Or weeks? The novelty of Dailus's strange stories still captured the miners. What else did they have in their days buried in stone, waiting to die?

"The wine." Xo pressed harder, and Dailus flinched away, trying to remember how the story began. He used more words when he began. Now, the stories took the form of summary, clumps of remembered words pressed between fits of shaking or coughing. Who would entertain Xo when Dailus lay on the furnace heap?

"The wine." Dailus squeezed the top of his nose. "There was a wedding in Canaan, and the ghost shaman—"

The tunnel brightened as one of the overseers looked in. "Hai—where's the ghost?"

"Working!" Xo called. "I'll send another."

"The masters want him."

Not the furnace men? Dailus started to push to his feet, but Xo grabbed his shoulder. "I want my stories." Xo bared bloody teeth.

Shaking his head—uncertain where his will left off and the tremors of his body took charge—Dailus muttered, "The masters. I have to go."

"We'll hide you, down below. Say there was an accident. We'll bring food and water, then you can tell us more. Never need to work." Xo pushed him down behind the baskets. "Nice, eh, not to work?"

Not to go outside, even twice a day? "The masters—"

Xo's hand smothered his mouth, knocking his head back. "Down here, I am master." Two other Cathayan miners clustered close, and Xo dragged Dailus in their direction. "Take him to a side chamber," he whispered. Toward the top of the tunnel, he shouted, "Soon—I find him!"

Dailus struggled, tearing at their hands, trying to find the strength to breathe, never mind screaming.

"Let him go," Tomor insisted.

"Why? Why let them take all our joy?" Xo hefted his pick.

An arm wrapped through Dailus's arms, pinning them while another locked around his throat. Tomor misunderstood: they kept him more to defy their Tatar masters as for his stories. Dailus kicked at them, but they dragged him backward, letting his feet scrape the ground. Pick in hand, Xo turned, already swinging.

Tomor grunted and dodged a blow that cracked stone. The miners cheered, urging on Xo in Chinese, a smaller chorus shouting in Mongolian.

Dailus got his feet under him and pushed backward, the Cathayans collapsing under him to the floor. "Here! I'm here!" He scrambled toward the surface.

Someone got hold of his foot, and he grabbed a stone, flinging it behind him. His attacker shrieked.

"Down there! Stop now! Stop fighting or we'll flood the mine!" Another, brighter light joined the first, then a cluster of them, illuminating the struggling silhouettes of Xo and Tomor.

The brawler turned, noticing Dailus. "No!" Xo shouted, swinging.

Tomor jumped, knocking into Xo's back. "Run—get out!" the Tatar gasped.

Dailus scrambled by, then heard the whoosh and thunk of a pick striking flesh instead of stone. Bones cracked, and a Cathayan voice shrieked.

"Stop fighting—last chance!" ordered one of the overseers.

Dailus pushed on, his hands and feet flailing against the floor. Behind him, other voices shouted, other blows fell, something crunched like a skull against rock. Water splashed over his hands, sweeping them out from under him. "No! I'm coming!" He made a last lunge, stretching the length of his frame, hands outflung, and grabbed a booted leg.

Sputtering, Dailus shook the water from his face and clambered the rest of the way. Over his head, the Tatar overseers directed a trough of water down toward the shouting, struggling men. The cheering and taunting became pleading. "They stopped fighting," Dailus said in Mongolian. "Please, stop the water!" He tugged on the man's del, but the overseer knocked him aside.

"Troublemakers. That vein was nearly done anyway." Two of the other men moved in to peel Dailus off the ground, one at each arm. "We know about the curse," the overseer said. "This is part of it, isn't it? You stirring up the men, bringing trouble, but now we can clear the curse."

"What curse?" Dailus barely felt the clean air of evening as they seized him.

"The ghost curse. The shaman told us. She said—" but the overseer broke off, staring upward. "It's coming! Hurry up!"

A distant flare caught his eye and Dailus, too, glanced up. In the deep blue of evening, the stars were falling. They streaked across the night, first one, then another.

"The Eternal Sky calls for his blood!"

Water streamed down into the tunnel, and the miners' shouts echoed. Dailus sagged. His blood? Just then, it ran colder than a mountain stream. He was about to be sacrificed to a pagan god. Would that make him a martyr? God was meant to see all, to know the death of a sparrow, but in the raw, red wound of a Tatar mine, Dailus had lost hope the Lord saw anything at all. In which case, there was no need for him to turn the other cheek.

Dailus dropped to his knees, twisting free of the men who held him. At least he would not die spread upon a heathen altar. He turned back to the tunnel, reaching up to grab the edge of the wooden trough, trying to stop the flood. If he broke it, more tunnels would flood and it might not stop drowning his own team, sinners all, and he was one of them. How had the overseer freed the water in the first place? There—a slat hung from a chain. Dailus fumbled it into place, cutting the stream.

"Get back here." One of the overseers snagged his arm, but Dailus kicked hard with his little strength. The man went down with a rush of breath. Dailus let go and flung himself down near the slanting floor of the tunnel.

"Come on!" he shouted down in two or three languages, reaching back. A wet hand clasped his and he braced himself, hauling Tomor up the damp and slippery slope. Together, they reached in again, then another, forming a rope of their arms to lead the others to safety. Dailus's shoulders screamed agony, his joints throbbed and he broke into a coughing fit.

"Get up, all of you! Out of the way!" The overseers waded through the miners, kicking the shaking men out of their way.

One of them held up his lantern, and Dailus turned from the light, his eyes streaming tears. "There he is," the overseer snarled. "A curse indeed."

"I give you curse!" Xo roared. Blood streamed down his face, much more than the effects of the poisoned mine. He hauled himself from the tunnel with his pick and gave it a mighty swing, burying it in the chest of the nearest overseer.

Around him, other miners scrambled to their feet, carrying stones to pound their overseers. Dailus pushed away as the man who had found him drew a cudgel and moved toward the mass of angry miners. Dailus fumbled for a rock of his own but it splashed into the flooded tunnel, shortly followed by a body. He stumbled back from the gaping entrance and found one of the wooden pillars supporting the elevated water troughs.

Hollering soldiers rushed into the valley from their posts along the gate, struggling to subdue the miners in the spreading darkness.

Dailus clung to the pole, then reached for the next one. He staggered along in the shadow of the trough, using the poles to drag himself forward. The gate loomed up ahead, miraculously open, its guardians streaming past toward the fight. Stars swept through the sky, and he did not care if they were real or just the poison seizing his mind. Though the open gate, he glimpsed freedom, the freedom at least, to die. Perhaps God had found this particular wandering sheep and would now lift him up to carry him home.

Then rough hands grabbed him and an edge of steel pressed to his throat.

CHAPTER FORTY-SIX

Clad in twisting squirrel skins and framed by flaming torches, Ming Lun stood on a hilltop over the narrow valley that sheltered the mine. Her position overlooked the heavy gate into the mine itself, currently open and unguarded. She considered rushing down there herself. Rough voices shouted and weapons clashed. Then a pair of soldiers dragged a corpse through the gate. Too tall and pale: even by this light, Ming Lun recognized Dailus. The heavens poured forth a glory of stars as if the Jade Emperor in his boat far above approved the plan. But if he had, then he had gone too far, for the Mongols drew knives to shed their prisoner's blood before he ever reached the shaman who awaited him. He flopped between them, streaked with blood and unmoving, at least by his own volition.

"Here! To me! The Eternal Sky must be appeased!" she called out, desperate to think of some way to prevent them. "Only by the proper rituals can the curse be stopped."

"Come down to us, shaman," one of the Mongols called back. "The curse is already happening! The miners are in revolt." The other soldier hauled Dailus up by the chin, stretching his neck back against a broad, armored shoulder, bracing him for the killing stroke.

Ming Lun slipped a short knife from her sash and took aim as the speaker for the soldiers moved into position. As it left her hand, she felt the blade slide wrong, and she ran after it, roaring incoherently as if overcome by her trance.

The knife struck the soldier, but skittered off the plates of his back armor, drawing his attention. In the gloom, she slithered on down the slope. The night grew in chaos all around her, and that meant danger. In response, Ming Lun cultivated stillness, an inner calm that guided her straight on, squirrel tails flailing around her, her fresh-made shaman's garb reeking of death.

She caught movement from the corner of her eye, and hoofbeats thundered in the valley. A streak of fire in the sky showed the rider's silhouette, short and unarmored. Ming Lun found the voice of the shaman and cried out, "See comes the rider of the sky to carry out the will of the Heavens!"

The soldiers swiveled, Dailus's feet dragging. In that stillness at her center, she felt he was already dead, by the poison of the mine or the cut of a soldier's knife.

Yusen barreled down upon them. "Slave!" he howled, his high, strange voice sounding otherworldly. "Wrist! Now!"

Dailus's body shivered, his head tossing as if to dispel a nightmare. He brought up his hand, the slave bracelet carving into what remained of his flesh.

Yusen leaned from the saddle and seized his arm at the shoulder, hauling him from the grip of the startled soldier and dragging Dailus across the neck of his horse even as they galloped past. He held the drakemaster with both hands, guiding the horse by thigh or by instinct; the dwarf was as skilled a horseman as any Mongol of the khan's army, better than most. It mattered not. Ming Lun would take him, once they had finished here. Still in the guise of the shaman, she shrieked and held her dagger to the sky. "Soon shall the Eternal Sky know peace!" She bounded back up the slope as fast as she could.

"Now?" whispered Bao Xing from her hiding place.

"Now," Ming Lun confirmed.

With a rush of wind Bao Xing flung up her silken robe, smothering the torches to plunge the hilltop into darkness, and the soldiers into wonder.

Ming Lun ran down to where the other horses waited. Bao Xing's cane clicked along behind her, but Ming Lun had already started back with their mounts. She dropped to one knee, preparing to help the other woman into her saddle. Instead, Bao Xing tapped the horse's leg. It bent its own knee and bowed to the ground before her.

"My husband also trains horses," Bao Xing remarked as she climbed aboard and took the reins.

A good thing the horse straightened, for that tone made Ming Lun sorely want to slap the other woman. Her husband beat and sent his slave to this place to die, only saving him when he found some benefit for himself. What had become of Ming Lun's detachment? Was it the night's failed plan that disturbed her calculated efficiency? Or the fact that the dwarf, the very man who had made this necessary, had also been the one to salvage it? She did not like to owe Dailus her life, and so she balanced that debt. No, there was no debt here. If Yusen had not galloped in, Ming Lun would have finished both soldiers with her blade and… her jaw tightened. How would she have taken the drakemaster from that place? She could carry him no more than a few steps, and he could not move on his own. If he still lived.

Ming Lun mounted the horse and hurried after the others. For now, she needed the dwarf and his horses, and so she followed the narrow defile Yusen had scouted, rode across a soggy meadow, then up again among the trees. Only Yusen's stubbornness kept them riding into the night—the mine overseers would invent their own story of what had happened, especially given the wild stars that flared and vanished overhead. When the Mongols found no sign of his body in the morning, they were more likely to imagine their prisoner torn apart by spirits than spirited away. Superstitious, fearful barbarians.

When they reached another meadow, higher and more enclosed than the last, Ming Lun called, "We must halt. At least for a moment."

Yusen turned his horse and rode back easily, one hand resting on the slave's bouncing body, almost as if he cared. "What troubles you?"

"That cannot be good for his head." She slid from her own mount and stalked nearer. "Surely we can give him one of the pack animals."

"We'd need to tie him on."

Bao Xing caught up, flopping on her horse almost as much as the drakemaster, but she halted along with the pack horses and dug into the baggage to pull out a small lantern.

Reaching Yusen's mount, Ming Lun cradled the drakemaster's head, sticky with blood, his hair matted. She crept her fingers toward his throat, searching for his heartbeat. The beard made that difficult.

"I can feel his breath," Yusen informed her.

Light flared from Bao Xing's lantern. In this new light, Dailus shivered. The arches of his cheeks and his long nose stood out plainly, more mummy than man.

"Do you know healing?" Bao Xing asked.

"Not enough for this."

"There is a monastery a little south, called Dragon Turns. The monks are renowned for healing." She faced the night, but the lantern revealed the gloss of tears in her eyes.

"If they are healers, why are you angry?" Ming Lun asked.

"I was there a long time ago, with my mother. They couldn't save her."

Ming Lun observed the other woman's grief and anger, even after so long. It might be useful later. Dailus's battered head weighed down her hands. He already felt cool to the touch. She scanned his body, but could see no obvious wounds, nothing she could bind or press. "Dragon Turns Monastery. How far is it?"

"If you know the way, we follow you." The dwarf picked up his reins, but Ming Lun swung back onto her horse and urged it closer.

"Give him to me—let him rest against my back."

"Better for the horses to even the weight."

Better for the dwarf to shut his accursed mouth. Ming Lun held out her hand. "Do you want him to live?"

"Then he will ride behind me," Yusen told her. "We need the horses."

They grappled with the unconscious man until he sat behind Yusen, long arm draped across the Mongol's chest, secured there by Yusen's small, strong hand. Travelling alongside her target gave Ming Lun the advantage of watching him, learning his strengths and weaknesses. Last time she tried to kill him, she had not known he was a light sleeper. This time, she would succeed.

They rode more slowly now, Bao Xing in the lead and Ming Lun following with the two spare horses, keeping watch over the others, but Yusen did nothing to jeopardize the drakemaster's safety, such as it was. The monastery could help him more than she could alone, and without Bao Xing, she would never find it. She began to think that Bao Xing would not welcome release from her odious husband, preposterous as that seemed. A pity for a woman who seemed the utmost of Han virtues to be bound to a barbarian. If Ming Lun ever sought a husband, the matchmakers would find someone just as undesirable, but at least he would be Han.

At daybreak, the dwarf agreed they could rest. Ming Lun jumped down from her horse, and took Dailus from Yusen's saddle, draping him against her chest then lowering him to the ground beneath a pistachio tree. She filled their waterskins at a stream, stripping off her squirrel skin cloak and rinsing her face and hands from the filth of the night. When she returned, Yusen sat on a rock overlooking the tree, chewing something as his restless, weary eyes roved the area, flicking to her and away again. Observant, wary, suspicious. Difficult traits in a target. Ming Lun held up a waterskin to him, then brought one to Bao Xing, who settled on a pile of saddle blankets. The horses cropped grass around them and snuffled at the fallen nuts.

Dailus lay in their midst, shivering, covered now with a silk robe embroidered with flowers. With a corner of the cloth, Ming Lun washed the blood from his face as best she could, then took out her sharpest knife and set to work shaving his chin.

Bao Xing giggled. "He has baby's skin, when it's not so dirty and hairy."

Ming Lun focused on her work, finding his lips, tracing the scar at his cheek, careful not to nick him. His eyes never opened, sliding beneath his lavender eyelids.

Above them, Yusen stood up, shielding his eyes with a hand, then he climbed the rough slope and crouched high above, looking around, but not revealing his head. When he slithered back down, he reported, "Soldiers on the mine road, but not this far. No sign of scouts." Glancing at Dailus, he grunted. "That's what he looked like when I took him. But not so thin." Then he peeled back the drakemaster's lip to reveal blood seeping around his teeth. Letting go, the dwarf moved back toward the horses and gave a soft whistle that gathered them around him like children, like her little dancers eager for a sweet. "We need to go. He won't last long."

Ming Lun stood up and pointed to the saddle blankets, causing Bao Xing to say, "Ai! Forgive me—these first." She rose unsteadily, smiling just as unsteadily while Ming Lun helped Yusen to get the horses ready. Rather than use the pack saddles they had ridden while in disguise, the dwarf uncovered the two largest bundles from their baggage, revealing two Mongolian-style saddles with high wooden frames and silver fittings. He gave one of these to Ming Lun.

"You ride well—from the dancing, but this will help."

For his own mount, he kept the pack saddle, and directed her to strap the drakemaster's feet to make their balance easier. His dangling feet looked huge and absurd, pale, battered and trembling like the rest of him. A ghost indeed.

"Which way?" Yusen asked, and Bao Xing described the path,

crossing the mine road at some distance from the mines, then circling under an arch of stone to a hidden spring. "How will we know it?"

"Dragon Turns." She shrugged. "I do not know enough words."

They rode on through the day with another short rest that showed Bao Xing tired and sore from riding. Ming Lun performed a series of stretches. Yusen showed no sign of fatigue at all, save that his eyes might be a little darker. Among the soldiers of his own people, the dwarf looked conspicuous, drawing their jeers for being so unlike them. Away from them, he was a Mongol from head to toe: powerful, determined, an excellent horseman and trail-wise scout, resourceful, tireless. As a girl, she had wondered how such a scruffy, ignorant people came to dominate the North and intimidate the Emperor himself. Now, being so close to one example, she could see an army of such men sweeping down—riding longer, harder, faster than anyone could believe, bound to their conquest, as one with their horses. First, they demanded surrender. When this was ignored, they utterly destroyed their enemy with fire, rape, and slaughter. Then the next city might surrender on rumors alone. The Mongols must be stopped before they moved on the South and broke the empire forever.

They rode out of the narrow band of sunlight remaining from a waning day into the shadow of a jagged peak, and Dailus's tremors worsened in spite of the silk bundled around him.

"When will we—" she began, then broke off as they rounded an outcrop. A fall of stones had broken from the mountain above, revealing a band of golden stone, and a creature that must be a dragon. Embedded in the layers of rock, the dragon's flattened bones stretched longer than the entire string of horses, its ribs cracked, its tail curling between long, heavy legs that ended with powerful claws. Over stunted forelegs, the vertebrae turned back, the hollow-eyed skull staring with a fixed grin of dagger-pointed teeth.

Along the ledge beneath the dragon's grave, a row of clay lamps and crude brass dishes remained from years of offerings. One of its forelimbs curved down, as if demanding more than balls of rice and sticks of incense. What could a dragon desire? Pearls, according to the old stories. Now, staring up at its wicked teeth, Ming Lun thought meat a more likely hunger.

Yusen rode by it, gaping upward, and finally muttered, "Our dragons are not so large."

An arch of stone stretched overhead beyond the dragon's bones, and they passed through, then abruptly down, a waterfall crashing in from one side, scattering water droplets on the path that skirted the stream. The red walls and tiled roofs of a monastery rose among thickets of willow in the moist, green valley. A group of young men in the plain robes of novices hurried up, bowing their bald heads, glancing at Yusen with pinched expressions, but offering signs of blessing. "All are welcome into the Buddha's compassion."

"Thank you," Bao Xing began, but Ming Lun urged her horse forward.

"We have a sick man, poisoned by the cinnabar mines. Can you help him?"

The leader turned toward Dailus. "We will do what we can. Bring him to the courtyard."

They rode on a little further, following the monks, then Ming Lun slid down and released the straps, letting Dailus fall into the arms of the novices. Yusen released the drakemaster's arm and paused to massage his shoulder, sharing a look with his wife, a look that spoke of things Ming Lun was not supposed to know.

"The stable is here." One of the smaller pointed, and Yusen turned his little herd to clatter over stones and sink into moss. Moving to the role she claimed as Dailus's protector, Ming Lun hurried after the novices. Already, they prepared a pallet for him along a sunny wall just by the entrance, and an elder monk emerged from the shadows of a building to join them, examining Dailus, tracing his hands down the long, pale limbs and pressing here and there before he sat back on his heels.

Ming Lun settled with him.

"He is very poorly off, you know this. But there is hope. This corner gathers sun and warm breezes to carry away the poison. We will prepare medicines that can be offered in healing soups. We will measure and track his pulses."

"Tell me how to help, and I will do my best."

The monk nodded gravely, then moved away.

Ming Lun gazed at the drakemaster, her hands folded in her lap. This attachment was a role, she reminded herself, a way to stay close to the dwarf and to gain knowledge of the weapon, nothing more.

Then his eyes flickered open, with a glimpse of jade, but drifting, and she was not sure if he saw her there beside him. Then he breathed, "Do you still dance?"

She stroked his cheek. "I will dance for you." Her throat ached just a little.

Ming Lun had been broken. Her role had become her, like a costume she could not remove. But her plans, her part, her place in the empire of the Son of Heaven, all slipped away in the quiet green depth of his gaze.

CHAPTER FORTY-SEVEN

Zhencai flattened his fingers out, then curled them into a fist again, watching his thumb wrap smoothly up and over, skin wrinkling between the thumb and first finger. A short pucker remained where the wound had been. He sensed the slight strain of the muscles there, the smallest disruption in the qi where the scar pierced its pathway.

Satisfied, he gave the sign of blessing. Across the small yard, his brother monk matched his gesture, then sprang to the attack. In a flurry of blows, they fought across from one corner to another and back. Zhencai's iron hand struck, countered, struck again, his legs launching him forward, back, to the side, swinging up into a kick that the other monk barely blocked. His sparring partner, a man half his age, narrowed his eyes and Zhencai took a careful breath, ready for the furious attack that followed. He dodged, countered, slipped away, ducked, landed a blow at the back of the man's knee that dropped him to the ground, and, when he rose, Zhencai had withdrawn to his corner, again giving the sign of blessing.

The other monk, breathing heavily, waited a long moment before responding, then dropped the sign almost immediately. "Your novice is hopeless, brother. He cannot center his qi. He cannot even find his qi, not at meditation, not in the fighting yard." The monk gestured with his chin across the practice ground to where Andao stood on the top of a short post—the shortest post in the forest of training equipment. Andao's willowy frame wobbled, his long arms flailing, then he plunged from his perch. At least he had learned enough to tuck his limbs and roll rather than break his arms in the fall.

"No man is hopeless." Zhencai watched Andao scramble to his feet, glaring at the post, then aim a kick at it, a kick that flicked from his ankle and involved none of the rest of his leg, never mind his center. It was true. For this, at least, his novice was hopeless.

Around them, a half-dozen monks practiced, some sparring, some developing an iron flesh technique, one standing atop a pillar taller than Andao, on one foot, the other crossed easily at his thigh, hands spread, gazing at the mountains. Zhencai wasn't sure he could climb such a pillar any more, but his thighs remembered the stance, and his center held the view from the top of the stairs at Cloud Mountain, ringed with other peaks and held up as if on the palm of the Buddha, offered to the heavens beyond.

"You both told us that he would never be a monk, and I can see why. He lacks discipline. He holds no sense of duty, except a persistent attachment to the world. If he cannot find his center, he will not only never be a monk, he will never learn to defend himself in the way that he must." The monk wiped his sleeves and checked the wrapping on his legs.

A monk should not cultivate pride in his martial skill, certainly not enough that to be beaten at sparring inspired such remarks. Zhencai considered offering him another lesson in humility.

A very young novice entered the ground with a chime, striking a single tone which resonated through the yard, then offering the sign of blessing. The monks ceased their practice, growing still between one breath and the next, and bowing. Even Andao managed this much. The novice walked over to stand in front of Zhencai. "Honored brother." He bowed. "If you have healed, you are invited to join the abbot for tea."

Zhencai returned the bow. "Honored son, I am humbled to do so." He raised his hand to summon Andao, but the novice frowned.

"This invitation is for yourself, honored brother."

"Oh." This slight stung more than the other monk's deliberate provocations. Andao approached, eyebrows raised, ready for his master's command, and now, Zhencai must send him off like a puppy. Like the puppy he ever would be.

"Master?" Andao bowed slightly.

"You have trouble with balance because you are weak at the core." Zhencai slapped his own firm stomach. "Practice. Jump every water channel in the monastery."

Andao barely sagged: at least he mastered his expression better than he had when they first met. He bowed and turned away, setting his feet and leaping the nearest channel, landing with both feet a little too hard.

"Not just here, in the public yard as well," Zhencai called after him.

Andao landed the next jump with a rush of breath and did not acknowledge.

"I follow," Zhencai told the novice, and they moved from the practice ground toward the inner temple and the private chambers of the abbot and the senior monks. When they first arrived, Zhencai stayed in one of the long, light buildings at the front of the monastery, accepting treatment for his hand—drinking strange soups, and applying herbal wraps. Once the flesh healed, he moved among his fellow monks, joining their daily practice to return to his strength and undergoing spiritual treatments to seal the damage to his qi as much as possible. That any scar still marked his qi suggested that the wound had been deeper or more difficult than they had believed.

They entered a small, mossy yard facing a structure built into the side of the mountain, its red walls turning green where they met the damp stone. Inside this tea house sat the abbot on a straw mat, legs crossed, eyes lowered. Zhencai bowed deeply, then formed the sign of blessing. "Amito fu, honored father."

"Amito fu, younger son." The old man waved him closer and Zhencai knelt before him as the novice prepared the tea things. "I have read your monk's paper—" he indicated the area at Zhencai's breast where he carried the document, "with the seal of my learned brother at Cloud Mountain. I have meditated upon his passing."

Zhencai gave a slight bow. He, too, meditated on the loss of the abbot, and of his brethren. In any other man, it would be called grief.

"I have heard of your journey to find us, and also of the questions you have brought."

Zhencai blinked at the bluntness of this beginning. He expected to sit a while or to speak of the dharma before they spoke of their other concerns.

"Even had I not heard of these things, I have felt them among the brethren. When we sit before the great Buddha and recite our mantras, there are stutters, an imperfection of form and focus. In the practice ground, a lack of balance. I prayed that these elements would dissolve as do all illusions of the flesh. It has not been so." The old man took his cup of tea, but he merely stared through the steam into the yard beyond.

"Forgive me, honored father. I had no intention of causing such a disturbance." His own hot cup singed his fingers, but he drew up the iron qi into his hands, and held it still.

"The wound is not in you, although you carry its evidence." The abbot turned, his rounded profile as subtle as a Buddha carved in ancient stone. "All those who come here seeking to be healed bring the world in with them. It is why we have an outer yard, to contain the world and isolate it. Because you have been travelling the world and it has infected you, we brought you to that yard for your healing. Because you are also a monk and know the illusions of the world, we then brought you inside, closer to the dharma, to complete your healing." He took a sip at last, and Zhencai did as well, the watery tea searing his throat. Another concern of the world.

"With us, at the feet of the Buddha, we hoped to return you to your unborn, undying state, in union with the dharma. Instead, the world clings to you. You wear it as a woman wears perfume. It cannot help but turn the heads of your brother monks."

The base of his small, round teacup fit perfectly in to his palm, its interior turned pale green by the tea inside. Zhencai felt that small. He might have curled into that cup, beneath the notice of the abbot, beneath the notice of the Buddha, utterly bound into the ways of the world.

"What can be done, honored father?"

The abbot took another draught of tea, holding it in his mouth, swallowing at last. "Aside from your wound, you carried into this place two things of the world. Two things which must be shed if you are to be reconciled to the Buddha and return to the eightfold path to Nirvana." He settled with a subtle movement suggesting the gathering of qi, as if he confronted a great foe or a spiritual problem.

Zhencai gathered his own qi, drawing himself out of that tiny cup, acknowledging that his center contained nothing and everything—it could only reflect the truth. He contained exhaustion. The world disrupted the spiritual life he had worked toward. It stabbed into the heart of the spirit, just as the woman's knife had infected his hand.

"You carry with you a scroll which contains not only the source of great suffering, but also the taint of magic, the stain of false pathways so closely bound to the world that they cannot be turned to the service of the dharma or the spreading of the truth. You believe the things on this scroll are not merely illusions, and that they will spread suffering throughout the world. Honored son, the world is suffering. It is made of suffering, it is made for suffering. To hold compassion for the world does not mean to take it upon oneself to dispel this illusion of suffering."

Zhencai bent his head. The abbot told him nothing he did not already know, nothing he had not heard from his own abbot, nothing he had not said to some novice at one time in his care. But it was easy to speak of suffering as an illusion from the mossy yard of a mountain monastery. Harder to say so in the burning city of Kaifeng. Harder to see beyond the illusion in the pagoda garden graveyard of one's brother monks, with the disemboweled corpse of one's abbot spread and bleeding on the ground. The abbot passed beyond the world of suffering. Many citizens of Kaifeng passed beyond it as well. But many others lived there still, and the Mongol armies spread the suffering daily through the breadth of China. Master Deng, the false monk, taunted him with his lack of spirituality. Perhaps Master Deng had been a demon, a tempter like those who tried to entice the Buddha back to the world. If so, then Zhencai had failed the test.

"Honored father, you remind me of what I used to know. The scroll carries the suffering of the world. An illusion of suffering, an illusion of the world." He took a deep breath. "What is the second thing?"

"You know this as well." The abbot set down his cup and ran his fingers along the prayer beads tucked through his belt. "Your... novice."

Zhencai bit down on this truth like a toothache he meant to overcome. Had the abbot seen the signs that Zhencai had noticed? If Andao held not his own qi, but the qi of the earth itself, he was bound up in magic indeed, never to be turned to the truth.

"Your novice has no wish nor will to become one of us. You entered the monastery to shed attachments, and you have become attached to one without a center, one in whom the qi is ungoverned and unfocused. The masters of disciplines here have examined and worked with him. Despite his diligence in seeing you here, this novice does not see that he weakens you. His presence erodes your spiritual discipline and that of the other monks. I thought to suggest sending your novice to undergo the same rituals as the others. He would be old for such things, but a willing spirit could bend his qi to discovering faith. I do not believe that his spirit is willing. I do not believe that he can hold his qi long enough to learn the proper way to draw water, much less to open himself to the dharma. He will not take even the first step upon the eightfold way."

Zhencai sat beside the abbot, swallowing bitter. He had taken on the boy over his own misgivings, in service to the world, not to the Buddha, not to the dharma. He wondered who could teach the boy anything, and settled that he, himself, must undertake to teach him, even knowing that he was already dangerously flawed: Master Deng had seen that, and Master Deng was not even a monk.

"Release your novice back to the world, honored son, and your worldly obsessions with him. Focus on detachment, and send him away."

A wave of grief passed through Zhencai, but he observed this evidence of his own attachment. How could he seek for Nirvana while he clung to such attachments? Had he done anything for Andao but shown him a few blows? Encouraged him to work toward the iron hand discipline for which he was so clearly unsuited. Led him further from his own attachments to his people and to Kaifeng itself—encouraging detachment from the world? No, merely building another attachment to Zhencai as master, a thing he was not and had no claim to be.

The abbot removed his string of prayer beads. "Join me."

Zhencai removed his beads as well, letting each one rest, then slide through his fingers, letting them go as he must let go of Andao, as he must let go of the scroll and the mystery that bound him to the world. He had a higher purpose than that. He was a monk not an archivist, nor an adventurer, a seeker not of answers outside, but of those within. Let him return to the scripture and the prayer, to the drawing of water and the fetching of wood that would guide him back onto the eightfold path.

Footfalls pounded near, and Andao's voice squeaked, "Master!" as if he had begun to call out, then stifled his own impulse.

The abbot turned his head, a deep and endless void reflected in his eyes, a center which was everything, which was nothing.

Zhencai rose and paced down to the yard below. "Novice, you have broken my meditation, and that of the abbot as well." He spoke very softly, barely a breath.

"I know, but, Master—"

Zhencai thrust up his hand to forestall words. "It is the time for eating bitter."

Andao's keen brown eyes searched his face, then the novice blurted,

"She's here—she arrived five days ago. The woman who stabbed you, the one who's after the scroll."

A vehicle to carry the world back to the world and leave the spirit in peace. "Then give it to her."

"Who will she give it to? How many more people will die while you all hide out in the mountains?"

The abbot sat in serenity in his tea house bounded by stone and moss and sky. Compassion did not mean that he must try to cure the suffering of the world, only that he must accept it and show how to move through it. Easy, for those who did not live in the world.

If Zhencai turned away from the monastery, he had no other way to the eightfold path save through the suffering world itself.

So, then, he should remain and return to the spiritual life. Detach himself from the world, from Andao, from the weapon and the suffering it could bring. The abbot offered him a place. Use the strength of his Iron Hands to cling to the dharma.

Andao stood behind him, his breath ragged, his heart consumed by worldly suffering. Between them, Zhencai balanced as if on a pillar as slender as a breath, as tall as any mountain. Above, the stillpoint he searched for, and below, the thousand, thousand other souls for whom peace was the ultimate illusion, and compassion just a word that meant they were alone.

He breathed in the revelation, feeling as if a veil had been lifted from his eyes. What if the attachment to truth were just another illusion? What did it mean to eat bitter, if not this? Detachment itself was an illusion—it must be—as long as a man were still alive.

"Amito fu, honored father. I will remove the tarnish of worldliness from this place. I choose the path of suffering." He bowed and left the only life he had ever known to follow his hopeless novice back into the world.

CHAPTER FORTY-EIGHT

Finally able to sit up and hold his own soup bowl, Dailus sipped quietly and watched Ming Lun dance. His mouth still tasted of metal, but watching her made it easier to ignore. He devoured the intensity of her movement, the purpose with which she stomped each foot and carved or smoothed or drifted her hands through the air. Dailus's fingers and toes felt numb, and he found it hard to imagine running, never mind dancing. At times watching her made his eyes sting. As twilight came on, she shifted from the quick, sharp style she had been using to a fluid sequence of movements similar to those he had seen Cathayan monks or soldiers practice. The Tatars had no such grace: they limited their precision to the use of their horses when they ruined great swaths of countryside. Had they ridden in to ruin Lithuania, after Yusen shot him and hauled him away? His master scouted the way for the soldiers to follow, but Dailus did not think they followed that time. Anya and Matteus were safe, somewhere… and so was their mother.

A fit of shivering overwhelmed him and Dailus gripped the bowl with both hands. Marietta was a good woman. What would she think of him lying here day after day, watching a heathen dance? He knew exactly what the priests would say—but he had too long felt God's absence. Unless God had sent a heathen to save him from the abyss into which he had fallen. Or the Devil had sent her to tempt him into another.

A handful of other patients rested in this courtyard, some alone, some surrounded by the family members who had brought them. In the gathering twilight, two monks moved through the scanty trees toward the gate. The gates would soon close against the night—these two must have someplace urgent to go if they wouldn't wait for morning. One of the two appeared tall and gawky, clumsy. For a moment the light of the temple revealed his silhouette: the Jewish monk! Dailus had seen him that morning, jumping around like an oversized frog. The shape of his nose and the set of his lips put Dailus in mind of the Jews—certainly he did not look Cathayan except for his skin.

He blinked and found Ming Lun watching him in the midst of a turn. Then she executed a spin that did not belong in the dance, her split skirts swirling out around her as she swept her gaze over the courtyard. With a single sharp breath, Ming Lun broke the dance to sprint across the yard. Already two novices drew one large gate closed and moved toward the other. The pair of monks hurried their pace to arrive before the gates close—but they could not move faster than the dancer. She leapt a sleeping child, startling the girl's parents from their healing prayers, and the father cried out.

The pair of monks glanced back, then broke apart as if at the sight of a charging bull, or a Tatar warrior. The older one dropped immediately into a fighting stance, shouting, "Go!"

The Jewish monk put on a burst of speed, running for the gate.

"Bao Xing! Yusen! Don't let him pass!" Ming Lun cried out as she launched herself at the monk.

Dailus gawked. Had the poison progressed to hallucinations? Surely she wasn't assaulting a monk, an old man no less. A knife shone in her hand, and the monk slid beneath it, turning his own hand back to strike hers. Her arm shuddered at the impact, then she shifted direction, exactly as she would in a dance, thrusting her knife along the path of the monk's arm toward his unprotected chest.

The monk grasped her elbow with a sudden twist and brought up his foot, knocking her away.

"Amito fu, honored brother," one of the novices began, "Please—" but the Jewish monk plowed into him, stumbled, and arrested his flight. Two other figures entered the narrow opening at the gate—one clad in flowing gowns, walking with a cane, the other short and fast and unmistakable. Yusen.

The bowl fell from his trembling hands to crack against the pavement. Dailus flashed to the night of his escape from the mine, when he imagined the Lord would carry him away like a lost sheep. Stars fell like Tatar arrows across the sky that night, Ming Lun wore a cape of squirrel fur, and a single command pierced his fog of pain. Yusen ordered him to offer his wrist, and he obeyed. If not for that habit of obedience, a soldier's knife would have slashed his throat.

For the first few days, Dailus had attributed the presence of his master to his own disorientation, another in a long succession of nightmares. The hours between that moment at the mine and opening his eyes to Ming Lun's face held nothing but a quaking agony. She had saved him, as she had once before. But she had done it with Yusen's help. It was not God who carried him away that night, it was one of the very riders of Hell.

Dailus's knees shook and his feet ached. Pain throbbed in his joints—he did not remember rising, but he would not give up his height, not now.

Across the yard, Ming Lun and the monk fought in a flurry of movement, both missing more blows than they landed. The Jewish monk feinted one way, then tried to simply vault past the dwarf's reach, a mistake Dailus wished he could have warned him against. Yusen leapt after him, landing a hard blow at the monk's gut that tumbled him to sprawl on the ground. The dwarf planted his foot on the young man's chest, standing over him, sword drawn.

"Honored brother, a woman!" bleated one of the novices, but the old monk showed no sign of caring. He sank suddenly, then pushed off of his hands to knock her backward, tumbling a blade from her grasp. She slipped in close, her fingers jabbing for his throat, only for him to twist out of the way, aiming a blow at her knee. Their breath escaped in short, even bursts, carefully controlled, with that same precision.

"Ming Lun, what's happening?" the other woman demanded. She looked familiar, but he could not place her. Their presence felt preposterous, like an allegory he did not grasp the meaning of.

"The diagram of the weapon." She spun, dodging a blow. "He has it."

Dailus lurched into motion, pulling his blanket around him, only his forward momentum preventing him from falling headlong. An image of huge wheels, gears and spokes reared up in his memory, crossing a pattern of stars. What did this other woman know about the weapon? As Dailus crossed the ground, Yusen yanked open the downed monk's tunic, then rolled him onto his stomach.

The Jewish monk curled and attacked, barreling into the dwarf. The whole scene struck Dailus as so ludicrous it should be part of the Feast of Fools, dwarf, Jew, monks, women—the world gone mad. Until the Jewish monk's tunic flared out from his movement and revealed a familiar scroll tucked at his waist. The metallic taste in Dailus's mouth doubled as if he returned in that moment to the poisonous mine.

The sound of scuffing feet on mossy stones and the impact of blows on flesh echoed around Dailus as he tottered closer. Yusen caught the Jew's flailing, unpracticed blow in both hands and pushed him back, but he had half the taller man's weight and they both stumbled. The other woman thrust her cane to jab the Jew's shoulder, drawing a cry and forcing him back, still within the confines of the gate, practically shoving him into Dailus's face. The Jew's loose tunic flapped against Dailus's hand, and he reached in beneath the fabric to grab the scroll.

His head swimming, Dailus slumped to the ground, clinging to the scroll with both hands, hunching over it.

"Amito fu! This must stop! This is a holy place, and a place of healing." A voice thundered, backed by the solid stamp of a hundred feet. A very old monk in bright robes led a company of younger monks with the wrapped legs and bare arms of warriors. They stopped and, as one, took a pose of readiness. Their hands swept into a gesture in front of them, a slice of the hand through the air before their faces, then back, their hands moving easily from blessing to threat.

The monk fighting with Ming Lun shifted away, putting several quick steps between them, glancing at the assembled monks and their leader, a wince fleeting across his face.

Ming Lun swayed and struck a pose as well, as if she had just executed a difficult dance and expected their admiration. The hand that shifted toward her back held a short blade.

"Holy Father," said the other woman, moving slowly forward, then bowing very deeply. "Please forgive this trespass against the peace of your monastery. My companion merely sought the return of something that had been missing."

The shadows shifted, and Yusen released the Jewish monk, stepping closer to Dailus, his sword still at the ready. His shoulders squared, his back to Dailus, his arm slightly lifted. A posture of defense, ready to protect his property against any danger.

Bitterness soured Dailus's throat. His joints rebelled and would not obey his desire to escape the dwarf. He lay there, trembling. God forbid the Tatars ever get control of the weapon! Racked with tremors, pain shooting through his limbs, Dailus curled himself around the scroll. By God, if

Yusen would have it, he would have to carve through Dailus, flesh and bone until blood soaked the scroll into a sodden pulp.

***

Bao Xing stood at the center of a frozen constellation of fury. The abbot confronted her small, strange party, with the strength of the monastery behind him, and Bao Xing had only her trust in Ming Lun to sustain her position.

"Do you suggest, lady, that this monk, this Zhencai of Cloud Mountain, is a thief?"

She glanced over at the old monk, breathing heavily, a thin trickle of blood from his mouth and another staining his chest. If the monk were a thief, what did that make Ming Lun? She had held her ground against the warrior monk and called for their help to stop his accomplice. "I can only say, honored father, that the scroll he carried contains knowledge most fearsome and much desired."

"He took it from me, honored father," Ming Lun said, still bowing. "Please forgive me for dishonoring your monastery."

"And what of our patient? What has this thing to do with him that he seems willing to die for it?" The abbot opened his hand.

The old monk's accomplice stood several paces away, with Yusen before him, sword drawn and eyes fierce in spite of facing a man twice his size. Behind him, the drakemaster lay shaking from head to toe, his breath coming in wretched little sobs.

Ming Lun hissed and rushed across the yard, but the abbot gestured and four of the warriors moved to block her way.

The abbot stared at each of them in turn. "Please remove yourself, lady, and your objectionable companion. You as well, Zhencai, and your novice. Too much of the world has entered through our gates upon your heels."

Ming Lun's opponent pressed his lips together, then raised his hand in blessing. His every movement slowed, his shaven head bowing, then he turned. His companion backed a few steps away from Yusen, his face furrowed into a frown almost comical. "Master, what about the scroll?"

Zhencai paced by, passing the tableau of Ming Lun confronting the warrior monks. The young man drooped after him, but pointed at Yusen. "We're not going far! And we won't let you have it!"

Ming Lun feinted away from the gate, then slipped around toward it as the four monks shifted position to maintain their blockade. As she leapt toward the fallen drakemaster, four other monks hurried up, then four more escorting two of their elders, the healing monks in their wrapped robes carrying packets of medicines. These two knelt beside the drakemaster, touching him gently. He cried out in any case and curled the tighter, batting at their hands.

Ming Lun gave another hiss, sustained like the note of a snake about to strike.

Bao Xing tapped her cane to get the other woman's attention, but she only darted a glance before she resumed prowling the barricade of monks, any vestige of the calm dance mistress swept away.

"Honored father," said Bao Xing, "May we be permitted to wait outside, as we have done, for our companion's recovery?"

The abbot closed his eyes briefly, and gave the sign of blessing. "We will extend our compassion to see that he is healed as quickly as may be."

"Thank you, honored father." Bao Xing bowed again, then walked over to intercept Ming Lun's path, though she hesitated to actually step in front of her. "Ming Lun? We must—"

"Leave him? And the scroll? How can you even suggest it? You were the one who could not be certain we should even trust the monks to heal him."

Did she worry more about the man, or about the scroll—the scroll they hadn't known she knew about?

Bao Xing smiled faintly. "I believe we can trust them to do their best to see that we depart here as soon as possible." She turned carefully, as Mistress Luo had taught her, and walked out the gate. Yusen fell in beside her and Ming Lun trailed after, her footfalls nearly silent.

At their backs, the great door swung shut and a bar slid into place. To one side in the narrow valley that led to the monastery centuries of water and weather carved into the stone to create a long series of steps with a deep ledge at the top, a natural porch where Yusen set their camp. The five horses tethered nearby pricked their ears, and a campfire's glow illuminated a stony cove of ancient fish and broken monsters. They undulated in the stone—schools of tiny fishes here, larger ones further along, and a vast array of round bones in the shape of an enormous hand. At one edge, a trail of vertebrae intruded from another ledge as if left behind by a careless visitor. No wonder this place had a reputation for healing—so many dragon bones would make powerful medicine.

The two monks expelled from the monastery lingered, their faces as stony as the dragon bones themselves, though the younger one shifted restlessly as Bao Xing approached. Yusen and Ming Lun spread to either side of her, by some silent agreement, like imperial guards in the face of a threat. Ming Lun sank into a posture that invited attack—unless she meant to pounce first. The older monk, Zhencai, regarded her impassively, but the wiry muscle of his arms looked taut, glistening with sweat, ready to meet her.

The young man flung himself down the steps. "What is your interest in the scroll? And who is that man they are healing?"

Zhencai gave a soft grunt, and the young man stopped short, though his hands kept moving a moment longer, underscoring some point he still made inside of his head.

"The man is my slave," Yusen stated, "And none of your concern."

Bao Xing rested the cane lightly on the next step up. "Join us at our fire, brothers, and we can speak of this together."

Yusen growled, and Zhencai's glance flicked in his direction, his lips drawn down. Disgusted by Yusen's Mongol heritage, or by Yusen himself?

"I am Bao Xing. The observatory of my father and grandfathers overlooked the Monastery of Cloud Mountain," Bao Xing said.

The monk's eyes flared, capturing the firelight. He carved the sign of blessing with one solid hand, then walked to meet her at the fire.

"I'm not a monk," the other one said. "My name is Li Andao—Kaifeng is my home."

Yusen circled beyond their reach to a position near the saddles, sword held before him, like a statue of a warrior on the pathway to an emperor's grave. His army destroyed both Cloud Mountain and Kaifeng, but the monk and his companion showed no malice, not yet. Laying her cane before her, Bao Xing settled onto a folded blanket in what had become her customary place these last few days, inviting the others to use the log that lay opposite, but Zhencai and Andao sank to the ground while Ming Lun stood with her back to the stone, her gaze fixed on the monastery gate.

CHAPTER FORTY-NINE

Zhencai watched the elegant lady before him, searching for any sign of the bereft child he had seen years before, weeping at the death of her mother and clinging to her father's robe as he asked the monks for their prayers. Like most in the area, the astronomer's family made their own offerings to the dead, but sought the serenity of the monastery in troubled times. If anything, the woman resembled more the woman who had died, a slender beauty whose occasional visit to the monastery always caused a lapse in discipline among the novices—and sometimes among the brethren as well. How did the daughter of such parents come to travel with a Mongol and a… a very dangerous woman. All women were dangerous, the astronomer's daughter only concealed it more carefully.

"Will you answer our questions now?" Andao's patience had expanded during their travels, but not so far as to encompass this strange gathering.

The woman regarded him with curiosity. "I am deciding who should be asking and who answering. How can I be certain you are who you claim?"

"Mongols came to Cloud Mountain under the half-ox moon. All of the monks were slain except myself," Zhencai said. "How did the observatory escape destruction?"

Bao Xing tipped her head. "I offered myself to the khan to distract those soldiers from the observatory. They looked no further than my face, and left my father's tower alone."

The Mongol soldier's glare aimed at Zhencai, admitting no wrong in the slaughter at Cloud Mountain, but when Bao Xing spoke of the khan, the Mongol drank her in. Small of form he might be, but great of qi, an undisciplined energy that burned in his face.

"I saw the monastery in flames, brother," Bao Xing said. "How did you survive?"

"I performed my duty in the sarira temple that day. While I was there, one of the monks woke up." He described what he had seen, offering his story, inviting hers, but it was the dancer who grew suddenly still. Gazing at her, he said, "You know of this."

"Of monks who claim to reject the world, then obsess about how to preserve themselves? I have heard of this." The dancer stalked closer, crouching as if to warm herself at the fire, but she watched them all with the suspicion of a cat. "It is how the Order of Celestial Purity hoped to remain in power until they found an emperor they had faith in. Your monk, Master Deng, is a member of the order."

"Celestial Purity?" Bao Xing frowned. "I have seen those characters recently."

"Draw them," the Mongol prompted. His Chinese was coarse and thickly accented. Zhencai meditated on the Buddha's admonitions about compassion, but the sound of the Mongol's voice and the scent of fire built tension in his muscles, gathering his qi as if he prepared for battle.

Sliding his sword into its scabbard, the Mongol stepped up and drew a smoldering stick from the fire, offering it to her. As the glow died from its tip, she made a few strokes with the burned end on the floor of the ledge, and the Mongol caught his breath. "The Minister of Archives, Guowei. I saw this on paper in his room."

"Perhaps you are correct." She clipped her words. Zhencai did not think she believed him.

"Why is he here?" Andao pointed at the Mongol. "Are you spying for the Mongols, both of you?" He faced the dancer and Bao Xing in turn. "Why else you would travel with one of them?"

The dancer spun into a martial stance. "Dare say that again, foreigner, and you shall not see the dawn."

"I am no more foreign than you—my family lived in Kaifeng for centuries. When it's safe to return, we will live there still."

"And yet you are no monk—what are you?"

"I could ask you the same thing! You're no dancer. What do you want with the plans?"

"To keep them out of enemy hands."

"So you asked a Mongol for help."

She sprang into action, leaping the fire, causing Andao to scramble to his feet. Before he'd even extended his lean frame, Zhencai stood between them, his iron hand just touching the dancer's chest, feeling the thunder of her heart, his other hand extended behind to keep Andao back.

"Please!" Bao Xing rose unsteadily, her cane knocked away in the movement. "Please stop. None of us can use the device, not the Han people and not the Mongols either. We cannot use it without burning thousands of our people and killing Kaifeng all over again. They cannot use it without slaughtering their army."

The Mongol might appear to have retreated from the argument, but Zhencai noticed the direction of his move, to the side away from Bao Xing, giving plenty of room to draw his sword.

"If no one will use it, then why are we all after it?" Andao demanded.

"Someone will," said Zhencai. "Master Deng did not wake after one hundred and sixty years merely to take a walk to the city."

"If he is a member of the Order of Celestial Purity, has he found the new emperor worthy?" Andao said.

"A worthy emperor would not abandon half of his nation," the Mongol said. "Your emperor would immediately use the weapon if he thought he could stop the khan."

The dancer slid back from Zhencai, giving a careless turn of her head as if to shift the hair from her face, or to remind him of the deadly ornaments in her hair. "Nor would the khan hesitate if it fell into his control."

"That is why we must stop it," Bao Xing insisted, her delicate hands pleading, palms up, to them all. "We must be sure that neither the emperor nor the khan can use it. If they would slay each other, let them do it slowly, and let the people of the north find their lives in peace."

Zhencai offered the sign of blessing. "Amito fu, lady. See where we have met?" He raised his hands, and they all looked, as if none of them had noticed. They gathered in an open-ended cave with a high roof of stone, and a back wall teeming with the bones of dragon fish and dragons. In the flickering light of the fire the bones seemed to stir against their prison of stone, as if they stretched to alertness after a very long rest. Like the dead monk, Master Deng, who walked away, and drew Zhencai like the Buddha's hand. But Zhencai had not been the only one drawn by him and by the scroll he sought. That these three parties should all come together, and in such a place, could only be the turning wheel of fate.

"Dragon Turns monastery. We came to get aid for the drakemaster," the dancer said.

"As we came to gain healing, both for the body and the spirit. Why here? Why all of us?"

Andao chewed on his lip, frowning furiously as he considered his master's questions. "Because we are all in need of healing? No, because the healing that is required is greater than any of us." His face cleared.

The dancer cocked her head and smiled briefly, like a bow plucked to launch an arrow. "The dragon is the symbol of the emperor. It is auspicious to meet here in his service."

The Mongol growled, and Zhencai shifted his position. "Dragon bones are used in healing, and dragons teach us to contemplate more deeply." He finished his turn, his hands spread to encompass the dragon bones in the wall. "Those who would seek wisdom must travel deep. They must enter the caves to meet the dragon. Once, a young man studied all there was to know of dragons. He read of them, and painted them, he learned the legends of them, and travelled to all of the places he might find more. Seeing this, a dragon was impressed with the young man's dedication, and so, the true dragon descended to the young man's bedside—but he woke in a panic, terrified to see a dragon in the flesh, and the dragon was forced to retreat to the sky.

"The dragon is wisdom, and it is found within. To meet the dragon in the cave, one must master one's own fear. One must face the darkness, and the truth." He drew his right hand around into the sign of blessing.

For a moment, the firelight flickered, and the hiss and crackle of wood was the only sound. "We are together here to face the dragon. This weapon is too much for man, too great for any man. There is no being of this world with enough wisdom to use it well. The emperor, you say, the khan, you think. Search within the caverns of your heart and see if you believe that to be true."

The dancer's gaze traced the dragon's form, then rested on the Mongol across the fire. He folded his arms and stared back at her.

"No," Andao whispered. He cleared his throat, and spoke more strongly than Zhencai had expected. "If none of us is wise enough to use it, then we must make sure that it cannot ever be used."

Zhencai gave a nod. "This is our duty, but we do not know where the weapon is."

The lady's pale-moon face slipped into sadness, her brows furrowed.

"Nor do I. My research convinced me that they built it, that they tested it, even, but I know only that it is in the mountains." She indicated the mountains all around them, mountains that ranged for a thousand li.

When the astronomer's daughter began to speak, Zhencai's hope swelled. With her knowledge and their own, they would locate the device and destroy it, and he could retreat from the world to seek the spiritual balance he had so long desired.

"They left no maps?" The dancer perched with her back to the stone, the empty eyes of dragon fishes peering over her shoulder.

Bao Xing tucked her skirts in preparation to sit, and nearly overbalanced, but the Mongol leapt to her aid, taking her hand to lower her to the blankets. Could the Mongol also hold some sense of compassion? Yet how could any being of compassion participate in the burning of Cloud Mountain and the ruin of Kaifeng?

Andao cast about and found the cane where it had rolled during the argument. He picked it up and approached in his usual sloppy rush, then his steps slowed and dragged. He turned the cane slowly in his fingers, frowning down at it. "This cane, lady. Where did it come from?"

"My several times grandfather. My father gave it to me." She held out her hand expectantly, but Andao did not give it back and the Mongol edged forward.

"They were astronomers, all of them?" He held up the cane in the firelight. "Did your several times grandfather know about the device?" Andao rotated the cane, firelight catching the carved mountains, bridges and trees that wrapped its length from one brass fitting to the other. "It shows the mountains—I've seen this ridge from the wall at Kaifeng." He tapped a finger near the bottom. "It's a map, isn't it? It shows how to get there."

"Of course. Guowei tried to steal it: he must have recognized it." The Mongol pounced and yanked the cane from Andao's hands to give it to Bao Xing.

She bowed her head over it, studying it.

"But it's round." The dancer crouched at Bao Xing's other side, head cocked. "How can you tell where to begin?"

"The Order of Celestial Purity!" Bao Xing looked up at the Mongol, then gave a little start as if she had not expected to find him so close. "Not

Guowei's chamber—it was in the inscription on the armillary sphere at Kaifeng, when I came to translate."

The Mongol sank back on his heels. "It was destroyed. Before I left the army, they were already breaking it up; even without the drakemaster, General Munkjar still has the molds to cast more firedrakes."

The dancer swiped her finger through the charcoal characters written on the stone. "More weapons to destroy our cities. The blood of China will grow the finest grass for your horses."

"Your emperor invited us, and the will of Heaven allows us to stay."

"Yusen rides with me," said Bao Xing, "to see that this machine is destroyed." The Mongol slapped his thighs in agreement, but the dancer held up her finger blackened by charcoal.

"How can you know what hides in a Mongol's heart?" the dancer asked.

Zhencai kept her in his vision, careful not to stare. She had not told them who she was or how she trained or how she felt about the device the rest of them had agreed to destroy. "Do not underestimate his heart," Zhencai murmured.

"Did I suggest he had a heart?" The dancer wiped the stain from her finger. "No more than any other Mongol. They destroyed the device that held the clue, as they have destroyed so very much."

At their midst, Bao Xing gripped the cane, and her eyes shimmered. The Mongol sat beside her, his dark gaze upon her.

"What grieves you, lady?" Zhencai asked softly.

She shook her head. "One of the rings in the device was fixed, and I thought that was strange, because it meant the viewing tube always pointed the same way. It had a marking on it, showing the Dark Lance ringed by a wandering light, just like what's happening now. When it finishes, the power of the Lance will be at its most terrible. If Master Deng reaches the weapon first, that's when he'll use it. My father—" she broke off, huddled into her silks, no longer the elegant lady, but the girl whose house lay in the path of fire. Zhencai formed the sign of blessing. The farmers and citizens had known the Mongols were coming—this next doom would arrive without even a rumble in the ground.

"You said the viewing tube was fixed on something—what could you see?"Andao's voice broke in upon the lady's grief and her companions' quiet sympathy.

Her shoulders rose and fell. "In Kaifeng, everything that does not look at the river plain looks at the mountains."

"The mountains aren't all the same, lady." Andao reached out and traced the carvings on her cane. "Some of them have these jagged cuts and some of them are smooth. Cloud Mountain had the double peak, one for the monks, and one for your father. Dragon Turns looks like a dumpling splitting open at the top—the sides are round."

"They're just mountains—they're not like stars! I have not studied them to know their patterns. If my memory were a book, I would hand it over and let you find the mountain I saw."

Zhencai settled into a cross-legged posture that made his old legs ache after the evening's exertions, but he set aside the concerns of his flesh and remembered the lessons of his spirit. Forty years a monk. Many things he had not yet learned, but this, he knew. "Lady, will you permit me to find that book?"

"How?" She almost laughed, but it would be more fragile than the butterfly's wing, brief and frail as beauty ever was.

"Empty yourself. Empty your sorrow, your fear and your pain. Give them to me." He employed a firm, but gentle voice, letting his hands lie on his lap, fingers just touching. "Lay them here, to vanish in the wind."

She blinked at him, then took a posture resembling his own, the embroidered toes of her tiny shoes protruding from beneath her skirts. The fire lay between them, sparks drifting up from time to time in the swirl of smoke. The Mongol prodded it with the blackened stick and a veil of sparks like a night of tiny stars briefly surrounded him.

"Do you see the fire? See through the fire." He took a deep breath and expelled it slowly. "You are looking back, lady, looking beyond." Another long breath. "There is nothing within you, nothing around you. Let the darkness fill you."

She sighed just a little. "It is full of stars."

"It is a dark passage and you can see beyond, but the mountain is blocking your view. You are the stars and the sky. You are the darkness and the light. You are the mountain, and the mountain is within you. Draw upon the scroll of memory, lady, and show us the mountain you see."

She opened her hand, and the Mongol pressed the stick into her palm. The blackened stick scraped across the ground for a very long time, or for a moment. Sparks drifted between them, bright writing on a scroll of smoke. Andao's whoop of delight shattered the moment. "Master, I see it—I know where to go."

Tears trickled from the lady's eyes and Zhencai's heart swelled with compassion. "The Dark Lance rises," she whispered. "We don't have much time."

CHAPTER FIFTY

In the courtyard of the Dragon Turns monastery, a senior monk knelt before Dailus, laying out a few small bundles. "This is Thunder God Vine—" he tapped a bamboo tube with a cap at one end, "for the joints. Rub it in when you need increased vigor." He raised a cautionary hand. "Do not ever take it in your mouth—wash it from your hands when you have used it."

He stared until Dailus gave a nod, then he set his hand on the next, a cloth pouch. "This is green tea with ginger. It is also for the joints, but you may drink it daily. And this—" he poked the smallest packet, "is Yan Hu Suo powder, from the root to the flower. It will aid with the internal wind that besets your liver. You may add it with the tea, or take it by itself."

"Thank you, honored brother," Dailus said, and managed a bow. The powder he had taken earlier must be working, for he barely trembled now, and a novice had rubbed Thunder God Vine into his joints before helping him dress. He wore something like the monks' own robes, made to suit his stature, and of a pale green fabric instead of the red or beige the monks favored.

The monk continued to stare at him. "The abbot believes that your companions have unbalanced the monastery with worldly concerns. I am not sure this imbalance should take precedence over the health of a patient."

Dailus took a moment to work out his meaning, first from the unfamiliar words, next from the veiled worry those words implied. Was he ready to leave the monastery? Would the Thunder God and ginger tea be enough to sustain him?

The monk's glance fell to the scroll, bound in heavy cloth, that Dailus would not allow to leave his side. "If you allow them to take that away with them, you might remain here until you are more fully healed."

"Thank you again, honored brother—but I can't. I, too, am concerned about the world."

"In that case, may the world show you compassion." He raised his hand into the sign of blessing. "Amito fu."

"You, too."

The monk inclined his head, then rose smoothly and moved on to another patient. Leaning forward, Dailus gathered the medicines into the traveling satchel they had provided and tied the scroll's wrapping onto the strap. Back home, the monks wore thick robes of dark colors and spoke about sin and corruption. If his liver failed him, resulting in an internal wind that shook his bones, they would take it for a sign that he was marked by sin and outcast of God until his repentance—likely accompanied by a substantial donation at the shrine of one or another saint. He pushed himself to his feet, with a slight throbbing in his knees and ankles, but nothing like the agony he carried from the mine. As the day progressed, the pain would return. How long would the pain haunt him?

Movement by the gate caught his attention, and he lost track of his thoughts—a not uncommon problem since the mine. Ming Lun waited outside, the novices warding her off, though she did not approach. When he stood up, she smiled, adding a little bow when he walked toward her. Bao Xing, the willowy beauty, had informed him of their plans the day before, and asked him to join the cause, as if he were not already committed. The destruction of this weapon would be his penance for the weapons he had made. His slave bracelet hung as the earthly reminder of his promise.

The novices bowed him through the gate into a narrow valley with a groove running down one side. Fantastical creatures grew from the rocks, reminding him of the thousand Buddhas he had seen, then he spotted the horses, with Yusen checking their saddles and tugging the knots of makeshift rope bridles. The sight of his master chilled him, but he would have to accept him as part of the group. Without those horses, the quest would be over.

"I am glad to see you on your feet." The dancer's smile played about her lips, as she had smiled that day in the drakemaster's workshop, claiming she wanted to find if he were just as hairy down below.

Dailus smoothed a hand over his cheek. "Thank you for bringing me here, and for shaving that terrible beard."

She laughed behind her hand. "This is better. Have they given you medicines?"

"Some, enough, I hope." He patted the satchel. "Green tea, ginger, some kind of flowers, Thunder God paste."

"Thunder God?" Her brows furrowed.

"I know, it's poisonous—I shouldn't taste it."

"Yes, but also—" she broke off, lowering her gaze.

"What else? He didn't say anything."

She took a step away, tipping her head. "It can make a man have no babies."

Dailus's cheeks warmed, and he suddenly missed the beard. He swallowed. "I already have two—I'm not likely to have any more without my wife around."

"You would not be the first foreigner to take a Chinese wife."

His throat felt thick. "I can't do that—it is against God."

Ming Lun turned away, the coils of her hair gleaming in the sun and moved swiftly toward the horses. "Come. The lady says we have little time."

He watched her walk before him, her every movement grace and power. Would he even see his wife or children again? If God had forsaken him, what was the point of obedience? Except the radiance of Heaven, the comfort of that place beyond pain, would be denied him forever. When Dailus closed his eyes to pray, he pictured the bright and pale angels of his youth, backed by their radiant wings, but standing in groves of celestial willows, overseeing fountains that ran beneath arched bridges, past chapels with pillars of red, where the monks wore red as well and wished him compassion rather than penance. Heaven had left the clouds and come to this green valley to be watered by mountain streams and honored by a woman's dance.

"I will ride first, as scout," Yusen told one of the two monks who stood by his precious horses. "You next." He pointed at the Jewish one. "Then my wife. I know you will have need of her cane." The little man noticed Dailus's approach, but said nothing.

Bao Xing tapped the knee of the third horse, and it bowed for her to mount. She had been given one of the two saddles, while two of the horses wore the sort of frame used for packing supplies. Yusen's wife. That was a story Dailus still could not quite believe.

"I'll walk," said the young monk. "Someone has to." Andao, that was his name.

"I am used to walking," the older one replied: Zhencai, a sturdy man at least a dozen years older than Dailus.

"I can't allow my elder to walk. And my master."

"They argue," Ming Lun whispered. "All the time." She pointed toward the brown pony behind Bao Xing's. "I think this one is yours."

Dailus eyed the animal. "They're all his."

"For now, we must trust him. He did bring me to you, and to this place."

"Why?"

She gave a shrug. "Because he is dishonored before his khan and his people. Even more so than before. His worth lies in you."

That tightened Dailus's shoulders and he gripped the satchel to his side with one arm. Heat flooded his hand as she stroked his fist with her fingers. "Ours are the last two horses," she whispered. "When there is a good moment, I can lead us away from here—from him."

"Bao Xing says that we need the cane and that young man to find our way to the weapon."

With a sharper breath, Ming Lun replied, "Bao Xing is under the sway of the Mongol. What if they're here on behalf of the khan?"

What she said made sense: why else would someone like Bao Xing be married to an unpopular dwarf—and apparently reconciled to the marriage? "And the monks?"

"That young one's no monk. He is not even Han."

"I knew it!"

Bao Xing glanced back at his sudden excitement, and Dailus lowered his voice. "He's Jewish, isn't he?"

"I don't know this word, but I have heard him say it. What does it mean?"

Both the question and the horse made him feel off-balance as he mounted. In the Church, Jews were held responsible for the crucifixion, but he would have to explain the entirety of his faith in order for her to understand, and even then, the stories would be received as Ghost Shaman tales. Instead, Dailus focused on the practical. "The Jews make money off of other people's work. They are merchants and bankers, moneylenders. I didn't know they had spread to Cathay."

She dipped her head in a slight nod. "He speaks more of study than of selling."

"That, too. They write all kinds of unholy books and spread them around. Their women even know how to read."

Easily swinging up on to her mount, Ming Lun glanced at him sidelong. "Even their women."

"They are a strange people." Dailus could read only a few words pertaining to contracts for materials or hired work. The churchmen loved their words almost as much as the Jews.

"Hup!" Yusen nudged his horse and started them out of the valley, the bone dragons watching them go with empty eyes. Dailus crossed himself, dodging those black glares. Immediately, Yusen turned up a narrow path likely made by goats. Dailus gripped his reins and saddle both. The horse jogged his joints so that they seemed to rattle inside.

"Why up?" he asked through clattering teeth.

Yusen turned in his saddle, gesturing at the mountains. "Scouting. To find the right peak." The little man looked perfectly at ease sideways, in spite of the ever-steeper slope. The horses kicked aside small stones that plunged downward, and Dailus forced his eyes away from the edge. Zhencai marched steadily along, keeping a little apart from the horses while his apprentice flopped on his mount. The young man looked back and offered a lopsided grin, pointing from himself to Dailus as if they shared something. Between them, Bao Xing leaned a little forward, utterly focused on the act of riding. She kept her seat well, not with the ease of her husband's long practice, but far superior to Andao's novice floundering. Really, it was a wonder none of them fell.

At his back, Ming Lun rode gracefully astride, her dancer's thighs providing all of the strength and balance she required. That thought brought an ache to Dailus's loins and he turned away. Maybe the Thunder God Vine would reduce that ache to a wistful memory and let him keep his heart and mind on God, and on his wife.

The landscape fell away as they topped a ridge. In every direction, mountains carved dark shapes onto the horizon, growing very tall and misty at his back, a few crowned with snow. Ahead and to the right, valleys merged into the hazy distance. To either side, pine forests fringed the slopes and other spiky trees leaned into the air, daring a fall of a thousand feet or more. Crows soared overhead at first, then below, dark, familiar forms never meant to be seen from such an angle. As they came around a great stone, a herd of white goats scattered uphill, even the tiniest lambs bounding up a near-vertical slope. Dailus clung to his reins as if he could force the animal to be just as steady.

When the riders emerged onto level stone, Dailus's horse skittered past the others, and Yusen called out to him, "Turn her head! Tightly, tightly—like a circle! Drop one rein so she turns."

Nausea stung Dailus's throat as he dropped the rein on one side and pulled. The horse snorted, ears flattening, but he hauled it around in a circle and it slowed its pace, tossing its head in protest until it stood, ill-tempered, a horse-length from the edge. His heart thundered, the joints throbbing from his fingers all the way to his spine.

Yusen grinned and nodded. "Just so."

Dailus reined in the urge to charge the dwarf straight over the ledge. "I am not yours to command, not anymore."

The grin vanished. For a long moment, Yusen stared back, then he turned away.

"Are you well?" Bao Xing spoke loudly rather than move her horse any closer.

"Fine. Hungry." Dailus found the dropped rein and eased his grip.

"Yes, yes. We need food soon." Her lips pinched and she looked around as if expecting to see a marketplace or a convenient shrine to steal from.

Turning his mount with no apparent exertion, Yusen galloped across the ledge and up the ridge, drawing his bow and leaning forward. At the sight of the bow, Dailus's hand clamped to his leg, to the scar from just such an arrow, but the dwarf wasn't even looking toward him. Instead, he shot ahead of them just as he disappeared over the top.

"What—"Andao began, then the sound of hoofbeats returned, and Yusen appeared at the top of the slope, leaning far back and allowing the horse to choose its own path down. On the saddle ahead of him draped a small white goat, blood spilling around the shaft of an arrow at its side, head and legs dangling.

Trotting easily back, Yusen switched to Chinese to ask, "Where now?"

Andao stared around them, shoulders drooping. "I have no idea."

Dailus, too, looked around at the endless ridges, slopes and valleys. For a time, Dailus allowed himself to hope the quest could be fulfilled, his guilt eased by preventing another slaughter. Now he could see it was hopeless. Master Deng knew where to go. If he found the machine in good repair, he could choose his time and target, while they wandered the mountains forever and never recognized the way.

CHAPTER FIFTY-ONE

Yusen did as he always had when he did not know the path: he worked on what he knew. When the mind worried, the body must be fed.

Hobbling Tsang near a grassy verge, Yusen hauled the dead goat to an overhanging rock to prepare it for cooking as the dancer watched. Either she was hungry, or she was thinking of something else entirely. Either way, he would not trust her. He slashed the goat's throat and pushed its head toward the edge to let the blood drain out. In a less promising environment, the blood, too, should be their dinner; today, he made it an offering for the land and sky in this place where they came together. While the blood trickled down, Yusen took account of his group. Who among them could do any work? The dancer, certainly. The slave once had the bodily strength of two men, but now he trembled like a baby. The old monk, even after a long day's walk, performed a series of ritual stretches and movements.

"Zhencai, we need a fire." Yusen flicked his gaze over their surroundings. "Down there, among the tall stones." Which would block the wind and disguise the fire's light.

The elder monk regarded him blankly, then started gathering materials. His apprentice slithered down and staggered from Uul's back while the horse gave a disdainful snort. Bao Xing, meanwhile, tapped Khukhree's leg, then dismounted carefully. He would make a rider of her yet. Yusen gathered the horses, holding the reins and tapping Zun's leg so that the slave could dismount. The giant still stumbled away from the horse's back until the dancer, springing down from Ech, caught his elbow. When they found the dancer waiting in Mouth of the Mountains, Yusen doubted her claims of attachment to the slave. Now, seeing her tender glances and supportive grip, Yusen only yearned for someone to look at him that way.

He stomped over to catch the reins of the other horses and brought them to Tsang. She would look out for them.

Stripping off his del, Yusen focused on his work, ignoring the stares of the others at his bare, thin chest. The latest scar throbbed at his left shoulder, but he ignored that, too. He gutted the goat, leaving the slash open to stuff in hot stones for roasting. Slinging the dead animal over his shoulder he brought it down to where Zhencai laid the fire as efficiently as Yusen himself might have done it. He had chosen his assistant well. Andao fidgeted with his sleeves, broke twigs off the few branches they had found, and shuffled against the stone, walking in little patterns.

"Heat some stones and fill the goat's cavity," Yusen ordered, already turning away

The monk's soft voice stopped him. "I have not cooked meat."

Yusen pivoted on his heel. "How can you be so strong if you don't eat meat?" He forgot his bloody arms and bare chest until Andao's eyes flared wide.

"I am a monk." The corners of the old man's eyes softened. "It is not the world that sustains me."

Yusen snorted, chuckling as Andao emulated his master's posture, even managing to tear his gaze from Yusen's childish body. "And you? Do you cook?"

"It is the Sabbath. I should not even be riding." Andao's hand strayed toward his bare scalp.

"What has this Sabbath to do with riding?" Yusen marched back to the fire, rearranging the stones to heat the ones most suitable. His hands left bloody marks.

"This day is holy. It is a day of rest."

Yusen shook his head. "Look around you. There is hunger and pain, there is climbing the mountains, there is searching, planning, hunting, scouting—there is no rest." He spread his arms. "This is why all the land is holy, and high places most of all, where the land reaches up to touch the sky."

Andao's restless body froze, long nose pointing toward the north like a coursing hound.

"When these stones are hot," Yusen directed, "pile them in the goat. When the hair falls off, is cooked."

Zhencai grimaced, but gave another nod.

Moving beyond the fire, down the slope opposite where they had ridden up, Yusen cocked his head and listened. He heard nothing, but the air smelled faintly of moisture, so he proceeded down the trail until he found the pool the breeze promised, a greenish cleft of water trapped by a stone after the last rains. Scraping off as much blood as he could, Yusen filled a waterskin and used it to wash his arms and chest.

A muffled slide of movement hissed behind him. Yusen spun about, crouching, hand to his knife.

The dancer stood on the path, her garments swaying in arrested motion. She smiled, beguiling and unconvincing. "Forgive me. I thought you might have found water." She spoke Mongolian too well.

Yusen held the blade sideways before him, not a threat, but a presence. "Yes, but not for drinking. How is the drakemaster?"

"Weak. It is too soon for him to travel."

"He'll recover. He has before."

The ornaments in the woman's hair shivered a little with a faint musical sound. "I suppose you would know; you have known him longer than I."

"He will stay alive until he can go home." He replaced his knife.

"Does he still have a home, after your people visited?" She softened her words with a twist of a smile.

"What Batu Khan has done with my information, I can't say. They had no defenses, weak archers, and more temples than fortresses. Some horses, but not good ones. Batu Khan might have swept the whole of that country to the sea like a woman sweeping crumbs."

The drakemaster appeared on the pathway behind her, gaunt, his green eyes flaming as if with fever. Yusen's chest constricted, his breathing suddenly sharp in his throat. Yusen shrugged, hooking his thumbs into the waist of his trousers not far from his knives. "I have had no home for most of my life, and it does me no harm."

"I have never had one," she replied, "not if you mean any home smaller than my country." She shifted, allowing the drakemaster to descend and join her. His hand clamped the satchel he carried over his shoulder, his slave bracelet standing out alongside the scroll. He towered over her as well, but she stood firmly, shoulders square, chin raised, more like a Mongol than a Chin. Yusen's damp skin prickled with gooseflesh. Two against one, with the pool and the cliffs as their allies. In two strides, he could be dead.

"Is there water for washing?" the slave asked in Chinese.

"Yes, but not for drinking," the woman said. "It might be boiled to make tea—if the Mongol has not fouled it with blood. Or does the blood stand in when you cannot get milk for your tea?"

"Oh, no, the tea stands in for blood." Yusen grinned back at her, pushing toward the trail and the fire and his horses beyond. The slave slipped aside, knees bending and head sinking in a bow, then his body clenched and he straightened again as Yusen passed by. Yusen bounded uphill, testing his dexterity in a series of jumps like the goat he had shot down earlier. Already above them, he dodged side to side as if playing goat, or dodging arrows, or knives. The woman despised Yusen, and her attitude or her presence encouraged the slave's independence. The two of them together made a dangerous pair, at least for him.

Yusen had no allies save his wife, and even she must be suspected because her loyalties remained Chin. Did he and Bao Xing need the slave's knowledge, if they could get the plan? Bao Xing could understand all of these things. But they did not know the mountains.

When Yusen reached the shadowed stones, the old monk had already filled the goat with hot stones and now sat poised upon a boulder, watching. His apprentice stood as if still frozen, but Yusen realized after a moment, that he was moving almost imperceptibly, his toes digging in and shifting him slightly against the stone, his face a mask of concentration. Tempted to shout and see him startle, Yusen refrained.

Silhouetted against the broad, clear sky as if emerging from it, Bao Xing descended the slope in stately grace. Her silks hung limp, and her hair had lost its shine, but her face still glowed and the drape of cloth revealed hints of her body, the sash snug at her waist, the folds of silk at her neck where he glimpsed the string that held his first gift.

Yusen placed his back to a large stone—the dancer and the slave would return shortly and he had no intention of being exposed. Over her arm, Bao Xing carried a swath of blue fabric and held it out to him—his del.

"You will want this as the evening cools."

He shrugged it on, warmed by the fact that she had thought of him, then she faced Andao, but Zhencai touched a finger to his lips and pointed to the young man. She settled both hands on her cane, tracing Andao with her eyes as if she were reading a poem. Would she ever trace her husband that way?

A hard truth settled in Yusen's gut. Another scholar, as tall as the last one, but younger. "What is he doing?" Yusen asked, keeping his voice low.

Zhencai said, "Since we left Kaifeng, he has been learning. In the city, he would be as any other man. Here, he seeks deeper, a knowledge that cannot be found merely in books. He opens himself to the world."

"He is like the emperor's statue," Bao Xing murmured, "the one surrounded by frogs that drop little stones from their mouths to indicate the direction of an earthquake."

How could bronze frogs know where an earthquake happened? Likely she had seen it in a book. What if the young man had read the same books she had? Yusen pressed his back to the stone. He shivered as if the shadow of a sword passed over his head. He had claimed a wife to his family's honor, he would not give her up without fighting, but this fight he did not know how to win.

Andao set his fingers on the ground, facing the cliffs over a deep valley, his eyes fixed on the distance.

Abandoning his own safety, Yusen climbed to the top of his stone, clinging with one hand while he squinted in the direction of Andao's scrutiny. A plume of dark smoke rose from a valley, and he saw the silvery sheen of water. "Smoke, lots of it, by a river. It's only the mine."

"Smelting mercury from cinnabar." She sighed, her woman's nature taking hold, then brightened, giving a little tap of her cane. "The device needs mercury, to keep the wheels turning without freezing. It's got to be close to the crimson shrines."

"They break the qi," Andao murmured.

"Excuse me?" Bao Xing edged nearer to him, and Zhencai sprang lightly down from his perch.

"You spoke of the qi," Zhencai prompted. "You can feel it."

"Can't you?" A hint of Andao's animation returned. "It's like a carpet over the earth, with... patterns." He waved one hand. "You're right about the mercury, lady, I saw that on the scroll. We need to study the scroll again."

Footsteps scuffed up the path and the slave and the dancer returned, walking slowly. "You need the scroll?"

"Please."

The slave regarded the young man, then gave a nod, and the three of them settled down with the scroll laid out before them. The dancer moved through a series of stretches, as if to distract the slave from his discussion.

The smell of burning hair and dripping fat drifted from the goat, and Yusen climbed down to carve chunks for eating. The monk recoiled, going off to find some dirt to chew on instead. Yusen speared a chunk of meat on a knife and carried it over to Bao Xing. She took it delicately, blinking at the meat while the juices ran down to her fingers. It disgusted her. Like everything about him. Yusen studied the scroll instead, with its complicated drawings of machines and patterns of stars. Above it, on the stone, someone had drawn the shape of the mountain Bao Xing remembered. "That's where we need to go?"

"Yes. Could you move over a little? The light is fading," the young scholar muttered, his hands moving again as if to erase Yusen's shadow, or Yusen himself.

Yusen leaned until his shadow fell directly over Andao's.

Andao gave a twitch and half-turned toward him, but Yusen pointed to the mountain. "I know where that is. My wife spoke of the mines. This mountain can be seen from the ridge behind the mine. I saw it when I scouted for a way to reach the drakemaster."

His pale-brown eyes widened. "Can you take us there?"

"I don't know the path, but I know the way."

"What does that mean?"

Yusen spread his hands. "I can't say what canyons or rivers may block our travel."

"Andao can." Zhencai opened his eyes. "He can see the carpet of the earth. Tell him which thread must be followed."

Yusen smothered any sign of excitement. "*The carpet of the earth*" could be another of their poems, but he did not think so. His hand tightened on his belt, alongside the hilt of his dagger. The young man was not simply mad, he was a geomancer—the emperor's secret sorcerers, poised to strip the Mongols from the earth they so treasured, or so the army had been led to believe. The khan pursued the legend unmercifully, allowing the slaughter of any who might harbor that skill. Yusen had one right here, at his mercy. Could that offer the key to win the khan's approval, and earn his silver belt? If he could return from this journey with the drakemaster and a geomancer, maybe with a weapon so great the Chin would have to surrender—his place would be sealed at last, his family's honor redeemed.

"I will find the thread," Yusen told them. "We'll follow it together."

CHAPTER FIFTY-TWO

As she rode at the end of the little party, deeper into the mountains, Ming Lun suppressed her skills in favor of her dancer's guise. She smiled, laughed, relaxed toward the Mongol. Every morning, she applied the Thunder God ointment to Dailus's knuckles, elbows, shoulders, knees, ankles. She rubbed gently, gazing into his eyes, offering to treat his hips likewise. He still refused, but he took longer each day to look away. In a vial of her own, she slipped a bit of the ointment every day, with his voice echoing in her ears, reminding her to wash off the poison. The monk regarded her with heavy admonition, but Bao Xing treated her as a friend. Bao Xing was the knot that bound them, smoothing out their friction with her quiet wisdom and graceful ways. If the lady noticed that Ming Lun spoke to her about the Han people and sang about the wonders of the south, she did not remark on it. Given time, Ming Lun could sway Bao Xing from destroying the weapon to give her full loyalty to the Son of Heaven. In the palace of the emperor, she would be prized—and her odious husband easily forgotten.

Yusen paused at each rise, studying the landscape before he pushed onward. At last they mounted a hill where the profile of a familiar mountain rose onto the horizon—a familiar mountain none but Bao Xing and Yusen had ever seen, and she only from a distance. Andao floundered down the slope—always on foot now, in spite of slowing them down. Whatever he claimed he saw could only be seen from there.

The sighting heartened the travelers, and Dailus urged his mount forward. Their days in the mountains gave him strength and greater control over his horse. He would need it to make their escape. Still, every night he shook, and his breath tripped with pain, though he tried to hide it. Would he survive the long ride south? He might—if they found aid at the Temple of the Lark. At Dragon Turns Monastery, she had left a note to be carried by the next patient traveling east, telling the larks that she had found the plan.

In the meantime, she could not single-handedly care for both of them and their horses. Instead, she rode with a Mongol whose skills kept them safe and well-fed—skills won in a lifetime of revealing the secret ways of other nations to the armies of the khan.

"A road!" Andao ran down—or rather, stumbled and continuously managed not to fall—plunging into a field of tall summer grass.

The ponies cropped bites and chewed as they jogged after. Yusen galloped in pursuit of their guide and emerged from the grass beside him. To Ming Lun's eye the low path in the grass could have been any livestock or wildlife trail, a mere depression where animals pushed through the grain. Wheat mingled with the stalks, and the depression cut straight across the land toward a notch in the far valley wall. A few stones nearby had the squared edges of mason's work.

"It moves the right direction," Bao Xing remarked, but looked to her husband to choose.

Andao bounced on his toes, then shuffled into the grass on the other side of the packed earth. He stuffed his hands under his arms, not looking up the road.

"This path troubles you," Zhencai observed.

Andao shrugged in that direction, but did not free his hands. "It looks like a good path, it goes the right way."

Yusen gazed about him in all directions. "The ridges are high. We'll save time if we take the road." He took his reins more firmly. "I'll ride ahead. Wait here." With a click of the tongue, he set his horse in motion, galloping down the road, keeping low along her neck, her tail streaming out behind.

Bao Xing gazed after him, her horse straining that direction, but she turned it deftly back to the group. "Are you a geomancer?"

"There's no such thing anymore," Andao replied, blinking. His hair had begun to grow in, though Zhencai still shaved his own head, and the young man looked fuzzy and ill-formed. "I've heard stories, and the scroll refers to them, but how could I be one?"

"Why would you think him a geomancer?" Dailus dropped his reins, massaging his hands.

"He feels the way of the land, the threads, as Zhencai said," Bao Xing explained, patient as ever. "He could only do this on foot, in contact with the land."

Ming Lun watched the small horseman dwindle in the distance.

"Does Yusen know? The Mongols have slain hundreds trying to slay the geomancers."

Andao lurched backward, bumping into Zhencai's horse.

The monk set his hand on the young man's shoulder. "It is why they burned Cloud Mountain. Forgive me, Andao."

"What? Why? I don't understand."

"I have suspected for some time that you are a geomancer. I should have been more cautious."

"You're saying the Mongol suspects me because of you."

The monk's lips thinned. "If this is so, then I am sorry. I was concerned to know the truth. I hope I have not placed you in danger in doing so."

Andao stalked away, free of the circle of horses, then pivoted and squared his shoulders. "You never told me? What am I supposed to do, if it's true?" Then his eyes grew round. "The Mongols only killed the ones that were left—it was the Buddhists who claimed the temples and seized the enclaves, a century ago or more. That's what the histories say."

"Monks do not kill if there is means to avoid it." Zhencai's horse pranced under him, sign of the rider's tension.

Andao stood very still. "The geomancers were driven into the mountains, often in winter, far from their homes, their ancestors' shrines destroyed, their place in the world stolen forever—you don't think that's killing?"

"There has always been tension between the Way, and the truth," Zhencai said. "The Way is obsessed with the world, the flesh, earthly things that mean only suffering. The Way is illusion, magic is illusion, to believe in it is to be deceived."

Dailus interrupted, "Wait a minute, your monks drove them out and took all of their land and temples?"

"Long ago. My brethren, not my monks. Do not speak as if I sent them from their homes."

"But you sit here defending those who did."

"I defend nothing! I say what I know, that is all." Zhencai's horse jolted into motion, galloping down the road, tossing its head as he tried to gain control.

"Turn her head!" Dailus called, then kicked his own mount in pursuit.

Ming Lun concealed her amusement, trotting gamely after him with the others, except Andao, who stood still gaping, whether at the revelation about himself, or at his master's confessions, she could not say.

"I shouldn't have asked," Bao Xing murmured as she came up alongside. "It was foolish."

"You are always asking questions. Sometimes, it is enough to watch for the answers."

"You are more wise than you believe, Ming Lun."

Up ahead, Yusen spun his mount, catching Zhencai's reins and hauling the wild horse back under command. "What happened?"

"There was an argument," Dailus said, glancing back. "He fought with his apprentice."

Yusen shook back his long hair, almost like a horse himself. "I thought monks were above anger."

"It is not your concern," Zhencai snapped, taking back his own reins though the horse snorted and twitched.

Yusen leaned toward him, pointing. "We all listen as if you are the source of wisdom and greatness when really, you are no bigger than me."

With a little cough, Bao Xing drew their eyes. "Husband, what did you find?"

The dwarf drew a deep breath. "You will not like it." His gaze fixed on the distant figure of Andao, trudging toward the riders. "But the road is safe now, from what I can see."

"'Now?'" Bao Xing echoed.

"What happened here was done a hundred years ago or more." He cut a glance toward Ming Lun. "And not by Mongols."

From behind, Andao called out, "Just go on! I know the *way*."

Yusen raised his hand in acknowledgement and turned the group for the road.

"Greedy monks are all over the world," Dailus said. "In my country, there is an outcry every few years about the wealth of the church."

"We are not greedy," Zhencai growled, then he made a series of gestures that ended in the blessing, as if he were trying to dispel the belittling Yusen had delivered. "And the Way, the study of geomancy, is not a faith. It is all how to be in the world, how to lead others. It has nothing for the spirit. It offers knowledge without compassion, always seeking for the future, never truly present." He said no more, his eyes drawn upward as he caught sight of the path ahead.

The shadow of the cliffs darkened their path save for the gap that led beyond. Stone doorways cut the cliff, some with lintels or painted arches, but the doors themselves lay heaped on the ground. A series of broken posts or footings thrust out from the cliff as well, showing where people had climbed to carve these openings, or to place their occupants. The cliff towered with tombs and every single one of them stood broken, but not a fragment of bone remained to be seen.

Bao Xing made a gesture to ward off evil, but tears shimmered in her eyes. "Why? why ruin all the graves? These can't have all been filled with gold—and even if they were, where are all the bones? So many ancestors, gone."

Dailus made a gesture of his own, vertical and horizontal across his chest.

"The flesh is an illusion," murmured Zhencai, and Ming Lun shot him a withering look.

The stubborn old man did not know when nobody was listening. Ming Lun's childhood, growing up in an orphan's home, severed her from all of this, but she knew what it meant, the connection of your ancestors, binding you into the history of the Han people and the soil of their land. To destroy graves invited disaster on one's own head, never mind how it broke the hearts of those who survived. Angry spirits might linger where their graves had been ruined.

"There may be another way, if we ride along the cliff." Yusen pointed east across the meadow toward the towering cliffs beyond. His horse stood squarely on the road, sidelong, blocking the gap.

"Where are the people?" Bao Xing flicked away her tears. "There is a road, and wheat as if animals pastured here, and the tombs of generations. Where are their houses?"

Yusen's chin dipped, and, for the first time, he lost his certainty.

"Through the gap," Ming Lun replied. "Where the road goes. You say it is safe, you say it will be shorter, why, then, do we linger here?"

"I said also that you would not like it. None of you."

"What about you? You won't be affected, yet you fear to lead us there?"

He darted a glance to his wife, and his throat worked, then, without a word, he turned his mount and rode into the sunlight beyond the gap.

Ming Lun edged up after him, joining Bao Xing, her curiosity pressing against her chest, and so they entered together, as once they had entered Kaifeng, with its smoldering houses and weeping women.

The weeping and burning here had happened long ago. The sloping back of the cliffs towered grey with ash to either side as if they rode into a fire pit. A few grains of wheat survived outside that barrier, but here, empty furrows marched in rows, their soil pale, dry, crumbling. Wind sifted across the field, sending trickles of earth into tiny eddies to trickle away again into the dust. The first ruin stood among these fields, a partial wall with a bit of roof, the rest of it, the side facing the center of town, lay cracked and burned. Ahead, a stone bridge lay crushed into the bed of a river where a trickle of water gurgled among the broken stones. Beyond that rose the town, a series of cracked foundations and barren yards.

A scream echoed from the cliffs as Andao entered the gap, then fell to his knees, moaning. Zhencai dragged his horse around, tumbling down from his mount and urging the young man up onto it, hauling on his arm until he complied. Their fractious voices jangled in the empty place, and Ming Lun left them, kicking her horse and passing the others, splashing through the stream onto the uneven paving stones of a vacant yard. In most villages of her experience, wood formed the houses, with tiled roofs, but square-cut stone and fieldstone dominated here, the plaster cracked and falling, made gray with age or with whatever calamity had befallen. No, not Mongols. Their firedrakes blasted flame and stone through a central core, but this destruction radiated outward, as if the firedrake shot from the air into the heart of the town.

Ming Lun rode deeper. The place smelled of ash, but nothing of pine or farms or animals. A few stumps of burnt trees lay like shattered urns. Pillars that should have been red jutted up behind a wall that might once have been a shrine. Twisted shapes of metal curled among the stones of a broken tower. A dragon made of bronze, its body half-melted, appeared to struggle in the shade of the ruin. The horse's hoofbeats echoed among fragmented walls as she reached the center of the village. Symbols marked the stones of the courtyard, some of them she recognized, others unfamiliar to her, placed at intervals. If not for the broken and missing stones, they might form a circle around a hollow center. No, not hollow, sunken—a mass of melted bronze.

A heap of metal fittings at a blackened patch of ground suggested some device that had gone up in flames. At each corner of the square, other distorted objects cast long and writhing shadows on the ground. Over the ruined well hung a bent frame absent of the pump it might have held. The streets radiating out had a pleasant symmetry, the broken houses marked with names and symbols like those on the ground. The bar patterns of the I Ching appeared here and there, smudged with soot and cracked by heat.

"Jian Ho." Dailus rode up beside her, shivering a little. He needed another dose of his medicinal tea.

She raised her eyebrows, and he continued, "Jian Ho, my assistant in casting the firedrakes. He drew symbols like this. To protect me." Dailus swallowed, his foreign skin as cracked as the ruins all around them. "The Mongols killed him for sorcery."

"On the day you defended me."

He nodded slightly, a ruffling of his pale hair. His satchel rested against his side, the scroll bound tightly to it, and he brought it closer with his arm. "The weapon did this, didn't it. This is the power it has."

"Is that what you think?" Two hundred people might have lived here, perhaps more in those ruined farms on the outskirts. The breadth of the plain around them stood vacant and gray, with nothing green or living outside of themselves, even after more than a hundred years. "The Mongols want it. They want to use it against us."

"We have to destroy it before it can be used again."

"Ride away with me," she whispered. "Now, while they are all distracted. We cannot risk the Mongols learning how to make this happen. If Yusen ever sees that device and lives to tell of it, the khan will find a way. He is a scout, he remembers everything—you've seen that."

Dailus worked his fingers into his hair, his expression bleak. He opened his mouth, then stopped.

Across the square with its mysterious symbols and melted bronze, a series of tilted steps lead to the base of an absent temple. Against the wall stood a ghost of darker gray, the image of a woman, her arm raised as if to shield her gaze, a shadow cast by an absent sun.

CHAPTER FIFTY-THREE

The world seemed frozen around Bao Xing, like ice which has been shattered and frozen again, arrested in an image of violence. With twilight, the steady breeze increased, rushing over stone and soil and howling through empty windows. Some of the walls carried shadows of people long gone—women bending over their work, children leaping, men carrying tools. Shadows too ordinary to be paintings, shadows the color of ash. Yusen sat his horse absolutely straight while Andao huddled on Zhencai's mount.

"I do not know how to help him. We must go." The old man's poise eluded him now, as if he had taken on his apprentice's wild energy.

"Where? How?" Yusen sounded as hollow and gray as the landscape around them. "This is the mountain Bao Xing saw, this is the valley between the two peaks. They fixed the circle on that device to remember what had happened here, not to lead us to the cause of it."

The horses had drawn close together, heads lowered, as if the unearthly calm of the place weighed on them as well. All was gray and cracked, melted, ruined and dead. The Dark Lance struck here with indiscriminate fire, burning so fiercely that no life, even now, had ever returned. What if Yusen were right, and the fixed point that drew them here served only as the marker for a mass grave?

"Not every turn of the seasons brings new life." Zhencai made the sign of blessing, his hand preternaturally steady, as if he made it so by the strength of his will in defiance of the flesh. He, too, had survived a slaughter to come here, believing together they could find a way to stop it, before they even knew what devastation the weapon could bring.

Bao Xing descended from a long line of astronomers. They had assisted in the construction and, marked the desolation all the way back in Kaifeng. Surely they did not want this to happen again.

"The Eternal Sky is not always benevolent," Yusen said. "The monk is right. We should go, back the way we came." He twitched his chin toward the distant wall where the ancestors of these absent villagers had once been interred. The villagers themselves had no descendents to honor them, none but this strange band. To burn incense here would only add to the layers of ash that guarded the dead. To think that her many-times grandfather had even a very small part—

"My cane…" she fumbled with the straps that held it and pulled the cane into her hand, shaking as if she, too, had breathed in mercury. "He said it was a map."

His face lighting with sudden hope, Yusen caught the cane, his small hand steadying it between them. "Are you able to read it?"

Andao bent into himself, the heels of his hands pressing into his eyes, useless for finding their way. The effect of the weapon lingered here, overpowering him.

"I can try," she answered.

"It will take time. Even if we were safe here, there is nothing, to harvest or to shoot, and I would not trust the water."

She saw worry pinch his brow—not the excitement that drove him during combat, or even the pain that flickered from his injuries, something deeper and more carefully hidden. "That's why you didn't want us to come this way."

"This place is dead." His dark hair stroked his shoulders as he shrugged. "There is nothing here for us, and this place makes us too exposed. I am a good scout and a poor general. We should not have come."

"Then we go back, back to the valley outside, to follow the cliffs as you said."

"With the tombs? What is better, to be inside where so many have died, or outside where their ancestors have been stolen? My people are nomads; we do not surround ourselves with relics." His glance dropped to her throat, to the amulet she wore. A relic? Pressed flat and cleaned of char. What fire had he saved it from? She had assumed it was taken as booty during some raid on a foreign city, but what if it had some other story?

Relics and ancestors. She gave the cane a gentle movement, drawing his eyes back to her. "They made a pathway. My many-times grandfather and the others, they wanted the location to be known if it were needed. I believe there is a path, and that we will find it,when Andao has recovered. You brought us to the right place, to the very mountain—it's not your fault that the place is—haunted."

"The men who made this weapon had to know what it did, see the effects. Even if they aimed for an abandoned village, or told the people to leave."

The oppressive weight of the place clearly affected him, too. People had obviously died here. When the buildings burned and fell, when the land flared into ash, the farmers had been home with their wives and families, the scholars had been studying, the shopkeepers settling accounts, the geomancers reading the earth for signs when they should have been reading the sky. Chang Mailou's book spoke of an argument between those who felt the weapon should be dismantled, and those, like Dengho, committed to preserving it. Looking at the desolated town, Bao Xing thought she knew what had happened to the dissenters, and their families.

Her stomach knotted, and Bao Xing doubted she could eat anything even if they found food. The Dark Lance must be nearly circled, filling with its malevolent strength. "We cannot go back—there is no time."

Yusen nodded, his thumb rubbing over a carving of trees.

"Perhaps they have found the trail." Zhencai pointed.

Beyond the village, two dark shapes hurried away, obscured by dust, the sound of their hoofbeats barely audible beneath the howl of the rising wind.

"They're trying to escape!" Yusen kicked his horse, cutting after them, but he reached the bank of the river and stopped, earth crumbling beneath his mount's hooves as he tugged her back from the edge. Turning aside, he galloped back to where Ming Lun and Dailus must have crossed some time ago and plunged down the slope, then up on the other side, the horse's hooves raising a cloud of ash.

Escape? Ming Lun stealing the man she maybe loved from the watchful eye of the man who claimed to own him. "So let them go!" Bao Xing called after him, and he halted so sharply his horse reared as he faced her across the ruined bridge.

"They have the plan! She is an imperial spy, she doesn't care about him, she wants the weapon for the emperor! Or is it only power in the khan's hands you fear?" His hair whipped around him, his eyes dark and yet blazing before he turned and galloped on.

"Do we follow?" Bao Xing wondered aloud.

Zhencai formed the sign of blessing. "I only know we cannot stay here."

Replacing the cane, Bao Xing guided her horse more carefully down the bank to splash across the stream. Zhencai followed, setting his bare feet carefully as he lead Andao's mount.

"If she is a spy, lady, then much would be explained."

"She can't want our people to die, any more than we do."

The monk said, "Death is part of the cycle."

"Look around you! There is no cycle, not here—this isn't the middle of anything, this is the end." They skirted the village and kept to the barren farmland. Far ahead now, a cloud of dust showed Yusen's progress and another, larger one, that must be Ming Lun and Dailus. Bao Xing squinted after them, unsure what to hope for. Yusen claimed the dancer didn't care about the drakemaster, but he might not be the best judge. As for Ming Lun being a spy, that sounded like Yusen's usual suspicions. Yet he had so often been right.

They had crossed beyond the village moving toward a flattened farmhouse when Bao Xing said, almost apologetically, "She is no spy, or she would have known you cannot take a Mongol's horses without a fight."

Zhencai gave a little huff of agreement.

"Something's wrong," Andao muttered. "It all feels so wrong."

Startled by the sound of his voice, Bao Xing reined closer. "What is it?"

"Pulling, from the east."

The direction they were riding. Bao Xing looked ahead. Ming Lun had chosen the shortest route to the ridges of the rising summit, perhaps hoping to be lost among them. A series of jagged stones thrust up there, shadowing the riders beneath as Yusen gained on them. At the top of the ridge a bright light flared, enormous and glowing. Bao Xing's mouth went dry.

"Is that the Dark Lance?" Zhencai breathed behind her.

"No! It can't be!" If it were, Yusen rode directly beneath its glowing, terrible eye. The ground rumbled, shaking loose the stones at the top of the broken wall.

The distant cloud of dust shimmered with startling light and clarity, the two horses suddenly visible as they passed into the beam. Two horses. No riders. Ming Lun hadn't ridden away at all.

"Where are they?" she called above the rumbling.

"There!" Zhencai pointed. Two small figures hurried down the road back into the gap. Rather, one of them hurried, the other stumbled to a halt.

A shadow swept the ground before her, and Bao Xing looked up. Overhead soared a pale, flickering shape. Her horse reared, and Bao Xing fell as the thing swooped. She covered her head, remembering every story she had ever heard about hungry ghosts and ancestors torn from their tombs. Heat flared to one side, and fire blossomed on the ground nearby, then snuffed out. Whatever flew above her rained orbs of fire.

"Bao Xing!" Andao waved his arms. He, too, had been thrown and now knelt by a rock as the shadow rushed overhead again, spewing bouts of flame.

Between them, Zhencai sat cross-legged, prayer beads in hand, eyes closed.

Bao Xing stumbled then crawled until Andao's hands reached out and pulled her into the hollow by the stone.

"This ground is safe, solid." The young man held her, both of them trembling. "Master, please!"

The monk paid no heed.

Beyond, the fireballs landed nearer and nearer to Zhencai. One of them brushed past his bald head, and he flinched as a red welt appeared against his skin. Andao clenched his jaw, then broke free of Bao Xing and started to scramble toward his master. Before he got there, Dailus loomed up, grabbed the monk's arm and dragged him down.

Another fireball smacked the ground, sending up plumes of smoke from the spot where Zhencai had been.

"What do they smell like?" Dailus shouted as Zhencai shook off his hands. The others stared as the drakemaster folded himself into their hollow. "The fireballs, the incendiaries, do they smell like Kaifeng?"

Bao Xing forced herself to breath deeper, one hand pressed over her thundering heart, trapping the amulet. That stinging, acrid scent, unlike a natural fire.

"They do," Andao replied.

"They're not ghosts, they're—machines, sails of some kind, they're launching incendiary devices." His jade eyes shone bright.

Another shadow slipped beneath the ghosts, and Ming Lun dropped down beside him. "Idiot! We could have been gone."

"And they could have been dead," he shot back. "Did you see those things?"

"Ghosts." Bao Xing peered upward. Along the ridge, the two ghosts soared back, but two more soared out, flickering with light, and she ducked back again as fire streaked down the sky. "Where's Yusen?"

Andao replied, "He changed course when the fires started falling, riding toward the slope, but I don't know where he is now." He scrambled out to the ruined wall nearby and looked around. "The horses are running wild, toward the far side. He's not with them. " A fireball cracked into the wall, and he shrieked, swatting at flames on his clothes. He dropped full-length onto the ground and smothered the flames as he scrambled back to join them.

"Ghosts can't be stopped, but men with devices can," Dailus said. "If I can get up that ridge—"

"I'll go." Ming Lun leapt to her feet before the others could say a word. She ran lightly in an erratic course, and the ghosts, swinging in wide circles, dropped their fires short or long of her.

Bao Xing took in the faces of her companions—Dailus's excitement, almost straining toward the danger; Andao's confusion; Zhencai's flash of anger followed by the impassive face of meditation and the quiet drone of prayer. "What if he is dead?" she whispered.

"Then you are free of him," Dailus answered grimly. "And so am I."

The amulet burrowed into her palm. Free. Widowed of the husband she never wanted, and yet...he was not without honor, nor without compassion. He kept them fed in the mountains, he rescued Dailus when the mine overseers would have killed him. She did not want him to die before she knew who he was, who he might have been without the khan's taunting and Munkjar looming over his life. He had brought her the stars when she thought she had lost them, brought her words when she longed for them, and let her practice her poor embroidery on the flesh he so despised. He taught her the freedom of a horse's hooves.

"The ghosts are going home," Andao said. "I think I can walk there."

Zhencai broke off his prayers and opened his eyes. "You would follow a ghost to its tomb."

"I would follow the *way* to find the *truth*."

"I did not ask for a student."

Their eyes met, then Andao said, "I could not have asked for a more patient master." After searching the ground, he stepped out from the hollow, his bare feet sinking a little in the dry earth. He had gone only a few paces when Zhencai rose to follow.

"Can you do this, drakemaster?" Bao Xing asked.

"Slowly. And you? You've lost your cane."

She nodded. "It ran off with my horse. Together, then."

He took her hand on his elbow, and they stood up together, balancing each other, and walked toward the ridge. Andao chose a path more carefully than Ming Lun had, but still it curved across the field to meet the rising wall beyond. He backtracked and moved forward again. Zhencai paced after him like a walking meditation. Sunset lent the glow of life to the dead world around them, then, half-way up the ridge, a single lamp shone. They walked the unsteady ground, then an increasingly solid, narrow track up the slope. A spatter of blood marked the stones, and Bao Xing caught her breath. Dailus gave her a glance, speculative, then paused. "Look down," he told her.

Below, the careful, shuffling trail of Andao's steps showed clearly, pale white against the gray of the dead earth, forming the character that meant the ground, that which went beneath. "The ghosts and the fires weren't magic."

Bao Xing merely shook her head and pressed onward until they came into the circle of the light. On a long rod, a man held a glowing lantern, a sphere of bronze pierced by many tiny lights. He lifted this over Andao's head and turned it to see him from all angles, but the light never spilled a drop of oil nor blew out in the breeze. Magic again?

Two others stood behind him, one with a hand atop Yusen's head, his other hand gripping a knife that kept her husband in his place. Even kneeling with his hands bound, a trickle of blood crossing his cheek, the Mongol lost none of his ferocity. His dark eyes found hers, and Bao Xing found herself smiling.

From behind a standing stone, Ming Lun emerged, accompanied by a few others.

"It is as you said." The man with the lantern bowed to Andao. "Please forgive our harsh welcome. Usually, the flying ghosts are enough to deter our rare visitors. But this is the first time we have a visitor who is also our kin. Come inside." He led them behind the stone, and into such a valley of wonders that an entire library would be needed to capture it. The sight so amazed her that Bao Xing did not even look at the sky.

CHAPTER FIFTY-FOUR

"My dear God," Dailus breathed.

They emerged from a narrow passage into a valley still lit by the setting sun. Sloping tiled roofs and pillars surrounded a series of courtyards where strange equipment stuck out of wells, and symbols etched the stones. From a ledge a little higher, two men wearing sails of white sprang into the air above this village, and their sails carried them in a spiral to a field down below. Two waterfalls streamed over the cliff at one of the narrow ends, framing a series of buildings clinging to the wall with carved and painted wooden props that looked too thin to support them. The pair of rivers spilled down into the valley, merging and driving a series of waterwheels at the heart of the village. From one of those mill yards, sparks flickered as the wheel turned—grinding? striking? The resonance of bronze echoed all around him. Opposite the village, terraces carved the entire mountainside into a series of gardens, fields, and farmyards full of chickens. On a pinnacle just below the sheltering wall, stood a square tower topped with devices he could barely make out. One of the terraces held dozens of frames of fabric that flickered in the breeze. People moved among them, hanging more and taking others down.

"There is no temple," Zhencai observed.

The leader swung his rod in an arc over all, the spherical lantern chiming gently. "The world is our temple, Brother. We see no need to worship like those who would not welcome us."

"Master Wei, what is to be done with the invader?" One of the guards kept a hold of Yusen's neck.

"I see no reason to preserve him."

"Please, Master Wei." Bao Xing took a small step forward. "He came as our guide in the mountains, to help us—" she broke off, and Dailus gripped the scroll across his body with a shake of his head. No matter how extraordinary this place might be, they couldn't be sure its people could be trusted.

"We are searching for understanding, and he has brought us this far. Please don't kill him." She spread her hands.

"We seek understanding as well, but we do not share it with those who mean us harm. We may be sheltered in our valley, but that does not mean we have no knowledge of what goes on outside." He gestured toward the guard who tightened his grip, drawing a sharp breath from Yusen who stared straight ahead.

Dailus's belly tightened. Would his master, his tormentor, be slain right here in front of him, after so long? Why did the thought no longer delight him?

Bao Xing lowered herself to her knees and bowed deeply. "Please spare him, Master Wei. Please, please." As she abased herself three times, a pendant swung free of her gown, and Master Wei stooped down, lowering his spherical lantern.

"What is this?" He pointed to the strange amulet, a round plate of bronze topped with a filigree of brighter metal. An astrolabe. Dailus wanted a closer look at that himself—he had only seen one before, among the items one of the nobles brought back from the Crusades many years ago.

"It is a traveler's device for knowing the stars. It was a gift from the Mongol, Master Wei. He is my husband."

Master Wei snorted, a sound that ruffled his mustache. "The Li tomb is not yet finished? Throw him in there and lower the stone across the door. I think even he will not squeeze out of that."

The guard gave a short bow and hauled Yusen along the trail that cut across the slope. At the far end of the valley, opposite the twin waterfalls, a series of tombs like little doors marked the slope and wall. Yusen began to protest, but the guard lifted him and gave him a shake the way a dog chastises a puppy.

"This is the Valley of the Sages, isn't it? I've read about that." Andao's hands spread to take in the valley.

"Your messenger tells us you are a geomancer, but newly discovered. Will you tell me how you came to the ghost town?"

Ghosts again. Had they arranged the entire display to frighten those who believed in their legends, like the flying men? Dailus scanned the rim of the valley, searching for signs of their defenses.

"We followed a mountain, Master." Andao helped Bao Xing to her feet. "The lady Bao Xing is an astronomer's daughter. She brought us together on our search because she had seen this mountain through the device at Kaifeng."

The leader's face hardened. "The invaders destroyed Kaifeng, did they not?"

Dailus's tremors began in his limbs, his joints aching quietly. Were they about to reveal him as the architect of the ruin of Kaifeng? Ming Lun rested her hand on his arm, her thumb gently stroking his wrist.

"My husband brought me to that place, Master Wei, to see the armillary sphere and translate its message," Bao Xing said, still determined to bring Yusen into everything.

"Its message," the leader echoed softly, studying her. All of the inhabitants they had seen so far wore short robes and trousers of dark grey, but edged in trims of red, blue or gold and decorated with bits of embroidery, drab compared with Bao Xing's travel-worn silks, but somehow regal. "Come and we will speak more of this." He held out his lantern, starting out on the same path as Yusen's guard, then following a series of sharp turns down the slope to one of the courtyards. A stream flowed along a narrow trench, interrupted by a contraption of wooden paddles all bound together in a line. It put Dailus in mind of a long, thin water wheel, staked into the ground, with another wooden apparatus attached to the end on the bank. Master Wei whistled, and a boy hurried out, jumped atop the apparatus and stomped up and down. The paddles lurched into motion, their rotation pulling water up to fill a narrow trough that cut into the stone.

"Dailus!" Ming Lun tugged at him, and he abandoned the machine to cross a narrow bridge into the courtyard. The water the boy was pumping flowed alongside, then through an opening in one of the buildings.

"This is the traveler's house. Baths will be prepared." Master Wei indicated one side of the yard. "The women will find their comfort here, while the men can use this chamber. We prefer to be cleansed of the dust of that place as soon as possible." He flicked a glance at Andao, who nodded vigorously.

"I do not require such vanities," Zhencai said. "A bowl of water will suffice."

Master Wei raised the lantern. "Cold water, no doubt."

At another whistle, a woman emerged from the far building. She received his whispered command, then departed. After a few minutes, she returned more slowly, carrying a two-handled low bronze bowl which she set on a pedestal at the center of the yard. Master Wei gestured for the travelers to follow him to the pedestal. "A bowl of water." He placed his lantern in a stand, and set a hand on each of the bowl's handles. "You have come here as seekers. This one, this monk, would say that he is seeking the truth beyond a world of illusions." He stroked his hands against the handles. "The world is all: it is one substance and the Way arises from it."

The bowl began to hum, an eerie, rising sound, and the water within shivered. "The Way arises from all that is natural and right. Like water, it is a hidden virtue, it makes the land good, and flows to all, without struggle." The water in the bowl rose up in a continuous spout, shivering and streaming upward, the bowl singing around it until the water stood beyond the rim, as high as the heart of the man who summoned it.

Dailus's mouth went dry: a bowl of bronze, exquisitely made—he could hear the perfection of its tone—and a man who made it magic. The silver strand of water shimmered between them, a miracle, and he had seen it. In this valley lived men who raised water with a song and boys who raised it with their feet. They had the skill to cast such a vessel, and to make a lantern sphere that never spilled—what else? What more could they hold in this tiny place? "Master Wei," he said, softly. "Will you teach me to fly?"

The man's hands shook, and the water fell back with a splash. Master Wei leaned on the handles of the bowls, laughing. "To fly? Of course, and I am eager to hear what knowledge you possess." That was dangerous ground, but the leader passed it quickly, much to Dailus's relief. "I am sure the astronomer's daughter will wish to climb to the tower, but we may need to find her a servant or a cane to assist."

Bao Xing lifted her eyes from the shivering, silent bowl. "My cane was bound upon my horse, Master Wei. I would be most grateful for its return."

"It may be found. If so, I will see to it. And you." Master Wei turned to Andao. "We have heard of a certain learned people of Kaifeng, a people who are not Han, but are still of our nation. The geomancer must be born of the land, and his people must be born of it for many generations. Their graves must be in the land, and their way is to always seek deeper."

"If you mean that he should ask many questions, then it is so," Zhencai said, but not unkindly. His apprentice grinned at him.

"My people came at the request of an emperor long ago, and were granted leave to settle in Kaifeng. Our graves are there, and our books are often buried there as well," Andao began formally, then his hands broke loose. "Is that how this happened to me? Because of how long we've lived here—there? My father wanted me to become a rabbi, a teacher, but I always had trouble studying in the school, it was easier for me—"

"Outside," Master Wei finished, nodding.

"Yes! Even the monasteries are easier because sometimes they don't have walls all the way around. That's why I was surprised, a bit, that I couldn't—I'm not a very good student for Master Zhencai."

"He wanted you to draw your qi from within."

"But it is not within, Master Wei," Zhencai said. "He did not find it until he searched the earth." Making the sign of blessing, the monk bowed. "He needs teaching I cannot offer. Teach him well."

"You honor and surprise me, Brother, if you can admit this."

When Zhencai straightened, his body sank into the stance of his readiness to attack, and Master Wei stiffened. "But know this, Master," Zhencai said. "If any harm comes to him from this teaching, to his body or mind or spirit, then I shall once again become the teacher, and share with you some lessons in suffering."

"I doubt your order would approve."

"I shall do it with utmost compassion." Zhencai released his posture.

From the corner of his eye, Dailus saw Ming Lun relax as well. She claimed a woman on her own needed skills to survive—but she had skills far beyond need. Even his hazy glimpses of the duel between Zhencai and Ming Lun had shown him that. She wanted the scroll for China; he had almost let her take it, along with himself. Would the south be like this, humming with genius, fresh discoveries around every corner? He would not have seen this unless he turned back to help the others. There was something of magic in Andao's connection to the land, that, too, he could see, but surely learning the secret of a bowl or a wing could be no cost to his immortal soul. He imagined himself strapping on his sail at the top of a church tower and leaping into the embrace of the sky, a man made angel, brought home by the grace of God to soar above the astounded faces of his family and friends. His palms itched for a stylus to sketch everything he saw.

"In the meantime, the baths are ready." Master Wei flicked them toward their respective halls, then smiled at Zhencai. "A bowl of water." He bowed and departed.

Dailus and Andao shed their garments and sank into a warm pool fed by a trickle of water from the channel and heated from below by gaps in the brick structure—Dailus crept around the room searching them out until Andao told him the trick of it. The young man scrubbed his stubbly scalp and especially his feet.

"What did you feel, out there?" Dailus asked.

Rubbing between his toes, Andao hesitated. "It felt slippery, as if I would fall at any moment. I grew sick to my stomach. The qi of the land is gone from there—that's why nothing grows. Did you notice the birds?"

"Birds?"

"Some of the buildings had bird nests, new ones, but the birds lay dead and skeletal inside. Newer than the catastrophe, I should say, but still very old. That place was poisoned for a long time. The men here, the sages, they must have laid the tracks I followed beneath the dead earth. That was the only place I felt safe. Balanced." He scrubbed his hands with a rough stone. "If the lady is right, then Master Deng will use the Dark Lance against the Mongols. He'll burn the entire Yellow River Valley, just like that."

Dailus ducked under the water and emerged just enough to scrub his hair. He studied Andao's distinctive profile. "You're a Jew."

"You've heard of us. My father says we have people all over the world."

"That's true." Dailus stopped himself from saying more. The Jew had magic, but from what Master Wei said, it had nothing to do with his Jewishness. Every lesson the Church ever taught about the Jews ended with depictions of their greed and their evils, but, like most people in Lithuania, he had never even met one. He thought of Master Wei's bowl of water, the spout rising from the substance—everything emerging from the one. He travelled here with a Jew, a monk, a lady, a Mongol united in their purpose to prevent another dead land like the one they had passed through.

"Are there many Jews in your country?" Andao asked.

"Not many."

"Sometimes I lose track of the Sabbath, since we've been traveling." Andao gave a nervous laugh. "I shouldn't admit that, I suppose. Everyone is so different, so many different beliefs, and Zhencai… he kept talking to me about qi and compassion and illusion. On the day of atonement, I'll have so much to think about." He wiped his hands down his face.

Dailus considered his own atonement, the years in purgatory his travels would mean, the fiery words of the priest at his many transgressions, the likelihood he would go to Hell simply for being here, for bathing in the same pool with a Jew and not feeling the least desire to convert the error of his companion's faith. Yet his most terrible crime, creating the weapon that killed Kaifeng, would be glorified because only heathens had died. Only infidels, killed by the Crusaders, only Jews and Gypsies and witches who died to please his own God.

He let the water lap up against his throat. "Do Jews go to Hell for the things you do wrong?"

"Hell?"

"It's a place of eternal suffering. Torment." Like hearing the screams of the women stolen from Kaifeng.

"Oh, no. Atonement means you have a chance to work harder, to do better, to perform, they're called Mitzvahs. Good things." Andao cocked his head. "Will you be going to this Hell?"

Dailus stared into the water, through his own distorted reflection. It didn't matter if Ming Lun thought him a fool, if Yusen saw the device and remembered every bit of it. This quest was still a worthy, or a hundred thousand heathens would die. "I guess I am." But first, he would learn how to fly.

CHAPTER FIFTY-FIVE

Sitting meditation in the Valley of the Sages filled Zhencai's mind with the swoop of winged men and the clatter of devices doing what men had always done for themselves, so he walked. After washing his face and hands in the singing bowl—an act that felt defiant—he walked around the courtyard until his traveling companions emerged from their respective chambers, clad in clean garments and smiling, aside from the dancer, who did not smile so far as he knew. He drew up his qi, an act which had become automatic whenever she was present. Both women wore their hair in elaborate twists and pins, though the number of these had diminished over the course of their journey. Yusen's absence felt strange. His deep and tightly bound qi drove the others in a way that Zhencai found both enlightening and disturbing. If the little man held more respect among his own people, he would be a force among them. Zhencai was fortunate not to be imprisoned along with him, representative of another regime which had overthrown the Taoists and claimed their lands and temples.

Dailus matched Andao's wild enthusiasm, both of them staring about, the young man's eyes nearly as wide and round as the foreigner's.

"That bowl! Is that a geomancer's tool, do you know?" Dailus pounced on the bowl, touching, tapping, finally lifting it up to study it from all angles.

"The geomancers' primary tool is the compass," Bao Xing offered, "but it has a series of rings to make determinations about what is most auspicious, similar to the armillary sphere but to study the earth instead of the sky." She hid her face briefly, then lowered her hand, the movement a bit awkward as if it were a habit she struggled with. "My father had a book about them."

"I wish I had that book," Andao remarked.

A gong sounded. At the open wall that lead into the streets, Master Wei stood flanked by guards with crossbows trained upon the companions. Zhencai and Ming Lun dropped into postures of attack, while Bao Xing's delicate balance faltered, and she caught Andao's arm.

Dailus clutched the satchel with the scroll, and he must have reapplied his treatments for he walked steadily two paces forward. "What is this? We thought we were guests."

"What is this?" Master Wei held out Bao Xing's cane, propped between his hands to display the carving.

"My cane—" Bao Xing said at the same moment that Andao blurted, "The map—" and both stopped immediately.

"Your cane is the map. I see. How did you come by it? And quickly, if we must clean up your blood I should rather take care of that before nightfall."

"My many times grandfather carved this cane and left it in our family. My father gave it to me." Bao Xing stepped up beside Dailus. "Andao's examinamination suggested it might also be a map."

"We cannot allow you to keep this. I shall have another brought for your use." Master Wei kept it close at his side, though Bao Xing frowned, her eyes still upon it. "You came here by looking through a device. How much do you know?"

"There is a ring upon the Dark Lance, and we don't have much time before what happened out there—" she indicated the cliffs that separated the valley from the ghost village, "happens again."

Master Wei's round cheeks puffed. "How can you be sure that it will?"

"Because Master Deng awoke." Zhencai turned his iron hand from warning into blessing. "How many sleepers remain?"

One of the guards gave a little twitch, but the Taoist leader stared at him like a stone Buddha without compassion. "There were at least five. The founders suspected there might be others. And some did not sleep. The Order of Celestial Purity has not simply rested until now."

"Then why haven't you stopped it?" Bao Xing clenched her fist. "You know of the sleepers and their plans, you know of the device, and what it can do—why let it exist at all?"

"Would you burn a library, lady, because it contained dangerous books? It is not knowledge that is dangerous, it is those who do not balance knowledge with good governance. The Order concluded they should not use the Dark Lance. They are men of reason, and I believe they will again reach the same conclusion."

"People died, Master, when the Dark Lance scoured their village. You live with their deaths on your doorstep every day."

"They remind us of the need for balance. Instead of seeking understanding without judgement, those who lived in that village believed that they could name this knowledge as wrong and thus destroy it. The knowledge they sought to suppress destroyed them instead. Balance. That is why our founders retreated. Here in this valley, we are seekers, discoverers. We do not claim the wisdom to judge, and if you and your companions believe that you possess that wisdom, then we must ask you to leave."

"I don't have any wisdom!" Andao ran forward, bowing. "I have no wisdom at all, just ask Master Zhencai. But I do need knowledge. I need to know what it is to be a geomancer and how to use that skill in balance. Please, don't make me go."

Dailus clung to his things, but frowned furiously, and Bao Xing's eyes lifted toward the astronomy tower she had earlier been invited to use.

Bao Xing brought her focus back to the Master, to the cane he still held, and to his armed guards. "Will you allow us to remain, Master Wei? To be seekers among you, if only for a short time?"

"So long as I see that you do not cause dissension or enforce judgement within our community, you may remain." He folded his arms, with her cane on the inside. "I hope that, as you stay among us, you will come to understand the way of balance."

"Thank you, Master Wei." Bao Xing made a sharp bow over her folded hands, her hair ornaments clinking. She did believe she could judge, as Andao believed he could not. As for Zhencai? He believed in compassion, and detachment from the world, yet the monks of Dragon Turns, and these sages, had both tried to convince him this meant refraining from action. But the Buddha witnessed suffering and was moved by it. Detachment did not mean they should enable suffering.

"You will wish to climb to the tower. Some of these men can escort you." At his gesture, the guards lowered their crossbows, sliding them onto their belts or slinging them across their backs. "Each of our enclaves of knowledge has the resources to nourish both body and mind. Hanliao is master of flight and will show you the way of it." A stocky, muscular guard stood forth, bowing to Dailus, who bowed back. "As for yourself, Andao, I will bring you to the center."

Andao wriggled like a puppy.

"What knowledge do you seek, lady?" asked Master Wei, giving a slight bow to Ming Lun.

"I am a dancer. I seek only the ground to practice my art."

"Then perhaps it is as well for you to remain here. I will instruct the servants to bring you food as you need it. As for you, Brother, I assume you seek enlightenment. I do not think that, even here, you will find it."

"Then I will seek it in myself." Zhencai bowed and blessed him. "And for this I need only a pathway to walk on, and the nourishment of the spirit."

Master Wei laughed out loud, plucking at his mustache. "In that case, you can remain here as well, except when you're roaming around, but I'll still have the servants bring you rice from time to time, unless you reach nirvana before supper. Come, fellow seekers, and grow in knowledge." He spread his hands, drawing the others away, Bao Xing on the arm of a young guard, Dailus already speaking in a low tone to his guide, and Andao trotting after Master Wei, up the slope toward the center of town, the handle of Bao Xing's cane still trapped over the master's shoulder. Bao Xing glanced after it, then back at Zhencai with an urgent flaring of her eyes before she gave attention to the guard who led her.

In moments, the courtyard contained only Ming Lun and Zhencai. She cocked her head to raise an eyebrow at him. He took a deep breath, centered his qi, and approached, though not within easy range. Dropping his voice very low, he said, "I do not imagine you intend to remain here, lady dancer."

"That guard nearly jumped when you mentioned the sleepers." She matched his tone, her sharp gaze darting about the place.

"A monk may walk in many places where a woman may not go. A monk might seek the solace of a long rest, from one old man, to another."

"You think they have a sleeper here?"

"Most likely one of the founders Master Wei spoke of. If we are to continue, we need that cane. Bao Xing has won us the time to take it back."

The corners of her mouth edged upward. "Does not an old man need a cane?" She let her face fall into a mimicry of wrinkles as she bent forward and gave a ratcheting sigh of exhaustion, the very image of an ancient.

Zhencai's qi warmed his limbs, his hands pressed together as he faced her. A worthy adversary, and a challenging ally. "An old man may not have the grace to acquire it."

"I hope you do not achieve nirvana for at least a little longer."

"Not until the Dark Lance passes." He made the sign of blessing, and she an elegant bow before she vanished into the shadows of the deepening twilight. She must learn where they were taking the cane, while he could bide his time to make his search. When a pair of servants arrived to lay out a simple meal, Zhencai explained that Ming Lun's stomach troubled her, and so she had found her way to the latrine.

He inquired about a walking circuit of the village, then ate lightly and set out, in his old, worn garments, hands at his back, for the ledge and bridges the servant described. All along the path stood stone pillars topped with their special bronze lanterns, although the stones themselves varied in type. Narrow tubes of bronze stood alongside the pillars, feeding into the lanterns, as if the lanterns would drift away without being tethered to the ground they worshipped.

The trail brought him down below the graveyard, but he paused to search out the Li tomb, the only one of the rock-cut tombs with its door placed sideways. Zhencai followed a workman's path to peer into the gap at the top of the door, a slab of stone nearly as tall as himself and as thick as a two hands laid together. "Mongol?"

A sharp breath greeted this. "Monk."

"The others are studying."

"She's at the tower, then," the Mongol rasped.

"Have they brought you water or food?"

A sound of derision. "They have not even unbound my hands."

Zhencai straightened. "I will return."

He trotted back down the path to the bathhouse and found Ming Lun settled by the low table devouring her meal. "The guards are vigilant at this hour, but I know the right direction, and you?" She dipped her fingers in a rinsing bowl and shook them off.

"I found the Mongol. He's hungry."

"So are the orphans of the people he's killed."

She reached for a flask of wine Zhencai had ignored, but he slipped this away along with a half-bowl of beans. He might also have taken the skewer of meat remaining from her portion, but she snatched it up, chomping into it.

"Lend me a knife."

"What makes you think I have one?"

He flicked a glance over her body, the ornaments in her hair, the sleeves cuffed at her wrists and the belt at her tunic. "By my count, you are wearing at least five, and have three darts in your hair along with a garrote."

Her lips turned up. "What does a monk want with a knife?"

"He wants to show compassion."

With a turn of her wrist—a dancer's turn—she slipped a short blade into her hand and offered it to him, hilt first this time. "Slit his throat with it. That's the most compassionate thing you can do."

Zhencai tucked the wine flask into his tunic and took the knife. "What happened on the ridge, before the rest of us arrived?"

Her casual posture turned stiff. "They stopped firing, and I convinced them that Andao came in need of their leader."

"The Mongol had already stopped them by attacking first."

Ming Lun sat up and took a handful of pistachios. "Any larger man would have been seen long before he reached them—he knows little of stealth."

"Did the attack require stealth, or merely distraction?"

She cracked off a shell in her fingers. "He would've done anything to stop them dropping fire on his wife. You don't suppose he imagines that she cares for him?"

"The practice of meditation may help you detach yourself from emotions and outcomes."

"Oh? As you do?"

Zhencai made the sign of blessing and turned away. He was already at the far gate when a pistachio tapped his shoulder, and he forced himself not to look back.

Once he had delivered the scant meal, and reached through the narrow gap to cut the Mongol's bonds, Zhencai considered his next path. The village had no temple, he knew that already, so where might he find a sleeper, a man who had been waiting for more than a century between the ruins of his old home and the pathway to the weapon that had caused it. The sleeper must be protected, as Master Deng had been in the sarira temple, from both the weather and marauding animals. In the last light of the day, Zhencai examined the village more closely, now that he knew what he needed to find. Would everyone know about the sleeper? Unlikely, so the location must not be in the village proper.

Zhencai walked toward the village. Small houses, well-kept, with tile roofs and red pillars, lined a circular plaza. People moved to and fro, doing the work of the evening—though none of them carried water or cut wood, defying the ancient advice to the Buddhist, to return to simple things. In the Valley of the Sages, nothing was simple. When he examined the lanterns placed at intervals on their stone pillars, he found that the flames inside danced atop narrow pipes, and every pair of houses had an apparatus which could be tread upon to bring up water from the streams. Machines brought them water, and pipes brought them fire. The water flowed through shaped channels, carefully laid out. He recalled some visiting monk describing the excesses of the geomancers, channeling water into the patterns of the other elements. All was illusion. Water could at any time overflow its banks, devouring the machines they labored in creating and the structures they used to bend the world to their will.

As he crossed the plaza, some of the inhabitants stared, as if they'd never seen a monk before, a distinct possibility. Zhencai offered the sign of blessing. A woman hurried her children away. Metal inlaid the stone of the round plaza in a series of nested rings with characters repeating the names of the elements along with names of stars and the symbols of the I-Ching, the random coins that claimed to predict the future. But only the present mattered. So why fret over the location of the sleeper—a figure from the past—in hopes of subverting the future? Zhencai walked the circles of the plaza. They felt loose, giving slightly beneath the pressure of his foot, or shifting, ever so subtly, forward or back. Or was it simply that he perceived this entire village as an enemy, and tried to track its movement to be ready for attack? Illusions again. He paced toward the surrounding land and the source of its twin waterfalls, crossing a bridge over the united waters where they plunged down a narrow chasm, then underground beneath the sheltering wall of stone. Waterwheels marked the river up to where the two streams parted into waterfalls, one tall and narrow, the other a thundering cascade down a series of ledges, its water twisting back into curls and waves. Between the two waterfalls, the home of the geomancers themselves clung to the cliffs with a series of pillars, struts, and balconies. Gabled rooftops glazed with blue rose in ranks up the stone, and a few men moved upon the bridge that gave access to the structure. It resembled the isolated monasteries of the mountains. How many of those had once been enclaves of geomancers instead? Andao occupied this one, learning to dedicate himself to the world and sever his spirit all the more. Would he learn the arts of magic and divination, arts forbidden to the Buddhist? Andao's ungainly presence no longer haunted Zhencai's steps. He had never sought an apprentice, and he was not the teacher Andao needed. Just as Zhencai had always said.

Sunset gleamed on the water, and the blue-black night swelled overhead. He crossed farm terraces where firelight shone in little houses, and passed a foundry full of silent tools, the workers all gone home. In a fluttering field of drying silks, he startled a girl checking the cloth, and bowed to her before moving on. Barking dogs grew louder at his approach, then faded behind him. Where the servant had directed him down, across the widest bridge which, he was informed, gave an excellent view of the waterwheels, Zhencai moved upward on a narrow track away from the village. At one side, this track split toward the tower where a dim light marked the lowest story, accompanied by the murmur of voices and the quiet groan of metal instruments.

The waterfalls grew louder, and the air grew moist. In a small hut, a guard slept with a device for a pillow. Would he dream mechanical dreams? Zhencai walked quietly past.

His path ended at a smooth face of stone with a dropoff toward the waterfall. Had he been completely wrong? Perhaps he had missed a turning, or the trail had been worn away by water or sheared off in a landslide. The stone showed no sign of damage, and he was certain he had missed nothing. He looked up and down, and saw a shadow, an indent in the stone, just big enough for a hand or a toe.

Sliding his foot down into the opening, Zhencai lowered himself, keeping his hands on the stone edge of the trail he had followed. He slid the other foot down, wondering for a long moment if there would be another foothold, then his toes notched in and he sank slowly down the cliff, the waterfall pounding in his ears until he was climbing beneath it, clinging to the damp stone.

His toes struck a broad surface, and Zhencai let himself down onto a ledge. The crimson light of sunset here struck murky patterns through the sheet of water, and he walked into the dancing reflections, draped with red splashes as if he were drenched in blood. Ahead, the ledge widened, ending at a carved wall where a curious waterwheel stuck into the back of the stream, turning. A narrow chain led from it to a series of metal attachments gone green with age. And there, at the corner of the shelf, on a silk cushion, sat a woman, eyes shut, hands lightly folded. A second cushion sat before her with a bronze bowl beneath a triangular arrangement of rods

Not an old man after all.

The device on the wall led in wheels and rods to a dial that showed a pattern of dots and strings. Moving in, Zhencai examined it and recognized the constellations, a disc turning very, very slowly at the behest of the waterwheel that kept it in motion. Among the patterns, the Dark Lance looked small and unassuming, the rest of the Celestial Palace much more grand.

But how to wake her? It should be one of the others, Dailus with his mechanical mind, Bao Xing with her knowledge of the stars, even Ming Lun with her speed and wit, not a failed monk already aching from the short climb down.

Master Deng must have had a similar device in that bare patch on the wall of the sarira temple, but it had been long gone, causing him to oversleep. Instead, Zhencai's careless attempt to re-set the stone had triggered whatever mechanism awoke him. It seemed plain enough that this woman's design involved the movement of the stars and the singing bowl that rested before her. Zhencai prodded the frame around the bowl, but it resisted his attempt to move it. Instead, he turned to the discs of the heavens. He nudged the outermost disc, bringing the Dark Lance closer to the top. With a click, a rod notched into a slot on the next disc, drawing it into alignment with the one behind. The whole disc of stars swung downward with a clatter, and Zhencai jumped back. He had broken it. His qi burned behind his breast. But the waterwheel still spun, and one of the rods nearby jerked back and forth. A sound hummed beneath the pounding of the waterfall, growing louder by the moment.

Within the frame, a thick beater rubbed the edge of the bronze bowl, dragged around in a tight circle so that it never moved from the rim. The bowl sang a low note that filled the cave and seemed to build in Zhencai's bones. And, for the second time, he watched a sleeper wake.

She wore a simple gown of dark silk, her hair bound up with gemstones, but in plain settings, nothing ostentatious like those of Bao Xing. The gems winked with a shiver of movement, stirring the large, red stone that rested on her forehead. Her head lifted, tilted slowly this way and that, and she raised her hands, rotating them in gradual circles, flexing her wrists and elbows. At last, her eyes flickered open, and her hand touched her lips

Master Deng had drunk from the offering bowls before he spoke. Zhencai hurried to the waterfall and gathered water in his hands, carrying it back to her. She sipped a little but more ran down her chin, and she moved her hand toward the bowl. Freeing it from its frame, the rod spinning uselessly as he yanked the bowl from beneath it, Zhencai filled that and returned, the cave echoing in the absence of the hum.

She drank for a long time, taking a second bowl when he offered it, but this one she did not finish. "I did not expect a monk."

"No more than I would have expected to be here, lady. There are others more worthy and more able to speak with you than I."

"Yet you are here, and they are not. Who are these others?"

"A bronze-caster, an astronomer, a warrior—" he let out a puff of breath, "perhaps two. And my apprentice. A geomancer."

She raised her eyebrows. "A geomancer apprenticed to a monk?"

He gave a nod of acknowledgement. "That is how the wheel turned."

"A strange turning indeed. Six companions. Five would seem more apt, five for the five elements. Six is not auspicious. I wonder if one of these companions is false."

One was the enemy, indeed, and yet vowed to their cause. Zhencai settled before her, hands resting on his knees. She studied him. "You are not of the valley," she said, "yet you are not surprised by me."

"You are not the first sleeper I have seen, lady. I was there when Master Deng awoke, though his device had been removed."

She frowned, then ran her fingers along her cheekbones and forehead, as if remembering how the expression felt. "I am no sleeper, I am a dreamer. I wake once in every cycle of the sky, so that—" she took another swallow from the bowl, her eyes once more upon him. "Master Deng, you say. What else have you learned?"

What else should he tell her? What side would she be on? He once told Andao that he had no side, but after departing Dragon Turns, after meeting the dragon in the cave, he knew that had been an illusion. "I have seen the diagram of the Mandate of Heaven."

Her fingers strayed to the red gemstone at her forehead. "Master Deng. I presume he is Deng Ho, the Mandarin who began the project. Monks have rarely been the friends of Daoists, brother."

"You fear my intent. Lady, I fear yours."

At that, her lips curved up, just a little. "I wake every twelve years. I hear the news, how the empire is faring. And I walk to the bridge. I have never found it open. But then, Deng Ho has never, to my knowledge, awoken before." She glanced at the fallen celestial disk. "Has a firing already occurred?"

"According to our astronomer, it will be soon."

"Against whom?"

"Against the Mongols."

She pressed her fingertips together. "A small tribe of horsemen. Surely not worthy of such attention."

"They have grown very strong, lady. The emperor invited them to defend against another invader, and they have become the invaders themselves."

"That is why you seek to destroy them?"

Zhencai shook his head. "I would prevent the firing, lady."

"You would cast judgement. Rather than allow the Mandate of Heaven to work its course."

"This is not the Mandate of Heaven, lady, this is the pride of man, seeking to control the stars, to force his own outcome."

She bowed her head over them. "Yes, brother. That is precisely what this is. I will need a good meal if I am to help you. You cannot cross the bridge alone, or without at least some knowledge of the Way." Her smile as she raised her head shone brighter than the most beatific of Buddhas. She held out her hand to him.

Zhencai's muscles tightened. Last time he touched a woman, it had been in anger, this was different, and yet—

The patter of the waterfall shifted, and he swung about even as the guard raised his crossbow. "Lady, you are not to speak without your warden. Master Wei will come soon. For now—" the guard's stare focused on Zhencai, "I will keep your secret."

"I chose to tell him." The woman struggled to her feet. "It is time."

"That is not for us to judge." He snugged the crossbow to his shoulder.

Zhencai lunged toward him. The guard's cheek still bore the imprint of the device he slept with, the one that had summoned him here, no doubt. As Zhencai burst toward him, the guard shifted, training the weapon on Zhencai. But Zhencai swept out his foot, hooking the man's ankle. They slid together, the guard pinned against the damp stone wall, his weapon in Zhencai's face.

A frail hand interceded, drawing the weapon aside.

The bolt hissed past Zhencai's head into the woman behind him. Zhencai's iron hand slammed into the guard's chest. The man swung his crossbow down again, at Zhencai's ribs. Zhencai spun out of the way, knocking the guard's legs out from under him.

The guard got a mouthful of the waterfall as he plunged through into the spray on the next ledge. Red spilled from the ledges, and the body tumbled, swirling into the river where Zhencai saw it no longer. He scrambled back from the edge before he too succumbed to the water's pressure.

Blood flowed in the cave as well, streaming from the woman's chest. She coughed, and blood filled her mouth, but her hands thrust toward him, her eyes dark and urgent. "To heal, it was meant," she coughed a gout of blood.

As if his iron grip could force the life back into her, Zhencai wrapped his powerful hands around hers, trembling and thin. She pressed something into his palm, then she coughed her last, her emaciated body slumping against the wall, her hands sliding from his.

The hope that had been born of her offer of aid died with her.

Zhencai opened his hand to see what had been so important. A large, round gemstone, cut in fine facets, the red of good fortune. The scroll showed gems like this in the array directing the power of the stars. Had she worn it all these years to remember her legacy of death? Why give it to him?

The guard had said Master Wei would come soon. Zhencai considered what to do about that, but nothing in the cave gave any sign of his own presence. What would Master Wei make of the scene—the dead dreamer, the missing stone, the fallen guard? The obvious story required no other participants: a thief trying to take advantage of his knowledge, only to fall.

It was the Buddha's joke, reminding him of the illusions of the world—the illusion of life, the illusion of hope. Zhencai blessed the body and spoke the prayer of closure then, disillusioned, climbed wearily away.

CHAPTER FIFTY-SIX

Over their shared supper the following night—after a day of dancing, and watching all across the town—Ming Lun leaned close to hear Zhencai's tale of the dreamer, how she woke and how she died. She took note of everything the old woman said in between; anything might be important. When Ming Lun asked to see the gem, he eyed her blankly, until she laughed and demurred. They were barely allies, held together by the companions who were not there. While the villagers seemed tense, and Master Wei stalked through town with greater vigor that day, they simply fell silent when their visitors drew near, imagining their secret was kept; all the more secret now, with the death of the dreamer.

Zhencai lay down his chopsticks. "I will go rest. You, I presume, have other plans."

"They are so agitated today, I doubt I shall achieve much—but sometimes, such feelings interfere with vigilance."

"Indeed." He gave her a nod and walked to the chamber across the yard.

After a few more sips of wine, Ming Lun yawned and let down her hair, swishing it back from her head. She moved slowly inside, sliding the door shut behind her. Once there, she removed the outer layer of her garments, revealing close-fitting dark leg-wraps and a shorter tunic, easy to move in. Not so different from the monk's own garb, save that hers were dark, and his bright.

The noise of the divided river remained constant, but the sounds weaving through it died down: the clanging hammers at the metal mill and the wooden paddles pumping water and churning vats of cloth. The light of the magic lanterns sank low, just enough to guide someone to the privy. She waited until the smells of cooking dissipated, and imagined the astronomers in their tower waking to join the night. Then, braiding her hair to keep it back, she rose.

Pulling the lower corner frame from one of her rice paper windows, Ming Lun slipped out through the gap, tugged the corner back into place, secured it with one of her hair pins, then ran lightly up a goat's track on the near side of the river. Cicadas thrummed in the night, falling silent as she passed, starting up again after. When she could, she followed the streams upward to avoid the silences.

With the cliff at her back and the Sages' bridge just below her, she waited. Two men guarded the bridge at all hours, though she thought this was new since the visitors arrived rather than a habit of people who lived in a secret valley among their own. Which might explain the guards' lack of training for such an activity. They lolled about, sometimes at either side of the bridge, but often drawing together at one end or the other, near the lighted globes. Tonight, they leaned together on the railing, their backs to the cliff—for what danger could ever come from that direction?

One of the men took a long clay pipe from a wrap at his side and started to pack it. "The new astronomer is very pretty. Do you think they'll let her stay?"

The other man laughed. "Everyone's noticed. Rare enough to get visitors, but a lady like that? If you think you've got a chance, you're sleeping deeper than the founder."

The guard jabbed his pipe at his companion. "I cannot believe you said that, and Jiushen dead with her, no less."

"You're right. I'm sorry." The other man glanced away for a while, then remarked, "Jiushen was the rude one, anyhow."

"It's a good thing you don't believe in ghosts." The pipe-smoker leaned over the waterfall and shouted, "Jiushen, if you're down there, I always liked you just fine!"

While both men had a good laugh, Ming Lun crept nearer, clung to the rail nearest the cliff, and sidled along it, her back to the thundering waterfall, her toes gripping the slippery stone. She kept her arms long, her knees bent so the balusters concealed her even more. If they did glance back, they never noticed her. In a few damp and strenuous moments, she stood across the bridge, still holding to the rail. The Sages' palace rose in five layers, with a wide balcony at the lowest. Like so much of their valley, the cliff, balconies, and buildings carried a tracery of metal and other inlays, often in the form of characters—words for strength, flexibility, movement, rising and falling. Some sort of tribute to the waterfalls? She expected to see wooden struts and carved holes in the cliff face to support the whole thing. Alongside these, she found metal beams, gears, and devices concealed by the bulk of the structure, at least when viewed from below. They provided a ladder alongside the layers. Absent the algae that slicked the waterside surfaces of the bridge, the metalwork here gleamed dully in the moonlight, as if the geomancers had novices to climb the palace with every passage of the moon to keep the metal clean and oiled.

Curious, like everything else here. And, like most of the valley, not her concern. These people chose to divide themselves from China. The emperor sought their aid, she knew that much, but if his messengers ever found the geomancers, they failed to intervene in the fate of Kaifeng or the rest of the North. One hundred and sixty years in hiding. Detaching themselves from the world just as much as any monk. For hundreds of years, the Buddhists and the Daoists bickered over the Truth and the Way—and neither side noticed or cared if the Han people died around them. So be it.

Ming Lun clambered over the rail and glided toward the first layer of the palace. Dim light showed at the windows, and voices murmured. Over the door, a wooden plaque read "wood".

A narrow stair bypassed the interior and led upward to the next level, so Ming Lun took it, finding an identical door labeled "fire", with brightly lit, flickering windows to either side and, presumably, continuing at the front of the palace. Even from here, the heat warmed her.

She kept climbing. Like Yusen, she must scout the place before she knew where the dangers lay. No, not like Yusen. She had been doing this for years, through human observations and contacts. Why would she want to be anything like him? Ming Lun froze upon the stair, her head just at the level of the porch that rimmed the next layer of the palace, where the doors stood wide open, the windows as well. A faint mist rose from the damp structure, probably from the heat of the fires below. Why would they have arranged their palace in such a fashion?

Light streamed through the open door, and voices as well. "Tell me about earth, Andao."

"Earth is the center, the ground from which all springs, and to which all returns. Earth is balance, substance, and knowledge. Its color is yellow, its nature is yin because it is receptive." Andao's voice, more confident than she had ever heard him before. "Earth connects all the living beings of the world."

Master Wei, warmly, "Indeed. You told me you studied well, and I can see the result, even so quickly."

"I've read ahead to the other elements as well, Master, I hope that's alright."

Of course Andao read ahead, and interrupted the master to tell him so. But here the impatience which made him a poor monk apparently made him a ready pupil. She remembered standing among older girls in the dance hall, taking a perfect pose while they wobbled or slouched. For her own way, Ming Lun had been just as fine a pupil. Keeping her head low, in a crouch, she ascended the remaining steps, then pressed herself into the shadows against the cliff.

Inside, Master Wei faced Andao across an indoor garden, without any plants to speak of. Plots laid in curves or angles showed various textures of rock and dirt. He held out his hand in a fist, palm downward. At his nod, Andao put out his hand as well, and Master Wei dropped something into it. "I give you a seed," he intoned, with the air of ceremony. "All that any man can ever give you, Andao, is a seed, and it is you who must determine where to plant it. Please, step forward."

Cradling the gift, Andao sucked in a breath, then stepped onto the first patch of dirt. He suppressed a yawn, but his expression revealed the truth, and Master Wei said, "Focus, Andao. Connection is our tool and our weapon. It can also be our downfall. You aren't ready to practice while the others are present—their drawing of the chi would confuse your own efforts."

"Sorry." Andao scrubbed his hands across his eyes and separated his feet, squaring his shoulders, head up as he drew another, deeper breath. She knew that posture—he had learned it from Zhencai, and Master Wei's lowering brow suggested he saw it as well.

"Tell me where you stand."

"The earth has known fire, and it has no life. No chi."

"And what—"

"It's from a volcano," Andao blurted, and Master Wei's eyebrows notched upward, then a smile twitched his mustache. "It transferred its chi to fire."

"Keep walking."

Andao paced from one area to the next, describing the qualities of the ground where he stood. Charts of earth covered the walls, with samples of minerals tucked into shelves that ran beneath the windows. Cushions of silk turned the shelves into seating as well, and bins of scrolls occupied the corners. Larger specimens decorated the walls, including a huge chrysanthemum stone, one of the most beautiful she had ever seen. A drawing of a lo pan, the strange compass employed by the geomancers, occupied the central position and, above that, hung Bao Xing's cane as if it were no more than another example of a different earth. Excellent. No need to take it tonight—it must be at least two more days before the Lark would be ready.

Andao's voice, steadily describing qualities of earth and stone slowed and filled with question. He stood between two patches of earth, his right foot sinking slightly into one of them, his left foot about to depart the previous one, and he was staring downward, his profile clear.

"Master…"

"What do you seek?"

"Fertile ground." He opened his palm before him, the seed rolling gently.

"I have given you the seed, Andao. What you do with it is not for me to judge."

The young man drew his left foot to join the right. "It's hard to find the chi when the earth is so shallow like this," he muttered. He bent down, prodding the earth with his finger and dropped the seed inside the hollow he had made.

Master Wei probably thought he was concealing his surprise. "If you are not ready, Andao, then so be it. Many novices take several nights before they can move the chi, even in a place with such clarity as this."

Andao shook his head vaguely, as if he simply wished for silence. He patted the ground over his seed.

"You are certain? There are eight more grounds you have not felt."

"Is this wrong, Master? You told me to let the earth reach into me like a growing thing. Master Zhencai always told me I move too quickly. I—" He broke off, his eyes growing even more round, then he lifted his hand. Beneath it lay a soft, green sprout. It coiled up between his feet and curled over, putting forth a leaf. Andao stroked it with the tip of his finger. "Thank you, Master, for the seed."

Master Wei stared down at him, wet his lips, then said, "You are welcome." He tore his gaze from the plant and gestured toward the other regions of the garden. "It is still worth the effort to walk the remaining plots, then the minerals." He swept his arm wide, to indicate the wall of shelves.

"All of them?" Andao's shoulders slumped.

Master Wei laughed. "Not all tonight, but we will make a start of it. When the Weaver rises directly above the valley, I'll let you rest."

When the Weaver rose above the valley. Ming Lun, too, was smiling as she slipped back down the way she had come. Soon, the Lark would be ready, and so would she.

***

For three days, Dailus lived and breathed flying. He slept in a scoop of fabric in the kitemen's pavilion, restless. Ming Lun carried word that she was searching for the cane. Andao seemed inclined to remain there, as well he might, and without him, the cane became even more critical to finding the weapon. The sages deliberately kept the companions apart, offering them wonders and knowledge—and deflecting them from their quest. Zhencai alone they did not bother. He sat perfectly still, scowling and staring at the river. One of the village's few warriors had fallen to his death in the stream, and Zhencai insisted on speaking prayers for the dead man—prayers that none of the sages cared for in the least.

Dailus could not carry the scroll when he worked with the kitemen, so he had hidden it in the rafters of the covered deck, a hiding place few were tall enough to reach.

Last night, the guardians roused everyone in the kitemen's hall because they had seen a light—a forbidden light—at the ridge and assumed one of the kitemen was responsible because of its height. The light went out shortly after, and no sign was found of whomever had lit it.

So Dailus woke sourly to the excited chatter of the others, then cleared his mood when he remembered the day. Normally, they only flew when ghosts were needed to scare the occasional herdsman or treasure-hunter who came up to the ruined village. Today, he, at least, would get to fly. Today! Dailus rubbed his eyes with aching fingers. Very little Thunder

God ointment remained in the tube, and he must remember to ask Hanliao how to get more.

"Do you fly today, ghost?" Hanliao used the same term Dailus had heard so often since coming to China, but the kite master grinned when he said it. The Valley of Sages brimmed full of dour and serious scholars, but here, among the ridges, dwelt nothing but joy.

"Yes! How are the winds?" He floundered out of his cotton sling-bed, nearly falling, but righting himself. Sailors slept in such things, but how they got out without banging their heads every time, Dailus could not fathom.

"You must read the winds yourself. But eat first."

After rubbing his medicine into his joints and meticulously washing off the residue, Dailus joined the others for their meal of beans and millet. Although his mouth no longer tasted of metal, neither had food reclaimed any of its flavor, nor flowers their scent. Still, as he said his own Grace over his meal, he thanked God that his hands no longer shook so hard that he could not guide a brush or a tool.

Up on the ridge, they watched a few vultures circle the ruined village. Dailus towered over the birds, as if he were soaring already. "This time," Hanliao told him, "It is all up to you. But we will make a tether for you to find your way home." His teeth gleamed in a brief smile, then he stood watching the preparations.

Dailus opened the spherical lantern one of the others carried up, resting it carefully so that the mechanism of rings that kept the flame upright would not slide. He smoothed out a sack made of delicate paper. Next, he lit the wick in the tiny pouch of oil attached to the sack by strings at its open end, and held the closed end loosely in his hands. Two mornings ago, Ming Lun knelt beside him while he held the lanterns, apparently as fascinated as he had been, though she whispered that, in the South, the cities were full of such wonders. She had promised to return to witness the morning's flight. The paper sack rippled, then swelled into a globe, glowing faintly with the light, warming his hands. He waited until it pressed against his fingers, as if it longed for freedom as much as he did, then he let it go.

The paper lantern rose up steadily, drifted out over the ruined city, and rose a little more. Delicate and bright, the shape wafted higher on the currents, then turned away toward the deeper mountains, passing over the broad, empty fields.

"So?" Hanliao prompted.

"So the breeze is light, but steady—not so strong I can't control it, and it blows toward a safe landing."

"Will you fly?"

"Captain, I will." Dailus grinned, then bounded up to fetch his wings.

***

Ming Lun managed to eat breakfast with her usual languor in spite of the way her palms and feet itched to move. Zhencai, her only companion, ate little since the death of the dreamer. She, herself, had accomplished her mission that morning—one of them—beneath the light of the Weaver when Andao and Master Wei finally went to bed. She must confirm whether she had achieved another during the night. Tempting to reveal her victory, but she refrained, knowing he carried his own loss so heavily. To be so near a source of knowledge, only to have her die leaving nothing but a pretty stone. It must be nearly as crushing to him as his earlier defeat of her had been. Sometimes, studying him, she felt the bite of the ropes they used to bind her and the ache of the arm he had broken. That time, he had won, and taken the scroll as his booty. This time, he did not even know he was fighting.

"When will you be able to take back the cane?" Zhencai asked.

"Very soon, it will be in our hands. I thought a monk would know more of patience."

The old man was in no mood for a jest. "A monk may have patience, but the world has little. Our enemies may already be there."

Ming Lun kept her slight smile. "I will bring food to the Mongol today," she announced, taking a few items from the table.

"Again? One might imagine the Buddha's compassion has taken root in you." A cup of tea steamed his weary face. "I trust he enjoyed the mooncake."

"I am to watch Dailus launch his kite today. The graveyard is not far from my path."

"In that case, I shall find a place to sit meditation where I cannot hear the machines of their world."

"If such a place exists."

He bowed his head and made the sign of blessing, then rose. "Have you had word from the astronomer's daughter?"

"She sleeps by day so that she can be awake at night, watching."

"Given your own habits, that cannot be too difficult for you."

Ming Lun smiled. "Well, Brother, they seem reluctant to have even myself pierce the silence."

"In such a noisy place, I can understand that sentiment." He looked toward the waterfalls. "The water tends to muffle the world."

She forced the smile to stay on her lips. If the message she sent had been received, the waterfalls would be a dangerous place, in ways he did not understand. "It is louder where they funnel into the ground. There are ledges near the chasm where you can barely hear yourself think."

"That sounds perfect." He bowed to her again, then departed, the beads already swaying in his hands as he slid his fingers over one and another and another.

When he was gone, she slipped into her own chamber, finding the things she had hidden there before. This would not be a day to be caught unprepared. She took all of her knives and her pouches—the few that remained—and the second mooncake she had prepared in its wrapping, though she hoped she would not need it. Leaving Bao Xing's cane wrapped, she tucked it inside her tunic at her back. It would be awkward to carry that way, but she dare not leave it behind. She must be ready at any moment.

A gong rang the Hour of the Dragon, still early for someone who had been busy sliding in windows to steal back the cane. Handling it gave her twinges of guilt. Bao Xing had been escorted to the tower, and kept there. No doubt the other sky-watchers occupied her, so that she hardly missed her freedom. Still, the cane belonged to her, from her family.

Ming Lun had no family and no heirlooms to treasure. Zhencai spoke of detachment as a great virtue, but from what Master Wei said, a person could not become a geomancer without attachments. Clearly, Bao Xing treasured her attachments, even those imposed on her by others. Ming Lun considered simply ruining the map on the cane, blaming it on rough treatment by the Taoists or while it was bound to the horse. That could be sufficient to please the larks, and Bao Xing could have her cane back. It might compensate her for other losses.

She steeled her resolve and departed, smiling, nearly dancing, for any who saw her, walking like a girl in love about to see her beloved perform a great feat. The disguise fit far too comfortably, a fact that knotted her jaw and made her spine feel as rigid as the cane she carried. Dailus represented a failed mission—a mission she chose to continue to fail though she chose not to consider why. But by the Hour of the Snake, it wouldn't matter. She hurried up the steps and ledges while wives set out with washing and men carried buckets of coal to the foundry. A few graves had little bowls of beans or paper offerings in front of them, even in this place of worldly rather than spiritual concern, and she wondered how the Li family felt that their tomb contained a Mongol.

The Li tomb smelled faintly even as she approached it, of human waste and sweat, of the man imprisoned there. The tang of vomit merged with this, new since yesterday. Ming Lun approached as she had before, as if nothing had happened. As if nothing would happen. A herdsman passed not far off with a little group of goats, and Ming Lun knelt by the stinking tomb to call out, "Mongol."

From very near the gap, subdued grunt. "That mooncake was no good. I had only a bite, but the taste was wrong. I purged myself in case of poison."

Ming Lun's heart fell. It would have been a kindness if he need not live through today. "Ai! That's terrible. I had one myself, and it was fine. I brought another—"

"I can't eat in here." His fingers emerged, holding him close to the stone, his eyes glinting through the gap. "I can barely see the sky."

The Eternal Sky, the Mongols' all-encompassing god. "You have to eat something," Ming Lun reasoned, sliding her hand along her pouches, sorting her inventory in her mind.

"Will they keep me forever?"

"They have not spoken of setting you free." But the fact that they made no provision to feed him or clean his cell suggested the truth, and they both knew it.

His head tipped, his forehead resting on his hands, his small, grubby fingers still clinging to the stone. "If I could see her again," he breathed.

Ming Lun opened her mouth to answer this prayer he surely had not meant to speak aloud. She could answer with spite, in words that robbed the small invader of his foolish hope. She pressed her lips together. She need not be cruel when her victory was so close at hand, or was it more cruel to allow him to be hopeful?

Long ago, in the chamber where she learned to dance, her mistress told her stories, how this dance portrayed a princess longing for her love, and that dance showed the joy of nature, and another one presented the marriage celebration. She thought them all so romantic, so full of promise for what might come—not for herself, of course, but then, who knew? She remembered lying awake, dreaming of a love worthy of dancing.

The trilling of a lark broke her reverie. Ming Lun had already chosen. When she lit the signal last night, she had chosen. The Mongol was the enemy, a small and sometimes worthy one. She had tried to kill him kindly; she had no other solace to offer. Her people would win, and his would lose. But she did, in fact, have a gift that she could leave him, to let him wrap himself in hope before her victory came down upon him.

She pulled the wrapped cane from her tunic and lay it on top of the stone. "They took this from her, and I have gotten it back. They will not think to look for it here."

His hands wrapped around it, drawing it down into the darkness beyond. When he spoke again, his voice cracked. "You have more honor than I knew. Eternal Sky shine blessings on you."

Ming Lun backed away, then fled. What blessings? The blessing of her people's freedom, of her nation's survival, her emperor's triumph and new radiance to come. The blessing of her own small part in so much glory. Then why did her throat ache? Surely, if Yusen could have chosen one treasure to be buried with, it would be that. Or would he, like the emperors of old, want his wife beside him, smothered in the darkness of his grave?

Ming Lun ran. Yes, she betrayed him. She could not outrun that truth, but he was Mongol, she was Han. His wife was Han. The thousand, thousand people his khan had conquered and killed and enslaved were Han: she must not lose sight of that.

Her feet pounded the smooth stone path, and her legs pumped, her muscles stretching as she leapt up the ledges. Along the ridge, she saw the kitemen waiting, only one of them preparing his ghost-kite of silk and slats. His fair hair tumbled in the breeze, his skin tanned by the sun, but still conspicuously brighter than the men around him, as he stood at least a head taller than most of them. When he turned, his jade eyes lit with pleasure, and Ming Lun's heart fluttered at her ribs, a lark searching for a way out. She forced herself to look at the ruins below, to remember why she did all of this, for every woman of the Han people who struggled beneath a Mongol brute, for every child of the Han people who sobbed at the loss of his parents, and every father slaughtered and left for crows. Her people possessed the power to stop it, forever. How much more terrible would it be if they failed to use it?

"You came." He grinned, laughed, looked away, his face falling again as it always did. He was remembering her, that wife so far behind him. After today, he could go home to her. The words pressed against her heart, but she did not speak them. Let him find out, in due course. For now, let him fly—high above trouble, far from the ground.

"I would not miss you dancing with the wind."

His hand lifted, hesitated, then touched a strand of her hair that had worked loose and tickled at her cheek.

"Stand back."

The kitemen's leader, Hanliao came up before him, holding a belt that resembled her own, with a buckle to hold it snug, and a few items attached. "The honor of a kite is in flying. If your kite should fail to honor the sky, we give you a knife to cut yourself free, a cord to bind your wings, a spark to light your way home." He bowed and stepped up to slide the belt around Dailus's waist.

Four men helped him raise the enormous kite at his back, and he tied himself against the frame, his fingers shaking—not with pain, she thought, but with excitement and that warmed her against the wind.

When his broad shoulders and narrow waist had been secured, he slipped his hands into the grips, flexing his fingers, his hands scarred but powerful. The men steadied him as he prepared. He gazed over the landscape, those jade ghost eyes stirring her all over again. His square jaw and long nose looked so different from the other men's rounded features, and curls of wheat-colored hair danced around his face. Who else but a ghost, for an orphan and a murderer?

Once again she found him occupied, unable to hold her back as she sprang up to her toes, caught her hands in the tangle of his hair, and kissed his mouth, breathing him in, refusing to close her eyes to the astonishment in his, to the desire she could see that she stirred in him. She broke away and danced back a few steps. The men around him roared with laughter and approval, gripping his tether to prevent their delight from fouling his flight.

"Go!" she cried. "Fly!"

His jade eyes flashed in her direction, then he faced the cliff and leapt into the wind's embrace.

CHAPTER FIFTY-SEVEN

As his feet left the ground and found the sling of cloth to support them, his arms straining against the tug of the kite at his back, Dailus thought for one dizzying moment that he should have waited for the power of the kiss to fade. He fought for control of the kite as it soared upwards, the men below him shouting and hollering—in joy or terror, he could not tell. Was he flying or falling? Had Ming Lun's kiss given him strength to soar, or distracted him to his death? He pulled to the right, and the kite dipped, dodged, and straightened. The wind whipped tears from his eyes. Giddiness swelled in his breast, and he howled with laughter into the sky.

Nowhere in Lithuania, nor in all of Europe could such a joy be found. It forged an alloy in his heart with the soaring joy of that kiss—forbidden, sinful, to celebrate a heathen's passion, a heathen sage's art. Sorcerous, maybe, but he did not care.

His garments pressed against him, cloth twisting and fluttering. He tipped, turning like the vultures he spotted from afar. Ruined farms marked the land below, but here and there among them, he glimpsed patches of green. The land would not be dead forever, the earth would not be defeated, even by the scorching of the stars. Sunrise stretched long shadows from the peaks and ridges, shadows that seemed to creep along the cliff sides like dark fingers withdrawing upward on the slope that lead into the Valley of the Sages. Dailus shifted his weight, tipping the kite. For a moment it nearly tore from his hand, bucking then sliding a little too fast downward.

The shadows were moving. The shadows were made of soldiers.

Dailus shouted, immediately made hoarse by the battering wind. Where were the warning systems, the wires and the watchers who had launched the fire-laden ghosts against his own small party? Watching him, the flying ghost, but he had no way to warn them. If he let go to wave his arms, would they even understand? If he tried to land too quickly, the kite would scrape him off on a ridge or flip him to plummet to his death.

Instead, he soared closer to the intruders, finding his balance, dipping over them until he saw their leather armor and the spears and bows they carried. Not Mongols: Chin. They carried small casks and paper-wrapped balls, up toward the lake above the village where the waterfalls began. If he waggled his wings or held steady over this small and deadly army, would the kitemen notice? He had to try.

Pitching closer, Dailus nearly tipped as he dodged a pinnacle that concealed the stockpiles of Valley incendiaries—but the stockpile was gone, the white-wrapped bundles carried away by the intruders. One of the hurrying soldiers glanced up at him, the darker shadow racing along the ground, then he unslung the bow he carried and took aim.

Dailus shifted his weight again, trying to draw back his circle, but not rising. The arrow itself might be the warning they needed. He entered the shadow of a ridge, and the archer released. Dailus flinched, twisting to dodge the weapon. The arrow sliced fabric, but his sudden shift tilted the kite, then his wingtip cracked against stone and his kite swung sideways, scraping down, silk tearing, his back slamming the ridge.

Yanking his arms free of the grips, Dailus fumbled to free his feet from their sling, but the kite wrapped him as he fell, battering against stone, then sliding down and coming to a rest at last, his face swathed in white silk, his skin stinging from a thousand scrapes. The breath whuffed out of him.

Dailus gasped, trying to force air into his chest, at least to draw breath enough to thank God he lived. The thin spars of the kite prodded him, along with the stones where he landed. When he could, Dailus pulled the fabric from his head, gulping breaths, dazzled by the sun in his face. He wiped a trailing bit of string from his forehead and found a trickle of blood as well. Even damaged, the kite slowed his fall so he did not feel any broken bones. With shaky fingers he found the knife the kitemen insisted he carry, and he cut the bindings at his waist and chest, struggling free of the broken spars and torn shroud. On his knees, Dailus gaped up at the dizzying slope above him. He had struck one of the narrow pinnacles midway up the barrier ridge that protected the valley. Where was the army? An arrow cracked against the stone over his shoulder.

Dailus scrambled up and ran across the slope, his feet stinging, the knife still gripped in his hand for all the good it did him. What had the kitemen seen? How much could they tell from his flight and from his fall? Please God, let their warriors be ready. But they depended more on secrecy and on their displays of mystic-seeming power to send visitors away—they were not prepared for invasion, certainly not for invaders who knew the hidden pathways.

A line trailed along the ground next to him, and he realized the tether still showed him the way back. He gave the cord a tug, the signal that he had survived the fall—it held taut, but no one tugged in reply. Keeping low, he hurried across the slope, angling upward. When his feet slid on the crumbled stone scree, he clung to the line and kept his balance. The invaders must have moved on high enough not to notice him, or not to care. One fallen ghost could do little to stop them. He had nothing but the clothes he had been wearing, the little knife that got him free, the cord at his belt. It could be a garrote, or a trip line—it could bind hands. It gave him something to do with his fears, and he wondered if meditation did the same for Zhencai. If he ever saw the monk again, he would ask.

At last, the ledge he had leapt from loomed above him. A series of hand and footholds brought him up, peering over the deserted launch platform.

The mountains echoed with cries and the ringing of bells. Bloodied corpses scattered the slopes, bristling with arrows, but many others ran, and a crowd pressed together in the heart of the valley where the central plaza held markings like a giant compass with too many rings. Above them, on the rim near the waterfalls, stood the invaders, raining down arrows, while the handful of warriors—most of them the kitemen Dailus had come to know—tried to shoot back.

The enemy soldiers spread out along the rim, not deep, but they did not need to be, a force of maybe two hundred men, well-armed. Between the waterfalls, the enclave of geomancers roused. Men hurried from the buildings that clung to the cliff face, gathering onto a balcony that seemed barely large enough to hold them.

To the right, where a viewing platform cut into the cliff, Dailus heard voices. A screen of flowering trees separated this official stage from the kitemen's workshops and homes. He lifted his eyes to the kitemen's pavilion where his things were kept—including the scroll.

Leaping up, Dailus ran across the short space and slithered down the stairs into the pavilion. He clung to the second pillar from the back and thrust his hand into the space between the rafters. Empty. The scroll was already gone.

Dailus reeled. Then he found his satchel and dragged it up onto his shoulder. What next?

The voices grew louder. Dailus dropped down into the grass beneath the flowering trees and peered up through the foliage. On the platform stood a handful of soldiers and a man in a long grey robe with a breastplate and helmet. "—such a nest of traitors, captain," he was saying, then he shifted his gaze and inclined his head, as if in answer to a bow.

"I had not envisioned such a force, Minister."

Dailus dug his fingers into the earth to keep himself grounded. Ming Lun's voice. She moved nearer, her back to the Valley of the Sages.

Ming Lun. The knowledge struck him like a blow. The others had united to stop the weapon, if they could. He had even thought he had won her heart, but her heart had already been lost, to an emperor, a cause, a country. It seared him more sharply than her kiss.

The Minister replied, "We were already on the march, and the Mongols are not far behind us. I saw no need to divide our force. What are they doing down there, gathering themselves to slaughter?"

"They are a strange people, Minister. They wish to understand the world, but not to participate in it."

"Which may explain why they refused to aid the Son of Heaven. We knew of them, of course, but not their precise location." He smiled, a gracious expression that left Dailus more worried than before. "The emperor will hear of your service, Ming Lun."

"My service is not yet done, Minister." She lifted her hand, then drew down into a graceful bow and brought up the other hand with a flourish, as if presenting a ceremonial blade. On her palms for his approval, lay the scroll. "This document details the device, my lord Minister. It may aid you in your work."

He settled it in the crook of his arm. "Indeed. You will wish to witness this. Come, turn around." He gave a flourish of his hand in invitation. Slowly, she complied.

"It seems a loss, my lord, not to take advantage of their knowledge."

"That is why we will not use fire, but stone and bamboo are resistant to flooding. As is bronze. I brought a portable firedrake, but it seems fitting to use the native devices."

The earth gave a low rumble, and Dailus looked back. Near the waterfalls, the soldiers worked, placing the Sages' incendiaries. On the balcony between the waterfalls, the gathered geomancers turned together. The balcony slid free of its cliffside and descended toward the village, the thin struts that supported it pivoting to guide the balcony downward until it occupied the middle section of the largest bridge. The geomancers scattered to either side, toward the stone pillars that surrounded the town. Andao, his hair growing in curly, stood out among them as he moved with another man in the direction of the tower. Again, the men stopped and turned. On the pillars between them, the bronze globe lanterns burst into glorious light. Between these markers, the geomancers spread their hands.

A whisper of movement drew Dailus's attention, and Zhencai slipped up beside him, crouching beneath the trees. "I knew she was not to be trusted," Zhencai breathed.

The words struck a shaft to Dailus's heart. "What now?"

"Bao Xing."

The tower stood on a low rise outside the perimeter of lanterns and geomancers. None had emerged from it while Dailus watched, but he could see a few people moving at the top. Please God they had archers inside.

The bowl of the valley gave a low moan that echoed upward.

"Magic," snarled one of the men on the platform—the Minister Ming Lun had recognized. "Now! Do it now!" He waved his arms.

Across the valley, the soldiers on the rim bunched together, then jogged away toward the ghost town, leaving tiny flames behind them. Curious: the Minister had said they would not use flames. Too late, Dailus understood, but his protest was lost in the explosion that followed, the stone of the waterfalls bursting outward and pelting the village below. People shrieked, and the entire valley rocked with the damage as more stone rumbled down the mountain slopes. The lake above rushed downward, sweeping away the buildings and stairs on the cliffside, tumbling the bodies of the dead and the living alike.

The rumble shook where Dailus and Zhencai crouched, and rocks bounced to crash among the kitemen's houses and into the graveyard below. "Yusen's down there. The tower is high—it'll hold."

Zhencai gave a nod, and the two men slid and scrambled downward.

The earth still rumbled as water poured in, rushing the streets, slamming into the outermost houses. When the central stone came down, the village would vanish beneath the waters. Even now, cracks opened in the ramparts of stone where the geomancers' palace had been. They had no time. When his feet hit the path and a shout behind him warned him they had been seen, Dailus hesitated—to run for the tower and the stable rock beyond meant safety. And for Yusen, trapped in the tomb, certain death whether by avalanche or drowning.

He ran on, Zhencai keeping pace despite his age and stature. A pair of soldiers scrambled down to meet them, and Zhencai sprang ahead, his extended leg slamming into the lead soldier before the man could throw his spear. "Go!" he shouted.

Dailus sprinted past, hearing the uff and smack of combat. At the Li tomb, an arm thrust into the gap above the slab. "Let me out! Please!"

The ground gave a heave, and Dailus stumbled as one of the grave markers shifted from its place.

A spear flew over his head as he went down, and he rolled, bringing up his little knife. The soldier lunged to reclaim his spear, but Zhencai moved faster, landing hard on the soldier's back with a telltale crack of bone. Blood streamed from the soldier's gaping mouth. Dailus clambered back up and snatched the soldier's spear, a shaft set into an iron cap as long as his forearm with a wicked tip. Dailus jammed the tip between the slab and the tomb wall and heaved with all his might. The slab groaned against stone. The ground tremored again, and he worked with it, prying into the tomb. With a long, grating movement, the slab inched outward.

A cloth-wrapped stick tumbled out, then Yusen scrambled through the opening, barely big enough, even for him. His dark hair hung in limp matts, his blue del stained and spattered, his skin gone sallow. Collecting the bundle and hugging it to his chest, the Mongol swayed on his feet, leaning against the tomb as he tipped his face to the sky. Finally he looked down, then straightened immediately, his breath sucked in.

Dailus still crouched as he had finished, with the spear in his hands.

"Why?" the dwarf rasped. "So you could kill me yourself?"

"Because no man should die a prisoner." Dailus turned away. The sight of his master in such a miserable state inspired nothing but pity. "Zhencai!"

The monk gave no sign of having heard. He paused between two soldiers, then lashed out at one with his fist. The man dodged, lifting his spear, but Zhencai caught the shaft and shoved it downward, planting the point as he swung his body around it and knocked the men down. He let go, dropping to his feet and sprinting back to Dailus. "The earth."

"I feel it." Beneath the ominous rumble of the water's rise came a slither of something else, then a shock that tingled the hair at the back of his neck.

Two dozen yards below, one of the geomancers stood between two lantern pillars, his feet placed carefully on stone. Pulling, Andao had said of the sensation in the ghost village before they were attacked by kitemen. Dailus's feet and knees trembled with the suction.

"They are gathering the qi—we must move!" Zhencai shouted above the rising moan.

Keeping the spear, Dailus launched into motion, diagonally upward, toward the tower. They would never make it.

Behind him, he heard a muffled curse, and glanced back to find Yusen struggling to keep up. Zhencai caught the Mongol's arm and pulled him along. The bridge at the chasm cracked and collapsed into the rising water even as they approached, forcing them uphill.

"You!" A Chinese voice, but the Mongolian answered: "Son of a snake! Guowei!"

On the platform high above, a group of faces peered down at them. One of them was Ming Lun's, her hair still shimmering in the sun. Steal from a comrade, spy for an enemy, betray a village. Anything for the emperor.

Dailus turned away. "Come on!" He planted the butt end of the spear and leapt the chasm, then turned back to toss it to the others. Yusen caught the spear one-handed. Spear in hand, he looked up the long stair toward the platform where the Chinese minister glared down at him. Dailus did not know what lay between Mongol and Mandarin, but the swelling fury needed no further explanation—nor must he be foolish enough to stop for it.

Zhencai tapped the Mongol's shoulder as he sprang past and leapt the gap, almost slipping, but catching himself, pitching forward to run up the other side. "Bao Xing." He pointed toward the tower.

Yusen stumbled into motion, planting the spear and flying into the air over the gap, limbs flailing. He struck the ground hard on the other side, tumbling. He pulled himself up again, panting, the spear forgotten, the other bundle still clutched in his grip. He pressed a hand to his shoulder, wincing as he lurched after them.

The valley's moan rose into a deafening sound that ached in Dailus's teeth. Already, a dozen or so soldiers converged on the tower's base.

"Yusen!" Bao Xing called out from the top of the tower, her silk sleeves fluttering.

Clenching his jaw, Yusen started forward. Almost immediately, he lurched sideways and nearly fell.

"Can you even fight like this?" Dailus blurted.

The Mongol shot him a deadly glance, his teeth framed in a snarl, but his eyes glazed with pain and fear. "She needs me."

Dailus glanced up again, thinking. "Can you climb?"

Yusen's brow furrowed, right hand still gripping the opposite shoulder. Dailus thought the Mongol might weep, an idea that stunned him more than anything else that day.

"I can," Zhencai said. "Tell me the plan." He strode forward, and the others followed as best they could.

"I have a cord, strong enough to hold me on a kite. If we tie off an end at the top of the tower, and one down low, she could slide down it."

The monk put out his hand and took the coil. "This means you must guard."

Dailus gave a nod. He glanced at Yusen, still uncertain. "If you go uphill—those trees should be strong enough. Zhencai will throw you the end, and you—"

"I understand," the Mongol snapped, then he changed course up into the fields, angling toward the trees Dailus had indicated.

On guard. With a knife, a field of drying fabric and a packet of ginger tea? Then the last rampart of stone at the end of the valley cracked, and the two waterfalls became one, a monster roaring directly into the valley.

High on the rim, soldiers cheered. In the village, citizens screamed. And, in the narrow band between, the geomancers raised their arms. Like the standing pillar of water trapped in its little bronze bowl, the floor of the valley shivered, sang, and rose with a howl of stone, thrusting upward, scattering dirt and gravel. The pillar of earth gleamed with veins of ore and echoed with power as the geomancers raised their valley to the sky. What power they called upon, Dailus could not know, save to whisper a prayer as he watched the pillar thrust ever higher, taking the heart of the village and all of its inhabitants with it. Bands of metal wove through the stone, gleaming with inlaid characters, themselves forming even greater words wrought into the very earth itself. The geomancers had tamed their world, and now it obeyed them, just as Yusen's horses raced to their master's. Soldiers fell, shrieking into the collapsing tunnels and streams as the Valley of Sages rose once more into legend.

CHAPTER FIFTY-EIGHT

For the moment, Dailus realized, Zhencai needed no guard at all: the miracle was enough to distract any reasonable man. As the pillar thrust upward, the water roared in around it, and the wall of the valley, where the waterfalls had been, crumbled inward, cracks streaking down the face of the naked stone; bits of buildings, wood, and bronze machinery tumbled after. The remaining bridges toppled, taking a few soldiers with them. More soldiers plunged into the cracks opening before them.

The ground still trembled beneath his feet, but Dailus shook himself into motion. A ring of water surrounded the sage's pillar, eating into the remaining earth of the valley itself. It crumbled toward the graveyard opposite, the terraced farms and the hillside of the astronomical tower where he stood. As he ran toward the tower, the edge of stone below broke away, tumbling into the frothing water. A few bodies slid down with it. Another body slid toward it, stirred, and pushed upward, lanky arms flailing. Andao!

Dailus ran into the lines of laundry. He yanked up the tall stake at the far end and ran back, flinging it ahead of him to rattle down the slope then grabbing the lower pole as the rope with its washing sailed by.

Andao struggled to his hands and knees as the end of the laundry skittered past him, grabbed the rope, and pulled himself onward. He needed only a few steps to find his footing. Dailus hurried ahead, pointing toward the tower, and their paths converged, Andao slowing to match him.

Tears streamed down Andao's face, and he smeared them away to no avail. "Master Wei pushed me. When the great work began, he—" Andao choked in a breath. "Master Wei saw Zhencai and Yusen. I revealed the wrong attachment." He nearly fell, then, but Dailus steadied him, and they shared a glance. Andao's half-smile shone through the tears. "I failed him."

"Could you do that?" Dailus pointed up at the stone pillar that shadowed their way.

"It's taken them a hundred years to lay the work for that." Andao took another long sigh. "She's still in the tower?"

Four soldiers remained at the base of the tower, pounding on its door with a stone baluster from the nearest bridge. More worked their way down from the valley's rim toward the stand of trees where Yusen waited.

"Zhencai is climbing the back of it. We need to draw off the soldiers. I have no weapons, nothing—not even the scroll any more. All I have is tea."

Andao brightened in spite of his tears. "You have tea? What's in it?"

"How should I know?"

Andao stuck out his hand expectantly, and Dailus pulled out the pouch of tea. "They've seen us." The tower door cracked beneath the soldier's onslaught and someone shouted inside, followed by the clash of weapons. But two soldiers broke off and headed toward them, raising their spears.

"This is very fertile ground," Andao remarked. "Let's hope for the best." He turned—another of those precise movements as if the direction he faced were critical, then opened the tea pouch and tossed it into the wind. A spear flew toward them, and Dailus leapt aside—into a lush and growing mound of vegetation. "Thorns would be better—or bamboo," Andao remarked.

Dailus handed over the bamboo tube that once contained his ointment, then picked up the spear as the soldier rushed him, knife drawn.

Dailus spun the spear, knocking the man in the side and sending him sprawling.

Andao pivoted again, holding the empty bamboo tube, then sank to his knees. Passing him, Dailus lunged forward to finish the assault and the soldier stirred to rise from the unsteady ground. Before the soldier could get his feet under him, he shrieked and his back bent as if the effort of rising proved too much. Blood blossomed all over his body, stains on his trousers and arms, then shoots of green pierced straight through his flesh. The soldier's body jerked and shifted as the bamboo swelled and mounted skyward, shredding the impaled man in a welter of gore.

"Holy Father!" Dailus scrambled back from the dead man, feeling sick, but he had no time for awe or horror. Using the spear as a prop to move faster, Dailus sprang up the slope and scrambled onto the solid stone of the tower's base. Four other soldiers, running ahead to aid their fellow, scattered, screaming. Bamboo struck upward through their feet, tainted by the poisonous Thunder God Vine. They writhed and howled, but hung dead in moments, pinned by the fast-growing shoots.

When the man at the door turned, Dailus whacked his head with the spear and sent him to his knees, but caught the man's shoulder before he could fall onto the deadly earth, settling him to the step. No one deserved that.

The blood-streaked bamboo rustled, and Andao emerged from the thicket like a timid deer, his face a mask of dread. "Perhaps not bamboo." Turning aside, he vomited.

Shouts and orders came from above as the Minister's party hurried toward the tower. Dailus regarded his suddenly dangerous companion, relieved to be out of bamboo. "We have to go."

Andao gave a dazed nod and followed him into the tower. They hurried up stairs that bent back and forth between the floors, seeing bloody corpses of soldiers and astronomers, some still tangled in their bedclothes from their day's rest. Footfalls thundered after them.

The tower trembled as a great crack opened across ground below, severing the tower from the upper fields where Yusen waited. Bronze astronomical instruments stood all around them or rocked where they had fallen with the shaking of the earth. Across the platform, Zhencai stood by the wall. Dailus caught a glimpse of Bao Xing as the monk lowered her. She held a band of silk across the stretched cord, one had gripping either end, her eyes large in her unpainted face as she rushed away over the crevice that gaped below.

Another soldier lay coughing on the floor beside a fallen bronze instrument.

Zhencai swiveled, already bringing up his hands for attack, then his eyes softened. "Andao. The Buddha blesses our meeting."

"You may not think so later," the young man mumbled.

Dailus nudged him forward, and Zhencai pointed down the length of the silken cord. "She landed."

In a flutter of silks, Bao Xing fell into the field terrace below the trees where Yusen waited. He took her elbow to draw her out of the way, then raised a beckoning hand toward the tower.

A handful of soldiers, with the captain at their head ran forward on the far side of the gap, straight toward Yusen and Bao Xing. "Look out!" Dailus shouted.

Yusen shouted and ran into the field, springing back down with a hoe which he swung at the advancing soldiers. They broke apart around him, three moving up toward Bao Xing, the other two, swords drawn, aiming for the cord that was the only escape from the tower.

Howling, Yusen spun about.

For a moment, Dailus felt sure Yusen would go after his wife, to save her, and let the cord be cut. The Mongol glanced at his wife, then up to where the three stood atop the tower in its landscape of crumbling stone—and lunged back to defend the cord. Bao Xing shrieked and kicked, but one of the others had her onto his shoulder before she could escape. Yusen, his back toward them, kept on, a sword cracking the handle from his weapon, then the hoe carved into the swordsman's stomach and stuck. Dailus flinched as if the tool struck his own spine.

Zhencai slapped a band of cloth over the cord. "Andao, you next."

The young man paled, glancing down at the widening crevasse where wheat and stone and a few goats plunged into the gap. "If they cut the cord, I'll fall—"

"Then hurry—the Mongol cannot hold them back for long, and you must escape." The monk pulled him closer and pressed the cloth into his hands. "Hold fast."

With a wail, Andao slid down the line, legs flailing.

"He still knows no discipline."

"Oh, he knows something," Dailus told him, remembering the bloody stalks of bamboo still growing through the dying men.

The remaining swordsman stumbled on the unstable ground and grabbed the cord to stop his fall. Startled, Andao let go too soon and fell into a crumbling field, digging in his hands and toes as the earth slid beneath him. Above him, Yusen brought his hoe down into the head of the fallen soldier. Two men, carrying Bao Xing, hurried toward higher ground, their companion turning toward the cord. From his lower ground, Yusen hacked into the man's legs and left him screaming as he dropped low and slid partway down. Yusen slammed the head of the hoe into the ground and clung to it, extending his feet toward Andao, who managed to grab hold and clamber up toward safety.

"Hai! Stop there," shouted a voice from the stairs.

"Now—go now!" Zhencai ripped off his belt and flung it over the cord.

"Not without you." Dailus grabbed the other side of the belt, both men clinging to it as they leapt the parapet and swung down over the abyss, flying again, but dangerously fast. The old man squinted into the wind as they soared, fierce as an eagle, then they struck ground, letting go and falling aside.

"Cut the line! Cut it!" Even as Dailus shouted, the cord slithered away into the air, and a man yelped at the other end. With a great crack, the tower shuddered. Its base shifted sidelong as the floors above crunched down. The tower collapsed, the instruments spinning off into the abyss.

"Can't we simply die right here?" Andao pleaded.

"Easily," Yusen answered. "If the earth doesn't swallow us first, they have archers."

Yusen yanked up his hoe, nearly overbalanced, and searched the ridgeline. The men with Bao Xing scrambled up to where a dozen more stood waiting for them—the captain and Ming Lun among them.

"And we have nothing—no weapons, no horses, no scroll, no cane," Andao said.

Dailus pushed to his feet, aching all over. "We have to stop them reaching that machine."

"We don't even know where to look!"

Whatever weakness he had seen in Yusen had vanished in the time since they parted. In spite of his haggard appearance, the little Mongol glared as steadily as ever. He reached beside him for the wrapped object he had been carrying and stripped the cloth away, to reveal the cane.

"Which way?" Zhencai asked.

Yusen pointed along the row of trees that separated the fields. "Harder for the archers to take us. Lead on, geomancer."

Andao trembled. "After all this—"

"You can, you will, or we will die." Yusen held out the cane, aiming at Andao's chest. "Choose your own death if you wish, but not my wife's. If this is where they're going, then I go, too."

With a shiver of his lean figure, Andao drew himself up and started down the path that Yusen had chosen. When the first arrow flashed into a tree by Zhencai's hand, they all sprang into motion—Dailus and Yusen toward the back. Yusen paused, leaping into a field only to rejoin them on their diagonal course carrying a curved pruning blade as well as his bloody hoe, its handle already broken off. The hoe he kept close to his chest, still favoring his left arm. Dailus reached out for the other weapon, his slave bracelet shifting against his arm, but the Mongol held tight, shooting him a narrowed glance.

"Why do you still wear that? Men with tools to build tombs could have struck it off."

"I won't be free until—" He bit off the words. Until his Mongol captor died, he thought, or at least, until he was humbled, but even then it wouldn't matter. He had a mission to fulfill here, on his oath to God. Until Dailus had the freedom to walk away from what he had done to China, he was not free and he knew it.

"You tried to poison me, even in the tomb. Don't think I don't know it."

"What? I never went near the tomb until this morning, and that was to get you out." Dailus put on a burst of speed to outstrip the Mongol, but his trembling muscles and aching joints defied him.

"I can smell it on you, the poison. That cake she gave me had a bit of the same smell."

Smell? Dailus groaned. Once again, his suspicious little master let his imagination run free. And yet Yusen turned away from his wife to give the three of them time to escape from the doomed tower. What smell could he share with a mooncake? He couldn't even smell a thing—then he thought it over. "You said 'she' gave it to you? Ming Lun, the dancer?"

"Your lover."

"Hardly. Thunder God Vine, the ointment the monastery gave me. It's poisonous if you eat it. She helped me apply the medicine—she probably saved some of it to poison you. She stole the scroll and gave it to your Guowei."

"She brought me the cane. Why poison me in a tomb?"

"Because she could come back for the cane any time she wanted. Did she offer you more food?"

Yusen kept silent, then held out the harvesting blade, hilt first.

Dailus gripped it a little too tightly. "She deceived us all."

Zhencai glanced back with a gentle gaze. "It does not mean she did not care."

"She led them to the valley so everyone would die!"

They mounted the ridge, coming suddenly into the sun with the mountains marching away before them, and a glimpse of golden desert far beyond, a landscape as rough and empty as Dailus's soul.

"No," Zhencai said, "Not everyone. She sent me to a hollow to meditate—a place far from the strike." Then he tipped his head toward the sky. "I heard our ghost would ride a kite out of the valley. That signaled the soldiers to come in—once you were safely gone."

Dailus balanced there between earth and sky, aching in both body and soul as he absorbed Zhencai's words. Ming Lun's kiss still lingered against his mouth, the sweetest, sharpest pain of all.

CHAPTER FIFTY-NINE

Yusen estimated the remaining soldiers would take a few hours to cross the crevasses and pursue them—if they intended to. A pitiful band like this one, no bow, no swords, no horses would hardly be worth hunting. Guowei had taken everything of value; everything Yusen cared about had been stripped away: everything but his anger.

He urged them on, in spite of their injuries and exhaustion, until they reached the shelter of a shallow cave where he finally let them rest. His bones settled deep, and he longed to simply collapse along with the slave and the geomancer. His wife had never complained through the long days of riding, though he could see her twinges of pain and heard her sigh of relief when she dismounted. They touched for an instant, beyond the void, then he steeped himself in battle. He defended the others, knowing that without him, they were dead. There was no time for another choice. When he turned back, she was gone. She wore only a light silk sleeping gown. He pictured her among the soldiers, surrounded by men who worshipped her as they worshipped any of their gods. Yusen wore the blood of three men, and it had not been enough. Could he have moved faster? With a bow, he might have taken them down, all of them, and saved her.

Dripping with other men's blood and aching to his heart, Yusen announced, "I will go for water."

"That way." Andao flapped his hand. "And down. Look for blue flowers."

The slave pulled open his bag and found a water skin, then offered another that had been bound at his waist. His eyes looked hard as stone. Did he brood over his lost love's betrayal, or over his dependence on Yusen himself? Tucking the short-handled hoe into the back of his belt, Yusen took the water skins, though a bolt of pain shot through his wounded left shoulder. It had been healing well, or so he thought. On top of sleeping in the stone tomb—rather, trying to sleep with the cries of his burning family echoing around him in the dark—wielding a farm tool two-handed against armored men had been too much.

"I will come with you," the monk offered.

"No need." Yusen turned away, but the monk fell in step with him, deliberately shortening his stride.

"I walk also for meditation."

"Very well." Yusen longed to bathe, but it would not wash him clean of the memory of darkness, lying alone and bound, away from the sun, forced to sleep in the cage where he shat and pissed and vomited. Buried alive.

Marmots whistled and scurried away among the tumbled boulders, and Yusen considered how to catch one without a bow and no supplies or tools to make snares. All four men would be hungry, tired and sore; even the monk who seemed beyond the flesh. In a few minutes, a patch of blue flowers bobbed among old grasses , and they found a spring bubbling up that broadened into a pool among the rocks. Yusen sniffed at it, dipped his hand and brought it to his mouth. "Clean. With an avalanche, you must be sure."

Zhencai sank to sit beside the pool, favoring his knees as if the mountain walking did not, in fact, serve him well. "You know many things."

"I am a scout." Yusen submerged the first waterskin to fill it.

"It allows me to see how your people have come to conquer so much."

Yusen lifted the full skin from the water. The words sounded almost like a compliment. "We have many strengths. This is one of them."

The monk took the waterskin. "Most men, even Mongols, would go mad in the darkness, in a tomb where they have been left to die."

Pushing the second skin under the water, Yusen prayed his arms did not tremble. In that tomb, severed from wind and sky and beauty, cramped and smothered as if they had bound him in a felt, he had prayed for madness.

He roughly pulled the waterskin back up, wincing as his left shoulder throbbed.

"You have survived this, and worse. You have a deep, unwavering qi and a powerful Buddha spirit. A powerful heart." Then the old man gave a breath of laughter. "Do not fear, Yusen. I will not tell the others." He rose, bowed, and walked back toward the others.

Yusen pressed the heels of his hands into his eyes to stop them burning. He plucked the hoe from his belt and lay it aside. When he mastered himself, he removed his belt, preparing to bathe. He longed to step into the spring and submerge himself, an act forbidden by the Khan's laws, the fouling of natural water.

A powerful Buddha spirit? It meant nothing, not to him.

His left shoulder throbbed, and he peeled back the cloth of his del to see the wound, still closed with Bao Xing's careful stitches, but red and angry. No good, and he had none of his scout's portion, the supplies he always carried on a mission. His medicines would have been on Tsang's saddle. The Sages had caught at least one of the horses, but what of the others? Did they run free in the ghost town, or had they all been swallowed up by the floods and avalanches of the valley? Yusen said a prayer for them as well. No wife, no horses, no bow.

Kneeling on a hollowed stone, he squeezed the waterskin over his head, drenching himself over and over again, letting his del be washed by the runoff down the slope. At least the gashes to his leg proved less troublesome, another layer to the scars that recorded his life.

What did he have? A great Buddha spirit, and a great heart. A farm tool, the Eternal Sky above, and a guide who could read the earth below. For now, that must suffice. He filled the water skin one last time, and dressed himself, pushing back his hair. Finally clean, he mounted the slope back to his company walking as tall as if he had never known the shadow of the sword.

Andao and Dailus passed a water skin back and forth, drinking deeply, as they studied the cane. Zhencai sitting quietly alongside.

"You saw this Guowei among the enemy?" the slave asked.

"Leading them, yes, along with a captain I also knew." Yusen lowered himself cross-legged to the ground, cradling his left elbow to keep it still.

"But we still have the cane," Andao pointed out. "Without it, they have no map, unless they know another way."

"Guowei has already had it. Long enough to study it, to take a rubbing. He knew it was valuable before we did." The cane was not all he had taken an interest in. Had Bao Xing's capture been Guowei's idea? "He knows the way, likely better than we do. If he is here, with such a great force, then the khan will know something is happening. Guowei's rebellion is revealed, and he must act soon."

"And so many people will die." Andao nudged the cane, rolling it gently.

"I wish we had a faster way," said the slave. "If we follow the same map, they'll slaughter us—even with half his soldiers killed he has the advantage. And he has Ming Lun."

"The dreamer who could have told us another way is dead," Zhencai said. "Along with the one who killed her."

"That night, in the hall of Geomancers we heard a chime." Andao faced his teacher. "Master Wei talked for a long time about secrets, about the importance of sheltering our knowledge, even at the cost of our lives." His young face looked thin, his gestures harder than they had been. "I just wanted to learn what he had to teach me. Now, so many of them are already dead, and their knowledge died with them. As for the rest—will they even survive up there?"

"On their island in the sky?" The slave shook his head. "They don't have the resources. I think they only did it to make sure nobody else could steal their thoughts."

Zhencai grunted. "Philosophers." He straightened his spine and made the gesture of blessing. "We have a story about a thief who comes in the night to a hermit's house. The hermit has very little, but the thief has even less. He takes the hermit's second best robe, the only spare clothing he owns, but the hermit wakes and the thief is surprised. The thief runs away, and the hermit chases after him, catching the terrified man. He removes his best robe and presses it on the thief, who escapes into the night.

"The hermit walks home, but he sees the moon is full, silver and round, perhaps the most beautiful moon he has ever seen. 'Ai!' says the hermit, 'if only that thief were still here. I wish I could give him this moon.'"

The old monk repeated the sign of blessing, but it felt like the hard edge of his hand aimed directly at Yusen's breast. Why should the monk first praise him, then cut him so deeply. "That story made no sense. Why give up everything, then wish to give up even more?"

The slave made a sign of his own, that furtive gesture across his breast he so often used when he thought Yusen wasn't looking. "It's like the book of our god," the slave said. "Our great teacher said that, if a man should strike your cheek, rather than strike back, you should turn the other cheek."

"So you can be hit again." Yusen slapped his thigh. "No wonder the khan rules so many if this is how you think."

Andao threw up his hands. "If the geomancers shared their ideas, imagine how many would die! How great would the wars be then—why have we come all this way if not to bury this idea of harnessing the stars as a weapon? A man thinks of something, something that might be wonderful—but another man will steal his thoughts and twist them. He takes that idea and changes it into something terrible. You didn't see what I did back there—I know how the earth lies, what it hides and how it grows, and I used that to kill. No wonder he threw me down. Master Wei knew I would be a thief, he saw it in me!"

The slave reached out, his bracelet clinking against the cane as he caught Andao's hand. "I did the same at Kaifeng, when I broke bells to cast weapons."

Yusen said, "What if we knew nothing? I should be at home now, riding. My wife should be reading in the archive, and then the Eternal Sky should rain fire and burn us all. She lives for knowledge, but to have knowledge is to take action because of it."

Andao shrank into himself, drawing back his hands. "To be a geomancer is to understand connection between things, between people. Master Wei could see that it was your wife who held us together. That's why he was so free with access to the tower. He thought if she remained there, then the rest of us must be divided."

The slave looked thoughtful, but Andao's words settled warmly into Yusen's belly. Master Wei sought to break their connections, and the first one he had severed was that between Bao Xing and Yusen himself—as if it mattered. As if it might even matter most of all. He pulled the hoe from his belt and checked its edge. If he must be a sower of men, he would sow them hard enough to never grow again, and he would win her back. "Where do we go?"

Andao took a deep breath and let it out slow, then another, mirroring Zhencai, who, since he told his strange story, sat quietly and said nothing at all. Finally, the geomancer took up the cane and gave it a turn. "Here, there is water from the ground. This is the other end of the chasm, where the river emerges, and the cane shows a bridge." Two smiling figures stood on the bridge, as they were often depicted in the paintings, but one of them held a little square—a compass—and the other held a star. "These mountains are the start of the ridge that leads to the mines." His fingers sketched them into the air beyond, "But the cane wants us to go the other way, to follow a ledge along this valley, by this sharp peak, and look for the Buddha. And pray the soldiers are far enough ahead that they won't see us following."

Zhencai stretched his back and made a series of careful twists. "I believe I am going to miss the horses."

Yusen missed them already, as if he had lost his right hand. He pushed himself up, though his feet ached already. "Wait here. I'll scout the route ahead."

"They already have too long a start." Zhencai rose as well. "We'll go together."

The slave groaned as he rose, but he tucked the handle of his pruning blade into his belt and gave a nod. Andao led the way, seeking the river, while Yusen angled uphill and found a tall stone to climb. Dry brush and grasses signaled they should expect little rain, and also showed a cloud of dust moving to the northwest, a troop of soldiers with spears that glinted in the sun—perhaps thirty of them, five of them mounted. Five. Guowei had stolen his horses.

Even the finest archer could not reach them from here, nor would he risk his horses in trying. Did Ming Lun ride in a place of honor? He would risk an arrow for her when he found himself in range. He could not make out Bao Xing, but one of the horses moved between two others, toward the back of the troop. Likely, that was her. Or did she ride in front, with Guowei? What if Yusen pursued her only to find that she had no wish to be rescued?

Across the plain, a swath of greener vegetation meandered along with the river, swinging east against the far ridge; beyond that, only mountains. He made his way down to the others.

"Guowei is a few hours ahead with about thirty men."

"Thirty is not so many," Andao replied, but Zhencai merely stared at him, and Yusen asked, "How many will you kill?"

Andao turned a little green and resumed his march. They trudged along, resting far too often, draining the water skins before they reached the river to fill them again. There, they drank for a long time and splashed water to cool their faces.

A few twisted trees grew along the river, offering some shade against the mid-day sun, and the rumble of his own stomach told Yusen it was past time for eating.

"Look." Andao dug his fingers into the mud of the riverbank and pulled up a plant by its thick root. "These are edible. My grandmother used to gather them. She knew all about plants and their properties."

The slave's shoulders slumped. "Ming Lun gathered them, too."

They dug out enough for everyone to chew on something as they walked. The roots squeaked between Yusen's teeth and tasted sharp on his tongue, but they helped to ease the ache of his empty stomach. Along the way, trampled grass and muddy tracks showed where the soldiers moved ahead of them, but the mud had already dried. Guowei's lead stretched by the moment, with every time the slave leaned against a tree, his skin shivering as if he tried to contain his tremors.

"At least we are on the trail," Andao said, but he could not muster any of his gestures save a little flop of his hands.

"If we move any more slowly, it doesn't matter if we ever arrive," Dailus murmured, "we won't be in time to stop them."

"We will find a way," Yusen said firmly, then stared at Andao until the geomancer started walking again.

At last, with the sun sinking low and their stomachs growling, the more since they had run out of roots, they saw the next marker. With the fire of hope springing at his chest, Yusen surged ahead to the curve Andao described, and the others quickened their pace behind him.

Where the river turned aside, a carved archway pierced the ridge, leading toward the walkway shown on the cane, a narrow path jutting from the side of the cliff itself. Yusen arrived at the shaded entrance, then stopped short and thrust out his arm. "Stop!"

Andao stumbled, his feet slipping, but Yusen grabbed his arm, dropping low and leaning backward as Andao's foot dangled over a void, a long, tumbling fall onto rocks far below. The archway opened onto nothing but a string of square-cut holes with the stumps of wooden supports sticking out of them, freshly hacked. The wooden walkway lay in pieces scattered down the slopes. Andao slumped at the archway staring at the ruins of the path.

"What is it?" The slave called, leaning on Bao Xing's cane. The sight burned at Yusen, who had suffered so much to bring it back to her. He moved to take it back, but the slave could walk faster this way. Let him keep the cane for now if it meant they would sooner reach Yusen's wife.

"The walkway is gone. They've cut it down." Andao drew up his knees, his head drooping.

"No!" The slave came to the verge, gazing across the span of empty cliff until it curved away at the far end. "That's it then. We're done."

"No," Yusen insisted. "There must be another way. Andao, can't you find a way?"

"Not unless I know what to look for."

Zhencai squatted, focused on his apprentice. "You have said that knowledge is the key, and connection. What else do you know? What else is connected?"

Sagging, the slave leaned on the precious cane. Suddenly, he held it aloft. "Cinnabar burns to produce mercury, which the device needs a lot of. If we cannot follow the trail the cane sets out for us, can we follow the cinnabar mines?"

Andao's eyes grew, and he grinned as he took the cane in his hands. "Yes, of course. The mercury of the lake that houses the device. The veins permeate this ground." He passed the cane back to the slave. "So, we look for the crimson shrines, the places where cinnabar comes to the surface. This stone is full of caves and passages—one of them must lead the right direction."

Eyes to the ground, Andao walked away from the river. "We're looking for low plants with yellow flowers and soft, thick leaves. Or crimson shrines."

Yusen scaled higher on the slope, searching ahead, until the slave shouted from a narrow ravine. "Crimson shrines? This way!"

Around the verge, a series of red sticks poked from the ground, close together like thick grasses. With their red pillars and deep grooves, they resembled the Chinese shrines to their ancestors. Closer to, the stone growths looked like the dripping blood of an injured sky. These so-called shrines honored no god Yusen cared to worship. One of the spires rose almost as high as his head, edging a gash of darkness in the earth.

Andao studied the area while his toes dug into the earth, then he nodded. "This way."

The slave lowered himself to his knees. "It looks like the mine."

Not to Yusen. The broad passages of a mine lay open to the sky, from which even the miners could return every night into the air. No, this looked like the tomb, and Yusen hated it already.

CHAPTER SIXTY

"I saw two men in that valley whom you did not kill," Guowei observed as he led his horse down from the end of the wooden path. One of the soldiers held his stirrup as he re-mounted.

Ming Lun vaulted into her own saddle unaided, nudging her mount forward to give the captain room. Two men whom she did not kill: the Mongol who wouldn't eat poison, and Dailus, who should have been well outside the valley. He had returned, the fool—then rescued the man he hated more than anyone in the world. Well, more than anyone besides Ming Lun herself, now that he knew the truth. She tossed her head, her ornaments shivering. She carried seventeen ways to kill a man and, on those two, she had failed. Guowei robbed her of face to say so out loud.

"Nothing to say to me? I'm not surprised. Still, you have done well in guiding us there, and in bringing the plan. I have no doubt it shall prove most useful." He turned a charming smile on her, and Ming Lun smiled in return, the same false smile he taught her. Her horse clattered over a fallen stone, and the nearest soldier shouted and thrust his spear. His troop—less than a fifth of the soldiers who started out—jumped at every creak or splash.

"What shall I say to you, Minister? It was more useful to preserve them alive. Alone, I might not have found the sages, nor retrieved the scroll." She allowed herself to lose face with this admission. "I have used those whom I required."

"That, too, does not surprise me." They rode down a winding slot of stone toward glints of water, a few soldiers walking ahead with the captain. "Our associate informed me of what he deemed to be rash behavior."

"He asked for proof of my worth, Minister. I provided it."

He laughed, long and bright, a melodious sound that made it easy to believe Bao Xing would love him. Did she ride at the back of the troop, quickening to the sound of his laughter?

"While you, Minister, allowed me to prove it in a less direct fashion." Ming Lun inclined her head.

"Given your history, Ming Lun, your loyalty is beyond question. I am grieved that he felt it necessary to test you. No woman who has suffered so directly at the hands of the Mongols would willingly aid them."

"That is a subject I prefer to avoid."

They rode on in silence for a short span, then he said, "You rode with the lady Bao Xing before the valley? How did she fare on the journey?"

Ming Lun dispelled her irritation before she dared speak. She thought of Zhencai, admonishing her to remove attachments. "She fares better than I would have thought, Minister. She rides rather well astride, and shows a good nature, even to her husband."

Guowei focused far ahead. "She is a woman of refinement, in spite of her country education. She would strive to uphold any marriage given her, I have no doubt."

"The dwarf is not dead yet, but, as the monks would tell us, life is impermanence."

Again, he laughed, flicking his glance in her direction, warm and encouraging. She considered whether she would bed a Mandarin. They were beyond her station among the servants of the Son of Heaven. She might enjoy it—a rare thing, in her experience—but it would merely complicate a relationship already strained.

"When we have the opportunity to rest, I look forward to speaking with her." He glanced back. "For now, it seems best to allow her to collect herself. This must have been a very difficult time for such a lady."

And there went any thought Ming Lun might have had of seducing him: beauty triumphed over all.

Gaps and openings pierced the thinning stone to the outside, then the wall subsided into rubble and opened a vista clear down to the river's course. In a deep canyon, the river rushed around an island from which rose a great knob of stone carved with Buddhas. The Buddhas started near the bottom, among the ledges and trees, connected by stairs and wooden walkways. Tall Buddhas and carved columns flanked caves likely full of Buddhas as well. A few enormous ones sat high up in the stone, crowned by a fringe of trees. Their trail led to a thick spine of rock connecting the mountains with the Buddha mound, a natural bridge riddled with caves and topped with pillars of stone: the only route to the island. The river ran so fiercely above it that if a swimmer or boatman were not battered to death on the rocks, they would be rushed straight past the island to where the river broadened in the distance.

"By all the celestial mansions," Guowei sighed, "the Mandate of Heaven shall be fulfilled."

They leaned back as the horses picked their way down the grassy slope. The hollows in the stone and the shapes of wind-wrapped pillars called to mind the ghost village, and Ming Lun suppressed a shiver. "You've seen the result of this weapon, Minister. One hundred sixty years later, the land has barely begun to grow again."

"The Middle Kingdom has survived for thousands of years not by turning aside from a difficult way, but by our belief that we shall survive a thousand more—what else does it mean that we possess the Mandate of Heaven to rule this land? We are given the means to do so, but we must see very far ahead, as the ancients did, as the astronomers of the emperor's court do today. Such a barrier of wasteland will deter the next barbarians who seek to ruin us—if any barbarians remain." Guowei stroked his chin. "The Emperor might create a map of the barbarian realms, and use it likewise, to foul their lands. Destroying the grass that feeds their ponies would be a great blow."

Like the ponies they were riding right now. "A great blow indeed, Minister." They had taken Yusen's horses and his bride. Demolishing the bridges would not be enough to stop him. "Have you considered that the lady Bao Xing may not share your conviction about using this weapon to serve the Mandate of Heaven?"

"Like all women—except, evidently, yourself—the lady has a tender heart. But, unlike most women, she also possesses great skills of reason. I cannot imagine her sojourn with the dwarf has given her much greater love for the Mongol race."

The track narrowed, and Guowei kicked his mount ahead as they moved into single file. Bao Xing had pleaded for the life of her husband in the Valley of Sages. Love for the Mongol? Perhaps not. Respect or admiration? Even Ming Lun found the persistent and practical dwarf worthy of that.

At the ridge that joined the mountains to the Buddha mound a row of dark stones set as close together as teeth blocked the way. On a pavement of broad flagstones, a low altar stood before the wall of stones, and the paving beneath it showed a pattern of arcs as if the altar shifted out of the way to allow passage, but what of the towering stone pillars beyond?. Zhencai's sleeper had told him he could not reach the weapon alone, nor without knowledge of geomancy. Still, the designers could not expect all of their number to have sorcery. What other knowledge might serve?

Guowei gestured to one of the men. "Move that thing out of the way, would you?"

"Minister—" Ming Lun began, but the soldier went to the altar and shoved against it. The flagstones opened beneath his feet and he screamed as he fell through. With a horrible grinding noise, the screaming ceased and the flagstoneslid back into place. A few bubbles of blood seeped from the edge.

Guowei's horse snorted and retreated from the altar while he tried to master it. Ming Lun slid down from her own mount, going to catch the Minister's.

The soldiers ahead of them stopped while Captain Cho turned on his heel. "Minister! Is the place set with traps? If we are delayed much longer, the Mongols will overtake us—"

"We shall handle them in due course." Giving Ming Lun control of the horse, Guowei slid down to the ground. From a leather pouch on his saddle, he drew out a sheaf of notes, written on various scraps of paper new and old. He balanced this on his palm and thumbed through it quickly, frowning. "Let me see the plan."

A soldier took charge of the horses, leading them away after Ming Lun untied the scroll from the saddle. She unfurled it onto a stone, but she knew already what the words said—many strange and arcane things about the device, and nothing of how to get there: one of the ways the Order, or their enemies, had tried to conceal the weapon. "The dreamer in the Valley of Sages implied there would be gates to prevent trespassers from reaching the weapon. Do you wish to consult the lady Bao Xing?"

Dropping his book on top of the plan so he could compare the one with the other, Guowei nodded.

Ming Lun filed between the soldiers to the back of the line. Mounted between two men, Bao Xing managed a pale, radiant beauty even without her paints, her hair hanging loosely over her shoulders. She flicked a glance at Ming Lun then toward the mountains, as if the Buddha mound held no interest for her. "Minister Guowei requests your assistance."

"Did he request yours as well? Or you his?" Bao Xing swept the hair back from her face.

"Together, we serve the Son of Heaven, and, through him, the Han people."

Bao Xing compressed her lips. "Together you will slay thousands."

"Thousands of Mongols, lady. Before they can do our nation any further harm. Come and speak with the Minister. Even if you are right, I can no more stop this wheel turning than the mouse can stop the flood." She took Bao Xing's horse and led it forward, then offered her hand to help the lady down.

Bao Xing ignored her, tapping the horse's leg to dismount. Her thumb traced over one of the silver ornaments on the saddle, then she faced Guowei, offering a long bow. He returned the gesture with one equally long, and the lady's lips compressed.

"Please forgive my men if they have handled you roughly, lady. It was our intent only to see you to safety in that dangerous place."

"Dangerous because your men seeded the embankment with bombs."

"Lady," he said, hands spread, "I do not think you are averse to the cause of the Han people. Allow me to share it with you."

Her moment of fire subsided into a wary interest. "How?"

"I invited you once before to join us, to sing with the larks for our freedom from the falcons. This device represents a great wonder created by people like your father, and like us—you and I, and all of those who value learning. All who seek the wonder of the sky, and search for answers upon the earth. The Mongol shadow spreads across our land, between us and our stars. Your aid could greatly reduce the suffering of our people, even these good soldiers who seek only to serve. We must find our way." He gracefully indicated the Buddha mound. "Surely you, as well as I, would like to avoid further bloodshed."

"Indeed." She darted a glance at Ming Lun, then turned to the scroll and traced her fingers across the open pages of the book. "May I?"

"These are my notes, lady, the record of my quest." His hands invited her, and she took up the book, slowly turning pages, ever so slightly smiling.

Ming Lun harbored no desire to witness the mutual seduction sure to follow on this exchange of courtesy. Somehow, she wanted the proud lady to remain proud, unbending, to stay atop her husband's horse and refuse to aid his enemy. Instead, Ming Lun prowled toward the earth bridge they had accepted as natural, until it devoured a soldier. She found a stone about as large as she could throw and tossed it onto the smooth patch where the soldier had been. The patch groaned aside, and slid back again, with a fleshy crunch.

"What are you doing?" Guowei shouted. He stepped toward her and stopped.

"Finding the way. If we had a geomancer, he could do this, but the geomancers are trapped on their little island. You believe they have written everything down, because it's what you would do. These people were not Mandarins."

"Some of them were," Bao Xing offered. "They fought among themselves: the geomancers, the astronomers, and the Mandarins."

Ming Lun accepted that. "Even if they had written everything down, there is no assurance that you, Minister, have read it all. So the question is, who prepared the bridge? They did not want shepherds and mountain goats crossing over."

"But they did want their colleagues to find a way." Bao Xing tottered closer, and Ming Lun caught her arm as one tiny foot slid until they stood together in the shadow of the slick stones. Bao Xing pulled free.

"I cannot do this alone," Ming Lun murmured.

"Lead your rebellion to their greatest weapon? You expect me to help you."

Ming Lun snapped her fingers, drawing Bao Xing's startled glance. "You want to get inside as much as I do, if for other reasons."

Bao Xing lifted her chin, and the smile that returned to her lips had an altogether different character. It felt as familiar as Ming Lun's own. "Together, then."

"For now." Dropping low, Ming Lun studied the path, noting the patterns of wear, the slim gaps around the standing stones. Even if she could reach them, they leaned slightly forward, curving toward her like giant claws, impossible to climb, even for her. Just as clearly, they moved. As the pillar of stone that elevated the Sages?

"All of these stones can move, lady. There must be some way to clear the path." Ming Lun observed the scraped markings and smooth patches showing that someone else had recently passed this way. Was it possible that Dailus and the others had gotten here first? Maybe, with Yusen's wilderness wiles and Andao to find the way. Her heart quickened and her throat felt dry. She should point it out to Guowei, if he had not noticed. She pressed her lips together and did not speak.

"Given the compass inscribed on the altar, this test must have been designed by the geomancers." Bao Xing stepped a little nearer, careful not to impinge upon the smooth stones where the soldier died. "The compass shows the directions but nothing more. They can't expect everyone to know geomancy, not if astronomers and Mandarins must also reach the weapon."

"Zhencai's dreamer said we must know of geomancy, not that we must practice it."

"There may have been sorcery in the creation of the test."

Ming Lun looked down with her. Five hollows marked the surface of the altar in a circular pattern. Five again, like the layers of the geomancer's palace. "Why is it always five?"

"For the five elements," Bao Xing answered immediately. Her hand hovered over each hollow in turn. "Fire, water, wood, earth and metal. I remember that from my father's library."

"We just need to fill the hollows?" Ming Lun cast about her for some dirt.

"We need to fill them in the proper order. There is a productive and a destructive sequence, but I don't know what it is."

"My notes on geomancy begin with that narrow bamboo," Guowei said. "I fear they are rather scant. The Mongols have destroyed every work regarding geomancy that they find. If the geomancers had ever responded to the emperor's messages, we would have been rid of the Mongol scourge already."

Bao Xing flipped through Guowei's notebook starting from the bamboo sheave, but her frown only deepened.

"Wood is first," Ming Lun said. "Then fire."

Bao Xing cocked her head. "How do you know that?"

"The layers of the Sages' palace. Each is dedicated to a single element.

Earth is in the middle. Earth is connection and balance." She deposited her handful of soil into the lowest hollow.

"And after that?"

"I do not know, lady. I did not climb that high." Ming Lun turned back to Guowei and the soldiers. "Wood? And fuel for a fire."

"More wood," Guowei said. "For the cycle to be productive, the ash becomes the earth. Captain, the tinder box."

The captain stepped forward hesitantly, leaning to hand over their fire-starting kit, then he retreated hastily.

Ming Lun placed a handful of twigs in each of the two hollows to the east of the earth, adding a bit of finer wood treated with tallow to the fire hollow, but she did not light the fire, not yet. "That leaves metal and water."

"If ash becomes the earth, then water grows the wood." Bao Xing pointed to the northern most hollow.

From her waterskin, Ming Lun filled the hollow. One hollow remained empty. The only metal she carried was in her weapons, and she was not about to give them up.

"Minister? We are still in need of metal."

Guowei sighed, then drew a few coins from a pouch at his belt.

"That's perfect, Minister," Bao Xing said. "Coins are used in divination with the I Ching." She pointed to the small dashed markings on the inscribed compass. Smiling, he placed the coins in her hand. She lay them in the hollow.

"Come away, lady." Guowei guided her to safe ground, leaving Ming Lun standing by the altar alone.

"Try it," he ordered. He closed the book and retrieved the scroll, holding them close, with the lady at his side.

Ming Lun found the two stones in the tinder box and struck a spark. It kindled in the hollow, then, after a moment, bit into the twigs. Flames arose with a curl of smoke that reminded her of the night she had been a shaman. A low rumble issued from beneath the altar. It pivoted slowly and Ming Lun paced with it. Her being vibrated as she moved, focused on this, that she could die at any moment. She had never felt so alive. Ahead of her, the towering claws of stone sank slowly into the ground, curving down beneath where she stood until only the pattern of their slots remained, a double layer, carefully arranged into one of those I Ching patterns from the compass, a fortune she had no means to interpret, but so far, a good one.

Guowei stared at her expectantly, and she reached out a foot to tap the slab where the soldier had died. Nothing. She pushed down on it, and finally stepped fully on top of it. "I see a pattern of stones," she called back.

"Go on, we'll be right behind you," Guowei told her.

"I must go, too, Minister," Bao Xing said, "Unless you would care to provide your knowledge."

The Mandarin folded his hands over the book, frowning, then bound the straps of the scroll and held it out to her. "Will this serve you as a cane, lady?"

Bao Xing moved forward, crossing the slab with its rim of blood, leaning a little on the scroll's bar, until she stood beside Ming Lun again. Before them spread a grassy area with a series of smooth, flat stones. "Easy," said Bao Xing. "These stones mark the shape of the Celestial Palace." She pointed toward an arc of stones at one side. "These are the Celestial weapons. That is the Dark Lance, the malevolent pattern that guides the device." The stones she indicated took a diagonal course across the path. "We'll need to mark the way for the soldiers. Minister, have you a seal?"

Guowei approached cautiously, stepping over the place where the guardian stones had been and held out a small case, remaining on their side of the barrier.

Bao Xing removed the carved stone seal from the case, stamping it into the thick red ink, then stamping the first stone, the scroll tucked under her arm. "I'll need to go first," she said, and Ming Lun nodded, though the idea of the unsteady, slow-moving beauty taking the lead worried her. The astronomer's daughter knew the stars as Ming Lun did not—she had to be the one—but Ming Lun moved one step behind, balancing as if for battle. Her heart sank a little. Andao might have gotten the companions through the first gate, but none of them could have crossed this bridge, not without knowledge of the stars. Why did that sadden her? Did she truly want them to win, even at the cost of certain victory over the Mongols?

Bao Xing moved across three stones toward the outside, then leaned to mark the next one and stepped onto it.

The ground shivered under Ming Lun's feet. "Stop!"

Bao Xing withdrew, but a seam opened across the path as the edge tipped down. Her eyes flared, and she launched herself back. Dropping to a lunge, Ming Lun seized Bao Xing's flailing hand and pulled her onto the path, wrapping her other arm around to steady them both on a single stepping stone as the ground ahead shifted. The ground shoved upward at the center, both sides tipping down, pebbles rattling from the path and dropping half a li into the raging water below. The pebbles tumbled through the broken skeleton of a man on the way down, the skull shattered on the rocks below. The two women clung together as the center sank down again, the edges rising to come flush with the top of the bridge.

Behind them, with a rush of stone, the gate swept upward, back into place, and Guowei flinched. A soldier halfway across the gap flew upward at the thrust of the stone, then tumbled, screaming, into the water below. Beyond the gleaming black stones, the other soldiers cried out. "Ai! Be quiet. Are you men of war or of weakness?" The captain shouted, though his voice sounded no more calm than the others.

"Minister, the altar tipped—the elements are gone," the captain said a moment later.

"Just replace the elements and hurry up about it," Guowei called from their side of the gate. "Bao Xing, are you injured? Have you lost the scroll?"

"Merely frightened," Ming Lun answered, feeling the thunder of the other woman's heart.

Bao Xing finally let go, still trembling, the scroll crumpled between them. The seal lay at her feet, and Ming Lun bent to retrieve it. "Not the Dark Lance, then?"

Bao Xing shivered and shook her head.

"The Dark Lance is inauspicious. I wonder if they mean for us to find an auspicious route?"

"Yes, that might be." Bao Xing swallowed, still so close that her breathing ruffled Ming Lun's hair. Together, they retreated to the solid ground they had left behind.

"I am pleased you are not injured, lady, but I believe I should keep the scroll." Guowei held out his hand.

Ming Lun glanced at him. "She needs it for balance."

With a groan, the gate sank once more into the ground, revealing the frightened clump of soldiers on the other side, though the horses raced away along the mountainside with marvelous grace.

"Come on then." Captain Cho stiffened his spine and marched across. After a moment, his men followed, but none lingered where the pillars would emerge. "Could she use this, Minister?" Captain Cho moved up a little closer, holding out a spear.

Guowei smartly broke it off on his knee and handed over the section without its blade. Not completely trusting, then, even of beauty.

Bao Xing accepted, though her hand lingered on the scroll as she returned it. Resolutely, she turned to the way ahead. "I don't know what to do."

"It hinges at the middle. Any path to either the left or right may shift the balance. Might we find the center and cross over?" Ming Lun squatted low and studied the ground. "But if that is not the solution to the riddle, then they will have another trick awaiting us." Then she thought of Zhencai's dreamer and the admonition that you could not go alone. "Unless we are meant to balance, one to either side. Is there a pattern that goes in two ways at once?"

"There is the Celestial Kitchen, but it is so… Yin."

"Is it auspicious?"

"Peaceful." Their eyes met. "But we would need to separate, to go both directions."

Bao Xing stood taller, but did not have the same muscular build. Ming Lun judged they would be about equal. "Carefully, and at the same time, yes. And then Guowei and his men must do the same."

"There must be another way," Captain Cho muttered.

"Even if you could swim upstream to reach the mound, there must be thirty caves and stairways. It would take a very long time to search them all—and all would be as fraught with traps as this bridge." Guowei pressed the scroll between his hands. "Have you a plan?"

"Yes," Ming Lun answered, more confidently than she felt. To Bao Xing, she murmured, "Yes?"

"There." Bao Xing pointed to a stone as she edged away toward her side. "That's where to begin."

Ming Lun stood at her appointed place, and they looked at each other, then Bao Xing nodded, and they stepped forward. The first stones sat well within the area they had passed on their first attempt. Bao Xing marked her stone, then tossed the seal to Ming Lun. It fell a little short, but Ming Lun retrieved it. The round stone seal, typical of the Mandarins, had a horse carved in its handle, perhaps for the year of his birth. She marked her stone, puzzled by the characters of the seal itself.

"Two ahead, one to the outside—do you see it?" Bao Xing called.

Again, the women stepped forward, separating, onto the section where Bao Xing had stumbled before. Ming Lun felt a little shiver in the ground, but no more. She let out a long breath and noticed Bao Xing doing the same.

"Two ahead, one to the inside. Ready?"

Ming Lun nodded, and each raised a foot—the one clad in a slipper that showed its embroidery through the grime of travel, the other bare, broad, and calloused. Together, they stepped forward. Bao Xing giggled, Ming Lun smiled. She marked her stone and tossed the seal expertly into Bao Xing's outstretched hand. They took one last step together beyond the stones.

"What next?" Bao Xing's excitement only made her the more lovely, a hint of color entering her cheeks and her eyes keen.

"Trees." A thicket of young trees grew almost together across the path. "These are too small to have been a part of the Order's plan." Ming Lun strode ahead, and Bao Xing called, "Be careful!"

The ground underfoot felt uneven, but not in an unnatural way, nor did she detect any stones that moved. Ming Lun walked through the shade onto a broad platform against the wall of the Buddha mound. A series of Buddhas stood and sat before them, some in shadowed niches, and some fully revealed, including one very large with an engraved stone monument set before him. She prowled the edges, but found no way off the platform, and returned to where Bao Xing examined the monument. "It's a poem. One of the classics, I think. *'Heaven and earth are floating'*," she read aloud. " *'War horses ride in the mountains.'* "

"What do we need to do?"

"Three characters are missing. *'I lean on the rail,'* then nothing else." Bao Xing reached down to the lap of the next Buddha, which was full of little stones, and held up a carved stone with the character for 'peace'. "We need to complete the poem, as a Mandarin would."

Ming Lun cocked her head to read the lines. "I don't know poetry."

"Nor I," said Bao Xing. "Women are not allowed to study for the examinations. We need Guowei."

Ming Lun ran to inform him. In pairs, as evenly matched as they could be, the Minister and his men crossed carefully through the star map. He settled his scholar's hat more firmly on his head and smiled down at her as he walked. "It is, after all, a thing for educated men." He glanced over the poem, then sifted his hand through the marked stones to find the three characters and place them in the hollows. "'*I lean on the rail, as tears flow.*' Rather sentimental, Du Fu, isn't he?"

With a sigh of old hinges and a breath of stale air, the Buddha's niche receded behind him, leaving a peaked opening into the side of the mound.

"Excellent!" Guowei stepped forward.

From a dark niche, one of the Buddhas stirred and jumped down before them. "Well done. Educated men indeed. I was half afraid these women would do the job. Nothing but trouble, women."

Hand to his chest, Guowei stumbled back but had the grace to catch Bao Xing as she wobbled. Ming Lun stood her ground. "Master Deng."

"It's you." The scrawny old man looked her over. "I should have known you would keep me waiting."

"How did you cross without a partner?"

Master Deng said, "I hired a counterbalance. He has received his compensation."

She caught the direction of his glance, toward a cave a little higher and a series of notches which might be used to reach it. Another of the statues—the figures she had taken for statues—leaned back from the stone with his feet dangling and flies buzzing at his dry eyes and open mouth. A spike held the corpse to the wall.

"I suggested the way might be through the cave. It is not." He stretched his scrawny neck to study Guowei. "And you are?"

"Guowei, Minister of Archives, Master of the Temple of the Lark. I trust you are with the Order of Celestial Purity?" Guowei bowed. Master Deng accepted the bow without answer.

"Minister of Archives. Well. You'll do." He glared at the finished poem. "I hate poetry. Always did. Come, then. We have Mongols to kill." He turned on his heel and stalked inside.

CHAPTER SIXTY-ONE

In the darkness of the caves, Zhencai focused on his breathing, long, and slow, in and out. Timing his breath with his footsteps, centering his qi, then allowing it to flow with each breath. Ahead, something splashed into a pool, then Andao's voice echoed in the narrow corridor. "I did say we would find water, didn't I?"

"Just find the way out," Yusen snarled. His anger grew as they moved in darkness, and even Dailus with his makeshift torch was not enough to soothe him. Anger. He once accused Zhencai of harboring so much anger that they were identical, but Yusen's anger covered his fear. Zhencai's covered his worldliness. In fact, the more Zhencai moved through the world, the more he wondered how many of his brethren could maintain detachment outside the peace of a monastery. Easy enough to avoid women, to avoid anger, to view all things with equal compassion when all the things one encountered were the same. Until the Mongols came.

"Slave, another light!"

"I've nothing else to burn," Dailus answered. "Unless you're offering." A scraping sound accompanied a flare of light as Dailus dragged the back of his blade along the wall, striking sparks that made his pale eyes look nearly empty, his teeth gleaming, his scalp trickling blood.

The passage briefly illuminated showed rough, natural walls, slanting and difficult to navigate. Up ahead, the passage jogged downward, but Zhencai glimpsed another opening to the right before the sparks died.

"Please don't kill each other, not here in the dark. I'm just tired, that's all." Andao sighed.

"Work on your breathing," Zhencai said to Andao, hoping the others would consider it too. "It will help you to center."

"Work on finding a way out of here," Yusen muttered.

Andao's footfalls moved forward, unnaturally steady. Yusen clomped after him, then Dailus, both men breathing in tight gasps. Zhencai maintained his focus because he had to—because someone must remember to breathe, even in the stifling air of the dark cavern.

Yusen cried out and Dailus shouted something in his own language, a long stream of fury that could only be cursing. Both men went down in a scraping of limbs and a smacking of flesh against the walls.

"Get off me, slave!"

"It's not my fault I take one step for three of yours."

Scrambling sounds, then a small form that could only be Yusen bumped into Zhencai, who put out a steadying hand. The Mongol batted it away with surprising accuracy, given the darkness.

Another careful splash from Andao, then a crack against stone and Dailus howled curses. He had struck his head. Again.

"For once, I have the advantage over you," Yusen observed.

Metal slammed the wall with a shower of sparks as Dailus struck the back of his curved pruning blade into the stone above Yusen's head. In the last sparks, Yusen's eyes gleamed with an edge of white, his body rigid.

Ahead, Andao yelled, and a tumble of stones ended in a splash and a muffled cry.

Zhencai froze. "Andao!"

"Here, master. I'm alright, I just fell, the water is deeper." Sloshing sounds filled the cavern.

Taking another deep breath, letting it out slow, Zhencai again reached out and laid his hand on Yusen's shoulder. He stepped up in the darkness, side by side with the Mongol who still had not moved. Zhencai leaned down and whispered, "This is not all that you are."

Yusen took a convulsive breath. "No," he answered, on a hitch.

Zhencai squeezed and let go, sliding past. Dailus crouched in the path, his head lower than Yusen's just then. Zhencai took another deep breath and squatted by him, feeling the agitated rhythm of his heart. "Do your people have stories of the underground?"

"It is the path to Hell." Dailus employed a term Zhencai did not know. "Tartarus is another name for it, the place of suffering and torture—like the Tatars, the horsemen from Hell."

"Perhaps it would help you to pray."

"What do you know about it? The damned Tatar dragged me from my home, dragged me here—just when I thought I was free, he beat me half to death and had me thrown in the mines. Then what? He came to fetch me back again, like a wedding present to impress his pretty wife."

"To stop the weapon, slave! To stop them killing all of us." Yusen's strident tone echoed.

Dailus pushed back to his feet. "I have a name—I had a home and a family. My people are a thousand miles from here, what do I care if all of you heathens should blast each other with flames? It'll send you straight back to Hell where you all belong." Dailus slashed his iron tool against the wall, making a rain of sparks as he lunged forward. In the scatter of light, Yusen snatched out his hoe and shifted back, the weapon thrust before him.

The sparks failed, and Yusen cried out as flesh smacked against flesh—Dailus kicking or tripping over him—then another streak of sparks, this time from Yusen's hoe clashing with the opposite wall. Dailus staggered back, struck the wall and spun about, his breathing harsh. "Have at you, dwarf!" he shouted. "I'll take your head off."

"If you can find it!"

Someone crashed into Zhencai—then pushed him back with a small, wiry arm, trying to keep him clear of the duel. Zhencai pressed the Mongol out of the way, flattening them both against the wall as the wind of Dailus's approach rushed them.

"Get off!" Yusen shouted. "Get away!" He struggled against Zhencai's body.

The drakemaster's curved blade glanced off Zhencai's chest, low, at the level of Yusen's head, the tip carving into Zhencai's side along his ribs.

Enclosing the pain, Zhencai swallowed his injury, sliding his fingers along Dailus's arm and clasping his wrist before he could lift the blade again. His qi warmed with anger, but he molded it with his breathing and stepped forward. Dailus tugged against his grip, and Zhencai summoned his qi to iron, his hand forging a second bracelet for the drakemaster's arm. Catching the drakemaster's elbow with his other hand, he jabbed sharply, forcing the weapon up as he planted his feet, then drove him away from Yusen.

"Let me go, monk—just let me finish this!"

Zhencai shifted his grip to draw the taller man's head down to his, his wheaten hair brushing Zhencai's lips. "While you were flying, he was buried alive."

For a long moment, they pressed together in the narrow passage,

Dailus's arm and his weapon trapped against Zhencai's chest, the slashing wound beginning to burn.

Zhencai released his qi, released his grip, sliding a half-step back to prepare in case the words only conjured deeper anger.

"The gift of the geomancer is connection, between all things of the earth, including the men who walk it," Zhencai said. "Your anger severs Andao from the qi that he must follow."

After a moment, a sharply drawn breath, Dailus said, "Those beads you carry. How many are there?"

"One hundred and eight. For the sutras of the Buddha." He pulled the loop of beads from his belt and pressed them into Dailus's free hand. The drakemaster gripped them tight, tendons and muscles shifting in his powerful hand, still taut with anger.

"It's too many," he said, "but it'll do."

Zhencai left him there, hearing the soft murmur of that foreign tongue, shaky at first, then sliding into the rhythm of prayer, the beads clicking.

"For once the slave is right," Yusen muttered as Zhencai approached, "you should not have interfered." His hand touched Zhencai's chest, the left-hand side, tracing the rip in his tunic. "How bad is it?"

"It is merely suffering." Zhencai used the sign of blessing to turn away the Mongol's hand.

"Merely suffering," the Mongol echoed. "Do you know what suffering is? It's having the world torn away—even the light, even the sky." His voice edged toward breaking.

"Dailus, too, has lost his world."

Yusen did not answer, and Zhencai moved on, drawing his hand along the rough wall, leaning to dodge the rough ceiling.

In the darkness beyond, the echoes changed, dripping water in a larger space, that opening he had glimpsed. Just below, to one side, a muffled sound of misery.

He moved carefully forward, then sank down near Andao's warmth. He extended his hand to touch Andao's arm.

"Will they kill each other, master?"

"We can hope that moment is in the past, and not in the future."

"The present again," Andao sighed. "It's just as before: fear is the present."

"Then it is fear we must embrace."

The young man leaned a little into his touch. He spoke so softly, Zhencai settled closer to hear. "You are all following me into the dark, and we might never come out."

Zhencai merely breathed, making his breath loud and even.

Andao sniffed again; his shoulder trembled under Zhencai's touch. "I was a thief to steal the knowledge of the sages. I wish they could have given me the moon."

"They did not give it to you, you must find it."

"I can't find anything," Andao moaned.

"Try again."

"Nothing has changed!"

His shout broke the murmur of Dailus's prayers, the silence of Yusen's fear. The close passageway reeked of sweat and unwashed men. It reminded Zhencai of the training grounds at Cloud Mountain, when a dozen novices strove to conquer each other, to conquer themselves. Zhencai breathed slowly in, and out. "Geomancers know connections. Your world stirs with fear and anger, a dangerous qi, too yang, too harsh." Zhencai tried to articulate what he sensed. "Bao Xing was our yin, our balance, you have told us so."

Andao's shoulder rose and fell in a longer breath, then, with quiet wonder, "Yes."

"Try again." Zhencai rose. "And I will work toward balance." Pain sliced over the ribs on his left side. His hand pressed against the wound, finding, in the fabric of his tunic, the small thing a monk always carried.

Yusen's voice rose into the darkness. "How long are we going to sit here?"

With a hiccup of laughter, and no humor at all, Andao said, "How will you balance that?"

"With light." Zhencai moved back in a series of precise steps until he could feel the small and solid presence of Yusen, more recently washed than the others and yet more redolent of sweat.

The Mongol shifted in the dark before him, catching his breath. "Has your apprentice gotten us lost?"

"He is seeking the way, but he must seek it in silence. Can you give him that?"

Yusen rumbled like a tiger in a cage.

"I can offer you light, but only for a moment. In that moment, you must envision all the light that you need. It will be brief as joy, brief as life."

Hope flared in the Mongol's voice. "You have a torch? Why haven't you lit it before now?"

Zhencai stood very still before him. "It is an instrument of enlightenment, but, for you, only a very small one. You must let it be enough."

"It will be better than nothing."

Zhencai found his iron and stone striker. From the pocket inside his ragged tunic, Zhencai removed the scroll that showed he was a monk: the only connection he had to his brotherhood, his entry to any monastery in China and beyond, the name of his abbot, the key to his peace. "Give me your hand."

Yusen's fingers touched his arm, higher, until he took the little scroll in a careful grip. Zhencai struck a few sparks that lit the space between them, showing the pale, old white of the paper and the narrow gold band of its tie.

"What is this?" Yusen drew his hand back a little.

"It is my monk's paper." Zhencai leaned in and struck another spark, lighting the edge of the scroll with a lick of flame, flaring in the dark gleam of Yusen's eyes and shimmering on his dark hair and on the blood that streaked Zhencai's tunic.

The Mongol snatched his hand away and killed the flame against his tongue, plunging them again into darkness. "I won't take the moon. Not from you." He pushed it back against Zhencai's chest.

"It is what I have, and it is mine to give."

"You gave enough." Yusen's breath trembled. "I'll remember the moon, and the joy. And the star." The word he used for star was "xing" and Zhencai had no need to ask which one.

"This way!" Andao called.

At the back, Dailus scrambled to his feet. "Thank God."

"We'll have to go through the water, but it isn't deep."

"Follow him, Dailus. Keep low." Zhencai replaced his monk's paper in the little pocket next to his heart, along with the sleeper's stone, reminders of the spirit, and the world.

"I'll go last," Yusen said. "I will know if you fall."

Zhencai took his place in their procession, each step tugging at his wound. It was not deep, but sharp and long.

"It slopes down." Andao's voice emerged from the inky black. "Then right." His voice strengthened as they walked. They slithered down into the water and grunted as they stumbled or struck the stones that intruded from above.

After a while, the texture of the wall shifted from rough to crumbly, sometimes flaking against Zhencai's hand.

Dailus gave a cry. "Something touched my hair."

Zhencai looked up reflexively—a gesture of no use in the dark—and yet, he dimly traced the outlines of tendrils from above. Roots. He touched the ceiling, bringing down a little shower of stones and dirt. The passage darkened again.

"What was that?" Yusen echoed with curiosity rather than concern.

"What we needed," Andao said. "Light." The sound of crumbling and a little shower of earth.

"I see nothing, not anymore."

"Wait, just wait."

The sound of their breathing filled the cavern along with the musty damp of earth. Andao stood still, his hands close together, growing steadily more visible.

"Sorcery," Dailus murmured.

Andao's grin flared in the pale, greenish light. "No. Glow-worms." He lowered his hands, displaying a double handful of earth riddled with larvae. "They don't like to be disturbed, that's why they stopped glowing before. They like a different kind of dirt, made from a different kind of rock." He held out his glowing hands to illuminate the pitted texture of limestone. Overhead, a few gaps in the rock permitted a crowd of roots, and little clusters of glowing worms.

Zhencai reached up and gathered a handful of his own, bringing the little creatures close, and thanking the Buddha spirit in them. Dailus scooped some into his hand, holding them at arm's length, his lips curled in revulsion. Yusen fitted his hands and feet into the natural hollows in the walls and climbed up to reach them, then smashed a handful against his del, leaving a long smear of dead glowing creatures.

The drakemaster recoiled, pulling back his own handful as if they were at risk, and Yusen hopped down again, smearing his hand a little further to clean it, and to spread the glow. "I may need both hands." He spread his palms, the left one glowing faintly.

With an echoing sigh, Dailus said, "Where next?"

The cavern opened out into a handful of passages, some wide, some narrow. Andao turned slowly, his face illuminated by the lives he carried, then nodded his head, indicating an opening a little off the floor. "Here."

Dailus gave him a dubious glance as Andao approached the chosen entrance. He clambered in on his knees, banging his elbow in a sharp impact that briefly made his hands lose their glow. Yusen simply caught the edge with both hands and climbed easily inside.

"I hate him," Dailus muttered, then he followed.

The passage wound and cramped and opened so abruptly into a larger way that Andao tumbled out, spilling his glow worms across the floor and painstakingly gathering them again. Dailus exited more carefully, looking up. "These are tool marks. This passage was a mine."

"Or a tunnel," Andao agreed. "From the cinnabar mines, to transport the mercury they needed. Mercury feels slippery, somehow. Cinnabar as well, but not as much."

"If the lake is as big as the scroll claimed, they needed thousands of gallons—hundreds of miners to dig out the ore, and hundreds of workmen to build the device and the cavern where it's hidden." Dailus shook his head. "Sometimes, I fear we are chasing shadows. How could they have kept something like that hidden, and for so long?"

"Most likely, the miners were prisoners." Yusen flicked a look at Dailus.

"Who died before they could tell anyone," the drakemaster finished. "What about the workmen? The carpenters who built the structure, and the foundry men who made the works. Surely they went home and told their wives what they were making."

"The scroll didn't say." Andao chewed on his lip. "The Order seems not to care much for workmen or peasants. Only the emperor matters." He started walking again, footfalls echoing, glowworms casting their strange light in a little patch around him. They walked two abreast in the corridor, keeping Yusen's short strides from fouling Dailus's longer ones. Zhencai began to release the grip he held upon his qi, the present lit not only by the glow worms, but also by the ease of their movement, and the hope that they drew close to their goal.

Ahead, cut stones filled the corridor from one side to the other with a stone slab door at the center, crossed with a bar fitted into a pair of iron braces.

Dailus and Zhencai poured their handfuls of glow worms into Andao's and each took an end of the beam to lift it off, then Zhencai clasped the handle and hauled the door open. Something clattered to the floor.

Andao gasped, and Yusen crouched, yanking out the hoe he carried at his back.

With an oath in a foreign tongue, Dailus performed his own sign of blessing, swallowing hard, turning away.

"Here is your answer," said Yusen.

Zhencai stepped around the door. In the greenish glow of the worms in Andao's trembling hands, he saw gaping eyes and grinning teeth, sunken cheeks and claw-like hands, legs tangled, clad in rags. For as far as he could see, corpses lined the hall beyond, some collapsed on their faces, some clustered at the wall, their hands still clinging to the stones. Some of the dead clung to each other in despair, or in rage, skeletal hands gripping antique knives or the parched skin of long-dead throats. Stringy hair on old skulls showed cracks in the bone. Two or three gripped the loose bones of others in their decaying jaws, sucking out the marrow of the dead. Skin stretched over barren faces and broken chests, parted with injuries or carved more deliberately with knives.

A hundred men had died here in the darkness—screaming and pleading and starving, battering the walls and door for their escape. They had beaten each other, maimed and killed, and gnawed in the dark on each other's bones.

When they opened the door, one of the dead had fallen through, collapsing his brittle ribs with a whiff of dried meat. His pleading at the door had been answered, a hundred and sixty years too late.

CHAPTER SIXTY-TWO

"Which way?" Dailus's voice came out as a hoarse whisper. He coughed, wet his lips and asked again.

Andao stood stiff as the cane he carried at his back. "Through," Andao replied, and there was no need to ask through what.

Through the room of the dead, because people who could do such a thing must be stopped. Steeling himself, Dailus faced the chamber. Zhencai stood at Andao's side, breathing. A ridiculous thing, not any deliberate attempt at comfort and yet, comforting all the same. Sometimes, in the darkness, the only thing they had was Zhencai's breathing.

Beyond them, in the chamber, something ripped.

"Stop that!" Andao leaned forward, hesitating, then stepping over the bodies.

Yusen tore a long strip of dry cloth from the clothing of one of the corpses. "We need light more than they need dignity." The smear of crushed glow worms across his chest cast his face in an eerie light and made it look as if his chest were glowing. Quickly, he bound the strips of cloth at one end of a shaft of wood, an old tool, perhaps or a bit of furniture.

Outrage warmed Dailus's face, and he strode forward, the prayer beads clinking at his hip, but the fury ebbed with every step. Irritating, offensive, utterly practical Yusen cared not at all for the old bones, but focused on the needs of the living. Had Dailus cowered beneath his master's shadow for two years and never known him? When Wang Lin Yo struck Dailus down and might have killed him, Yusen's intervention saved him, speaking of duty, discipline and honor, full of passion. He had clasped Dailus's hand to the saddle of his beloved horse and kept him there with a grip that marked his slave with his own blood: the Mongol ignored his own injury in his urgency to see to Dailus's care.

Now he extended his duty to all of them, as if these four—the remainder of their already small company—were his soldiers. A good scout, but a poor general he termed himself. Dailus envisioned him taller, broader, clad in a general's armor to take the place of brutal Munkjar, or lazy Batzorig who couldn't be bothered to scout a monastery before he slew the occupants in case they might be geomancers. Yusen would never make such a mistake, not if his duty to the khan were at risk. He had as much as told Dailus that Jian Ho was innocent, but that there was no stopping Munkjar's idea of justice. He was no general... but what a general he might have been.

Dailus prowled into the room, reaching to tap on the lanterns that still hung down until he found one that gave a dull echo, then he pushed up on his toes to lift it from its hook and carry it back to Yusen. "Oil."

The Mongol's eyes glinted white, then he gave a nod and took it, dripping the contents onto the two torches he had already made. "Zhencai, we need a spark." Then he looked again to Dailus. "Weapons. Those knives, at least."

Gritting his teeth, Dailus searched the bodies, reluctant to pry a murder weapon from the bones of its target. He found a dozen blades of different lengths. They hadn't been polished in a century, but they would do for stabbing if need be.

Yusen exchanged a torch for a few of the blades, tucking short knives into his boots and two longer ones into his belt. "What do you fight with?"

The monk raised his hands. "I practice the iron hand. I will take no blade."

With a little shake of his head, Yusen got to his feet. "You, geomancer?"

"I'll take a knife, I guess. I haven't—I don't really fight."

Dailus swept the room again, trying to see as Yusen saw, not a chamber of the dead, but a storeroom full of resources. He picked up a few shards of bamboo and silently walked them over. Andao's face in the greenish light looked drawn, and he did not take the shards. "Underground. They won't grow."

Casting about, Dailus found a pouch, putting in the bamboo and a few other odds and ends—seeds, tea, beads that had fallen from their rotten string. He tucked the pouch into Andao's belt. "In case you find fertile ground."

The golden light of fire danced around him, brightening the sickly dried-up flesh of the dead workmen. He squinted for a moment as his eyes adjusted. Overhead, a low rumble of sound moved constantly, as if they were underneath the river. The walls and ceiling showed bands of darker stone and brighter markings, metals, tarnished with age. They resolved in his vision into characters both large and small, inscribed into the walls and ceiling. "What is all of this?"

Depositing his glowworms past the corridor of death, Andao tracked the marks back again. "Geomantic writing, naming, bonding and connecting the stuff of the earth. They infused different stones and metals into the chamber to strengthen and protect it."

Focused on the dead men who surrounded them, Zhencai formed the sign of blessing, repeating a few words over and over. A dark stain and a gash marked his tunic from the center of his chest down to the left, and Dailus's heart fell. "Did I do that?"

"A small enough hurt. Better than one of you dying before you see through each other's illusions." Zhencai blessed Dailus then, his eyes crinkling a little. "Keep looking."

"Did you feel that?" Andao scampered forward, dodging the bodies.

Dailus paused. A tremor in the earth, slight, but definite.

"Hurry," said Yusen. He tossed another torch to Zhencai who took it and lit it from the first as they started toward the far end.

The corpses thinned at the center of the room, then a dozen or more all pressed against a door at the far end where the floor sloped up. Yusen pushed the corpses aside with his foot, clearing the ground before the door. Dailus lifted the latch and pushed, but the door did not give. The room had been barred at both ends, to keep the workmen inside while they died. Two big iron hinges held the door at one side, but they looked rusty, pitted with age. Dailus handed off his torch, then heaved up against the hinges. Nothing happened but that his arms and back ached.

Yusen took all of the torches, holding them aloft like a demon of fire as the other men set the hoe and pruning blade against the ancient hinges, levering them up and back. The door groaned, scraping against its lintel, and finally the lower hinge bent back, leaving a narrow gap, and a wedged door. Stepping back, panting, Dailus studied the door more closely. A soft noise echoed beyond it, then Yusen caught his arm and breathed, "Footsteps."

Hurriedly, they doused all but one torch, and gave that to Andao, who pressed himself to the wall at the corner furthest from the gap. The footsteps grew louder, followed by a voice in Chinese, "Who's there?"

"Ghosts," answered another, with a laugh.

"Let's go back. This is pointless."

The footfalls retreated. In their wake, Yusen beckoned Dailus and Zhencai down to his level. "I may fit." He tipped his head toward the narrow gap. He pulled the hoe from his belt and laid it beside the door, then lay down on the floor and peered through. He tested the size of the opening, and removed his long knives as well. After a moment, he wriggled through, turning sideways to wedge his shoulders and hips through the gap, scraping the floor and sides, then expelling a breath and pushing harder before he finally dragged himself through. A smear of blood marked the floor.

Yusen's hand reached back through and groped, then grabbed the handle of his hoe and pulled that after him. "There is a bar across the door. I'll try to lift it," he whispered through the hole. Metal scraped on metal outside, accompanied by a soft grunt of effort, then a crash.

"Son of a snake," Yusen gasped.

Footfalls and shouting. "Lights out!" Yusen hissed, then lighter steps ran away.

"There! Halt!" someone shouted, and the heavier treads picked up speed.

Andao smothered the torch, plunging them into darkness as the soldiers ran by, accompanied by the glow of their own light.

"Was that the dwarf?"

"Can't be!" More shouts echoed past.

"Now," said Zhencai.

All three of them together shoved the door open, pushing the bar which still hung by one end, then pulled the door shut again and propped the bar against it, leaving it just as the guards might have seen it.

Running the opposite direction, their bare feet swishing rather than pounding, the three made for a glow beyond all glow-worms. Patterns of light danced on the walls of the corridor at that end, as if sunlight fell on a river. Dailus, outstripping the others, stopped short and put out his hand, but Andao shook his head, taking the hand and pulling him across the way. They stumbled into an alcove alongside a sculpture of a long-faced sage smiling as if he appreciated the silvery, dancing light. Dailus gazed beyond, at the scene that gave the sage so much pleasure, the scene that took his breath away.

They stood on a narrow ledge forming a half-circle at one side of a vast cavern lit with a hundred lanterns, but also, at the top, open to a slice of the sky, as if they were in the gallery of a great cathedral and the nave stood open to the Lord. The light of all those lanterns glinted from a shimmering silver lake that made Dailus's mouth sting just to look at it: mercury. A series of narrow square pillars broke the surface of the lake as if a dock or bridge once spanned it, but had crumbled long ago into the mercury below. A landscape stretched out with streams of mercury lapping the feet of tiny terra cotta mountains. Miniature bridges crossed these ribbons of silver, and glazed pagodas perhaps as tall as his ankle marked the riverside. Tiny houses or buildings grouped around little squares of ground, including a palace glazed in red and gold, and a half-circle bridge: Kaifeng, in replica. More tiny houses dotted the country around, with pale herds of miniscule sheep. The model extended for an acre or more, like the playthings of a child so wealthy he could own an entire country, at least, from the mountains out to the edge of a silvery sea bounded once again by the native stone. The terra cotta map contained the dull shadows of men, their limbs outflung, like those on the walls in the village of the dead.

Across this miniature landscape, a dozen soldiers strode like giants, moving a few buildings, removing the palace at Kaifeng, but mostly placing tiny groups of round, white markers. The gers of the khan's great army, surrounded by the herds of his horses.

Dailus turned from the shimmering lake and the fragile world it watered with its poison. At the heart of the lake rose a dark, square island busy with movement. A handful of soldiers illuminated more lanterns that showed the tower of the great device.

Sturdy as a church, the tower rose four stories, topped by a platform with a peaked roof of its own, though this was pierced and edged by a series of instruments with the glint of bronze and something brighter. Glass? Dailus wished he had his kite to fly to the tower and view its instruments up close. The plan on the scroll showed this area as the union of the astronomer's art with the geomancer's: collecting the power of the stars above. This activated the Golden Serpent, the circle of radiant energy with its golden threads that ran throughout the device for no purpose Dailus recognized. From the examples of bronzecraft he had seen, he knew the workmanship would be extraordinary, every surface embellished with poetry and proclamations, every brace supported on the backs of tigers and dragons, every device given a name to inspire: the Emperor's Crown, the Dragon's Pearl, the Brazen Star of Fire.

On the third story, beneath the level of the instruments, to one side he could make out the shadow of the dials, great thick, round slabs carved with figures to mark the days, and others still for every hour. Here, the skills of the Mandarins organized the power of the geomancers and the knowledge of the astronomers, harnessing their achievement to an array of controls and measurements. The image from the scroll overlaid reality, filling in the parts he could not see. The stack of dials stood at center. Behind them rode a huge gear with spindles that would turn the dials, and a pair of water wheels with a mechanism of little buckets. At the back of this platform, facing the miniature countryside, stood a more delicate apparatus of pipes and chains and gears, and a few handles that would crank the mechanism around, pointing it toward any place on the map below.

On the second story, thick beams supported the wheels and the central shaft that joined the dials with the instruments on top. A hum of voices and the clatter of soldiers' light armor echoed in the chamber as they went about their work. From the tower itself, a chime sounded periodically, marking time.

The scene shifted as the great wheel groaned into motion. A cheer echoed among the soldiers. Silvery mercury rose in the little buckets, gleaming into the shadows. A broad patch of white light appeared on the landscape below, highlighting a soldier who put up his hand to shade his eyes, calling to a voice from the tower.

The light narrowed, then winked out, followed by a whirr of metal. A new yellow light flared into life with a thrum through the air that made Dailus's hair quiver. The soldier shrieked, sparked, and flared with a brilliant glow. Dailus turned sharply, covering his eyes. The stench of scorched meat reached him, the silence after the shriek pressing against his ears.

Andao sank to his knees, gasping, under the gentle pressure of Zhencai's palm. The Jew whispered something Dailus did not understand, but knew for a prayer. He sank down at the geomancer's side, his knees trembling.

"Apologies! I am sorry, so sorry. Forgive me," called a voice from the tower, resonating with a sound of metal as if the speaker used a horn. Four words asking forgiveness, instead of the auspicious three—even Dailus knew that. On the map, the pale shadow of the soldier remained, just like the shadows in the ghost village.

From beneath the balcony of stone where they hid, a languid, familiar voice called, "If you want the power to pass through to the realm rather than simply strike the map, you've got to reverse the focusing stone—you've got it backwards." Master Deng, directing from afar. "Get it right. Once you lock the dragon lever, it cannot be reset until the dial comes round again."

A pause. "Thank you, Master Deng, for sharing the wisdom of the ancestors," Guowei's voice echoed from the island. "Now all can see the strength of the Mandate of Heaven. I praise the genius of our ancestors, and the skill of their labor in making this device possible. In making it possible for us to remove our enemies from the Middle Kingdom forever." The voice rang with conviction, but the cheer took a moment to build, and was accompanied by the careful rush of feet as soldiers stepped lightly among the miniature buildings to leave a wide ring around that point of light.

One of the soldiers moved too quickly, overbalanced, and stepped aside to one of the pillars in the lake to steady himself. The pillar dropped beneath him, and he shouted as he splashed into the mercury, gagging and clawing his way to the surface. A golden shimmer streaked across the surface, and the cavern warmed in an instant with power.

The soldier's face and figure streamed with silver, but the golden streaks pinned him, jolting his body half out of the lake, lights flashing from the silver-cloaked edges of his armor and sword. The flailing hands jerked, and he sank again, never to rise. Dailus clamped a hand over his mouth, his stomach churning as if it were he who drowned in poison, struck by the power of a dangerous star. The Golden Serpent indeed.

"The strength of the Celestial Palace is nearly full. When the gong strikes for the Hour of the Dog, we must be ready to enact the glory of the Son of Heaven and reclaim his kingdom from the dogs who have stolen it. In two more cycles of the chime, the Han people will rise again!"

Another cheer greeted this, more whole-hearted than the last, and the soldiers got back to work, filling the land with Mongol camps to flame.

"Where is Yusen?" Dailus whispered.

Andao shook his head. Zhencai leaned, then edged carefully forward from their alcove. "I see Bao Xing," he said, almost a sigh. "She sits below, having tea with the dancer, and the old man, Master Deng. Seven soldiers surround them, at ease, like escorts."

"What can I do?" Andao said. "I can't fight them, and I don't know anything about the stars."

Dailus touched his arm. "Bao Xing knows the stars, and I know the machine. What *can* you do?"

Setting his fingers on the floor, head bent, Andao remained still a long moment. "The cavern must have weaknesses, bad earth, bad stone. It may contain elements that would help us, better earth or other connections. I can't locate them from here; I'll need to find solid ground. When I learn this place," he met Dailus's eye, "we can bring the cavern down and crush the weapon. But it might take me longer than two cycles."

Dailus nodded. "In that case, I need to get to the island—or Bao Xing does—to figure out how to stop that thing."

Andao drew forth the cane and passed it to Dailus. "For the lady, with my compliments."

The carving dug into his palms. "Can we be sure she still plans to help us?"

"Certainty is an illusion," said Zhencai. "But I will go with you. Seven is not so many. Assuming the dancer does not join the battle. She does not fight with honor."

"What's the most you've ever fought?"

"Six."

"You weren't injured at the time," Andao murmured.

A banging sound echoed through the cavern, then a soldier appeared, breathless, and bowed toward the island. "Captain!"

"Just cross," a shadowy figure shouted back.

The soldier hesitated, then stepped to one of the pillars, then another and another, in a bouncing pattern of corners across the lake. Dailus leaned closer, but the soldier's long tunic concealed his feet as he leapt, and Dailus couldn't tell which pillars he chose. Dailus sagged as the soldier reached the island, speaking softly to the captain who greeted him. Those pillars formed the only bridge to the island, and Dailus had two chimes to find his way. Even testing the pillar with the cane or some other object would cause it to sink, and conjure the killing energy. His joints ached and his muscles trembled, but he could not afford to get this wrong. One wrong step would plunge him into the lake to choke on silver poison and burn with golden fire.

CHAPTER SIXTY-THREE

Ming Lun set down her cup, watching the soldier cross the mercury. Something in the rhythm of his movement appealed to her, but he did it badly. Master Deng had demonstrated the crossing several times for Guowei and some of his soldiers, but she and Bao Xing had been taken to a chamber equipped as a kitchen and told to make tea. Bao Xing sat quietly breaking bits off an ancient brick of tea and wiping out the dust from the cups, so it fell to Ming Lun to shovel the coal and fetch water with a foot-pump like the ones they had seen in the Valley of the Sages. Had their brief partnership changed anything? Bao Xing no longer watched her as if she were an adder about to strike, a fact that should not have concerned Ming Lun at all, and yet, when she returned with a bucket of water, the other woman's smile pleased her. Perhaps, as Guowei believed, she was merely a woman, if a little too touched with Yang energy. Long ago, Bao Xing sought friends, and looked at her. Was this how to be friends, to make tea together in a stranger's kitchen? Crossing the bridge had been more familiar, an act of adventure which might win great risk, or great reward.

Now they engaged in idle conversation with Master Deng while Guowei prepared the great weapon to destroy the Mongols once and for all. When the soldiers had died in light and silver, their dazzling deaths haunted the inside of her eyelids. Thousands more people would die like that, their bodies gone in a flash, their ghosts haunting the ruined land for hundreds of years. The north would become a wasteland where even a Mongol pony would starve. Bao Xing harbored some naïve belief that they two could destroy the weapon—fending off all of Guowei's soldiers, divining the purpose of every aspect of the device—and thus save the Han farmers and citizens who would die along with their Mongol oppressors, but ruining the weapon would not end the war, it would merely remove the one advantage the emperor possessed. Even Dailus rejected the use of the weapon against a people he hated.

Ming Lun turned her tea cup in her palm. A few tea leaves drifted in it, inviting her to divine the future. There would be other weapons to assault the oppressor without so much damage to the land and its people. If the device could be stopped. Naïve and noble. For two women surrounded by soldiers? Impossible.

Ming Lun's leg twitched, and she forced it still. She hated sitting. Hated tea. Hated idle conversation perhaps more than anything.

"Do I presume correctly that you are the Mandarin mentioned in the journal of the astronomer Chang Mailou?" Bao Xing inquired, raising her eyes just above the rim of her teacup, a practiced coyness.

"That idiot left a journal? Ha! I should have known. He was always a simpering fool, eager for my favor, then dismayed to find it might have consequences." Master Deng swished his tea and tossed it down his throat. "That's good, that tea. My hireling bought inferior tea at the last market we passed, and I've had to make do for a week in the wilderness." He raised his cup. "This, on the other hand, came from the emperor's own supply." He grinned, a ghoulish expression on his thin face. "Another, if you please."

Bao Xing reached for the pot and poured. In spite of being clad in only a nightgown, she covered her hands with a fitting modesty, and managed grace and tranquility, quite like a member of the emperor's court herself.

Something was happening with the soldiers. One of the patrolling men had returned and gone to Cho with an urgent message. Captain Cho kept it between himself and his messenger, but he twitched his sword in and out of the scabbard, and finally crossed the pillars back to shore to approach the officer who directed their own circle of guards. Ming Lun stood up, stretching extravagantly, watching him move across the pillars. She had missed the start of the pattern, and of course it was backward. What had the soldier said to make Cho return to land?

"Guowei likes you—and no wonder, if I were a younger man, I'd take you for myself," Master Deng said. "You'd be my first wife, in this new life—I assume my other wives are already dead; though one was such a harpy she might've learned the secret to our sleep just to vex me."

Bao Xing smiled behind her hand. "You honor me, and my poor astronomer father. It is because of him I so enjoyed reading the journal. But Astronomer Chang, as you say, seemed to lack wisdom. I am not sure he understood fully the great device you created here."

"Of course not. Only a handful of us knew the whole thing—even that scroll doesn't have every detail." He leaned back on a pile of old cushions, releasing a shower of dust and coughing as he waved it away. "That was me, my plan." He thumped his thin chest. "To ensure that not just anyone could work the device." Bao Xing leaned forward to offer his tea, and he stared down the neck of her gown. "Did you really imagine you'd be able to do it?"

"No, Master Deng, not I." She glanced away as the soldier and the captain approached their little gathering.

"That drakemaster then. I could tell he'd taken in the whole diagram. You could almost see him turning it around in his head." He waved a hand over his own head.

Ming Lun remained standing, stretching through a series of poses, the last of which left her balanced several feet from where she started, fingers held above her head. Captain Cho stood so close to the officer that their chest armor clinked softly.

"—saw the dwarf. I need two of you to go to the surface and look out for the Mongols. The Mandarin claims that the dwarf could not have communicated with our enemy, but we cannot be sure."

"The Mongols were at least a day behind us, Captain," murmured the officer. "They might have made up the distance, but we destroyed the trail to get here."

"They persist like rats chewing a corpse—they won't let go of this." The captain twitched his sword again, brow furrowed. "We should have done something about those horses. If they see them they'll search."

Guowei's Mongol pursuers were drawing close. The captain's head swiveled her direction, and Ming Lun pitched into a forward bend that left her rump in the air, draped in the thin fabric of her trousers, one leg still raised. She moaned with pleasure, as if she found the pose infinitely satisfying.

The captain cleared his throat, then dismissed his officer and stalked back toward the lake. Inverted, Ming Lun looked back to the dark hollow where the stairs ascended to the gallery, a carved archway into darkness, and movement, and a glimpse of wheaten hair. The dwarf, the drakemaster. They should not be here, yet when the great device was used, this might be the only safe place left in the whole of the North. One of them was here to destroy it, the other, perhaps to claim it for his own empire. Another risk, and one the Son of Heaven could not afford.

Two women alone against the soldiers could never succeed. With the drakemaster, and even the dwarf—who would certainly fight the Han soldiers…the odds improved.

Did the Son of Heaven truly wish the Mongols defeated so badly that he would condone the slaughter of his own people?

She snapped herself back up again, and Master Deng applauded.

"He said you were a dancer, I wasn't sure if I should believe it. Entertain us!" The old man's sweeping gesture took in himself and Bao Xing, as if she were, indeed, his concubine.

Thinking furiously, Ming Lun sank to her knees and bent backward, then slowly drew herself up. "Will you whistle me a tune, Master?"

Master Deng hooted, clapping his hands like a child. "Women were never so saucy in my first life. We had a few here, you know, one with a talent for gemstones, as well as for dancing, but she allowed her emotions to overwhelm her. She refused to follow through on her duty, started cutting stones we didn't need. Gemstones and dancing—isn't that just like a woman."

He must be speaking of the dreamer Zhencai had discovered and the stone she gave him, but it made Ming Lun think of the woman who had taught her—dancing, and other skills.

Ming Lun started dancing, humming to herself, moving in small circles, her arms weaving, dancing for an audience only she knew about. Once more, she made herself a dangerous distraction. She danced on the verge of her dream of a free China, free of the Mongols and the men who made their weapons, but the Mongols, too, had honor in their way. She danced upon the edge of death—she could step in either direction. Which way should she choose?

In a burst of speed, Zhencai ran across the space of ground between, leapt, nearly silent, and slammed into the back of one of the soldiers who stood watching her. His force knocked that man into his companion, sending them both to the ground with a sharp crack and a yelp of pain. The four remaining guards spun to meet him, surrounding him, swords drawn, and he moved like a hurricane, twisting, turning, bouncing lightly off his feet. His hard hands shot out, striking a cheek here and thrusting into an exposed armpit when the soldier raised his sword. Now that his skill was not aimed at her, Ming Lun took a breath to admire it.

"Captain!" Master Deng scooted back on his cushions, then Dailus rose up behind him, pressing a knife to the old man's throat. She had not known him capable of this. The moment the captain returned to shore, Dailus would be a dead man.

"The path across the pillars, master, tell me."

The old man tipped back his skeletal head and laughed into Dailus's face. "You really think I waited a hundred and sixty years for this moment only to let some yin-balanced foreigner steal my glory? I'd rather die."

"Are they stars? Is it a constellation?" Bao Xing trembled on her tiny feet. "Or is it geomancy?"

Dailus withdrew his knife and reached back, pulling out her cane and tossing it to clatter on the floor by her feet. In that moment, Ming Lun was on him. Launching herself over Master Deng's slouched form, she caught the fist around Dailus's blade and drew his arm back behind him, carrying them both to the floor.

"You cannot win this. Thirty men oppose you, and they hold the greatest weapon ever made."

Those jade eyes locked to hers, then he rocked his hips and shoved his long legs against the ground, tipping her over. She rolled with him to fetch up against the cavern wall, Dailus pressing her down. Her palms went moist and her stomach clenched.

"We have to—or thousands will die. Thousands of your people."

"And thousands of Mongols." She twisted about, caught his knee and squeezed until he dropped to the side. She flipped him off of her, pinning his right arm with her knee. "You hate them, too."

"There are ways to stop an army without slaying those you fight to protect." He pushed back and kissed her.

Startled, she let her knee slip, and he caught her wrist, wrenching her arm behind her.

"Use the boat, you idiots!" Master Deng shouted. "On the far side there's a boat!"

From the corner of her eye, she spotted Zhencai as he slammed an opponent against the wall, leaving him with only three, but he did not see the dozen more filing their way across the pillars, too caught-up in their terror to heed Master Deng's words.

Ming Lun dropped her weight, spinning Dailus to the ground, the breath knocked from his lungs, his knife clattering across the floor.

A slender form barely noticed, Bao Xing stood back, cane in hand, watching the men cross the pillars. She'd never make it across that way—was she fool enough, or desperate enough to try?

Another of Zhencai's opponents went down, then three more rushed in to take the fallen soldier's place. Blood streaked the monk's tunic and trickled down his thigh.

Dailus worked his way to his knees, panting. She caught him, dropped him with a knee against his chest and setting a knife tip at his eye. "Do not move."

"You would kill me." Those eyes stared back at her, his lips turned, his lean frame shivering beneath her. Then his gaze flicked away, his lips compressed as if to hide a smile, as if he had seen something she did not. She refused to be distracted.

"You cannot defeat the Mandate of Heaven. It is already set in motion." She steeled her arm, the vision of blood streaming from that eye giving her strength to hold perfectly still. "There are worse fates than the cinnabar mine."

"Worse than having to kill me yourself?"

Was there no pattern in the constellation of choices which allowed him to live? Thirty soldiers, the device already in motion. Did he not understand the meaning of futility? Or was there something else, something she, herself, did not understand?

A shriek and a splash rang out behind her, then the pulse of energy that made her arm hairs tingle. Another shriek. The third time, she heard the whistle of the arrow just before it took down its man. The dwarf had found a bow.

***

Joy surged through Dailus, first at her hesitation, second at the sight of Yusen flitting across the gallery, bow in hand. Two years ago, even two weeks ago, Dailus would not have imagined he would be glad to see his master, gladder still to see him armed.

Soldiers shouted and ran. Another splashed into the mercury, triggering the strike of the golden flame.

"Even if I let you free—even if you kill them all, you'll never cross the pillars—Master Deng will never tell you how." Ming Lun sounded distracted, as if it were herself she tried to convince.

"Get that dwarf!" roared the captain.

Only a handful of soldiers could try cross the pillars at once and Yusen picked them off, every splash spooking the others. Two returned to the island rather than fall, one reached for a floundering companion only to take an arrow to the back so they both fell. Spears flew from below Yusen's position to clatter uselessly against the gallery floor.

A chime sounded, ringing clear though the cavern across the shouts and cursing, across the running feet and the smack of Zhencai's fists. Dailus felt that chime in his bones. One more chime and the gears would turn, sending down the power of the stars to blast the country. Time ran short.

He caught Ming Lun's wrist and forced the knife from his eye as he rocked her aside, using her automatic shift of balance to pull himself up. She spun against him, swiping his other knife even as he reached for it. Strong and beautiful, and deadly.

Another arrow hit its mark, a soldier reaching out for Bao Xing. It struck his shoulder but did not stop him. She jabbed at him with her cane, and his hasty withdrawal tipped him into the mercury where the golden flames streaked up his body. He spasmed and dropped. Bao Xing stumbled back, out of the mercury spray.

"This stops now," said the commanding voice from across the lake. Guowei appeared at the corner of the second level, holding a lantern. It illuminated the gleam of bronze. A smaller flame crackled, then a rush of heated air. Dailus knocked Ming Lun so they both sprawled on the carpets, tumbling apart. A firedrake, small, but powerful. The stone it launched crashed near Yusen's leg, spinning him sideways and cracking the stone. He fell from the gallery to the floor below, the bow torn from his hand to bounce away into the lake. Scrambling to right himself, Yusen drew one of his boot knives. He staggered up, off-balance, his leg streaming blood, but three soldiers converged on him, striking him down with boots and fists. Blood sprayed in the air.

Dailus found himself praying, whispering the words over and over, but each impact jolted him as if it were against his own flesh. The furious soldiers concealed Yusen's small form—he saw only the pumping of their fists, the pull of their legs. Blood flicked from their boots as they pulled back to strike again. He glimpsed a patch of blue fabric, blue like the Eternal Sky, then it, too, washed with red.

Andao, alone of all of them, remained free. Like Yusen, he had hidden talents—unlike Yusen, he had no boldness in using them. And Yusen was getting beaten to death.

Guowei's voice echoed across the lake. "Bring him here—let him witness the destruction of his hopes. Let him be the last barbarian alive in all the North."

One of the soldiers dragged Yusen to his feet, his hands bound, the left side of his face a mass of blood. He staggered, trying to find his balance, doubled over. His left leg twisted under him, and he tumbled to the stone. Beaten as he had beaten Dailus. Why was there no satisfaction in any of this? Because Dailus had been punished as a slave is, a man whose master wants him to recover, to work, to succeed. These men beat Yusen to break him, to ensure that he would never again stand or walk or ride.

One of the soldiers grabbed Yusen's leg and heaved him onto his shoulder. The soldier marched up the lakeshore toward Dailus and the pillars of stone, Yusen dangling like the dead goat once draped his own saddle. The soldier crossed the lake unsteadily, stumbling onto shore on the other side. Yusen slid from his grip, but he got a hold of Yusen's hair and dragged him up three flights of stairs, leaving a bloody trail in his wake. Jian Ho had been dragged like that, beaten senseless, bound in felt.

Zhencai stood at bay, his back to the wall and four soldiers arrayed before him. He, too, bled from several wounds, and hunched a little to the left, the wound that Dailus had delivered in the darkness, hoping to kill another man. Bao Xing wavered by the lake, lashing out with her cane at anyone who came near. Thirteen soldiers on their side of the lake. Four more in the middle, plus the captain and Guowei himself. Ming Lun was right—they could not win.

"Throw the foreigner into the lake," Guowei commanded, from the safety of his weapon. "The monk, too. Unless one of you would like the honor of slaying a Shaolin. And they have another companion—find him."

Five more soldiers swarmed to Zhencai, the knot of them jostling to see who would get his chance at the Shaolin warrior. Nine. Seven might have been possible, but nine, for a man who could barely keep his feet?

The other four came toward Dailus and Ming Lun sprang back to her feet, breathing heavily, knife in hand.

The thought of the mercury flooded him with dread as he remembered the acrid stench of the mine, then his days of recovery at Dragon Turns, wracked with pain, shaking so hard he could not feed himself. The only solace had been Ming Lun's dancing.

Ming Lun's dancing. Dailus imagined he could see her from above, dancing over a lake of mercury. *The Dance of the Mandate of Heaven*, that near-martial combination of stomps and pivots when her grace and strength had first commanded his gaze. In his mind's eye, he saw the same pattern, the hopping steps the soldier had taken. The one person who knew the way, who had betrayed them all for her emperor. Zhencai observed that the signal for the last attack had been Dailus's flight. Could they yet sway the dancer's heart?

The soldiers grabbed his arms, hauling him up. Dailus said, "Ming Lun. The Mandate of Heaven must be fulfilled."

She tipped her head. "For the glory of the Son of Heaven."

Was he wrong about her, about the conflict he read in her form when she fought with him? Dailus chose to have faith. "For the astronomer's daughter. Dance it for me, Ming Lun. Dance it for life, one last time."

Ming Lun met his eye, her own widening, then her lips curved into a smile. The soldiers' grip tightened as they hauled him toward the lake, and Ming Lun began to dance.

CHAPTER SIXTY-FOUR

So much blood, Bao Xing thought as they dragged Yusen away. So much blood, and he was so small. How much more could he lose? By the time they brought him to Guowei's side, he must be already dead. Even a man as stubborn as her husband could not live forever.

She clenched the cane in her hands—unless she could reach the island, she could do nothing at all. She could not save her husband, and she could not stop the machine from killing so many others. Then Ming Lun danced toward her, mad and grinning. "Come, Bao Xing, a last dance for those who would die. Join me!" She swished her hands before her, executed a turn to face the soldiers who brought up Dailus between them. "Just for a moment, please, for you are decent Han soldiers. You would not want me to deny his dying wish? Please, great warriors, please let him watch."

Three times. Was she so moved by the foreigner that she had gone mad at last? But the soldiers shrugged and watched her move, as they always did, holding Dailus with hands and swords. Somewhere behind, she heard the grunts and strikes of battle, as Zhencai fought for his life against one, and another, and the next. He could not last. Life was impermanence. Would he greet his Nirvana with his open heart?

"Just tip him in and be done," Master Deng advised. He tottered about in the tea room, scowling at the disorder and blood. "And you, Guowei!" He cupped his hands at his mouth. "The dragon lever! Don't forget!"

"Here, lady, watch." Ming Lun stepped up before her, and her eyes flared. Her voice shifted lower, with the intensity of command. "Watch, lady. I can teach this to a child, but you must learn it fast, and learn it now."

She stomped and struck a pose, then turned and stomped again. Two steps, stomp, pivot, step and stomp. The khan hated this dance, Bao Xing recalled, when she performed it at the ger, and her young students rolled their eyes. *The Dance of the Mandate of Heaven.*

And Bao Xing understood.

She moved more slowly, watching Ming Lun's feet, the pattern of steps and stomps. Short and inelegant, the dance repeated, and Bao Xing was dancing, too. She pasted on a smile as once she painted her face, and imitated the stomp with a rap of her cane, letting her little toes peek from beneath her bedraggled silk. Step, step, stomp.

"Yes, lady! You see, it is never too late."

Ming Lun began to clap with her dance and turned in counterpoint while Bao Xing moved the opposite direction, balanced as they had been on the bridge, matching each other's speed. And Bao Xing stepped over the first pillar, out onto the shimmering silver lake. Stomp. Each step was a pillar avoided, each stomp a pillar to choose. Her heart trembled and she gripped the cane as if it were her balance and she could, by her slender strength, force it to be still. As if it were Yusen's life and she could hold it safe beneath the great Eternal Sky. The mercury hummed and lapped the edges of the pillars. Shouts, the clash of weapons and of fists. Bao Xing borrowed the focus of Zhencai and set aside everything she could not afford to hear.

The hands of a dead man, still stroked with silver, lay upon the bank, the rest of him submerged, as she stepped onto the island and made herself breathe again.

Ming Lun's dance shifted, her foot lashing out to take one of Dailus's guards in the side. Sliding a pick free from her hair, she rammed it into the spine of another man as she spun around him. Dailus snatched the sword from the dying man and hacked into one of his two remaining guards. The blade stuck as the man fell, gurgling blood. The fourth man stumbled back to avoid the body, only to find Ming Lun already there, her blade piercing his breast. As he dropped, she shared a smile with Dailus, then she was in motion again, a dancer of death.

Zhencai fought from his place by the wall, and Ming Lun fought her way through until they stood, back to back, with knives and feet and fists. Dailus pulled a weapon from a dead man, and came to the pillars, carrying a spear in his other hand. Bao Xing turned for the tower stairs as Captain Cho clattered down them, sword in hand.

"Ai—what are you doing here?" Captain Cho demanded.

Bao Xing raised her chin and took a few perfect steps forward. "I have come to see how I might assist Guowei. There are those on shore who would see this venture fail."

"He'll be pleased to hear it, lady." The captain offered a slight bow and stepped aside, then shouted, "You! The foreigner's on the bridge!" He lunged past her.

No time. Ming Lun, Dailus, Zhencai, even Yusen—all of them meant for her to be here, to stop the greater evil.

She started up the stairs, avoiding the stained wood where his blood had fallen. Another shout from Captain Cho as Dailus sank down, braced on two pillars while he swept at the captain's feet with his spear. The captain dodged, jumped, then flailed his arms as he fell.

Bao Xing hurried to the next level where the huge wheels turned. She lifted her cane, gaze flicking over the mechanism to see where best she could thwart it. A tracery of metal embellished the wooden parts, emitting a hum like the lake of mercury.

"Lady Bao Xing, so good of you to come." Guowei's elegant voice reached her just as his hand clamped over her arm. "This is merely mechanics. But watch." He plucked a pin from her hair and tossed it against the towering wheel where it struck the embedded metal. The hairs tingled on her neck, and the pin buzzed with a bolt of golden flame. She flinched, inadvertently drawing closer to him, imagining what would have happened to her if she touched it, even to try to stop it.

Guowei cradled her against his side. "Once the device is operational, the dragon lever ensures that it will remain so. A clever trick, no? You will want to see the instruments. The apparatus for aiming the device is quite ingenious." He pulled her toward the stairs. She tripped to keep pace with him.

She stumbled up the stairs with his propulsion, and he held her upright at the top. She stepped onto a platform dominated by the huge round dial at one side. A narrower dial marked with dragons clicked along as well, and she could see the lever latched within it, completing the circle. A rod at the back would connect when it came around again and flip the lever open. Until then, the machine was set, beyond human power to stop it. Intricate gears and tubes drew the star's power from above, through the gap in the roof, and aimed it, through the directional apparatus at the map down below. A cut gem set on a swinging arm there, ready to shift into place and transform the beam.

The humming grew louder here, as if the mass of metal amplified it, and she could feel it in her teeth. For a moment, the thing awed her, as if she were once again a child in her father's observatory, seeing the vastness of the heavens encompassed by the workings of man. But heaven was never meant to be mastered.

She dropped her gaze. "Minister, I—"

Two more soldiers, and Yusen between them, on his knees as if he must be made even smaller. His breath hitched unevenly, blood oozing from his lips. His head tipped to one side as if he had not the strength to hold it up. At the sound of her voice, he lifted his head, his dark eyes upon her, a sheen of pain clouding his features. She remembered the intensity of that gaze, from the first night in the khan's great ger to the day of their wedding to the moment he took her hand to guide her to safety during her escape from the astronomical tower in the Valley of the Sages.

Bao Xing looked away, to the bronze workings all around her. Her eyes burned, and her throat felt too tight even to breathe again. Two more soldiers idled nearby, swords drawn. The device gave a groan of wood and the click of gears turning. On the map down below, a circle of white light covered the area from the mountains to the Mongol capital beyond Kaifeng, encompassing temples, towns, farms and armies. When the light shifted gold, the North would die.

Guowei chuckled lightly. "I can see the device excites you. When I saw you in the library, when I knew what you were reading, I thought you might be the worthy bride for me, one who could aid me in my work, at every level."

Guowei offered her all she had ever dreamed of: the joy of books, the greatness of the heavens, the quiet pleasures of court, the sweetness of plums, the glory of a free China. Her father's dream wedded with her mother's, but Bao Xing was already married.

She brought her eyes back where they belonged, to that gaze, dark with pain and distance, hungry, and hers. "There are things you cannot learn from books, Minister," Bao Xing said, "and love is one of them."

"Love, for that?" He laughed again, but neither so lightly, nor so pleasantly. "As if love meant anything outside of poetry. You cannot be serious."

Setting down her cane, Bao Xing knelt there in the tower, feeling the wheel move below her, the instruments moving above, centered in the place between earth and sky, in the place where men could exercise their power. The strength of the stars hummed all around her, trapped in a cage of power, bound into a terrible harmony from which there could be no escape.

Yusen's lips parted, battered and bloody, his breath rasping. Her husband gave her stars and words, the freedom of horseback and the devotion of his body and spirit. He abased himself to support her. He stood by her, risked everything for her, learned from her and taught her in equal measure.

Bao Xing met his eye, unflinching. She could not stop the great device or the men who controlled it, but she could shine her own light to a heart too often trapped in darkness. "By all the stars in the heavens, and all the horses here on earth, Yusen is my husband until the day that I should die."

His face glowed, his chin lifting, eyes bright, and she saw what she had never thought to see: his smile, bright as the great Eternal Sky.

Just for a moment, she felt herself like one of the kitemen ready to soar.

"Until the day you die," Guowei echoed. "Or he does." He took two strides across the platform and seized Yusen by his bound arms. One of the soldiers dashed out of the way as the Mandarin flung the Mongol over the edge.

***

Dailus grabbed the rail as the body flew, launched from above, landing hard against a little mountain range and tumbling down with a crunch of bone and a streak of blood. Yusen lay in a heap, face down, his boot stirring ripples in the river of poison that wound out to a silver sea. For once, the Mongol was a giant, dominating the miniature landscape, crushing a tiny terra cotta city, its pagoda rolling slightly in his wake. His body spasmed and shuddered, glowing beneath the white light of the waiting weapon.

Upstairs, Dailus heard Bao Xing's cry of grief.

Pounding up the next few steps, Dailus spun about on the middle level. He still carried his spear and knife. The vast, turning wheel stood before him, the stack of dials slowly rotating. Cheerful figures of flute players and dancers stood upon the dials, waiting to greet the new hour, the Hour of the Dog when the Yellow River from the mountains to the sea would burn. High up, near the ceiling, he could see the chime waiting to be struck and the pin approaching in a smooth, inexorable way. Guowei stalked overhead, two other men guarded the apparatus, two more stood by the dial just at the top of the stairs. Bao Xing kneeling at the middle, weeping.

"I cannot decide what is the greater pity," Guowei murmured, "that such an intellect is wasted on a woman, or that such beauty is wasted on a Mongol's whore."

The diagram from the scroll overlaid the vast construction, with rows of orderly characters explaining it all, explaining how a device invented to heal could be transformed to killing. Dailus reached out with the spear to thrust it between the gears. It gave a sudden hum and raced with golden fire that singed his hand as he dropped it and stifled his cry. The spear gave off a little curl of smoke, and his hand still trembled. The gears ticked on, drawing the chime ever nearer. It could not be stopped that way. If he would stop the device, he must break the Golden Serpent, but how?

Grabbing the spear, warm and heavy in his hands, he surged ahead, not stopping when he reached the top and rammed the spear through the first soldier. It took more strength than he imagined, and he tumbled after, the spear swept from his grip as he sprawled.

Bao Xing lifted her head, and pushed to her feet. Guowei reached for her, but she snatched her cane and swung it hard toward him.

He deflected the blow easily, shunting the cane toward a supporting pole where it snapped in two, a few fragments of cinnabar scattering the floor.

"Must I do everything myself?" a querulous voice demanded, and Master Deng tottered up the stairs, holding a small crossbow.

As the second soldier sprang to his master's defense, Dailus slammed into him. The man tumbled and caught hold of the sighting tube, making a deadly contact with the metal. Golden light flared down his body. He shook and danced with a smell of charred meat as he dropped to the floor.

Master Deng's bolt launched, and Dailus twisted away as the bolt carved a furrow across his shoulder. He sprawled full-length rather than strike the fire-webbed bronze. "Too high," Master Deng muttered as he cranked back the bow for another shot.

"Minister!" called a voice across the lake. "I have the boy!"

Sidelong, across the landscape spattered with Yusen's blood and marked by his broken body, Dailus spotted Andao, clutching his stomach, bent at the feet of the officer who had gone out earlier. The young man retched and gasped for breath. Their last hope captured, kneeling for the sword that would take his life.

"It is over, then." Guowei wiped his hands on a delicate cloth which he tucked back into his robe. "A child, a dwarf, an old man and a slave. Sad to say, my dear, you appear to be the most competent of the lot. Did you really think such a strange alliance could subvert the Mandate of Heaven? The stars are on our side." He smiled faintly down at Bao Xing.

She looked up at him, her beauty more pale and fragile than ever, then slashed the broken cane toward his unprotected side. Guowei dodged the blow. He slid free his own sword, with a shake of his head, his eyes full of pity as he brought it down.

Bao Xing turned sharply, flicking out her silken sleeve. It lashed at him, the blade slicing through fabric, just missing her.

His lips gone hard, Guowei reached out his free hand and caught her wrist, the sword rising between them. "Such a waste," he said, "that you—"

She met his stare and shoved the broken cane into his throat, stopping his voice with a spill of blood, his eyes still wide. The sword slid from his grasp to clatter to the floor as he clawed at his ruined throat.

The Mandarin crumpled. His two soldiers hesitated to touch Bao Xing, and Dailus roared, bringing up his knife, making himself the obvious target. He grabbed the step-stool for a shield, catching the first sword cut so hard it bit the wood and chipped off slivers. Dailus slumped to the floor at the last moment, leaving his long legs sticking out. One of the soldiers tripped and staggered, hands waving as he tumbled down the stairs.

"No, no, no," Master Deng chanted. With a metallic ping and a whoosh, a bolt snapped over Dailus's head and into the beam.

When they started for him, Bao Xing clambered across the floor and pulled herself up on the wooden brace near the sighting tube that, any moment, would channel the strength of a star. "What can we do?"

But Dailus could not answer, for a sword leapt to his throat. He caught the man's arm, struggling to keep the blade away. The soldier slammed Dailus's left arm into the rail, knocking loose his step-stool shield. The soldier's other hand swept up with a short dagger and Dailus put up his hand to stop it.

The blade struck hard against the slave bracelet he still wore and scraped away along it. Dailus grabbed the man with both hands and lifted, pulling him off the ground, then tipped him over the rail. The soldier let go, hands groping for purchase, and slipped into the silvery lake below.

The buzz of the golden fire swarmed behind him, but Dailus ignored it, stalking back toward Master Deng.

The old man fumbled the crossbow, losing his last bolt to the floor below, then glanced up with his skeletal grin, like the miners and carpenters who died down below. "It is too late. The Dragon lever is locked and all of your companions are dead. What do you even have to fight for?"

"For life," said Dailus, "for freedom."

He lunged, but Master Deng hooked the crossbow onto the rail and leapt over, then dropped lightly to the ground below, running for the upturned boat. Dailus grabbed the chipped stepstool and flung it over the side, knocking him down.

A soft and desperate sound turned Dailus around.

Bao Xing stood at the sighting tube, tracing it with her eyes, hands outspread and helpless. It would slide upward into place on that pivoting arm, locking with the one above to channel the Dark Lance's fire through the gemstone in between. Could he even reach it? If he did, he would succeed only in burning to death. Ming Lun had been wrong—they could defeat the soldiers, and cross the lake of mercury. And yet she had been right as well: they could do all of that, and still not win. With the merciless precision of clockwork, the device ratcheted toward destruction and he had no idea how to stop it.

CHAPTER SIXTY-FIVE

Sensing the rush of wind as his assailant moved, Zhencai dropped to his hands beneath the slice of a blade, then kicked hard into the swordsman's knee, sending him out of the fray. At his back, Ming Lun twisted in a dancer's turn and carved her short blade into a soldier's gut. For a moment, their eyes met, she grinned, and danced away. They had fought each other before, and now they would die together.

Another soldier thrust, and Zhencai caught the man's arm across his shoulder, pivoting and wrenching back. Something popped, and the arm went limp in his grasp as he swept the soldier down. The maneuver left him facing the lake and the miniature landscape when an unmistakable body fell from the tower and tumbled into the dangerous light. Not dangerous yet, not until the clock struck one more time. When he offered to burn his monk's paper for Yusen's comfort, the Mongol turned him down, claiming he had given enough, but it was Yusen who gave everything.

Then the officer strode into view, shoving Andao before him. The young man collapsed and remained huddled on the ground.

A soldier interrupted Zhencai's view and landed a solid blow at his hip, but with the flat of his blade. Zhencai twisted away, reclaiming his qi, searching for detachment. They fought, turned, met, and repelled each other, both breathing too hard. Was this the man who would slay a Shaolin?

Not far off, the officer leaned toward the island, shouting for the attention of someone who did not answer. His sword rested on Andao's shoulder, ready at any moment to slice into his throat.

Zhencai had allowed Andao to follow him, to undertake this foolish quest. Andao did not even understand enough about Nirvana to welcome the chance to achieve it, and Zhencai could not help him.

The next soldier aimed a blow at his chest, and Zhencai barely responded in time to deflect the blade. The soldier's fist around the hilt still slammed into him, crumpling his monk's paper and digging in the sleeper's gift, the ruby dark as her flowing blood. Zhencai gasped a breath, then found another. "Ming Lun!"

She spun about. "What?"

"This—they need it, for healing." He pulled the stone from his hidden place.

"You trust me?" She dodged a blow with automatic ease.

"I trust your aim."

Ming Lun gave a nod that might have been a bow. In a spin, she swept the stone from his hand and dropped low, sliding past the few remaining soldiers, and those already dazed.

"But you're a lark like us!" The officer protested. He swung away from Andao, who suddenly rose to his knees and spread his hand, flinging something at the officer, scattering a handful of particles at the soldiers.

Did the boy's brief time as a geomancer make him think he would win this war with dirt?

First one soldier, then another wailed and cursed and twisted, slapping themselves, losing their weapons. One of them stumbled out of the way of Zhencai's attack, apparently without noticing as he flailed. The soldier's skin was crawling with ants. Ants! Andao had summoned ants to be his army. Zhencai laughed aloud.

"Bao Xing!" Atop the tower, the woman turned, and Ming Lun paused. She took a deep breath. It was just like the bridge when she threw stones at him and Andao, only a little bit further. That was the past. In the present, she would only have one try.

"Catch!" And the red stone arced through the air toward Bao Xing, but the lady did not put out her hands.

Zhencai dropped his opponent, adding a sharp blow to the man's neck.

Ming Lun's mouth opened, her brows the image of fury, then Bao Xing pinched up the edges of her gown and raised her skirt as a lady never should. She made a basket of silk, and the gem winked as it landed.

***

Utterly confused, Dailus watched as Bao Xing scooped the ruby from her skirt. "If only we could change it, instead of destroying it. Master Deng told Guowei to change the focus."

"Because it killed the soldier—it struck here in the cavern when he had it wrong instead of transmitting through the map to the world." But she didn't mean to burn Yusen's corpse to ashes, did she? If they didn't figure out how to stop the machine, the rest of her world would be in ashes in any case.

"Red is the color of joy, they did not make this machine to kill, they made it to heal." She rolled the gem between her fingers, and a tear slipped down her cheek. "If I could touch it, I could align a different star, a more auspicious one."

"Right now, lady, we need to stop it. We don't have time to make things better." Brave words, given that he hadn't even worked out how to touch the mechanisms without dying. Would he preserve the device just so they had an outside chance of saving Yusen—whatever was left of him? Even if he broke the Golden Serpent, the dragon lever remained locked until the gears rotated all the way through the firing cycle.

Dailus leaned in close to the controls before them, the array of knobs and levers that altered focus and direction, enabling the device to aim at different locations on the map below. The thin gold lines that connected them all. The circle of radiant energy, the Golden Serpent. Ironic that so much gold sat within a great lake of its enemy, quicksilver. Quicksilver! He dropped to his knees, staring at the lake. But the lake, too was part of the serpent, and he could not touch it—not with his hands.

Dailus grabbed Guowei's sword, the slender blade so sharp it cut a lady's gown. He clutched the dead man's sleeve and sliced off the excess fabric, letting the arm flop back onto the floor, the sword clattering beside it.

"What are you doing?" Bao Xing watched him curiously.

"You said you can chose a different star, lady. Get ready to do it."

"But—"

He was already running down the stairs, sleeve in hand. A pair of dead soldiers lay on the bank, still smelling faintly of burnt meat. What a time for his sense of smell to return. Before him spread the mirror-surface of the deadly lake, the quicksilver that had nearly been the death of him already. He held his breath as he leaned in and scooped the silken sleeve through the mercury, letting it fill. He carried the heavy pouch back up the stairs. His knees trembled, but he forced himself to keep going. The machine ticked overhead, the chime now a slender two prongs of the gear short of its moment. Another tick.

Dailus sprang up the last few steps, stumbling over one of the bodies and sliding in a slick of blood. The red gemstone lay on the floor where Yusen knelt until he'd been thrown over the side. Bao Xing was nowhere in sight, but a line of tiny footprints limned in blood led to the final stairs, the narrow way to the instruments over his head. "Lady!"

"Here! I am ready."

He pinched the bottom of the silk between his fingers, mercury sliding over them, coating them in silver as he poured the liquid along every golden thread he could see. It oozed thickly down among the dials, filling the engraved characters that labeled them and dropping among the gears below. Thick and silver like the blood of heaven. For a moment it merely rested, bubbles on the surface, then the gold curled and peeled up into the globes of mercury, just as they had when he gilded the khan's greatest firedrake. The humming all around him died to nothing.

Had he broken the serpent? He found one of the dropped knives and tapped a gear. No sparks, no frisson of power.

A final click and the sighting tube pivoted as the gears shifted. "Now, lady! Do it now!"

Dailus grabbed the knob that controlled elevation and cranked it back, then pulled the lever that Guowei employed to draw the focus of the huge device. For a moment, he trembled, not from the mercury that poisoned him nor from the power that hummed in the machine—but from the power that rested in his own hands. He once more commanded a weapon that could bring down walls and cities, a weapon that could incinerate an army and ruin a land for centuries, a weapon more terrible than anything short of the seven seals which God would break to unleash the apocalypse.

Dailus stood again in the place of God. Last time, outside the gates of Kaifeng, he stood there blind, wanting only the chance to go home, not thinking of the homes he would ruin and the lives that he would end. He swallowed hard. Did he trust himself to choose wisely? Would his aim, just as before, be true? Somewhere on the map below lay the village where those two boys played, and his straw blessing moved in the breeze to bring them his good wishes. Somewhere near Yusen's left foot, if he did not miss his guess.

Overhead, the device thrummed in a lowering pitch, making the hairs rise on Dailus's neck, setting his teeth and bones aching—the same sound that marked the blast of yellow light that slew the soldier.

"It's still going to fire," Bao Xing called from overhead. "You've aimed it at the Mongols, Dailus—you must make it stop! Even with the right star, we don't know what it might do!"

"Not at the Mongols," he said under his breath, "just the one."

"Stop!" She cried again, then he heard the patter of her feet as she ran for the stairs.

He needed three hands and another handspan of reach. Snatching the gem, he darted toward the array as it shifted slowly into place, the higher tubes and mirrors re-aligned at Bao Xing's command from the instruments above. He spun a circle, and Zhencai's prayer beads clinked at his hip. Taking the loop from his belt, Dailus moved to the rail nearest the map.

Doubling the string of beads, he reached up and caught the beads over one of the protrusions. Using the beads for balance, Dailus stepped up to the top rail, then he leaned out and barely kissed the end of the tube, grabbing the yellow gem in his teeth. The tube shifted upward and he stuffed the ruby in the socket as the tube elevated above him. The tube notched together with the array that brought down the stars. The prayer beads slid free.

Dailus wavered on the rail. Bao Xing caught his arm and yanked him to his knees on the platform as the chime struck a single pure note that echoed in the cavern. The great device buzzed. From above came a roar like an avalanche, then a bolt so bright they had to look away. The broad circle of light aimed straight for Yusen's fallen body, sprawled across the heart of the territory the Mandarins would burn. The image glowed beneath Dailus's eyelids as he prayed: Yusen pinned in a circle of brilliant crimson light that flared and died away.

From the display down below came the tinkle of tiny instruments. Dailus blinked open his eyes, peering downward. A parade of mechanical figures emerged along one of the broad rings. They danced with the sound of bells and the striking of a miniature drum, joyously celebrating the Hour of the Dog. The dragon dial moved as well, and the lever dropped open, preparing the machine to be re-set and fired again. The machine's ominous hum died away, leaving them in silence.

CHAPTER SIXTY-SIX

Bao Xing gripped Dailus's arm, letting her fingers dig in. "What have you done? I know he wounded you, but could you not let him die in peace? There was more to him than what he did to you."

He winced, but lay his hand over hers. His fingers dripped with gold-flecked globes of mercury. "Lady, I hope—I pray—we are both redeemed today." He swallowed, his pale throat working. "You chose an auspicious star, and the stone it focused through was red."

The healing stone Zhencai had from the sleeper, the stone Ming Lun tossed up to her too late, or so she thought. She let go of him, but he kept her hand a moment longer, and she noticed she was trembling. "Your hands," she whispered. "The mercury."

"It can harm me no more than it already has, lady." He withdrew his touch and flicked away the drops to spin and strike upon the floor, silver on crimson.

He rose to his knees, while she crawled to the rail, staring down. Bao Xing held her breath, expecting to see a shadow burned into the landscape where Yusen had been, a small shadow that failed to capture the outsized truth of him. He lay there still, unburnt, curled on his side, blood pooled around him.

"There's a boat," whispered Dailus. "On the far side."

She nodded faintly, and stumbled to the stairs, too shaky to stand. Just as when she was a child in her father's tower, she sat and bumped down the steps, then hurried, clinging to the sides of the tower to steady herself. She stopped short at the view across the lake where she and Ming Lun shared tea with Master Deng. Dailus clattered down behind her, his long limbs made the more awkward by the poison that moved through him, then he, too, stared.

In the comfortable alcove, a bamboo forest grew from the carpet, with the soldiers trapped inside, staying well back from the new-grown stalks. Andao and Ming Lun worked over Zhencai, who sat on the floor between them, allowing them to staunch his blood.

"Trees?" Dailus called.

Andao looked up with a shy smile. "Power doesn't have to kill." Then his smile fled, replaced by something stern, something of the look of Zhencai. "I found three ways out including the path we took in getting here, but there are no weaknesses in the stone, Dailus. The geomancers reinforced it with words and minerals of strength, just as we saw in the corridors and on the platform when they fled to the sky. They meant for it to last forever. I'm sorry."

However Dailus replied, Bao Xing did not hear. She rounded the island to the far side where a bowl-shaped leather boat lay upside down on the stone. She grabbed its rim and struggled to lift or turn it. The world blurred around her, and she blinked fiercely, the boat sliding from her grip. She knelt to try again, then Dailus knelt beside her, easily rolling the craft onto its bottom and pushing it onto the lake. He held the boat with one hand, and offered her the other, helping her inside.

Silently together, they made the short crossing to the miniature landscape beyond.

***

The smell of burning flesh always brought him home. A white glow surrounded him, the sky too bright—had the fire dazzled his eyes, or was it the glow of the white felt gers themselves? And then he knew. He drifted in the great Eternal Sky. Pain pulsed through his body, but surely that, too, would soon be ended. The light turned red as it consumed him, sweeping him with a tingle of power like the coming of a storm. The pain overwhelmed him, and his mind rushed to darkness.

When he returned, the smell of burning flesh had diminished. Faces formed in the white, and he knew that he, too, had been caught in the burning gers—the whiteness was the felt above him, falling to smother him, and the red was the light of the fires that devoured his family. Voices filtered through, the angry voices of the soldiers, then quiet voices, close by, his skin shivered with the memory of pain, and with the stroke of ghostly hands.

"Mother?" His tongue felt stiff, his own language foreign, as if he had been speaking too long in other tongues. She answered, but he could not hear her.

"I was dreaming as we died," he told her. "I dreamed that I sat in the ger of the khan. I was his guest, and we ate a great feast, with dancing and music." A man's voice thrummed after his own, too deep to belong to one of his brothers, but they were all dead, now. Munkjar chopped off his father's head. He had seen that, hadn't he? Munkjar carrying away his father's head.

"I saw the most beautiful woman in the world, and I married her." He laughed, remembering his wedding day, marveling at it, her face once more before him, radiant. "She married me. She was wise and kind, like the breeze of summer that tells you to move the herds into fields of flowers. You would have been so proud."

He caught his breath, and his joy turned sour. "I wanted to honor you, to honor our name." His voice felt hoarse from the flames.

"I was cruel. I hurt her. I hurt so many people." His ribs felt too tight, his lungs seared. "I was such a coward, scared of everything."

His father sounded worried, his mother distraught, but he had to tell them the truth. They had to know that, even in his dreams, he was no worthy son.

"I stole a man from his home and made him my slave. Everything I had was earned by him. I just—I wanted to honor you." His voice nearly failed him, and he forced himself to say the last of it, the worst of it. "You would be ashamed of me, if I had lived that dream."

He thought for a moment that he saw his dream-bride, that she was holding him and easing his pain. And he wept as he thanked the Eternal Sky for bringing her back, one last time.

***

Dailus broke off his translation, wiping a hand over his face. "It's too much! I can't—I shouldn't even hear this." He pressed the heels of his hands into his eyes.

Bao Xing cradled Yusen in her lap, holding him close against her heart. "Thank you," she said. "Thank you, thank you."

"No!" Dailus pushed away, standing in the plains of the miniature world, stained with Yusen's blood. Glow worms crept across the scenery, whole and healed. A tiny pagoda rolled by his foot and he kicked it hard across the mountains to splash into the lake with a silvery sheen.

Back on shore, Ming Lun stood watching, waiting. Dailus stared back at her. He had forgiven her, hadn't he? He had forgiven her when they fought, when she wouldn't kill him and he kissed her, half in desperation, half in lust, for who could blame him then, in the moment of battle? *Forgive us our trespasses as we forgive those who trespass against us.*

Andao stood uncertainly near her, wavering as always. "There are Mongols coming. Lots of them. I let the soldiers out, on the condition they left right away." He flashed a grin. "I told them I had more ants."

Dailus gave a nod. They had to go. He drew a shaky breath, and forced himself to return to Bao Xing. "We need to destroy the device before the Mongols arrive."

"Yes." She stroked the hair from Yusen's face. Dried blood flaked away, revealing nothing but bare, whole skin. Healed, in the crimson stroke of light, like the glow worms he had crushed against his chest. But he did not wake. "Will you—I cannot carry him," she whispered.

Staring down at the small, crumpled form, Dailus stooped and gathered his master into his arms, his slave bracelet rubbing Yusen's back. Yusen, too, had a name. He drew him tight and carried him to the edge of the landscape, stepping over the border of mercury, back into the world. Dailus deposited Yusen at Zhencai's side.

The monk sat stiffly, a cloth bound around his middle and another wrapping his shoulder. "He is not dead?"

Dailus shook his head. "The red stone healed him, but he hasn't woken up."

"Perhaps he does not wish to."

Sitting back on his heels, Dailus made a little space for Bao Xing to join her husband, and he thought of the things Yusen had said, rambling in Mongolian, about the fire and his family, about his wife, and his fear and his shame.

He leaned into Yusen's still face. "Wake up, Yusen! Wake up—you have a duty."

Bao Xing turned her tear-streaked face to Dailus with sudden fury. "You leave him be!"

No longer the porcelain beauty, caught up in the life of the mind, Bao Xing had found her passion on their curious, dangerous quest. Dailus said, "No."

He rested his hand on Yusen's chest, over the slow beat of his heart. "Master, wake up!"

The dark eyes flickered open, and Yusen caught his breath, glaring at Dailus, all trace of his anguish gone in that blink. For a moment he glanced around as if searching for trouble, then he eased up to his elbows, and found Bao Xing. At her breast, she wore the astrolabe, the old amulet he had given her. Yusen caught his breath and let it out slowly. He reached out as if to touch the amulet, and drew back. "All the stars?" he whispered, not meeting her eyes.

"And all the horses," she answered.

He gazed at her in awe. His hand grew more steady as he touched her necklace, her tumbled hair, her cheek, his thumb brushing gently over her lips. She closed her eyes, catching his hand to keep it close, her lips pursed against his palm. Dailus turned away, thinking of how to destroy the great device, thinking of anything but love.

Slowly, Yusen sat up all the way then found his feet. "There must be tools around here, yes?"

"By the kitchen, there." Bao Xing blinked a little, letting him withdraw his hand, and pointed back.

He walked stiffly, shaking out his arms, tipping his head to one side, then to the other as if he had slept too long on stone, or just arisen from his tomb. Again. He returned after a moment with a hammer that looked enormous in his small fist, another tool tucked into his belt.

"Hand," he ordered, staring at Dailus.

Dailus held it up, fist clenched, the slave bracelet settling into its place, a chink of bright metal showing where the accursed thing had saved his life. Yusen caught his hand in a soldier's grip, hands wrapping each other, the grip of a comrade, then knelt, bringing his arm down to rest upon the ground. He plucked a chisel from his belt and struck the bracelet free with one ringing blow, then pulled it away and flung it into the silver lake to sink forever. For a moment, he knelt there still, his black hair hiding his face, a penitent.

Dailus breathed over his master's bent head—but Yusen was master no longer. "I forgive you," Dailus said.

Yusen's head dipped a little lower, and Bao Xing smiled, open and warm.

"Have you all forgotten the Mongols?" Ming Lun inquired.

"Of course not." Dailus stood up, his arm feeling lighter—no, his entire being lighter for the loss of that pound of metal. Freedom, at last, was his. "There's a model firedrake on the island. I can use it to bring down the tower into the mercury. Ming Lun, will you help me?"

"Assuredly."

"Do you know what happened to the plan, or Master Deng?" Andao asked.

For a moment, the dancer hesitated, one foot raised. "He left by the third way. I believe he took the scroll with him."

"You don't think they're going to try again."

"Like this?" She waved her had toward the huge map and tower, then shook her head. "But the fight to free the Han people is not over." Her eyes met Yusen's, both dark and strong, then she dipped into a bow, and bounded lightly over the pillars back to the weapon.

Dailus followed more slowly, his long days accumulating in his bones the way that rust built in the joints of old metal. On the second level of the tower, the bronze firedrake remained, aimed at the gallery where it had taken Yusen down. Dailus recognized its shape, the rough pattern of horses that galloped along the side, and the unique side-facing breach. They had cast his own model into this miniature. Likely Guowei stole it just to prove his mastery over the Mongol's weapons. Near Guowei's body lay a bamboo tube of black powder.

"That is one of your firedrakes?" Ming Lun ran her fingers lightly down the side. "It is a beautiful monster."

He glanced at her sidelong. "An apt phrase. Help me carry it down. If we destroy the lower struts at the back, the tower should topple into the lake behind. It will smash the instruments against the stone on the way down."

Together, they brought the firedrake to the shoreline where the soldiers died. He nestled the bronze vessel alongside the wooden struts and set about loading the device. He used too much powder and stuffed the end of the bore with cloth bound around stones. He was not aiming his model, he was exploding it, using the very force of his creation to destroy another. Two beautiful monsters, sent to their grave together. "We'll need a long fuse, so we have time to run."

Ming Lun squatted beside him, their backs to the others as they worked. She unwound the cord at her waist and offered it up. "Will this do?" He doused the cord in oil from one of the lanterns, then continued his work.

When the wick lay ready, Dailus took the loop of its length into his hand. Together, they crossed the pillars most of the way, until the cord ran out. It lay across the stones in a curious path, leading to Dailus's last firedrake, like a child grown up full of rage, waiting to spew its fire. Ming Lun stood one pillar beyond, then held out her hand. "Go on. Whoever lights this fuse will need to be quick about finishing the path."

Dailus held the lantern in one hand, and the last of the wick in the other. His knees and ankles trembled a little, just standing there, while she stood casually, as if she could wait all day.

"The third way out—you know where it is?"

She gave a nod, then pulled something from a pouch, a stone seal which fell heavy in his palm. "Guowei brought this. It is the khan's personal seal. He'll want it back." She gave a little shrug.

"You aren't coming with us."

"The emperor still needs me." She finally met his eye. "This was not the way to win our war. We will find another." She took a deep breath. "Master Deng crossed back after you took the boat. I saw him, but he lost me in the caves. He still has other plans."

Dailus sighed. "I'm sure he does."

"I will find out about them. The Son of Heaven will rule again one day, but not like this." She indicated the landscape with its shadows of the dead.

"You aren't coming," he said again, his throat aching.

"You were the only man who ever wanted me, who ever watched me for myself." Her eyes gleamed. "And even you won't love me."

"I didn't say that," he answered, too sharply. "I said I could not marry you."

Her brows arched upward, a smile lighting her face. Mercury shimmered between them, then she leapt lightly toward him, resting her toes on two of the pillars, she pushed up toward him. Dailus leaned in and they kissed, light and hot, and over too soon. "Know that when I dance, I dance for you." She slid the wick from his fingers and the lantern from his hand, shifting away so he could pass her and find his way to safety.

Dailus concentrated on the movements of the dance and finally reached the shore.

"Do you really think she'll do it?" Andao said.

"Yes." Then his smile turned rueful, "But can we see the chamber from the third path, just in case?"

Andao gave a nod. "This way."

Yusen helped Bao Xing to her feet, drawing her hand to his shoulder and holding it there as they followed Andao. Zhencai pulled himself up and joined Dailus, moving awkwardly, shaking his head. "Being in the world has improved neither my flesh, nor for my spirit."

"But the world would be in flames, if not for your flesh and your spirit," Dailus told him, and the old monk made his sign of blessing.

Together, they climbed the stairs and took a narrow path that ran along behind the device, with occasional windows out into the main chamber. At last, the corridor turned aside and angled upward. Dailus stopped at the last window. From here, the device loomed over its miniature world, poised for destruction. Beyond it, he could make out Ming Lun balanced over the stones. She held the lantern, looking up, but if she looked for him, or at the great device she once imagined would save her people, he did not know. His mouth went dry, waiting.

At last, she brought her hands together, her face illuminated by the lantern, and by the spark that flared and crept along the fuse. She lay it down and stood a moment, watching the flame move toward its ending, stone by stone, creeping up.

"Go," Dailus whispered. "Run."

At the last moment, she did, springing away, dancing and turning over the pathway and vanishing as the cave exploded once more with light. The ground rumbled and Zhencai caught his arm, tugging at him.

Time itself suspended as if the explosion devoured the workings of the clock and broke the hours. The tower flared, then it, too, twisted with a flash of gold and a groan of metal. The huge armillary sphere on top swung sideways to crash against the wall, its rings bending, its dragons writhing as they fell. Sighting tubes and gears whirled up, freed from their springs and levers to clash against stone. One of them swung in through the window. Dailus leapt back and ran, Zhencai moving ahead of him, up, up into the dark. Then their feet were splashing. He tried to pause, but the tumbling water rushed his feet out from under him, and he slid along a narrow passage of stone, plunging suddenly out into the light.

The sound of breaking wood and groaning metal echoed after him and fell silent at last as Andao reached down a hand and drew Dailus to the bank of a small pool. A stream gushed down from the wall of stone, and he could hear the river on the other side. An exit, yes, but even a man who knew it was there would be hard-pressed to get back inside that way. Beyond the shallow pool where they landed, the stream meandered through a narrow grassy meadow.

Bao Xing sat on a large stone, shivering from her dip in the chilly water, and Yusen shed his del to drape it over her shoulders, wearing only his trousers. He had revealed his thin, scarred chest as if he no longer cared. Andao paced the rocky ground where they stood, and Zhencai sat in a posture of meditation, watching his apprentice, strangely at ease.

"There are other centers of learning," Zhencai said. "Other places where the knowledge you need can be found."

"Other places to learn about the world at the same time that I hide from it? It's not right to detach from someplace that needs me." Andao swallowed. "That needs us."

The old man's hands spread open, palms up. "Detachment is an illusion."

Andao's pacing ceased, his hands gripped together. "Will you come with me?"

"I cannot follow the Way, but I can help you find yours."

Andao grinned, his hands freed to embrace the whole of the world around them.

"What about you?" asked Bao Xing, glancing at Dailus. "What will you do?"

"I'm a thousand miles from home. I don't know how I'll ever get back," Dailus answered, but he stood taller, his chest lifted, as if the very air he breathed were changed. He stood free in the open air, and choices lay before him.

Yusen stepped away from the water, scanning the peaks that surrounded them and the valley where the stream had brought them out, then stuck his fingers in his mouth and whistled. Head cocked, he listened.

After a long moment, he whistled again. Across the stream,

something moved, galloping into view: Tsang, and all of her companions. She splashed through the water, her mane streaming out behind her.

"It's like magic," Dailus grumbled.

"Mongol magic," Yusen answered. They stood side by side watching the horses run. "I am a prince of the blood of Chinggis Khan. If I can convince them that I am no traitor, then I can get you a tablet to ensure your safe passage back home."

"You'll need this." Dailus held out the seal Ming Lun had given him. "Guowei stole it from the khan. The arrogant bastard was that certain he would win."

Yusen closed his fist around it. "I can give you a horse better than any you'll find in your own land."

"Smaller, too," Dailus observed as the horses approached.

Yusen's hand dropped to his hip, as if searching for a weapon, a way to punish his slave for that remark. He came back instead with a golden pin, topped with a single pearl. "I found this where she fought. Where she danced."

It fell into Dailus's palm, sharp and beautiful, precious as memory for the long ride home.

E. C. Ambrose writes knowledge inspired adventure fiction including *The King of Next Week*, also from Guardbridge Books; *The Dark Apostle* series about medieval surgery (DAW), and the *Bone Guard* archaeological thrillers as E. Chris Ambrose. In the process of researching her books, Elaine learned how to hunt with a falcon, clear a building of possible assailants, and pull traction on a broken limb. Her quest for real-world detail has taken her from the steppes of Mongolia to the deserts of southern California.

Elaine's short stories have appeared in *Fireside*, *Warrior Women*, and *Fantasy for the Throne*, among many others, and she has edited several volumes of *New Hampshire Pulp Fiction*. A graduate of the Odyssey Writing Workshop, Elaine has returned there to teach, as well as at conventions and writer's groups across the country. She has judged writing competitions from New Hampshire Literary Idol to the World Fantasy Award.

Elaine dropped out of art school to found her own wholesale gift business. Former jobs include professional costumer and part-time adventure guide. In addition to writing, Elaine incorporates weaving, dyeing, and felting into unique garments. To learn about all of her writing, check out RocinanteBooks.com

More historical fantasy from Guardbridge Books.

The King of Next Week
also by EC Ambrose

When a captain trades his cargo of ice to bring home a djinn bride, his life in post-Civil War coastal Maine will never be the same.

"Historical Fiction at its best" — Beth Cato

The Elephant & Macaw Banner
by Christopher Kastensmidt

Adventure in Colonial Brazil,
A pair of heroes face the monsters of Brazilian folklore.

"A fantastic romp… with epic battles, creepy creatures and wonderful set pieces." — Aliette de Bodard

Death by Effigy
by Karen L. Abrahamson

Mystery, Magic, and Marionettes in 19th Century Burma. A traditional Burmese puppetry troupe is more than meets the eye: these puppets hold living spirits.

"A wonderful blend of conspiracy and playful spirits, with a pair of unique detectives, and no strings atached." — Steven Poore

All are available at our website and online retailers.

http://guardbridgebooks.co.uk